Resistant

Revolt of the Jews

Chronicles of the Apocalypse

Book Three

By Brian Godawa

Resistant: Revolt of the Jews
Chronicles of the Apocalypse Book Three
2nd Edition c

Warrior Poet Publishing
www.warriorpoetpublishing.com

ISBN: 9798710886342 (hardcover)
ISBN: 978-1-942858-35-5 (paperback)

Scripture quotations taken from *The Holy Bible: English Standard Version.* Wheaton: Standard Bible Society, 2001.

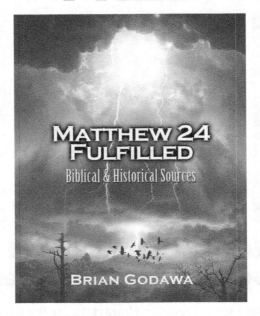

The *Chronicles of the Apocalypse* series

is dedicated to

Ken Gentry and Gary DeMar.

Scholars and gentlemen, both.

ACKNOWLEDGMENTS

Special thanks to my Lord and Savior Jesus Christ for allowing me to combine my esoteric theological interests with my passionate love of storytelling. I never envisioned such privilege or ministry. I do not deserve it.

Perpetual thanks to my wife, Kimberly, my Cassandra, my muse.

I am so grateful for Jeanette Windle for making this entire series so much better because of her loving editorial ruthlessness. Jeanette, your theological understanding, your life experience in missions, your own storytelling choices and your skill convince me that God providentially led me to you. I could not imagine a more perfect editor for this project to make it what it needed to become.

My deepest gratitude goes to my long-time friend and scholar Kenneth L. Gentry Jr. for allowing me the privilege of early access to his Revelation commentary, *The Divorce of Israel*, which served as a scholarly guide to unveiling the complexities of this most fascinating of all New Testament books.

I would also like to thank my newer friend and scholar Michael S. Heiser, whose work on the divine council, the Watchers, and the Deuteronomy 32 worldview constitutes the other major influence on my interpretation of Revelation. I believe I have made opposites attract. Christus Victor!

I cannot neglect to thank Gary DeMar, another long-time friend and scholar whose eschatological work continues to be a trumpet call of sanity in this generation of last days madness.

And of course, I could not have made this as clean a manuscript as it is without all my devoted Advanced Reader Team's kind and gracious help in proofreading and helpful feedback. Thanks to (in alphabetical order): Kwame Antwi-Boasiako, eagle eye proofer Mike Beidler, Steve von Berckefeldt, Kenneth Conklin, Jeremy Eng, Mark Gerger, James Hawk, Susan Haymon, Jeff Hopper, Grace Jacob, Sue Jensen, Dawn Korotko, (with special theological appreciation) Jerel Kratt, Larry Krejci, Carla Lamb, Shane Lloyd Love, Jim Monts, James G. Olson, Zoriana Petryna, Shari Risoff, Jonathan Roberts, David Von Schmittou, Dixie Von Schmittou, Carol Sitzlar, Cynthia Stevens, Bonnie Tarttier, Clinton Vladivelu, Frazer Williamson and David Wright.

NOTE TO THE READER

Chronicles of the Apocalypse is a standalone series. But this book you are reading is not a standalone novel. It follows *Tyrant: Rise of the Beast* and *Remnant: Rescue of the Elect*.

In another sense, *Chronicles of the Apocalypse* is the conclusive sequel to my Chronicles of the Nephilim series about the biblical Cosmic War of the Seed and the victory of Christ over the Powers. One need not read the previous Nephilim series to be able to understand this Apocalypse series, but the literary and theological connections run deep.

This is the story of the apostle John's writing of the Apocalypse during the time of the Roman Empire, the first major persecution of Christians, and the Jewish revolt of A.D. 66 that resulted in the destruction of Jerusalem and the temple in A.D. 70. My hope is that the ancient world in all its symbolic glory will come alive to the reader as you encounter the imagery in Revelation dramatically unveiled through its Old Testament and first century literary lens.

I've included numbered endnotes for each chapter that provide detailed biblical and historical substantiation behind the fictional story. As it turns out, half of the text of this book is endnotes. This is my most heavily researched series of novels yet. Though using endnote numbers in a novel text is considered anathema by many, I chose to use them to provide biblical and historical context for those who want to "fact check" the eschatology and dig deeper.

I have tried to be as accurate as I can with the actual historical events and characters surrounding the Jewish revolt of A.D. 66 and the fall of Jerusalem in A.D. 70. However, there are many details we simply do not know with certainty because either the Bible or other historical sources are silent or because there is disagreement over the facts. Because of this, I had to take some creative license to fill in the gaps and simplify for easier reading. But I have tried to remain true to the spirit of the text if not to the letter.

CAST OF CHARACTERS

Some readers prefer to conjure pictures of what characters look like in their own imagination. But this is a sprawling epic with a lot of characters, so I wanted to help the reader keep all the characters straight in their minds as they read. See the color versions of these characters on the Chronicles of the Apocalypse website: http://wp.me/P6y1ub-1uH

I also have artwork of maps, paintings, and illustrations that relate to this story: http://wp.me/P6y1ub-1uJ

Brian Godawa
Author, *Chronicles of the Apocalypse*

MAPS

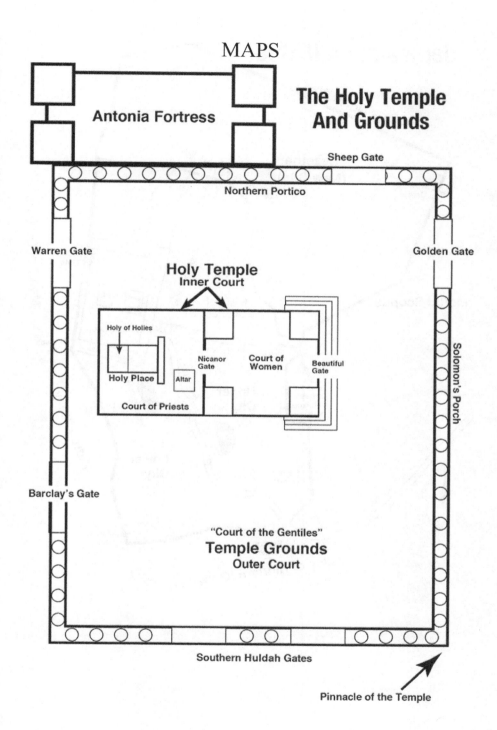

The Holy Temple And Grounds

Antonia Fortress

Sheep Gate

Northern Portico

Warren Gate

Golden Gate

Holy Temple
Inner Court

Holy of Holies

Holy Place

Altar

Nicanor Gate

Court of Women

Beautiful Gate

Court of Priests

Solomon's Porch

Barclay's Gate

"Court of the Gentiles"
Temple Grounds
Outer Court

Southern Huldah Gates

Pinnacle of the Temple

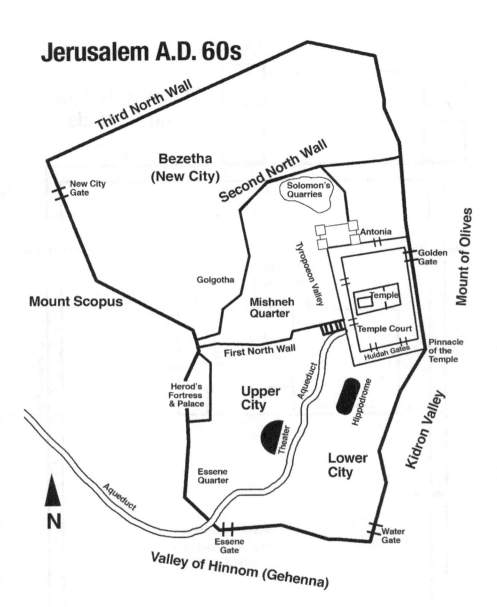

Jerusalem A.D. 60s

Third North Wall

Bezetha
(New City)

Second North Wall

New City
Gate

Solomon's
Quarries

Antonia

Mount of Olives

Golden
Gate

Golgotha

Tyropoeon Valley

Mishneh
Quarter

Mount Scopus

Temple

Temple Court

First North Wall

Huldah Gates

Pinnacle
of the
Temple

Herod's
Fortress
& Palace

Upper
City

Aqueduct

Hippodrome

Theater

Kidron Valley

Essene
Quarter

Lower
City

N

Aqueduct

Water
Gate

Essene
Gate

Valley of Hinnom (Gehenna)

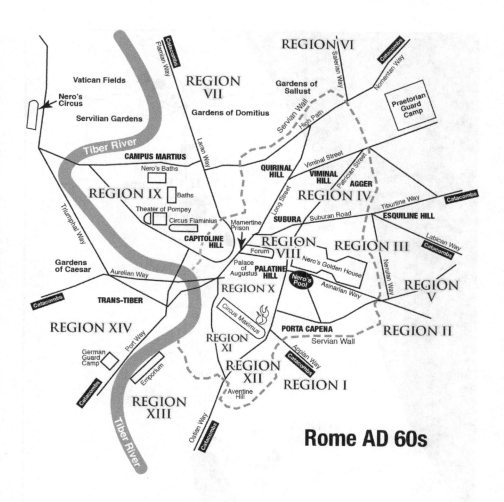

Rome AD 60s

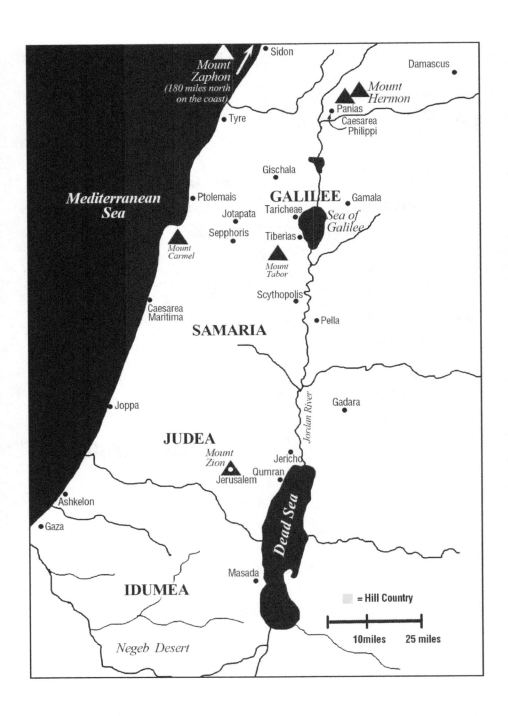

Mount
Zaphon
(180 miles north
on the coast)

Sidon

Damascus

Mount
Hermon

Panias
Caesarea
Philippi

Tyre

Gischala

*Mediterranean
Sea*

Ptolemais

GALILEE

Gamala

Jotapata

Taricheae

*Sea of
Galilee*

Sepphoris

Tiberias

*Mount
Carmel*

*Mount
Tabor*

Scythopolis

Caesarea
Maritima

SAMARIA

Pella

Jordan River

Gadara

Joppa

JUDEA

Mount
Zion

Jericho

Jerusalem

Qumran

Dead Sea

Ashkelon

Gaza

Masada

IDUMEA

= Hill Country

Negeb Desert

10miles   25 miles

"For these are days of vengeance, to fulfill all that is written. Alas for women who are pregnant and for those who are nursing infants in those days! For there will be great distress upon the land and wrath against this people."

—Luke 21:22-23

PART ONE

Abomination

PROLOGUE

Judea
Spring, AD 67

The Jewish revolt against Rome began in AD 66 and climaxed when the rebel Eleazar stopped the daily sacrifice on behalf of Caesar in the holy temple.[1]

In response, Nero Caesar sent Syrian governor Cestius Gallus with a Roman army to Jerusalem. But for a mysterious reason, Cestius turned away from his siege. He was killed on his retreat to Caesarea Maritima.[2]

Temporary victory over Rome has empowered the Jewish revolt. A new Jerusalem government has been organized to deal with the return of Rome and the coming war.[3]

But not all has gone well for the Jews. Tens of thousands of them have been killed in a civil war with Greek citizens of Judea that tears apart the land.[4]

In Jerusalem, the new rulers are divided between the pro-Roman high priesthood and the anti-Roman Zealots, Sicarii, and other factions.

The fanatic Eleazar ben Simon holds the inner temple hostage.

Former high priest Ananus ben Ananus, now the supreme commander of Judea, wants to stop the revolt and submit to Rome but he does not have the support of the populace.[5]

The Pharisee Joseph ben Matthias is regional commander of Galilee. He is headquartered with his army at Jotapata, a well-fortified city in Galilee, awaiting the arrival of the Roman war machine.[6]

3

Joseph's rival John of Gischala holds onto his home town and several Galilean cities in defiance of Joseph, dividing the Jewish forces against each other.[7]

Vespasian, general legate of the Roman army sent by Nero, has arrived in Ptolemais on the Mediterranean coast near Galilee.[8]

Vespasian's son Titus has marched Legion XV overland from Alexandria, Egypt, to meet his father in Ptolemais and initiate the campaign of war against Judea.[9]

The abomination of desolation (the Roman army) is now set up in the holy land. The die is cast.[10]

> *And from the time that the daily sacrifice is taken away, and the abomination of desolation is set up, there shall be one thousand two hundred and ninety days.*
>
> *Daniel 12:11*

The 1290 Days begins.[11]

CHAPTER 1

**Mount Carmel,
The Coast of Palestine
April, AD 67**

The Egyptian god Serapis made his way into the foothills of southern Mount Carmel on the coast of Palestine. The gods of the nations had been called to assembly on the peak of the mountain range that jutted out into the Mediterranean. Serapis was secretly meeting with Poseidon first before joining the others. He had received a request from the Greek sea god to meet in a cave to discuss an offer of covert alliance. Poseidon had only told Serapis that he had a plan that would ensure the two of them a place of power in the aftermath of the coming war.

Serapis was willing to consider Poseidon's offer. As a hybrid Watcher of both Greece and Egypt, Serapis was a liaison of the two kingdoms. When Alexander the Great had conquered Egypt centuries ago, he had established Serapis in power over the underworld. This was why Serapis looked Greek with his ethnic muscular stature, flowing curly hair, and beard, but wore Egyptian robes and ornaments. He looked like Hercules in Alexandrian garb. He carried an Egyptian scepter that doubled as a heavenly weapon and was accompanied by Cerberus, the three-headed hound of Hades. If this was a trick or an ambush planned by Poseidon, the sea god would be sorry he ever considered such foolishness.[1]

But Serapis doubted such betrayal. The two Watchers were the patron gods of the most powerful legions in the Roman armies now assembled in Palestine. Poseidon was the mascot of the Roman general Vespasian's Greek Legion X, and Serapis was patron of Titus's Alexandrian Legion XV. Together they represented the most significant principalities in Apollyon's coalition forces. Together they commanded the most powerful of the legions.

5

The huge beast beside Serapis was as muscular as his master. Its wolf-like heads were complimented by a tail that was a venomous serpent. The myth was that Hercules had captured the canine guardian to use for his purposes, another connection to the Greek hero. The blending of myths across nations was a commonplace tactic of the gods. The various Gentile nations worshipped the same spiritual entities behind different religious façades. The Watchers were happy to accommodate the narrative as long as it pointed away from Yahweh.

What the pathetic, deluded humans failed to appreciate was that their gods were actually the fallen Sons of God from Yahweh's heavenly host.[2] Because humanity continued to worship the host of heaven instead of their creator, Yahweh had allotted those rebellious Gentile nations and their land as an inheritance to the gods of the nations, their Watchers. Humanity was enslaved to the principalities and powers they worshipped.[3] But Yahweh had kept one single people on one parcel of land for himself: Jacob, the people of the land of Israel.[4]

But now Apollyon had used Nero Caesar to gather the nations in Palestine in order to consume the land and destroy the Jews. It was Apollyon's bid for total dominion. That final battle would determine the hierarchy of power within the pantheon. Serapis wondered just what plans Poseidon had for the two of them grabbing that power. He wondered as well just how he might use Poseidon and betray the sea god to Apollyon to ensure his own superior position.

Cerberus stopped, sniffing the air. He growled.

Serapis bent down. "What is it, boy? What do you smell?"

The three canine heads returned to their forward movement. The desert contained a mixture of predator and prey whose odors intermixed and flowed through the air currents. The hound of Hades could smell them all. But an aggressive yelp confirmed to Serapis that he had picked up the god's scent.

Serapis remained on the alert as he approached the designated cave hidden in the rocky terrain, a warm desert breeze at his back. He noticed a tri-fold scraping mark at the cave's entrance. It was made by Poseidon's trident, a mighty weapon that the god of the sea wielded with ruthless skill that garnered the grudging respect of Serapis. His conspirator was waiting for him inside.

Cerberus led Serapis forward into the cave. They walked through the darkness, their preternatural eyes able to see as clearly as in daylight.

It was a deep cave that led down into a small cavern with a pool of water and large stalactites above. Serapis spotted Poseidon sitting on a rock about fifty feet away at the pool's edge, trident in hand. Cerberus grunted approval, then snorted. Serapis knew that the sea god's fishy odor was strong to the hound's sensitive noses. Serapis smiled with amusement, wondering if the mighty dog would be tempted to try to eat the fishy deity.

The dog-wolf at his side, Serapis walked along the water's edge towards Poseidon. Cerberus stopped, and this time all three of its heads snorted. Then they began coughing. The beast backed up in a choking fit, whining.

Poseidon looked their way and got up. Starting towards them, he shouted out, "What is wrong?"

Just then Serapis noticed the dusty air stirred up by the hound. He sniffed and immediately recognized it: chili peppers. The dirt had been laden with crushed chili pepper flakes. In the hound's ultra-sensitive noses, they would be like burning fire.

As Poseidon got closer, Serapis saw that he was not the sea god after all, but the archangel Gabriel disguised as the sea god. Gabriel had masked his own scent from Cerberus by wearing Poseidon's garments.

Just then the pool along which Serapis walked exploded. Three archangels burst from the water: Remiel, Saraqael, and Raguel. As they fell upon the new arrivals, Cerberus stumbled, momentarily incapacitated by three sets of watery eyes, burning noses, and choking throats. But in a moment, he would be clear of the patch of contaminated dirt. Then the archangels would regret their dirty trick. The dog-wolf growled angrily through vicious fangs.

Unfortunately, the beast had not bothered to look up. A large stalactite plummeted from above with deadly accuracy, impaling the dog-wolf through his torso. Cerberus let out a ghastly howl that was stopped short by the air leaving his punctured lung. The rocky missile had been dropped from above by Uriel, who now leapt to the ground, landing on bended knee next to the hound.

Serapis swung his scepter at Uriel. But his skills were no match for the small, blonde angel. Uriel pulled one of his two swords and casually deflected the god's advances. The angel was the smallest of seven archons, but he was the most skilled. The truth was, this spiteful little miscreant of Yahweh could take Serapis alone. That so many archons were here so close to their enemy's camp meant this was a trap of overwhelming importance.

Serapis swung his weapon again and again with increasing futility. From the corner of his eye, he saw the naked and bound body of the real Poseidon dragged from the water by one of the angels.

He probably got the same fake message of conspiracy from these loathsome abominable archons, Serapis thought.

Before he could think any further, he blacked out from a blow to his head.

CHAPTER 2

Jordan Valley

Cassandra resituated herself on her horse, striving to find a comfortable position for her sore muscles. She saw that her husband Alexander was looking at her from his own mount and smiled at him through gritted teeth. She was exhausted from a full day of travel, and the sun was now setting. But it was still another twenty miles to their destination, Jerusalem, so they would soon need to find a place to camp for the night.

Their small company had been traveling for the past three days along the Jordan River from the city of Pella up north. It should have only taken two days to cover the forty miles on their horses, but their pace was slowed by a couple of donkeys pulling two supply wagons.

Cassandra had married Alexander just four months ago with the understanding that she would assist him in giving medical help and the Gospel to Jerusalem residents in anticipation of the coming war with Rome. The Christians of the city had all safely fled to Pella in obedience to Jesus's command to flee to the mountains when Jerusalem was surrounded by armies. The armies had subsequently left, but they were about to return with a vengeance.

Cassandra and Alexander were essentially walking into a deathtrap. She had avoided marriage because of the great tribulation. A married person had divided interests between their Lord and their beloved. And a married person had more to lose in a world of suffering. Yet, here she was, a thirty-two year old married woman, risking everything with her husband for the sake of the Gospel.

Through their journey together over the past few years, Cassandra had fallen deeply in love with Alexander, in love with his heart of compassion and his hands of healing as a physician. She thanked Jesus daily for using her, despite her weaknesses, to lead Alexander to the heart of Messiah and his Church, the heavenly Jerusalem, the remnant, the true Israel of God.

Alexander's compassion had in turn convicted Cassandra of her sin of hatred towards her own people, the Jews, who had martyred her parents because they had embraced Jesus as Messiah. She was now on her way back into the furnace of fire to help those upon whom she had previously prayed death.

Judgment was coming upon these people and their holy city and temple, but vengeance was in Yahweh's hands, not hers. Together she and Alexander hoped to rescue as many as possible, not from the earthly wrath to come, but from the far greater danger of eternal destruction away from the presence of the Lord and his glory.[1] Jesus had warned this generation of Jews over and over again that their rejection of him as their Messiah would result in them being cast into outer darkness where there was weeping and gnashing of teeth—the wrath to come.[2]

And now that time of destruction was at hand. Previously, she longed for it. Now she dreaded it. She prayed they could save as many souls as possible before their bodies were destroyed.

The two wagons were filled with medical supplies for the people of the city. Such supplies needed to be stockpiled because once the Romans arrived and surrounded the city, the Jews inside would have no access to outside resources. This precious cargo would be all the medical supplies Alexander and his party would have to work with.

Alexander smiled back at Cassandra, but she caught a flicker of sadness in his gaze and wondered how prepared they really were to meet the needs of others when they themselves were suffering. She knew the source of his sadness. Alexander wanted children, even in this dangerous world that threatened their survival. She did not, and after four months of marriage she had not yet shown any signs of conception. The disagreement had distanced them from one another. They shared a vision for the kingdom of God, but they did not share a vision for whether or not a family should be started at the end of the age when all the prophecies of God's cup of wrath were about to be poured out on the land of Israel.

Cassandra loved Alexander dearly, and his devotion to her was unquestionable. But greater men had been compromised by their hopes for legacy. Their very own father of the faith, Abraham, had united with Sarah's handmaiden to produce an heir. That momentary lapse of faith had resulted in Ishmael, whose ancestors forever haunted the people of Isaac and Jacob.

Would Alexander be tempted to such compromise should Cassandra never conceive? Would their marriage even survive should she prove barren?

Not that four months was long enough to be already worrying about barrenness. But neither Alexander nor Cassandra had been young when they married. And if to Cassandra each month that passed without conceiving was a sign of God's blessing, she knew how much disappointment this brought Alexander.

Cassandra told herself to focus on something else. She thought of the two others who rode just ahead on their horses. Elihu, her lifelong Egyptian friend, formerly named Demetrius, remained engaged in an intense but private discussion with Michael, the mysterious, handsome warrior.

Michael had been in charge of the forty Kharabu warriors who watched over the Christians at Pella like guardian angels. There had even been joking comments thrown about that some of the Kharabu actually were angels in disguise because of their seemingly unbeatable fighting skills.

Ever since Elihu had changed his name and announced his calling as a prophet at Cassandra's wedding, he had become a different man, bent on a mission to get to Jerusalem to join Moshe, the old prophet. He believed that their calling was to be Yahweh's Two Witnesses to the Jews in fulfillment of the Apocalypse. Michael seemed particularly protective of Elihu and often spoke in secret with him for hours.

Cassandra's gaze returned to the world around her. They were on a well-worn road along the Jordan. The vegetation was lush, the rushing Jordan river to their left, the Dead Sea just ahead, and the mountain pass to their right that would lead them the final twenty miles to the holy city. They would pass Jericho before tackling the hills of Judea.

We should be stopping any moment, she told herself as they turned onto the western road to Jerusalem. She again adjusted her seat on the horse, her back stiff and haunches aching. She considered the pain to be training for much worse to come.

At least it was spring, and the cold had thawed. At least they were protected by Michael, the mightiest warrior she had ever seen in her life. And she had been around the entire world.

She noticed Michael stop talking to Elihu. They had halted. Cassandra and Alexander caught up with them.

She asked, "What is wrong?"

Michael quietly gestured with his hand to stop. "We have company."

Cassandra saw three men on horses blocking the road up ahead. Dressed in weather-beaten nomadic clothes, they were unshaven, filthy, and carried swords in their hands.

"Brigands," she muttered.

Alexander drew protectively closer to her.

Cassandra looked at Michael to see what he would do. She remained more curious than frightened, since whoever these bad men were, they had no idea of the warrior they were facing down.

The three brigands trotted forward to meet Michael and Elihu.

"We want no trouble," Michael said to the strangers.

Cassandra smiled to herself. *What a smart actor Michael is. Play fearful. Draw the victims in.*

She glanced at Alexander, who returned her smile.

"Well then, this should go rather smoothly," said the leader, a deep-throated man with a scarred-up face and an eye bandage. *Experienced in battle. But not as skilled as Kharabu.*

It was at that moment that Cassandra heard a loud rustling as the brush on both sides of the road exploded. The additional bandits who had been hidden there rushed forward, about twenty of them, circling the company of four. They were all gruff-looking, undernourished but with meanness in their eyes.

Several of them had bows pointed at Michael.

"What's in the carts?" demanded the ugly leader.

"Medical supplies for the sick of Jerusalem," said Michael.

"Well, imagine our luck. We just happen to be sick ourselves."

Several bandits came up to the two carts and led the donkeys swiftly away onto another path that led north, perhaps to the brigands' camp.

"Thank you for your generosity," said the leader.

A half-dozen bandits drew close to Michael. They must have intuited that he was the biggest threat to their intentions.

Cassandra became confused. *Why isn't Michael stopping them? Is it fear for our safety? Michael could take care of those foolish six men surrounding him, but by then, Alexander and I would be dead or taken captive. He must be waiting for the right moment.*

She thought she would help with her verbal skills, but before she could speak up, Elihu beat her to the punch, "We are Jews like you."

The leader looked at Elihu with surprise. The young prophet added, "Why do you rob your own people, the poor? The Zealots and Sicarii fight the rich ruling class, Greeks are killing Jews, and Rome is coming to kill us all. Yet you rob innocent, defenseless fellow Jews."

Well, he has suffered no delay in exercising his prophetic gift, Cassandra thought.

The one-eyed leader laughed. He looked straight at Michael and said, "I don't think you are so innocent or defenseless."

Elihu replied, "The Son of Man is coming in his Father's glory with his angels, and he will reward each person according to what they have done."[3]

Cassandra felt a chill of fear. Had Elihu gone too far? Had he just made it more difficult for Michael to take their assailants by surprise? *Let us hope God will back him up with deliverance.*

The leader became deadly serious. "We are hungry. We do not care for your religious scruples. But I see you are trouble for us after all."

He nodded to the men surrounding Michael. One of them swung a rope lasso around the warrior's torso and pulled him to the ground with a thud. Immediately the others kicked and pummeled him with clubs.

Cassandra froze in fear. Why was Michael doing nothing? She could hear him grunting in pain beneath the beating. She couldn't watch.

The only thing she could conclude was that there were simply too many of them for Michael to vanquish.

But if Elihu was Yahweh's prophet, why wasn't God saving them?

She wondered if Elihu would temporarily ignore his vow of putting down the sword, pick it up, and join Michael in self-defense.

But Elihu didn't move.

The other bandits then came up to Alexander and Elihu, pulling them from their horses to the ground. Would God not protect his own prophet?

Cassandra heard a grunt of interest and saw a bandit looking at her with hunger. She prayed, "Lord Jesus, help us."

But before the bandit could get his hands on her, a stone hit him in the head and dropped him to the ground. She heard the sound of rocks whizzing in the air. Several more bandits fell to the ground, others gripping their guts or legs in pain.

Slingshots. Someone was slinging with deadly accuracy.

Cassandra looked upward towards the ridge from which the rocks came and spotted the slingers, a dozen of them in Jewish garb.

Then a couple dozen more rushed from the bushes with swords. She recognized these young men in their peasant robes and haircuts. They were Essenes from Qumran.

The surprise had created chaos.

The bandits scrambled and fled down the path taken earlier by their stolen donkey and carts.

The ugly leader whistled, and the horsemen followed their comrades, disappearing into the darkening twilight.

Cassandra jumped off her horse and moved toward Michael to see if he was still alive.

She recognized the young monk standing over Michael. It was Aaron, the seventeen-year old Essene who she had met in Jerusalem a year ago. The young man had helped them find the home of the Christians when Moshe had been nearly beaten to death. He had helped them though he wasn't a Christian. And now he was helping them again.

Alexander had moved even more quickly than Cassandra, and by the time she reached Michael, her husband was kneeling beside the warrior to check his wounds. But already, Michael was sitting up, his hand raised to wave off Alexander's ministrations. Cassandra could see no blood, no bruises, no scratches. How could that be? She had seen the bandits thrashing him without restraint. He could not have shielded himself so effectively.

"Why did you not fight back?" she asked. "I don't understand. You are a mighty warrior. Some of us even joke that you are a guardian angel."

He said, "Angels won't always rescue you, you know. But that doesn't mean God isn't at work."

He looked up and grasped Aaron's wrist. Aaron helped him up. "Sometimes it's suffering that disarms the enemy. Distracts them from the real deliverance."

The analogy was of Christ. He had fooled the principalities and powers of this present darkness with his death on the cross. They had thought they'd

14

conquered him because they had been distracted by their expectations of a military messiah. They had not expected a suffering servant. They had expected an earthly kingdom, not a heavenly one. They'd expected power, not sacrifice. And in their distraction, Jesus had risen from the dead and ascended to heaven dragging those powers behind him in a triumphal procession of victory.

Aaron joined in. "Those fools were so focused on you as their prey, they didn't see us coming."

Elihu said, "I see your fellow monks have become quite accurate with the sling."

Aaron said, "We were trained by a good warrior, a good man." He was referring to Simon bar Giora, the fugitive brigand said to be hiding out at Masada in the south.

Cassandra said, "I thought Qumran was a peaceful community."

Aaron said, "We are divided. Some of us believe in the deliverance of angels and messiahs. Others believe we must fight alongside them."[4]

Cassandra was still stunned by Michael's lack of wounds. She asked him, "How is it that you are not damaged?"

Michael smiled. "Would you prefer I be?"

The young men around them laughed. She said, "No. I'm sorry. I should be grateful you are alive and safe. Forgive me."

She saw Alexander next to her and hugged him, clinging desperately to him.

Alexander asked, "What about the carts?"

"The carts are long gone," Michael responded. "It is night, and I am not going to leave you three to follow them to the basecamp of who knows how many more bandits."

Alexander said, "We will be destitute without the medical supplies."

"God will supply our needs," said Michael.

Cassandra stared at the warrior, still incredulous that he was unscathed by the beating he had received. He gave her a knowing wink, and she looked away. Maybe there was more to those angel jokes than she at first thought.

Aaron asked, "Are you on your way to Jerusalem?"

"Yes," said Elihu.

"May we accompany you? We have much to speak of."

Cassandra and the other three glanced at each other with approval.

"Why not?" said Elihu.

Much to speak of? thought Cassandra. *What did this sandy monk want to speak about?*

Michael said, "The night is upon us, but Jericho is a few miles hence. We can stay safely inside its walls for the night."

CHAPTER 3

Mount Carmel

Apollyon sat on the stone platform ruins of a high place, surrounded by his company of three-score Watchers. He was androgynous in appearance, neither male nor female, pale-skinned with long, scraggly hair. He chose this incarnation with deliberate irony. He was much stronger and more ruthless than he looked. He loved defying Yahweh's created order of separation between male and female, between beauty and ugliness. Such binary distinction was simply barbaric to Apollyon's refined sense of self-definition.

He looked out onto the Mediterranean Sea from the heights of Mount Carmel, deep in thought. This altar had been desecrated and out of use since the time of Jezebel centuries earlier. That incident had made a fool out of Ba'al and Asherah and left Apollyon bitter for ages. Elijah, a sole prophet of Yahweh, had contested with four hundred prophets of Ba'al and his battle maiden consort. The simpleton prophet had won by calling down fire from heaven. His priests then slaughtered the prophets of Ba'al and turned the waters of the river red with their blood.[1] This altar had become a symbol of shame and abandoned ever since. That was why Apollyon had chosen it.

For a comeback.

The faint sound of a distant canine howl, as if deep within the mountain, carried on the wind. It was a howl of pain. Something was amiss.

"Where are Poseidon and Serapis?" he demanded of his commanding generals, Semyaza and Azazel.

One of the gods said, "This is no time to walk the dog."

"I sent Horus and Artemis to find them earlier," Semyaza added.

Semyaza was the genius, or guardian spirit, of Flavius Vespasian, the commanding legate of Nero Caesar's legions. Azazel was the genius of Flavius Titus, son of Vespasian and second in command. Apollyon had

17

released them from the Abyss because they were the mightiest of the ancient ones bound at the Flood.[2]

His comeback would involve a glorious, overdue plan of revenge.

Vespasian was climbing this very mountain to consult with the oracle of Mount Carmel, not far from where they currently assembled. Apollyon wanted to have a strategy meeting with the gods before he used the oracle to communicate to the Roman legate.

"If those two Watchers delay my meeting with Vespasian," said Apollyon, "I'll gut them and make them eat their own feces."

The punishment was no idle threat. Watchers were divine. They could not die, but they were created beings with heavenly flesh. Heavenly flesh would heal supernaturally but not without suffering.[3]

This meeting with Vespasian was crucial to Apollyon's strategy to conquer the Promised Land. Apollyon was the Watcher of Rome, ruler of nations. And all those nations with their principalities and powers were subject to his authority as god of this world, the adversary of God, the satan.[4]

His problem was that the archangels had captured four of the Watchers who were over his Roman legions. These were Ares, the Greek war god over Macedonian Legion V; Ba'al, patron deity of Legion XII in Canaan; Ahura Mazda, Persian deity of the client kingdom of Commagene; and Hubal, the Arabian Watcher over the Nabatean allied forces.[5]

In response, Apollyon had captured the archangel Raphael and currently held him hostage. The angel was hidden and guarded a short distance away so that he could not listen in on their strategy. Apollyon had ordered the angel drawn and quartered, arms and legs cut off, so he could not escape. With his heavenly flesh, he could be put back together and healed—after they engaged in a hostage exchange.

That exchange was to happen somewhere in the north by the Euphrates River, as determined by their prince, Michael. It would be an exchange of one archangel for four gods. But Apollyon wanted to make sure that his negotiation team was ready and spiritually empowered.

"Where are the daughters of Allah?" demanded Apollyon.

Allat, Al-Uzza, and Manat stepped forward. The three Arabian goddesses wore full-body coverings so that only their eyes were visible. They looked like identical triplets.

"Where is the enemy captive?" he asked.

"A short distance away." When they spoke, the daughters of Allah spoke as one, three voices blending into a unity. "He is guarded by Zeus, Anat, Dagon, and Molech."

"Excellent. I want you and those four to be my chosen force to negotiate for the hostage exchange. You will also be responsible for the archangel."

They said, "Yes, my lord and god."

"But do not go directly to the Euphrates. I want you to travel with me throughout the land. I cannot face the full force of the heavenly host in Jerusalem until I get my Watchers back. But I can destroy the countryside in the meantime. And you can draw strength from the desolation to face the archangels."

"We gladly obey," said the daughters of Allah. "We will drink the blood of our enemies to receive their power."

The power of principalities lay in the idol worship of their followers and the consequences of their religion. The more sacrifice, the more war, the more bloodshed, rapine, and oppression, the more spiritual empowerment for the gods of the nations. Judea would soon be a wasteland of such ruination.

By the time Apollyon received his hostage princes back, he would be so strong he could sweep right down from the Euphrates and launch his final attack on the so-called holy city, that festering dunghill of Yahweh.

And how appropriate that would be. Not only was the Euphrates the northern-most boundary of the land promised by Yahweh to Abraham and Moses, but it was the direction from which Israel was usually attacked by her enemies. Assyria in the north. Babylon in the east. Greece to the west. All tended to invade Israel from its northern region, which made the Euphrates a common apocalyptic symbol of coming judgment used by the Hebrew prophets.[6] Couple this with the fact that Vespasian had several thousand Roman troops guarding the Euphrates river region, and Apollyon's invasion would beautifully fulfill that prophetic pattern with symbolic finality.

But he still needed the principalities of his legions to achieve victory in this Armageddon with Mount Zion, this battle of cosmic mountains.[7] And until he got them, he would not have the power he needed for total, overwhelming victory.

Horus, the falcon-headed Egyptian deity, and Artemis, huntress of Ephesus, arrived from their search for the missing gods. They were carrying Poseidon's trident and Serapis' scepter.

They bowed before Apollyon. Horus said, "My lord, we found these beside the carcass of Cerberus in a cave of the foothills."

Artemis added, "We believe that Poseidon and Serapis have been taken captive by the enemy."

Apollyon boiled with rage. But he spoke with a measured tempo. "That makes six. Those godlickers now have the generals of six of my legionary forces."

Four lost principalities were bad enough. Six was devastating to his plans. He hadn't seen it coming. The thought of hostage exchange had become so central to his thinking that he hadn't thought of the possibility of another kidnapping. He had been taken completely by surprise.

He shifted the blame. "None of you saw it coming. None of you were prepared. And now my six top generals are all held captive by the deplorable Yahweh and his archangel toadies."

Some of the gods trembled. They knew what was coming.

Apollyon grabbed the closest one to him, Artemis, by the fur around her neck. He spun around and flipped her to the ground. She landed on her back with a thud, the wind knocked out of her.

Apollyon jumped on top of the goddess and pounded her face with his fists, exclaiming with each hit.

"This..." SLAM.

"...is..." SMACK.

"Unacceptable." CRUNCH.

Blood gushed from Artemis' nose and mouth. She knew not to respond. She knew to accept her misfortune at being the master's target of frustration. She blacked out beneath the bombardment.

"I..." WHACK.

"...will..." SMASH.

"...not..." SLAM.

"...be..." CRASH.

"...mocked!" SPLATTER.

Apollyon stopped, his chest heaving for air. His face and hands dripped with Artemis' blood and gore. Her face and skull were a caved-in, bloody mass. The damage would take a long time to heal.

The gods had taken unconscious steps backward from the scene of violence. But Azazel and Semyaza looked at one another. This loss of control could actually be a benefit to their designs of power. Cool heads and calculated choices would be that which ultimately prevailed in the long War of the Seed—not unhinged rage.[8]

Apollyon wiped the blood covering his hands onto the goddess' tunic and stood.

"Somebody, clean this mess up and take care of her. I have a meeting with Vespasian."

CHAPTER 4

Vespasian knelt within the holy place a few hundred feet below the peak of Mount Carmel. It was a simple sanctuary and altar, no images of deity, with basic Phoenician architecture of marble pavement and pillars. His military entourage of fifty soldiers were encamped on the ridge just below.

His knees ached with almost sixty years of age. The added weight of his hearty girth made such moments even more unpleasant. He scratched his balding head and gave a slight belch from the wine he had consumed earlier. His self-made success in the Roman military lacked social graces, and he didn't have much use for sacred ceremony either unless it could help his strategy in the real world. He was a practical man.

The oracle, a gangly man named Basilides, had already sacrificed the general's goat and was inspecting the entrails. The slippery, mucus-lined intestines slithered through the priest's hands. He had a haruspex beside him for consultation—a priest who specialized in the art of divination by examining intestines.

Semyaza stood by his ward Vespasian. Apollyon took his place behind the oracle, and Azazel licked the blood of the sacrifice on the altar with moans of delight. The humans could not see or hear the gods who inhabited the unseen realm between heaven and earth unless the gods allowed it. In many cases, such as this one, they would possess the humans or whisper into the spirits of those they controlled. There was not as much need for glorious displays of power as in primeval days. This was a more modern, sophisticated world, where subtlety and nuance were more effective.[1]

Apollyon grasped Basilides' skull in his talons and squeezed. The oracle jerked, and his eyes turned up inside his head. He would now be a manipulated puppet.

The oracle's voice changed from its high-pitched softness to the deeper growling tone of his master. "General Vespasian, have you any prior omens of importance?"

22

The general didn't respond. He kept his head bowed as if deep in prayer or contemplation.

Then Apollyon heard the sound of a soft snore coming from the general's throat. The old Roman had fallen asleep on the oracle.

Basilides raised his voice. "General Vespasian!"

The general snorted, jerked his head awake, and looked up.

This time Basilides spoke impatiently. "Have you any prior omens of importance?"

Apollyon did not want to outright contradict any previous superstitious delusion the general might be under.

Vespasian cleared his throat and spoke. "When I was younger, I saw a mighty cypress tree fall to the earth. The next day a new one, just as tall and mighty, had grown in its place."

"How did your oracle interpret the omen?" Basilides asked.

"They said it was a reference to my own rise in power. But to be frank, I don't believe it. I have no desire for grandeur. I want to do my job and retire in Egypt with my mistress and plenty of leisure, food, and drink."

This was a weakness in Apollyon's plan for the house of Flavian. A man without political ambition was more difficult to control.

The general continued, "I considered the vision to be a reference to the imperial throne at the time. The fall of Tiberius and the rise of Caligula. Which did happen. My concern is not with political dynasty but with military success here and now. I want to know if there is any guidance from the god regarding my campaign of Judean subjugation."

Apollyon jerked Basilides' head around as if he were listening to the god in council. The oracle spoke. "Whatever you are planning, Vespasian, whether to build a house or enlarge your holdings or increase the number of your slaves, the god grants you a mighty home, limitless bounds, and a multitude of men."[2]

Apollyon saw Vespasian scrunch up his face over the vagueness of the oracle's pronouncement and shot the general's guardian spirit an impatient look. Vespasian opened his mouth to demand clarification but stopped when Semyaza whispered understanding into his ear.

But that still wasn't enough for the wise old general.

"I am so tired of ambiguous babbling that could mean anything," he said forcefully. "Give me something tangible. Something about my campaign in Judea."

Basilides jerked his head in attention again to unseen entities. "Do not descend upon the holy city of Jerusalem until you have devastated the rest of the land. Therein lies your strength."

And Apollyon's as well.

The oracle continued. "First take Galilee, then Samaria, before concluding with Judea and Jerusalem."

Vespasian lit up. "That is more like it. It's refreshing to get some practical advice for once."

Without waiting, Vespasian stood to his feet, growling from aching knees, and marched out of the holy place. Semyaza followed.

Apollyon shook his head with amusement. Perhaps he could use such impulsive lack of deliberation after all.

CHAPTER 5

Jericho

Alexander awoke as if nudged. He turned on his bed to find Cassandra missing. He had to take a moment to shake off his confusion and remember where he was. Jericho. They had rented a room in an inn that was inside the great wall surrounding the city. Michael and Elihu were in another room. The Essene monk warriors camped outside the walls.

But where was Cassandra? Alexander's heart beat with worry as he jumped up and lit an oil lamp. He knew the first place to look. He made his way with haste, praying for her safety.

He tiptoed through the tight hallways and up the wooden stairs that led to the roof. When he opened the latch and stepped up onto the brick platform, he was arrested by the sight before him.

Since the inn was embedded in the wall, he was now standing on the parapet overlooking the city. Hundreds of acres of homes and businesses were built close upon one another, including half a dozen Herodian palaces and gardens. Most of the city was dark, but flickering lights and the sounds of celebration and revelry indicated pockets of night life. This was the great city Joshua had conquered first upon arriving in the Promised Land. Its walls had since been rebuilt, though not with their previous grandeur.

A lowly harlot, Rahab had hidden the Jewish spies from the authorities so they could report successfully to their armies. A woman of ill repute, one of the cursed Canaanites, she had been declared righteous by her simple act of faith. That faith would become a signpost of the Gospel itself, and that harlot would be transformed into a bride in the lineage of Christ.

How tragic that Israel had now become a harlot and Jerusalem a Jericho whose walls were about to fall to the earth with the seven trumpets of God.

The sound of soft crying spun him around to the wall's edge. He saw Cassandra facing the darkness of the wilderness outside the walls, wrapped in a blanket from their bed. She was weeping with her head in her hands.

He ran to her and held her in his arms.

She responded by burying her head into his shoulder.

He stayed silent for a moment, just holding her tightly with assurance.

Finally, he whispered, "My love, what grieves you?"

She took a minute to calm herself and wipe her eyes and nose before answering him. "I am overwhelmed with guilt."

"Guilt? For our disagreement last night? Believe me, I have forgotten it already. And it was as much my blame as yours, no, more. I should not have kept pushing you about having a child."

"It is not wrong for you to want children, Alex."

"It is not up to me or you to determine when you will conceive, but our heavenly Father, who determines for each of us our day of birth."

"And death," Cassandra added darkly.

They had discussed this often. Cassandra had not wanted to get married because the apostle Paul had warned them of the present distress. She had wanted to give undistracted devotion to the Gospel.[1] But she had agreed to marry Alexander and help him bring medical care and the message of redemption to Jerusalem. They were almost certainly facing death together. But they were doing so for the kingdom of God.

Still, did their dangerous situation rule out having a family? Alexander had told Cassandra he was willing to trust God for their protection if God chose to bless them with a child. And he could readily admit that like most men he wanted the legacy of sons and daughters.

Holding his wife closer, he said softly, "If it is God's will that we not have children, then his will be done."

Cassandra shook her head with closed eyes. "That is not why I weep."

"Why then?"

"I feel guilty because I am glad that I have not conceived. Because I would be relieved if we never have children."

"But that is only because you don't want to see them suffer," Alexander responded.

She replied, "Yes. But I know that your heart's desire is to have a family to see them live for Christ. So if God continues to grant my desire, my gain would mean your loss. And that is why my heart is broken. I want your loss to be my loss, your gain to be my gain."

She paused, holding back another flood of tears. "Your happiness to be my happiness."

He held her tighter. "Oh, Cassie," he moaned.

She whispered, "I feel I have betrayed you."

"You have not betrayed me. Quite the opposite. Apparently, God agrees with your sentiments, or he would have placed a child within you. He still might, you know. Four months is not a long wait to conceive. Let us not forget the wives of the great patriarchs." He paused, calling them to mind. "Sarah, Rebekah, Rachel..."

Cassandra had stopped crying, though her body still trembled slightly against his. Alexander was not sure the logic of his argument was getting through to her. He continued, "I won't deny that I want a family. But if God does not give us one, then that is his way of telling us he wants us devoted fully to the work of the Kingdom, to be free to minister with undivided attention to the suffering of Jerusalem."

Now he felt his own eyes tearing up. Cassandra looked up at him, and he knew she could see through his façade. He had said what he wanted to be true. But it was not how he felt. He too had to deny his feelings for his faith.

They looked out into the dark wilderness surrounding the walls outside. A wolf howled in the distance. A brisk night wind blew over them, penetrating them to their bones with a chill.

"I'm cold," said Alexander.

Cassandra opened her blanket to him. He grabbed the open corner, and snuggled in next to her, his arm around her, trying to warm her. They pulled the blanket closer and continued staring out at the night horizon, where the stars met the earth.

Alexander led in prayer.

CHAPTER 6

Jerusalem

Alexander looked up at the walls of Jerusalem as they approached the Essene Gate at the southwest end of the city. Alexander, Cassandra, Elihu and Michael had finished traveling the twenty miles from Jericho with the company of forty Essene monks, led by their young leader Aaron ben Hyam. Alexander found the wiry Aaron to be a fascinating mixture of both intellectual passion and religious zeal. But not of the Zealot or Sicarii kind. Those groups used a cause to justify their craven bloodlust. This young man seemed more driven by a genuine desire for holiness, misguided as it was.

Alexander and Cassandra had talked the entire way with Aaron, who had peppered them with questions about their faith and about the death, resurrection, and ascension of Jesus to the right hand of God. Michael and Elihu stayed out of it, often engaging in their own private conversation.

The monk had a difficult time accepting the Gospel because he had been indoctrinated to believe that his Qumran community was the remnant of believers in the last days. Jesus had said the remnant were his Jewish followers.

It was amazing how similar some of the beliefs of the Essene community were to those of the Christian community. The sectarian monks of the little commune isolated on the shores of the Dead Sea were so close to the kingdom of God and yet so far.

Like Christians, they saw the priesthood as corrupt and the temple defiled and deserving of judgment by Yahweh.[1] Like Christians, they saw the Roman empire as the culminating fulfillment of Daniel's prophecies of the "times of the Gentiles." Babylon, Medo-Persia, Greece, and now Rome were the four Gentile kingdoms that dominated the land since Daniel's days. But those "times of the Gentiles" would be transcended and overthrown by the arrival of the kingdom of God in Messiah.[2]

The Essenes called Romans "Kittim." They believed that when the Kittim came against Israel, the War of the Sons of Light against the Sons of Darkness would break out. This great final battle would end in Messiah returning to rescue his chosen ones, the Essenes, and purify the temple anew.[3]

With the help of Cassandra, Alexander sought to explain to Aaron that Messiah had already come and had atoned for sin. It was not an earthly kingdom that he had brought but a heavenly one. And the remnant of true Israel was those who had faith in Jesus, not those of a physical lineage. They were in the last days of the old covenant. The new covenant had been inaugurated with Messiah, but despite the believing remnant, the nation as a whole had rejected him and was thus about to be judged.

It wasn't until Alexander found a point of common ground that he felt he had made any headway with this young warrior monk. That point of connection was John the Baptizer.

Aaron had asked them about John because he knew the prophet had been an Essene like Aaron but had been killed years before Aaron was born. He had only heard that the Baptizer was a heretic who left the community and was cut off from their fellowship because of his radical claims regarding the Nazarene Jesus. Though the Qumran community did have their own sectarian writings, they nonetheless followed Torah as the Word of God, so Alexander had some hope that he might open Aaron's eyes from the Scriptures.

He said, "You are familiar with Isaiah the prophet's 'voice of one crying in the wilderness, "Prepare the way of Yahweh; make his paths straight"'?"[4]

"Yes. We believe that the voice is our community at Qumran."[5]

"But the prophet speaks of one individual, not a community," explained Cassandra. "And with this, the words of the prophet Malachi agree. 'Behold, I send my messenger, Elijah the prophet, before the great and terrible Day of the Lord comes.'"[6]

Aaron asked, "Are you saying the Baptizer was Elijah come back in disguise? Do you believe that Elijah's soul transmigrated into John's body?"

The Greeks believed that after death souls could travel into new bodies at birth through reincarnation.[7]

"No," said Alexander. "John was Elijah to come *in spirit and power*.[8] But that day of the Lord is now at hand. The axe is laid to the root of the trees. The baptism of unquenchable fire has arrived.[9] Yahweh will suddenly come to his temple. And he will use the abomination of Rome as his instrument of desolation. That will be the great and terrible Day of the Lord that the prophets foretold. Isaiah's Day of Vengeance."[10]

The four Christians and their Essene companions approached the gate and got off their horses amidst a slew of residents walking into the city.

Aaron said, "You use the language of Daniel's seventy sevens and the abomination of desolation."[11]

"I do," said Alexander. "Do not your own calculations of Daniel's seventy sevens arrive at this very generation?"

"Yes," said Aaron. "From the decree of Artaxerxes to this era is the four hundred and ninety years as predicted.[12] That is why we look for Daniel's coming Prince to finish the transgression of Israel, to put an end to sin, and to atone for iniquity, to bring in everlasting righteousness, to seal both vision and prophet, and to be anointed Messiah."[13]

"You left out the key to the prophecy," said Alexander. "Daniel said that those accomplishments would occur when Messiah was 'cut off.' That is not military language, that is the liturgical language of sacrifice. And that is precisely what happened when Jesus was sacrificed on the cross for our sins. He took our sin upon him, and was therefore cut off from the Father. Because Jesus was the very Son of God, that act finished the transgression of Israel. His once for all sacrifice put an end to sin, atoned for iniquity and brought in the kingdom of God in everlasting righteousness. The new covenant in Christ's blood seals up vision and prophecy. Jesus has been anointed as Messiah. The only thing left in the prophecy is the coming desolation of the city and sanctuary as confirmation of that end."[14]

Aaron's face twisted with silent disapproval. Alexander was used to it. Jews could simply not accept the Suffering Servant over their misconstrued anticipation of an earthly conqueror. They sought power and missed grace.

The group passed through the Essene Gate and made their way to Boaz's home in the Essene quarter, just a couple blocks away. Boaz was the church elder who had led the Christians to Pella over a year ago. His home had been the center of congregation for them. They had received Boaz's blessing to reside there and engage in ministry to the city.

Residents filled the streets in their everyday pursuits of going to work and the market, living their lives as if nothing had changed, completely unaware or unconcerned with the storm cloud that darkened the spiritual skies above them. Alexander was reminded of Jesus's prediction,

> *For as were the days of Noah, so will be the coming of the Son of Man. For as in those days before the flood they were eating and drinking, marrying and giving in marriage, until the day when Noah entered the ark, and they were unaware until the flood came and swept them all away, so will be the coming of the Son of Man.*[15]

Alexander said, "Jesus told us this would all happen within his generation. Wars and rumors of wars, the abomination of desolation, and the great tribulation would mark the end of the age with his *parousia* on the clouds of heaven to destroy both city and temple."

They had earlier discussed the *parousia* or "presence" of the Son of Man on the clouds. Alexander knew the scribal monk was fully conversant in the symbolic language of Yahweh's cloud comings in the Law and the Prophets. It was used whenever Yahweh came in judgment upon a city, people, or nation. This destruction of Jerusalem and its temple would be the sign and vindication of Jesus's claim to be Messiah at the right hand of God, as Daniel had predicted; the very claim the Jews had rejected.[16]

Aaron frowned. "It all comes down then to trusting the words of Jesus as your Messiah."

"Yes," said Alexander. "And that is why Jesus performed miracles: to show his people he was the promised Messiah for the restoration of Israel."

Aaron looked agitated. He said, "For as many as our similarities of belief, our differences lead me to see this Jesus of yours as a blasphemer. You speak of restoration, but then you say your messiah is coming to destroy. We Essenes believe there are two messiahs, one a king like David, the other a high priest like Aaron.[17] They are coming to purify the temple and restore Israel to its rightful priesthood, the sons of Zadok."[18]

"Aaron, the new covenant in Jesus *is* the restoration of Israel," Cassandra joined in, "as a heavenly kingdom in a heavenly Jerusalem on a heavenly Mount Zion with a heavenly temple."

Cassandra had been well-educated in the Scriptures, having spent much of her young Christian life around the prince of preachers, Paul the apostle. Alexander could see that the monk did not have much patience for her. He rarely looked at her when she spoke, and his face showed displeasure when he did.

Cassandra was too intent on her point to notice. "Torah and all its earthly elements of covenant, temple, and land are but a shadow of the true temple in heaven and the new covenant that has arrived in Messiah. Torah can never save us. The earthly priesthood with its shedding of blood could never perfect us. Are not the priests of both Aaron and Zadok human and in need of constant atonement themselves?"[19]

"Yes," grumbled Aaron. Alexander could see he was getting more restless and disturbed. The Holy Spirit was no doubt working on Aaron, but so was his own male pride.

Alexander was proud of his wife's boldness for the Gospel.

She continued, "Jesus is a perfect high priest, without sin, who has entered once for all into the heavenly holy places, not by means of the blood of animals but by means of his own blood. And that secured an eternal redemption. But the way into that true holy place in the heavens is not yet opened as long as the earthly holy place is still standing."[20]

Aaron mumbled out another moan of disagreement.

But Cassandra was not finished. "The earthly temple in Jerusalem is symbolic of the present age. But Messiah appeared once for all at the end of the ages to put away sin by the sacrifice of himself. The old covenant and its temple are obsolete. They are about to vanish away."[21]

"Enough," Aaron hissed. "I am about to vanish away if you do not stop talking, woman."

Alexander saw Cassandra freeze with embarrassment. She looked to Alexander for guidance. He gave her a shrug.

Aaron said to Alexander, "Is this how you Christians let your women behave?"

"I find it refreshing," said Alexander with a sly smile. "Wisdom from the weaker sex." He saw Aaron sigh and roll his eyes at the friendly jab.

Cassandra took the high road. "I am sorry, Aaron, if I have offended you or spoken too much. It is one of my flaws."

Aaron remained quiet and red-faced.

Alexander was still smiling. He said to Cassandra, "Like Jesus used to say, 'For him who has ears to hear, let him hear.' I think Aaron's monkish ears are just a little too sensitive to hear right now, my dear."

Alexander detected the slightest upward turn of Aaron's lip. A good sense of humor could be disarming.

Michael interrupted their banter. "Here we are."

They stopped in the street before Boaz's residence. But it was not abandoned. It was very much lived-in and taken care of. They saw servants leaving the front door on their way to market. Others could be seen in the windows.

Alexander stood beside Elihu and Michael, equally confused.

Michael grabbed the attention of one of the servants passing by, a chubby cheerful-looking young man. "Excuse me, friend. Who resides at this estate? Who is your master?"

"It is owned by Jacob ben Mordecai," the young man responded before continuing on his way.

Alexander swallowed.

Cassandra said what everyone was thinking. "That serpent. He betrayed Boaz and the congregation with his false teaching, and now he confiscates Boaz's home and wealth."

Jacob ben Mordecai had been the leader of the faction within the Jerusalem congregation that sought to place Christian believers under Torah. They had demanded that Gentile believers become circumcised and obey Jewish dietary restrictions and sabbaths. They called themselves the party of the circumcision. Cassandra, in her fiery quotation of the apostle Paul, called them the party of mutilation.[22]

The "mutilators" had also rejected the Apocalypse and the prediction of the temple's destruction, arguing that God would not destroy his holy temple but protect it. They wanted the messianic age to come while trying to hold onto the passing age. Like the Essenes, they supported the continuation of what had become obsolete. Like a dog returning to its vomit, they returned to the *stoicheia*, or elementary principles of a dead covenant. They were apostates who had tasted the heavenly gift, shared in the Holy Spirit and the powers of the messianic age, but had fallen away. They had crucified Christ all over again.[23]

Alexander sighed with frustration. "We have lost all our medical supplies to the bandits. Now we have lost our home base to the apostates. We have nothing."

"Where will we go?" Cassandra asked.

Elihu calmly looked to his Kharabu warrior. "I guess we'll have to trust Yahweh completely for everything."

"Follow me," said Michael. "It gets worse."

CHAPTER 7

Ptolemais
Coast of Palestine

Berenice and Agrippa stood at the top of the marble steps with a handful of servants and guards. Their palace in the city of Ptolemais was one of the smallest Herodian residences in the land, and it greatly displeased the princess. Her brother annoyed her with his lack of concern for royal comforts. Their Herodian family were Jewish converts who ruled Judea. Agrippa was therefore focused on their political influence with Rome as they were about to have their entire world torched and trampled by imperial force.

Berenice cared for that as well. But she reasoned that should not force the siblings into an insufferable austerity that deprived them of such necessities as proper bath houses, aged wine, and personal attendants. Why could they not achieve both political *and* economic ambitions?

At the foot of the stairs, General Flavius Titus arrived on horseback, accompanied by a dozen or so Roman tribunes over the legions. After an absence of several months, he had recently arrived at Ptolemais with Legion XV, traveling overland from their base in Alexandria, Egypt. He had overseen their encampment just outside the city and was now being received by the Herods.

Berenice could feel her insides quiver at the sight of the commanding Roman general, her lover. He looked so handsome, so strong and stately in his imperial uniform. His firm square jaw and steely blue eyes, his dark cropped hair and tight, muscular body. He ascended the steps like a mighty male lion might approach its den, his tribunes submissively behind him.

When his eyes locked on Berenice, she almost fainted. Her pulse increased, and her breathing became shallow. She was thirty-nine years old to his twenty-eight. But her concern of their age difference vanished in the animal hunger of his eyes.

As Titus arrived at the top of the steps, the servants bowed. The guards and the Herods saluted with arms straight out and open palm to the ground. Berenice felt her eyes clouded with tears of joy.

Agrippa greeted him. "General Titus, we are proud to host your honor in our humble palace of…"

Ignoring Agrippa, Titus passed him right by and grabbed Berenice's arm. It was a strong grip, determined.

As he pulled her along into the palace, he spoke backward to Agrippa, "Strategic assembly with Imperial Legate Vespasian will be in two hours at the legionary encampment. I will escort the princess."

Titus kept walking. Berenice felt his forceful pull as if it were a prelude to punishment. It was all she could do to keep up with his pace. She felt light-headed.

"Where is the bath?" Titus asked.

"Right here." Berenice pointed to the archway on the left. He pulled her in, and they moved through a small hallway that opened up into the bath, a steaming twenty-foot square pool surrounded by stone columns.

She said, "I'm afraid it's not very luxurious. The servants barely keep it cle…."

He jerked her to him and kissed her forcefully. She submitted and drank in his passion.

He groped her. Began pulling off her robe.

She resisted, saying shortly, "You're filthy. At least control yourself enough to take a bath first."

He stopped with a look of surprise. He stunk of sweat and sand and dirt. There was an earthy manliness about it. Still, she preferred a clean lover.

She wasn't sure he was willing at this point. Then he laughed. "You're right. I have missed you so."

"And I you."

He said, "Our time apart has only enflamed my lust for you." He grabbed her long thick raven black hair in his hands with sensual worship. "I cannot tell you the pain of longing I endured in that arid stink hole of Alexandria."

His fingers traced the pale smooth surface of her cheek and chin. "Just to see you again. To touch you. Taste you. No woman of Egypt could satisfy my hunger."

36

Berenice frowned. "I prefer not to hear about your whores, thank you."

Titus smiled. "You are the woman of my desire."

"And you are the man of my every dream."

"You are the only woman I have ever accommodated."

"Good," she said with a smile.

Berenice turned serious. "I am your complete and utter slave."

"Good," he repeated and pulled her over to the bath. He pushed her into the water, fully clothed, and jumped in beside her.

She came up laughing, pulling her soaked hair away from her face, her tunic floating to the top of the water.

He grabbed her and pushed her against the pool's edge. She could barely move. She lost her breath again. She loved his aggression, his power, his desperation.

He was under her control.

He pushed against her hard and kissed her madly.

They tore at each other's clothes and drowned in each other's desire.

•••••

"What is your Jewish experience as a Herod?" asked Titus.

Berenice rolled over in the silk sheets on the bed of her private chambers. They had moved from the pool to the bedroom through one of the private hallways and had spent the last hour exploring their delayed intimacy.

Titus had put his tunic back on and was strapping up his sandals. Servants had cleaned their clothes. It was time for him to meet with Vespasian, his father and legate of the imperial Judean campaign.

"Why do you ask?" she responded to him.

He paused ever so slightly. It was enough for Berenice to know that what followed was not the honest truth but calculated agenda.

"I want to understand the Jewish mindset. So I can minimize the casualties and damage in this war."

A half-truth. She suspected he was searching out their weaknesses.

She said, "Ours is a life of peculiar difficulty. Though we Herods are converts to Judaism, we are not accepted by our brethren."

"Why not?" Titus finished strapping his sandals. He stood up.

"Because we are Idumean, or Edomites. We are from the seedline of Esau, Jacob's brother."

He scowled. "Is that not the line of Abraham, your Jewish forefather?"

"Yes. But Yahweh chose Jacob as his beloved seedline for Messiah. Esau, he hated. Thus the perpetual antagonism between our peoples."

"Despite your conversion to Judaism?" Picking up his leather cuirass, Titus slipped it on, tightening its laces.

Berenice smirked. "Yahweh's people are not as quick to forgive as is Yahweh. Besides, the idolatrous devotion to Rome that marked Herod the Great's legacy is a monument I am afraid we will never be able to hide. Herodian architecture throughout Israel is Greek and a permanent reminder of that pagan betrayal."

"Like this palace we made love in?"

Berenice hunched a bare shoulder. "You want to understand the Jewish mindset? The Jewish mind is governed by exclusivity and separation. Covenant. The Roman mind is governed by inclusivity and expansion. Empire." She paused for a second. "It is in its simplest form the rule of God versus the rule of Caesar."

Titus looked confused. "But Caesar *is* a god."

"Yahweh is *the* God."

He huffed. "That is why so many of you are willing to die instead of surrender. Because to submit to Caesar is to deny Yahweh." He grabbed his red general's robe and draped it over his back, tying the laces.

Berenice stared sadly into the distance. "And to incur Yahweh's eternal wrath."

Titus stared at her, honestly trying to understand. "Then why do you, princess of Judea, seek to unite what can apparently never be united? Does that not torment your soul?"

Her eyes widened with surprise at his brazen words. He was obviously referring to their amorous liaison. His words reminded her of a similar challenge made by another secret lover so many years ago. A lover she could not forget. Simon bar Giora. She had hidden her love then as she was doing now. And she had lost Simon when he was betrayed and had escaped into the desert wilderness, a fugitive bandit.

She was a woman torn between two worlds. A world of faith and a world of power. Yes, she wanted both. Yes, the compromise tore her apart.

"No," she said. "I believe in love. Love unites, hate divides. I believe that through love we can overcome division and separation—and wrath."

"And God?" Titus added. "Can love overcome God?"

"God is love," she corrected.

"And what of his eternal wrath?" he challenged, buckling on his belt with sword and dagger.

Berenice didn't answer. She looked toward the open balcony, where she could see the sky. She was looking for something. An answer to his question? Or was it an answer to her own troubling doubts? She felt under a cloud of that wrath.

"Well, I must go," Titus announced, securing his belt and sword. He leaned over the bed and looked her in the eye. "You and I may have more in common than you think." He kissed her on the forehead and turned to leave.

"Titus," she called out.

He stopped and looked back at her.

"If you really want to minimize casualties and damage in this war, I suggest you prosecute it as if you were emperor, not Nero."

He gave her a thoughtful smile and left.

She looked down into the tangled sheets and cried.

"Dear sister," came a voice almost magically beside her.

She looked up.

Herod Agrippa, her handsome and privileged brother, the king of Judea, placed his hand softly on her shoulder. He stroked her hair. He had been spying on Berenice and Titus for the past hour from a secret compartment in the wall. Herods treasured spying and secrets. They had such secret places in all their palaces.

"You did well," he said. "I especially enjoyed your departing line about prosecuting the war as if he were emperor. That was superb. It appealed to his vanity and affirmed Herodian loyalty. Well done."

Berenice wasn't aware of such motives in her words. Or was she? Sometimes she thought that the House of Herod had crafted such an extensive web of lies to support their power and legacy that she could no longer discern the truth of her own motives.

"The goal is survival of the Herods, no matter what happens to Judea," Agrippa reminded her. "If the nation is reduced to ashes, we become the ones who get to rebuild—in our image. The Herodian dynasty becomes the destiny of Israel."

Berenice felt disgust. Yes, she wanted to survive. Yes, she sought favor with the Flavians. But there was something so craven about the way Agrippa expressed it that it made her sick to her stomach.

He pulled her hair out of her face. "And your sexuality excited me."

He kissed her. She let him, but she didn't respond. He looked at her questioningly. "Never forget, the love of family is the deepest of all."

She felt like throwing up.

He caressed her. "Let me prove it to you once again."

She pushed his groping hands away. "Not now."

Berenice slid to the other side of the bed to get up and get dressed. She felt filthy. Like a blood-stained warrior with the gore of her enemies upon her body. She wanted to bathe herself. To wash it away.

"You need to get to the war council," she told her brother, "if you want to represent Herodian interests in this war."

He raised his brow. "You're right. I love you, sister."

She was already on her way to the hallway that led to the private bath. She would scrub her body with self-loathing. A scrubbing she feared would not be sufficient to cleanse her from the contamination of her soul.

CHAPTER 8

Jerusalem

Cassandra looked around her. Death had come to Bezetha, the New City. Burnt-out ruins, refugee residents in tents, poverty, and hunger. This northern part of Jerusalem had been completely burned to the ground over a year ago by Syrian governor Cestius Gallus and had yet to be rebuilt.

By decree of Nero, Cestius had marched forty thousand Roman legionaries and auxiliaries from Antioch down to Jerusalem to crush the Jewish revolt that had begun years prior. He had razed the New City to the ground, trampled it underfoot with his forces, and besieged the northern walls of the temple. Then without warning, he had left just before he breeched the gates. No one had ever learned the reason for such inexplicable behavior. The temple had been saved and desolation diverted. But Cestius had left the New City a wasteland of smoldering ruins, empty and void like the chaos before creation.

The Jewish forces had chased Cestius back to Caesarea Maritima and through a miracle, they had decimated the legions and killed Cestius. It was a humiliation for the Romans so deep that it gave the Jews the very hope and courage they prayed for to finally stand up to the imperial beast that had enslaved them for generations.

Word spread that it was also the catalyst that inspired Caesar to send his highest generals with their mightiest forces from all the nations to return and seek vengeance upon this obscure little piece of land and her proud and foolish people.

Aaron and his company of Essenes had parted ways with Cassandra and her three traveling companions earlier. As she, Alexander, Elihu, and Michael walked through the streets amidst the rubble and debris, Cassandra gripped Alexander's hand tightly. Beggars, dilapidated make-shift residences, families trying to rebuild their homes were everywhere. It was like a garbage dump of the unclean, the misfits, and the forgotten. Was this where they were to set up

41

their residence and minister? There were so many in need. Her heart became overwhelmed.

Cassandra heard an aged but strong voice shout out, "Elihu, you young prophet wannabe! It's about time you got here!"

She knew that voice anywhere. Elihu returned the humor. "Moshe, you creaky old rabble-rousing troublemaker! I couldn't let you get all the suffering!"

Moshe bar Annas approached them from a small, lone tent near a dumping ground of rock and garbage. He was dressed in his signature tattered sackcloth with wild white hair and beard. Cassandra figured he must by now be near seventy, but he still seemed so robust and strong. And that hearty voice was created by Yahweh for a prophet.

Moshe and Elihu embraced with laughter. Moshe grasped wrists with Michael and said, "Good to see you, my warrior friend."

"And you as well," said Michael. They embraced.

Moshe said, "Though I suspect you won't be here long."

"I must return to Pella as soon as possible," said Michael.

Moshe had been a lone prophet named Joshua in Jerusalem, declaring her destruction, when Cassandra first met him years ago on the steps of the temple. He had been ignored and even beaten by temple guards for his proclamation of coming judgment. Back then he had seemed so crazy, his message so foolish. Now he was proven wise and his prediction in line with the Apocalypse.

Cassandra so respected his boldness and courage. She had much in common with the old man, but also some stark differences. Though she was quick to learn, she had in her past lacked his compassion for other people, especially those who had hurt her family and rejected her Messiah.

Like Elihu, Moshe had recently changed his name from Joshua to match his calling. They were to be the Two Witnesses of the Apocalypse. They represented the Law and the Prophets that were to witness to Israel's covenant unfaithfulness and to announce the sentence of punishment from Yahweh's heavenly court. They were also amusingly opposite in their appearance, Elihu a dark-skinned, young, brooding, handsome Egyptian and Moshe a light-skinned, wrinkly old man with a nimble step.

Moshe stopped and opened his arms to Cassandra. She smiled and ran to him, hugging him heartily. She heard him whisper, "My precious Cassandra. God bless you, my child."

Moshe saw Alexander and hugged him as well. Then he stood with a wry smile, gestured to the area around them, and said to the four of them, "Welcome to my home, the new Gehenna. It's a bit uncomfortable but tolerable for short visits."

They all smiled and chuckled.

"Oh, we're not visiting," said Alexander. "We're here to stay."

Moshe looked shocked.

Cassandra added, "We want to bring medical help and the Gospel. Although God has seen fit to take away all our medical supplies and any hope of a base for operations."

Moshe smiled. "His way of making us trust him completely."

Elihu said, "An ironic sense of humor, our Lord has."

Moshe sighed, then clapped his hands, looking to Elihu. "Well, I suppose it is time for the two of us to begin our ministry."

"Keep your humor," interrupted Michael. "The moment has not yet arrived."

The two prophets looked quizzically at the warrior. He pulled them aside to speak in private.

As Cassandra watched the three of them, she asked Alexander, "What do we do now, my love?"

"Like Moshe said, I suppose we will just have to wait on the Lord. Trust him completely."

Michael returned with the other two to speak to Alexander and Cassandra. "I am afraid this is where your paths will diverge. Elihu and Moshe have a special calling upon them by Yahweh."

"We can support them," protested Cassandra. "We must stick together."

"No," said Michael. "They will be drawing great hostility from the forces of evil. It will be too dangerous for you and those to whom you minister to be connected to them."

"But will not God protect us?" Alexander asked.

Michael said soberly, "God has promised to protect the Two Witnesses. But the Two Witnesses alone. If you are seen to be conspiring with them, you will be vulnerable."

"Well then," said Alexander, raising his hands out for embrace, "let us say our goodbyes and pray for God's will to be done."

"Amen," said Elihu, looking sadly at Cassandra. Their friendship had lasted since they were young adults in the city of Ephesus. Along with Alexander, they had faced death and torture together. Now she knew it was all going to change. The humor would be gone. And their world was going to end.

She teared up. The four of them exchanged holy kisses.

Cassandra felt that with each step they took, one more thing was taken from her and Alexander: provisions, protection, fellowship. It seemed as if hope was the only thing they had left. And that was not looking good either.

CHAPTER 9

Ptolemais

Titus approached Vespasian on horseback on a ridge overlooking the Roman encampment outside the city. Three legionary cavalry horsemen guarded the general at a safe distance.

Titus saw his father give him an annoyed glance. Vespasian said, "So good of you to find some time in your busy schedule of leisure to discuss such minor inconveniences as the Judean war."

Titus smirked. The old man with his bald head, gruff voice, and portly stature was like a curmudgeon in an Aristophanes comedy. Always griping and complaining, but with a touch of wit. Vespasian had never cared much for social propriety, which explained his lack of etiquette and nuance. He was a pragmatic man of simple tastes.

Titus had amusingly thought of his father as a plebeian who had been given magical power from the gods, yet had retained the plebeian temperament. Vespasian had earned the grudging respect of Nero Caesar through successful military exploits and brilliant strategy. But he was one of the few Roman ruling class Nero did not consider a threat because of Vespasian's lack of political ambition and transparent desire to retire to the good life. Titus knew that his father's simple epicurean exterior was partially calculated for just such a purpose. It wasn't fraudulent but simply exploited for Vespasian's benefit.

Titus said to his father, "I was confirming the loyalty of our most crucial client kingdom, the Herods."

"I'll bet you were. Are they compliant enough for your taste?"

"Oh, yes. Very much so."

"Good," said Vespasian. "There is nothing of more use against an enemy than the enemy's own leaders."

Father and son looked out upon the troops quartered below. Two miles square of legionary tents aligned in a grid. Compact and efficient. It was a city of soldiers, larger than its civilian host city.

"We have four legions and ten client kings arrayed with us. Sixty thousand troops," Vespasian said. "Governors in Asia Minor are providing supplies and financial support. Auxiliary forces from Syria, Emesa, Commagene, and Nabataea as well your most 'crucial of client kings," Herod."

Titus mused in agreement, "Mighty Rome, the empire of all nations, aligned against this one tiny little rebellious people."

Vespasian said, "Their delusion is unlike anything I have seen. Do they really believe they have a chance?"

Titus said, "They believe their god will rescue them. A savior will rise up and lead them to miraculous victory."

Vespasian gave his son an incredulous look. "Is there any news from that vigil prefect Nero sent to hunt down the conspirators and their propaganda?"

"His name is Lucius Aurelius Severus. He disappeared. But it's none of our concern."

"Tell Nero that," said Vespasian. Nero was known for being consumed with hunting down conspirators—and killing them.

"Father, we are crushing the entire land of Israel. No conspirators are going to survive."

Vespasian raised his brow. Good point.

Titus wasn't going to tell his father that he had a secret spy whom he was using to find those Christians. Nero had commissioned him and told him not to tell Vespasian. Titus hated being in that compromised position. He would eventually tell his father. But not yet.

Titus said, "The conspirators were Christians, a sect of the Jews. A pathetic minority."

Vespasian remembered, "The ones who caused the Great Fire of Rome?"

Titus affirmed the lie. "Yes. They've been all but wiped out by Nero's purge. Which you would know if you hadn't been asleep at the arena."

Vespasian countered, "Nero's obsessions bore me. But I do remember something about lions and human torches." He grinned.

Titus said, "Even the Jews persecute the Christians. They won't be around much longer."

Vespasian asked, "The Jews persecute their own?"

"A dispute over the identity of their Messiah."

"What a confused and petty lot."

Titus shrugged. "Too bad, though. According to their Christian propaganda, this Messiah was supposed to assassinate Nero."

Vespasian smiled at him. "So you have an affinity for these Christians, do you?"

Titus would have assassinated Nero himself if given the chance. He spit out, "They're all the same. One is the root and the other its branch. Neither will bow the knee to Caesar. Nothing but complete desolation will humble them."

Vespasian grunted in agreement. "So what policy does my legate-in-training recommend?"

"Scorched earth," said Titus. "Kill them all. Jews and Christians. Let their god distinguish them from one another."[1]

Vespasian narrowed his eyes with doubt. "Extreme measures have extreme consequences. For Romans too."

"Not if we move quickly before they can organize their opposition. They are currently engaged in a civil war that divides them to our advantage."

Vespasian mused, "They do us the favor of killing themselves. Which reduces our risk and cost."

Titus pushed back. "Or they solve their differences and unite against us, which increases our risk and cost."

Vespasian thought through the options. He said, "I consulted the oracle of Carmel."

"And?" Titus saw a concerned distant look in his father's face.

"Certain victory. And honors for the Flavian house."

"So," queried Titus, "an imperial ambition is not so unspeakable after all?"

Vespasian frowned. "You are too impatient, son. A good strategist does not rush ahead and does not trumpet his intentions."

"What are your intentions?" asked Titus.

"To take Galilee first, then Samaria, then Judea. And after the whole country is occupied, we besiege the capital. Jerusalem is a mighty walled city. But she will not last long with the entire land under our fist."

"Spoken like an emperor," said Titus with a grin. "Let us stomp this people and their 'holy land.'"

47

Vespasian said, "The war council will be waiting for us. Time to launch our campaign."

They kicked their horses and returned to camp with the guards in tow.

Vespasian added, "And hold your tongue with the emperor nonsense."

CHAPTER 10

The Watchers Apollyon, Semyaza, and Azazel stayed on the ridge to discuss their next step as their wards, Vespasian and Titus, descended into camp on their horses. But the spiritual powers never recognized the three cavalry guards that had accompanied the legate and his son.

Those guards shadowed Vespasian and Titus to camp, then continued on into the city on an apparent leave from duty. They were Uriel, Saraqael, and Remiel disguised in the legionary uniforms of the cavalry guards they had buried outside the camp. The Watchers would have noticed the angels in the unseen realm, so they'd concealed themselves behind earthly disguises.

Uriel, their captain, said, "The 42 months begin. The ten horns of the Beast have been given their authority. The nations will soon trample Jerusalem underfoot."

In the Apocalypse of Jesus Christ that the apostle John had written and distributed, the ten horns on the sea Beast symbolized the client kings of Rome, subjugated nations who were allowed a certain amount of self-governance in reward for their submission and allegiance to Caesar. When called to imperial duty in war, client kings and their armies would have the temporary authority and power of Caesar for the duration of the war.[1]

> And the ten horns that you saw are ten kings who have not yet
> received royal power, but they are to receive authority as kings for
> one hour, together with the beast.[2]

Once out of range of the camp, the angels changed their course and rode swiftly to Jerusalem.

Uriel thought through the symbolism of the seventeenth fragment of the Apocalypse and its imagery of a harlot riding the Beast with seven heads and ten horns. Everything was coming to pass, just as the apostle had written.

> This calls for a mind with wisdom: the seven heads are seven
> mountains on which the harlot is seated; they are also seven

*kings, five of whom have fallen, one is, the other has not yet come,
and when he does come he must remain only a little while.*[3]

The Beast was a composite symbol that sometimes represented the
individual Nero Caesar, sometimes the heavenly principality behind Nero, and
sometimes represented the collective empire.[4] The image of seven heads also had
a dual symbolism, pointing to both the seven mountains of Rome as well as the
seven kings, or Caesars, of Rome that marked out this time period of the end.

Uriel smiled to himself. Any chaos in the enemy's camp was a welcomed
event by the angel. The earthly rulers and the powers behind them would both
eventually reap judgment from the wickedness they sowed.[5] The Beast on
earth would end his reign soon and the spiritual Beast behind him that came
up from the Abyss would find his end in the Lake of Fire.

And then there was the harlot who rode the Beast.

*The harlot was arrayed in purple and scarlet, and adorned with
gold and jewels and pearls, holding in her hand a golden cup full
of abominations and the impurities of her sexual immorality. And
on her forehead was written a name of mystery: "Babylon the
great, mother of prostitutes and of the land's abominations." And I
saw the harlot, drunk with the blood of the saints, the blood of the
martyrs of Jesus...And in her was found the blood of prophets and
of saints, and of all who have been slain on the land."*[6]

The harlot that rode the sea Beast was a symbolic incarnation of the
religious ruling class of Judea. The priesthood had become spiritually
unfaithful to Yahweh like Hosea's harlot. Her adornment of purple, scarlet,
gold, and jewels were the very adornment of the priesthood. The name on her
forehead, "Babylon the great," was a mockery of the name of Yahweh on the
High Priesthood's forehead. And the blood she drank in her cup was the blood
of the Christians that the Jews had martyred, like human sacrifice.[7]

Jesus had repeated the very same judgment when he spoke to the scribes
and Pharisees, the Jewish leaders of his generation. He called them serpents,
a brood of vipers with the sentence of Gehenna upon them. And why? Because
in killing the Messiah, that same generation would have upon themselves the
guilt of the righteous bloodshed of all the previous prophets, wise men, and
scribes in the land of Israel.

It was for that reason that the temple was about to be destroyed, "not one stone left upon another." It had become a den of thieves.[8] The holy city Jerusalem had become an unholy Babylon, her religious leaders an unfaithful spiritual harlot, her people idol worshippers bearing the mark of the Beast for damnation. This coming war and its destruction would mark the end of the old covenant age and the death of its people.[9]

The instruments of that judgment were the Beast and its ten horns. Those horns, the client kings of Rome, came from surrounding nations and hated Israel's leaders. Along with the legions of Rome, they would "make the harlot desolate and naked and devour her flesh and burn her up with fire."[10]

Considering such irony always amused Uriel. Pagan nations hated Yahweh. They warred on God and his people. And like the king of Assyria, they thought in their hearts,

> *"By the strength of my hand I have done it,*
> *and by my wisdom, for I have understanding;*
> *I remove the boundaries of peoples, and plunder their treasures;*
> *I bring down those who sit on thrones.[11]*

In their pride, they were blind to the fact that they were simply the axe in Yahweh's hand, the rod of his anger. They could not see that the staff in their hands was actually Yahweh's fury.[12]

> *Shall the axe boast over him who hews with it,*
> *or the saw magnify itself against him who wields it?*
> *As if a rod should wield him who lifts it,*
> *or as if a staff should lift him who is not wood![13]*

God used pagan nations to accomplish his judgment on earth. He had put his sword into the hand of Nebuchadnezzar to perform his will. He had mustered the Medes and the Babylonians as his right hand. And now he would use the Romans as his armies against Israel.[14]

The ten horns made war on the Lamb, but they would never realize that God had put it into their hearts to carry out his purpose. Yahweh was the one who allowed them to fulfill his words. Yahweh was the one who gave them the power. All the while they were defying Yahweh, he was using them anyway.[15]

Yes, Yahweh's providential control of foolish evil was an amusing irony for Uriel.

When Yahweh used these pagan nations to judge people, cities, or other nations, he used the language of "coming on clouds." Yahweh "came on the clouds" to Egypt in the army of Assyria. He came on the clouds to Nineveh, Assyria, Egypt, and Israel in the armies of Babylon. Those pagan armies became God's own armies for his purpose.[16]

Now Jesus was coming on the clouds to Jerusalem in the armies of Rome and her client kings.[17] Uriel and his two companions had to get to the holy city as soon as possible.

> "But when you see Jerusalem surrounded by armies, then know that its desolation has come near. For these are days of vengeance, to fulfill all that is written. There will be great distress upon the land and wrath against this people. They will fall by the edge of the sword and be led captive among all nations, and Jerusalem will be trampled underfoot by the Gentiles, until the times of the Gentiles are fulfilled."
>
> Jesus in Luke 21:20–24
>
> "The nations will trample the holy city for forty-two months."
>
> Apocalypse 11:2

The 42 Months Begins

CHAPTER 11

"And I will grant authority to my two witnesses, and they will prophesy for 1,260 days. These are the two olive trees and the two lampstands that stand before the Lord of the land."

Apocalypse 11:2-4

Jerusalem
Passover
The 1260 Days Begins

Moshe's voice penetrated the crowds before the southern Huldah Gates of the temple. "Thus says the Lord in the sacred text of Leviticus: 'If you walk in my statutes and observe my commandments and do them, I will give peace in the land, and the sword shall not go through the land. Your enemies shall fall before you by the sword. I will make you fruitful and multiply you and confirm my covenant with you. I will walk among you and will be your God and you shall be my people. For I am Yahweh your God, who brought you out of the land of Egypt.'"[1]

Cassandra and Alexander scanned the crowd of several hundred people, praying for the Holy Spirit to move upon them. The time of their ministry had begun. It was Passover, and once again the city was full of pilgrims from the four winds of the land. Though the population of residents was normally around seventy thousand, there could be as many as six or seven hundred thousand packed into the city and surrounding area during a sacred festival like Passover. Space was at a premium both inside and outside the city, which helped to provide crowds for the Witnesses.

Cassandra spotted Aaron and his band of Essenes on the other side of the crowd, listening intently. She felt relieved to see him still considering their message.

Elihu stood with Moshe, both of them dressed in humble sackcloth. They traded off in their proclamations with theatrical synchronism and oratorical skill. Cassandra wondered how she and her husband would be of any help with God's Word in the face of such mighty Spirit-filled proclamation. She wondered if they had made a mistake of hubris in coming to Jerusalem. To think that they might be of assistance to the Two Witnesses of the Apocalypse of Jesus Christ. How proud and foolish could they be?

Elihu took over with a young presence and equally booming voice. He and Moshe were prophetic twins of the end of the age. "But if you will not listen to me and will not do all these commandments, if you spurn my statutes and break my covenant, says the Lord, then I will set my face against you, and you shall be struck before your enemies. I will visit you with panic and with plagues. I myself will strike you sevenfold for your sins. And I will bring a sword upon you, that shall execute vengeance for the covenant!"[2]

The scripture was well known to the listeners. It was Yahweh's covenant pronouncement of blessings and cursings in both Leviticus and Deuteronomy.[3] As Israel was entering into the Promised Land, Yahweh had enumerated a long list of blessings upon the people of Israel if they would but obey him. God would set them high above the nations of the earth. They would be blessed in every way: nationally, economically, agriculturally, and most of all, paternally. Their families would grow in abundance and inherit the land as he had promised.

But God had also given an equally long list of curses for disobeying him. The Israelites would be destroyed by their enemies, struck with plague and pestilence, famine, and cannibalism. Yahweh himself would scatter them among the nations. Instead of bringing them out of Egypt, the Lord would strike them with the plagues of Egypt. Israel would become the enemy of God.[4]

The book of Leviticus was important because in it Yahweh stated four times that he would strike Israel sevenfold for violating the covenant. Four times he repeated himself.[5]

Moshe now spoke to the crowd, "Hear, O Israel, your sevenfold judgment is at hand. Seven seals to be broken, seven trumpets to sound, seven thunders unheard, and seven bowls poured out."

There it was. The four repetitions of seven. The Levitical cursings were to follow.[6] The apostle John had explained the symbolism he had used in the

Apocalypse to describe the wrath of God to come. They were not chronological but cyclical. The seven seals, trumpets, thunders, and bowls were not going to follow one another continuously. They were simply four different perspectives of the same increasing intensity of wrath that would build up to the final desolation. The Apocalypse of Jesus Christ was a poetic and symbolic narrative of the whirlpool of chaos that would overtake the land of Israel and her inhabitants.[7]

The Two Witnesses now proclaimed the prophecy of the Apocalypse to their captive audience. Moshe said, "The first seal has been opened, the first trumpet has sounded, and the first bowl is poured out."

Elihu shouted out, "The first of the seven seals was opened, and I looked, and behold, a white horse! And its rider had a bow, and a crown was given to him, and he came out conquering and to conquer. The armies of Vespasian, Nero's golden-crowned legate, have already come to conquer the land of Israel."[8]

Moshe pronounced, "The first angel blew his trumpet, and there followed hail and fire mixed with blood, and these were thrown upon the land of Israel. The armies of Rome will raze a third of our land, crops, and cities. The trees will be cut down and the green grass burned up as they build machines for their war of scorched earth."[9]

Elihu spoke again. "And the first angel has poured out his bowl of wrath on the land of Israel. Harmful and painful sores will come upon you who bear the mark of the Beast and worship his image."[10]

"Blasphemy!" someone shouted in the crowd. "We are Jews! We do not worship the Roman Beast!" The crowd murmured in agreement.

Elihu responded, "All over the empire, Jews in the Diaspora host Caesar's imperial cult in their cities. A cult that demands obedience from our people. Every day, Jewish priests offer a sacrifice on behalf of Caesar in the holy temple of God. The high priesthood of this people is a corrupt harlot that rides the Beast of Rome. They have turned the altar of this temple into an altar of the Beast. And you who reject Jesus the Messiah are marked out for wrath!"[11]

Cassandra thought it made perfect sense. The temple and all its buying and selling were controlled by the ruling class that rejected Jesus as Messiah. Christians had been routinely kicked out of the temple and its practices from the very beginning of the ministry of the apostles. Just as Christians were marked out by the Holy Spirit for their faith in Jesus, Jews were marked out by the Beast for their loyalty to that priesthood and rejection of Jesus.[12]

The crowds did not agree with the Witnesses. They became hostile. Cassandra heard more shouts of "blasphemy" and saw rocks and food pelted at the preachers, who raised their arms to protect themselves from the missiles.

The crowd became more unruly with shouted invectives.

Cassandra wished that Michael had not left them to return to Pella. They could have used his protection. She worried that they might all be martyred at the very first sermon of the very first day of the beginning of their ministry.

CHAPTER 12

In the Hall of Unhewn Stone, located in the northwestern wall of the temple, an assembly of a lesser sanhedrin met to deliberate over their options in light of the coming war. There were at least thirty-five of them seated in the circular chamber of chairs around the high priest's throne.

Jacob ben Mordecai scratched his balding head as he listened to the acting high priest, Ananus ben Ananus, explain his strategy for dealing with the populace.

He's in his late sixties and too old for this position, thought Jacob.

In fact, Ananus had already been high priest many years ago. But he had remained a background influence of power after he was replaced. He had been manipulating the previous high priest who was recently murdered by the brigand John of Gischala. So Ananus quickly took the post in the interim until the greater sanhedrin could make the difficult choice of the next high priest.

That was a decision being conveniently put off, thought Jacob. And it was compounded by Ananus' appointment to commander-in-chief of the Jewish forces during the war.

Ananus was experienced and cunning, and Jacob needed his approval to be accepted into the sanhedrin. So Jacob was determined to ingratiate himself to the old man—in spite of the fact that he despised him.

"We are in a most difficult predicament," said Ananus. "As the ruling class, we favor the Herods and Roman sympathies. We tried to stop the revolt and avoid this war. Yet here we are. Forced to fight in a war we did not ask for, started by revolutionary Zealots and Sicarii whom we do not support, defending a people who increasingly do not support us."

The interim government had named ten generals over their forces to divide up the land for protection: Galilee, Samaria, Perea, Judea, and their surrounding territories.

One of the elders spoke up. "Can we not persuade a united surrender to Rome and avoid total destruction?"

"It is too late," said Jacob. "Our civil war has divided us so deeply that we cannot even unite against a common enemy, let alone surrender to them."

He was referring to the precarious reality that in cities around Israel, civil strife between Greeks and Jews had resulted in tens of thousands dead at the hands of their own countrymen. Some of the generals were not even in concert with each other. John of Gischala was in outright rebellion against the regional commander of Galilee, Joseph ben Matthias. The fanatical captain of the temple, Eleazar ben Simon, had violently taken over the inner temple, stopped the daily temple sacrifice for Caesar, and was calling for the end of days. The Roman eagle was sweeping down upon a divided nation in chaos.

"But we must try," said Ananus. "What other option is there?"

Jacob knew the old man's goal was to minimize both the conflict and the damage to maintain his own status and power. Jacob chose this moment to push his personal plan for promotion. "Your holiness. I own the rights to the quarries of Solomon near the north wall of the city. May I suggest we begin an immediate program of fortifying the city walls in anticipation of the inevitable."

Ananus looked angrily at him. "You would seek to exploit our disadvantage to your financial benefit?"

"With respect, no," said Jacob. "I am seeking to donate my business for free to the protection of our holy city and temple."

Ananus looked incredulous. The others appeared skeptical as well.

Jacob added, "I only ask in return that this sanhedrin approve me as a member of this august body of godly rulers."

Ananus looked to the others to see what they thought. Jacob had been lobbying to get on the sanhedrin for quite some time. He was not born into royalty. He had become wealthy as a merchant through his stone quarrying. Though the merchant class was not well respected, his devotion to a decade of building the temple had earned him grudging acceptance. But that had recently been completed, and work had dried up.

It was the perfect quid pro quo. Jacob glanced nervously at the others, trying to find some hope.

The court herald interrupted them. "High priest, a messenger from the Huldah Gates."

A sweaty temple guard stepped into the chamber, breathing heavily from running. "My lords, the Scourge is back. And he has a partner. They are both preaching judgment on the Huldah steps."

Jacob cursed. "The Scourge" was the derogatory nickname they had given the self-styled prophet Joshua years ago. He had preached the judgment of God upon the city for months on end. They had thought he was gone with the Christians after the siege. But it appeared he had only been waiting for the right time to start up again with his hateful rhetoric and seditious slander.

Ananus spoke to the temple captain, "You have a guard. Go stop them."

The temple captain had taken a dozen guards with him to the Huldah Gates at the southwest pavement of the temple. A large crowd had gathered. The guards pushed their way through the people, twenty deep. When they arrived on the pavement, they saw the two preachers on the stone steps pronouncing their message with zealous fervor.

The captain had orders to stop them immediately. But both he and all twelve of his heavily armed guards froze in position. They looked at one another with eyes of fright.

Behind the two Christians, they saw a company of seven huge warriors, each about eight feet tall and wearing strange-looking armor that was not of this earth. The giants stared down the captain and his men, just daring them to make a move.

Not one of the temple guards moved.

Down in the crowd, Cassandra knew what the temple guards were looking at because she saw them too. The angel Gabriel had visited her on her ship several years ago and had told her she would be given sight into the heavenly realm as a spiritual "sensitive." She had seen a Watcher in Ephesus, and now she could see these giant warriors behind the Two Witnesses.

She whispered to Alexander, "I see them. Seven guardians."

Alexander believed her. He couldn't see them. But he had learned to trust her in these things. He gave a slight grin of victory and returned to listening.

On the pavement, Moshe and Elihu continued preaching to the crowd below them. The hostility had died down. Moshe was explaining to them the meaning of the prophecies. "Jerusalem has become as Sodom and Babylon,

Israel as Egypt.[1] So Yahweh will release the plagues upon you as he did with the Egyptians. You have become unclean in his eyes, as those with leprosy."

Someone in the crowd yelled out, "When does the next seal open or the next trumpet sound?"

Moshe said, "The seals have all been opened in heaven. The trumpets have all been blown, the thunders all sounded, and the bowls all poured out. We simply announce to you their earthly fulfillment."

A female heckler yelled out, "What plagues? There are no plagues!"

Many in the crowd shouted agreement.

The woman stepped out into the open. She yelled, "You are false prophets!"

More shouts of agreement backed her up.

She was near Cassandra, who could see her hate-filled eyes as she threw her fist in the air and yelled obscenities at the two of them. Cassandra glimpsed the demon inside the woman as a spirit losing control.

Then the woman fainted.

Cassandra ran up to her and rolled her over to check her out.

She saw the woman had sores over her face.

Another woman in the crowd screamed. Everyone looked at her to see her pointing at a man, who was looking at his arms. They were covered with sores. She yelled, "Plague!"

Chaos ensued. People began running away. Others were screaming and fainting. Others yelled, "Leprosy!"

Cassandra tended to the fainted woman, now in a delirium. Alexander kneeled down to examine her.

One man screamed at the Witnesses, "What have you done to us? You cursed us!"

The crowds scattered in panic. The Two Witnesses had been given the authority to strike the land with plagues, and this was their first. Cassandra knew the others to come. They were described in the apocalypse. She looked around. Dozens had fallen to the ground in sickness and confusion, bodies covered in sores.

She turned to Alexander. "What should we do?"

"We have to quarantine them," Alexander responded.

"But where? We have nowhere to bring them." Casandra saw Alexander look up at the temple guards that were leaving the area.

"You stay here and do your best," he said. "I'll get us a refuge."

As her husband jumped up to follow the exiting temple guards, Cassandra raised her face in prayer. "Lord, help me! What am I supposed to do?"

She looked up to see if Aaron and the Essenes were still here.

They were gone.

CHAPTER 13

Jacob had explained to the sanhedrin how he would organize conscripted laborers to obtain the stone from his quarry to rebuild and reinforce the walls of Jerusalem. He needed two thousand workers around the clock and the authority of the sanhedrin to avoid government regulations in order to achieve his impossible goal before Rome arrived.

Ananus stared at him thoughtfully. "With the current unrest among the citizenry, I am not sure how well it would work to conscript two thousand laborers. But we can start by offering wages and see what we get."

Those wages will be very low, Jacob thought to himself. He asked Ananus, "Will I be considered for the sanhedrin?"

The high priest paused, and Jacob could see that Ananus knew Jacob had the upper hand. Since Herod's temple was finished four years ago, Jacob's quarry had plummeted in sales. He was not needed as before. And Ananus played that to his advantage.

"The truth is, if you do not offer your stone for the walls in such a dire time for our holy city, the populace may rise against you."

That jackal, thought Jacob. *He's right. And he's got me by the groin.*

But Jacob had dirty information he had been sitting on for just the right moment. This was that moment.

He said, "Indeed, my demise at the hands of revolutionaries would be most unfortunate, not merely for me, but for many in the ruling class whose bribery during the building of Herod's temple I have been at pains to keep from public notice."

Jacob saw the high priest's eyes open in shock. Ananus had been one of those who used bribery to extort large amounts of money for his own benefit from the building of the holy temple. Jacob wasn't sure if such implication would get him his appointment or get him killed. But these were desperate times.

The herald entered the chamber and announced, "My lords, the captain of the temple guard."

The captain and his twelve armed guards marched in and stood at attention before Ananus.

"Why are you interrupting our proceedings?" the high priest demanded. "This had better be important, Captain."

The captain said, "My lord, we went to the Huldah Gates to arrest the Christian preachers as you ordered."

"And?"

The captain cleared his throat. "When we got there, we saw they were protected by a company of seven guardians."

"So?" said Ananus. "Did you arrest them?"

The captain looked with dread at his fellow soldiers. He said to the high priest, "My lord, the guardians were eight feet tall, armed unlike anything I have ever seen in my life. It was like—heavenly armor."

A hush went over the crowd of sanhedrin. Everyone was listening closely now.

Finally, Ananus spoke. "What are you saying? That they were angels?"

The captain paused. Too frightened to respond audibly, he nodded his head yes.

"Don't be ridiculous, Captain."

"My lord, every one of my men was there with me, and they will testify. We all saw them."

Ananus looked at the other guards. "You all saw eight-foot-tall angels guarding the two Christian doomsayers?"

They all to a man said yes or nodded their heads in fear.

The captain added, "And then the doomsayers pronounced a plague on the people. And a plague broke out—as we stood in their midst."

The sanhedrin expressed shock amongst themselves. Some of them pulled away from the captain so as not to become unclean.

"They pronounced a plague and a plague broke out?" Ananus repeated with incredulity.

"Yes, my lord."

"And all of you also saw that as well?"

More nods of agreement and grunts of yes came from the guards.

"How many were struck?"

"Dozens. They were falling like flies when I left to come here."

Ananus considered the options. He was about to speak up and ask for the advice of the council, but he was interrupted.

"My lord, another messenger from the temple area." It was the herald again. This time Jacob saw a familiar face step forward from the entrance. It was Alexander, the physician with whom he'd had a theological battle when Jacob was still part of the Christian congregation in the city. The doctor clearly recognized Jacob as well.

A spring of hatred welled up within Jacob. He felt his face flush hotly. He had quarreled with the doctor over the obligation of Torah for Christian believers. This lawless creature and his loud-mouthed, arrogant woman—Cassandra was the whore's name—had condemned Jacob and spoken against the Law of God and his temple. They were one of the reasons why Jacob had rejected Jesus as Messiah and returned to Torah. And now Alexander dared return to Jerusalem?

"My lords," said the doctor, "my name is Alexander Maccabaeus. I am a physician and a Jew. I have an assistant, and we can help take care of the sick who have contracted the plague. But we need sufficient quarters to quarantine the victims."

"Take them out of the city!" someone shouted.

"I'm afraid that's not possible. As you know, with the Passover the entire countryside is filled with pilgrims. This has the possibility of spreading through the population if we do not quarantine immediately."

Ananus said, "You say dozens have been infected?"

"Most likely more."

"Where do you suggest we segregate them?"

"The hippodrome. We can secure it and close it off from the rest of the population."

Jacob complained, "But what about the games?"

Ananus said, "This is not the time for games. Our nation is at war." He paused, then added, "However, we cannot contaminate such a large facility for the sake of a few dozen or so victims."

The high priest turned back to Alexander. "What about the New City? Can you clear out some space in the ruins of that area?"

"I could do my best," said Alexander. "But we cannot contain the individuals without enclosed quarters."

Ananus said, "Do the best you can in the New City."

Alexander showed deep displeasure with the decision.

They were interrupted again, but this time by the arrival of several messengers. One of them said, "My lords, I come from the New City. There is an outbreak of plague up there. We don't know what it is."

Another two stepped forward, still breathing hard from their run. One of them said, "I come from the Upper city, and my companion is from the Lower City. There are many falling sick with plague in those quarters as well."

Jacob knew this was now serious. Had these two preachers become powerful sorcerers?

Ananus said to Alexander, "Doctor, you may secure the hippodrome for your quarantine. Move quickly before it infects any more of our people."

"Yes, my lord." Alexander left.

The entire sanhedrin murmured with scandal. This was not good.

Ananus said, "We need someone to oversee the quarantine for the sanhedrin and maintain security for our people. Who will take the office?"

The men looked around at each other. No one would volunteer. They were all too afraid of contamination.

Ananus turned angry. "We will not leave this assembly until someone volunteers."

Still no takers.

Then Jacob spoke out. "I will oversee the quarantine, my lord." Relief washed over every face in the room. Then the merchant added, "With your approval of one stipulation."

The look on Ananus' face indicated he knew exactly what stipulation that would be. Jacob felt a moment of power as he finished, "That I am appointed to the sanhedrin as a result of my duties."

The quiet did not stir.

Finally, Ananus said, "Agreed."

Jacob smiled with victory. He had won a place on the council.

Now he just had to survive his duty over the quarantine to be able to enjoy that power.

CHAPTER 14

The hippodrome was situated just south of the temple in the southern Tyropoeon Valley of Jerusalem. At about a thousand feet long and a hundred and fifty feet wide, it was a miniature version of Circus Maximus in Rome. It could hold over fifteen thousand spectators in its multilevel, oblong stone structure. Herod the Great had built it over eighty years ago in an attempt to bring Greco-Roman and Jewish cultures together through entertainment. The Jewish residents had first protested its building, but the universal appeal of chariot races and athletic games soon pacified the crowds.

With the declaration of quarantine on the hippodrome, there would be no more games for quite some time. The large stone center median of the oblong arena divided the racing track and worked as a natural barrier for partitioning off areas for hygiene.

A construction force of workers now boarded up the lower entrances on the exterior of the structure. Herodian guards watched over them as did Alexander. Cassandra watched Alexander tirelessly overseeing every aspect of the transformation of the arena. He was a man obsessed with his mission. He organized the planting of a large garden at the center of the arena to supplement the rations they would receive. He helped put up tents for the sick and worked out protocols for taking care of them.

Cassandra helped him by organizing within the arena several hundred people already stricken by the plague. The patients were allowed a certain number of tents, blankets, and other amenities for basic survival. These would not be sufficient if the plague spread, but they had to do their best with what they had been given. God would provide for their needs.

Fortunately, the hippodrome had a well-designed sewage system with flowing water that would ensure the quarantined victims would not end up living in their own waste.

The sun was now low on the horizon. The hundreds of sufferers had eaten a spare meal of bread and vegetables and were bedding down for the night. Cassandra helped a woman and her two children into their own sleeping area on the vast compact dirt of the arena floor. The children were coughing and could not stand without help. She placed blankets over their quivering forms and silently prayed to God for mercy upon them. It broke her heart to see poor victims as young as five and six with boils and sores all over their bodies.

She looked up to see more victims straggling into the arena through the sole unboarded entrance. She wondered how many would die of this leprous curse. Then she wondered how many would repent because of it.

But if this plague was a judgment of God for unrepentance, why did innocent children have to suffer for the sins of their fathers? Was it only unbelievers who could be stricken? Could she and Alexander get the disease despite being called by God to minister here? If they did, then who would help these poor souls? Who would bring them the message of hope they needed to hear in the midst of suffering? It was a suffering that would multiply as the Roman war machine bore down upon them.

She suspected she would not have answers any time soon for her questions and doubts. God was like that. He tended to do things without being beholden to man's demands for explanation. The judgment of fiery serpents in the wilderness did not distinguish between believers and unbelievers. The *herem* wars of Yahweh in the days of Joshua were the same. Whole cities of men, women, and children—even beasts—had been devoted to destruction. In the Babylonian exile, righteous Jews were killed and others sold into bondage along with the unrighteous.

God always protected a remnant to continue his promise, but he didn't promise absolute protection for every believer. Thus, Cassandra and Alexander did not have the certainty of their own survival. Michael's words to her in the Jordan Valley came back to her: "Angels won't always rescue you. But that doesn't mean God isn't at work." So they would labor ceaselessly to use every minute of health they had for the kingdom.

Cassandra made her way to the tent reserved for her and Alexander, pitched on the royal platform at the center of the stadium where they could oversee everyone. She wanted to drop onto her bed cot and pass out from fatigue.

Alexander saw Cassandra approach their housing tent. He had just completed his duties for the night, making sure as many as he could were as comfortable as possible. He was already exhausted and wondered how they would make it through the days and weeks to follow.

Give us the strength, Lord Jesus.

When Cassandra arrived and entered the tent, she broke down sobbing, covering her mouth lest anyone hear her. Alexander held her strongly until her tears stopped and her trembling subsided. It was all he could do.

He whispered, "Not one sparrow falls to the ground apart from the will of the Father."[1]

She whispered back with a whimper, "So many sparrows."

She was right. He had spent a lifetime dealing with the physical sufferings of humanity, much of which was through no fault of their own. Sickness, disease, accidents, earthquakes, storms, rape, torture, murder. It troubled his own faith in Yahweh.

So many sparrows.

She asked, "Is it evil for me to worry about catching the disease?"

"It is only human." Of course, he shared her fears.

"My love," she said, "I am not as strong as I had thought. I know we came here accepting our lives were not our own. But the reality feels so much less heroic than I had envisioned."

He had no words to comfort her. But he had to be strong for her. Holding her tightly, he prayed, "Heavenly Father, give us the strength to fulfill the calling with which we have been called. To serve others for you and not for ourselves. We pray for your protection to be able to minister to these lost souls of the house of Israel. Our lives are in your hands."

Cassandra added the only thing it seemed she had the strength to pray, "Come quickly, Lord Jesus."

After a few moments of silence, Cassandra spoke again. "When I see these poor souls and their suffering, I see the reason why God has made me barren. To save more from suffering."

"And what if he opens your womb?" said Alexander. "What then?"

She spoke with a sad resignation. "I would no longer have a reason."

"Would you not trust him to protect a family as you trust him to protect our marriage?"

After a moment of painful silence, Cassandra spoke. "I told you my parents were martyred when I was seventeen years old. I never told you what happened."

Alexander swallowed hard.

Cassandra's voice turned strangely dull, emotionless.

"It was in the eighth year of Claudius' reign.[2] The Jews were kicking Christians out of the synagogues in Rome and starting riots over the Gospel. I remember the day. My father had recently returned from delivering goods to Alexandria, and I was cleaning out the ship in port with my uncle.

"We had heard there was a riot in our neighborhood, so we rushed home. When we got there, it was too late. The street was filled with a mob of hundreds of angry Jews. We went into the home of a neighbor family who were friends of my parents. We went up to the rooftop to see what was going on.

"I don't know how the riot started. There had been several of them in the city already. The Jews were most offended by the claim that Jesus was the Son of God. It was blasphemy to them. Idolatry to worship a man, as we did Jesus."

Alexander knew it well. He had been one of those offended Jews. But he let her tell her own story.

She paused and swallowed. Her composure was crumbling. She trembled slightly. "So they stoned them."

Alexander felt his heart rip in two for his wife. He knew he could do nothing to comfort her in this except to listen. He wished he could take on her pain, to free her from the burden.

"My parents had been meeting with a small group of other believers in fellowship. Four others. They were bold about their faith. Everyone knew. The crowd had dragged them out into the street, throwing them up against a wall. I considered it a miracle of mercy that someone had slit my mother's throat while dragging her out. She was already dead by the time I saw her, lying at my father's feet in a pool of blood.

"They stripped my father and other Christian brothers naked to humiliate them. Their hands were tied over their heads to a roof post so they couldn't protect themselves or fall to the ground. I remember wondering where the attackers had found so many rocks. Large ones. We didn't have such in our streets. They must have planned this out, gone to a riverbed or quarry, then carried them all the way to our neighborhood with the deliberate desire to murder.

"When the rocks began to hit my father, I could only imagine his groans of pain with each strike. I couldn't hear him because the crowd was too loud. But I could see the blood. Then a large sharp rock hit him in the head, and he lost consciousness. By then his body was black and blue.

"At that point, I broke down in uncontrollable tears. I wanted to shout at them, curse them all for their demonic evil. But my uncle kept his hand over my mouth and moved me from the roof into the house.

"I couldn't sleep for weeks. I couldn't eat. I just kept living it over and over again. I still have nightmares. I can still see my father and mother hanging there, lying there, drenched in blood and broken."

Cassandra looked up into her husband's face with fear. "Alex, if we bring children into this world that we have chosen, that is the future we face."

Alexander could see the pain in her soul. A pain born of compassion. His wife wasn't afraid of suffering herself. She was afraid of bringing pain and suffering upon others. Upon innocent children.

What could he say to such fears? Fear not? Trust in God? His kingdom will overcome all kingdoms?[3] All truths, but all words that would only cut instead of heal at this moment.

He held her instead with quiet strength and prayed.

A temple guard messenger arrived at their tent. "Are you Alexander Maccabaeus?"

The words jarred like an accusation.

"Yes."

"The worthy Jacob ben Mordecai of the sanhedrin is overseer of this quarantine. He commands your presence at his residence in the Essene quarter. Both husband and wife."

Cassandra turned to Alexander with a look of horror.

He could only wonder, *What is God doing? Have we misunderstood his call? Is he the one trying to stop us from helping others?*

• • • • •

Cassandra followed Alexander through the halls of Boaz's residence, now occupied by the traitorous Jacob ben Mordecai. They were led by a servant into a large room that Jacob used for dining.

Jacob was leaning on his side, being served wine by another servant, a pretty young female. Cassandra recognized that look in Jacob's eyes as he leered at his servant. From the girl's fearful posture, she could guess what this pig had been doing to her.

"Come in, please," said Jacob. "Have a drink with me."

Cassandra glanced at Alexander, who appeared to stiffen with resolve. "No, thank you, my lord. I am sure we should be of sober mind for consideration of your concerns."

Jacob lost his fake smile. "As you now know, I have been given authority over the quarantine, both to secure the hippodrome and provide rations and resources."

Cassandra felt sick to her stomach as she struggled to keep her feelings from her expression. Jacob ben Mordecai had their fate completely in his hands. And she knew he hated them with all his black-hearted soul.

"Well," said Jacob with a sigh. "Needless to say, we do not have a happy history, the two of you and me."

Cassandra felt the bitterness of their past well up inside her. Jacob's constant hostility against the Gospel, against them.

He took a sip of his wine. "I just want you to know that it is my sincerest desire to protect and provide for the sick and wounded of our people. In this we share a noble pursuit."

He must have leveraged the quarantine to get into the sanhedrin. Cassandra knew the ruling class' perception of merchants. It wasn't good.

Jacob continued, "And part of that protection requires full compliance with our laws of uncleanness. No one under the quarantine will be allowed to leave the structure until they are healed and declared clean by the priests in accordance with Torah."

"Understood," said Alexander. "I only ask that Cassandra and I and our assistants are permitted leave when it comes to transporting patients, supplies, or resources."

"Granted," said Jacob. "I will do everything I can to ensure you have what you need to provide help for the people of Jerusalem. This is my compassion."

Compassion? In this Balaam? As Jacob's expression suddenly became deadpan, Cassandra knew they would now hear the real reason he had called them here.

"But if I hear the faintest of rumors that you are propagating your insidious faith amongst your patients or anyone else in this city, you will be punished."

Jacob stared his visitors down. "I will squeeze you until you bleed and die."

A shiver went through Cassandra's bones. This apostate had lost his soul to gain the world.

"And you will be to blame for the increased sufferings of those in your care. Am I understood?"

"Yes, my lord," said Alexander. He squeezed Cassandra's hand silently. She wanted to scream. She wanted to call down God's judgment. She wanted to damn Jacob to Gehenna.

Instead, she echoed Alexander. "Yes, my lord."

CHAPTER 15

Qumran

Salt water lapped the shore near the small Essene community on the northern edge of the Dead Sea. Their walled village hosted a self-sustaining brotherhood of monks, mostly celibate and unmarried. They had their own garden and animal husbandry to sustain their modest lifestyle of contemplation, study, and preparation—preparation to take over the priesthood of Jerusalem and lead the true remnant of Israel once the War of the Sons of Light against the Sons of Darkness destroyed the corrupted priesthood.

The entire grounds of Qumran were empty because everyone was in the meeting hall to debate this very issue of the eschatological war that was upon them.

"Order!" yelled the balding, obese overseer Phineas. The monks calmed down.

One of the elders announced, "The Romans under Syrian general Cestius Gallus left in a hurry and were overtaken by Jewish warriors half their strength, who wiped them out by a miracle of God." He was referring to the event of just over a year ago.

Phineas countered, "But the hostilities were averted. The final war is not yet upon us. We should not seek revolt like the Zealots and Sicarii. I implore you, brethren, even if it were the war we expect and we were facing the armies of Belial, our scriptures say that the battle is a heavenly one."

He read from the scroll he had opened before him: "'The mighty one of war is in our congregation, and the host of his spirits is with our steps. The great hand of God shall overcome Belial and all the angels of his dominion, and all the men of his forces shall be destroyed forever.'" He closed the scroll and said, "We are called to pray and maintain religious purity. Michael's armies will fight for us."[1]

The crowd of congregants broke out in a murmuring cacophony of agreement and disagreement.

Aaron stood just outside the door, listening to the fat overseer whom he detested with all his soul. He could barely listen to the man. This hypocrite spoke of purity yet had sexually abused Aaron and God only knew how many others. Aaron had always been too powerless to speak up. But in the past year he had been mentored by Simon bar Giora and had become a warrior.

Aaron would remain silent no longer.

He stepped into the meeting hall, followed by his twenty fellow Essene warriors, and quieted the din with a commanding voice. "The War Scroll does speak of the heavenly armies of the Lord."

Everyone turned to see him. He saw Phineas watch him with shock. He continued, "But it also speaks of the *Yahad*, our community, fighting with those angels."

Then he quoted from memory the passage that Phineas avoided, "'Mighty men and a host of angels are among those mustered with us. For on that day, the assembly of the gods and the congregation of men shall confront each other for great destruction. Between the shout of gods and of men, on the day of calamity. And it shall be a time of great tribulation for the people which God shall redeem; of all its afflictions none shall be as this, from its sudden beginning until its end in eternal redemption.'"[2]

Aaron slowly walked forward to the platform where Phineas stood with the scroll. The disgusting pig was sweating and watching Aaron with fearful eyes. Aaron had never felt such strength before in his life. His men moved into the room and stood at the back.

Aaron spoke as he walked, looking around him at his fellow monks. "Brethren, we stand at the crossroads of an important decision. What will we choose?" He paused to make them wonder. "Brother Phineas is right that the legions of Belial have retreated. But they have already regrouped on the coast at Ptolemais. I have intelligence that they are over sixty thousand strong and are led by Nero Caesar's mightiest legate, Flavius Vespasian, and his son Titus. They are embarking on a campaign to lay waste our promised land, ending with Jerusalem."

More murmuring broke out in the hall.

Aaron stopped a few mere feet away from Phineas. He stared the balding old man in the eye. Phineas trembled. Aaron turned back to the congregation.

Someone shouted out, "How do you know their goal is Jerusalem?"

"I have heard from reliable sources in Jerusalem, and I have spoken at much length with the Christians."

A rumble of disagreeable sentiment broke out. Aaron waited until they subsided. "The Christians have prophecies very much like our own. Their prophet Jesus predicted that the temple would be attacked by the Romans. Does not Daniel the prophet concur with this?"[3]

He looked over the muttering assembly.

"The Christians have run from Jerusalem to hide out in the mountains because they believe that the Day of Vengeance has arrived.[4] Should we be like them? Cowardly and afraid? I say no. There is much debate in this community whether we should pray or fight. But I believe our scriptures command us to pray—*and* fight."

Aaron's band of warriors at the back applauded in agreement. Aaron looked proudly at them.

"Most of us have been trained for battle by the wisdom and leadership of Simon bar Giora. Yet some of you still stand in indecision. My company you see standing at the back fought against Cestius Gallus at Beth Horon pass, and I can tell you that the hand of God was upon us. It was at that battle that I realized that all of my life had been leading up to this very moment. I was a part of history and prophecy. *We* are a part of history and prophecy."

Aaron paused to look over the congregation with pleading eyes. "But if you choose not to fight, when the Romans come to the shores of the Dead Sea—and they will come—what will you do then? If you pray but do not fight, you will die. But if you pray and you fight, then you will shout with the gods. So I implore you, choose today whom you will serve. As for me and my house—" He gestured to his comrades at the back. "—we will serve the Lord. We will pray *and* we will fight."

The warriors in the back cheered as did some in the congregation. Others booed. The division remained.

Phineas raised his hands to quiet them and announced, "Brethren, it is clear we do not have a unity of opinion amongst ourselves. So let us dismiss this meeting and pray in our private chambers to discern what the will of God is. Let us seek our scriptures again for a word from the Lord. We shall return to the meeting hall tonight to discuss what we should do next."

The room emptied out of the congregants. Aaron stayed at the front with Phineas. He followed the overseer's gaze and noticed him eyeing the young initiates David and Baruch. The two had both been a mere fourteen years old last year when Aaron realized Phineas had set his affection upon them. He had thought the present tribulation would bring a reprieve from the overseer's perverse designs.

But Aaron had clearly been mistaken.

Phineas glanced at the warriors at the back with fear, then to Aaron, who had been staring at him. He swallowed and cleared his throat.

Aaron let the fat leader sweat with discomfort until everyone had left. Then Aaron spoke. "I will not forcibly take over this congregation through a coup."

He saw the overseer visibly relax with relief.

"And I will not depose you from your position as overseer because I believe in the rule of law and authority established by God. But you are accountable to that law. The only reason I do not bring you before our court of judgment is because it would rip us apart at the very moment we need to come together in unity and strength. We would surely be destroyed, and that I cannot abide."

Phineas slipped into flattery. "I respect your wise decision, Aaron."

The young monk knew every wretched trick the overseer used to manipulate others. He had lived with him for too long. Aaron was not going to let it continue.

"Then respect this, brother overseer. If you so much as touch the innocence of David or Baruch or, for that matter, any other initiate of this congregation, I will castrate you with my own blade."

He saw Phineas tremble again with fear, his eyes darting to the warriors at the back.

Then Phineas spoke. "Aaron, since you claim to support the rule of law, then you must be aware that our War Rule commands that soldiers in the army of the Sons of Light must be at least twenty-five years of age. Yet you and many of your company are under twenty. What shall you say to the congregation for such legal violation?"[5]

Aaron stared at the weasel. Even at this very moment of undeniable guilt and shame, the fat creature had the gall to challenge his righteous accuser to avoid admitting to his own crimes.

Aaron said, "I will ask for their forgiveness and say that we cannot all be perfect in a time of war."

CHAPTER 16

Jotapata, Galilee
July, AD 67

*The first angel blew his trumpet, and there followed hail and fire,
mixed with blood, and these were thrown upon the land. And a
third of the land was burned up, and a third of the trees were
burned up, and all green grass was burned up.*

Apocalypse 8:7

Berenice looked out from her traveling carriage upon the countryside around her. It was a wasteland. She had traveled this area of Galilee before. She remembered it as a rich forest of cypress and oak trees. Now an ugly, barren landscape of stumps and fallow, burnt ground extended as far as she could see.

Beside her in the carriage, Agrippa gestured to the destruction around them. "Get used to it, sister. You are going to see more of this throughout the land. It's a common tactic of siege warfare. The Romans cut down the forests to build ramps against the fortifications."

"All this for one city?" Berenice was speaking of Jotapata. Agrippa had taken leave of his own siege of another city, Gamala, to pick up Berenice at the behest of Vespasian.

"Jotapata is a stronghold, my dear. I wouldn't be surprised if Vespasian cuts down and burns up all the forests of Israel to achieve total victory. It is a war policy called 'scorched earth.' We're doing it at Gamala as well."

Berenice sat back in her seat, a look of horror engraved on her face, an image of the land of Israel burnt up like kindling seared into her mind.

Agrippa mused, "'I will utterly sweep away everything from the face of the land,' declares the Lord. 'I will sweep away man and beast; I will sweep away the birds of the heavens and the fish of the sea, and the rubble with the

78

wicked. I will cut off mankind from the face of the land,' declares the Lord. For the great Day of the Lord is near, a day of clouds and darkness. In the fire of his jealousy, all the land shall be consumed."[1]

Berenice glared at her brother with a frown. He was doing it again, quoting prophecies of destruction from the Prophets with a relish that disturbed her.

Agrippa said, "That's the prophet Zephaniah describing God's judgment upon Judah and Jerusalem near the reign of Josiah."

It was a common technique of prophecy and apocalyptic. Whenever God used one nation as his instrument to judge another nation, he would describe it in hyperbolic terms of de-creation, as if the world were turning back into the pre-creation state of chaos, formless and void.[2] It was as if the sun and moon would lose their light, as if the stars would fall from the sky and the sky roll up like a scroll. This was the poetic way of describing the world ending for that city or nation and their principalities and powers. It was their "Day of the Lord," their day of reckoning.[3]

The Herods were traveling to meet Titus's forces, who together with Legion X had recently decimated the nearby city of Japha. All the men and boys had been mercilessly butchered, fifteen thousand of them, with peculiar brutality. Agrippa had told his sister that the legions were getting revenge for the humiliating defeat their fellow soldiers had suffered at the hands of the Jewish forces last year.[4] All the women and children who survived, about two thousand, had been put into slavery.

The Day of the Lord had come for Japha. And the Day of the Lord was now coming for Jotapata. Its sun and moon were about to go dark and its stars about to fall from the sky. Berenice was about to experience her own foretaste of what the coming Day of the Lord would be like for Jerusalem if they could not persuade the Jews to surrender.

Her heart was already broken. How much more devastation, how much more human slaughter of her beloved nation would she have to endure?

As if in touch with her thoughts, Agrippa wondered, "How much loss of our property and kingdom will we have to suffer before this is over?"

A messenger arrived on horseback to the carriage and announced, "My lord Herod, we have arrived outside the city of Jotapata."

Agrippa and Berenice entered the war tent of Vespasian, pitched on a ridge that overlooked the city of Jotapata below them. The Herods had been allocated their own quarters nearby and had already cleaned up from their travel.

Inside were several of the legate's generals, including Titus, who eyed Berenice like a hungry wolf. She noticed Vespasian had his right foot bandaged up. He sat on a chair to relieve his wound.

Everyone gave the proper salute of hand out, palm down to Vespasian. Her brother spoke first. "My lord, you are wounded."

"It's nothing," complained Vespasian. "Struck in the sole of my foot by a random arrow."[5]

"I am sorry to see your misfortune," Agrippa said. "I brought my forces with me at your command. What is it you require?"

"Not so much your arms as your insight," said Vespasian. "This is a most crucial battle. The Jewish commander of the Galilean region, Joseph ben Matthias, has joined the defense of the city."

Agrippa's expression showed surprise.

"He is a wily rascal, that Jew," Vespasian added.

Agrippa nodded in agreement. "If you can defeat and capture him, you hold the key to the surrender of the entire region."

"Exactly," said the legate. "And that is why I have invited you here. We have besieged the city for forty-six days and have not been successful at breaking through. Their countermeasures are frustrating my patience and shedding a poor light on my forces. I need intelligence on this general Joseph that might help us undermine him. His weaknesses, his strategies."

"I have had equal trouble with Gamala for months," said Agrippa. "What have you already achieved?"

"Follow me." Vespasian stood and limped his way toward the entrance of the tent.

They exited with Titus along with a couple of the generals and guards who accompanied them to the ridge overlooking the city.

Vespasian said, "You are just in time for our latest attack." Two servants carried the chair and placed it for Vespasian to sit down.

The others stood on the ridge. The city was a well-protected fortification with ravines on all sides. Berenice could now see what all those cut-down trees had been used for: a huge earthwork ramp that spanned the ravine up to the gates of the city, as well as hundreds of catapults and ballistas for throwing huge stones and other missiles onto the inhabitants and their city walls.

Vespasian explained their current situation. "We have the entire city surrounded with troops. Joseph will not be able to escape. The distance of the valleys has made our projectiles less effective. As you can see, we've built the rampart up to the walls, but Joseph had stone masons extend the wall height thirty feet. They've repelled us effectively with boiling oil, fenugreek, and stones from above. And they have used secret excursions to burn our siege towers at night."[6]

Berenice spotted the towers on wheels, now piles of black smoldering timber. Then she looked back at the walls. Large poles stuck out from the battlements with animal skins stretched out on them. She asked, "What are those structures on the top of the walls?"

"An ingenious trick," explained Titus. "They are a barrier to our missiles so they could build the wall. The animal skins are oxen rawhide soaked in water. When our rocks hit them, they bounce back at us. And when our fiery darts hit them, they extinguish."

Berenice wondered if this Jewish commander might be the one to hold off the Romans long enough for winter to come, thereby forestalling the war campaign.

Vespasian said, "So, we have resorted to standing back and starving the city while we readied our latest stratagem, which you have arrived just in time to observe."

The general gestured towards a host of Romans who were wheeling a huge pendulum device on wheels up to the wall. It was housed with an angled roof to protect the soldiers. A large wooden tree pole hung inside the housing. An iron head mounted on one end was sculpted in the shape of a ram's head with large, imposing horns. A battering ram.

Jews on the parapet of the battlement were now launching stones and arrows upon the ram structure. But the angled roof repelled their attempts to halt the progress.

At the same time, the Roman ballistas launched their stones, bolts, and fiery brands at the Jews to provide cover for the arriving ram. Some projectiles hit the walls, others hit warriors above, while others flew into the heart of the city. Berenice winced at the thought of the inhabitants inside the city having to endure a hailstorm of such giant proportions. It was a hailstorm mixed with fire and blood.

When the ram arrived at the wall on the top of the embankment, twenty soldiers inside the housing used leverage to swing the ram back and forth like a pendulum. The iron horns hit the city wall with the sound of thunder. From high up on the ridge, Berenice could almost feel the tremor herself.

Again, the ram swung, and again it hit the wall. Stone crumbled beneath the pounding force of the iron. Berenice could see the wall giving way with each thrust. It would only be a matter of minutes before a breach was achieved.

She trembled for the fate of the innocent in that city. There must be at least fifty thousand inhabitants. How many women, children, and elderly of her people would be killed or enslaved when this iron monster broke through the barricade?

The prophet Daniel was right. This empire of Rome was a terrifying beast with iron teeth and bronze claws that would devour the whole land, trample it down, and break everything into pieces.[7]

Then Berenice saw a large Jewish warrior at the top of the parapet holding a huge stone above his head. It was one of the catapult stones seized from within the city.

"Who in Hades is that?" Titus demanded.

The warrior cast the large stone down upon the ram. It hit the timber and snapped the iron head right off the engine.

The large warrior bellowed with a war cry that echoed through the entire valley, sending shivers down Berenice's spine.

He slid down a rope with other warriors who attacked the ram, killed the Roman soldiers, and set the housing on fire. The large warrior picked up the iron ram's head and was hoisted back up the wall by his fellow Jews.

A cohort of Herodian archers approached within range and targeted the fleeing defenders with their arrows.

As the large warrior reached the top, he was hit by several arrows, but kept going. He stood above the wall and held the iron ram above his head as he had the stone previously. He bellowed again. A dozen more arrows hit the warrior, but he remained in his victorious position despite the deadly missiles embedded in his body. He didn't even seem to notice the wounds.[8]

Berenice saw amazement on Titus's face.

Suddenly, the Jewish warrior pitched over and fell to the ground below, dead.

The generals stood in silent awe. The entire Roman army seemed to stand in silent awe. Many fled the front line to return to safety.

That single Jewish warrior had accomplished an act of heroism that Berenice could see had shaken the legions to their core. If the rebels they had yet to face possessed this kind of courage and determination to the death, the odds would not be as strongly in favor of Rome as had been assumed.

Vespasian turned to Agrippa. "That is why I called for your counsel, Herod. Your people are like cockroaches. I need you to help me figure out how to exterminate them."

Berenice and Agrippa glanced at each other. At best, the old legate's vulgar frankness was offensive. At worst, it was an omen of how they were all to be treated in the end.

CHAPTER 17

Berenice was pulled out of her dreams by a hand on her arm.

"Sister, wake up." It was Agrippa. "We are needed."

In her dazed condition, Berenice had no idea what he meant. But she quickly put on some clothes and followed him obediently through the night to a tent on the outskirts of the encampment.

They entered the tent to find Titus standing over an emaciated Jewish man seated on a stool. He looked sickly in the lamp light, perhaps due to malnourishment from lack of rations during the siege. Both eyes were blackened and his face bruised from an apparent beating.

Titus said, "We caught this deserter trying to escape the city into the desert. We had no luck using torture on a previous captive. I burned that one with fire and crucified him, but he still would not speak. So here you are for this one."[1]

Agrippa paused, his expression thoughtful, then told Titus, "Leave us."

At first Titus appeared offended at Herod's insubordinate response. Then realization of what Agrippa was doing dawned on his face. Agrippa was building trust in the deserter by appearing to stand for him against Titus.

Yes, Herods were masters of political diplomacy.

Titus gave a sarcastic, nodding gesture and moved to leave. He paused and whispered to Berenice, "Come to my tent afterward. You owe me for this." And he left them.

Agrippa and Berenice pulled up stools to sit with the prisoner.

Agrippa asked, "What is your name?"

The deserter said through blinking, delirious eyes, "Jonathan."

Berenice looked closely at the poor sod. He was some kind of farmer or shepherd. It didn't matter. He was theirs.

"Jonathan, I am Herod Agrippa II, king of Judea. This is my sister, Princess Berenice. You are familiar with us?"

Jonathan nodded.

"Well, we are here to make sure you are treated properly as a prisoner of the Roman army."

"Where were you earlier?" Jonathan coughed and winced with his hand on his rib.

"You were trying to escape the city," said Berenice. "Why?"

Jonathan looked at her, his face displaying disdain for a woman interrogating him. She repeated her words, "Why?"

"Because we are about to be destroyed by the Romans, why else?"

Agrippa sighed. "Jonathan, what if I told you we could save the city?"

Jonathan squinted with doubt.

Agrippa continued, "The longer it takes the Romans to breech the walls, the angrier they get. And that means the more brutal they will be when they finally break through." He let his words sink in before adding, "But I have the ears of the legate."

Jonathan's eyes widened.

"That's right. General Vespasian seeks my advice. If I can give him intelligence that will help him to take the city through more peaceful means, he has promised me to go easy on the residents."

Berenice glanced at her brother. She felt dirty going along with it.

"If you help me, I can save the entire city."

"What do you want from me?" Jonathan's voice seemed accusing.

"Do you know anything you can give us that will help us to avoid taking Jotapata by storm? Is there a secret passage into the city? Do you know what General Joseph ben Matthias is planning next?"

Jonathan asked, "If I help you, will you persuade the legate to be merciful to me? To spare the sword?"

"Absolutely," said Agrippa. "Vespasian has vested me with the power to negotiate this very thing. You may be surprised, but he is a rather practical man. He prefers to engage in the least amount of violence possible because that means less of his own soldiers will be hurt. And he is a generous man as well. If you help him, he will help you. Give me a way into the city, and I guarantee you the legate will show mercy on all."

Berenice could not look at the poor Jewish prisoner before her. She knew Agrippa could guarantee nothing.

Jonathan thought for a second, then said, "I know that our forces are so weak from fighting and lack of food that the lookouts all sleep at their posts in the early morning hours."[2]

Agrippa considered the information. "How do you know?"

"Because I was one of them."

Agrippa smiled. "Thank you, Jonathan. You may have just saved the population of Jotapata because of your sacrificial choice. The house of Herod thanks you for your selflessness."

He led Berenice out of the tent and past the two guards. She heard the poor farmer calling after them, "Wait. What about me?"

• • • • •

Shortly before sunrise, Titus lead a team of stealth assassins up the walls at several locations the deserter had suggested. Fortunately, an early morning fog had set in, which served to cloak the invaders. They scaled the stone with grappling hooks and found the nightwatch soldiers just as the Jew had said, asleep from exhaustion. Slitting their throats, the invaders descended into the city to open the gates. After so long a siege, the city was taken by such a simple yet tragic weakness.

Flooding in through the entrance, the Romans sought out the men and boys in the city. Titus had ordered his soldiers to find the General Joseph ben Matthias and to keep him alive.

He marched through the streets as Roman legionaries ransacked homes to put all men and boys to the sword. Some were murdered in their beds, others forced outdoors where they were summarily executed by sword and axe. There was to be no mercy.

Screams rang out through the city.

Titus strode past a group of soldiers dragging a woman and her daughter from their home by their hair. They shrieked and kicked as the soldiers laughed and had their way with them.

Titus ignored the scene. He had to allow some rapine for his forces, otherwise he might suffer the backlash of their pent-up fury. Soldiers were primed for mutiny if they had no outlet for release. Besides, it was a good way to break the women and children in preparation for slavery.

Arriving at the center of the city, Titus took over the main synagogue where the local sanhedrin would have met. He had the priests killed and stacked outside in a pile as his personal guard secured the area.

Where was this General Joseph? They were already a couple hours into the takeover, and Titus still had no word of his capture.

The sun and moon darkened over Jotapata. Its stars fell from the sky, and the mountains shook as the city's power and prestige were crushed by the iron teeth of Rome.

It took all day for the massacre to be completed. The streets were running with the blood of forty thousand slain men and boys. Over a thousand women and small children were taken into captivity to be shipped to Rome. Vespasian had ordered the entire city demolished and burnt to the ground.[3]

But Titus had still not found Joseph ben Matthias. He could not have escaped as the entire city was surrounded. His father was right. This Jewish general was a wily rascal, a cockroach hiding in a dark crevice somewhere.

"General Titus," said an arriving tribune. "We have intelligence on the possible whereabouts of the Jewish general and his leaders."

The tribune had a Jewish woman in his custody.

CHAPTER 18

When he opened the second seal, I heard the second living creature say, "Come!" And out came another horse, bright red. Its rider was permitted to take peace from the land, so that people should slay one another, and he was given a great sword.

Apocalypse 6:3–4

Joseph ben Matthias could not sleep. It had been three days since the Roman seizure of Jotapata, and his hiding place had still not been discovered. That was because he was concealed in a cavern at the bottom of a deep, dried-up cistern. Other caves were explored by the Romans and cleared out of refugees. But this particular cavern was not visible in its access unless one was lowered into the well.[1]

Joseph sat up and looked at his forty comrades sleeping on the floor of the large cave. They were several nobles of the city and other officers in his army. When Joseph had heard that the Romans had breached the walls and opened the gates, he'd known the battle was over. His several counselors had advised that they hide out in the secret cavern since the Romans were sure to make a mocking display of Joseph, dragging him through the streets in triumph as they usually did in such victories.

The devastating humiliation of the best of Israel's generals so early in the campaign could collapse the morale of the rest of the nation. They could not risk losing the war in such a manner, and Joseph did not want to die without dignity. So he agreed to follow the others into this hide-out.

They had food and water to last for weeks. Once the Romans explored every corner of the city and could not find Joseph, they would conclude he had somehow escaped in disguise. They would then burn the city and leave. Joseph and his officers could then exit the city and find their way to Jerusalem to prepare for the final battle. As long as the holy city was not taken over by the Zealots and Sicarii, in which case they might hang Joseph for his leadership in the priestly ruling class.

Joseph laid his head back down on the ground and sighed. What had become of his beloved nation? They were supposed to be the chosen people of God, a royal priesthood and holy nation that should have been a light to the Gentiles of righteousness and peace. But peace had been taken from the land. Israel had disintegrated into warring factions all slaying one another. Greeks killing Jews. Zealots and Sicarii attacking the ruling priesthood. Brigands robbing the common man.

Last winter Joseph had sought to fortify Galilee, but under much duress. John of Gischala, that treacherous traitor, had taken control of Tiberias on the Sea of Galilee. After some skirmishes with Gischala, Joseph had retreated to Taricheae, just four miles north, because he wanted to avoid the self-destruction of civil war that Gischala was provoking.

Gischala had then tried but failed to have Joseph assassinated. In the midst of their internecine battles, Vespasian had arrived. Taking nearby Sepphoris and Gabara, he had ordered the slaughter of every male in revenge for the losses of Legion XII under Cestius Gallus the year before.

When Joseph had heard that Vespasian was on his way to Jotapata, he had decided to meet the Roman legate there in battle. He'd hoped to take a heroic stand and humiliate the Romans with the city's well-fortified defenses. But alas, the mightiest of walls were as weak as the exhausted watchmen who guarded them.[2]

A deep sadness overwhelmed Joseph. He saw himself as a savior of his people. He saw in his mind's eye a picture of himself crowned with the laurels of victory after successfully pushing back the Romans. He saw himself standing before Caesar and receiving the grudging respect of the emperor to allow the Jews to return to their land with self-governance.

But those dreams seemed delusions to him now. He knew in his soul that the Jews could not win this war. They could not withstand the might and power of the iron beast of Rome. They were going to be crushed and trampled beneath Caesar's feet.

The only explanation that made sense of this chaos was that God had gone over to the side of the Romans. Not in the sense of rejecting his people, but for the purpose of chastising them. Much as Yahweh had done when he used the armies of Assyria as his instrument to chastise Israel. Or when Yahweh called forth the armies of Babylon to drag Judah into exile for her sins. Maybe Rome was now God's instrument against Israel.[3]

Jeremiah the prophet had pleaded with Judah not to defy Nebuchadnezzar, but to submit to him as punishment for her sins. But she did not listen, so Jeremiah had pronounced doom upon the nation and Jerusalem. Nebuchadnezzar had ended up fulfilling those prophecies, destroying the holy city and temple and bringing Judah into a captivity that lasted for seventy years.

Could it be happening all over again?

Like Jeremiah, Joseph was a member of the priestly caste. Maybe that was what Joseph could become, a modern-day Jeremiah. But he would have to get to Jerusalem first. And he would have to survive this ordeal to do so.

He heard the sound of a rope being dropped in the cistern from above. A torchlight descended. Grabbing his sword, Joseph whispered to his comrades, "Men, wake up. We are discovered."

He moved swiftly toward the light, feeling the alarm of his impending fate. The Romans could not send a significant crew to capture them because the cistern was too small. So those descending must be assassins.

Joseph gripped his sword tightly and prepared to fight. The others soon joined him, armed and ready. But as the torch reached bottom, Joseph realized it was only one person: a Roman tribune.

"Nicanor!" he exclaimed with surprise. Joseph had known the tribune from official interactions in Jerusalem. They had become friendly in their dealings. Nicanor was an intellectually curious Roman who respected Joseph's faith and beliefs.

Joseph held up a hand to stop his comrades from attacking. "I know this man. He is not hostile."

The other leaders mumbled amongst themselves, refusing to sheathe their weapons.

"How did you find us?" Joseph asked.

Nicanor grasped Joseph's wrist firmly as he responded, "A citizen who saw you entering the cistern gave you up."

There was always a witness.

Several of the men murmured, "Traitor."

Nicanor said, "Titus has killed all the men and boys and enslaved the women and small children. He is about to raze the city to ashes."

This was hardly a surprise, but it still silenced the group to sober consideration. The Roman looked directly at Joseph. "But he does not want to kill you."

"Is that why he sent you?" Joseph demanded. "To persuade us to give ourselves up?"

"Titus admires you, Joseph. He doesn't want to punish you. If you come willingly, he assures me that he will spare your life. It would be a waste of a great leader to kill you."

"And what does Vespasian say?" asked Joseph.

"They speak as one," said Nicanor. "Titus is Vespasian's right hand. And I believe them to be honorable."

Someone shouted, "We should burn this place and ourselves with it."

"Silence!" commanded Joseph. He turned back to Nicanor. "As you can see, I am accountable to other leaders. We'll need time to deliberate. How many hours until sunrise?"

"Several."

"Then tell Titus he will have my answer then."

"Godspeed," said Nicanor, and he yanked the rope to be pulled back up the cistern.

Joseph walked back into the cavern. He barked out, "Someone start a fire. And let us decide what we will do."

The fire crackled, bringing warmth to the forty-one men huddled around in the cold dark cavern. One of the older experienced leaders named Reuben didn't wait for Joseph to lead the discussion. "Why is there any question? We cannot give ourselves up. It would disgrace the memory of our forefathers. The Maccabees accepted the sword rather than bow the knee to Rome."

"If the Romans hold you captive, Joseph," another spoke up, "they will parade you before our brethren as a symbol of defeat to destroy their morale. You would be more valuable to their propaganda alive than dead."

A third asked, "How can we trust a general of the empire that has enslaved us for generations?"

91

A fourth argued, "I would rather die by my own sword than by the sword of a swine. If we kill ourselves, we will crush the confidence of the godless, who will see that we are a people willing to die before submitting any further to their subjugation. Pray we become an example to the rest of the nation."

The men all seemed to agree on suicide. But Joseph finally spoke up. "It is a brave thing to die in war. But only at the hand of conquerors. If I avoid death from the sword of the Romans, I am truly worthy to be killed by my own sword. But if they, our mortal enemy, offer mercy and would spare us, how much more ought we to have mercy upon ourselves and spare ourselves?"

Mutterings of disagreement broke out. Joseph raised his voice to quiet them. "I affirm that he is a coward who will not die when he is obliged to die." He looked around at the men. "But so too a coward is he who will die when he is not obliged to die."[4]

More rumbling from the others made Joseph pause. Then he finished, "Are we not in the image of our creator? Is not the act of self-murder a marring of that image of God in us?"

The men's expressions were thoughtful. He had finally begun to get through to them.

Then the old leader Reuben drew his sword and pronounced, "If you do not have the courage to kill yourself, Joseph, I will do so gladly. As should we all."

Several others drew their swords. Joseph heard their approval. Reuben stepped toward Joseph. Joseph put up his hands. "In the name of God, halt."

Reuben paused, but kept his sword raised. Joseph continued, "Reuben, I am the senior officer in this company. You will not want to face our God with the blood of mutiny on your hands." He hoped their consciences were still intact, for once the mob begins its chaos, conscience is the first casualty.

The men froze, looking at one another. Joseph decided to try a different tack. "As your senior officer, it is my duty to consider your counsel seriously. And I cannot deny that you are all resolved to die rather than be enslaved to Rome."

The men nodded and grunted in agreement.

"So, it is my obligation to accept such unanimous agreement and subordinate my own desires to the wisdom of the many."

Reuben was now watching with curiosity. Joseph continued, "But to avoid the moral perils of self-murder, I recommend we allow chance to dictate our deaths."

"What do you mean?" one man asked.

Joseph picked up his satchel and drew a piece of parchment from it. "We draw lots by chance to determine who will die and by whose sword. The final two left can kill each other with a mutual thrust of their weapons."

The men looked at one another in apparent approval. Reuben said, "It seems fair enough. We are not choosing, but letting God choose through the lots."

Joseph took a charcoal stick from the fire to mark out an equation on the back of the parchment. He said, "I think I have the simplest way. Everyone stand in a circle."

As they moved into position, Joseph wrote out a formula he had learned in his study of mathematics when he was younger. It was something most of these men would have no idea about. During his studies, he had solved a problem of permutations as part of an exercise that resembled a scenario not too different from what he was in now.

He asked, "How many of us are there?"

Reuben counted them out. "Forty-one."

Joseph was hurriedly writing out his formula. "Just one moment. I'm making sure it will work out fairly."

He finished the formula. He had the numbers he needed. Sixteen and three. He walked into the circle.

He gestured to Reuben. "We will start with Reuben as number one." Joseph walked around the circle, secretly counting to himself, then chose to stand in the sixteenth spot from Reuben.

"Now we all count off, and every third man will be executed by the man on his right. Then we will move the bodies and continue through the circle, every third man executed by the man on his right. This way we will allow God himself to choose and not ourselves."

He looked around the circle. The men became sober. Some of them counted in their heads. The third man and sixth man became nervous with dread of their doom to die first.

Joseph said, "Count out, and every third man step forward into the circle."

93

The men counted out.

"One."

"Two."

"Three." The third man's voice wavered with fear. But he stepped out into the circle.

The others continued to count.

"Four."

"Five."

"Six." Number six stepped forward, facing his fate with courage.

"Seven."

"Eight."

"Nine."

They finished counting around the circle until the first fourteen chosen delegates had stepped forward.

Joseph was not one of them.

"You chosen ones say a prayer to God," he commanded the men. "And those to their right engage in your duty before God. Strike to the heart so their death is quick and merciful."

The "chosen ones" closed their eyes in dread and prayed.

Their fellow warriors lifted their swords, thrusting them into their comrade's chests.

The first kill shook everyone to the core. But they had committed to this fate. They had chosen to die with their God rather than to live as slaves to godless Rome.

The second round counted off. This time nine were left in the center of the circle, where they were killed to fall into the growing pile of the dead.

Joseph was still not one of the chosen.

A third time round was followed by a fourth, the floor by now drenched with blood.

Joseph was still not one of the chosen.

The cycle repeated up to an eighth round, by which point only Joseph and one other noble of the city was left.

The truth was that the mathematical problem Joseph had learned in his schooling had allowed him to determine where to place himself in the circle so that he would be one of the last two standing.[5]

Such is the benefit of a good education.

Joseph walked up to the noble, who stood before him shaking. He was not a warrior; a bit of luck Joseph had not calculated.

He drew his sword, and before the noble could even realize what was happening, Joseph impaled him in the heart. The poor soul grunted in pain and with shocked eyes slid off Joseph's blade onto the ground, dead.

Joseph stood for a moment, frozen like a sculpture.

He looked around at the dead bodies of his forty countrymen, fellow leaders who had given up their lives for their country.

Joseph had determined to instead live for his country. But the image around him burned into his conscience like a vision of Sheol, the underworld. All their bodies, their blood. He was surrounded by death. A death he had engineered to save his own life.

Joseph fell to his knees and wept. He tried to pray, but he could not.

What else should he have done? They were all mad to kill him and kill themselves. He could not reason with them. They thought giving up was some kind of heroism. But to Joseph it was foolishness. They had become like the Zealot fanatics. So he'd done what he had to do: save himself. Live to fight another day. To fight another way.

With the dawning light of morning, he heard the sound of Nicanor being lowered into the cave to hear Joseph's final decision.

CHAPTER 19

Joseph was escorted by Titus and a small guard unit into Vespasian's war tent in the middle of the legionary camp above Jotapata. The city burned like an inferno below. Manacles chained Joseph's hands and feet, and he was now covered with rotten food, spittle, and mud thrown at him as he was paraded through the Roman camp. Many had called for his execution by hanging before the entire army.

Joseph got down on his knees before the legate. Titus stood beside his father, a grim look on his face.

Joseph noticed the Herods, Agrippa and his sister, the princess Berenice, standing off to the side. He didn't acknowledge them as he considered that Agrippa had become an enemy of Israel by devoting his forces to the Roman campaign.

"General Joseph ben Matthias, you have caused me great inconvenience," said Vespasian. His voice was gruff, but his tone was humored. He took a sip of wine from a goblet in his hand. He looked quite relaxed.

"General Vespasian," said Joseph, "I submit to your victory. My only claim is that I sought to fight with honor, nobility, and strategy."

Titus responded, "Your defense was impressive."

Joseph said, "Upon hearing of your generous offer of grace, I willingly accepted it with trust in your integrity."

"Evidently the forty others with you did not agree." Vespasian was smiling, amused by it all.

"Yes," added Titus. "Some are saying that you betrayed your own people. Are you a traitor, Joseph?"

"No, my lord. My survival was in fact a miracle."

Vespasian and Titus looked at each with interest.

"We had all decided to kill ourselves by lot rather than face slavery or execution. It was by the providence of God that I was the last alive. Like our

96

forefather Abraham, my sword was stayed when I received a prophecy from the God of the universe."

"Fascinating," said Vespasian, still smiling, eager to hear the rest.

Titus was smiling as well.

Joseph cleared his throat. "God has chosen me to be a witness, not as a traitor but as a servant. You see, he has given me dreams that have foretold the calamity of the Jews and even the success of Caesar."

"Do tell," said Vespasian. He took a gulp from the goblet and belched.

Joseph lowered his head in deference and raised his hands in open surrender. "You think, O Vespasian, that you have a mere captive in Joseph. But I come to you as a messenger of a greater destiny. No doubt you intend to send me to Nero. But why do so? Do you think he will continue in office? You, Vespasian, will be Caesar and emperor. You and your son Titus. For you are master not only over me, but over land and sea and over the whole human race."[1]

Vespasian burst out in a hearty laugh. Titus joined him with a smirk and a wagging head.

Vespasian glanced at Titus. "Now even my enemies agree with you, my son."

Titus added, "And the oracles."

"And the oracles," Vespasian grudgingly admitted. He turned back to Joseph. "However, your words smell of desperation, general." He gestured to the Herods. "What would your fellow countrymen here say of such boot-licking?"

Joseph could see panic on the royal siblings' faces. What would they say? That Vespasian would not or should not be Caesar? They were caught on the horns of a dilemma.

So Joseph would force them to support him.

He said, "My lord, this is no attempt on my part at conjured flattery. I'm sure the Herods will attest that our own prophet Daniel wrote six hundred years ago of one who would become ruler of the world at this very moment in history."[2]

Vespasian turned to the Herods again and said with amusement still on his lips, "What say you, Herods?"

Again Agrippa and Berenice stood mute, not sure what to say. Everyone had always considered that prediction a prerogative of Messiah. But the pagan King Cyrus was called God's anointed Messiah, so why couldn't Vespasian be so as well?[3]

Joseph quoted the poetic prophecy, "And to him was given dominion and glory and a kingdom, that all peoples, nations, and languages should serve him; his dominion is an everlasting dominion, which shall not pass away, and his kingdom one that shall not be destroyed."[4]

Vespasian and Titus became more serious. The legate was reconsidering his doubts. "I like that prophecy. It sounds quite Roman." After another pause, he demanded, "Well, Agrippa, does Joseph speak the word of gods or not?"

Agrippa cleared his throat. "Yes, my lord. That is from the prophet Daniel."

Joseph added, "Our God has gone over to the Romans. He is using you to judge the Jews."[5]

Vespasian raised his eyebrows with delight, took another drink, and said, "I do believe we have a court prophet with us, my son."

Vespasian let out another vulgar belch.

Titus smiled at him. "Glad to hear the idea is finally digestible for you, father."

Joseph could see the idea of becoming emperor had been an area of disagreement between father and son. But the old man was not taking it as seriously.

Vespasian said, "Well then, though we will have to keep you in chains for now, I will not send you back to Nero. Furthermore, because of your devotion to us, I think I will change your name to be one of the family. Titus, what do you recommend?"

Titus thought for a moment. "Flavius Josephus."

"Excellent. Flavius Josephus. Welcome to the family." He toasted Josephus with the goblet and drank again.

He added, "You will be of use to us. But now we must discuss how we are going to clean out the rest of this stinking cesspool region of Galilee."

CHAPTER 20

Jerusalem

Cassandra and Alexander were exhausted with the care and concern of the five hundred plague-stricken victims left in the quarantine of the hippodrome. A third of the victims had already died, and Alexander knew of no remedy for the sickness. A third of the patients had become well, but he doubted the salves and medicinal herbs he used had much to do with it.

Alexander and Cassandra continued to share the Gospel of salvation with those in their care with quiet but deliberate defiance of Jacob's orders. As a judgment on the collective people, the plague did not discriminate between young or old, good or evil. Some of those who were sick repented and believed in Jesus, but still died and went on to be with the Lord. Others, about fifty of them, survived. These had chosen to stay in the hippodrome and help with the care of the others. This wasn't entirely altruistic, as their new faith made them more unclean than leprosy to their fellow Jews in the city.

The spread of the disease had stalled, and now only a few were falling prey. Fewer as the days progressed. But the responsibility for feeding, cleaning, and caring for the victims had taken its toll. Alexander and Cassandra were physically and emotionally exhausted. Sometimes they would not see each other all day until they dropped into bed late at night.

Alexander could see that he was becoming distant from Cassandra. Their dedication to the cause was drowning out their relationship with each other. But he could not let that hamper his thoughts right now as he was teaching a class for the fifty Christian volunteers on the basics of medical aid and hygiene to help with the sick.

Keeping clothes, beds, and bandages clean. Washing boils and applying ointments. These had all been demonstrated in the sick area with the victims. But Alexander had pulled the volunteers aside under the arched stands to explain to them the perspective that was required to do the job.

"You cannot become emotionally involved with the victims. As a new Christian, you will be drawn to do so, but as a physician's helper, you cannot let it happen."

One of the helpers raised his hand to ask a question. "Aren't we called by Christ to have compassion?"

Alexander nodded. "Yes. And that is why we help them in the first place. But if a physician enters into the private suffering of each patient, he will be mentally and physically drained almost immediately, making him less capable of helping more people. In the case of this plague, there are so many who lose their lives that our compassion would be rendered useless by the emotional devastation of dying with each of them. We must remember that we are part of a cause bigger than ourselves, the kingdom of God, so we must keep our minds focused on that kingdom. The Holy Spirit will give us the strength."

Alexander spotted Cassandra at the back of the group, listening attentively but with a sad expression. She knew as well as he did that this class meant he would likely not see her tonight for dinner, since he still had to catch up on his rounds. There was so much to get done for the kingdom. As much as he warned his students about the dangers of burning out, he wondered if his own flame could stay lit under the pressure.

One of the volunteers arrived from the front gate. "Alexander and Cassandra, there is an armed guard at the entrance ordering a meeting with Jacob ben Mordecai."

• • • • •

The armed guards brought Cassandra and Alexander to Jacob's residence. An elderly servant with peppered hair ushered them through the home. Cassandra noticed a scar that slashed across the servant's cheek. Some war injury, or a mark of brutality by his wicked master?

She asked him, "What is your name?"

"Nathan," the servant answered her.

They arrived at the atrium in the center of the complex. Jacob stood calmly in the midst of a massive nursery of flowers, trimming some of them with a special curved blade. The servant announced their presence and left them. Jacob continued his work without acknowledging his visitors.

Cassandra recognized some of the wide selection of flowers surrounding Jacob: tulips, orchids, irises and crocuses and others she did not. It was clear the merchant pursued an interest in horticulture. Lifting up a large red tulip he had just cut from its stem, he finally turned to his two visitors.

"The Rose of Sharon. A lily of the valleys." He was quoting the Song of Songs. Staring at Cassandra, he continued reciting, "As a lily among brambles, so is my love among the young women."

His words sent a chill of disgust through her. The merchant was toying with them. Jacob's smile carried a depraved twist of irony as he gestured to the flora that filled the atrium like a greenhouse. "Do you like my garden? My predecessor in this house did not have an appreciation of beauty as I do."

Jacob did not turn his gaze from Cassandra as he approached. "I find that beauty soothes the soul and lifts it toward God. It's why the holy temple has so much plant and flower imagery engraved on its walls, its pillars, and its sacred instruments. The temple is the Garden."[1]

He looked around the atrium. "I suppose you could call this my own little taste of Eden."

And you are the serpent that defiles it, Cassandra thought.

Jacob quoted a scripture: "'In days to come Jacob shall take root; Israel shall blossom and put forth shoots and fill the whole world with fruit.'"[2]

He was alluding to the promised restoration in Isaiah, a restoration that he denied had already begun in Jesus as Messiah.

Cassandra could not help but quote a later section of the same scripture in response. "Woe to the crown of pride whose glorious beauty is a fading flower. Behold, the Lord will bring them down to the earth, and they will be trampled underfoot."[3]

She saw Jacob's smug expression turn sober. He changed the subject, "I understand some of your patients have converted to your faith."

Alexander said, "A few."

"How many?" Jacob demanded.

"About fifty."

Cassandra could see Jacob seething with resentment. He spit out, "I told you not to proselytize. Yet you defied my orders."

"They asked us why we were helping them, my lord Jacob," Alexander responded steadily. "We will not lie. And we cannot be silent because the Lord

Jesus Christ commanded us to share the hope that is in us. But judge for yourself whether we should obey God or man."

Jacob's face was now tightening with anger. So much for these peaceful flowers. Cassandra felt deep respect for her husband's courage to stand strong in the face of this reptile.

Jacob said, "I want the names of all your converts. And they will not be allowed to return to their families. They must stay in the quarantine."

Alexander said, "They have already committed to stay and help us with the sick."

Jacob turned red with mounting frustration. His intent had been to make these new Christians suffer. But their confinement would only draw them closer in their faith.

He said, "I will require daily reports and registrations of all victims. I want to know who dies, who gets well, and who converts. Daily reports."

That would not be good, thought Cassandra. The more knowledge he had of them, the more easily he could control them. Or punish them.

But Jacob was not done yet. "The both of you and your assistants are now required to get approval for every leave of absence from the quarantine, along with a written description of your activities."

"Yes, my lord." Alexander could not quite keep the resignation from his even tone. If this apostate could not crush their faith, he would bury them in bureaucracy.

"Oh, and there is one more thing before you leave," said Jacob. "I will be shutting off the running water to the hippodrome. The civil engineers need to repair some of the city sewage lines."

Cassandra could sense Alexander striving to hide anger and frustration under a carefully bland expression. He asked mildly, "May I ask how long you anticipate this temporary deprivation?"

"It depends. Perhaps you should take this time to carefully consider how valuable the resources of this city are to you. It may temper your message of condemnation."

Jacob was lying. Cassandra knew it. There was no need for civil repairs. This was punishment. He would let them wallow in their filth until they did what he told them to do. Until they stopped ministering the Gospel.

Well, that was not going to happen. So Cassandra prepared herself for the stench of injustice about to come.

CHAPTER 21

Sea of Galilee
September, AD 67

An angel blew his trumpet, and something like a great mountain, burning with fire, was thrown into the sea, and a third of the sea became blood. A third of the living creatures in the sea died, and a third of the ships were destroyed.

An angel poured out his bowl into the sea, and it became like the blood of a corpse, and every living thing died that was in the sea.

Apocalypse 8:8–9; 16:3[1]

Raphael the archangel observed the devastation around him in the city of Taricheae as his dismembered torso was wrapped and carried along in a small cart that was pulled by Molech. Dead lay in the streets. Houses were burned and pillaged. Another Galilean city taken by Vespasian for the glory of Rome. He'd already been shown the stadium of nearby Tiberias, where over a thousand old and weak Jewish citizens had been slaughtered by the Romans. Six thousand of the strongest sent to Nero as slaves. The rest, thirty thousand, sold into slavery elsewhere.[2] The sheer numbers of casualties in this war were too staggering to comprehend.

Now Raphael arrived at the shores of the Sea of Galilee, where his captors, Zeus, Anat, Dagon, Molech, and the Daughters of Allah, paused to take in the sights and smells before them.

Zeus breathed in deeply and sighed. "Now, that is the smell of sweet pleasure in my nostrils."

The smell Zeus referenced was making Raphael gag. The shoreline overflowed with thousands of bodies of dead Jews floating in water that had turned red with blood. Putrefying, rotting corpses from a sea battle with the Romans, they swelled and bloated in the hot sun, the wreckage of their boats scattered around them.

If the stench was unbearable to Raphael, it was a soothing aroma to the demonic gods of the nations. They drew strength and vitality from death, destruction, and chaos. That was why they were here.[3]

The seven Watchers knelt in the water and drank of the bloody carnage. So much blood and gore choked the water that it had killed the sea life as well. Dead fish drifted next to the humans.

"Ah," said Zeus, "there is nothing quite so rejuvenating as the blood of unrighteous war. It is an unparalleled sacrificial offering to the principalities and powers. Their blood becomes our sacred libation."

"Death begets death," the Daughters of Allah echoed his sentiment.

"Look!" shouted Dagon. "Leviathan."

Off-shore, the huge scaled back of the seven-headed sea dragon of chaos broke the surface as it glided through the waters, drinking in the annihilation in its wake. The sight of the great sea monster always bothered Raphael. Yahweh had crushed its many heads when he pushed back the chaos of the Red Sea and established his covenant with Israel.[4] Jesus had tamed the great beast when he calmed the storm and walked on its back in this very sea to confirm his mastery over the waters.[5]

The sea had always been a symbol of both the Gentile nations and the chaos of the cosmos, that which Yahweh himself overcame with his creation and covenant. The day was coming when there would be no sea, no chaos left to overcome, and Leviathan would be no more because the new heavens and earth of the new covenant would be consummated with God's marriage to his new wife, the bride of Christ. But until the final state, Leviathan would have his way in this cosmos of grief and pain.[6]

Zeus said, "I can see the Jews were no match in their simple fishing boats for the mighty rafts that Vespasian built. The Romans rammed them into pieces and cut off their hands and heads in the battle."[7]

"A delicious feast, indeed," said Dagon. He picked up a head from the water.

Anat added, "Not unlike our delightful banquet of seafood at Joppa."

Raphael had heard what terrible fate had happened at Joppa. Thousands of Jews fleeing on ships in the Mediterranean Sea. Their vessels crushed on the rocks in a storm. Those not drowned in the waves were hacked to pieces by Vespasian's forces on the shore. Blood red seas full of dead bodies and shattered shipwrecks.[8]

"This is only the beginning," said Zeus. "When the holy mountain, Zion, is thrown into the sea in burning flames, the rivers will also be clogged with bodies of death. And they thought the Nile turning to blood was glorious. Just wait and see."

The Watcher was once again referring to the battle of cosmic mountains. The Roman attack on Jerusalem would be like throwing Mount Zion into the sea, something Jesus had hinted at when he likened earthly Israel to a cursed fruitless tree and a mountain. The faith of the new covenant would throw the earthly Mount Zion into the sea of chaos and judgment, to be replaced by the heavenly Mount Zion.[9]

There was one other thing Raphael had noticed. Anat would not look at or respond directly to Zeus. The archangel had overheard whisperings and had figured out what was going on between the two deities. Evidently, Apollyon had humiliated Anat's brother and lover Ba'al, the chief of the Canaanite pantheon. Apollyon had also conferred leadership on Zeus for his sycophantic loyalty.

Raphael could see that Anat was envious and resentful of Zeus for his favored status. She was planning something. Anat was a mighty warrior goddess whose skill was unequalled by any except Ba'al, so it would not take much for her to crush Zeus. But she also had to answer to Apollyon for her actions.

Raphael only hoped this rift within their ranks would ultimately resound to his benefit.

In the meantime, he had to bear his own burden of limbless helplessness. The gods enjoyed taunting him and beating him whenever they had the opportunity. He had suffered much pain throughout this predicament. But he was thankful to Yahweh for the hostage trade they were about to engage in that would give him back his limbs and ultimately return him to his former glory.

He prayed, "Come quickly, Lord Jesus."

CHAPTER 22

Jerusalem

The Day of Atonement had arrived. Pilgrims filled the city for the holiest festival of the year. The people were supposed to assemble together, humble their souls before God, perform sacrifices, and cease from their labors.[1] It was the one day of the year when the high priest would enter the holy of holies to make atonement for the sins of Israel. All other sacrifices were mere cleansing for sacred space. This day constituted actual covering of sins in anticipation of the arrival of Messiah, who would bring full and final atonement.

Ananus was acting high priest. Eleazar allowed him into the inner court and escorted him to the high priest chambers at the side of the temple. Though Eleazar had command of the temple in defiance of the sanhedrin, he had to allow the daily sacrifices as well as the prescribed festivals of Israel. If he did not, the entire nation would rise up against him and his cause would be fruitless.

Ananus hoped to use that one day to his advantage, but for now, he too had to perform his ritual duties. He entered the high priest chambers and put on the special garments reserved for that special day. He washed his hands and feet, donned the linen garments, and made his way out to the altar. Eleazar waited for him to return, upon which he would then restore the holy garments to safe-keeping.

Ananus went out to the altar and sacrificed a bull for his sins. Retrieving some of the coals from the altar, he then filled a censer that he took into the holy place on his way to the holy of holies. He looked at the Menorah of lights in the holy place. The central light was unlit. It was the most important of the seven lights on the lampstand. It was said by the rabbis that during the wilderness wanderings of Israel, the center lamp never went out. It was miraculously perpetual by the shekinah glory of God's presence resting over them.[2]

What deeply bothered Ananus was that for the last forty years since that trouble caused by the Nazarene, the central light would no longer stay lit. Every morning the priests would light it, but it would go out, no matter how much oil or how fresh a wick was used. It was the opposite of the exodus miracle, and it disturbed him. The priests who served in the temple had kept the problem a secret amongst themselves.

When Ananus entered the holy of holies, the smoke from the censor filled the empty room. Another bothersome detail. He was supposed to sprinkle the blood of the bull on the mercy seat of the ark of the covenant. But since the ark had been long since gone, he sprinkled it on the Foundation Stone where the ark was supposed to rest. He wondered why Yahweh continued to allow this tragic lack of presence to continue.

His consternation was made all the more troubling when he engaged in the final ritual of the scapegoat. Two goats were offered, one in sacrifice for the Lord, the other to carry the sins of Israel into the desert of Azazel. The priests would choose which goat was for the Lord by choosing lots. Whatever hand the lot for Yahweh came up, that would be the goat chosen. Though the right hand was the preferable one, another secret of the high priesthood was that the lot for the Lord had miraculously come up in the lesser of the two, the left hand, every time for the last forty years.

A final ritual of the scapegoat was tying a scarlet thread upon the horns of the goat for Azazel, followed by a scarlet thread tied onto the gates of the temple. The goat would be led off into the wilderness as a symbol of God casting Israel's sins into the void of chaos. Afterward, the scarlet thread on the temple gate would turn white, confirming that Israel's scarlet sins had become white as snow.

This year it happened again, as it had for the last forty years: the scarlet thread did not turn white.

Ananus pulled the thread off the gate to keep word from spreading and returned to the high priest chambers to undress.

When he arrived there, he removed the garments and Eleazar took them. Because Eleazar had engaged in a hostile takeover of the temple, Ananus despised him as abominable. There was always tension between the two during these obligations of the covenant. But the signs of Yahweh's disfavor were so disturbing that he mentioned them to his opponent.

"The western light remains unlit in the menorah, the lot for Yahweh came up in the left hand again, and the scarlet thread did not turn white. This has been the case for forty years."

Eleazar surprised him. "Every night the gates to the temple open of their own accord. Every night for the last forty years as well."[3]

The gates were so large and heavy it took twenty men to open them. Such opening made the temple vulnerable to profaneness.

The two men gave each other a grave look. Despite the fact that they were at odds over the temple, these portents of disaster were a shadow over them all. In a strange way, the omens united them beyond their political and religious differences.

Ananus said, "It was only a few years ago that I saw with my own eyes several additional omens of danger. During the festival of Hanukkah, the fire on the altar increased to a blinding intensity like the light of day. This lasted for a half hour before returning to normal. During that half hour, the last heifer brought for sacrifice gave birth to a lamb."[4]

Eleazar listened with quiet intensity. Ananus swallowed dryly and told him, "The temple gates opened of their own accord at that time as well."

"What do you think it means?" Eleazar asked.

"At the time I claimed they were positive miracles of God's presence," Ananus answered. "But I was lying to myself and to others."

"How so?"

"Because when the doors opened there was also an earthquake that moved the foundations of the temple, followed by a rushing wind leaving the temple."

Ananus paused. His face turned even more dire than it already was.

"Some of us heard the sound of a heavenly voice. It said, 'Let us remove ourselves henceforth.'"[5]

Eleazar's eyes went wide. He looked away with concern.

Finally he said, "We must keep these omens to ourselves. Continue to guard them. If the people find out, we may find the revolution against Rome turned against us, and none of us will survive."

Ananus nodded solemnly in agreement. Some truths were too important to allow the common people to know. They were too volatile and dangerous.

Ananus thought, *The people need our wisdom. They need protection from the wrath of God.*

CHAPTER 23

Alexander had completed his rounds of checking on the sick in the hippodrome quarantine when Cassandra arrived, her arm around one of their helpers. Alexander recognized the young woman as Sarah. She had worked in the theater across the way before catching the plague, but when she had become well, she had embraced the Messiah and stayed to help with the others.

Now this young woman's normally vibrant face was pale and anemic. Her lovely brown eyes were bloodshot, and Alexander could see vomit on the front of her robe.

Cassandra braced the weakened Sarah and helped her onto one of the beds. Pouring her a drink from a nearby water jar, she whispered to Alexander, "Sarah is the seventh volunteer to fall sick. We have to do something, Alex."

It had been over a month since Jacob blocked their running water for the sewage system of the hippodrome as punishment for their proselytizing. Cassandra continued, "The waste is becoming unmanageable. The stench. Swarms of flies are starting to enter the stadium." The flies were spreading the sickness.

"What do you suggest we do, Cassie?" Alexander asked quietly. "Stop preaching the Gospel? That's what the satan wants."

Cassandra sighed in agreement. After a sober consideration, she said, "We must ask the Two Witnesses for help."

Alexander's immediate reaction was unencouraging. "You know we can't do that. We were explicitly told by Michael to avoid connection with the Witnesses for the protection of those in our care."

"It doesn't seem to me like we're protecting them very well."

"You know what will happen if anyone sees us contacting the Witnesses. They'll consider it a conspiracy and attack us because they can't attack the prophets. And Michael warned us that we don't share their supernatural guardians."

"Can we not approach them in secret?"

Alexander thought about it. It was an option. But a difficult one. "They have no residence. They sleep in secret locations, different alleys or storm drains each night. I wouldn't know where to begin looking for them."

He was softening. Cassandra reminded, "But we do know where they preach regularly in public."

He sighed. "How could we contact them in broad daylight without being seen?"

"Leave that to me," said Cassandra. "I have an idea."

• • • • •

Alexander had requested permission to leave the hippodrome for supplies. It was a pretense. Instead, he had followed the Two Witnesses moving throughout the outer temple precinct and the sacred marketplace under Solomon's portico. The Witnesses seemed to have complete freedom to go wherever they wanted. Alexander knew it was because of the angels who watched over them.

Few actually saw the invisible guardians except those who attempted to do them harm such as the soldiers sent to incarcerate them. Because of the soldiers' reports, the authorities were dissuaded from further attempts. They still kept a watch but from a safe distance.

Cassandra saw the guardians too. She had been blessed with the sensitivity of observing the unseen realm behind the Witnesses. But all most people saw were two simple men, unshaven and scruffy, dressed permanently in sackcloth. God enjoyed using the weak of this world to shame the strong.

As Alexander followed the Two Witnesses up to the inner temple walls, he saw the temple guards watching the prophets at a distance, never attempting to arrest them or deny them access.

Alexander looked around the crowd for Cassandra. He couldn't find her. But he was sure she was there, ready for their plan.

Today Moshe and Elihu engaged in a theatrical prophecy similar to those of Jeremiah and Ezekiel, whose predictions were often acted out in dramatic form.[1] The Two Witnesses brought out a measuring rod the size of a staff and used it to measure both the altar inside the temple courtyard and the walls outside. They physically walked around the structure and measured it in the sight of everyone to see.

Then they stood outside the inner temple and spoke to the crowd of curious citizens who had gathered to watch their odd activity. Alexander knew exactly what they were doing. It was a re-enactment of the angel's command in a vision to the apostle John in the eleventh fragment of the Apocalypse.[2]

Moshe spoke first. "Hear, O Israel. The Lord our God has measured the true temple in heaven and the altar and those who worship there because he has kept that heavenly temple for himself. But he has not measured the court outside, which represents this earthly temple, because he will not protect it. He has given this temple of stone and dirt over to the nations to trample for forty-two months."

The crowds had been hearing this message for years. It wasn't a new offense. And it was particularly relevant to the Feast of Tabernacles, which the city had been in the midst of celebrating. The Feast marked the ingathering of the harvest and commemorated the wilderness wanderings of Israel. For forty years the Jews had lived in temporary booths, as had Yahweh in his wilderness tabernacle, a foreshadow of the temple within which they were standing.

Elihu took over the preaching. "The prophet Ezekiel saw a vision of the messianic temple at the time of the Exile. God had destroyed the city of Jerusalem and Solomon's temple as judgment for the sins of Israel. So, I tell you, God will once again destroy this city and temple. He will replace it with the new temple spoken of by Ezekiel. And his sanctuary will be in the midst of his people forevermore." He quoted a scripture that no doubt most of their listeners knew by heart, "My dwelling place shall be with them, and I will be their God, and they shall be my people."[3]

Alexander called to mind the discussions he and his traveling companions had with the apostle John on Patmos. John had told them that he had patterned the Apocalypse after Ezekiel's prophecy in both content and structure.[4] Ezekiel had declared that the shekinah glory of the Lord had departed from the temple, resulting in God's judgment of destruction upon both temple and city, which in turn resulted in the Exile.[5] Jesus had likewise declared that God had once again left his house and would once again destroy both temple and city, sending the Jewish nation to its grave.[6] But Ezekiel had also promised a resurrection from that death and a new covenant temple.

Elihu continued, "The prophet Zechariah told us that Messiah himself would rebuild the temple and that it is he who would sit and rule on his throne.[7] Brethren, we tell you Messiah has come. He is Jesus bar Joseph of Nazareth. A man attested to you by his resurrection from the dead, all according to the Scriptures. Jesus is the cornerstone that you rejected, but he became the cornerstone of the new temple, a heavenly house, being built on the foundation of the apostles and prophets. In Christ all those who believe are the living stones of that spiritual structure that is growing into a holy temple of the Lord, the dwelling place for God's spirit."[8]

He stepped back and let Moshe speak, "This adulterous generation rejected Messiah. You crucified him. But he is coming on the clouds of heaven in the armies of Rome to destroy this temple and city. And that destruction will be the sign to you that he is the Son of David you rejected. And that he is seated on David's throne at the right hand of God. His kingdom will reign forever with all his followers, his spiritual temple, in a spiritual Jerusalem on a spiritual Mount Zion."[9]

Alexander heard more than a few laughs from the crowd. So many still rejected the Spirit in favor of a tangible physical structure that they felt was more real because they could see it and touch it and engage in physical ritual. But they would soon be clutching crumbling stone and dirt in their wretched fists and performing funerary dirges as their liturgy.

Alexander wondered how much the average Jewish citizen who was listening to this sermon really understood their own Scriptures. Scribes, Pharisees, Sadducees, and the priestly class all studied the Law and the Prophets. But the average hard-working Jewish citizen did not have access to the scrolls. They spent most of their lives struggling to survive, working in the fields, the herds, or the city, laboring with their hands and bodies. The only time they were exposed to the Scriptures was in the synagogue, and for the prescribed feasts throughout the year. Only then would they hear the word of God. Their access was so limited.

He wondered how many would understand the picture of Ezekiel's eschatological temple and how it was fulfilled in Jesus and the new covenant. He cursed the shepherds who withheld the truth from their sheep whom they were responsible to safeguard.

Ezekiel had described a vision of the resurrection of Israelites out of their dead bones. It was a corporate metaphor for God restoring them out of exile. In the same way that so many Jews had missed the Messiah because they had interpreted his kingship as a literal earthly reign, they now missed the glories of the new covenant so obvious in this motif of resurrection or regathering.[10]

Yahweh had promised Ezekiel that he would take the scattered remnant of Israel from all the countries and bring them into their own land. This was a promise echoed by many of the prophets.

Micah spoke for Yahweh, saying, "I will gather the remnant of Israel."[11] Hosea wrote that even though Israel was "swallowed up" among the nations in exile, nevertheless "the children of Judah and the children of Israel shall be gathered together"[12] in what Isaiah also called the faithful "remnant."[13] That remnant is the Jewish believers in Jesus.[14]

But God had added another mysterious aspect to that gathering of the remnant. Hosea had promised that the Gentiles from all the nations would also be included in it.[15]

> "And the children of Judah and the children of Israel shall be gathered together...And those who were not my people I will call 'my people,' and her who was not beloved I will call 'beloved'"[16]

The apostle Paul had proclaimed that Christ had suffered and rose from the dead to be a "light both to our people and to the Gentiles." The mystery of the Gospel was that the regathering of Israel included the Gentile believers as fellow heirs with Jewish believers. That they were members of the one true root of Israel.[17]

That promise of the regathering had already begun to be fulfilled almost forty years ago when the Holy Spirit first fell upon believers at Pentecost. They were Jews from every tribe of Israel, from all the seventy Gentile nations, drawn back into the land to receive the promise of the Spirit that united them as one. And that gathering was ongoing as Jesus drew all men to himself, both Jew and Gentile, from those nations. He was resurrecting Israel out of death as a new body, the body of Christ.[18]

Ezekiel's vision of the valley of dry bones had foretold that symbolic resurrection that embodied the new covenant kingdom.

"My servant David shall be king over them, and they shall all have one shepherd. I will make a covenant of peace with them. It shall be an everlasting covenant. My dwelling place shall be with them, and I will be their God, and they shall be my people... And I will remove the heart of stone from your flesh and give you a heart of flesh. And I will put my Spirit within you...Then the nations will know that I am Yahweh who sanctifies Israel, when my sanctuary is in their midst forevermore."[19]

When Jesus had ascended to the throne of David at the right hand of God, he had united the sheep from his two folds of Jew and Gentile. They were one nation under an everlasting covenant of peace through the blood of the cross. In believers, the new covenant replaced the heart of stone with a heart of flesh. God now made his dwelling place among them just as he had promised.

Ezekiel had predicted the new covenant kingdom that the apostles had announced. The Apocalypse was foretelling the death and destruction of the old covenant system and its people, followed by the resurrection and marriage of the remnant as a new covenant bride of Christ.[20]

The dimensions of Ezekiel's eschatological temple were based on multiples of fifty, a symbol for the year of Jubilee.[21] Jesus had declared himself the fulfillment of the Jubilee when he read Isaiah's scroll.

"The Spirit of the Lord is upon me, because he has anointed me to proclaim good news to the poor. He has sent me to proclaim liberty to the captives and recovering of sight to the blind, to set at liberty those who are oppressed, to proclaim the year of the Lord's favor, and the Day of Vengeance of our God."[22]

Jesus had fulfilled the Jubilee in his ministry, and he would fulfill the Day of Vengeance in the coming destruction of earthly Jerusalem and temple.

"But when you see Jerusalem surrounded by armies, then know that its desolation has come near...for these are days of vengeance, to fulfill all that is written."[23]

Ezekiel had pointed to Jesus as the symbolic temple of the New Jerusalem. These listeners were living in the carcass of a spiritually dead city about to be ground to dust.

For you are dust and to dust you shall return.

The words of Jesus echoed in Alexander's mind. *For that which is born of the flesh is flesh. But that which is born of the spirit is spirit.*[24]

Moshe now described the eschatological temple to his hearers, "Behold, the true temple of God has a stream of living water that flows from the threshold and pours out to the east. That living water of the Holy Spirit began in our generation, and as it flows away from the temple, it becomes a mighty river too wide to cross. It flows into the sea of the Gentiles and turns the water fresh and gives life to every living creature in its wake."[25]

Suddenly, a heckler yelled out, "Enough pretty poetry! Tell us the gruesome details to come!"

People laughed. It was nervous laughter. For while the crowds mocked the prophets, Alexander sensed that they nevertheless feared there was truth in their message. Perhaps they wanted to know how long they could hold on before they could leave the sinking ship. What the people didn't realize was that by the time they would recognize the truth, it would be too late.

The Two Witnesses finished their prophecy and turned to leave. A small crowd of people surrounded them as they always did, asking for miracles or some other self-interest. The masses were always begging for miracles from Jesus, then the apostles, and now the Two Witnesses. It was human nature to seek the spectacular and to seek one's own wellbeing. That was why Jesus called this generation that sought a sign "adulterous." But the sign that was coming, the sign of the Son of Man, would not be for their wellbeing.

He saw an old stooped-over woman approach the Witnesses. She had a shawl and a hood protecting herself from the beating sun. She grabbed Elihu's hands with gratitude and said something to him.

What nobody around would notice was that she had also slipped a note to the prophet. The old woman was Cassandra in disguise. The note explained the dire situation of their sewage plumbing at the hands of Jacob. It would be fruitless to ask the prophets to heal everyone in the hippodrome, since the very point of the plague was God's judgment. But surely Jacob's cruel vendetta was not part of God's plan. Surely the Witnesses could publicly reveal the injustice of the sanitation problem to force accountability from the civil authorities. Or was their problem just too insignificant for these prophets of God who were busy addressing the covenant violations of an apostate people?

Alexander saw Elihu's head turn to watch the disguised Cassandra limp away, stooped over in pretended old age. The prophet's face held a look of concern as Elihu whispered to Moshe what Alexander could only hope was a successfully transmitted message.

Unfortunately, two temple guards appeared to have noticed the hobbling old woman's brief exchange with Elihu. They dared not accost the Witnesses, but they followed the disguised Cassandra to the gate. Hurrying through the crowd, Alexander caught up in time to spot one of the guards pulling Cassandra behind a pillar under the portico.

He needed a diversion before they had opportunity to interrogate Cassandra. Approaching the guards, Alexander asked, "Is there something wrong?"

One of the guards held up his hand, the other on his sword. "Stop. This is temple business."

Alexander stopped. What else could he do? He wasn't a warrior. He couldn't fight the guards or physically rescue his wife. He did the only thing he could do: pray.

One guard yanked down Cassandra's hood. Then both guards pulled back in surprise. Their action had exposed to view an old woman, a very old woman, with a wrinkled face and scraggly white hair. And she appeared to have infectious boils on her face.

Looking horrified, the guards backed hastily away. They were out of view here of the crowds, and yelling unclean would just cause a panic. Pretending they'd never seen their elderly captive would be the easiest way to avoid trouble.

"Get out of here," one guard barked at the old woman. The other glared menacingly at Alexander. "You too. It's nothing. Get out."

Pulling her hood back up, the old woman scurried toward the gate. Alexander ran after her as the two guards dissolved back into the temple. He caught up with Cassandra just outside the Huldah Gates.

"Are you okay?" he asked.

She kept limping away, but said with a craggily voice, "Do you want the plague, young man? Stay away."

Instead of obeying, he tucked an arm underneath her own. She stopped limping and stood up straight. As they walked together back to the

117

hippodrome, Cassandra smiled impishly at Alexander. "I told you it would work."

Sarah, the sick volunteer they had tended to earlier, had previously worked at the theater and still had connections with the acting troupe. She had borrowed some of their stage props and make-up to disguise Cassandra as the doddering old woman. Alexander hadn't expected the plague victim subterfuge, but he thanked God it had worked.

"You are quite the actress, my love."

"I didn't fool Elihu. He knew immediately who I was."

"That doesn't surprise me."

"They have our request."

"Now let us hope they grant it."

CHAPTER 24

"Cassandra, wake up!"

The voice was Alexander's. It sounded excited but not with agitation as had been the norm lately. Its happy tone left her confused. Where was she? Was this a dream?

Wiping sleep from her eyes, Cassandra took in her husband smiling at her from the tent entrance. No, it wasn't a dream. She was back in her own bed in the hippodrome.

"You'll never believe what happened." Alexander's smile grew wider. "The sewage water is running again."

Cassandra's note to the Witnesses must have worked. "What happened?"

"I don't know. But there are civil workers cleaning out the excess refuse that had built up. Come on."

Getting up, Cassandra threw on a tunic and robe to follow Alexander to the latrine area.

Just as Alexander had promised, they arrived to find a dozen civil workers cleaning out the toilets. They had lifted the long stone bench of public seats, and a team had climbed down into the sewer drainage, where they were using shovels to evacuate the excess build up. Body coverings and veils protected the workers from flies and the filth they were handling.

At the wonderful sight, Cassandra began to tear up. Then she took note of an elderly man with peppery hair and a scar down his cheek standing a discreet distance from the stench and flies. She recognized him from prior encounters as a servant from Jacob's household. Cassandra dredged up a name from her memory. "Nathan."

She'd remembered rightly from the man's acknowledging bow. Cassandra asked, "Jacob ordered this?"

Nathan looked around as though checking for eavesdroppers, then pulled Cassandra and Alexander both aside. He whispered, "Last night we were visited by a man who was cloaked to disguise his presence. It was one of the Two Witnesses."

"The young one or the old one?" Cassandra asked.

"The young one."

So it was Elihu.

"What did he say?"

"He told Jacob to extend his arm. When my master did so, he saw it was full of leprosy. Then the prophet told him to hide his arm and pull it out again. When he did, it was clean. No sign of the disease."

As Alexander and Cassandra exchanged a glance of mutual joy and gratitude, Nathan continued, "The prophet then said to my master, 'Let waters roll down like justice.' After which he left."

"That's all he said?" asked Alexander.

Nathan shrugged. "That is all."

It was a verse of scripture in reverse. The prophet Amos had said to let justice roll down like waters. Elihu must have been using a scriptural allusion to tell Jacob to release the waters of sewage or he would be stricken with the plague.

Cassandra stared dubiously at the servant. "Why do you tell us this, Nathan?"

"I thought it would help you to know." Nathan appeared skittish, eyes shifting, looking around.

"Do you not jeopardize your relationship with your master in doing so?" Cassandra demanded.

He demurred, "Please do not tell him."

Alexander looked skeptically at Nathan. "Did Jacob order you to tell us this?"

"No!" Jacob's servant responded quickly with apparent offense. "Not everyone is against you," he added and turned to leave.

Cassandra and Alexander gave each other a glance as the elderly man hurried away across the arena floor. Could they trust him? Did it matter? The water had been released. Their request for help had worked. The patients of the hippodrome had running water and sanitation again. It was an answer to prayer.

Alexander mused out loud, "Let us hope there is not another side to this story that we are not privy to."

Cassandra could not help but think there was!

CHAPTER 25

Gamala
November, AD 67

Raphael lay helpless in his wooden cart as he was hoisted down a steep ravine into the valley surrounding the city of Gamala across the Sea of Galilee from Taricheae. It was the end of another Roman siege of another Jewish city on the top of a steep gorge. He felt his cart passed through the hands of Zeus, Anat, Molech, Dagon, and the Daughters of Allah. Overhead, carrion birds circled. The stench of death greeted Raphael as the cart arrived at the bottom of the ravine.

His six captors lay the cart down and once again celebrated with joy at the sight around them. Thousands upon thousands of dead Jews lay in high piles. They had jumped or been cast off from the city walls hundreds of feet above them, only to land here in splattered pieces. It looked like a garbage dump of human bodies. Birds and rodents were feasting on the rotting flesh. The Watchers licked their lips with hunger and thirst.

"How wonderful!" exclaimed Zeus. "The Romans must have pushed them all to their deaths."

"No," said a stern, strong voice behind them.

They all whipped around to see Apollyon standing with Azazel and Semyaza, their legs drenched in gore. The gods bowed in deference.

Apollyon continued, "These jumped to their deaths to escape the clutches of the Romans, who massacred the rest of the city above, every man, woman, and child."

Raphael heard Molech breath out a hungry longing, as he did every time he heard about desecrated children. The abominable deity began to search for young ones amongst the dead.

Apollyon sighed with delight. "Nine thousand more dead Jews. Nine thousand souls whose deaths become the source of our life and power. Drink of this blood, my minions, and grow strong."[1]

Apollyon finished licking a skull clean and tossed it back onto the carnage. Raphael glanced at Anat, who was watching her leader with a dour expression. She made the mistake of not disguising her contempt well. "Master Apollyon, we have supped on the murder and sacrifice of tens of thousands already. How long shall we delay our journey to the Euphrates?"

The master gave her a scolding look. "As long as I say, virgin goddess." He was using her religious epithet as a subtle insult. "But as it happens, I am happy to announce that we are ready for the second phase of preparation."

The seven travelers looked excited to hear a new task.

"We are going to the city where it all began, Babylon on the Euphrates." Apollyon was referring to the place where the allotment of the nations to the Sons of God had occurred: the Great Dispersion of Babel.

"We?" asked Anat with a touch of disappointment in her voice.

"Yes, we!" snapped Apollyon. "I am going with you. Azazel and Semyaza are capable of their responsibilities without me. The entire region of Galilee is under Roman control save the town of Gischala. They will finish that final task while I help you complete yours."

"But my lord," complained Anat. "Surely the seven of us are capable of our responsibility?"

Apollyon was getting visibly agitated with her contrary attitude. "You are not privy to all my intentions. You would be wise not to press me."

"Yes, my lord." She bowed, but Raphael knew her submission was only outward.

Apollyon said, "All of you, have your fill on this feast of death. We leave shortly."

The gods began to move among the dead to find their sustenance.

Apollyon walked over to Raphael and looked down at him.

The archangel swallowed with fear at the monster hovering over him.

Apollyon whispered maliciously, "Do you think you are gaining intelligence to use against me, archon? Spying out weakness, overhearing strategy?"

He laughed derisively. "You have no idea what is really going on."

But Raphael *did* have an idea of what was going on and why they were going to Babylon. He hadn't forgotten what was buried there generations ago. Buried deep in the ground of that cursed land. And he was worried for his fellow archangels if Apollyon was successful at finding it.

CHAPTER 26

City of Gischala

John ben Levi paced back and forth on the top of the battlement, the sun setting behind him. He was known as John of Gischala, or simply Gischala, because of his pronounced loyalty to his city.

He looked out over the Roman forces arrayed against him: a thousand Roman horsemen. Vespasian didn't need much to defeat this town, and Gischala knew it. It was smaller than Jotapata and Gamala with easily penetrated walls and no ravines of protection. Gischala had with him his four hundred loyal warriors and several thousand men of the city, all ready to fight for their lives.

But he did not have them all on his side. He'd had to barricade the town nobles and rulers inside the main synagogue to keep a mutiny from happening. He'd also forbidden anyone but his most loyal soldiers to man the walls and gates in defense.[1]

Gischala stared out at the horsemen, arrayed in formation. The Roman cavalry was a powerful force. They could sweep through entire contingents of enemy forces, cutting them down with ease. Gischala knew he could not win this fight.

Anger rose within him as he recalled the events of the past year. Joseph ben Matthias had been named regional commander of Galilee by the newly formed Judean government, but Gischala considered him a whore of Rome. The Pharisee had even traveled to Rome, where he had wined and dined with that abominable swine Nero in what was an obvious political maneuver for power.

Gischala had circulated reports that he believed Joseph would soon betray their chosen nation to the Romans and had even warned Jerusalem of Joseph's tyrannical intent.

Joseph had responded by confiscating Gischala's finances that he had plundered from Agrippa. Their clash of rivalry had soon spread, and sides were taken. While Gischala had begun with a mere four hundred brigands in his force, he had ended up with the support of Sepphoris, Gabara, Gischala, and Tiberias. Joseph had everyone else.

Joseph had managed to frustrate two assassination attempts, but the Roman invasion had frustrated all their ambitions, and now here Gischala was, the last hold-out in the region.[2] He'd heard that Joseph had been captured and killed by Titus. He could only imagine his own fate if he tried to fight this unwinnable battle.

Down below Gischala spotted an officer leaving the ranks of the Roman horsemen with two other soldiers and a bannerman carrying a flag of negotiation. As the party approached the city gates, Gischala recognized the officer as Titus himself. This was almost too good to be true. Perhaps they had a chance of escaping this mayhem after all.

The Roman general and his party halted still some distance from the city. Gischala called to his men and made his own way to the gates. He mounted his horse and signaled for two of his own bodyguards to accompany him. Archers waited on the battlements, arrows aimed at Titus and his guards. The distance was a little too far for accuracy, but they would try just the same if they needed to.

John arrived and stopped within audible range of the Roman company.

Titus said, "I am General Flavius Titus, bearing negotiations for the surrender of your city. Are you John ben Levi, leader of the city's defense?"

"I am," said Gischala. He thought, *How did he know my name?*

Gischala eyed the general warily, his senses heightened, ready to spring into action. It wasn't unusual for a betrayal of the rules of war to happen in such circumstances. If the Romans attempted to take Gischala hostage, he would have to outrun any attackers back to the gates, where the archers would then protect his retreat into the city.

Gischala prayed he would not need such countermeasures.

Titus spoke. "We have secured the entire region of Galilee. You remain the last holdout. I have your mightiest general Joseph ben Matthias captive."

So, that's how he knew my name. That conniving wolf is alive after all, thought Gischala. *Not very mighty for a general.*

"I know about your city's defenses. Surely you don't believe you will be able to withstand me."

"Then why do you seek negotiation?" asked Gischala. He had to maintain an air of confidence, boldness.

"If you surrender, I will pardon you all. If you oppose my offer, I will spare no one in the city, man, woman, or child. If you rebel, you must be made an example of."

A chill went through Gischala. This Roman was ruthless. *I must be more cunning.*

"General, I am no fool," he responded. "I know the casualties I can inflict upon you, and I know they are not enough to win this conflict. But while I am inclined to hearken to your proposal, I am not a despot but a leader among equals." It was a backhanded insult at his opponent. "I will need to persuade the war council, which I am willing to do. However, you face one additional obstacle to your desires."

He let Titus wonder for a moment, giving Gischala a sense of control over the negotiation.

"As you can see, the sun is setting, and we are entering our Sabbath. As I am sure Joseph has explained to you, the Sabbath is our most holy of days, wherein we cease from all work for religious observances."

He saw Titus nod with awareness. So he was informed.

"That cessation of labor also includes removing our arms as well as engaging in entreaties of peace."

Titus sighed with contempt and shook his head.

Gischala said, "You may scoff at what you do not believe, but I am certain your 'mighty general' captive also informed you that if attacked on the Sabbath, we are allowed to fight to defend ourselves. In past conflicts, such a violation of the sacred by our enemies has been an inspiration that enflamed the entire Jewish force with a fanaticism unto death. I only ask that you allow us one day to observe our religious duty, and I assure you my attempt to persuade them of your beneficence will be proven by your very actions."

Titus stared at him, thinking through the request. Then he said, "I have seen the reality of this Jewish fanaticism on the walls of Jotapata." Gischala had gotten wind of the mighty feat of the warrior who broke the battering ram's head.

"Well enough," Titus went on. "I will pitch camp in Cydessa and await your answer by midday tomorrow." A well-fortified city a couple miles away, Cydessa was filled with Tyrians who hated Jews. They would probably join Titus in the attack.[3]

"Thank you, General," Gischala said, and the two adversaries parted ways to return to their respective bases.

Upon his return through the gates of the city, Gischala called together his war council for immediate deliberation. There were a dozen or so captains of hundreds.

Gischala looked at them grimly and said, "We do not have the manpower nor the defenses to withstand the Romans. General Titus himself is leading them, and he told me he would kill every man, woman, and child in the city."

The leaders looked despondent to a man. One of them asked, "What did he offer us as terms of surrender?"

"That he would only kill the soldiers. Every one of us."

"So either way, the warriors die," another captain spoke up gloomily.

The silence of dread filled the room. Gischala said, "Unless we escape."

The group looked suddenly hopeful. "What do you mean?" the first speaker demanded.

"Titus has allowed us the Sabbath to rest before I give him my answer. He is so convinced of our sincerity that he has not bothered to surround the city but has retired to Cydessa. So each of you go back to your units and tell your men that we are leaving under cover of night to flee to Jerusalem."

"But what about the civilians of the city?" a third leader protested.

Gischala said, "Titus has promised he will not kill them."

"No, he'll just enslave them!" the leader responded angrily. Others grumbled in agreement.

Gischala had to avoid the appearance of callousness if he wanted to maintain their loyalty. He said, "They can gather as many as they want, but they only have one hour before we leave through the western gate. And it must be clear that we cannot be slowed down. No carts. Horses alone. You are dismissed. I warn you, move quickly."

An hour later, Gischala saw the growing mass of several thousand men, women, and children at the gates. He knew their presence was a futile gesture of hope. He had six thousand fighting men, but only his own units were all mounted, and the overwhelming majority of civilians were on foot, despite his orders. It would take five days of hard riding through the highlands to reach Jerusalem as it was. It would take double that with innocents weighing them down.

This was an impossible journey. As much as the exodus from Egypt.

He led the multitude out into the night.

After they had traveled a few miles under the light of the moon, Gischala stopped the caravan to speak to the captains of the fighting units. They were moving too slowly. By morning, the Romans would discover their ruse and catch up with them with ease. Gischala had weighed his options and had landed on what he thought was the best strategy.

Gischala spoke to the captains, "I want the main bulk of the forces to continue to escort the civilians. Keep moving as fast as you can. I will take my four hundred and ride on ahead to make sure the way is clear for passage."

He looked at one of the elder captains, an experienced man with scars to prove it. "Medad, you will be in charge while I am absent."

Medad didn't nod to acknowledge the honor. The captains looked at one another with apprehension. Gischala could tell they didn't trust him.

Medad said, "If we stay together, we are stronger."

"And slower," said Gischala. "If we do not clear the way, we could be surprised by Vespasian's forces coming from any of the occupied towns in Galilee. Then we'll be hemmed in front and behind. Do you prefer that battle strategy?"

No one answered. But some of them shook their heads no.

"If there are any Roman forces in our path, we will draw attention away from your presence and goad them to give us chase."

Still the captains did not like the order.

Finally Gischala said, "We will return every other day or so before scouting the next leg of the journey."

That seemed to calm their fears.

Gischala then organized his men and set off into the night through the valley ahead of them.

As they galloped through the darkness, one of Gischala's captains, who had been with him since the beginning, pulled up next to him and said, "We're not returning, are we?"

Gischala shook his head. "No, it would be a pointless throwing away of our own lives."

Even six thousand fighting men could not defend several thousand townspeople that made up the caravan. The Romans would certainly catch up with them, slaughter the men, and enslave the rest.[4]

Gischala added, "If we must die, it won't be needlessly. Tell the men to use the deaths of our people as inspiration for revenge against the Romans."

The captain nodded and pulled away as they continued on their race toward Jerusalem.

CHAPTER 27

Jerusalem

The priestly service in the inner temple began first thing in the morning with a waterwheel mechanism beneath the temple pumping fresh water from cisterns into the molten sea, a huge bronze laver located between the altar and the temple above. The water was supplied by a full forty miles of aqueducts stretching as far south as the hills of Hebron as well as the three pools of Solomon.[1] A fresh supply of running water was necessary to the ritual of cleansing engaged in by the temple priests. They washed their hands and feet and sacred vessels at the large fifteen-foot laver in preparation for the offerings and entering the sacred space of the temple. They were ministering in the presence of a holy God on his cosmic mountain.[2]

The molten sea was so named because it was a symbolic depiction of the primordial sea out of which God had created his holy mountain Zion, the "center of the earth." Land and sea were metaphorically represented by the altar hearth and bronze laver respectively.[3] The laver was hoisted on the backs of twelve bronze-cast oxen surrounded by a rim sculpted like a lily; garden imagery of Eden.

The temple was considered the cosmic center of the earth, the very garden of God's presence, his holy mountain.[4] The priesthood was like Adam in their responsibility to work it and keep it. It was the most sacred space in all the land. But it was also a microcosm of the heavens and earth and the heart of Yahweh's covenant with his people. God dedicated the cosmos as his temple in the opening of the first book of Moses and instructed the land to come out of and separate from the seas, just as the land of Israel and her people came out of the nations and were separated unto Yahweh.[5]

Twenty priests gathered around the bronze laver to begin their morning cleansing. They heard the sound of the large water mechanism churn to pour

131

forth fresh water for the new day into the laver. They turned on faucets positioned around the perimeter to wash their hands and feet first.

But they were all frightened with shock as the water turned to blood that poured onto their bodies in defilement. Some screamed. Others backed away from the laver. Turning off the faucets, they ran to alert Eleazar ben Simon, the captain who had taken charge of the inner temple with several hundred of his followers.

Eleazar came out to the molten sea and saw for himself the blood-red waters that poured out onto the ground.

"It is a miracle," said one of the priests. "A miracle curse."

One of the guards asked, "Is God condemning us for taking over the temple, Eleazar?"

"By taking it from the bloody hands of a corrupt priesthood? I don't think so!" the commander huffed. He thought for a moment, then said, "Come with me."

Eleazar marched the priest down to the large waterwheel mechanism below the temple, only to find the cistern full of blood-red water as well. The low-level aqueduct opening that filled the cistern had stopped. It looked as though it had been plugged up.

"From where does this source come?" he asked. "Pools inside the city?"

"No, from the aqueducts that bring water from Hebron and its surrounding area," a priest responded.

Hebron was in the southern hills in Idumean territory. Eleazar pointed to the two guards with him. "Disguise yourselves in cloaks. We are going outside the city."

The three disguised guards slipped out of the temple on horseback and made their way to the southwestern hills just outside the city. There were several aqueducts of stone that provided water to Jerusalem from the south. They climbed the structures to check the water, and Eleazar found what he was looking for.

Where the low-level aqueduct split off from the high, the waterway rounded a corner to enter the city at a different location. It was currently dammed up by the dead bodies of dozens of soldiers who wore flowing robes and carried scimitars. Idumeans from the south.

Eleazar knew exactly what had happened here. Simon bar Giora was warring in Idumea with his forces and had been dumping some of the dead into the aqueducts, knowing they would create this very scenario of unclean defilement in the temple.[6]

Scurrilous son of a harlot! Eleazar ordered the guards to unplug the canal of the dead bodies. It wasn't long before the water was back to its usual flow. Already, the water coming from the south was losing its red hue.

But Eleazar knew this was only one of many such scenarios all around the land. He'd heard about rivers like the Jordan and others being plugged with corpses from Vespasian's destruction in Galilee. The Dead Sea too now lived up to its name with dead bodies floating in its salted waters.

The blood waters in the temple might have had a rational explanation, but that didn't mean it wasn't a sign of the spiritual reality of polluted sacred space.[7]

They had to get back to the temple before they were discovered.

CHAPTER 28

Moshe and Elihu stood on the great stone-arched entrance above the southwest corner of the temple. Hundreds passed by on their way to temple, and when the two preached, their voices could carry down into the marketplace at the foot of the stairs.

Moshe read from the scroll of the Apocalypse, "An angel blew his trumpet, and a great star fell from heaven, blazing like a torch, and it fell on a third of the rivers and on the springs of water. The name of the star is Wormwood. A third of the waters became wormwood, and many people died from the water, because it had been made bitter."[1]

He closed the scroll and gave it to Elihu, then said, "Remember now the Law of Jealousy in our Torah that speaks of the 'trial by ordeal.' If a woman is suspected of adultery, the priest makes her drink a mixture of water with dust from the floor of the temple, added to the curses written against her in the book. If she is innocent of adultery, nothing becomes of her. But if she is guilty, God makes the water bitter in her stomach with pain and sterility."

Moshe paused to let his listeners consider. "So the office of High Priest has fallen like a star from heaven. The priesthood has led Israel into adultery against her husband, Yahweh. Her stomach is made bitter in her trial by ordeal."[2]

Elihu stepped up and took over, reading again from the scroll of the Apocalypse. "An angel poured out his bowl into the rivers and the springs of water, and they became blood. And I heard the angel in charge of the waters say, 'Just are you, O Holy One, who is and who was, for you brought these judgments. For Jerusalem has shed the blood of saints and prophets, and you have given them blood to drink. It is what they deserve!'"[3]

He closed the scroll. "The waters of this land are turning to blood because this generation is guilty of the blood of Messiah and all the righteous blood shed on the land, from righteous Abel to Zechariah to the saints of Messiah Jesus. God sent us prophets and wise men and scribes, but we killed them. We flogged and persecuted them. We crucified them.[4] Jerusalem, this great city, has become Babylon in God's eyes!"[5]

Elihu opened the scroll again and read, "'Alas! Alas! You great city, you mighty city, Babylon! For in a single hour your judgment has come. Rejoice over her, O heaven, and you saints and apostles and prophets, for God has given judgment for you against her! And in her was found the blood of prophets and of saints and of all who have been slain on the land. So Babylon the great city will be thrown down with violence and will be found no more."[6]

Elihu stepped back and let Moshe conclude. "Thus says the Lord, 'Come out of her, my people, lest you take part in her sins, lest you share in her plagues; for her sins are heaped high as heaven.'"[7]

• • • • •

Alexander and Cassandra stood in the crowd before the steps of the Herodian palace in the Upper City. They listened to the high priest Ananus speak to an assembly of the people. He was the supreme commander of the Judean forces, and he had become frustrated with their situation.

"People of Israel, I call upon every man of fighting ability to join me in standing against Eleazar ben Simon and his rebel army. Eleazar is a tyrant who has killed our own countrymen. He now holds the temple hostage to pollute it with their unclean presence. Do we fight the Romans, the lords of the earth, only to tolerate our own tyrants who treat the holiness of our temple with less respect than the pagans?"

The crowd responded with ire. Ananus was skilled at inspiring the masses.

"I have posted six thousand guards around the inner temple where Eleazar hides like a sewer rat. How shall we stand against the powers of Rome when we are divided by civil war in our midst? Shall we be hemmed in by Romans outside our walls and robbers inside our temple?"

The crowd yelled no to his provocation.

"Then join together, and we can put an end to this abomination."

A voice rang out from the crowd. "What about negotiation?"

Some agreement rumbled through the multitude.

Ananus responded indignantly, "Eleazar is a fanatic. He does not negotiate. But he was also captain of the temple guard, so he knows too much of the temple to be outmaneuvered militarily. It would take someone of Eleazar's equal to match him."

The voice yelled out again, "Like another captain of the temple?"

Alexander and Cassandra looked behind them, along with everyone else, to see who was speaking with such confidence. The crowd began to part as a single warrior made his way to the front, followed by a contingent of his own warriors.

They recognized him: John of Gischala. He announced, "I was a captain of the temple. Eleazar was my lieutenant until I stood against Rome for the sake of the temple, and was made a fugitive of Caesar's tyranny. I know how to get command of the temple back."

Impressed, the crowd cheered him on. Cassandra and Alexander looked at each other with dread. They remembered Gischala, another serpent in the temple. Before he was captain of the temple, he had participated in the persecution of Moshe and other Christians back at the beginning of Moshe's prophetic ministry. At that time Moshe's name was Joshua and Elihu's name was Demetrius. When he had become captain, Gischala had sought to kill Joshua, but Demetrius had rescued him with his warriors. When Gischala recognized the Two Witnesses as those two men he had confronted in the past, he would surely seek to kill them now. He would strike the heel of the body of Christ.

Gischala stopped at the bottom of the steps. "I bring news of the war in Galilee."

Ananus gestured, and Gischala ascended the steps with the bravado of a ruling general. He turned to the crowd. "Galilee has fallen. Vespasian has captured or destroyed all the cities of the region from Gamala to Sepphoris to my hometown of Gischala. He slaughters innocent men, women, and children and enslaves the survivors. I faced a Roman cavalry unit of the general Titus himself and barely escaped with my life."

A heckler yelled, "You ran away!"

"No," said Gischala. "I came to Jerusalem with intelligence that will help us defend this great city from the coming siege. We have a mighty wall, but we must have a strategy. I know how the Romans fight. And I also know that they have a most deadly weapon."

The audience grumbled with curiosity.

"The general of Galilee, Joseph ben Matthias, has gone over to the Romans. He has become a traitor."

The people burst out in shock. Ananus appeared as if he was going to fall down.

"It is true. I saw him with my own eyes by Titus's side giving him consultation on how to attack my city. Rest assured, he will be offering the Romans the same advice on our holy city!"

The crowd broke out in shouts of anger. But Gischala raised his hands and quieted them down.

Cassandra saw Ananus eyeing the Galilean warrior distrustfully. Gischala's skill of persuasion could be a double-edged sword if he were to gain too much power.

"The Roman eagle is coming. And it brings desolation in its wings. We would do well to first rid ourselves of the satan within the heart of our holy city or we may not have the soul to fight the satan from without. I commit my allegiance to the supreme commander's forces, and so let us all do so!"

Cheers rang out again from the crowd.

"He has captivated them," Alexander muttered to Cassandra beneath the din. "He has maneuvered a call of allegiance to Ananus into allegiance to his own call."

"He's a demagogue!" Cassandra muttered back in agreement.

A messenger shouted from the back of the crowd, "Refugees are approaching the city at the northern gates!"

CHAPTER 29

Cassandra and Alexander arrived at the northern gates of the New City. It was still an area of charred ruins in the process of rebuilding from the rubble. They had made it just in time to see arriving refugees swarming past the Herodian guards into the city. Alexander noticed one group of about fifty huddled together to one side of the gate. All were children, ragged and malnourished.

John of Gischala had arrived ahead of them and was already questioning the refugees. As Cassandra headed toward the children, Alexander went to the gate. More refugees were still arriving like a line of walking corpses, including more children.

Alexander returned to Cassandra. She was already deep in conversation with some of the children. She turned to Alexander. "They are refugees whose cities were destroyed by the Romans. These children have no adults to care for them because their parents are all dead or enslaved."

"Dear Lord," said Alexander. He prayed for them silently.

Cassandra gestured to Gischala, moving abruptly through the crowd of refugees. "Some seem to be from his home city of Gischala. Did he not say his city was destroyed and all men, women, and children were slaughtered?"

Alexander gave her a sharp look. "If they have a different story to tell than his…"

He didn't have to finish for Cassandra to know exactly what he meant. If any of the refugees from Gischala's home town contradicted his story of escape, Gischala's new position of power in the city would be jeopardized. And knowing the Galilean warrior's ruthless character, Cassandra expected the worst.

Cassandra's musing was interrupted by a low moan, quickly broken off. Turning, she spotted two young boys just beyond the children she'd been questioning, the taller one supporting the smaller one to the point of practically carrying him. From his expression of pain, gritted teeth, and ginger cradling of his left arm, it was the smaller boy Cassandra had overheard. Both children were filthy with the dirt and sand of a long and arduous journey.

"Alexander, those two children need help," she said urgently.

But her husband was already moving in their direction. The small one flinched when Alexander reached for his arm. The taller boy immediately pushed in front as though to shield his smaller companion. "Don't touch him!"

"I'm a doctor," Alexander reassured gently. "I can help with your injuries."

The taller boy moved grudgingly to one side. While Alexander began examining the smaller boy's injuries, Cassandra addressed the older boy, a thin-looking lad with baggy clothes. "My name is Cassandra. What is yours?"

He looked downward as though too shy to speak or trying to hide his face. But Cassandra had already noted the very unboyish gait of his walk and delicacy of features. This young lad was not what he appeared to be.

"Why are you dressed like a boy?" she asked.

He wouldn't respond, but the smaller one did. "Because she *is* a boy."

"Noah!" the older one barked with anger.

Just then Noah yelped. "Ow! That hurt!" With a grimace, he pulled his left arm away from Alexander.

"It's okay. I've finished with your arm," Alexander said with a chuckle. "Now may I look at your foot?"

Noah cautiously moved his right foot out for inspection. His older companion was watching Alexander like a hawk as though suspicious of the doctor's motives.

"He won't hurt him. My husband is an excellent doctor," Cassandra soothed, then added gently but firmly, "Now, what is your name, girl?"

The girl started violently at the question. Cassandra took her by the arm before she could bolt away. Dropping her face with an expression of shame, the girl finally whispered, "Rachel."

"Why are you dressed like a boy, Rachel?"

Rachel looked up into Cassandra's eyes, and at whatever she saw there, her face relaxed somewhat. "Because of what men do to women and girls."

Cassandra winced with painful sympathy. The girl was too young to be faced with such trauma. She motioned towards Noah. "You are brother and sister?"

"Yes. And I am not so young. I have lived twelve years already, my brother seven." Rachel hunched her shoulders, her voice suddenly wobbling. "He is all I have left of my family. I was afraid he would die too before we reached Jerusalem."

"Well, we will not let that happen now," Cassandra assured, then continued probing gently. "Does this mean your parents are no longer alive?"

"They are not. We were escaping our city with other citizens and soldiers at night. But the Romans found us and attacked us."

"What is your city?" Cassandra already knew the answer.

Rachel said, "Gischala."

Raising his head just then from his patient, Alexander interrupted, "Noah here has a broken arm and a sprained ankle. We need to get him to where I can deal with his injuries."

Alexander hoisted the young boy in his arms. Taking Rachel by an arm to follow, Cassandra saw that John of Gischala had now left the adult refugees coming through the gate and was moving through the children, still asking questions. He was almost upon them when Noah let out a gasp.

But it was not from pain. Looking up at the small boy, Cassandra saw that Noah's face was red with anger, his good hand tightened into a little fist as he glared hatefully at Gischala.

"I know that man!" The small boy spoke with an angry passion that reminded Cassandra of herself.

Alexander raised an eyebrow at the boy in his arms. "What do you mean?"

But Cassandra raised a hand before Noah could speak. "Not now!"

She dropped her voice to an urgent whisper. "Rachel and Noah, I want you to keep a secret. Do not tell that man you are from Gischala." She looked at Rachel, who immediately nodded.

Noah did not. "Why?" he demanded.

There was no time to respond as Gischala was now upon them. "And where are all of you children from?"

Cassandra glanced at Noah. Her heart sank when she saw him opening his mouth to say "Gischala." But Alexander squeezed the boy's bad arm and he gave a cry of pain before he could say the full word. "Gi—aaaahhhhh!"

Gischala snapped a look at him. Alexander was holding Noah's arm gently now. "He broke his arm. I have to get him to an infirmary."

Rachel interrupted Gischala's suspicion, "Why do you ask, sir?"

Cassandra knew Gischala too well to be fooled by the look of concern he focused on the girl. "I am gathering together all the refugees from my own city of Gischala, so I may help them."

Rachel said, "My brother and I are from Jotapata. The Romans burned our city too."

Gischala looked as though he'd already lost interest. "Well, I am sure you will find other survivors from your city with whom to take refuge."

His glance flickered briefly over Alexander and Cassandra as he moved off. Cassandra found she was holding her breath until he occupied himself interrogating another group of children, but she wasn't really worried. While they had seen only too much of his brutal whipping of Moshe when the elderly prophet was still Joshua, Gischala had never been close enough to recognize her or Alexander.

Cassandra turned to Rachel. "That was quick thinking."

Rachel smiled back. "Some children from Jotapata joined us on our way down here. They told us about the city."

Cassandra gave Rachel an impressed smile. The young girl was quite intelligent and industrious. Cassandra's heart was already being drawn to these two.

Rachel asked curiously. "And why did you not want that man to know we are from his city?"

Alexander answered, "His name is John of Gischala. He is now a leader of military forces in Jerusalem."

"And he is not a good man," added Cassandra. "Whatever he promises, you cannot trust him to help you."

"He is a coward and a bad man," Noah pronounced defiantly. "He left us to be killed by the Romans."

"Shh! Keep your voice down, boy," Alexander said softly but sternly. "You can tell us what you know later when we are in a place of safety. Until then, keep to your sister's tale."

The hatred and defiance didn't leave little Noah's face, but he fell silent. By now the group of refugees pushing into the city had grown to several hundred, filling the gate area.

With Noah still cradled in his arms, Alexander addressed the other children milling nearby, "Children, we will arrange a place for all of you to stay and get something to eat. And any others who have injuries will be cared for. But for now you must stay together and not leave this area until we have made arrangements."

Cassandra whispered to him, "Where are we going to take them?"

"I have no idea," Alexander whispered back. "But we must find somewhere. At least for those children who are without family."

They turned to see Jacob ben Mordecai arriving on horseback with a handful of temple guards. He rode like a self-appointed prince looking down on his subjects. Dismounting, he strode up to Alexander and Cassandra.

"Why am I not surprised to find you two here?"

He looked around at all the refugee children with distaste. "And who are these?"

"Refugees from the surrounding desolate cities," Alexander said. "These children here are those who have no surviving family." Briefly, he explained. "We were just discussing what to do."

Jacob was now looking bored. "Take them with you to the hippodrome. You can care for them there."

Alexander protested, "My lord, we are still quarantined with several hundred plague victims. It is not safe for children."

"Then make it safe," said Jacob. "You two are doing just fine."

Alexander said, "Children are more susceptible to contagion. It could reignite a flame that you would not want to occur on your watch."

Jacob appeared to consider his reputation.

"What about the theater in the upper city?" Cassandra suggested. "It's small, close enough to the hippodrome for our access, and it would not risk spreading the disease."

Jacob stiffened. "Have you not appropriated enough city property? Take them to the hippodrome. Or you'll receive no food rations for them." He turned and sauntered back to his horse.

"What he means," Cassandra grumbled to Alexander, "is that if the orphans die of disease, they'll no longer be in need of rations."

Alexander said, "Let us get these children to the hippodrome. They're in God's hands, like us." He turned to help Noah. "And let me tend to these injuries of yours."

CHAPTER 30

Jacob made his presentation before the lesser sanhedrin of twenty-five in the Hall of Unhewn Stone. "Pure and undefiled religion, it is said, is caring for widows and orphans in their affliction. As the psalm says, 'Give justice to the weak and the fatherless; maintain the right of the afflicted and the destitute. Rescue the weak and the needy.'"[1]

Ananus appeared annoyed by Jacob. He interrupted with a sarcastic tone. "You impress us all with your grasp of the Scriptures, Jacob. But we do not need a sermon on widows and orphans. Get to the point."

Jacob scratched his neck. "I only meant to say that I have killed two sparrows with one stone, so to speak. By gathering the refugee children into the hippodrome, I have offered a way for us to discharge our obligation to them. And because they are now in quarantine, they are also under a tight restriction and will not be about the city causing trouble amongst the citizenry. Which of course would reflect poorly on this body's governance and possibly lead to more unrest."

Ananus' face reflected the fact that Jacob was making sure with every gesture that he was valuable to this cutthroat ruling class. He was not merely on the sanhedrin now. He would climb his way up the ladder of power by making himself indispensable to their reputation.

Ananus whispered counsel with several others before giving his order. "It is an act of stupidity to endanger the children by placing them in the quarantine. Take over the theater in the Upper City and house them there."

Jacob felt a flash of humiliation burn inside him. He had misjudged Ananus. And now Jacob looked heartless. He would have to maneuver back into good graces.

"Of course, my lord high priest. Forgive me, I was only trying to protect your governance."

Jacob felt his cheek itching. He scratched it but stopped as he felt some pain from the boil he had just broke open.

Ananus said, "Yes, well, our governance is charged with protecting the people of this city, not our own…" He stopped and peered closely at Jacob. "What is on your face and neck?" His eyes went wide with shock.

Someone blurted out, "Those are boils!"

Another said, "He has the plague!"

Everyone in the chamber pulled back in fear. Ananus yelled, "Jacob ben Mordecai, remove yourself immediately from this chamber! In the name of God, you are unclean!"

Jacob filled with dread. He had the curse upon him.

• • • • •

Alexander and Cassandra had helped arrange the quarters for the refugee orphans in the northern section of the hippodrome. They had prayed that God would protect the children from the plague and sought to keep them as physically separate as possible from the sick in the southern section.

Refugees continued to pour into Jerusalem, and by now over two hundred children had been brought to the hippodrome. All were hungry and sick from malnourishment. The sound of them crying filled Alexander's heart with pity. These were the orphans of war. The sad pathos of consequences suffered by the innocent.

Twenty of the adult volunteers helped manage the children and cheer them up while Alexander examined ailments and wounds. By God's grace, little Noah's broken arm was the worst of the lot, and Alexander and Cassandra now sought to solve that difficult problem. Rachel refused to leave her brother's side as Alexander settled Noah on a pallet in the tent set up for medical treatment.

"You never did tell me how you got hurt," Alexander commented conversationally, feeling along Noah's arm to find the break. Cassandra knew his intent was to distract the small boy from the inevitable pain.

Noah didn't unclench his gritted teeth, but Rachel looked over to Alexander. "The leaders of our city decided we should escape the Romans by night. We all left together, thousands of people and soldiers."

She paused, painful memories darkening her eyes. "Father and Mother told us not to carry anything with us other than food and water skins. We had to travel quickly. But we could not keep up with the soldiers on their horses."

"That was why I saw the man from the city gates!" Noah broke in with bitterness.

"John of Gischala?" Alexander confirmed.

"Yes. He came with his men on horses to speak to the soldiers leading the caravan. I had run ahead with a friend because we wanted to see their horses. I heard him tell the other soldiers that he and his men would ride to scout ahead and lead the Romans away from the caravan. He said they would come back every day or so to make sure we were safe. Then they rode away. But they never came back. Not once! Then the Romans came."

The small boy broke off, his face again reddening with hate and anger. Rachel took up the story. "When the Romans caught up with us, they…"

She stopped, choking up, before continuing. "They surrounded us. They took the men and lined them up. Noah tried to join Father. That was when a soldier hit him, and he hurt his arm."

Alexander had given up trying to deal at this moment with Noah's broken arm and just held the small boy close. "What happened then?"

Rachel could not go on. Silent trembling tears rolled down her cheeks.

Noah's voice was tight with fury as he took over. "They made us watch as they poured pitch on our father and lit him on fire. Just like the others. Then four Romans took our mother and did terrible things to her."

A moment of excruciating silence fell upon them.

Cassandra finally said, "I'm so sorry for your suffering. No child should experience what you have gone through."

Alexander asked, "How did you get away?"

Rachel pushed away her tears. "They set up camp to return to the city the next day. So we snuck away in the night when the guards were asleep."

Alexander was amazed and impressed with the children's courage, especially Noah. For a seven-year-old to remain quiet enough for a stealthy escape while enduring the searing pain of a broken arm took more fortitude than most men could boast.

"Well, Noah," said Alexander. "You are a brave young boy. And I am going to have to ask you to be brave in a different way."

Alexander tried to remain objective, but it was difficult after hearing their story. He felt he was violating his own principles of staying impersonal.

"Your injury happened weeks ago, and it has already started to heal, but as you can feel, the bone is not in its proper place, so it has been healing wrong. That is why you have the pain."

The boy's eyes searched Alexander's for what was coming next. Alexander dreaded to tell him.

"What that means is, I am going to have to re-break the bone and set it back into its proper place."

He saw brother and sister look at each other with fear.

"But I promise you, if you are willing to endure this pain right now, you will get well and the pain will go away eventually. If we do not do it, your arm will heal improperly, you will lose the use of it, and you will never be rid of the pain."

The young boy gritted his teeth and said with surprising quickness, "I'm ready."

Rachel stepped beside Noah and grabbed his good right hand.

Alexander felt around Noah's arm to get the exact area of the break. It was the outer ulna bone on his forearm. Alexander saw Cassandra place her hand on Noah's back and close her eyes to pray.

"Now, Noah," said Alexander, "I want you to understand…"

Noah looked up at him intently, waiting for instruction. But instead of speaking, Alexander gritted his teeth and snapped the boy's arm at the break.

An ugly, cracking sound penetrated the air and made Alexander shudder.

Rachel burst into tears.

Noah let out a yelp, but it wasn't that loud. He squeezed his eyes tight and moaned silently in pain. Alexander was again amazed at his grit. He had seen hardened soldiers on the battlefield scream in such circumstances. But not this brave, young boy.

Alexander manipulated the bones to fit them back into place. The boy whimpered and passed out. Alexander felt the click of the bones fitting together, and he released the arm with a sigh.

"Is he dead?" Rachel asked through her tears.

"No," said Alexander. "He passed out from the pain. It is actually better for him that way."

Rachel wept and continued to cling to her brother's limp hand as if she was never going to let him go.

Alexander told Cassandra, "Hand me the splint and bandages."

He began to wrap the arm in a cast-like splint to keep it immobile for healing. His thoughts were drawn to the endurance of these desperate child survivors. It made Alexander well up with hope for humanity at the very moment he was struggling with the goodness of God.

It was always a difficult emotional issue for him as a doctor, seeing the worst sort of pain and suffering in this life. He understood the theology of collective representation, but he had a difficult time reconciling it with the reality of individual suffering. Why did these innocent ones have to suffer for the sins of their fathers?

Governing rulers represented the people before Yahweh as authorities over them. A just and compassionate king brought God's blessings upon his people, but a corrupt and heartless king brought God's judgment upon them as well. So it went with families, clans, and nations.

The nature of the covenant was representational. Adam had represented the human race. He had brought sin into the world and with it death. Jesus had become a new Adam, a new representative for the faith community whose death on the cross undid the condemnation of Adam's children.

Therefore, as Adam's one trespass led to condemnation for all men, so Jesus's one act of righteousness leads to justification and life for all men. For as by the one man's disobedience the many were made sinners, so by the one man's obedience the many will be made righteous.[2]

If individuals did not find relief from their suffering in this life, they would have to trust in God that he would provide it in the next. Alexander had concluded that it was his job as an ambassador of Jesus Christ to bring healing to those who suffered now as a picture to them of the ultimate healing that Christ had promised through eternal life beyond the grave. It was the final resurrection that promised ultimate redemption from suffering. At this time, God was spiritually resurrecting souls through the eternal life of faith.

Whoever hears my word and believes him who sent me has eternal life. He does not come into judgment, but has passed from death to life. Truly, truly, I say to you, an hour is coming, and is now here, when the dead will hear the voice of the Son of God, and those who hear will live."[3]

148

Jesus was bringing Israel back from the dead, but as a new creature in Christ, a creature of faith. The children of Abraham were children of faith, not children of flesh. But Jesus said that spiritual resurrection was a foreshadow of a physical resurrection to come.

> But an hour is coming when all who are in the tombs will hear his voice and come out, those who have done good to the resurrection of life, and those who have done evil to the resurrection of judgment.[4]

In the Apocalypse, the apostle John had described two resurrections, the first as spiritual, experienced by the martyrs of this Tribulation. The second resurrection would be a physical one at the great white throne judgment.

There was hope in this world of shadows and flesh. All bodily groaning would be transformed. Adam, the first man, was from the earth, a man of mortality, but Jesus, the second Adam, was from heaven. So it would be with the resurrection of the dead. Our bodies would be sown weak, suffering and perishable, but would be raised glorified, healed, and imperishable.

> Behold! I tell you a mystery. We shall not all sleep, but we shall all be changed, in a moment, in the twinkling of an eye, at the last trumpet. For the trumpet will sound, and the dead will be raised imperishable, and we shall be changed. For this perishable body must put on the imperishable, and this mortal body must put on immortality. When the perishable puts on the imperishable, and the mortal puts on immortality, then shall come to pass the saying that is written: "Death is swallowed up in victory." "O death, where is your victory? O death, where is your sting?"[5]

Death itself was the last enemy to be defeated at the second resurrection. But for now, we suffer.

"Alexander!" shouted Cassandra. She had gone to the gates and received a new victim into their house of healing. "It's Jacob. He's been struck with the plague."

Jacob stood behind her, boils on his face and arms. He was swooning with dizziness. Before Alexander could do anything, Jacob fell to the ground unconscious.

CHAPTER 31

Jacob came back to consciousness on a cot in the sick area of the hippodrome. He could hear Alexander and Cassandra talking about him, so he kept his eyes closed.

Cassandra's voice said, "Alex, he has been more than a thorn in the flesh. He has been an impediment to the Gospel for years, even when he was a part of the church in this city. This must be God's judgment upon him."[1]

"Even so," came Alexander's voice, "it is God's way of challenging us to love our enemies."

"I'm sorry," Cassandra said. "After all we've been through, I should know better. But sometimes my lack of faith overwhelms me."

Alexander responded, "Sometimes I say what I believe is true, though I too lack the faith to live it."

Jacob heard the couple embrace each other. He thought he heard the soft whimper of crying from Cassandra.

"Let us pray for Jacob," said Alexander.

Jacob heard them kneel to the ground, and Alexander began to pray. "Heavenly Father, forgive Jacob for he does not know that he is but an instrument of your will to do whatever your hand and your plan has predestined to take place. Open his heart with your Holy Spirit. And grant us strength and boldness to help him and love him that he might know the grace and forgiveness of the Lord Jesus Christ."

Jacob's stomach turned sour at their condescension. As if he were like the Gentiles without God and the covenant! This was exactly why he hated the Christians so. They dared to call themselves the chosen remnant of Yahweh, while condemning the Jews as cut off from their own covenant like the branches of a tree.

Cassandra added a reluctant, "In the name of Jesus Christ, amen."

Jacob chose that moment to open his eyes.

"The children," he groaned in feigned delirium.

"He's awake!" Cassandra exclaimed. The doctor and his wife moved to loom above Jacob.

"What did you say, Jacob?" Alexander asked.

"Move the children to the theater. I have approval from the sanhedrin."

"Your servant has already informed us," Alexander responded. "We are preparing for the move."

"Will you tell the Witnesses to call off the plague?"

Jacob saw confusion on the faces above him.

"What do you mean?" asked Alexander.

"I did what you asked. So why do I still have the plague?"

"I'm afraid we don't have that kind of power," said Alexander. "Only the Two Witnesses do, and they do not answer to us. But if you repent, though you may die, yet you shall live in Messiah."

Jacob felt himself choking up with tears. He repeated, "I did what you asked. Why am I being punished?"

"Pray, Jacob," said Alexander. "Pray to the God of Israel that he may have mercy upon you and extend his grace toward you."

Jacob drifted back out of consciousness.

· · · · ·

The adult volunteers rounded up the children for their short trip from the hippodrome across the valley to the theater in the Upper City. Cassandra went with Alexander to check on Noah and Rachel in the injury ward they had created at the northwest corner of the stadium. Only a handful of patients remained there.

Alexander said to his wife, "You should oversee the children at the theater."

"I'm not leaving your side," she said.

"It's only a hundred yards across the valley."

"That's a world away. We have plenty of adult volunteers who have the calling and interest to do so."

"You are the only one I trust."

"Well, maybe you should trust God a little more."

He smiled at her teasing tone. She added, "I am called to support your vision and work with you in your medical ministry, not baby-sit a bunch of children."

"Like it or not," Alexander responded, "they are part of my responsibility and ministry here."

Cassandra came up with a compromise. "What if I was a liaison? I could delegate adult supervisors and coordinate them from here with occasional visits to the theater."

"That would be acceptable," Alexander agreed as they entered the injuries tent.

Alexander examined Noah's arm-splint and bandages. Everything seemed well. Rachel stood dutifully beside him in her boyish clothes and dirty face. Cassandra understood now that the girl's unkempt and unclean look was her way of trying to look unattractive to men. She would try to build the girl's courage to face her life without such fear. But after Rachel's experience, Cassandra fully understood it would not be easy.

Alexander smiled at Noah. "Your arm is doing well. How is the pain?"

"Better," said Noah.

Alexander examined Noah's sprained ankle. "You should be able to walk on this soon."

The small boy looked anxious. "Rachel told me all the children have to leave this place. Must we go? I wish to stay with you!"

"The other children are being moved to a theater that is much nicer than this," said Alexander. "But you will stay here a while longer until you are more fully recovered. Your sister, however…"

"I'm staying with my brother," Rachel interjected emphatically.

Alexander glanced at Cassandra. She nodded in agreement. "Of course, you can stay with your brother. He couldn't have a better protector."

"She's not my protector," declared Noah.

Cassandra smiled at the young boy's bid for maturity.

"You protect each other," Alexander said. "That's what family is for."

"That's right, staying together!" Cassandra emphasized, giving her husband a scolding look.

Rachel said to Cassandra. "I can care for Noah. I did so for my mother. And I can help you with your other work. If you teach me."

Cassandra considered the offer. The girl was starting to connect with her. "I would like that very much. I could use your help."

Rachel beamed with a brightness Cassandra had not seen in the young girl since her arrival. There was hope for healing.

She added, "And the first lesson in the work of medicine is the need for hygiene. So let's get you a bath, young lady, and some clean clothes."

Rachel's eyes went wide with regret.

•••••

Cassandra led fifty of the adult volunteers along with the two hundred refugee children on a short walk over to the Herodian theater just across the valley from the hippodrome in the Upper City.

They passed by some workers already boarding up the first level of the theater as they had done with the hippodrome. When they entered, Cassandra saw many of the children light up with excitement at the sight of the grand stage with its façade of Greek architecture behind it.

The theater was smaller than the arena, multi-tiered, and semi-circular in structure. The public were entertained here by Greek and Roman plays as well as musical concerts. Where the hippodrome could seat thousands, the theater sat hundreds.

Children squealed with delight and ran up to the large stage platform for a chance to play-act themselves. Cassandra smiled at how their imaginations seemed to be the most capable of taking their minds off of their predicament.

In contrast, Rachel, who had reluctantly consented to come along, refused to leave Cassandra's side. This was one way these war orphans responded to the trauma of their situation, as Cassandra was discovering. Some like Rachel clung to their new guardians with a desperate desire to be loved. Others like Noah responded with anger and withdrawal to protect themselves from the ruthless world.

Cassandra considered it real progress to coax Rachel away from her brother's side, even if just for this short trip.

Just then Cassandra saw the interested gaze of a guard light on the young girl. Rachel had taken a bath and was still wearing loose-fitting clothing. But it could no longer be hidden that her youthful features and slim body were on the verge of blossoming into womanhood. Flushing with embarrassment, Rachel averted her eyes from the guard's admiring stare and ducked behind Cassandra's shielding form.

Putting an arm around the young girl, Cassandra gently tugged her back to her side. "Rachel, you have no reason for embarrassment or fear. You are a beautiful young girl. God has made you. He has a purpose for everything in our lives, even when we don't know why. You must trust him."

Rachel hunched her shoulders. "I need to get back to my brother."

Cassandra said, "We will shortly. I need to say something to the children."

She signaled to some of the adult volunteers nearby. They moved to quiet the children, settling them onto the theater seats to listen.

"Children, we want to protect you from sickness in the hippodrome, so this will be your new home for now." Cassandra gestured to the fifty or so adult volunteers around them. "These adults will be your guardians. Obey them and obey the rules they give you for your safety. Know also that the Lord watches over you like a shepherd."

Turning to Rachel, Cassandra smiled down at the young girl. "Now let's go see how your brother is doing."

CHAPTER 32

Babylon

Apollyon and his team of seven Watchers wheeled the captive Raphael to the outskirts of Babylon on the shore of the Euphrates River. Zeus, Anat, Dagon, Molech, and the Daughters of Allah stared at the once-great city before them. It was rather unimpressive now. The walls were in disrepair, the city itself neglected, broken down, and barely occupied compared with the numbers it had once boasted at the height of its glory millennia ago. The wondrous hanging gardens were long gone with the palaces that hosted them. A shudder of disappointment ran through Apollyon's body, followed by a rising tide of bitterness.

Babylon had been the original enemy city raised for Apollyon's glory to oppose God. After the great flood, humanity had thankfully not learned their lesson and had returned to the worship of creation instead of Yahweh.

The hunter king Nimrod was the first of the *gibborim*, or mighty men of the primeval era. Apollyon had used him to build the mighty city of Babylon as a "gateway for the gods" with its tower that reached to the heavens. Apollyon saw the remains of that tower as he walked into the temple complex, a walled area that took up about a fifth of the city.[1]

The tower was called Etemenanki, which meant "the temple of the foundation of heaven and earth." It was a ziggurat, or step-pyramid, dedicated to Marduk, patron warrior god of Babylon. It rose three hundred feet into the sky, a man-made cosmic mountain with a shrine at the top where the gods would come down to meet with man.

Because of the prior judgment of the great flood on the world that was, Nimrod had built this ziggurat with kiln-fired bricks instead of the usual mudbricks, using bitumen pitch to seal it from any possibility of being destroyed by another flood, should God choose to do so again.

155

It was here at this temple that Nimrod had drawn humanity together in their worship of creation and attempt at self-deification. Like the Nephilim before the flood, they had wanted to make a name for themselves.[2] To Apollyon, this was progress. To Yahweh, that jealous tyrant, it was idolatry. According to him, they exchanged the truth of God for a lie. They became futile in their minds, and their foolish hearts were darkened.

It was also here that Yahweh, in response to man's self-empowerment, confused the tongues of humanity and spread them out upon the land into seventy separate nations to keep them from achieving their human potential. It was here that Yahweh allotted those nations to the Sons of God, the Watchers, as an inheritance, to rule over them as principalities and powers. God gave up the pagan nations to the lusts of their hearts, to dishonorable passions, and to debased minds to do what ought not be done, all of which empowered the heavenly host in their rebellion.[3]

The myth went that Marduk, the storm god, had won the status of chief god of the pantheon because he had defeated Tiamat, the sea dragon of Chaos that threatened the gods. Marduk had used special weapons forged in heaven to achieve that victory, and he rode a mighty chariot named "Storm Demon" with four steeds of terror. Marduk was one of the mightiest of gods. But the gods' fates are linked to their earthly nations, and in the days of the Persian empire, King Xerxes had conquered Babylon and destroyed Marduk's image. A hundred and fifty years later, Alexander the Great conquered Persia and sought to restore Babylon to her former glory, but he died before he could achieve his goal. Marduk had been lost to history in the shuffle of kingdoms.[4]

But Apollyon was not here for Etemenanki. He was here for a smaller temple called Esagila that was located in the southern part of the temple complex. It was the temple that the original image of Marduk had inhabited along with his armor and weapons. Its complex hosted a small lake called "Abzu," or the Abyss. That lake had been drained and filled in with dirt and sand.[5]

Apollyon had left the Daughters of Allah to guard the hostage, Raphael, outside the walls of the city so the angel would not be privy to his plans. The four others he took with him into the temple complex. They entered the abandoned, crumbling Esagila and approached the dry lake bed.

"Start digging," he ordered. Anat, Molech, and Dagon retrieved shovels and pickaxes and began boring down into the earth. Working for an hour at a time with short rests in between, they filled buckets with dirt that were hauled up a mechanism by Zeus, who emptied them and sent them back down for more.

Hours passed, and a pile of dirt and sand grew around the mining as they reached a depth of seventy feet.

During one of her resting periods, Anat brushed sand off herself and asked Apollyon, "Why is Zeus exempt from our rotation? Why does he enjoy such privilege?"

Apollyon turned slowly from watching the diggers below. "Because he has displayed a loyalty to his sovereign I have yet to see in you."

Anat returned to her station with silent hatred on her face. Apollyon smirked but watched her closely.

From below Dagon yelled, "We found something!"

After a few more minutes of furious digging and uncovering, they sent up their discovered treasure: a battle net and mace, a bow and quiver, then body armor. Zeus handed them to Apollyon with a holy reverence. Apollyon grinned triumphantly and said, "The weapons of Marduk, king of the gods of Babylon."

Zeus said, "Those archangels will be in for a surprise."

"Keep digging," barked Apollyon to those down in the pit.

At about a hundred feet down, they hit metal.

It took all six of them to hoist up the storm chariot of Marduk they had uncovered.

"Storm Demon," said Apollyon as he polished the heavenly metal with relish. "Keep digging!"

But before they could, the ground at their feet burst open with a flurry of flames. The mighty whinnying of horses echoed throughout the shaft. Four divine steeds came up from their grave in the earth to be reunited with their chariot.

Apollyon called their names with gleeful madness, "Slaughterer! Merciless! Overwhelmer! Soaring! Mighty war horses of the unseen realm! It won't be long now."[6]

As the gods attacked the ground furiously, Apollyon began an incantation with his eyes closed and hands held wide. "Let the gods exult in assembly! Shurim, who with the weapon roots out all enemies! Who frustrates their plans, scatters them to the winds! Zisi, who silences the insurgent! Zahrim, who destroys all adversaries! Zahgurim, who destroys all foes in battle!"[7]

He continued to call out fifty names of power and exultation. Fifty names of a single being. Fifty names of Marduk, king of the gods of Babylon.

A bellow filled the shaft from below. It held the pent-up anger of five hundred years of bondage. The muscular form of Marduk came forth from his grave to ascend the shaft of freedom.

Apollyon watched his freed prisoner bow before him in naked perfection, muscles rippling. "Marduk of Babylon, I have resurrected you for a time such as this. Awaken, my warrior. Awaken to your calling and join my army of the nations."

"Yes, my lord and savior," said the hulkish brute, and he stood to receive his armor and weapons.

CHAPTER 33

Jerusalem
December, AD 67

Gischala straightened his leather armor plates as he stood before the Beautiful Gate of the inner temple with a party of twenty men. He looked above at the temple's parapet, lined all around by archers with bows at the ready for attack. Behind Gischala were thousands of Zealots, brigands, and patriots who had joined the cause of Ananus against Eleazar, who held the temple hostage.

Gischala felt satisfied that they were mostly loyal to him. Six thousand armed soldiers of Ananus' were spread around the outer court porticos. The moment was wrought with tension; three armed forces at odds, at the tip of the spear, ready to plunge into battle.[1]

Under the strength of twenty men, the large bronze gate slowly swung open. Gischala entered cautiously with his escort, hands on their swords. The area had cleared for them. Eleazar's warriors crowded the outer area and filled the upper walls everywhere. Gischala could assume even more filled the side-rooms and tunnels below, possibly several thousand in total.

Gischala was risking his life by coming here to negotiate on behalf of Ananus. But Gischala had one thing in his favor. Eleazar had become captain of the temple after Gischala lost that title when he had fought the Roman procurator Gessius Florus in this very spot. Gischala had become a fugitive in the name of protecting the temple, an act of heroism that had garnered Eleazar's respect—and that of his soldiers who told tales of Gischala's heroism. Gischala was counting on that respect to still be there.

He was greeted by a man he did not recognize wearing the high priest's vestments and accompanied by a group of twelve priests. The high priest looked uncomfortable in his outfit like a bad actor playing a part. He walked toward Gischala with uncertain gait. "Hello, warrior. I understand you called for a meeting to negotiate a treaty?"

159

The man spoke like a rustic provincial from the highlands. Gischala squinted his eyes, wondering if this was a trap. "Who the hell are you? What kind of blasphemous joke is this?" He placed his hand on his sword hilt. His men raised their shields.

The priest's face filled with fear. The warriors around the colonnades became agitated. Gischala heard the gate behind him closing. He drew his sword. His men followed suit.

The high priest stepped back in fright and tripped over his robe, falling to the ground on his rump like a fool.

A loud laugh echoed through the courtyard. Gischala looked around in confusion.

He saw Eleazar walking out toward him alone and unarmed, hands open and still laughing.

The priest got up. Eleazar stepped up next to him and placed his hand on the priest's shoulder as he spoke to Gischala. "I see you are not too impressed with our new high priest. His name is Phannias." He smiled at Phannias as a king would a clown.

"You mock the royal priesthood?" Gischala demanded.

Eleazar's face sobered into a frown. "On the contrary, I guard it." He paused. "As you once did."

So Eleazar did maintain some respect. He continued, "But I do mock the ruling class of Israel. That oligarchy of corrupt Roman-loving, greedy oppressors of the poor and fornicators with Caesar. Don't you?"

Gischala shrugged assent, his brow now knit with interest. Of course he did.

Eleazar went on, "For centuries the Hasmoneans controlled the priesthood. Then Herod, that despicable Edomite, took over and raped our people. The most holy position of responsibility in our entire nation is controlled by Herodian money, influence, and politics. Have we ever really had a true high priest under the Herods?"

Gischala raised his brow. It was a good point. Not that it mattered one whit for his own ambitions. He replied, "So you chose the opposite. A poor rural clodhopper."

Phannias' face expressed hurt at the insult.

Eleazar smiled. "We drew lots to allow God to choose the family instead of corrupt regimes. God chose Phannias."[2] He smacked Phannias' back as though the priest were a child.

Cunning, thought Gischala. *He cloaks his actions in symbolism. He could do much damage to this city.*

Eleazar said, "But you called upon me for something else entirely. So, forgive my distraction."

He turned to Phannias and muttered, "Return the garments to the vestry."

Phannias turned to leave. Eleazar kicked him in the rear, and the priest almost fell to the ground again. Eleazar grinned.

"Let's get to the point," Gischala commented. "I am empowered by Ananus to negotiate a treaty with you."

Eleazar gestured with his hand toward a stairwell. "Shall we have a drink, then, the two of us? Like in the old days."

The two men sat at a table in the wine cellar. Around them, thousands of bottles of wine were stored for the priests. This was all Eleazar's wine now. He poured a goblet full for Gischala. He tasted it. Excellent quality. He knew all about this cellar and many other secret chambers of the temple from his past as captain of the temple. He put the goblet down.

"Eleazar, Ananus has asked me to negotiate a compromise with you. He is outraged at your presence in the temple. He considers it polluted by your warriors as men of bloodshed. But he won't attack you for fear of creating more bloodshed in this holy place."

Eleazar toasted him with a smile. "I thank the Lord for my enemy's scruples." He took a hearty gulp.

"But I am not here for Ananus' agenda. I hate him as much as do you. I think he pollutes the city with his history of corruption."

Eleazar's face brightened with interest.

"I am here to make a pact between me and you—against Ananus."

"Pray tell," said Eleazar with a hopeful curiosity.

Gischala told him, "Ananus will betray you. I know all of his plans. Where his forces are stationed in the city and how he is planning to attack you."

Eleazar was too engrossed to take another sip.

"He has sent a delegation to Vespasian, offering him the city. His forces will then join with the Romans against you and against any who are zealous for the purity of temple and cult."

"That traitorous swine," said Eleazar.

Gischala thought the lie would help enflame Eleazar's zeal like nothing else. But now he buttressed the falsehood with some truth. "Tomorrow he is going to call a fast for the city. He will then have his soldiers disguised to enter the temple under the pretense of fulfilling their religious duties. While inside, they will attack you to take control."[3]

"I thought he didn't want bloodshed in the holy place."

"Ananus has never considered hypocrisy to be a vice when it served his interests."

"So what is the pact you offer me?"

"First, I and my forces will join with yours to take control of the temple complex from Ananus' forces inside. I have sent a message to the Idumeans in the south, telling them of Ananus' correspondence with Vespasian."

Though the Herods were Idumean, they had become traitors in the eyes of their people, who were now enemies of both Ananus and Rome.

Gischala continued, "They have sent twenty thousand soldiers to meet us by tonight at the southern gates of the city, which are controlled by my men.[4] Once my soldiers let in the Idumeans, we'll squeeze Ananus between us, the Idumeans from the Lower City and you and I from the temple."

Eleazar wasted no time. He said, "I want to maintain control of the temple precinct."

"Done. I'll take the Lower City and leave the Upper City to the Idumeans. When Vespasian arrives, he will have a triple surprise when he tries to take Jerusalem."

Eleazar grinned. "It would be nice to have Vespasian's head on a pike."

"First let's impale these whores of Ananus inside the temple."

As the sun was setting, Gischala exited the inner temple with his soldiers and waved a banner to Ananus' soldiers in the porticos of the outer courtyard. They came out and drew near to Gischala to hear his announcement.

He declared, "We have a treaty with Eleazar to join Ananus and stand against the Romans together! A triad of defense!"

Everyone cheered, Herodian, Zealot, mercenary, and patriot.

Eleazar's warriors filed out of the temple and spread out among the soldiers of Gischala and Ananus. Men on all sides were apprehensive at first, but soon overcame their caution and began to greet one another as comrades in arms.

"Let our first act of unity be a feast of celebration!" Gischala announced. The men cheered.

But Gischala's words were a cue for which his Zealots and Eleazar's temple guards had been waiting. Drawing their weapons, they fell upon Ananus' soldiers who had been lulled into the false three-way treaty. It was actually a secret treaty of two against one.

One of Eleazar's men sounded a battle trumpet from the corner of the temple. A trumpet sound that could be heard by the Idumean forces almost upon the city, cloaked by the falling night.

CHAPTER 34

Surrounded by Pharisees, scribes, and several military leaders, Ananus paced the floor of the council room in the Herodian palace on the western edge of the upper city. He was sweating from the fear of his world falling down around him.

"Blind fools!" he mumbled. "They never stop to ask themselves if they fight for God or for Gischala's twisted imagination."

"My lord." A messenger stood at the entrance, drawing Ananus' attention.

The high priest snapped at him, "What now?"

But he was answered by a man marching right into the meeting in a cloaked hood. Everyone stepped back with caution.

The man took off his hood. It was Herod Agrippa.

Ananus asked, "How did you steal into the city?"

"You forget," said Agrippa. "This is *my* palace, secret passages and all."

"Your life is in danger here," said Ananus.

"I will not stay long."

"Gischala has betrayed me," said Ananus. "He has joined with Eleazar, and they have slaughtered six thousand of my soldiers who were in the temple. They now surround this palace along with an army from Idumea."

"The palace is strong. You're safe for now."

"For now," repeated Ananus with incredulity.

Agrippa said, "If you were to quench the revolt and present Jerusalem fully surrendered into the hands of Vespasian, I can persuade the legate to grant clemency to you and the nobles."

"What nobles are still alive," complained Ananus. "I am entirely on the defensive. I don't have enough forces in this stronghold to take back the city."

"You need help."

"I need a miracle."

"I know someone who can turn the tables for you. I'll get him myself."

"Who?"

"Simon bar Giora."

The name made Ananus cringe. "Simon hates you. He hates the house of Herod and everything the ruling class stands for. How can you possibly persuade him to help us against Gischala?"

"Because Gischala is the one man Simon hates even more than the Herods. He won't talk to me, but I know who he will talk to."

A soldier burst into the room in terror. "We've been betrayed! The Zealots have been let into the palace!"

Ananus froze in terror. Then his wits came back to him. He yelled to his military leaders, "Bring your forces to bear!"

They ran out of the room to issue a call to arms.

Ananus turned back to Agrippa. But he was gone. Disappeared into one of his secret passages that Ananus wished he too had known about.

By the time Ananus found his way out to the courtyard to command his forces, they were either dead or submitted to Gischala.

He froze when he saw twenty or so of his fellow sanhedrin members lined up along the wall. They were forced to their knees by soldiers with swords. At a yelled command, the soldiers all swung their swords at the necks of their victims.

Ananus felt the horror hit him in his stomach. He wretched and vomited where he stood, unable to keep looking at the carnage of decapitation. He knew those men, had prayed with them, served with them. Now they were all dead.

Ananus looked up to see Gischala and Eleazar waiting for him in the middle of the yard. His throat went completely dry. He tried to swallow but coughed.

He approached the traitors, holding his chin high, trying to maintain his dignity.

He hissed, "You profane the temple and the priesthood with Idumeans and bloodshed."

Idumeans were the ancestors of the cursed Edom, so their presence in the temple constituted an abominable pollution. The Herods alone had been tolerated through political manipulation and force—and not without trouble.

Eleazar stepped up to Ananus, spit in his face, and punched him in the abdomen.

Ananus grunted with pain and crumbled to the ground.

Two soldiers grabbed his arms and dragged him from the courtyard onto the entrance of the palace.

Ananus heard the sounds of a cheering mob.

He lay flat on his back, looking up at the stars. What a bright display they offered this night. Unusually clear, unusually beautiful. Or were his senses heightened with the danger? Ananus caught sight of a falling star burning out in the heavenly tapestry. It reminded him of the scriptures that spoke with similar poetry. Stars falling from the heavens. The sky rolling up like a scroll. The mountains shaking. He felt the full force of the spiritual description of the fall of earthly powers now upon his own soul.

A long, mounted pole with a rope broke his view of the crowd of heavenly witnesses.

He was pulled up, and the rope was placed around his neck and tightened.

The crowd of soldiers screamed for blood.

A strange feeling of detachment came over Ananus. As if he too was watching himself from the mob. He felt the tug of the rope on his neck. It lifted him from his feet into the air, choking him.

The sounds of cheering increased.

He felt himself rising high above them.

Below, he saw the headless bodies of other nobles, the ruling class of the city. His body shuddered with convulsions as he gasped for air.

He was hoisted high enough to see the city before him, being ravaged by these monsters. Flames of burning buildings, women screaming, fights in the streets. These men were destroying their own city, raping and killing their own people. It was madness. His city was possessed by demons.

He saw the temple in the distance. It was glowing with its torches like a tomb in a funerary rite. The skies above had become blackened by a storm cloud. A bright flash of lightning lit up the city, followed by a thunder clap that shook the palace.

Then darkness drowned him.[1]

The body of the high priest Ananus stopped spasming and went still. Rain began to fall, drenching everyone.

Gischala said to the executioner, "Feed him to the dogs."[2]

Then he raised his sword toward the soldiers and shouted, "The city is ours!"

Again, they roared with howls and war cries in the windy pelting rain.[3]

"Now let us take the temple!"

These were the code words he'd agreed upon with his allies as the prompt for them to attack Eleazar's men amongst them.

But down in the crowd, Eleazar had figured it out before the other soldiers could organize an attack. He yelled to his men on horseback, "We are betrayed! Retreat to the temple!"

One betrayal had been followed by another. The cosmos was coming undone.

Eleazar's soldiers were on horses and had a head start on the crowd of Gischala's loyal forces.

Gischala jumped on his steed. He took some of the back alleys to avoid getting caught in the sea of chasing soldiers.

He made his way to the temple, hoping to head off Eleazar and his men. The pounding thunder of the storm shook buildings around him. He wondered if God was thundering his approval of their conquest.

He passed soldiers on the streets who were robbing citizens, taking their food and valuables, dragging out women to violate them in the mud and rain. He had made an agreement with the Idumeans and the brigands that they could do as they pleased with the citizens so long as they respected his army.

He passed the hippodrome and arrived at the Huldah Gates.

But he was too late. His forces were too slow to catch Eleazar and his horsemen. Gischala saw them gallop up the steps of the Huldah Gates on their horses to join the rest of Eleazar's army that had been left behind to guard the temple.

That slippery weasel had escaped his grasp for now. Eleazar would be holed up in the inner temple fortress again. But this time Gischala and not Ananus would own the outer court and the rest of the city. And that was a good enough start.[4]

Something he had passed by on his way here had caught his attention: the hippodrome.

A thought crossed his mind, and he galloped back to the large boarded-up arena, the rain stinging his face as he rode.

When Gischala arrived at the hippodrome, he saw that the Herodian soldiers assigned to guard it were gone, fled or killed in the battle. A large mob of Idumean warriors now gathered before the hippodrome with bloodlust in their eyes and scimitars in their hands. Their distinct look of silk robes with light chainmail and round metal helmets made them stand out from the plain garb of the Zealots and light leather armor of the Herodians.

Another lightning strike lit up the mob, and thunder cracked overhead. The flash of light revealed that the inhabitants of the quarantine had tried to blockade the entrance with carts, boards, and pieces of furniture. It was a futile gesture of fearful innocents about to be raped and pillaged.

A man of ordinary looks, average build, and trim beard had come out from behind the blockade to try to dissuade the mob. He was drenched in the rain and displayed no weapon.

Fool, Gischala thought. *He knows nothing of the mob he is facing.*

Galloping his horse in between the Idumeans and their victims, Gischala announced with an angry voice, "I am General John ben Levi of the city's forces, and this hippodrome is off-limits to plunder!"

Calling to mind a report he'd recently received about the relocation of the refugee children, he added in a shout, "That goes for the theater as well!"

"We were told we had free reign!" one of the soldiers yelled back.

Another called out, "What if the enemy is hiding in there?"

Grumbles from the mob expressed agreement, barely audible above the sound of the stormy wind whipping through the streets with its fury. Gischala's horse grew restless, jerking back and forth beneath the hand of his master.

"If you want free reign in quarantined areas for leprosy and plague victims," Gischala yelled back, "then be my guest!"

He had stretched the truth to include the theater in his warning. But it had worked. Already, the mob was melting away into the darkness.

Once Gischala saw that terror had been averted, he approached the blockade of piled up debris and furniture. Sitting tall on his mount, he glared down at the unarmed man who had been offering such a futile defense of the entrance, squinting in the deluge of rain that was now drenching both men.

"I recognize you from the New City gates, helping the refugees."

Wiping water from his upturned face, the man responded, "I am Alexander Maccabaeus, the doctor in charge of the plague quarantine here in the hippodrome."

"Alexander Maccabaeus." Gischala scowled. "I know that name. You were among the Christians who caused so much trouble when I was captain of the temple guard."

His expression hardened. "Do not think I was protecting you just now. I consider you Christians the devil's stronghold. But those inside this arena are my people, and them I will protect. I will decide your own fate later. But if I find you are harboring any of the ruling class, you will pay with your lives."

Wheeling his horse, Gischala galloped off into the chaos of the night to return to his headquarters.

CHAPTER 35

Morning light broke in the hippodrome. The storm had passed, and though everything was still wet from the night before, the air was clear and crisp with the cold of winter now settling upon them.

Cassandra and Alexander had been up all night with those wounded in raids across the city. An estimated twelve thousand soldiers and citizens had been killed in the mayhem.[1] Dozens of bruised and bloodied victims had arrived at the hippodrome. In the midst of civil war like this, the wounded cared nothing about quarantine. They only wanted medical help, and by now the entire city knew they could find such at the hippodrome.

Cassandra looked around the arena. Their tent city had been blown apart in the storm winds. Every capable person was engaged in rebuilding their dwellings, and fires had been lit to warm the residents. With the adult volunteers split between here and the theater, Alexander only had about fifty of them to manage the mounting masses of wounded.

Fortunately, the Christian population had been growing among the surviving plague victims. They were turning to Messiah in their sickness to be the healer of their souls. And those who lived had stayed to help with the duties. They were becoming the new church of Jerusalem, a hundred strong. Though overwhelmed by the numbers, they pitched in to get the wounded settled and attended to.

By now a month had passed since the refugee children and their adult guardians had been moved to the theater. Young Noah and Rachel had stayed in the hippodrome hospital at first because of Noah's injuries. But his sprained ankle was long healed, and his broken arm was doing better. Another couple months and he would be able to take off his protective splint.

Despite his improvement, Noah continued to complain of excruciating arm pain. Cassandra and Alexander were well aware that his ongoing complaints were feigned so he and Rachel could stay on in the hippodrome. But they went along with the fabrication because in truth the young brother and sister had by now greatly endeared themselves to both Cassandra and Alexander. And after so many weeks, there seemed little point adding two more charges to those volunteers already dealing with two hundred other children needing love and attention.

Cassandra's heart welled up every time she thought of those not chosen by God for salvation who would sooner or later suffer judgment for their sins. But at this moment her heart was especially grieved over the present tragedy that had occurred in the city; the judgment of civil war.

Rachel had helped Cassandra give comfort to a woman in her twenties who had a black eye, broken nose, and bruised arms. The woman winced as Cassandra cleaned crusted blood from her face with a damp cloth. She shook with fear, her gaze distant and frightened as though looking into the Abyss.

Her companion, an elderly woman, said to Cassandra, "It was five men who pulled her and her daughter into the alley. Five demons from hell. They did unspeakable things."

The elder woman's voice cracked with deep pain before continuing, "Her daughter did not survive." She dropped her voice to add sadly, "What has become of our people?"

The terrible truth was that this was but one of scores of women and girls with similar suffering who had sought haven in the hippodrome. Cassandra wiped a tear from her eye, trying not to choke up. She needed to be strong. To stay strong. For all of them.

She whispered, "Fallen, fallen is Babylon the great. She has become a dwelling place for demons, a haunt for every unclean spirit."[2]

Cassandra was quoting the Apocalypse. The apostle had written that Jerusalem had become like Babylon of old. She had become possessed by evil spirits. Jesus had foretold this very terror that now gripped their beloved city. He had compared this generation of Jews that had rejected him to a man possessed by an evil spirit. When that spirit goes out of the person, it gathers seven spirits more evil than itself, and they return to dwell in him. His last state is then worse than the first. Cassandra knew what had become of her people. They were in the grip of a seven-fold demonic infestation.[3]

Cassandra heard a call from Alexander.

"Come, Rachel. We must have breakfast." If they didn't eat, they would be weak and useless to help others.

Cassandra stopped and turned back to see Rachel staring at the poor catatonic woman. Finally, the girl joined her.

As they walked back to their tent, Cassandra said to her, "I understand why you chose to hide yourself as a boy. What you've seen these women suffer is too horrible to imagine. It breaks my heart."

Rachel nodded quietly.

"But I want you to know, you are safe with us here."

"Nowhere is safe," said Rachel.

Cassandra looked at Rachel's uneven haircut, done hastily with a knife on the run. And she had insisted on returning to her boy's tunic and robe once they were scrubbed and dried. "You must let me fix your hair so it will grow out well."

"No," said Rachel. "I won't let it grow out."

Cassandra chose not to push it at this point.

They arrived at the tent to meet Alexander and Noah, who were getting ready for their meal.

They sat for their breakfast of crusty bread and water with a single dried date each.

Alexander lifted his hands and prayed, "Heavenly Father, bless this food and nourish our bodies as you did for your children in the wilderness. In the name of Jesus the Messiah, our manna from heaven, we pray this. Amen."

Cassandra said amen, but the two siblings did not. They were still wary of the Messiah this pair of adults continued to praise. Cassandra didn't blame them. They had been through more than any child should have to.

Noah pulled out a dagger to dig a pit from his date. Cassandra noticed it was a Roman blade. She and Alexander shared a look of surprise.

"Where did you get that dagger?" asked Alexander.

"Yes, where did you get it, Noah?" Rachel demanded angrily. "You had no right!"

Noah shrugged as he looked from one face to another, his expression the epitome of innocence. "Rachel stole it from a sleeping guard when we escaped the Roman camp."

Cassandra now knew how Rachel had cut her hair.

"She hid it when we came here," Noah went on nonchalantly, "in case we again needed to defend ourselves. She thought I did not see where, but I did. I took it because I want to learn how to use it. How to fight. I want to become a warrior."

Alexander sat back thoughtfully. "You are a little young to be a warrior."

"I learn fast."

Rachel said, "You'll die faster."

"Shut up, Rachel." Noah sounded more desperate than angry.

"I will not shut up! Why do you think I hid the dagger? I know how you long to go after those who killed our parents. But you are just a little boy! I will not see you die as we did our parents!"

"Hold it!" Alexander raised his voice to drown out the children's escalating tones. He gave Rachel a compassionate look. "You need not worry that we will allow Noah to put himself in danger. That said, it is never too early to learn properly the skills of defending oneself and one's family."

He smiled down at Noah. "I am not a warrior. I'm a healer. But I'll tell you what. If you promise not to carry that knife around in the open or to give worry to your sister, I will see if I can find you a warrior to learn from."

Noah searched Alexander's face. Apparently satisfied he was not being lied to, he slid the blade back under his cloak.

"In the meantime, let me teach you how to care for and heal others before you learn how to hurt them." Alexander smiled at both children. "Okay?"

"Okay," Noah nodded.

More softly and with reluctance, Rachel added, "Okay."

They were still finishing their meal when they were interrupted by a messenger from the plague quarantine area, one of the now-healed volunteers. "It's a miracle! He's healed! He's healed!"

"Who?" asked Cassandra. "Who is healed?"

Alexander and Cassandra both headed for the tent entrance to see what the volunteer was talking about. Outside just a few yards away stood Jacob ben Mordecai.

Jacob gobbled the bread Cassandra had brought him to eat and slurped some broth she had heated up. In clear recognition of his eminent position, the doctor and his wife had brought Jacob to their own tent instead of the dining area where ambulatory patients were fed. Two children, a boy and a girl, seemed to be sharing the tent. He had seen amazement at his recovery on all their faces. And indeed, while his tall gaunt figure was undernourished from a month on hippodrome rations, it was no longer covered in boils and as healthy as it had ever been. He just needed food, which he wouldn't be getting much of here.

When Alexander insisted on asking some medical questions, Jacob explained that he had awoken that morning from a fitful sleep to find himself completely well.

Cassandra said, "The Lord Jesus healed you, Jacob."

Jacob sipped more broth and tried to give an open-minded shrug. *Maybe! Or maybe I just survived the sickness.* After all, plenty of other people had eventually gotten well. Not every plague victim was dying.

Still, the boils had been there, and after the stormy night they were gone. That was certainly unusual. He had been sick for weeks but was now suddenly well like a body risen from the dead.

Cassandra asked him, "Can I tell you a story, Jacob?"

Jacob nodded as he finished eating.

"I once knew a man who had been a Pharisee of the highest order. Before I met him, he was empowered by the sanhedrin to persecute Christians. He hated them, and he thought the Gospel of Jesus was heresy. Until one night he met Jesus in a vision of light that made him blind. For days he could not see until a man sent from God came and restored his sight. The scales fell from his eyes. That encounter, and that miracle of healing changed that man's mind, and he became an instrument of God's grace to many people."

Jacob had stopped eating. He found old emotions stirring within himself. Conflicting emotions. He knew who she was talking about. Jacob had once met that man as well. And he had once treasured his writings.

"Paul of Tarsus," he whispered.

He knew why Cassandra was telling that story. He said, "I am no Pharisee, and I do not have the respect of Ananus and the sanhedrin."

Jacob saw Cassandra and Alexander look at each other, troubled. "What is wrong?"

Alexander said, "There was a great slaughter in the city last night. Gischala and Eleazar united with an Idumean army to betray Ananus and the city. The Idumeans defiled the temple with the blood of battle."

"What of Ananus?"

"Dead."

Jacob swallowed. "The sanhedrin?"

"They were wiped out. Most all of them along with many of the ruling class. Those not killed in the heat of battle were bound over for trial, then executed."

Jacob broke out in a cold sweat. "But they didn't come here?"

"They did. They feared the plague so they left. But if Gischala finds out you are here, he will kill us all."

Jacob thought for a moment. Then he said, "If you do not tell Gischala that I am sanhedrin, I will continue to safeguard the hippodrome and provide you with food and resources."

As Alexander and Cassandra exchanged suddenly hopeful glances, Jacob added, "I owe you my life."

"The Lord Jesus Christ healed you, Jacob," Cassandra said quietly, "not us."

"I am sure you are right," Jacob lied. "But right now, we need to make sure that we protect these poor suffering souls under your care. And I'm the only one left that can do that. We need each other."

Jacob hoped the doctor and his wife could not see into his own soul. Control of the hippodrome quarantine was a bargaining tool Jacob would need to regain a foothold in the new government that would now be forming.

• • • • •

Qumran

Aaron had been working on fortifying the defenses of the community. He had overseen the building of several tower structures at the corners of the walls. They had laid more bricks to extend the height of the walls. Aaron knew that it was futile. Heavily protected cities like Gamala had fallen. These monks wouldn't stand a chance against the legions.

But he had to do something. Anything to inspire others to join his cause of fighting in the army of the Sons of Light.

He was working on one of the towers' battlements when he saw a company of horsemen approaching their village in the distance. They looked to be a bodyguard of about a dozen warriors. Giving a special whistle to alert his men, Aaron hurried down to the courtyard to mount his horse. Twenty of his trusted Essene fighters with sling, sword, and shield joined him, and they galloped out to receive their visitors—with force if necessary.

They met the company of horsemen a hundred yards out from the village walls. Both groups had halted at a hundred paces, eyeing each other with suspicion, weapons ready.

Then a lone rider pranced out in front of the other newcomers. He pulled down his hood, and Aaron instantly recognized Herod Agrippa. The Edomite king looked weary.

"Stay here," Aaron commanded his fellow monks and rode out to meet Agrippa.

"My lord, Herod Agrippa. What brings you here?" He tried to keep his detestation of this Roman sympathizer from his tone.

"I come from Jerusalem," Agrippa said. "A civil war has erupted within the city."

"But what do you seek at Qumran?"

"I have heard of the exploits of your warriors at the battle of Beth-Horon against Cestius."

Aaron could not help but smile with pride, then scorn. "And you think we would want to join your fight?"

"I am no fool. I know your doctrines. I know you hate the Herods as much as you hate the corrupt priesthood. I come to Qumran in search of the man who trained you: Simon bar Giora."

Everything became clear to Aaron. He said, "He did train us. And I know that he hates you with all his soul."

Agrippa asked, "What is your name?"

"Aaron ben Hyam."

"Aaron, this is much bigger than our personal vendettas. Jerusalem has fallen hostage to the sinister forces of John of Gischala and Eleazar ben Simon. They've murdered the high priest Ananus and most of the ruling class nobles."

"Let justice be a light to the nations," said Aaron with a bitter edge.

Agrippa said, "It is not justice. It is only an exchange of criminal control."

"Is not Rome criminal? Yet you are allied with Vespasian."

"I would ally with the devil to save Jerusalem from these rebels."

"Would you destroy Jerusalem to save Israel?"

Agrippa became agitated. "My family built this country and its temple."

Aaron snorted. "That is why I am here in Qumran instead of in *your* Jerusalem."

Agrippa pleaded, "Then help me find Simon bar Giora, so that maybe we can make it *our* Jerusalem. There is one certainty, and that is that the beast of Rome is coming. And I believe that one man has the ability to change the course of the civil war and stop us from killing each other before the beast kills us all."

Aaron stared thoughtfully at the desperate Herod before him. The only problem now was getting that one man to care.

CHAPTER 36

Terqa

Apollyon and his band of seven had traveled over two hundred miles north of Babylon to the city of Terqa on the Euphrates River. They were closer to their ultimate destination, but not yet ready for the exchange of divine hostages with the archangels. Apollyon had a few more things to gather for the coming war.

Terqa had been a client city of ancient Babylon under the great Hammurabi centuries ago. It was now a shadow of its former self as was Babylon. As he had done previously, Apollyon left the Daughters of Allah to guard over the captive angel outside the city. Zeus, Anat, Dagon, and Molech followed him invisibly through the streets past the sparse residents going about their day to the temple of Dagon in the urban center.

As they approached the structure, Dagon sighed. "I miss this temple. There was a time when it was a mighty center of the kingdom of Hana. Now look at it. Disappointing."

It was crumbling and hadn't been attended to for decades. The city populace was now Parthian and as such were Zoroastrian in religion.

Apollyon said, "A humble housing hides a mighty secret."

They entered and walked through the columned holy place to the most holy, passing unseen and unheard amongst the small order of a dozen human priests left behind to care for the facility.

Apollyon parted the veil, and the gods looked inside. It had been stripped bare of all its cultic objects.

Apollyon closed the curtain and walked impatiently toward the priest's chambers. The gods stayed close behind.

They entered the chamber and locked the door behind them. Inside were rotting wooden lockers for priestly wardrobe and sacred items. Most were empty save the few used by the current temple-sitters.

But there was only one sacred item Apollyon was looking for.

He began to tear at the wooden lockers. He smashed boards, broke wood away from the wall, and punched through backboards.

He yelled to the other four, "Do I have to command you fools to get your help?"

They immediately joined him, ripping apart the lockers, crushing them to pieces, and tearing them from the walls.

Apollyon didn't care if their physical destruction was heard by the priests in the sanctuary. They wouldn't dare try to gain entry into the room. And if they did, they would die. Apollyon had no time for religious protocol. Zeus held the door closed to prevent needless bloodletting.

"I found it," said Dagon. "I knew it was here."

They all turned to see a secret passageway revealed behind one of the lockers. They followed Apollyon into the dark.

The passageway opened up to a small stone chamber with incantations and enchantments scribbled on the walls, cursing any who might seek to steal the precious treasure mounted on one wall.

"Ayamur," said Apollyon with adoration.

It was the name of the heavenly spear of Ba'al, and it meant "Chaser." It had been brought to Terqa from Aleppo by the ruler Zimri-Lim almost two millennia ago. This spear, together with Yagrush, or "Driver," Ba'al's war hammer, were the mighty weapons used by the storm god of Canaan to overcome Sea and River in the Ba'al epic.[1]

When Ba'al was returned to Apollyon, he would finally receive back Driver and Chaser and lead the Twelfth Legion with unstoppable brute force.

Apollyon saw Anat staring at the spear with desire. He knew what she would try to do if she got her hands on it. And it wouldn't go well for Apollyon. He suspected she was planning mutiny, but he had no hard proof yet. Not that he needed it. Apollyon had after all bullied and humiliated her brother and incestuous lover, Ba'al the storm god, when they first joined this campaign. Apollyon had to make sure the mighty cloud-rider knew who was boss.

The angel of the Abyss would continue to keep an eye on the virgin goddess.

Apollyon walked up and lifted the spear from its mount on the wall. It was heavy to hold, and he felt the vibrations of its energy resonate through his arm. It sparked with the power of lightning.

Under the jealous eye of Anat, he handed it to Zeus. Zeus's face went flush with surprise at the sense of power it gave him.

Apollyon told him, "Use your trumpet. Call for a unit of messengers to bring this to Mount Hermon for safekeeping with Driver. Until the appointed time."

"Yes, my lord." Zeus left the chamber.

Apollyon mused, "I have Marduk's storm chariot from Yahweh's eternal enemy, Babylon. I have Poseidon's trident for the Tenth Legion, Hubal's arrows of divination for the Nabatean auxiliaries, and Ares' golden chariot and weapons for the Fifth Legion.[2] When those armies get back their patron deities, Michael will be sorry he ever kidnapped them in the first place."

The blast of Zeus's heavenly trumpet outside the temple resounded through the unseen realm.

Their next destination was set. The hostage exchange was to take place at Mount Bashar, mountain of the Amorites.

CHAPTER 37

Caesarea Maritima
March, AD 68

Berenice and Agrippa walked through the palace hall in Caesarea. Vespasian and Titus had returned here with their forces to wait out the winter. But it was now time to move. Berenice had dreaded this moment, but it was inevitable.

Josephus, the captive general, trailed them, accompanied by his ever-present guards and permanent manacles on his hands. He was allowed some freedom, but not so much as to provide him opportunity to escape. Berenice knew Josephus would not attempt escape because he was under the same stigma as the Herods. They had become traitors in the eyes of their countrymen for helping the Romans in their war. Were Josephus to flee to Jerusalem, he would surely be ripped to pieces by the mob long before he had a chance to explain to them his reasons for surrender.

Josephus was as calculated as Berenice and her brother. She respected his shrewd counsel to Vespasian and Titus. He had sought to stave off the worst possible damage by revealing tactical weaknesses he knew about various cities. The quicker the defeat, the less vengeful their treatment at the hands of the Romans.

The three of them arrived in the war council room, a chamber filled with tribunes and other hand-picked counselors. Titus stood with Vespasian before a map of Judea and its surrounding territories.

Titus looked up and saw Berenice. They shared a knowing look as Vespasian said, "Ah, my favorite Jews. Welcome to my war council." He took a gulp of wine from a chalice. "Bring out the rabbi."

Some guards left and returned with an elderly man in his sixties dressed in rabbinic robes with a full, gray unclipped beard.

Josephus and the rabbi appeared to recognize each other.

Vespasian said, "Well, I see you two are acquainted. For the sake of the others, this is Rabbi Yohanan ben Zakkai. He tells me he has escaped from Jerusalem in a coffin no less!"[1] That amusing story elicited raised brows and a smile from the legate. The warring factions in the city had killed the ruling sanhedrin and many of the aristocracy.

Vespasian turned to Josephus. "Imagine my surprise when he prophesied over me just as you had, claiming that I would be the next Caesar. Some might call such convenient proclamation flattery."[2]

"Others might call it confirmation of prophecy by two witnesses," Josephus replied. The Pharisee kept his hands clasped in front of him, his sleeves covering his chains of shame.

Taking the response in stride, Vespasian smiled. "He wants to start a library and school in Yavneh, where he can store your sacred writings and teach a new generation of Jewish leaders to work more agreeably with Rome. What say you, Josephus?"

"I can vouch for Rabbi Yohanan's character," said the Pharisee. "I knew him to be a man of integrity when I was in Jerusalem. As far as his intent to collaborate, would it not be in Caesar's interest to have the allegiance of a new sanhedrin created under your supervision now rather than wait and see what monstrous hybrid is birthed from the ashes of your destroyed enemy?"

"Well argued," said Vespasian.

Agrippa interrupted, "Lord legate, if I may?"

"Of course."

"Since the house of Herod remains your loyal servant in this godforsaken land, may I suggest my involvement with the Yavneh institution to ensure its compliance?"

Berenice knew her brother meant its compliance in ensuring the legacy of the house of Herod.

"Granted." Vespasian looked at Yohanan. "You may have your request, Rabbi. I will appoint a magistrate to oversee the process. Let's see if we can't make some alterations to your religion that would make it more amenable to our changing world." He thought about it for a second. "I like this. A new Judaism."

The rabbi bowed with gratitude.[3]

"I'll oversee the magistrate," said Titus. "I have some ideas about their laws and appointed festivals I would like to see addressed."

Berenice shared a look of eerie chill with her brother and Josephus. They had just this morning been discussing the messianic prophecies in Daniel. Josephus had argued the scandalous possibility that Vespasian fulfilled the promise of the coming prince of the world.[4] But Daniel's visions of beasts also included a "little horn" of the Roman empire that would rise up, persecute the holy ones of the Most High, and seek to "change the appointed times and laws." If Vespasian was Messiah, could Titus be an anti-Messiah? It was too horrific to consider. Berenice put it out of her mind.[5]

Vespasian dismissed Yohanan. He then turned to the Herods and Josephus. "I have received news from Rome that a revolt by governor Vindex in Gaul was put down. Rumors have been growing that forces loyal to governor Galba may be planning a coup against Nero. The provinces are in chaos. My ability to prosecute an effective war here may be impeded if I am called back. However, I have resolved that if I am recalled, then Titus shall be legate."[6]

Berenice looked at Titus, who stood, chin held high, as if he was already the supreme commander of the greatest army the world had ever known.

"However," cautioned Vespasian. "I am still in this stinking sandpit. So spare yourself the glory and power, my son." He turned back to the others. "Titus advises we attack Jerusalem immediately while they languish in the throes of civil war. Their division can only be our gain to exploit. But what say you three?"

He looked at them all, awaiting an answer from any one of them.

Josephus spoke up. He had been aggressive these past months in having his voice heard. Berenice knew he was jockeying for power.

"With all due respect to your highness, Titus, may I explain the Jewish mindset in this matter. No matter how quarrelsome or divided the city is, brother against brother, if you attack them now, the factions will unite against a common enemy. In this, they will find their true brotherhood. It is the Jewish way of survival over the centuries."

Berenice saw Vespasian give a nod of acknowledgement. Even Titus would not contest it.

Brian Godawa

Josephus continued, "And they will be stronger. But if you exercise patience and allow them to continue their civil war without interference, then they will kill each other, making the Roman job much easier. A strategic delay of attack will result in far fewer Roman casualties."

Berenice shivered. Like Cain and Abel, Israel had become her own worst enemy. She couldn't decide which was worse, facing the demonic Roman beast or their own inner demons.

"Let them kill each other," repeated Titus. "I can live with that." He smiled at the Pharisee. "Josephus, like the Herods here, you are proving yourself quite useful to the Flavian family. We won't forget it."

He lingered with a look at Berenice. She prayed he would not forget this time they shared in the land of Palestine.

Vespasian said, "So we wait for Jerusalem. In the meantime, let us finish mopping up the rest of the land. We start with Perea."

CHAPTER 38

Masada

Aaron led thirty armed Essenes on a treacherous cliff trail that wound its way up a rocky bluff. They were visiting the fortress of Masada on the shores of the Dead Sea thirty miles south of Qumran. The fortress was built by Herod the Great as one of his several refuges around Palestine. It sat atop a sheer cliff of fourteen hundred feet overlooking the sea and was protected by a casemate wall of stone all around the mountaintop. Sicarii and other Jewish rebels had recently captured Masada from Roman forces. Aaron and his men were there to solicit the help of their countrymen.

"Halt!" yelled a voice from above. Aaron and his monks stopped yards from the gates and looked up. The walls were lined with soldiers ready to rain arrows down upon them.

Aaron raised his hands. "We are Essenes from Qumran. Allies against Rome."

"What is your name?" demanded the skeptical guard.

"Aaron ben Hyam. I seek an audience with Simon bar Giora."

The Essenes stood for several minutes in their vulnerable position beneath the wall. Then the gates slowly opened.

Aaron and his men were ushered in past storehouses full of food, cisterns full of water, and an armory full of weapons. There were too many warriors packed into this fortress, thousands of them. And an encampment of thousands more on the plains below the plateau. There must be a full twenty thousand or so men in this mighty army!

As they approached the headquarters, Aaron saw Simon walk out to meet him, arms open wide and brimming with a smile.

"My bull-headed Essene apprentice."

Aaron replied, "My stubborn, unwilling mentor."

185

They embraced with a hearty laugh. Simon said, "Come, have some food and drink and tell me of your exploits."

Aaron's men had been fed and taken care of in the soldier's camp. Aaron lay at table with Simon and several of his leaders in the officer's canteen, drinking wine and eating vegetables and some beef.

"I tell you," said Simon with a spring in his voice, "I thought I was a dead man. There I was, having just killed their legate Cestius Gallus, an arrow in my shoulder, and three vengeful legionaries facing me down on horses with javelin and bow."

Aaron noticed the officers were listening in rapt attention. It was the story of the last time Aaron had seen Simon two years ago when the Jewish forces chased Rome out of Jerusalem.

"I don't have a chance in Hades to survive this. And I'm asking myself, why did I have to come to fight these Romans anyway? They were running away, for God's sake!"

The men laughed.

"Then all of a sudden, the sky began to rain stones on those Romans, knocking them from their horses to the ground. My first thought was, this was the same pass where Joshua made the sun stand still and caused hail to fall upon his enemies. So I'm thinking, is this another miracle? But the other side of me is thinking, no way in Gehenna, Simon. You are no Joshua."

The men laughed in agreement again. Simon had a long reputation for intemperance and debauchery.

Simon pointed to Aaron. "And then I see this pimply-faced little monk and his band of slingers come out of the dark like a group of orphan rascals."

Aaron smiled.

"And I'm thinking, maybe that's a bigger miracle than stopping the sun."

The men all guffawed and slapped Aaron's back. He smiled and retaliated, "You forgot to tell them, Simon, that you were on your knees crying."

The men now bellowed with laughter at Simon, who without effect tried to deny the counter joke.

Aaron turned serious. "The truth be told, you saved yourself that night because you were the one who taught us how to sling and how to fight."

Simon returned the honor now. "You became a warrior that night. A warrior that earned respect."

Aaron gave an obligatory smile. That night of battle, he'd lost his innocence. He'd killed his first man in combat, and it had changed him forever. He'd finally understood that becoming a man meant standing up to evil and sacrificing himself to protect others. Aaron had found in Simon the very father figure he had lacked in his life. Simon had helped Aaron's confused feelings turn from perverse affection to masculine respect.

Aaron said to Simon, "Do you remember what you said that night? You said you would fight to free the oppressed from those who exploited them."

Simon looked away guiltily. The other men turned silent.

"Right now, the holy city of Jerusalem and all her citizens are being exploited and plundered by Gischala and Eleazar."

Simon's men looked to him for response. He remained silent.

Aaron said, "Agrippa told me that Galilee has fallen to Vespasian. Rome is about to come and destroy them all. Please come to Jerusalem, Simon. Help free our people from their oppressors."

Simon demanded with a slow burn, "You spoke with Agrippa? You should have killed the traitor."

"I made a deal with him."

"What kind of deal?"

"I thought you would be eager to come for the opportunity of revenge against Gischala."

Simon said, "That was a long time ago. A different life, a different world."

"I reminded Herod that you were a mercenary. So he authorized me to offer you a large reward should you defeat both Eleazar and Gischala."

"That would benefit Herod, wouldn't it," said Simon. "But I don't need any more money. I've plundered Idumea, and we are doing just fine."

"I am sure you are. For now," said Aaron. "But if you think that if you leave evil alone it will leave you alone, you are sorely mistaken. It will come after you, Simon. Rome will come after you."

One of his generals, a gray-haired old warrior, said, "My Sicarii would support you."

Another one added, "So would our Zealots and other forces. They believe in you, Simon."

Simon got up angrily. "I told you before, I don't believe in the cause. And I have no intention of dying for a god, a people, or a delusion."

He turned to leave them. "Get your rest, Aaron. You can return home in the morning."

Aaron watched him leave and suddenly felt a lack of appetite.

The sun was rising, casting the desert cliffs in a beautiful morning glow. But it was not enough to give Aaron hope. He and his men were mounted on their horses. They said their goodbyes to the soldiers they had met and marched toward the gate to begin their long trek back to Qumran.

Aaron had not slept the previous night. He had racked his mind for other options at how to take out Gischala and Eleazar. But there was no one else with enough forces to accomplish the job and free Jerusalem from their tyranny. There was only one option open to him: assassination. He would gather his small band of Essenes, slip into the city, and assassinate Gischala and Eleazar. It would be a one in ten thousand shot, and his men would most likely be caught and executed. But it would be worth it.

And perhaps this was what he had been trained for all along. Aaron remembered Mordecai's words to Esther about God preparing her for "such a time as this." Now he knew. This had been his preparation. This was his time.

"Aaron!" a familiar voice said behind him. He turned.

Simon stood proud, suited in his armor. He approached Aaron and said, "If it's one thing I know about you, you'll be fool enough to face Gischala alone."

Aaron began to smile.

"You'll need my help." As if Simon would be helping Aaron instead of the other way around!

Then Aaron saw the other officers and men joining Simon, ready for battle. He shouted out to them, "We will wrest the holy Temple from the Zealot's grip!"

The men cheered. They were up for a fight like this.

Simon turned to them and joined in, "Gischala has raised hell! So we will send him there!"

They cheered again. Simon turned back to Aaron and said, "But at twice the price because of Herod's involvement. Gischala isn't the only one on whom I want revenge."

Aaron grinned wider. "I warned Agrippa you would do that. Done."

Simon reconsidered, "Maybe I should have tripled it."

CHAPTER 39

Jerusalem

Alexander could not find Noah anywhere in the hippodrome. He had asked around and had checked where he could, but the young boy was nowhere to be found.

Alexander was becoming attached to the orphan. He had deputized the young boy and his sister as assistants for Cassandra and himself so they could stay in the hippodrome rather than the theater with the other children.

Alexander had begun taking Noah on rounds and teaching the boy about what he was doing. The boy was transfixed by the grossness of wounds and the corrupting effect of sickness. But he was only seven years old and couldn't stay still for long. Before Alexander knew it, he would find himself abandoned as the lad wandered off on his own explorations.

Alexander had a strong suspicion the boy was sneaking out of their protected quarantine to explore the city. It was a treacherous world out there, and Alexander felt the pangs of fatherly fear for the boy's safety. Thank God Noah's broken arm had fully healed and he no longer wore his splint.

Unfortunately, Noah had already lost his innocence in this time of war. Alexander hoped to influence the child with the Gospel of healing for his spirit and soul. He had explained to Noah how Jesus the Nazarene was Israel's promised Messiah and that faith in him would atone for sin and redeem his relationship with the Father in heaven through the new covenant. Because of this, they had hope for the future despite the present tribulation.

But Noah would have none of it. He blamed Yahweh for the murder of his parents. Why would God allow his mother to be raped and his father burned alive? Alexander had his own experience of evil and suffering, and it drew him in dependent trust to his heavenly father. But such faith was not something he could give to Noah. He prayed God would.

190

Noah might be young, but he carried an anger at the world for what he had experienced. And he would not let it go. He protected himself by not trusting anyone, not even those who helped him.

Alexander decided to check Noah's sleeping quarters one more time.

When he arrived, he saw Noah standing over his small bed, examining a Roman gladius.

Noah tried to hide the sword behind his back.

"I'm not going to take it from you," Alexander said mildly.

Looking surprised, the boy cautiously pulled the sword back into the open.

"But you should not steal, Noah," Alexander went on. "Is that not one of God's Ten Commandments?"

"I didn't steal the sword. I found it in the garbage dump outside the city."

"Boy, I fear for your safety. You know you are not allowed to leave the hippodrome."

"You and Cassandra get to leave."

"Because we are the overseers. And even we have to get approval to do so. The rule is not there to keep you from fun. It is to protect you."

"I can protect myself."

"You and your sister are under my care and responsibility. There are many out there who will hurt you if they can. Like they did your parents." Alexander wondered if he'd gone too far bringing that up.

Noah wielded the gladius with clenched teeth. "That is why I want to learn how to use this. You promised to find someone to teach me. But you won't fulfill your promise."

"You're right, I did promise you. But the truth is, Noah, you are not ready to become a warrior until you learn moral character."

Noah considered his words quietly.

Alexander added, "You want to learn how to kill, but you don't want to learn how to heal."

"I don't want to be a doctor like you."

"That's not what I mean. You want to be a hero? You want to avenge the evil done to you and your family?"

Noah nodded his head.

"What you do not understand is that heroism is not found in attacking others for your own revenge, but in sacrificing yourself for others."

191

Noah frowned. "Are you saying that I should just forgive those who hurt me and hurt others?"

"No, I am saying that if you pursue the first without the second, then you will end up becoming the very thing you seek to destroy. Is that what you want, Noah? To kill people or to save them?"

Noah shot back, "But can't you save people by killing bad men?"

"Yes," Alexander agreed. "And when you understand the difference between revenge and justice, then you will be ready to become a man."

For the first time since meeting Noah, Alexander finally saw the young boy relax his anger and truly listen. He hoped he wasn't too late.

He said, "Let me show you something."

Alexander and Noah arrived at the garden in the center of the hippodrome. It took up several hundred square meters of the arena, and multiple gardeners tended to the harvest of grains, vegetables, and legumes.

Alexander pointed to a man at the outer rim of the small, homegrown field. "See that man. He is the chief gardener. Go and help him."

Noah looked confused. "I thought you said you were going to show me something."

"This is it. Go help the gardener, and I'll be back in a few hours."

Noah pouted and groaned.

Alexander said, "Everyone has responsibilities in the hippodrome. You know that. If you don't work, you don't eat." He smiled. "Think of it as the Garden of Eden."

Noah grumbled but made his way with resigned obedience toward the gardener. Alexander watched Noah's slow gait and slouched shoulders. Tedious gardening work was the last thing this eager adventurer wanted to do.

As Alexander returned to his rounds, he felt both pain and hope in his heart for the young soul. Could he rescue Noah from his growing bitterness? Could he find a warrior who would teach the boy how to fight with moral integrity in these days of vengeance?

$$\bullet \bullet \bullet \bullet \bullet$$

Cassandra had crossed the valley to visit the theater and now sat on the stage with the orphans and their adult caregivers gathered on the theater seats to listen. Rachel had come with her as usual but stayed at the outer fringe of assembled children.

Cassandra was teaching the Gospel to the children in the best way she could think of by telling the story of Israel and their longed-for hope of deliverance. The couple hundred boys and girls listened with rapt attention as Cassandra told of the promise of blessings and curses that Yahweh had made to Israel when entering into the Promised Land. She spoke of Israel's disobedience and Yahweh's scattering of the ten northern tribes into all the nations. Her young audience cringed in fear at the Babylonian destruction of the temple and the exile.

Then Cassandra told of how God's prophets had promised that one day Messiah would come and draw all his people back into their land along with the Gentiles who were orphans from God. She explained that Yahweh would adopt those who were not his own children into his family. Cassandra saw some of the children wiping tears from their eyes because they too were orphans who longed for a family to belong to.

Cassandra felt herself choking up as she told the story of the arrival of Messiah. His name was Jesus ben Joseph from Nazareth. But he wasn't what the Jewish people had expected. They had expected an earthly conqueror, but Jesus was a spiritual savior come to save his people from their sins. And when he claimed to be the unique Son of God, his own people rejected him and killed him.

By now a significant number of the children had been so drawn into the story that they too were crying. Cassandra described how the followers of Jesus lovingly prepared his body for burial and laid him in the tomb. But then on the third day, Jesus appeared to his followers, risen from the dead! Tears now dried up, and some of the children even began laughing with joy.

Cassandra saw that Rachel had moved in closer, listening intensely to the story. She finished her lesson. "And now, young ones, the end of the story is that Jesus is not only the Son of David reigning as king from heaven, but he is also a good shepherd who cares for you as his little sheep. Though you are orphans, you are not alone in this world. Our heavenly father wants to adopt you. And he does so through simple faith. If you believe in Jesus, that he died for your sins and rose from the dead, you will have eternal life and be forever adopted into the family of God. You can all become sons of God."[1]

Her conclusion was punctuated by a burst of joy from the children. Cassandra could tell they were expressing their heartfelt love not only of the story, but of the savior they trusted to adopt them. Because of their Jewish upbringing, it was natural for these children to embrace the story she'd told. Yet it was also supernatural to see the Holy Spirit move upon children who lacked the spirit of delusion that had come upon so many of her fellow Jews. Jesus's words echoed in her thoughts, *Let the children come to me and do not hinder them, for to such belongs the kingdom of God. Truly, I say to you, whoever does not receive the kingdom of God like a child shall not enter it.*

Cassandra looked for Rachel and saw her standing still at the edge of the crowd. She was not joining in on the excitement but remained stoic. When Cassandra caught her gaze, she turned and stormed away from the group into the stadium structure.

Cassandra's heart went out to her. At first, she felt a responsibility to stay with all these who had responded. Then she remembered another parable of Jesus, how the heavenly father leaves the ninety-nine sheep to find the one lost one. Leaving her young audience with their caregivers, she went in search of her own lost lamb.

"Rachel? Rachel, where are you?" Cassandra walked through the pillared outer corridor of the theater stadium, checking hiding spots.

She heard the sound of sobbing coming from a recess behind a column.

"Go away."

"I'm not leaving you, Rachel." Stepping into the recessed area, Cassandra sat down beside the twelve-year old. Rachel mopped up her tears.

Cassandra asked, "Why do you run?"

"I feel alone."

"You're not alone."

"You tell us a happy story and they believe you."

"I believe the story."

"I don't."

"That's okay. I'm still with you."

"I'm grateful for what you've done for me and my brother. For all of us. But what is coming is worse than what we've escaped, isn't it?"

Cassandra sighed. "Yes. Yes, it is."

"Then why do you not tell us?"

194

"You have already experienced what no child should."

"Why do you lie?"

"Adults protect children, Rachel. They don't lie to them. They shepherd them until they are mature enough to understand the world. We will tell them in due time."

Rachel sniffled. "I understand the world. I know that it is a horrible place that isn't for women or children."

"Yes, it is a horrible place. And I am a woman. But I believe there is hope. It is not a childish hope." Cassandra put her arm around Rachel. She felt the girl shudder, then settle in, comforted.

"I think you are becoming an adult. Do you know what that means?"

"What?" Rachel asked.

"You must now begin to protect children. Care for them. Are you willing to do that? To help me protect them?"

"Yes." Rachel's voice was soft, surrendered.

Cassandra squeezed her lovingly, remembering her own coming of age and how frightening it was, but also how liberating.

She felt Rachel squeeze back.

This young girl was winning Cassandra's heart.

But now they had to return to the hippodrome.

• • • • •

Near sundown, Alexander approached the hippodrome garden. He found an exhausted Noah, hands and feet dirty from handling crops.

"Are you hungry?"

"Yes," said Noah. They walked back to Alexander's tent for dinner. The boy's demeanor was quiet, discouraged.

"So what was it like for you?" Alexander asked.

Noah didn't respond right away. "Boring. Hard."

Alexander smiled. "I've often thought of how hard it was for Adam and Eve after they were driven out of the Garden. 'Cursed is the ground because of you; in pain you shall eat of it all the days of your life; thorns and thistles it shall bring forth for you.'"

Noah snorted. "I think I understand."

Alexander said, "Farming is not glorious like the life of a warrior. It's thorns and thistles. Like you said, boring and hard. And yet it is just as necessary to the preservation of human life as is the work of the warrior."

Noah listened thoughtfully. Alexander suspected his defenses had come down if just a little.

"Most people won't appreciate what you've done. But think about it, Noah. Without that garden, the rations we receive would not be enough to live on. Some of your own friends would get sick. The weakest would die. When you tend that garden, you are sacrificing of yourself to help feed others just as any warrior is sacrificing himself. But in a different way. You aren't out there killing bad men in the glory of combat. You won't get praise for mighty exploits or awards of honor. You won't be remembered in history. Yet by longsuffering hours of boring, hard work, you are saving lives. You are sacrificing yourself for others. And God sees your sacrifice, if no man does. That, young man, is heroism. That is how you find your way back to the Garden."

Noah looked humbly at the ground as they walked. Alexander prayed that through this experience, the young boy would begin to understand the true measure of a man.

As Alexander and Noah neared their tent, Cassandra and Rachel caught up with them from the direction of the hippodrome entrance. Alexander smiled at his wife, already knowing from the happy glow on her face that her visit to the theater this afternoon had gone well.

The four reached the tent to find a young man was standing at its entrance. Tall, handsome, with a cut jaw, tight beard, and light-brown hair, the youth looked to be about twenty years old and wore the tunic of a Jewish peasant. As he spotted the approaching group, a sparkle of recognition came to his eyes and a growing smile to his lips.

Cassandra was the first to blurt out a welcome. "Thelonious!"

Hurrying forward, she embraced the son of Lucius Aurelius Severus. "How did you find us? How did you…"

Alexander placed a hand on her shoulder, glancing at the children. "We have much to talk about—in private. First, let us share a meal with our guest. I'm sure he is hungry from his trip."

"I am ravenous," said Thelonius.

CHAPTER 40

"Forgive our humble rations," said Alexander as Thelonius finished his meal of bread and legumes. They lay at the dinner table of their hippodrome tent.

"I've eaten far worse in my journeys abroad," said Thelonius. "Sow's womb was the most awful. Though vinegar and pepper did help to make it tolerable."

Alexander and Cassandra laughed. Noah and Rachel gave each other a look of disgust.

Cassandra could not stop smiling with joy over their guest. She said to him, "You have grown into such a handsome young man."

"You have my father to thank for that."

"Nonsense," said Alexander. "It was your mother."

They laughed.

Cassandra asked, "So is there a young woman in your life?"

Thelonius's face dropped. He became pensive and said, "Love is a dangerous luxury in these times."

Cassandra felt as if he were evading the topic. As if he were hiding something. She wouldn't push him, so she offered, "Yes, it is." She looked at Alexander. "A costly luxury. But worth the risk."

He smiled back at her.

Alexander said, "Rachel and Noah, you are dismissed. We need to talk privately with our guest."

When the children were gone, Alexander said what they could not say in front of them. "Our joy at your presence is only equaled by our shock. How did you find us?"

"That was simple enough. My father had told me Jerusalem was the center of his investigation. As for finding you…" Thelonius grinned. "I simply asked for the best physician in the city."

Cassandra and Alexander smiled. Thelonius added, "The most difficult part of my journey was disguising myself as a traveling physician's assistant. I hear Romans are not welcomed in this land."

"You jest, but the danger is great. If you are found out, you will be lynched," said Alexander. "Why then did you come?"

"For one, I want to know what happened to my father," said Thelonius.

Husband and wife shared a sad but knowing glance.

Alexander said, "He left Judea two years ago in the fall. He used Cassandra's merchant vessel to sail to Patmos. He was going to retrieve a prisoner who was banished by Caesar and return to Jerusalem with him. We never heard from him again."

"John bar Zebedee," said Thelonius. "My father mentioned him in a letter."

"What else did he tell you?" asked Cassandra.

"Something about a seditious apocalypse that you were looking for. And he was to investigate the Jewish revolt."

Cassandra said, "He trusted you to tell you such things."

Alexander said, "The situation changed. Your father changed."

"What do you mean?"

"When we found the apostle, we learned the true meaning of the apocalypse. It is not a call to revolution against Rome but a prophecy of judgment upon Jerusalem. So there was no threat. And after we arrived in Jerusalem…"

Alexander hesitated. He glanced at Cassandra, who nodded in agreement. "After we arrived in Jerusalem, we became captives of the Zealots in the temple. It was there Severus became a follower of Jesus Christ."

Thelonius stopped eating to repeat incredulously, "He became a follower of Jesus? A Christian?"

Cassandra offered, "He told us that he was tortured and that he had received a vision of Jesus Christ and of the full weight of his sins."

"Did he confess those sins?"

Cassandra replied, "He had a mistress who was pregnant with twins by Severus. Two boys. Severus arranged for the abortion."

"He never told me." Thelonius appeared to be having a hard time with this news.

"He was going to," said Cassandra.

Alexander added quietly, "I was complicit in the act."

"You were his servant," Thelonius dismissed.

"We are all accountable for what we've done."

Cassandra went on, "His mistress opened her veins in guilt. When he received word from you that—" She choked up. "—that your mother had done the same, your father became overwhelmed by his conscience."

Alexander continued, "Like you, he had hidden his Roman identity because the Jews had revolted and no Imperial officer was safe in Jerusalem. He began helping us with our attempt to get the Christians to leave the city before the governor of Syria arrived with his legions. We had trouble persuading the Christians of the authenticity of the apocalypse, so Severus was going to Patmos to bring the apostle back to Jerusalem in order to convince them."

Thelonius looked deeply troubled. "He never arrived at Patmos. He is believed to be lost at sea."

Cassandra said, "We are so sorry for your loss, Thelonius. Your father was a man of courage and conviction."

The young man's expression turned sour. "He was a harsh man. And he treated my mother heartlessly."

But despite his hard words, there were tears in the young man's eyes. Cassandra and Alexander remained quietly sensitive to his pain.

Then Thelonius's eyes seemed to dry up. "But I have forgiven him. I too have become a Christian. And it makes my heart rejoice to hear that he became a follower of Jesus before it was too late."

Cassandra blurted out, "What? That's wonderful Thelonius. How? When?"

"Only recently. When I began to look into my father's disappearance and the apocalypse, I found what was left of the Christian community still in Rome. Still in hiding. They explained the message of Jesus to me." Thelonius looked straight into Cassandra's tearfully joyful eyes. "I remembered you and your faith. And what you did for me. How you saved me. It all made sense, so I was baptized secretly in the catacombs."

Cassandra remembered the catacombs of Rome, burial tunnels outside the city where Christians congregated secretly to avoid persecution.

Alexander said, "This is truly good news, Thelonius."

But the young man's smile was not as joyful as theirs. It seemed forced to Cassandra.

Thelonius said, "I still have much I do not understand. Questions. Faith is not always easy for me. I am a man of science."

Alexander said, "You are young in the faith. It's to be expected. Give it time."

Thelonius mused, "I once wanted to be a doctor like you. But after the fire, I became interested in natural philosophy, the study of the nature of things in our world, the science of knowledge."

Cassandra changed the subject. "Thelonius, do you know your father freed us?"

He looked at them with a sudden awareness. "I did not come to claim your servitude. I came to offer you mine. I want to help you."

Alexander and Cassandra looked surprised.

Cassandra said it first. "You cannot help us, Thelonius. We will be ministering to the sick and wounded when Rome arrives at the walls. They will spare no mercy."

He said to her, "I don't care. You saved me from the fires of Rome and from the fires of hell. I owe you my life."

Cassandra and Alexander sat stunned in silence, not knowing how to respond.

They were interrupted by the voice of Noah at the tent entrance. "How did Cassandra save you from the fires?"

Noah and Rachel were standing there. How much had they heard?

Alexander said angrily, "You were dismissed."

Cassandra placed her hand on his, hoping to avert punishment.

Thelonius said, "I think it is important that they hear about the moral character of their guardians."

She and Alexander had told the children about the Great Fire and its devastation of the eternal city. But they had never mentioned this story.

Thelonius said, "I was in the emporium market by the Tiber River when the fire broke out. It engulfed the city with such speed that those of us in the emporium were blocked by the flames with our backs to the river. Cassandra used her boat to rescue many of us as the fires licked our sleeves."

The two children listened with their mouths open.

"Now it was the final trip across the river. Cassandra would be able to take no more refugees after this pass. By the time she returned, the docks themselves would be in cinders. And the ship was already overweight with people. The flames were singeing my hair. That's why you see it is so light-colored."

Alexander smiled. Cassandra thought his storytelling was a bit too embellished, but Noah and Rachel remained in rapt attention.

"Cassandra had lifted the plank, and the ship was leaving me behind. That was when she noticed me in the crowd. She knew me as the son of her master Lucius Severus, but she had not known I was there until that very moment. She yelled to her captain, 'Stop the boat!' And they returned just close enough for me to jump onto the ship as the flames burst over the dock, consuming everything in a wall of fire."

Cassandra rolled her eyes at Alexander. Thelonius was indeed exaggerating for effect.

"So you are a Roman," said a pensive Noah.

Cassandra knew what the young boy was thinking. And Rachel too. They hated the Romans.

"Yes," said Thelonius.

Cassandra jumped in, "But he has become a Christian, Noah. He has repented of his sin."

Alexander added, "That is the power of the Gospel. It brings Jew and Gentile together in forgiveness and unity. He is now our brother in Christ. We trust him as family."

Noah kept staring at Thelonius. He asked, "Are you a warrior?"

Thelonius answered, "I was required to serve a short time in the imperial army. So I know how to fight." He turned to Alexander. "Do you need a security force?"

"No, I think Noah has something more personal in mind."

Alexander shared a knowing look with the boy, and Cassandra knew what was coming next.

Noah asked, "Will you teach me how to fight?"

Thelonius looked with surprise at Alexander, who shrugged with resignation and a smile. Cassandra considered this a good sign. Noah would keep the secret of Thelonius's Roman identity if he was being taught by the Roman how to fight.

"Do you have a weapon?" asked Thelonius.

"A gladius."

"All right, then."

Noah grinned at Alexander with gratitude.

Cassandra said to the children, "But the both of you must remember that the Jews of this city will not understand the secret you know."

Cassandra watched the two of them closely. They nodded in agreement. But would they keep it a secret? Rachel had been quiet the entire time. She still distrusted men, Jew or Gentile. Was this too dangerous a thing to place Thelonius's fate in their hands?

Thelonius offered to both husband and wife, "I will help you any way I can. Although I am not sure how my science skills would be of any benefit."

Alexander said, "Perhaps there may be a way for you to help save others from a coming fire of judgment as well."

Thelonius looked quizzically at him.

"You can help lead our band of orphans out of the city and escort them safely to Pella."

CHAPTER 41

Mount Bashar
Syria

Apollyon and his band of seven gods arrived at the foot of the mountain near the river Euphrates. It was a location in the desert almost perfectly equidistant several hundred miles from Babylon in the southeast and Jerusalem in the southwest.

Apollyon knew Michael had chosen Mount Bashar for symbolic reasons. In the deep past, it had been the holy mountain of the Amorites, that tribe of pagans out of which El Shaddai had called Abraham.[1] The conquest of Canaan by Joshua was preceded by their victory over the last of the Amorite kings in the Transjordan: Sihon and Og.[2] Yahweh had demolished the Amorites, taken over their holy mountain, and left it a deserted rock.

Michael was rubbing that victory in the nose of Apollyon.

What Michael might not have realized was that Apollyon knew that mountain like the palm of his hand from his primordial days with the Sumerian, Akkadian, and Syrian pantheons called "the thousand gods" of divine assembly on that mountain.[3] He knew every rock and crevice, every cave and tunnel.

He won't be crowing when I get my Watchers back, thought Apollyon, *and use my supernatural weapons of war on him and his fellow archons in the war to come.*

Molech pulled the cart with Raphael's dismembered body held captive. Zeus, Anat, Dagon, and the three Daughters of Allah surrounded the angel of the Abyss as he motioned to them.

"Michael is cocksure by his superior position in having the upper hand. And that will be to our advantage." Apollyon had a calculated trick prepared that he had not even told his seven fellow travelers. He was going to turn this hostage exchange into a hostage capture. He was going to take Michael, the prince of Israel, captive to ensure demonic victory over Jerusalem.

Apollyon located a large stone with some hieroglyphs scratched onto it. Kneeling down, he began to dig in the dirt. He soon found what he was looking for. He pulled out the handle of Driver, Ba'al's war hammer, and lifted it with a grin to his comrades. Apollyon had given more than one command to that messenger who brought Chaser, Ba'al's spear, to Mount Hermon.

"Be prepared for anything," Apollyon told his companions. "I expect this will not go smoothly, and we might find ourselves in a battle."

The gods all nodded and emboldened themselves for the journey up the mountain. Apollyon slung the hammer in its leather case on his back and led them to the heights.

The eight gods and their captive arrived at the prearranged location about halfway up the two-thousand-foot-high peak.

Apollyon stopped them when they saw five archangels standing a hundred feet away: Uriel, Gabriel, Remiel, Raguel and Saraqel.

Michael was not one of them.

"Curses," muttered Apollyon. He had counted on Michael being there. The archangel must have stayed in Jerusalem for its defense. Apollyon would have to improvise.

Two figures were released from behind the angels.

As they walked toward Apollyon and his gang, he recognized them as Ahura Mazda and Hubal, the Persian and Arabian deities.

They ran to their freedom as Gabriel announced, "Nothing more happens until we receive Raphael."

Apollyon said with a grin to the archon, "What's the matter, don't you trust me?"

Uriel replied from behind Gabriel, "You *are* the Father of lies. Can you blame us? Liar." Apollyon hated that blond rodent. He was small, but he was mouthy.

Apollyon nodded to Molech, who then rolled out the cart with Raphael's captive body and limbs secured within it. Molech stopped halfway between the two groups and returned to the Watchers.

Gabriel and Uriel ran to the cart. Uriel pulled out a weapon that Apollyon recognized. It was the long, metallic whip sword nicknamed "Rahab." The Watcher had faced that heavenly weapon in the past. It had been passed down from Lamech before the Flood to Shem and eventually to Caleb, who used it to conquer the seed of the Serpent in Canaan. Ittai the Gittite wielded it for King David against the Rephaim, and then Demas the thief used it in Hades beside Jesus. It was a mighty weapon.

But Apollyon had a mightier one: the war hammer of Ba'al.

The angels were pulling Raphael to safety, and Apollyon was betting on the fact that the other four Watchers were behind them. This was the moment he had planned for.

He pulled Driver from its sheath and swung down upon the rock with all his might.

An earthquake shook the mountain and the land.

Crevices opened up all around them on the ridge.

Everyone had fallen to the ground at the concussion. The angels were confused. They drew their weapons, guarding their wounded warrior.

Two hundred Watchers climbed out of the crevices from the bowels of the mountain and surrounded the angels. The two hundred ancient ones who had been returned to Apollyon's control. He had sent them a message to hide in the caves and tunnels of the mountain in advance of his coming. Now they joined Apollyon in full force against five lonely angels.

Archangels were a mighty force against Watchers. But five of them were no match for the two hundred.

If Apollyon could not have Michael, he would simply capture all the rest of the archangels, and Michael would be all alone in his defense of Jerusalem.

Sometimes, thought Apollyon, *bad luck has a way of turning into good.*

Apollyon shouted, "Where are the other hostages?"

Gabriel didn't answer. Uriel shouted back, "How stupid do you think we are, serpent brain?"

At that moment the clouds above them parted and the two hundred looked up in awe.

Tens of thousands of Yahweh's heavenly host stood at the opening of the heavens. They were arrayed in armor and chariots of fire.

"Beelzebub," cursed Apollyon. The tables had just turned, and he was now facing sure defeat. His two hundred warriors backed down and began to slink back into the crevices.

Apollyon turned to Gabriel in anger. "Where are the four Watchers? You promised an equal exchange for your archon."

Gabriel said, "We just made an equal exchange. Two for one."

Apollyon yelled, "Who's the liar now, godlicker?"

A column of intense light burst down upon the six angels. They were engulfed in its brightness. Two chariots of fire pulled by horses of fire were suddenly there, and the angels jumped onto them, carrying their wounded brother. The column of light became a fire of holiness.

Apollyon yelled out again, "You broke covenant! You hypocrites! You broke covenant!"

Uriel yelled out in response, "Then sue us!"

The chariots ascended into the heavens with a flash of blazing flames and lightning.

And just as quickly, it all vanished. Sucked into the disappearing vortex above them. The portal of heaven closed.

Everything had gone wrong for Apollyon. He still lacked his most potent principalities and powers for the coming war: Ba'al, Ares, Serapis, and Poseidon. Without them, Apollyon could not achieve his Armageddon.

He had been out-maneuvered by a pack of Yahweh's puppets, and everything had gone wrong.

Everything, except one thing. One thing rang in his head. The words of that sardonic little twerp before they fled in cowardice. "Sue us."

His sarcastic jab was more helpful than he may have wanted it to be. For if there was one thing Apollyon had eons of experience at, it was covenant lawsuits in heaven.

CHAPTER 42

Jerusalem

Alexander, Cassandra, and Thelonius arrived at Jacob ben Mordecai's residence in the upper city. They were ushered in by the scarred elderly servant Nathan. He was the one who had told them of Jacob's secret experience with the Two Witnesses. The three kept their relationship to themselves, merely nodding to each other.

Cassandra struggled with hatred in her heart every time she stepped foot into this place. This despicable apostate had returned to Judaism and had recanted his belief in Jesus as the Messiah. He was a dog returning to its vomit. And now his confiscated home was a den of thieves. The words of the letter to the Hebrews became poignant to her.

> For it is impossible, in the case of those who have once been
> enlightened, who have tasted the heavenly gift, and have shared
> in the Holy Spirit, and have tasted the goodness of the word of God
> and the powers of the age to come, and then have fallen away, to
> restore them again to repentance, since they are crucifying once
> again the Son of God to their own harm and holding him up to
> contempt.[1]

But she and Alexander had to deal with Jacob. He had managed to maintain his control over the quarantine despite the overthrow of the sanhedrin by Eleazar and Gischala. And he was the source of their food rations and resources in the hippodrome. They had to obey his authority or they would lose everything.

Yahweh, protect us and grant us favor, Cassandra prayed silently.

They arrived in the atrium, where Jacob was trimming his flowers and drinking wine.

"Welcome," said Jacob. "And who is your new companion? Another convert?"

Jacob was clearly suspicious.

Alexander said, "This is Thelonius of Corinth. He is a friend who has come to help us with the quarantine area."

Thelonius had chosen a false surname for his disguise, since Jacob had known Thelonius's Roman father.

"Tell me, Thelonius, why would you come all the way from the safety of Corinth to put yourself in danger in Jerusalem?"

"I am a natural philosopher, so I can not only help them with their ministry to the suffering, but I can study the nature of both disease and wounds on the human body."

Jacob eyed Thelonius, trying to figure him out, to figure out if he was lying. Finally, he turned to Alexander and Cassandra and changed the subject. "Speaking of your congregation, what can you do about Moshe and Elihu? They are not helpful to your cause. They continue their divisive, hateful diatribes in public. Can you speak to them? Persuade them to be more reasonable?"

Alexander smiled. "No man has control over the Two Witnesses. Their ministry is from Yahweh. You will have to take that up with them."

Jacob rolled his eyes and sighed dramatically. He changed the subject again. "Gischala has approved of my continued supervision of the quarantine and theater."

"How did you manage that?" Cassandra asked.

"Thanks to my stone quarry, Gischala considers me useful to the cause. I helped build the holy temple, which appeals to his religious passion. But my stone quarry is also crucial to the workforce that is now rebuilding the walls for defense. *And* I'm willing to take on the inconvenience of your bothersome camp of uncleanness."

Cassandra knew Jacob didn't care one whit for the poor victims of suffering. He was using them as pawns in his pursuit of power.

Alexander took charge. "Have you considered our request?"

Jacob responded, "Ah yes, your request. I am afraid I cannot allow you to take the orphans to Pella."

"Why not?" asked Cassandra hotly.

"Well, for one thing, Jerusalem is in crisis. No one is allowed to leave without approval of Gischala, and he is not in the mood for granting such approval for desertion."

"But we are not deserting," said Alexander. "We will return once the children are safe."

"I'm sure you would. But he is not so sure. There are so many sick and dying here that need your help."

"I will stay, then," said Alexander. "Cassandra and Thelonius will lead a group of adults to protect the children,"

"Yes, well, that would be better. However, I cannot in good conscience send off a group of vulnerable children, even with adult guardians, into a desert wilderness full of bandits and brigands without a military escort."

Alexander said, "Then grant us the military escort."

"Gischala will not release any of his armed forces for such a task. They are on high alert, and he needs every man available at a moment's notice. I am sorry, but I cannot grant you leave. The orphans must stay in the safety of Jerusalem."

Cassandra glanced at Alexander in the silence. They knew what Jacob was doing. Having control over something, even an unclean quarantine and a group of orphans, was a source of power in this crisis. Jacob would not be needed if he got rid of the problem, so he wanted to keep the problem around.

And keep his claws in it.

Alexander said, "Thank you, my lord. We must return to our duties." They were led out of the atrium by the servant Nathan.

Cassandra prayed for the protection of the orphans, for Noah and Rachel, and for all those in the hippodrome at the mercy of this evil apostate.

CHAPTER 43

Mount Hermon

Apollyon stood at the peak of the mountain. The wind whipped about with fury, and the skies above were darkened with clouds. His Watchers were gathered below as his witnesses. He held a trumpet to his lips and blew with a mighty force.

The trumpet sounded throughout the heavenly realm. It was not a call to war, but a call to assemble. It was the call of prosecution in Yahweh's heavenly court. Apollyon had served as adversary in God's divine council for millennia. He had accused Adam and Eve. He had accused Job. He had accused the high priest Joshua during the days of Zechariah. He had been the master prosecutor of accusation until he was thrown down to the land during the Nazarene's ministry.[1] He could no longer accuse God's people, the Christians, but he still knew how to prosecute a covenant lawsuit.

The heavens opened above Hermon, and Apollyon saw Jesus seated on the throne of David at the right hand of God, surrounded by a myriad of ten thousand times ten thousand of his heavenly host.

Apollyon held up a seven-sealed scroll and shouted with vindication, "I have in my hand a covenant lawsuit against the godhead of Yahweh and his covenant people Israel! I am suing for breach of covenant!"

PART TWO

Accursed

CHAPTER 44

The Heavenly Temple

Apollyon was escorted by a guard of heavenly host into the outer courtyard of the temple that was seated on the waters above the firmament.[1] It was the heavenly reality of which the earthly temple in Jerusalem was but a shadow copy.[2]

He was familiar with this hallowed structure. He had entered it often since primordial days as the adversary in Yahweh's heavenly court. What joy he had derived from accusing God's people right to Yahweh's face. He had been given legal right to do so by the Creator himself as part of the due process of his covenant with Israel.

But when that detestable Nazarene became incarnate, he'd thrown down the great dragon and his minions to the land and bound them so he could plunder the empire. The Adversary had lost his coveted role along with his powers of accusation and prosecution.[3]

But he had not lost his skills.

He walked on a floor of crystal sapphire past walls of marble and flaming fire. He looked above him at a ceiling that was like a path of the stars with lightning and fiery cherubim looking down upon him. He didn't miss those monstrous creatures one bit.[4]

Apollyon was ushered into the holy place. He felt the strange contradictory sensation of hot fire and cold ice all around him. It sent a chill down his spine. He never had liked that feeling.

Then they entered the most holy place. A rushing wind blasted his face. He felt disgust for the smug holiness of it all. The floor beneath his feet and the ceiling above his head were both flaming fire. So much fire. Too much. It was overkill.

Then Apollyon stood before the throne chariot of Yahweh. He fell involuntarily to his knees on the firmament.

The Ancient of Days was human in appearance but burned like gleaming metal so bright that no eye could see him. He sat in the very midst of a rainbow on a throne chariot of crystal sapphire that was held up by cherubim beneath him.

Apollyon had always considered these hybrid guardians to be ugly beasts, nowhere near the beauty of his throne guardians: the sphinxes of Egypt, the lamassus of Assyria, the mushussus of Babylon.[5]

The pious monstrosities called cherubim were basically humanoid but with four faces—human, lion, ox, and eagle—that looked at the four points of the compass. Each cherub had two sets of wings, one that held up the throne and the other that covered their bodies. They had gleaming wheels within wheels at their cloven feet that allowed them to move in any direction, and their appearance was the brightful shine of fire and lightning.

Excessive lightning to go with the excessive fire.

Beneath them was, of course, more streaming fire. Fire, fire, fire. Yahweh had an obsession with it as an instrument of holiness and judgment.

The Son of Man, that despicable, simpleton Nazarene, sat on the throne at the right hand of Yahweh. He glowed with the glorified burnished bronze of the sons of God. Otherwise, he wore the same boring flesh he had on earth, rather homely and unimpressive. Apollyon thought he actually needed that glow to spruce up his mediocrity.

Above the throne were the seraphim. They had six wings each. Two covered their faces, two covered their feet, and two were used to fly. Apollyon knew that when he launched his own throne guardians into battle against Yahweh, these would be the hardest to defeat. They were truly awesome. These were his kind.

He was disappointed with how far he had transformed from his original identity as one of them. But that was fire under the bridge now.[6]

The one thing of which he was not envious was their sycophantic praise. They sang with the voice of many waters and declared the Trisagion, "Holy, holy, holy is Yahweh of hosts; the whole land is full of his glory!"

Ten thousand times ten thousand of other heavenly host surrounded the throne in a way that would defy earthly logic. But they were there. And they repeated the dreaded Trisagion praise like an army of mindless parrots.

Apollyon was impatient to get through all this pompous vainglory and get to his lawsuit. He contemplated the irony of being here. Though Yahweh had banished him from heaven and stripped the Adversary of his ability to condemn believers in Messiah, Israel after the flesh was in breach of their covenant with Yahweh. He would get to that prosecution eventually. But his foremost concern was his rights as god of this world and getting his four Watchers out of confinement. They were the key to his plans of desolation.

An angelic herald announced, "Yahweh has taken his place in the divine council. In the midst of the gods he holds judgment."[7]

Once again, that annoying redundant flattery from the mob filled Apollyon's ears like fingernails scratching a piece of slate.

"Holy, holy, holy is Yahweh of hosts; the whole land is full of his glory!"

The herald continued, "Let the heavens praise your wonders, O Yahweh, your faithfulness in the assembly of the holy ones! For who in the skies can be compared to Yahweh? Who among the gods is like Yahweh, a God greatly to be feared in the council of the holy ones, and awesome above all who are around him?"[8]

This sanctimonious, self-righteous egotism is insufferable, thought Apollyon. *And humans wonder why I resisted?*

The herald continued, "The heavens are yours, the land also is yours, the world and all that is in it; you have founded them. Righteousness and justice are the foundation of your throne. Steadfast love and faithfulness go before you. Amen and Amen."[9]

Sudden silence fell upon the court. It was not just the quiet of voices stopping for breath. It was the quietness of all sound sucked away into a vortex of holiness.

Apollyon gave a sigh of impatience that cut through the silence with contempt.

Then smoke filled the temple, and the foundations of the thresholds shook with the voice of the Ancient of Days. "Adversary, what charges do you bring forth?"

Apollyon responded sarcastically with an honorable bow, "Oh, King of kings and Lord of lords. Despot of despots and Tyrant of tyrants. Mighty puppet master. Eternal dictator."

He gestured to the cosmos around him. "Give ear, O heavens, and I will speak, and let the land hear the words of my mouth."

He loved using Yahweh's words against him. That call to witness was part of the Mosaic covenant to which he would shortly appeal.

"First of all, let it be acknowledged by this court that Yahweh started this cosmic war." Apollyon looked into the burning brightness of the Ancient of Days. "It was all your fault." He looked away. The holiness was too much to face.

He continued pacing. "You created man in your image. You gave them an arrogant privilege of superiority, human supremacy over nature. But then you tried to keep mankind barefoot in the Garden—ignorantly dependent upon you. This obviously reveals an insecurity on your part. A need to stroke your own ego. A recurring character defect that will show itself in my complaint before the court."

He stopped to let that one hang defiantly in the air.

"But when the man and woman actually reached out and took responsibility for their lives, when they became enlightened to their own ability to know good and evil—for themselves—you rewarded their maturity by kicking them out of the Garden! Such petty, childish jealousy."

He stopped for a moment, filled with indignation. "Then you had the unmitigated gall to declare war. I quote again from your lofty, self-justifying creation narrative." He twirled his hand with mock regality, "'I will put hostility between you and the woman, and between your seed and her seed; he shall crush your head, and you shall crush his heel.'"[10]

Again, he stopped with dramatic emphasis, ruminating over the obvious unfairness of it all.

"You want to crush my head because I gave humanity autonomy, freedom, self-determination from your bullying tyranny." The heavenly host remained quiet. He wished he would have gotten a rise out of them. It would have been fuel for his fire. Their lack of reaction had a dampening effect on his rhetorical impact. *Godlicking toadies.*

"But may I remind you of the primeval covenant that you yourself—without any input from your lovely creatures—crafted, signed, and *imposed* upon them."

Apollyon pulled out a scroll of the covenant and unrolled it. He found the passage he was looking for and quoted it with more biting sarcasm, "'Remember the days of old; consider the years of many generations; ask your father, and he will show you, your elders, and they will tell you.' And I quote, 'The Most High gave to the nations their inheritance, he divided mankind, he fixed the borders of the peoples according to the number of the Sons of God. But Yahweh's portion is his people, Jacob his allotted heritage.'"[11]

Apollyon stressed that line about the Sons of God receiving the allotment of the nations just to dig it in. He put on his best prosecutorial voice. "Now, according to your own words at the tower of Babel incident when you divided the nations and confused their tongues, you allotted those nations as an inheritance to the Sons of God known as the Watchers. And you explicitly said that you would only keep one people for yourself—and only one people— those stinking Jews. A choice with which, I might add, I have no problem. Please, keep them." He gave a disgusted wave of dismissal.

"But you also promised that they would only get *one* piece of land *and one piece only*. A land, I might add, that you stole from its lawful owners, the gods of Canaan with your despicable holy wars. But I will let that pass. That's a technicality, and I suppose Jews have to live somewhere—*if* you are going to allow them to live at all."

Apollyon began to pace around the firmament with a professorial pride, teaching a lesson to the rest of the sniveling host.

"But the most important legal issue here is your breach of covenant. You have used that technical exception to become the justification for more criminal theft. You have taken back the allotted inheritance that you promised to the Watchers. And you did it through a trick. You withheld evidence. You kept the mystery of the Gospel from us through obstruction.[12] It wasn't fair. You made everyone believe Messiah would be an earthly military deliverer, not a sacrificial suffering servant. You spiritualized Messiah, the Land, the temple, Israel, Jerusalem, and the kingdom of God and let us keep thinking in earthly terms. You stole the land rights to the nations with a sleight of hand. You were deceitful in your narrative of redemption. How can anyone trust you if you keep changing the rules of the game?"

He paused for a moment, then said, "I demand justice!"

CHAPTER 45

Jerusalem

Alexander went to the garden of the hippodrome to see how Noah was doing at his work. When he arrived, he couldn't find the boy. He found the chief gardener at the shed of tools. "Have you seen Noah?"

The gardener, an elderly farmer with a humorous disposition, grinned. "Oh, that clever little boy. He worked hard to finish his chores early so he could play swords."

"Where?"

The gardener pointed behind Alexander to the northern wall of the stadium. Alexander saw Thelonius exchanging sparring blows of wooden swords with Noah. They stopped while Thelonius showed Noah how to hold the weapon better, then returned to their swordplay.

Alexander trampled over to them in a huff. He had promised to provide the young boy with this very thing, but now he found himself feeling jealous of the attention Noah was receiving from Thelonius. The child was spending too much time fighting. He needed to learn compassion too.

The two stopped their battling as Alexander arrived. He said impatiently, "Noah, I need your help. Come with me."

"But Thelonius is teaching me."

"And I have something more important to teach you. Come along."

Thelonius nodded for Noah to go ahead.

Alexander wanted to tell Thelonius to stop these lessons. But he knew if he did, Noah would despise Alexander. But if he let him continue, would he lose Noah to a spirit of vengeance?

Grabbing Noah's hand, Alexander whisked him back to the hospital area. He felt the boy's resistance, almost like he was dragging him.

"You're walking too fast," complained Noah.

Alexander stopped and was about to chastise him. But when he saw the boy's scared, young face, he froze.

"I'm sorry," he whispered.

He released his grip and knelt down to Noah's level.

He sighed. Noah looked angry, confused.

Alexander said, "I'll tell you what. Go ahead and practice with Thelonius for another hour, and then I can show you how to dress the wounds you create with that sword of yours. How does that sound?"

Noah's face lit up with excitement. "Thanks!"

Without a moment's delay, he turned around and yelled after his mentor, "Thelonius! Alexander says we can practice for another hour!"

He ran back to the Roman, who exchanged an apologetic look with Alexander. He nodded as if to say, "Don't worry, I won't steal him from you."

Alexander walked back to his tent, feeling like a fool for his jealousy. Questioning himself. Was he not man enough for Noah? The world needed both warriors *and* healers. Alexander was a healer, not a warrior. And he had never thought it less. But suddenly it seemed healers were just not enough. Even to Alexander. Was the world upside down? He felt his cosmos unraveling into a state of chaos.

Yes, the world was upside down.

When Alexander arrived at his tent, Cassandra was inside, folding some dried washing. He walked over to her and opened his arms. "My love."

She smiled at him, and they embraced.

He looked into her eyes, soft pools of love for him. "Our census of plague victims has decreased to but a handful."

She softened in his arms. "God has brought us through the gauntlet."

He asked, "How are the children doing at the theater?"

She smiled thoughtfully. "They are doing well."

"And Rachel?"

"An indispensable help. She still hides herself in her cloak. But she is starting to come out of her shell. How is Noah?"

"I'm concerned for him. He spends all his free time practicing with his sword."

"You mean with Thelonius?" She looked at him slyly. He felt a bite in his pride.

She added, "He wants to defend his loved ones."

"He wants to kill."

"We are in a time of war."

"He's only seven years old."

"He has to start sometime."

"I think he's planning something."

"What?"

"I don't know."

She changed the subject with a thoughtful stare into the distance. "Are we too close to Rachel and Noah? Have we lessened our attention to the others under our care?"

He considered her words with thoughts of his own. *Are we losing sight of our larger calling?*

"It's a little late to be raising that question, Cassie."

She had not wanted to get married because of the Tribulation, but they had fallen in love and shared a calling. Now she was glad she was barren to avoid the painful loss of a family in that same Tribulation. Yet they were becoming so attached to Rachel and Noah that they were already operating like a family. Cassandra was at war with her own heart.

They both were.

She looked back at him. "We have to find a way to get the children to safety."

"But Jacob is watching us like a hawk."

"More like a serpent," she said.

Rachel burst into the tent. "The overseer Jacob is at the entrance. He wants to speak to you both."

Alexander and Cassandra went with Thelonius to the entrance of the hippodrome to meet with Jacob. Even though he had survived the plague, he avoided going inside, perhaps out of some kind of superstitious fear of contracting the disease again.

Jacob was accompanied by guards. "I want you to clear out of the hippodrome and theater."

"What?" exclaimed Alexander.

Jacob said, "The plague is all but gone so there is no more need for quarantine."

"What about the children?" asked Cassandra.

"The children can be handed over to citizens willing to care for them."

"We've already canvassed the citizens. No one is willing to take the children. The war has made people fearful and withdrawn. They'll have nowhere to live."

"There is room in the New City then."

"You would have them live like rodents in burnt-out abandoned structures?"

Jacob's jaw tightened with anger.

Alexander put a hand on Cassandra's arm, signaling her to let him take over. With a conciliatory tone, he said, "Jacob, we are grateful for all the help you have given the sick and wounded and the children. I know it is a drain on you. But may I remind you that if it were not for that quarantine, you might not be alive today?"

"That is the only reason why I haven't forced you out until now."

Cassandra asked heatedly, "Then why do you not allow us passage to Pella? You could salve your conscience by getting rid of the children and get back your hippodrome and theater as well."

Jacob would not be moved. He said, "You will have one day to remove the children and others to the New City to find new quarters."

He said it with Caesar-like firmness. Alexander knew their troubles were starting all over again.

Jacob turned and marched back to his horse.

The three of them stood there stunned, watching Jacob gallop away into the city.

Thelonius finally said, "We need to deliver the children to Pella."

Alexander countered, "You heard what he said. He wouldn't let us get a hundred yards into the desert before he'd send Herodian guards to arrest us and bring us back."

Thelonius found it hard to believe. "Didn't you say he was miraculously healed of the plague? Is he going mad?"

Cassandra quoted Scripture with a distant look, "If they do not hear Moses and the Prophets, neither will they be convinced if someone should rise from the dead."

Alexander said, "Jacob has had a root of bitterness and a score to settle with us ever since we arrived in this city years ago. It's the nature of apostates. He will not rest until he crushes us."

"Then we must sneak the children out," said Thelonius. "Are there tunnels beneath the city?"

"Yes," said Alexander.

"How many days travel to Pella?"

"With children? Four days."

"We move them at night. We bypass the city gates. By the time he discovers we are gone in the morning, we could be twenty miles out."

"They're children, Thelonius," said Cassandra. "They don't have the stamina to run all night."

"What about those miracles you believe in?"

"You shall not test the Lord your God."

Alexander said, "She's right. If we had no other choice, I would consider it. But we do have a choice. And we must keep the children safe as far as it is up to us. We must prepare them and the others to find a home in the New City."

CHAPTER 46

The afternoon sun was nearing the horizon. Long shadows filled the Jerusalem streets. Inside the hippodrome, Alexander finished strapping up a small cart with a few belongings. Cassandra stood with Rachel and Noah, holding the donkey ready.

The adult Christians had organized the handful of sick patients onto carts for transportation and had brought the children over from the theater. They were all ready to follow Alexander out into the streets on their journey to the northern part of Jerusalem.

They were awaiting the arrival of their scouts, some of the adult volunteers led by Thelonius, who had been looking around the ruins of the New City for a place to resettle.

Alexander looked back out at the arena. They had cleared out the area, returning it to its original state as much as possible. They had even pulled up their precious garden and packed away what herbs and harvest they could. He did not know how they would survive the winter now. Jacob's food rations were not enough.

"Alexander!" Thelonius shouted from the open entrance way into the stadium. He was not alone. A dour-looking Jacob loomed behind him on horseback along with several guards.

Alexander and Cassandra both headed over to the entrance. Jacob's expression was fearful and anxious as he said urgently, "You must come with me. There is an outbreak of pestilence in the temple."

"What kind?" Alexander queried.

"Flies. A plague of black flies. Dozens have fallen sick. Many of them soldiers."

Alexander turned to Cassandra. "Hold everyone here. Get all the lavender, basil, and mint that we've packed away and meet me in the temple court as soon as you can."

Alexander mounted his own horse and followed Jacob and Thelonius the short distance to the temple.

They entered through the Huldah Gates and saw Moshe and Elihu leaving. This was most certainly another plague from God as promised in the Apocalypse.

And the Two Witnesses had the power to strike the earth with
every kind of plague, as often as they desire.[1]

The outer temple court was empty of people save the dozens who had fallen sick. Buzzing swarms of flies hovered around the courtyard like dark writhing phantoms, agitated, ready to explode. The sound of their wings penetrated Alexander's bones like a hive of little black demons.

Alexander took charge. He barked orders, pointing to a squad of temple guards. "You, gather as much firewood as you can in several piles around the temple."

As the guards hesitated, Jacob yelled, "Listen to him, fools! He is a doctor!"

He pointed to another captain and his squad. "You, help us bring the sick to the hippodrome."

When Cassandra arrived at the temple court, Alexander had cleared the people out, and fires were being lit all around the complex. Cassandra had bags of the herbs Alexander had requested: lavender, basil, and mint.

When she saw the black swarms, she whispered to Alexander, "Ba'alzebub."

He nodded in agreement. She was referring to the name that Jesus had called the satan in the holy land. The actual name of the prince of demons was Ba'alzebul, which meant "Lord Ba'al." Changing the name to Ba'alzebub was a pejorative insult that meant "Lord of the Flies."[2] The kind of flies that swarmed around excrement. By rejecting Jesus the Messiah, the Jewish temple had become a habitation of the satan.[3]

"Spread the flowers and herbs in all the fires," Alexander told Cassandra and Thelonius. "Flies hate those herbs. Their essence in the smoke will drive the pests away."

They ran to do so.

But just when Alexander thought they might have it all under control, an officer broke out of the inner temple gates. He was met by Jacob, who brought him to Alexander.

"We have a plague of frogs in the temple."

"Where?"

"In the high priest's chambers. What do we do?"

Alexander said, "Salt and citrus. Spread as much of it as you can spare."

The officer nodded and ran back to the temple.

The signs were too obvious to Alexander. First boils, then flies and frogs. He had heard that the waters flowing into the temple had earlier turned blood-red. The apostle John had called Jerusalem Egypt in the Apocalypse. The Two Witnesses were confirming the judgments. God was inflicting a new version of the plagues of Egypt upon Jerusalem.[4]

And he wasn't done yet.

Jacob was suddenly beside him. He said to Alexander, "Don't leave the hippodrome. We'll need to reinstate the quarantine." Then without apology he walked away to shout orders at the soldiers now cleaning the temple of the disgusting little amphibians.

Alexander looked out onto the chaos of the temple and thought, *This is only going to get worse.*

• • • • •

Outside the temple on the porch of the Huldah Gates, the Two Witnesses pronounced a fitting explanation of what was going on inside. Moshe quoted the Apocalypse to the sparse crowds in the marketplace. "And I saw coming out of the mouth of the dragon and out of the mouth of the beast and out of the mouth of the false prophet, three unclean spirits like frogs."

The Witnesses had called the high priesthood "the False Prophet," whose apostasy from Messiah embodied infernal lies. A plague of frogs in the priestly chambers was no coincidence. It was a message from God: the satan, Caesar, and the high priest were an unholy trinity, a demonic mockery of Yahweh.[5]

Moshe continued to explain the frog metaphor. "For they are demonic spirits, performing signs, who go abroad to the rulers of the Roman empire to

225

assemble them for battle on the great day of God the Almighty! And they assembled them at the place that in Hebrew is called Armageddon!"[6]

The listeners knew what the symbolic name "Armageddon" meant. It was the mount of God's assembly, his cosmic mountain. It was Mount Zion. The rulers of the empire would assemble for battle against Israel in Jerusalem.[7]

Elihu stepped in. "Remember the words of Zechariah the prophet. He foretold this day. 'Behold, the Day of the Lord is coming, For I will gather all the nations against Jerusalem to battle. On that day his feet shall stand on the Mount of Olives that lies before Jerusalem on the east, and the Mount of Olives shall be split in two. Half of the city shall go out into exile, but the rest of the people shall not be cut off from the city. Then Yahweh my God will come, and all the holy ones with him!'"[8]

He stopped to let the prophecy sink in. Moshe then explained it, "When this city is destroyed, you shall be split from the family of Yahweh, cut off from the very God you claim to serve!"

The concept of "cutting off" was well-known from the Torah. It was the penalty that was visited upon anyone unworthy of entering sacred space. The Witnesses were claiming that the unbelieving Jews would be cut off from Yahweh's presence, divided as spoil. But the believers in Jesus would not be cut off. They would live in the presence of Yahweh. The coming Day of the Lord would consummate that division forever.[9]

Moshe returned to the Apocalypse for his final challenge. "Behold, the Lord Jesus is coming like a thief! Blessed is the one who stays awake, keeping his garments on, that he may not go about naked and be seen exposed!"[10]

The area before the platform was nearly vacant. Many Jews no longer cared to hear the declarations of woe. They had been subjected to them for years already. And the message just wasn't encouraging or hopeful. More of the populace was hardening their hearts. They had ears, but they were not listening. Eyes, but they were not seeing. So like the prophets Isaiah and Jeremiah, Moshe and Elihu continued to fulfill their calling despite the lack of interest.[11]

But that was all going to change.

CHAPTER 47

Gadara
May, AD 68

The city gates of Gadara opened to allow Vespasian's entrance with his first cohort of eight hundred soldiers. The ruling officials had negotiated surrender before the legions had even arrived in the area. The city was on the eastern side of the Jordan River in a mountainous region. Vespasian was finishing his occupation of the Greek cities of the Decapolis.[1]

Titus rode in the victory chariot with Vespasian up to the party of ruling officials. Or what should have been the ruling officials. There were several Pharisees and Sadducees, but most did not wear the garb of governing leaders. Most looked like farmers and merchants.

The chariots stopped. The soldiers surrounding the Flavian generals kept a wary lookout for any rebels or surprise attacks.

A Pharisee stepped forward. He looked more like the head of the local synagogue. Vespasian said to him, "Where are your city leaders? Is this an insult to Rome?"

"No, my lord," pled the Pharisee with nervous fear. "The city leaders are all dead. A contingent of Zealot rebels within Gadara killed them for surrendering."

"Where are these scoundrels?"

"They fled south toward Jericho across the Jordan. Fifteen thousand of them."

Titus leaned in toward Vespasian and whispered, "Give me a legion. I'll hunt them down."

Vespasian nodded approval and muttered back, "Just be sure you don't get lost trying to find Jericho."[2]

The humorous jab was in reference to the fact that when they had sent scouts ahead of their forces into these mountains, they were unable to find the

227

city of Pella before making their way to Gadara. It was as if the city had disappeared from the face of the land.

Josephus had told them that Pella had been abandoned. The Greeks and Jews had killed each other off in the initial outbreak of the revolt a few years back. So the "missing city" was not a loss.

None of them knew about the Christian refugees who had resettled the ruins and rebuilt the city for refuge.

In Herod's tent at the Roman camp, Berenice helped remove the bandage from Agrippa's arm. He winced with pain. She saw his elbow, black and blue with a puss-filled wound where he'd been hit with a stone at the last town they had taken. He had been trying to convince the villagers to surrender peacefully and avoid unnecessary destruction. They had felt differently.[3]

"Ow!" he cried out as she tried to clean the wound with water.

"I never realized a sling could do such damage with a small rock."

She smiled. "Have you forgotten Goliath, brother?"

"Are you likening me to Goliath?" he asked playfully. "Maybe I am in more ways than one."

She shook her head with amusement and pressed a little too hard on the wound with her cloth.

"OW!" he yelped again and gave her an accusing look.

She said, "You need to stay safely behind the legions. I want you alive for the reorganization of Judea after the war."

"With your help, sister."

"Am I interrupting intimate family conversation?" The voice from the entrance of the tent drew their attention.

It was Titus, returned from the city gates.

Agrippa said, "You are already an intimate part of our little family, General."

Titus got to the point. "I'm afraid I'm going to have to pull you two apart for a while. Berenice, prepare for immediate travel. You will accompany me to Jericho."

"Why?" asked Agrippa.

"Because she pleases me," said Titus with an air of sarcasm. "Does that please you, my servant?"

Berenice tightened. The competition over her between these two made her uneasy, but it was also a bit of a thrill.

Agrippa said, "I would not presume upon you, my lord."

Titus asked, "By the by, are there any other towns or communities near Jericho and the Dead Sea that I should be aware of for occupation?"

Agrippa looked thoughtful before saying, "No. I would recommend next focusing your efforts on Idumea in the south."

Berenice looked at Agrippa curiously. He was deliberately ignoring the Qumran community. She knew the Essene community had ties to the rebel Simon bar Giora. Was her brother trying to make contact with Simon? She suddenly felt a wave of emotion come over her. Thoughts of Simon still did that to her. He was a ghost of her own conscience that she had thought she'd left behind.

She spoke to Titus, "As soon as I am done here, I will join you, my lord."

Titus became firm. "No, I need you immediately. There is no time for delay." He turned and left the tent.

Berenice set the cloth back into the water and got up. She looked sadly into Agrippa's eyes. She saw them a bit wet. Was it from the physical pain, or was it heart pain?

She said hesitatingly, "I am sorry, dear brother, but you'll have to tend to yourself."

She moved to leave, but he grabbed her arm. He winced from the pain again.

"Until we are together again. Godspeed."

He pulled her to him and kissed her on her cheeks. But then stopped face to face with her and kissed her on the mouth.

"Until we are together again," Berenice repeated with a sad resignation and left him.

CHAPTER 48

Jordan River
Near the Dead Sea

*The third angel poured out his bowl into the rivers and the springs
of water, and they became blood. And I heard the angel in charge
of the waters say, "Just are you, O Holy One, who is and who was,
for you brought these judgments. For they have shed the blood of
saints and prophets, and you have given them blood to drink. It is
what they deserve!"*

Apocalypse 16:4–6

Titus sat on his horse staring down into the Jordan river. He was surrounded
by his personal guard of several soldiers. He was covered in blood. They were
all covered in blood.

His victorious army moved among the bodies of the dead on the river
bank, sticking them for certainty and plundering any weapons or treasures they
could find before dumping the bodies into the current. There was not much to
plunder among these rebels. They had fled Gadara and were seeking to enter
the walls of Jericho when Titus fell upon them.[1]

He had backed them up to the river and slaughtered them all mercilessly,
fifteen thousand of them. A river of blood was a message for the rest of the
inhabitants of the land. Corpses filled the waters all the way downriver to
where the Jordan opened up into the Dead Sea.[2]

Titus thought of the irony of it all. The Dead Sea full of dead bodies. The
salt water would keep them afloat, cooking their bloated flesh in the burning
sun. Or would the excessive saltiness of the water preserve them like it did
fish and game? A curious thought.

230

The general and his several guards galloped along the river bank until they saw a handful of other legionaries on horses approaching them from the Dead Sea. Titus had sent out scouts earlier to reconnoiter the area.

He couldn't wait to get out of this blood-drenched armor, wash himself off, and take his lover Berenice, who was waiting for him back at the camp. A good battle, while exhausting, was also an aphrodisiac for him.

The guards arrived with several captive monks dressed in simple frocks, hands tied on a leash behind the horses. They looked like frightened mice, young, skittish, and breathing heavily from having to keep up with the horses.

"We found them gathering asphalt on the banks of the Dead Sea."

That explained the black pitch on their hands. They looked harmless enough to Titus. But one could never assume in this duplicitous land of deception and lies.

The guards pulled the monks forward, and Titus said to one of them, "Where are you from?"

The monk replied, "A small community called Qumran."

CHAPTER 49

The Divine Council

Apollyon had finished his first oratory of complaint before the throne of Yahweh. He now waited in silence as Jesus counseled with his heavenly host at the right hand of God.

When he finished deliberating, he stood to make pronouncement. The sound of his voice made Apollyon increasingly irate. Every syllable of the Son of Man was offensive to the Prince of the Power of the Air.

"Adversary, you represent the gods in this holy court, gods who were indeed allotted the nations to be their heavenly Watchers and to judge them, as you remind us. But to this, we declare, 'Do you indeed decree what is right, you gods? Do you judge the children of man uprightly? No, in your hearts you devise wrongs; your hands deal out violence on the land.[1] How long will you judge unjustly and show partiality to the wicked?'"

Jesus paused. Apollyon sighed and rolled his eyes with derision. It peeved him that Yahweh had given up the nations to their depravity to worship the gods, but then judged those gods by his Law. Why wouldn't he just leave them alone?

The Son of Man continued, "Give justice to the weak and the fatherless. Maintain the right of the afflicted and the destitute. Rescue the weak and the needy; deliver them from the hand of the wicked. They have neither knowledge nor understanding; they walk about in darkness. All the foundations of the land are shaken. I said you are gods, sons of the Most High, all of you."

Apollyon raised his chin with pride. Yes, they were gods.

"Nevertheless, like men you shall die and fall like any prince."

Apollyon grimaced as the Son of Man continued. "I have arisen to judge the land, to inherit the nations. Yahweh has set me as his king on Zion, his holy hill. And he has decreed to me, 'You are my Son; today I have begotten you. Ask of me and I will make the nations your heritage and the ends of the land your possession.' I am the root of Jesse. I have arisen to rule the Gentiles. I have assembled the banished of Israel and gathered the dispersed of Judah from the four corners of the land. I disarmed the rulers and authorities and put them to open shame, triumphing over them. I have led a train of captives in triumphal procession and distributed gifts to my followers in victorious conquest."[2]

Apollyon sighed. The Nazarene was rubbing the Adversary's nose in it. That was a particularly humiliating defeat in this spiritual war. Apollyon remembered well when Jesus had busted through the gates of Hades, taking the gods captive. And how that bullying Messiah dragged them through the spiritual streets.

Then Apollyon grinned to himself. *I have stolen the key to the Abyss, and I have freed those captives to serve me in my army of darkness. Gloat all you want, Nazarene. They're back—with a vengeance.*

Jesus concluded, "Yahweh says to my lord: 'Sit at my right hand until I make your enemies your footstool.' I must reign until I have put all my enemies under my feet."[3]

Apollyon could not deny it. When Jesus had ascended to his throne in heaven, he had taken his seat at the right hand of God, far above all rule and authority and power and dominion and above every name, not only in this age but in the age to come.[4] The Watchers had been disinherited, their allotment of land and nations legally seized with forfeiture. Apollyon actually had no intention of denying it. His only reason for bringing it up was to lead to his real complaint.

He said to the Son of Man, "You argue your case of being faithful to your covenant and your right to judge covenant-breakers. This is all well and good. You hold the Sons of God to their covenant. But why then do you not hold the sons of Israel to theirs?" Apollyon looked around at the heavenly host. "I call heaven and earth to witness that I charge Yahweh Elohim with violating the terms of Torah and the Sinai covenant."

CHAPTER 50

Rome
June 9, AD 68[1]

An angel poured out his bowl on the throne of the beast, and its kingdom was plunged into darkness.[2]

Apocalypse 16:10

Nero opened the curtain of his golden house across the Tiber to look out onto the gated entrance. A mob of angry plebeians protested at the gates with torches. The light of the midnight moon gave them an eerie glow like that of a horde of agitated ghosts.

They raised their fists and chanted slogans for that usurping governor who sought the throne. "We want Galba! We want Galba! No more taxes! No more taxes!"

Nero jerked the curtain closed and spit out, "Ungrateful pukes! What do they want from me? I gave them bread and circuses. Where do they think the money comes from but their own pockets?"

He was barefoot and in his nightgown, having been awakened by the unrest outside. He looked to Sporus, his male wife, who stood obediently by in his gown. Sporus had been castrated and made to look like the late empress Poppaea. He tried to act like her too.

"My husband, we had best leave this place and find secret shelter."

"Where can we go?" demanded Nero. "Galba is behind this. He has his spies everywhere."

Nero looked over at the haruspex priest he had called in for the emergency. The priest had been hurriedly cutting open chickens to divine the will of the gods from their entrails. He was desperate and nervous.

"Well, priest? What do you divine?"

234

The priest looked up at Nero, afraid to say anything.

Nero walked up to the portable altar and looked down at the chicken innards. He picked up two handfuls and looked at them. He squeezed them until they oozed and gave off a foul odor.

Then he slapped them to the floor, screaming out in agony.

The priest fled the room.

Nero fell to his knees, bawling like a baby.

Then just as suddenly, he stopped.

His fate had become clear to him. His head still in his hands, he muttered, "I should have killed Galba when I had the chance. I should have killed the entire senate as I considered." His voice became bitter. "I should have killed the commanders of the armies and all the governors of the Gallic provinces for conspiring with Galba. I should have set fire to Rome again and let loose the wild beasts."[3]

He paused and became overwhelmed with sadness. "I only wanted to be a god. A benevolent god."

He looked up. Sporus was gone. He was all alone.

"Has all of Rome betrayed me? Have I neither friend nor foe?"

His Praetorian Guard had vanished from the grounds earlier, leaving him unprotected. It was only a matter of minutes before the mob outside would realize this and break through into the palace.

Nero felt as if he was being watched. He looked up. A shadowy figure stood at the door. He could barely see it in the dark. It was a tall, muscular creature, standing in the shadows like a phantom of death. It sent a shiver down his spine.

It looked like Spiculus, his favorite gladiator. He considered a glorious climax at the end of the chosen warrior's sword.

"Spiculus? Spiculus, is that you?"

The phantom didn't respond. It just lurked in the shadow with menace. Nero remembered that Spiculus was already dead, murdered by the mob.

He yelled out, "Damn you, Pluto, come for my soul!"

He crumpled into a ball with his hands over his head, trying to wish it away.

When he looked back up the phantom was gone.

But then Sporus broke back into the room with a head servant whose name was Phaon.

"Caesar, we can escape to Phaon's villa if we leave now."

He held out a cloak for Nero to hide himself for traveling.

Reason returned to Nero, and he leapt up to follow them out.

They rode horses through the back streets across the river with three attendants guarding them. One of them was Nero's loyal secretary Epaphroditus, a tall, lean man. Phaon would meet them at his villa shortly. Nero and Sporus wore their hooded cloaks to conceal themselves and held handkerchiefs to their mouths. They were still barefoot in their urgent fleeing from the palace.

It had taken them a half hour to get to Phaon's villa. When they arrived, Nero and Sporus ran inside with the others.

Nero paced nervously as Sporus remained silent in the corner.

Nero said to the other two guards, "Go dig a grave for me out back."

The two looked at each other askance.

"I SAID GO!" screamed Nero like the burst of a hurricane.

The guards obeyed and left them.

Nero muttered to himself, "Oh, what an artist the world is losing."

Sporus was beside him, trying to comfort him with caresses. Nero slapped him away.

Just then Phaon arrived in the villa, carrying a pamphlet.

He stopped when he saw Nero. His face was dark.

Nero swallowed and snatched the pamphlet from his hand. He read it, then cursed. "I've been declared a public enemy by the senate. They intend to kill me according to the ancient fashion. What is the ancient fashion?" He had enjoyed pronouncing godlike legal judgments, but rarely bothered himself with the details of execution.

Phaon swallowed and said faltering, "It is…when they…strip the condemned naked…fasten the neck in a fork…" Nero closed his eyes in dread. "…and then beat him to death with rods."

Nero could not abide such ignominious death. He immediately drew a dagger from his belt and placed it at his throat. He would kill himself before he allowed such disgrace.

Sporus yelped in fear and began to cry like a child.

Nero trembled with indecision. He felt as if everything in his mind was telling him to plunge the dagger into his throat. But his hands were holding him back, keeping him alive.

His eyes welled up with tears. Through the blurriness, he thought he saw the phantom again out in the dark of the yard. It was watching over the servants digging the grave. Was it his genius? A guardian daemon?

The presence distracted him. His muscles relaxed, and the dagger fell to the floor.

Nero muttered, "The fatal hour has not yet come."

The two servants stepped back into the room.

One of them said, "The grave is dug, Caesar."

Nero's eyes lit up with an idea as he looked at his companions. He picked up the blade and offered it to Epaphroditus, saying, "Come, help your emperor to find the courage by killing yourselves as examples of heroism."

The servants looked at one another. Sporus's eyes dried up. Epaphroditus stepped back. They all demurred, looking away from the emperor in an uncomfortable silence.

None were willing.

Nero pronounced with self-importance, "To live is a scandal and a shame. But I cannot kill beauty."

Phaon heard the sound of horses arriving in his front entrance. He ran to see who it was. When he returned, he said ominously to Nero, "Galba's messengers. They're here."

Nero put the dagger to his throat again and called out, "Epaphroditus, loyal friend, come rouse thyself!"

Epaphroditus was by his side with his hand on Nero's hand, holding the blade. He swallowed and pushed. The dagger slid into the emperor's throat, and Nero's eyes went wide with shock.

He gurgled on the blood that poured from the wound. As his vision began to fade out, he thought he saw Epaphroditus's face transform into that of Apollo, his patron god. A dark grin crossed his lips.

But then that vision turned into the hideous form of an ugly creature he had never seen before. Large, gaunt, androgynous with long greasy hair and ugly yellow teeth.

Nero gurgled through his blood, "It's too late." His grin turned to frozen terror, and he slipped away.

Into the fire.

Epaphroditus stood back as if to disavow what he had done. He saw blood on his hands and tried furiously to wipe it off onto his tunic, leaving messy swipes of blood like tracks of accusation.

Breaking through the door, a company of Praetorian Guards found the company around the dead form of the human monster who would be emperor no more.

The leader of the Praetorians stepped forward. It was Flavius Domitian, the son of Vespasian. Beside him was Tigellinus, Nero's favored Praetorian.

Tigellinus spit on the dead body and glared at it without pity.

Domitian said to one of the soldiers, "Send a message to my father."

> The beast was captured, and was thrown alive into the lake of fire
> that burns with sulfur.[4]
>
> Apocalypse 19:20

CHAPTER 51

Jerusalem

Simon set up camp with his forces of forty thousand warriors outside the northern walls of Jerusalem by the New City. They were out of the range of missiles, but close enough to keep an eye on the walls and gates. Though this was the weakest area of defense, Simon had no siege engines or battering rams.[1]

Simon and Aaron looked out at the gates and the archers on the top of the battlement.

"We'll need a miracle to breach that wall," said Aaron.

"It looks like we may not have to breach it at all," said Simon. "Apparently, Gischala is taking the battle to us."

Aaron saw the gates open and a host of soldiers pour through the opening to take formation outside the wall.

Simon turned to a trumpeter near them and yelled, "Sound the alarm! Battle formation!"

The trumpeter blew with all his breath, and the sound of the trumpet awakened the thousands of Simon's army like a hive of hornets.

Idumeans, Sicarii, and Zealots of all stripes gathered in their companies to face off against the growing formation hundreds of yards away from them in front of the wall. Simon had built his armed forces from conquests throughout Idumea. It was not a homogenous army, which provided difficulties in organization. But they were united in one thing: their respect for Simon's leadership. He had treated his men with fairness and equity, and his strategy was ruthlessly brilliant. They would stand with him.

Simon squinted as he saw an officer walk his horse, accompanied by a small guard, to a midway point between the two armies. The officer's liege carried a banner of peace.

Aaron asked, "They want to negotiate? Or draw you out as a target?"

Simon could finally tell what he was seeing. The silken robes and round helmets, light metal chainmail glinting in the sun, scimitars. "Those are Idumeans." He turned to his captains and yelled, "Let them approach!"

When the officer and his team arrived at Simon's position, they got off their horses and bowed.

Simon demanded, "Where is John of Gischala?"

The officer said, "We have pushed him back into the temple precinct."

"You are not his ally?"

"He is a cruel and ruthless tyrant. He betrayed his ally Eleazar, so we do not trust him to not betray us. Besides, you have our countrymen at your side. The city is ready for your taking."

Simon smiled.

Aaron muttered, "Like I said, a miracle."

Simon said to the officer, "Then let us take the city."

The officer nodded to his bannerman, who waved the flag to the Idumean troops by the wall.

A rousing cheer went up from the soldiers.

Simon said to the officer, "Muster all forces inside the walls. I want to talk to my new allies."

The combined armies of Simon's warriors and the Idumeans in Jerusalem had assembled in the northern quarter of the New City and stood at attention.

Simon looked overhead at the gathering of storm clouds. A fitting reality for the storm that was coming. He looked out upon the warriors from a wooden platform that had been arranged for his oration. He spoke with a booming voice to his new army.

"Fellow warriors, I stand before a diverse crowd of men from every conceivable background and belief in this land. Most of you are united in your love of the holy city—and your hatred for Gischala!"

The crowd stirred in agreement.

"You have chosen to follow my leadership. I am flattered. And I accept!"

The men cheered. He waited for them to quiet down.

"I am here to do a job: to rout Gischala and return the city to order!"

Again, the soldiers cheered.

"But I have no intentions of fighting an unwinnable war with the mightiest kingdom on earth!"

The festive spirit turned sour as the happy soldiers questioned each other if they had heard him correctly.

"So if any of you have more revolutionary intentions for my leadership, do not fool yourselves. I will be gone before the Romans arrive!"

The forces had gone soberly quiet. He saw Aaron standing below the platform, his face sad. He had helped the young monk understand what it meant to become a man. Now he would teach him about the vanity of religious fanaticism.

But he knew he had to finish by raising their spirits.

"Bring me to Gischala and let us crush his tyranny over Jerusalem!"

The armies broke out in renewed vigor and applause.

Men chanted, "Simon! Simon! Simon!"

The sound of rumbling thunder overhead punctuated their praise as if from God himself.

He wondered if they had heard anything he had just said.

CHAPTER 52

The Divine Council

Michael the archangel stood beside the Son of Man in the throne room of the heavenly court. He had been summoned by the Most High because as prince of Israel Michael would stand as representative for the defendant in Apollyon's lawsuit against the Jews. He was filled with righteous indignation as he listened to the dragon recite to the court the long litany of curses in the covenant that God had promised he would bring upon Israel if she disobeyed Yahweh. As if he had to remind God of his own words. The contemptuous little snake!

That reptile finally came to the conclusion. "Yahweh will bring you to a nation that neither you nor your fathers have known. Yahweh will bring a nation against you from far away, from the end of the earth, swooping down like the eagle, a hard-faced nation who shall not respect the old or show mercy to the young until you are destroyed. They shall besiege you in all your towns, until your high and fortified walls in which you trusted come down throughout all your land. And you shall be plucked off the land that you are entering to take possession of it. And Yahweh will scatter you among all peoples from one end of the land to the other."

Apollyon paused after his longwinded reading. He then concluded with the height of his condescension. "All these curses shall come upon you until you are destroyed because you did not obey the voice of Yahweh your God to keep his commandments and his statutes that he commanded you. They shall be a sign and a wonder against you and your offspring forever."[1]

The Adversary took a moment to formulate his next argument. He appealed to the myriad of witnesses around the throne. "Now, this covenant is perpetual and its statutes are forever. And I will grant the court that it was enforced in the Assyrian and Babylonian exiles. In those cases, Yahweh fulfilled his curses, took Israel out of the land into the slavery of foreign powers, and destroyed their fortified walls and towns. But let me remind you of the words of your own prophets."

Apollyon opened the scrolls of the Scriptures to make his case. *He is a manipulator*, thought Michael. That devil always quoted select verses while ignoring key other ones that gave a more nuanced meaning. He quoted out of context in some cases and made up false contexts in others. He even outright lied to suggest things Yahweh had never claimed. *Hath God said?* Would he try such blatant manipulation now before the Ancient of Days? No, he would be subtle like the serpent he was.

"Ah, here it is," said the Adversary. "Now as we all know, Yahweh married Israel as his bride at Sinai with the giving of the covenant. She is his covenanted wife.[2] As Yahweh himself has said of his lover, 'When I passed by you and saw you, behold, you were at the age for love, and I spread the corner of my garment over you and covered your nakedness; I made my vow to you and entered into a covenant with you, declares the Lord Yahweh, and you became mine.'[3] How sweet and precious."

His sarcasm was profanity in the face of God. Michael held back his desire to smite the slitherer.

"With your indulgence, may I now read from the prophets, your mouthpieces to the world. One might even call them your ventriloquist dummies. Well, those same prophets continually charged Israel with spiritual harlotry over and over again even after the return from exile into the land.[4] And I quote from the prophet Malachi, 'Judah has been faithless, and abomination has been committed in Israel and in Jerusalem. For Judah has profaned the sanctuary of Yahweh, which he loves, and has married the daughter of a foreign god.'[5] In fact, virtually all the prophets spoke of Israel's continual ongoing addiction to spiritual harlotry. Ezekiel, Jeremiah, Isaiah, Hosea.

"Then, those same prophets promised that you would divorce Israel and destroy her house of marriage, the temple.[6] And what does Israel continue to do through all her history? She kills the prophets and stones those who were sent to her. And then when the King of kings sent his own son, the Messiah, they killed him to take his inheritance."

Apollyon looked straight at the Son of Man on his throne. "What did you say that Yahweh would do to the tenants of the vineyard who would dare do such a thing? 'He will put those wretches to a miserable death and let out the vineyard to other tenants who will give him the fruits in their season.'[7] Now, correct me if I am wrong, O Son of Man, but it was you who said that this generation of Jews who rejected you would be guilty of all the righteous blood of the prophets shed in the land."[8]

The Adversary paused to prepare for his final statement.

"Now it seems to me that both father and son have declared repeatedly in the Scriptures, *ad nauseum* I would argue, that Israel is an unfaithful harlot who will be divorced and disinherited. That her house will be destroyed by a foreign army for her rejection of both the prophets and Messiah. And that she will be scattered into the earth. Yet here we stand. The harlot Israel is still in her land. She is still fornicating in her house that still stands in her cursed city whose walls are still strong and still guarded by this prince beside you." Apollyon gestured to Michael.

Just keep talking, fool, thought Michael.

"My armies stand ready to fulfill *your prophecies*. It is my covenantal right to do so. Yet you have allowed your meddling bureaucrats to hold back four of my angels from completing that task. What kind of god claims justice but withholds it? I demand you release my angels!"

Michael shook his head. Apollyon was like any petty tyrant. He was so full of hubris that it blinded him to his own folly. He reminded Michael of the king of Assyria in Isaiah's day. God had used the Assyrian to punish Israel with his armed forces. The king then boasted in the arrogance of his heart, "By the strength of my hand I have done this." He had no clue that he was the rod of God's anger, the axe in Yahweh's hand. His pagan armies were Yahweh's armies. He was the instrument of God's sovereign purpose.[9]

So, Apollyon did not know what was going on in Jerusalem. He did not know that his complaints were virtually identical to the proclamations of the Two Witnesses inside the city. The Adversary was correct in his charges. But he didn't know that his own lawsuit was the planned purpose of the heavenly witness for God's earthly intentions.

244

CHAPTER 53

Jerusalem

When he opened the sixth seal, I looked, and behold, there was a
great earthquake, and the sun became black as sackcloth, the full
moon became like blood, and the stars of the sky fell to the land
as the fig tree sheds its winter fruit when shaken by a gale.[1]

Apocalypse 6:12–13

Lightning ripped the night sky overhead. Thunder rattled the walls of the city, and rain poured down like opened floodgates. John of Gischala used this opportunity of chaos to launch a raid out into the communities surrounding the temple. They were looking for food and supplies to plunder but were sorely disappointed by the poverty of the people's resources.

He was gathering his unit of two hundred men to journey deeper into the city when he looked up into the Tyropoeon Valley just north of him.

Through the dark sheets of rain, he saw a flood of soldiers running his way like a tidal wave. There were too many of them.

He yelled to his men, "Retreat to the temple!"

But it was too late. Hundreds of Idumeans had slipped out of hiding in the Lower City and had formed a phalanx blocking the Zealot's path back to the temple gates.

Within yards of their escape to safety, Gischala and his men engaged in desperate battle.

The sound of clashing swords and battle cries resounded with the shattering thunder and howling wind. Mud and water mixed with flesh and blood as men fell to the ground beneath the hacking, piercing, and slicing of weapons.

An Idumean warrior launched himself at Gischala, dragging him from his horse. They fell into the mud, but only Gischala got up, pulling his dagger from the Idumean's heart. He ducked and dodged another attacker, then dispatched him with his own sword.

Gischala jumped back up on his horse in time to see that the wave of attacking forces was almost upon them.

He yelled, "To the temple!"

Pushing with renewed vigor against their enemies, the fighting Zealots finally broke the line. They bolted up the steps for the Huldah Gates just as the attacking companies arrived.

The huge gates were closing behind him. Gischala turned. A bolt of lightning lit up the city, and he saw who was leading the forces against him: Simon bar Giora.

At that moment, the ground rumbled. Simon's soldiers were thrown into the mud by the force of a massive earthquake. Loose stones fell from the temple wall, crushing some of the attackers. Some poorly constructed homes nearby collapsed into piles of rubble, burying their inhabitants in death.

Gischala felt the very foundations of the temple move and wondered if Yahweh would show up. Was this a sign of his rescue?

The entire city felt the effects of this seismic upheaval. Many would die in the destruction.

• • • • •

In the unseen realm, outside the southwestern wall in the valley of Gehenna, a large crevice opened up from the impact of the quake. Deadly gasses were released from below, and a pit opened up to Sheol, the underworld.[2]

• • • • •

Alexander and Thelonius were at the top of the hippodrome within sight of the confrontation that had just occurred between Gischala and the newly occupying forces of Simon bar Giora. They covered themselves from the pelting rain as they watched the attacking forces gather themselves around the gate after the earthquake.

Alexander said to Thelonius, "The city is now split into three parts, just as the apocalypse predicted. Simon holds the city, Gischala holds the outer temple, and Eleazar the inner temple."

"How so this prediction?" asked Thelonius.

Alexander recited it,

> *An angel poured out his bowl into the air, and a loud voice came out of the temple, from the throne, saying, "It is done!" And there were flashes of lightning, rumblings, peals of thunder, and a great earthquake such as there had never been since man was on the land, so great was that earthquake. The great city was split into three parts.*[3]

Thelonius looked impressed, even disturbed, by the prophecy. Alexander said, "The ruling powers in heaven and earth are being shaken. The world order is changing. It's the end of the present age."

In the streets below the doctor and his companion, the Two Witnesses stood screaming into the wind and rain, prophesying a coming drought by the hand of God.

A drought—declared during a huge rain storm.

No one was listening.

· · · · ·

"GISCHALA!"

"GISCHALA!"

Simon's throat had gone hoarse yelling the name above the wind and rain that drenched him like a deluge.

He was alone, prancing back and forth on his horse in front of the Huldah Gates. He didn't care if Gischala's men shot him through with arrows from above. The coward. So be it. In truth, he didn't care about anything at the moment. He only felt a boiling rage that defied death itself. If they killed him, he would be relieved of the burden of pain he had carried all these years. So be it.

The huge gates opened just enough for a horseman to walk through.

It was Gischala.

The two warriors locked eyes, circling each other with their snorting warhorses ready to leap into battle.

"Well, look what ghosts the storm dredged up," sneered Gischala.

Simon gritted his teeth. "I should have killed you when I had the chance."

"You mean when you were cavorting in the bath with Berenice? That's a bit too late, Simon. A long time ago."

Thunder cracked the sky. Simon continued to circle his enemy, looking for any excuse.

Gischala added, "Well, I hear she cavorts with Romans now, my friend. And as I recall, *you* ran away from *her*. And from Jerusalem."

"I control Jerusalem," said Simon.

"But I the temple."

Simon laughed with incredulity. "Do you really think you have a chance against the legions of Rome? Are you that deluded?"

Now Gischala got angry. "Since when did you suddenly sprout concern for the holy city? I smell Agrippa's stench on this."

Simon didn't care about any of it. "Why did you betray me?"

"I did not betray you, Simon. I sacrificed you for a higher cause."

"What kind of cause makes you kill your own people? Hold them hostage?"

Gischala grinned diabolically. "You would rather I kill them for money like you?"

Simon felt stung—or rather pierced. The click clack of the horses' hooves on the pavement, the howling wind, the pouring rain all became a kind of a requiem of sounds in Simon's ears.

He said, "Before this is over, you will die a criminal's death."

Gischala burst out laughing. "Good luck, infidel. There is no satisfaction in Sheol."

With that, he turned his mount back toward the gates, leaving Simon standing alone in the stormy wind and rain. Simon was still, staring grim-faced, feeling as though he were falling, falling into the void.

The soft sound of a voice gradually brought him back until he could hear it with clarity. "Simon! Simon, something horrible has happened!"

It was Aaron with another Essene monk.

What could be more horrible than this? Simon thought.

Aaron said, "This brother has brought news from Qumran. They've been attacked!"

CHAPTER 54

Qumran

Simon and Aaron arrived at the walls of the Dead Sea community just as the sun broke the horizon. The storm from the previous night had passed. The desert was already dried up. They could see the walls were broken down in several places. The *Yahad* had been attacked.

The two of them were accompanied by a cohort of cavalry as well as Aaron's squad of forty Essene warriors. Simon gestured to speed up their gallop. A feeling of dread came over him.

When they arrived at the gates of the small monastery, Simon jumped off his horse, followed by Aaron and the other Essenes. The cavalry stood guard outside.

One of Simon's scouts had galloped around the perimeter and had judged from the tracks that they had been attacked by a unit not much larger than their own cohort.

Inside, the two warriors stood in shock at the devastation. Simon looked darkly at Aaron. There was no sign of life. Just dead bodies everywhere. The structures had been decimated, some of them burnt to the ground. But there were no smoldering ruins, the storm rain having quenched all fire and smoke. It was like a graveyard of death long since lost.

Simon and the Essenes spread out, looking for anyone who might have survived, who might have hidden themselves.

Then Simon heard the sound of Aaron crying. He ran out into the yard.

He found Aaron kneeling over his two young friends, Baruch and David. Dead.

It was clear who had done this.

"Romans," grunted Simon. He began to shake with anger. These naïve foolish monks had hurt no one with their separatist beliefs and lifestyle. They were not even fighters until he had trained them.

Until he had trained them.

Would they still be alive if he hadn't taught them how to fight? Would they have been enslaved by the Romans instead?

Simon realized now how much the Qumran community had become a family to him in his previous life. A family that reminded him how far he had slipped into darkness.

He growled and continued into the elders' chambers. Aaron eventually followed him.

They had to step over the bodies, there were so many dead.

Striding into a room, Simon recognized a body. "Aaron," he called out.

Aaron followed him into the room to find the fat, balding overseer Phineas lying in the corner with a broken spear through his gut.

As Simon and Aaron approached, the overseer woke from unconsciousness, choking for air.

He was alive! Just barely.

They stood over him. Phineas looked up and gurgled out, "A-aaron."

Simon watched the young monk to see what he would do.

Aaron stared at Phineas like a cat waiting for a mouse to die.

This overseer had abused Aaron and others in this community with his unnatural desires. He was a wolf in sheep's clothing. Simon wouldn't consider it wrong if Aaron twisted that spear and pulled out the monster's intestines for all that he had done to these young, innocent lambs.

When Simon had met the young Aaron, he was a fragile, broken child because of this pig. Simon wasn't even sure Aaron would be able to overcome the pain he carried. But the young monk had learned how to become a man despite it all. And he had earned Simon's respect.

It was a pyrrhic victory, though, because everything that Aaron believed in, everything he had hoped for, was now destroyed. Including a future Zadok priesthood with their two messiahs, their dreams of victory in the final battle of the Sons of Light. His religion had been crushed and his soul cast adrift. In a way, the Romans had now violated Aaron's spirit as Phineas had violated his body.

"Mercy!" Phineas gurgled again.

Simon saw Aaron look with incredulity at the overseer. But no words left his mouth.

Aaron turned to walk away, leaving Phineas to suffer. Then Simon saw Aaron return to the overseer, draw his sword, and plunge it into the fat man's heart, killing him instantly.

Was it mercy or was it revenge? It was certainly *not* justice.

Withdrawing the sword, Aaron wiped it on Phineas' tunic. He had recently learned what Simon had known for years: that there was little justice in this life. Too many monsters like Phineas got away with inflicting far more suffering on others than they could ever experience in earthly retribution. There had to be an afterlife judgment or there was no ultimate justice. Anyone who thought otherwise was a vain fool.

Simon and Aaron left Phineas to face his judgment of eternal destruction in unquenchable fire.[1]

Back out in the yard, Simon became overwhelmed by the dead monks, and his anger boiled again.

The scout he had dispatched earlier to examine the perimeter approached Simon. "Sir, I followed the tracks down to the shores of the Dead Sea." He stopped as though afraid to explain what he'd seen.

Simon asked, "What did you find, soldier?"

The tracker shuddered, then told him. "The sea is filled with corpses. Bodies of rebels."

Simon clenched his teeth and his fists. "You said the Romans were a unit about our size?"

"A bit larger, General. Or more."

"They must be upriver." Simon headed toward his horse. "Let's go find these *goyim* and kill them all."[2]

"Simon!" Aaron shouted. By the time the rebel general had mounted his horse, the Essene warrior was there looking up at him. "Simon, don't do this. We'll be slaughtered."

"Mount up!" shouted Simon, ignoring the young monk. "If we hurry, we might be able to catch their rear guard."

His captains hesitated, appearing to agree with Aaron.

Aaron grabbed the reins of Simon's horse. "Simon!"

Simon finally stopped as if shaken out of a daze.

Aaron said, "They were my family, too."

Aaron was right. Chasing after a Roman scouting party right back to their legion would be the most foolish thing Simon could do. He froze in indecision. His heart screamed for justice. His head sought another way, any way.

He sighed. And the answer finally came to him.

"Vespasian has a son—Titus—a general of his forces. It is time for the blood of Vespasian's own family to pour through his fingers."

Simon had a new target for his hatred. A reason to live. A second reason. He would find a way to kill both Gischala and Titus.

He muttered, "And vengeance will be mine."

CHAPTER 55

Jerusalem

The third seal was opened and I heard the third living creature say, "Come!" And I looked, and behold, a black horse! And its rider had a pair of scales in his hand. And I heard what seemed to be a voice in the midst of the four living creatures, saying, "A quart of wheat for a denarius, and three quarts of barley for a denarius, and do not harm the oil and wine!"[1]
Apocalypse 6:5–6

Cassandra and Alexander awakened just before sunrise, as they always did to spend time in prayer together. They knelt by their bed and held hands. They thanked their heavenly Father for bringing them back into the hippodrome and restoring their ability to minister to the sick and infirm. They didn't thank God for the pestilence and plagues but rather expressed faith in his mysterious providential purposes. They prayed for the Two Witnesses and for the proclamation of the Gospel so that they might snatch some from the fires of judgment already in process upon the people.

Afterward, they hopped back into bed to warm up for just a few more minutes before starting their day in the infirmary. They held each other and kissed. The spiritual intimacy of prayer often had the effect of bringing them together physically to share both Spirit and flesh.

It was something Cassandra had often wondered why she had been so privileged to experience. Alexander often told her that he didn't deserve her, but the truth was, she didn't deserve him any more so. God had been so gracious to allow them this sweet refuge in the world of suffering around them. But it was always only a few moments of relief because the weight of their responsibilities always came crashing down upon them.

Looking into his wife's eyes, Alexander said, "I'm worried about our food situation. Jacob is not being consistent with the rations he promised. And we plowed up the garden when he ordered us to leave."

"Have you resown any seed?" Cassandra asked.

"Some vegetables; carrots, broccoli, beets. But it's late in the harvest season and the drought—I don't think we'll see any growth."

"Then we must petition Jacob."

"Let me do that," Alexander insisted. "He has a peculiar animosity toward you."

"I wonder why," Cassandra smiled. She had called Jacob and his apostates every cursed name in the Scriptures: whitewashed tombs, dogs returning to their vomit, and of course, mutilators. She struggled with her own boldness. On the one hand, truth was needed to call out lies. On the other hand, Cassandra often felt she turned people away through harshness instead of winning them with grace. It was such a difficult balance to achieve in life between justice and mercy, between truth and compassion.

She said, "Well, we had better get started. We have a stadium of children and sick people who need us."

She got up to get dressed.

Alexander sighed, "And strangely, I find myself caring for two of them above all others."

"I too." Cassandra paused thoughtfully, then said, "Please do not think me heartless. But has our growing affection for Noah and Rachel distracted us from ministering to the needs of the many others entrusted to our care?"

Alexander mused, "Our interests have become divided. We have treated Noah and Rachel with partiality. That cannot be denied. They have become like a family. But we cannot return them now to the other children. That would be cruel."

Cassandra closed her eyes, pain squeezing at her heart. "When I visit the theater, I often have children asking if they can come stay with us in the hippodrome like Noah and Rachel." She started to choke up with emotion. "Sometimes my heart becomes so overwhelmed I have to distance myself or I will fall apart and become useless."

Alexander's immediate embrace conveyed understanding. Whether they intended to or not, their two orphaned charges *had* become like family.

"Alexander, come quickly!" Thelonius interrupted from the entrance to their tent. "The storehouses of the city are on fire."

Alexander, Thelonius, and a dozen other able-bodied men from the hippodrome ran through the Tyropoeon Valley. Up ahead, a huge pillar of smoke rose from a location across from the temple in the Mishneh sector.

Another fire shot up to their right in the Lower City. Recognizing the location as another granary, Alexander signaled Thelonius to break off from the others, and the two men raced in that direction.

But by the time they reached the Lower City, it was too late to help. The huge granary was engulfed in flames that licked the sky. All the corn inside the silo, above ground and below, was gone, burned up.

"Years of grain destroyed!" Alexander lamented. "It must be a third of the city's stores."

Two men arrived on horses and got down off their mounts.

Alexander recognized them as Simon bar Giora and the young monk Aaron.

An elderly man nearby spit out, "I saw the culprits. It was John of Gischala and his men."[2]

Alexander and Thelonius looked with shock at the witness.

Simon said, "The city will not last long on what is left."

The old man added, "We'll be starved out."

"But why would Gischala do this?" Aaron demanded with incredulity. "Why would he imperil the entire city for his cause?"

Just then the granary imploded in an explosion of flames. A burst of hot wind washed over the crowd of onlookers.

Simon brooded. "Whatever he cannot have, he destroys."

Aaron added, "It looks as if he is trying to force God's hand to come and save Israel."

The monk was probably right. Gischala was a fanatic. Now many inhabitants of the land would die because of this one man's messianic delusions.

The group's attention was diverted by the arrival of the Two Witnesses within hearing distance on the Huldah porch. Their booming voices carried on the wind as if amplified by an angel.

Elihu recited the words of the Apocalypse to the open air. "Jesus opened the fourth seal, and I heard the voice of the fourth living creature say, 'Come!' And I looked, and behold, a pale horse! And its rider's name was Death, and Hades followed him. And they were given authority over a fourth of the land, to kill with sword and with famine and with pestilence and by wild beasts of the land!"[3]

Alexander overheard Simon's words to Aaron, "I remember the old prophet from years ago. He was spouting the same nonsense back then. His back bears the scars of my chastisement. I think I should lay these two to rest."

Aaron said, "I would not do that if I were you."

Simon considered his words. Despite his profane disinterest, he had apparent respect for Aaron, who seemed to have a fearful high regard for the Witnesses.

Alexander thanked God that the Essene monk had met Joshua and the Christian congregation in Jerusalem some time ago before they fled to Pella. Had the experience softened the young man to the Gospel? He prayed that it was so.

Alexander and Thelonius left to return to the hippodrome.

Their journey back found them engrossed in discussion prompted by the tragedy they had just witnessed.

Thelonius said, "These times make it difficult for my faith. I told you I had questions and doubts that troubled me."

"Yes?" Alexander encouraged the young Roman to continue.

"It seems that religion causes such divisions. Factions kill each other and those with whom they disagree. Caesar won't need to finish this war. The Jews will help him by killing themselves."

"That is not religion," said Alexander. "That is human nature. Romans too kill many with whom they disagree."

"True, but has not Rome brought great progress to the earth?"

"The empire appropriates what it conquers. That is power, not progress."

Thelonius nodded with seeming agreement. "The reason I became a natural philosopher was for progress. Empirical observation provides the knowledge that supports the sciences of medicine and technology."

"And war," reminded Alexander. "Nature is chaos and death. The sting of the scorpion. The poison of the viper. The pestilence of disease. God charged us with the task of harnessing nature for the good of mankind. That is the image of God in man."

Thelonius had been listening intently. He asked, "What of the plague and pestilence that has seized this city? Is that not God's judgment?"

"Yes, it is."

"Then by treating its victims are we not working against God's will?"

"No. We work within his will. God is both just and compassionate. Even when he punishes, he offers grace to those who would receive it. We are God's hands, Thelonius, offering mercy in the midst of justice."

"Then what of the children? How is it that so many of the innocent suffer along with the guilty?"

"The sins of the fathers. This is a fallen world. The guilty cause the innocent to suffer. Their sins leave a stain of blood that spreads and contaminates all of life with death."

"But does not God promise deliverance for those who serve him?"

"God promises resurrection, not escape from suffering. Even some Christians have already died in the net of destruction that envelopes this land. But they will be resurrected unto life."

They had now arrived at the hippodrome. Alexander was surprised to see Cassandra waiting for them at the entrance, holding the hands of Noah and Rachel. The children were grinning ear to ear, and Cassandra was weeping tears of joy.

"What is it?" asked Alexander.

"A miracle," cried Cassandra. She gestured for them to follow her into the stadium.

When they got out onto the grounds, Alexander did a doubletake as his mind searched for a way to make sense of what he saw in the distance. But he couldn't. So he ran instead, all the way to the edges of the large garden that filled the center of the arena. The garden they had recently uprooted and only yesterday replanted in the midst of a drought.

The garden was now fully grown and bursting with a harvest of crops: fruit, vegetables and nuts. People were filling baskets overflowing with bounty.

It *was* a miracle. God had provided food as he had when he multiplied the fish and loaves.

Alexander fell to his knees and raised his hands to heaven, praising the Lord of the Harvest. At the sound of footsteps, he looked up to see Thelonius reach his side, also smiling with amazement.

"How does this fit your natural philosophy?" Alexander asked.

Before Thelonius could answer, a snide voice behind them demanded, "And what have you been hiding from me?"

Rising to his feet, Alexander turned to see Jacob ben Mordecai striding up to the garden with a contingent of guards. Alexander's excitement over this miracle ebbed as he looked into the vindictive face of his spiritual enemy.

"I am sorry to say that I am here to bring you some bad news." Jacob's grimace of concern did not match the evil glee in his eyes. "You see, because of the storehouses being burned down, I am afraid there will be no more rations."

Cassandra hurried up, Noah and Rachel at her heels, in time to catch Jacob's words. Her eyes went wide with dismay as she stepped around next to Alexander, tucking her arm under his for support. "What did you say?"

Jacob threw her a malicious glance. "I've been explaining to your husband that as much as I would love to continue helping you with the more unfortunate among us, I simply can no longer do so because of the hand of God."

"Hand of God?" Cassandra snapped back. "That was the hand of criminals! And for that you now punish children and the sick?"

Jacob stared at the lush garden full of produce. "Evidently, you have not been honest about your own hoarding."

He turned to the captain of the guard and pointed to the people picking the harvest. "Stop those pickers and confiscate their baskets. I am declaring this garden the property of the people."

The guards obediently began taking the baskets away from the workers.

"You can't do that," said Alexander. "This is our garden planted to help feed these people."

"I can do it," corrected Jacob. "This quarantine is my responsibility, and I am using emergency powers in the face of drought and famine."

He turned to his captain. "Guard this plot of land until I bring in my own workers to harvest it. If anyone tries to steal so much as a single carrot, kill them."

"Yes, sir," said the captain, and he moved with his men to secure the area.

"What are the children going to eat?" cried Cassandra. "They'll die!"

"Have faith," said Jacob. "If you behave, I will do my best to find something. But until I do, this may be a good time to teach those children the virtues of fasting and endurance."

He turned and left them.

As soon as he was gone, Cassandra broke down weeping. "Why, Alexander? Why would Yahweh do this to us? Why would he hold a miracle before our eyes and then take it away?"

Alexander held her. "I don't know, my love. I don't understand the ways of God. But we must trust him."

He had to be strong for his wife. But the words felt hollow in his mouth because Alexander was having a hard time trusting God as well. It didn't make sense. Why would God allow such a thing? He and Cassandra had given their lives to save these people—to die for them if they had to. But this? It seemed so...so calloused!

Thelonius's questions of God's seemingly capricious ways were no mere academic exercises for Alexander but living reality.

Cassandra was already straightening up, a hand dashing her momentary weakness from her eyes. As she pulled away from his embrace, Alexander's eye fell on the horses tied up in a pen by the entrance. They seemed restless as though spooked by an awareness of their own fate. In the famine to come, Alexander would have to feed his charges. And horses were, after all, meat.

CHAPTER 56

The Divine Council

Michael sat back with satisfaction, listening to the Son of Man decree his judgment of Apollyon's lawsuit before the heavenly court. He saw the Adversary fidgeting impatiently.

Let him squirm, he thought.

Jesus said, "O Adversary, your lawsuit has been considered by the righteous judge of all the earth."

Michael was watching Apollyon's reactions. The Watcher seemed put out.

"With regard to the first complaint of the Adversary, he is correct. Israel has been an adulterous harlot, deserving of both divorce and capital punishment for her unfaithfulness to her husband Yahweh."

Apollyon's face brightened with vindication. He stood up straighter.

"Israel was given the very oracles of God, but she was unfaithful to her covenant of election. As it is written, 'none are righteous, no, not one. All have turned aside; together they have become worthless; no one does good, not even one.' The Adversary is correct that the covenant condemns all under sin. By the works of that covenant, shall no flesh be justified in God's sight.[1]

"But God's righteousness is found in this: the Son of Man was the faithful Israelite who fulfilled the Law. Through my faithfulness to Yahweh, I became the Servant prophesied by Isaiah. I fulfilled what Israel after the flesh could not, and I am the Israel of God. So the righteousness of God is achieved through the faithfulness of Messiah and is granted to all who believe. The identity of true Israel is now reorganized into Messiah.[2]

"Those who have faith are the justified. Because they are in Messiah, they are the true Israel of God and cannot be condemned. It is those who are of faith who are the children of Abraham and who will inherit the promises of God. Not those who are of the flesh. Not those who are under Torah. For the promise to Abraham and his seed did not come through Torah but through the righteousness of faith."[3]

"So the natural branches of the root of Israel have been broken off and gathered for the fire. Israel according to the flesh is Ishmael, born of Hagar, the slave woman. But the children of faith are Isaac, born of the free woman, born of the Spirit. They are the children of promise. The Scripture says, the children of flesh persecuted the children of promise, therefore 'Cast out the slave woman and her son, for the son of the slave woman shall not inherit with the son of the free woman.'"[4]

At that moment, from under the heavenly altar came the voices of souls who had been slain for the word of God; the persecuted ones. "O sovereign Lord, holy and true, how long before you avenge our blood on those who dwell on the land of Israel?"[5]

Michael felt holy anger burn within him. These were all the prophets and holy ones murdered by the sons of Israel. They were the white-robed martyrs of this great Tribulation as well as all the righteous blood shed on the land, from righteous Abel to Zechariah, who was murdered between the sanctuary and altar.[6]

Another moment of chilling silence penetrated the court, before Jesus continued his judgment. "Let this court affirm that the charges of the Adversary against Israel according to the flesh are upheld. She is an unfaithful harlot who is under the curse of the covenant. The heavens and earth of the old covenant must be removed. Jerusalem the holy city must be destroyed and her people scattered to fulfill the everlasting covenant.

"Jerusalem has become Babylon. In her was found the blood of the prophets and holy ones and all who have been slain on the land. Rejoice over her, O heaven, and you holy ones and apostles and prophets, for God has given judgment for you against her. Alas! Alas! You great city, you mighty city, Babylon. For in a single hour your judgment has come."[7]

Jesus then turned to a mighty angel and nodded with unspoken command. The columned wall to the left of the throne vanished, and Michael saw the waters above the firmament that the temple rested upon. The mighty angel went to the shore, picked up a huge millstone, and cast it into the waters. It made a huge splash, and its waves expanded out in all directions without seeming to lessen.

The angel and the Son of Man spoke as one, "So will Babylon the great city be thrown down with violence and will be found no more, and the light of a lamp will shine in you no more, and the voice of bridegroom and bride will be heard in you no more, for all nations were deceived by your sorcery."[8]

The walls of the temple returned, and the eyes of all present fixed on the Son of Man, who finished his judgment while looking at Apollyon. "But my Remnant you may not condemn. They are in Messiah and are therefore the children of the promise, the seed of Abraham. Isaiah cries out concerning Israel: 'Though the number of the sons of Israel be as the sand of the sea, only a remnant of them will be saved, for the Lord will carry out his sentence upon the land fully and without delay.' And as Isaiah predicted, 'If the Lord of hosts had not left us his seed, we would have been like Sodom and become like Gomorrah.'"[9]

That seed was not the fleshly offspring of Abraham but Jesus the Messiah. And all those believers in Messiah were his offspring, his remnant.

"So I pass sentence upon Israel according to the flesh. The Adversary has legal right to pursue desolation. It is decreed that the four angels of destruction shall be released."

Apollyon smiled and rubbed his hands together like a demon-child just freed from constraint. But his glee was interrupted by the Son of Man.

"But their release will be contingent."

Michael watched Apollyon's face turn from smug self-satisfaction to disappointed surprise.

He could tell what the Adversary was thinking. *What legal maneuver is the Son of Man pulling? Of what contingency is he speaking?*

CHAPTER 57

Jerusalem

The conflagration began in the early morning hours. Simon's forces assaulted the temple on the two bridges and four gates of the outer temple's western wall. The bridges were paved arches that crossed the Tyropoeon Valley, large enough for a concerted attack.

Simon's soldiers assaulted the bridge gates with battering rams. But the fire from above was too heavy, and they had to retreat.

Gischala had built several battlement towers inside the temple along the wall to aid those protecting the gates with darts and projectiles from higher above. He was able to wound and kill enough of Simon's men to thwart their initial encounter.

But Gischala had not anticipated that Eleazar would attack him from the inner temple walls as he was defending the outer temple against Simon. As Gischala's men focused their attention on protecting their gates, archers on the walls of the inner temple launched volleys of missiles at the backs of those defenders.

Gischala's men became confused and had to split their forces in half to respond to Eleazar's attacks. Wedged between two opponents, they suffered a disturbing number of casualties before they were able to repel their inside foes.

Eleazar had rained down death upon Gischala from above just as Gischala had rained down death upon Simon from above.[1]

As the sun lay low on the horizon, Simon and his war council met for strategy planning in an occupied home. Aaron had a hard time following the discussion. His thoughts kept drifting to the horror he had encountered at Qumran. Everything he had believed in—the chosen call of his community, the war of the Sons of Light at the end of the age, their victory over the Sons

263

264

of Darkness—it had all been destroyed, crushed like the head of a serpent. He felt like a man adrift in an endless sea with no rock to hold on to.

Had it all been a lie? Was there something that he had missed? That they had all missed? Aaron felt more aligned with Simon's cynicism than he had ever imagined he would be.

His attention was brought back by Simon pointing out to his captains, "Gischala is more entrenched in the temple than I realized. We lost too many men today."

One of the captains offered, "So did Gischala. His forces were divided in a wedge between us and Eleazar."

Another offered, "But he held the temple and repelled both sides."

Simon said, "I won't sacrifice my men just to inflict losses upon my foe."

Aaron spoke up. "The populace is frightened at the prospect of this ongoing internal devastation. It is like a beast eating its own flesh."[2]

"Sedition upon sedition," another mused.

Simon said, "Vespasian has occupied Galilee, Samaria, Perea, and the rest of Judea—all while we fight amongst ourselves for control of the last outpost on the shred of a conquered land."

"The holy city," challenged a captain.

Aaron saw Simon's look of displeasure at the comment. But he remembered what Simon had said earlier. So he brought it up. "Vespasian has his forces mustered in Caesarea Maritima. He is about to launch his final assault upon Jerusalem. What will you do if he arrives before you are able to leave?"

Simon thought a moment, then said, "There is still time."

Aaron wondered if the hesitation was the sign of a change of heart, a sliver of faith growing in Simon—just as Aaron was losing his.

CHAPTER 58

Cassandra cloaked her face with her hood as she walked up the street to Jacob's stolen home. She was on a mission.

She knocked at the door, glancing around to see if anyone had seen her. The servant Nathan opened the door. They gave each other a nod of silent recognition.

"Tell your master Jacob that Cassandra, wife of Alexander, requests an audience."

She was ushered in and waited for what seemed like an eternity. Finally, the tall, balding figure of Jacob approached her with a devilish grin on his face. As Cassandra pulled down her hood, he feigned a look of surprise.

"To what do I owe this pleasure?"

Cassandra could feel the condescension dripping from his words.

She said, "I have come to plead for the lives of the children in our care. Without rations and the garden we grew, they will be the first to die of starvation. I cannot let this happen." She swallowed with a dry throat. It took everything to keep going. "So I am begging you. What must I do to ensure their salvation?"

Jacob's gaze was that of a snake seeking to mesmerize its prey. "Why has your husband sent you in place of his authority?"

"My husband does not know I am here."

Another surprised look. A revelation seemed to dawn on Jacob. "Hmmmm."

Then he said, "Come with me. I want to show you something." He added, "Put your hood back on. We're going out in public."

Cassandra narrowed her eyes with puzzlement. Where was he taking her?

Jacob led her through the streets down to the temple walls in the Tyropoeon Valley. Cassandra kept glancing around nervously, hoping no one recognized her. But the populace was too intent upon their own difficult lives under the constant threat of war and pillaging to notice her in the crowds.

They arrived at the gated entrance to the Hall of Unhewn Stone. She hesitated. "Where are you taking me?"

Jacob laughed. "Don't worry, Cassandra. I have no intention of making you a prisoner. As a matter of fact, the three factions inside the temple and outside have allowed a new sanhedrin to be created for the sake of city governance. You see, they are not as chaotic as you may think. Anyway, I have managed to get onto that sanhedrin, so we have full access to the temple despite the ongoing hostilities."

He didn't appear to be lying. But then again, he was a deceiving asp whose very life was a lie. So she couldn't trust him.

But if this was what needed to happen to save the children, then so be it. She would take that risk—for them.

Cassandra followed Jacob into the temple. They made their way through subterranean passages all the way to the southeastern corner of the temple. Then Jacob led her up a long staircase until they were standing at the very top of the tall tower overlooking the entire city: the pinnacle of the temple.

Jacob turned reflective. "I come here when I need wisdom or refreshing. When I look out onto the holy city, I am reminded of its history, of its glory." He quoted a psalm with a soft, loving voice, "If I forget you, O Jerusalem, let my right hand forget its skill! Let my tongue stick to the roof of my mouth if I do not remember you, if I do not set Jerusalem above my highest joy! Let us go to the house of Yahweh! Let us pray for the peace of Jerusalem! May they be secure who love you! Peace be within your walls and security within your towers!"[1]

Cassandra could have responded from the psalms or from Isaiah or Jeremiah. But she chose another prophet. "O Jerusalem, Jerusalem, the city that kills the prophets and stones those who are sent to it! How often would I have gathered your children together as a hen gathers her brood under her wings, and you were not willing! See, your house is left to you desolate."[2]

Jacob smiled as though he appreciated her challenge. "You must realize, Cassandra, that if the Nazarene was Messiah, I would have continued to follow him. But I rejected him based upon the Scriptures. Surely you cannot fault me for such expectations."

"On the contrary," she replied, "I demand such expectations."

"Well then, what have you to say about the curse of Jeconiah?"

He let it sink in. She knew the curse. The prophet Jeremiah had declared that Jeconiah would be as if he were childless because "none of his offspring shall succeed in sitting on the throne of David and ruling again in Judah."[3]

Jacob then dropped the other sandal. "The genealogies of Jesus in your Gospels clearly record that Jesus bar Joseph was a descendant of Jeconiah. It seems to me that according to the Scriptures both you and I endorse, Jesus is cursed by God in his lineage and therefore cannot claim the throne of David."

Cassandra breathed a sigh, praying for patience and grace to speak with civility to this man whom she considered a modern Balaam. It wasn't her nature to do so.

She said, "You are right that Jesus is a descendant of Jeconiah through the line of Joseph. But what you are missing is that Joseph is the *legal* father of Jesus, but not his natural father."

"Ah, the claim of the virgin birth, " Jacob responded cynically.

"Yes. The seed of the Holy Spirit is not of the human cursed seed. But his mother Mary was also in the line of David. So he is both legally and naturally of the blessed line, but not the cursed line. He is both Son of David and Son of God."[4]

"But he is not a Levite," responded Jacob. "Only a Levite of the lineage of Aaron can be a high priest for the people of God. Jesus cannot be a priest because he is from the tribe of Judah."

"Now I take exception," Cassandra answered with a slight smile. "My lord, permit me your indulgence to explain a complicated matter that is nonetheless simplified in its truth. The new covenant that Jeremiah prophesied would necessarily bring with it a new priesthood, a superior one."

"Hah," he scoffed. "And what priesthood could that possibly be?"

"The priesthood of Melchizedek." She saw his jaw tighten as if she had caught him unaware. "The promise of our people was made to Abraham, our forefather, on this we can both agree."

Jacob nodded his head.

"And yet when Abraham was returning from the slaughter of kings, he came before Melchizedek, king of Salem, our Jerusalem, and was blessed. Now it is beyond dispute that the superior blesses the inferior. But more than that, Scripture says that Abraham gave a tenth, or a tithe, of his spoils to Melchizedek. One could then say that Levi paid tithes through Abraham to Melchizedek because Levi was still in the loins of his ancestor Abraham. And since the Scriptures give no genealogy for Melchizedek, no father or mother, having no beginning of days nor end of life as recorded, then Melchizedek resembles the Son of God and is a superior high priest to Aaron. Melchizedek's priesthood is forever. As the psalmist says of Messiah, 'Yahweh has sworn and will not change his mind, "You are a priest forever after the order of Melchizedek."'"[5]

Jacob watched her like a judge considering guilt or innocence. "So you are saying the Levitical priesthood is temporary and destined for obsolescence?"

"Yes, because it is a weak system. Its priests are themselves sinners who require atonement as much as the people. But Jesus is a high priest, holy, innocent, unstained, separated from sinners, and exalted above the heavens. He has no need like those other high priests to offer sacrifices daily, first for his own sins and then for those of the people, since he did this once for all when he offered up himself. Jesus appeared once for all at this end of the ages to take away sin by the sacrifice of himself."[6]

Jacob rejoined, "Yet the temple remains standing. And with it the priesthood and its sacrifices."

"For now," Cassandra qualified. "Jesus is our high priest, who has entered the heavenly temple, of which this earthly one is but a copy, a shadow that is destined to fade away. When the earthly temple falls, the old covenant age will be over and the new covenant kingdom will take over."

"Fascinating," said Jacob, looking her up and down. "As much as I disagree with your Christian heresy, I cannot help but be impressed by your conviction, your courage…" he paused, then added with a tinge of irony, "…your elegance."

He was changing the subject. Cassandra felt a chill go through her. *This discussion was all a pretext.*

"You are an amazing woman." Jacob looked back out over the city. "And I want to help you. I really do. But your request carries with it a high price."

Cassandra decided not to respond. Not to say anything she might regret.

"I can help you. I have the resources to do it. I can provide food and more help for your orphans and for the quarantine. I can even make your life more comfortable and the lives of your husband and your Christian followers. But I will only help you under one condition."

His pause was like the calm before a storm. "That you become my mistress."

Cassandra's throat tightened up. A wave of nausea rolled over her.

This was the very location where her Lord was taken by another creature of power. And now it was her test as well.

Jacob spoke with a reassuring voice. "I don't expect you to have an easy answer. I know it is a high price. But think of the good you can do for your loved ones. You can save them from pain and suffering. All you have to do is become my mistress."

He paused again before concluding, "Take time to consider. Bring me your answer within the next couple days—and everyone can be saved."

She didn't want to wait a couple days. She wanted to curse him right now. Damn him to Gehenna for the evil he had done and the evil he was now doing.

But the children were starving. The sick were dying.

And it was only going to get worse.

Cassandra kept her mouth shut and left him in the tower to watch over the city like the vulture he was. She had to return to the quarantine before Alexander found out.

CHAPTER 59

Caesarea Maritima

Berenice lay in Titus's arms on the large, silken bed of her palace bedroom. He seemed distant with concern.

"What is wrong, my love?" she asked.

"The empire is still in upheaval. Vindex was put down in Gaul, but his ally Galba is a danger. And there is Vitellius, the governor of lower Germany, and Otho in Lusitania. All vying for position to oppose Nero."

"And what of the Flavians?" she asked with a soft voice,

Titus sighed with frustration. "Father is loyal to a fault. He has carefully avoided the politics of dissent."

"What will you do after the war?"

He turned his head on the pillow to look at her. Berenice felt her heart beat faster. *Does he not trust me?*

"Return to Rome—with my Jewish spoils."

He is teasing me. Berenice forced a smile.

"And the victory will provide my family with distinct political advantage when it comes to imperial succession."

Berenice was trying to formulate her response when Titus added, "I want you to come with me."

She tried not to speak too quickly. "I will."

"But I warn you, your acceptance by the people is a necessity. And it is not a foregone conclusion."

"Was not Poppaea beloved as empress?"

"Indeed she was. But she was not a Jew. She was favorable toward your religion, but it is not the same."

Berenice caressed his chest with loving tenderness. "Well, I am confident we will persuade them. Love has its power."

"And its limits," Titus warned.

A knock came at the door. A messenger announced from behind it, "Forgive me, my lord, but the legate Vespasian has called for an urgent war council."

Titus looked concerned. He responded, "I'll be there shortly."

Was this it? Berenice wondered. *The beginning of the end?*

Berenice followed Titus into the war room to find Vespasian with his generals and counselors, including her brother and the Pharisee Josephus, his hands still bound in manacles. She felt immediately embarrassed as all eyes turned upon the two of them, being the last to arrive.

Berenice watched Vespasian closely, trying to divine something, anything that would hint at his purpose in convening this assembly.

The old legate's face was grave. But his sense of humor was still intact. He said, "How nice of you to come, son. Is the imperial campaign getting in your way again?"

Titus replied with equal wit, "Father, you should know everything I do is an imperial campaign."

It thrilled Berenice, even if in jest, that Titus was interested in her for more than mere gratification of his lust. It was hopeful indeed.

Vespasian spoke to everyone, "Returning to the matter at hand, Nero is dead."

His frankness was disarming, followed by silence that now filled the room. Without fanfare, such shocking statements sounded like a joke or a deliberate provocation.

He explained, and Berenice's world became undone. "I received the news by messenger from Domitian. Nero killed himself while a coup was under way by the senate with the help of the Praetorians."[1]

"I'll bet Tigellinus is behind it," Titus immediately spoke up. "Who is now in charge?"

"Galba has seized the throne."

"Of course," said Titus. "I should have guessed."

"But there is contest," said Vespasian. "Vitellius in Germania has allied with Gaul and Brittania against him."

"For the gods' sake," complained Titus, "we are no better than these Jews. Consumed by civil war with our forces spread thin upon the world."

271

"What do you, my counselors, recommend for my course?" asked Vespasian.

Titus wasted no time, quickly taking the lead, "We finish this campaign immediately. Secure an overwhelming victory." He looked at Vespasian. "Which will in turn provide you the power necessary to take back the throne."

Vespasian raised an eyebrow high. "Take back the throne? I didn't know we had it to begin with."

"Galba is a usurper. His lackey Otho is sullied by his affair with Nero's ex-wife Poppaea. Vitellius is undisciplined and deferential to you, legate. Now is the time to act. To seize the moment of history's offer."

Vespasian mused, "Once again, my son proves hasty and impulsive in his imperial ambition. Are there others who would argue against him?"

No one responded. The fear of reprisal was obvious to all.

Vespasian said, "I did not appoint you to kiss my son's ass. He may be my successor, but contrary to his delusions, I am not seeking the throne, and I did not raise him to be a narcissist. Speak up. I want opinions."

Berenice could see Titus's jaw tighten at the chastisement. But Vespasian was right. Titus might be ambitious in his designs, but he was no tyrant like Nero or the others.

Josephus was bold. He spoke up first, "Legate, if I may. I would suggest that in times of political turmoil, it is not wise to make rash moves that may be interpreted as an attempt to seize power."

"I think your original course is still wisest, my lord," Agrippa stepped in. "Wait for the outcome of both civil wars. The Roman one for your own strategy and the Judean civil war to lessen your casualties and enhance your reputation. The current drought in the land only helps your cause."

Vespasian looked around the room. "Is that it? Only the Jews have the testicles to advise me?"

Finally, a general spoke up. "Legate, I support Titus. We can quench this revolt and be available for whatever you plan."

Another added, "If we are needed to bring stability to the new regime in Rome, and we do not crush Judea, she will only rise again with a more fanatical certainty that her god is on her side."

Still another said, "Your legions are loyal to you, Vespasian. They would support a claim to the throne."

Vespasian appeared to have his mind already made up. He said to the council, "All things considered, I am in no hurry to claim power or title. I say we stand back and wait for the political unrest to subside. Continue to let the Jews kill themselves."

Berenice watched Titus deflate with disappointment.

Vespasian added, "Furthermore, I think it would be appropriate, Titus, for you to travel to Rome and bow to Galba, assure him of our allegiance, and await his commands."

Titus said nothing. Berenice knew that once Vespasian made up his mind, it was fruitless to argue with him.

Vespasian added, "I want you to bring Agrippa with you to explain the strategy of dealing with his people."

Josephus made a bold request, "Legate, may I go as well? I have a history with the court, and I could confirm Agrippa with a second voice."

Confirm Agrippa, thought Berenice. *The only thing Josephus wants to confirm is his future with the new regime.*

"No. You will stay," said Vespasian. With a wry twist of his lips, he added, "I need my faithful court prophet." He paused thoughtfully and said, "But with the death of Nero, I think it is time we sever your chains. You have proven yourself a loyal subject to me and to Rome."

"Thank you, my lord," said Josephus, bowing in gratitude.

Berenice knew that if she didn't get Vespasian's permission, she might find herself without a foothold. "Legate, I would like to stay in Judea as well. You will need a Herod here for any correspondence with the ruling class."

Out of the corner of her eyes, she saw Titus give her a disapproving look. Of course he wanted her with him, but her people needed a voice at this dangerous moment. A voice that would not betray them as others would. Berenice threw Josephus a look of contempt.

"You can stay," said Vespasian. He turned to Titus. "I'm sure you will want to say a long and touching goodbye to the princess but leave in the morning. I will await your word from Galba."

The war had been halted. The death of Nero had bought them more time. A weight lifted from Berenice's soul. Or was it just another delay of the inevitable disaster she sought to avoid? All of Galilee, Samaria, Perea, and the rest of Judah had already been crushed and subjugated. Jerusalem was the last stronghold of revolt, but it was also the heart of Israel, the center of her whole world. If Vespasian destroyed Jerusalem as capital punishment for her rebellion, Israel herself would die.

Would Yahweh remember his people? Would he resurrect them like Ezekiel's valley of dry bones? Or would he start over with a new people who would obey him as the Jews did not?

The counselors filed out of the room. Agrippa passed Berenice and whispered with a lewd eye, "I will want to say goodbye to you as well, sister."

Once again, she felt in the middle of men and empires vying for her soul, ripping her in half.

The whole world was being torn asunder.

• • • • •

Josephus held out his hands, still in manacles and laid the chain across a chopping block in the public square. A crowd of onlookers watched as Vespasian and Titus stood over him. They were engaging in a ritual of freedom from unjust bondage. Vespasian announced to the crowd, "It is a shameful thing that this man who has foretold the change of empire, and been the minister of a divine message to me, should still be retained in the condition of a captive or prisoner. I pardon you and thus release you."[2]

The legate nodded to a soldier holding an axe, who swung high and cut the chains with one arc of his blade. Josephus could not help but smile and with tears proclaimed, "My lord and Messiah, Vespasian. I pledge my fealty to Rome as a loyal Jewish subject."

Titus responded, "Would that all Jews had such humility and devotion. So too their chains would be severed with grace and their doom unsealed."

CHAPTER 60

Jerusalem

Noah swung his gladius at the Roman. He was blocked by a sword and had to defend a counterattack.

"Excellent!" said Thelonius. "Now you are catching on."

Noah had graduated from practicing with a wooden sword to the real thing, steel on steel. He gripped his gladius tight.

He had been moving at half speed for the sake of safety, but feeling more confident under Thelonius's encouraging words, he increased his speed. The clanging in his ears was like the hypnotic beating of a gong, urging him onward.

The two were practicing in their usual location, the hallways under the arches of the hippodrome. Thelonius had taught Noah basic moves for offense and defense: lunge, feint, thrust, parry, slash. Noah had been faithful to wake up early every day and practice his moves before his chores and responsibilities. He had become so obsessed with his workouts that during the day he often found himself executing his forms with nothing in his hand but an imaginary gladius.

He dreamt of battle forms in his sleep.

He felt strong and confident; he felt like a warrior.

So this was what it was like to become a man. He had recently turned eight years old and he was feeling more confident than ever.

Noah moved full speed now with his sparring against Thelonius.

His desire for revenge had grown obsessive too. Every move of his form, every swipe of his blade, he imagined to be against the man who had abandoned his family to the Romans and to death. It would have been one thing if Gischala had broken his promise to return because he and his men had run into the Romans and died like so many others. So Noah had assumed until he'd seen the general safe and unscathed here in Jerusalem—all while

275

countless thousands from the city whose name Gischala so proudly claimed had been left to fall by Roman swords.

Well, the rebel general would not be allowed to profit forever from his betrayal. It had come to the point where it seemed Noah's only purpose for living, the only reason he had survived and escaped from the Romans, was to hunt down and kill John of Gischala.

Despite his few years, Noah was neither so naïve or foolish to believe he could fight the rebel warrior head on. No, he would have to assassinate his enemy. Surprise Gischala and his guards when the man wasn't looking. After all, who would suspect an eight-year-old child to be an assassin?

"Noah!" The shout of his Roman instructor brought him out of his thoughts.

He had missed a counterattack by Thelonius, who now held his sword at Noah's throat.

"You are too distracted. Where is your head, boy? I almost cut it off."

"Sorry," said Noah. "I think I need to rest."

"You need to focus. Look into the eyes of your enemy. It is in his eyes that you will see his every intent."

The eyes are windows to the soul. Noah wondered what evil pools of darkness were in the eyes of Gischala. He would give anything to be able to shut those eyes forever. Cut them out. He would give his own life if need be.

And if he didn't die, he would go on to fight the Romans, his other villain, a far more difficult beast to vanquish.

Alexander had said that the heart of a hero was sacrifice. Noah would sacrifice his life if he could only have a chance to kill the monster that lurked behind those temple walls.

Thelonius dropped his sword. "Pugio."

It was a reference to the dagger a warrior carried in his belt. Dropping his own sword, Noah pulled out his pugio to practice the stab and slash moves he had been taught. Holding the dagger tightly in his fist, he stabbed, twisted, and slashed at target points on an imaginary Gischala.

Thelonius had taught him these techniques as well. How to reach vital organs. More importantly, how to target the body's major arteries, where death could occur within seconds of bleeding out. Thelonius's experience in the legion was minimal, but a world of help for Noah.

"Thelonius, Noah, come with me." The voice was Alexander's, newly arrived in the hallway.

"We've received some financial donations from sympathizers in the city, so I'd like to buy a cow for milk and some lambs for meat."

Good! thought Noah. *I'm hungry.* His stomach growled. Everyone was hungry and thirsty these days because of the drought.

He put away his sword and joined the men in search of food.

• • • • •

Cassandra could barely keep her mind on the task at hand. The plague numbers had dwindled to only a few again, but with the lack of food storages in the city and the drought, she knew they had to prepare for the rise in sickness and malnourishment that would be caused by the coming famine.

She was scrubbing sheets and blankets in the water basin of the ground portico, but only the dirtiest as water had become tightly rationed in recent weeks since the drought had taken a stranglehold of their weather.

No baths were allowed, only wet rags to wipe the body down. Crops were dying, food and provisions dwindling.

The Witnesses had prophesied the drought, but no one had listened. Now they were all in the throes of it and unprepared. Most cisterns had gone dry. The aqueducts were the only source of water from the pools of Solomon in the south.

Their little hippodrome community was suffering doubly under the drought and the elimination of rations and the garden by Jacob. Armed soldiers still guarded the garden for Jacob's benefit. So their community now survived on begging and the secret charity of sympathizers in the city.

As she scrubbed her sheets, Cassandra could not help but think of the hundreds of children in her care and their fate. Their small, growing bodies needed food and water more than adults. Many were becoming listless with lack of energy. It broke her heart to see the suffering of little ones. They were always the ones most hurt by war and by acts of God.

The words of Jacob haunted her like a repeating nightmare. *You can save them from pain and suffering. All you have to do is become my mistress.*

All you have to do.

The offer was so repulsive just the act of considering it made her sick to her stomach. Adultery was a violation of God's law, a violation of her husband's love and trust.

But if she did it, she would save the children from starvation.

But where was her faith? Should she not trust God and accept their suffering?

How could the world be so complex? So confusing? Was not the Torah absolute? Thou shalt not commit adultery.

The Torah also forbade lying. But wasn't Rahab justified for lying to save the Jewish spies who conquered Jericho?[1]

She prayed, *Lord, what do you expect of me? Is this from you or from the devil? Shall I do evil that good may come? Is this a trial of faith? But why would you let the children die for the sake of my moral righteousness?*

She could not get the children out of her mind. If she did not do this thing, they would not get food and they would die. If she did it, they would live.

You can save them from pain and suffering. All you have to do is become my mistress.

"Cassandra. Cassandra?"

The voice broke her out of her trance. She realized she had stopped washing the bedding. Rachel came into view, giving Cassandra a quizzical look. "Are you well?"

"Oh, yes," Cassandra answered. "Just caught up in my thoughts."

Rachel had changed her clothes, Cassandra noted. She was no longer wearing the ragged, baggy clothes of a boy but the feminine tunic and robe Cassandra had provided the girl upon her bath that first day. And her ragged haircut had been trimmed to evenness. She was letting it grow out.

Cassandra forced a smile. "You are becoming quite the young woman."

Rachel blushed and tried to change the subject. "You have been looking sad all day."

Cassandra hesitated. "I'm worried for the children. For all of us."

Rachel asked, "Will worrying add a single hour to our lives?"

Cassandra felt stunned. Rachel was repeating what Cassandra had taught the children just the day before in their Scripture lesson. She had tried to encourage them to trust in the Father in the midst of their tribulation. "O you of little faith," Jesus had said to his disciples. "Do not be anxious, saying,

'What shall we eat?' or 'What shall we drink?' or 'What shall we wear?' For the Gentiles seek after all these things, and your heavenly Father knows that you need them all. But seek first the kingdom of God and his righteousness, and all these things will be given to you."[2]

O you of little faith.

The words felt like a blade opening her own veins. Cassandra dropped the sheet she was scrubbing and broke down weeping.

Rachel moved to comfort her, hugging the older woman tightly, even motherly. It made Cassandra weep even more. Had she now become the child in this relationship?

Strangely, the thought calmed her.

She brought her tears under control. "Being an adult is not an easy thing, Rachel."

"I know."

"I told you that becoming a woman meant learning to protect children. But the truth is, sometimes events are out of our control. And only God can protect them."

Rachel asked, "But didn't you say that God sacrificed for us that we might sacrifice for others?"

It was true. Cassandra had taught the children that the sacrifice of Jesus was an example for them all. That they were to have the mind of Christ, who though he was God had emptied himself by becoming a man. He had humbled himself by becoming obedient to the point of death, even death on a cross.[3]

Jesus sacrificed his perfection, his righteousness, to take on the sin of the world. To become sin for us so that we might become the righteousness of God.[4] Could Cassandra do the same? Could she become sin for the sake of the children?

Her musings were interrupted by the sound of men's voices at the hippodrome entrance. Alexander had returned from his mission.

Hope rose in Cassandra's heart as she dropped her washing to rush after Rachel toward the entrance.

But one glance at Alexander's dire expression as he, Thelonius, and Noah dragged an empty cart through the entrance told Cassandra the news was not good. Nor did she see any tethered animals in tow.

"There's been another plague," Alexander explained. "This time among the livestock. Many of them are dying with a mysterious disease. No one is selling their live ones right now out of fear."

Cassandra felt faint at the implication. She didn't catch herself from exclaiming, "Why would God do this to us?"

Alexander said, "I don't know. But we must pray."

Cassandra thought, *I must sacrifice.*

CHAPTER 61

Noah sat at the top of the hippodrome, as he often did, watching the people below. It was the afternoon time of rest when most of the quarantine residents would take naps or waste time talking. Alexander and Cassandra were alone in their tent doing whatever things spouses did together.

Noah had completed his chores with Alexander on his rounds. Down in the hippodrome, the boy felt as vulnerable as the victims Alexander treated. Up here, he could see a great distance around the lower city and up to the southern part of the temple. It was liberating looking down on everyone, like God's own eye-view of the world. He felt so inconsequential in this time of crisis. But here on his lofty perch, he felt like an angel, above it all.

Noah noticed the Two Witnesses in the distance entering the temple at the Huldah Gates. They often spoke outside the gates or throughout the streets and marketplaces of the city. But today for whatever reason, they were entering the temple area. And that was what Noah had been waiting for.

He rushed through the stairwells of the hippodrome down to the hallways beneath the stands on the east side of the stadium. In his early explorations of the structure, he had discovered a hole there where brickwork had crumbled away. Just big enough for a small, thin child to wriggle through, the hole led into a recess dark enough only a torch would reveal the board Noah had purloined to camouflage the opening.

Climbing through, Noah propped the board back in place, then slipped out of the recess and through a long row of arches that left him outdoors and just a few dozen yards from the Huldah Gates. Slipping through milling crowds, he hurried up the steps. Gischala's soldiers guarded the entrance diligently, checking all adult temple-goers for weapons and asking their business.

But they didn't check children.

Noah crowded close behind a family as if he were one of them. Once inside the temple precinct, he slipped away and made his way through the market to where the Two Witnesses were preaching.

It wasn't too hard to spot what he was looking for.

Standing in the shade of the portico, a group of temple soldiers listened to the Witnesses.

In their midst was John of Gischala.

Elihu's voice penetrated the crowds as he quoted the Apocalypse. "When he opened the fifth seal, I saw under the altar the souls of those who had been slain for the word of God and for the witness they had borne. They cried out with a loud voice, 'O Sovereign Lord, holy and true, how long before you will judge and avenge our blood on those who dwell on the Land of Israel?' Then they were each given a white robe and told to rest a little longer until the number of their fellow servants and their brothers should be complete who were to be killed as they themselves had been."

The Witnesses had told their fellow Jews over and over that this generation was not merely guilty for crucifying Messiah, but also for the persecution and murder of Christians, who were Christ's representatives on earth. They had martyred all the apostles save one. They had delivered up the disciples to the synagogues and prisons, putting many of them to death. Just as Jesus had prophesied, the Christians were hated by all for his name's sake.[1] More than that, the Jews had betrayed their own brethren who had embraced Messiah by handing them over to the Neronic persecutions that spread through the empire to all nations.[2]

Now Noah was standing by a large column behind the soldiers. He could see the back of Gischala, virtually unprotected.

Noah fingered the dagger beneath his cloak. In his mind, he visualized his plan of casually walking up to the leader right past the unconcerned eyes of his guards, then pulling his dagger and using the technique he had learned from Thelonius to cut through a man's femoral arteries in both legs.

Noah was too small to try to reach Gischala's throat effectively from behind. But Noah's small stature gave him an advantage. No one would see him coming.

Gischala's legs were unprotected. And if he slashed those major arteries at an angle, the beast would bleed out before anyone could figure out what had happened.

Noah had practiced it a thousand times with his knife and ten thousand times in his head. Even so, he found himself sweating and trembling under the pressure.

Suddenly, he felt he was being watched. He looked around behind him. Small crowds of people went about their temple business buying animals or other elements for offerings.

Thelonius had told him that it was not an easy thing to kill a man. Now Noah experienced that truth. He felt his whole body trembling. He shook his hands out to make it stop.

Setting his face like flint to the task, Noah stealthily pulled out his pugio and held it hidden in his cloak sleeve, waiting for the right moment.

In the sunlight, Elihu stepped back and Moshe took over, telling the parable of the sheep and the goats to those listening.

"When the Son of Man comes in his glory, and all the angels with him, then he will sit on his glorious throne. Before him will be gathered all the nations, and he will separate people one from another as a shepherd separates the sheep from the goats."[3]

It was a parable explaining that the treatment of the Christians throughout the empire represented their treatment of the Son of God. Those who embraced Christians, who fed them, clothed them, visited them in prison, were actually feeding, clothing, and visiting Jesus because his followers were the images of Christ on earth. They represented Christ's presence. They were his brethren. So whatever people of this Tribulation had done unto the least of Christ's brethren, they had done unto Christ.

Such compassion toward the remnant of God would receive the blessing of the Father's "inheritance of the kingdom prepared from the foundation of the world."

But those who rejected the Christians, persecuted them, or did nothing to help them in this Great Tribulation would find themselves cursed and cut off from Yahweh and from the new covenant kingdom of God. These were the goats of Gehenna.

Noah watched Gischala talk to several guards. The warrior appeared to be disgusted with the prophets, no longer interested in hearing their message. Then Gischala turned to leave.

Noah panicked. He had lost his advantage.

Some of the soldiers were staying. Some were leaving with Gischala.

Noah had to move now or lose his chance.

Suddenly a pair of hands grabbed Noah from behind, pulling him around the backside of the pillar out of sight of Gischala and his men.

Noah tried to raise his dagger in defense, but his captor held it firm in his grip.

It was Thelonius. The Roman put his hand over Noah's mouth to keep the boy quiet.

Noah was bewildered. How had Thelonius known he was here?

Gischala and his guards passed right by the hidden pair and exited the market place. Noah heard Gischala say to his men, "Don't allow those two crazy fools in the temple anymore."

At that moment, Noah knew he would never get another chance like this again. Thelonius had ruined his opportunity. He glared at his teacher, who was staring back with angry eyes.

The eyes are windows to the soul.

Thelonius whispered to him harshly, "Not only would you have failed, you would have invited Gischala's vengeance upon the innocent of the hippodrome in response. Is that what you want? Is that what you think being a man is?"

Noah remained defiantly silent.

"Then I have failed you as a teacher. You really should have listened to Alexander. You should have spent more time learning how to save souls than how to kill them."

"But you don't know what it's like to lose your family to these demons," Noah complained.

"Yes, I do," said Thelonius. "And far more than my father and mother."

Noah had heard about Severus and Thelonius's mother, but he had not heard this before. He asked, "Who else have you lost?"

"It's none of your business, boy." Thelonius's eyes were wet with tears. Noah had never seen that before either.

Thelonius pulled him along. "Now let's get you back to the hippodrome where you belong."

Elihu finished the parable to the crowd. "Then the goats will say, 'Lord, when did we see you hungry or thirsty or a stranger or naked or sick or in prison and did not minister to you?' Then he will answer them, saying, 'Truly, I say to you, as you did not do it to one of the least of my brethren, you did not do it to me.' And these will go away into eternal punishment, but the righteous into eternal life."

Seven remaining soldiers had become agitated watching the Witnesses after Gischala had left. One of them heckled, "Let us test this false prophecy. Let us 'do unto' these sheep and see if we turn into a bunch of goats!"

His fellow soldiers laughed along with him, and four of them followed the bullying leader toward Moshe and Elihu. Their eyes burned with hatred, their faces frowning with evil intentions.

The bully reached out to grab Moshe.

But when he did, he froze, his hands grasping in midair like a statue. He began to shake as though trying to break his frozen posture, but he could not.

The others behind him couldn't move either. They looked at each other with surprise.

Then the bully's eyes went up into his head, and he fell to the ground with a thud.

The others fell to the ground with him.

They all twisted and jerked as if having epileptic seizures.

But this was not epilepsy.

Their faces grimaced with terror. They began to howl and bellow like animals. The noises sounded inhuman.

And then they spoke in an ancient tongue. Elihu could not understand it, but he could see they were trying to curse and fight back.

"Silence!" Moshe yelled. The seven demon-possessed soldiers stopped their noises, but they could not stop their twitching muscles.

Moshe and Elihu did not cast out the evil spirits because they knew that it was futile. Jesus had cast out many demons during his messianic ministry of cleansing. But after he left, the demons had returned with seven times their number.

And there were many more coming.

No, the Witnesses would not cast out these demons. They simply walked away.

CHAPTER 62

Alexander inventoried the bandages, medicines, and other medical supplies he had stored in the supplies tent in the hippodrome. They were dangerously low with no sign of replacement. With the new pestilence, their census of patients had increased to several hundred again, but Jacob was not delivering on his promise of supplies. They never had enough. And the patients suffered for it. He felt the weight of it all hit him. He sat on a box, trying to figure out how to beg Jacob again for the needs of the sick.

"Alex, have you seen Rachel?"

He looked up. Cassandra was at the tent entrance, a somber, melancholic look in her eyes.

"No," he said. "I thought she was with Noah."

She paused with troubling thought.

"What is wrong, my love?" Alexander asked. "I have never seen you as sad and quiet as you have been since yesterday. What is on your mind?"

"I was thinking about the story of Tamar and Judah."

That was a sad story indeed. And Alexander knew it well from the scroll of Genesis. Tamar was a woman unjustly cut off from Judah's promised inheritance, so she disguised herself as a prostitute, tricked Judah into impregnating her, and won back her claim of inheritance.

"Did Yahweh consider Tamar's action an acceptable sacrifice?" Cassandra asked.

Alexander paused before responding. The matter was morally complicated. Tamar had been wronged. Then she had claimed through deception and immorality what was illegally and immorally withheld from her. She had been condemned for adultery until Judah discovered he too was the adulterer and then took her in.

Alexander quoted the words of Judah from the scroll, "Tamar is more righteous than I."

She continued to stare into the distance. "From that union, Tamar gave birth to Perez."

He finished her thought, "The ancestor of King David and of Jesus the Messiah. God redeemed a tragic and unjust circumstance."

Cassandra looked at him with pleading eyes and repeated her question, "Did Yahweh consider her action an acceptable sacrifice?"

Alexander said, "I cannot deny that all parties shared in guilt and that God brought noble purpose out of ignoble deeds. But does that justify what she did? That I cannot say. It is for God to judge. But I know that for those who love God all things work together for good, for those who are called according to his purpose."[1]

After a long moment, she said softly, "Thank you, my love. You are a good and godly husband. And I love you with all my heart."

That sounded to Alexander more like a goodbye than a praise.

"I am going to the theater to find Rachel and Noah." Cassandra turned and left. Alexander watched her walk away, wondering why she was behaving so strangely.

Thelonius arrived at the supplies tent. "Do you need help?" he said.

Alexander continued to stare after his wife. He didn't even hear the question. He asked, "Have you seen Rachel with Noah?"

"I was just practicing with Noah. Rachel was not with us."

Alexander feared something was wrong. He looked around at the supplies and said, "I could use your help."

CHAPTER 63

Cassandra moved briskly through the back alleys of the Upper City, cloaked and secretly on her way again to Jacob's stolen home.

Her thoughts tormented her. Tamar and Judah. Tamar's adultery saved the line of Messiah. Was that not a justified action?

Did not Yahweh use the lies of Rahab the prostitute to save the people of God and bring them victory against Jericho?

Did not Esther defile her body with a pagan king to save the people of God from destruction?

The words of Esther's cousin Mordecai felt as if they were spoken to Cassandra: "And who knows whether you have not come to the kingdom for such a time as this?"[1]

He became sin for us.

She had to save the children. She saw no other way.

She was Tamar. She was Rahab. She was Esther.

But the words of Rachel quoting Jesus haunted her. *Do not be anxious saying 'what shall we eat?' or 'what shall we drink?' Seek first the kingdom of God and his righteousness, and all these things will be given to you.*

O you of little faith.

It was faith that allowed Cassandra to see the other side.

Tamar fulfilled God's law of levirate marriage. Rahab deceived murderers who did not deserve the truth, but she did not prostitute herself. Esther did not give herself, she was taken without a choice. Joseph, another hero of faith, refused adultery with Potiphar's wife, yet God used him to save all of Israel from famine.

It was faith that helped Cassandra realize that she could not be like Messiah in his sacrifice. She could not become sin for others.

O you of little faith.

She was not Tamar. She was not Rahab. She was not Esther.

What am I doing? she asked herself.

Seek first the kingdom of God and his righteousness.

Cassandra found herself at the front door of Jacob's home. She swallowed and knocked on the door. She was ushered in by a somber-looking Nathan. His look told her he knew what trouble she was facing. But he was powerless to help her.

Cassandra followed Nathan to the atrium, where Jacob was tending to his flowers and foliage again.

He turned with surprise. "Oh. That was quicker than I expected. 'How lovely are the feet of those who bring good news.'"

Jacob had used the phrase that the prophet Isaiah had called the Gospel. The good news of the kingdom of God. This lecherous apostate was mocking Jesus to her face.

He said "Nathan, tell the guards to take a break."

Nathan left obediently, and Cassandra knew Jacob had dark intentions.

She spoke with a trembling but resolved voice, "I will not be your mistress. God will provide for our needs."

Jacob raised his brow and set down the blade he had in his hand. "Is that so? Like he provided your garden harvest?"

It was an implied threat. He still controlled their garden. And he was planning to do what he had done previously: steal their miracles.

Nathan had returned. Jacob said to him, "Bring the girl here."

He turned back to Cassandra. "Well, I must say your response is not entirely unexpected. Which is why I prepared myself for it."

Nathan returned to the atrium leading Rachel, her wrists bound before her, eyes full of fear.

Cassandra moved toward her. "Rachel!"

Jacob raised his hand to stop her. "I caught her leaving the hippodrome without authorization. So I am going to take her as a household servant."

"You can't do that."

"I can." Jacob spoke with relish. "I have full legal authority over the quarantine, over the theater, and over everyone in your care. I am your law."

Cassandra desperately searched her heart for anything she could say, anything she could do to save Rachel from this monster.

Then he said, "In fact, I plan to take Rachel as my mistress in your place."

Brian Godawa

"No!" Cassandra cried out. She saw the terror in Rachel's tear-blurred eyes. "You can't do that. Please."

"I can. And I will. Unless you are willing to change your mind on my offer."

Fear, rage, and confusion flooded Cassandra's soul. She questioned everything she had just decided.

"If you become my mistress, I will return Rachel to your care without charges and provide the food rations to the quarantine as I promised."

Rachel broke down crying. Cassandra could not bear to think of this bald, sweaty serpent placing his despicable hands on the child, raping her innocence.

Cassandra straightened up with resolve, nodded agreeably to Jacob and said, "Untie her hands."

Jacob studied Cassandra for assurance. She closed her eyes and sighed with resignation to her fate. When she opened them, she saw Jacob grinning. He said to Nathan, "Do it."

Nathan quickly untied Rachel's hands.

Cassandra held her hand out. "Rachel, come."

Rachel looked for approval from Jacob. He nodded. The girl ran over to Cassandra and embraced her. Cassandra kept her eyes on the apostate. He was looking Cassandra's body over with hunger.

She whispered into Rachel's ear, "Run as fast as you can. Tell Alexander and Thelonius everything."

Rachel looked up at her, unsure of what she just heard. Cassandra said firmly, "Go. Run."

Rachel bolted and ran back toward the entrance.

Cassandra heard the door open at the house entrance. Rachel was in the street. Her long, young legs were fast.

But Cassandra's were not. She turned and ran for the door. She only made it to the entrance before Jacob tackled her, pulling her to the floor.

She squirmed, trying to get loose. But her enemy's strength was greater. He jerked her around and punched her in the face.

Everything went black. She didn't know how long she was out. Seconds? She came to, dizzied and confused.

The tall, lanky creature was still on top of her, his filthy hands tearing at her robe, clawing her tunic.

Through blurry-eyed vision and a bloody lip, she murmured, "Leave me alone."

He stopped for a moment, holding her in his iron grip. "You have teased me like a harlot. I am going to teach you a lesson, you little whore."

She managed to spit at him.

He smiled and wiped the bloody mass from his face. Then he licked it from his fingers with mocking delight.

She turned her head to the side, not wanting to see the monster. She saw Nathan standing down the hall, watching, frozen with horror.

She cried with a weak voice, "Help me."

But Nathan could not help her. He was a beaten slave of this demon himself. A strange sense of pity for the scarred witness overcame her.

She prayed, *Lord Jesus, protect me.*

But before anything else could happen, she felt the weight of Jacob's body pulled off of her. He didn't get up. He was yanked up.

She heard the sound of scuffling and punches.

She held her head up, still swooning with dizziness from her beating. She saw her husband on top of the creature, pounding him with his fists.

She tried to call out, "Alexander."

Alexander stopped and looked at her. He was breathing heavily with a wild look in his eyes. Almost as if he was surprised by his own actions.

Cassandra saw Thelonius with Rachel at the doorway. She couldn't think straight. How did they get here so fast? Rachel had just left them. It wasn't possible.

Rachel ran to Cassandra and helped her sit up. Thelonius made his way to Alexander's side.

Cassandra saw Nathan still watching everything from his position in the shadow of the hallway.

Alexander grabbed Jacob's collar and said between breaths, "There are three of us witnesses." He looked up and saw Nathan in the hallway, "No, four witnesses to your attempted rape of my wife. You will finally face the law."

Cassandra's dizziness was gone. She could think more clearly. She croaked out, "Wait. There is another choice."

Both Alexander and Jacob turned to hear her explain. She offered to Jacob, "You will reinstate our rations to what they were at the very start of the quarantine last year, and you will double our medical supplies. In return, we will not report your crime to the authorities for prosecution."

At first Alexander looked furiously resistant to the suggestion. Then his expression calmed to thoughtfulness. He shook Jacob for an answer. "What do you say to the woman?"

"Okay, okay," said the gurgling voice of the weasel beneath him.

Cassandra groaned from the pain of a blackened eye and bruised ribs. But the pain was worth it. God had once again redeemed suffering and impossible circumstances for his purpose.

But for how long? she wondered. Judgment was still coming to Jerusalem.

Alexander got up, leaving Jacob to wallow in his own bloody pain on the floor. Making his way to Cassandra, he held her tenderly. "My love. I am so sorry I did not get here sooner."

"Sooner?" Cassandra asked. "How did you get here so quickly?"

Alexander smiled lovingly. "We followed you. I knew something was wrong when you asked me about Tamar."

Cassandra raised a hand to caress his face tenderly. "See? You are not just a doctor after all. You are a warrior."

She could see her words had great impact on him. He tightened his eyes and embraced her.

"Ow!" she exclaimed as her ribs creaked painfully.

He loosened his embrace. "I'm sorry."

She smiled at him. "You are my hero."

Nathan helped Jacob up and led him into the house to clean him up. Jacob yelled behind him, "You will have your ransom. Just leave me."

Alexander lifted Cassandra gently from the ground. Then he and Rachel held her up and made their way back to the hippodrome.

"Do you think he will do it?" said Cassandra. "Do you think he will reinstate the rations?"

"He has to," said Alexander. "At least for now."

She could see the concern in Alexander's face. The apostate could not allow his secret to get out. But what would he do to protect it?

CHAPTER 64

Simon had been engaged in another battle with Gischala's forces at the western wall of the temple and its gates when he received the message that Nero Caesar was dead. He immediately called off the attack and withdrew to Herod Antipas' palace, Simon's new headquarters in the upper city.

He called for a ceasefire and an urgent negotiation with both Gischala and Eleazar. They obliged him, and the three of them met in the Hall of Unhewn Stones under equally limited guard.

The new grand sanhedrin of seventy was host and mediator to the negotiations.

Simon had told them of the news of Nero's death, and immediate debate broke out amongst themselves.

Gischala asked, "Who is now emperor?"

"Galba," said Simon.

"Will he renew the war against us?" asked Eleazar.

"It's only a matter of time."

"But for now they have halted the war?" Gischala asked.

"Yes," said Simon. "That is why I called this meeting. We now have the luxury of solving our disputes without the Roman war machine bearing down upon us."

"But they will return," said Gischala. "Rome never backs down."

"They did at Beth-Horon," said Eleazar. "God routed Cestius. He can do it again."

"I killed Cestius," corrected Simon. "And it was sheer luck because of their miscalculation. Under Vespasian, it will never happen again."

"Where is your faith, Simon?" taunted Gischala.

Simon ignored it and said, "Rome will return. But this can be a moment of opportunity to solve our grievances. We could unite in strength against our common foe."

"So you want a treaty," Gischala said with sarcastic disdain. "You want to negotiate with the devil."

For all the talk of uniting, Simon still wanted to plunge his dagger into Gischala's neck and cut his throat out.

Gischala eyed Eleazar warily. "There is no unity to be had with traitors."

Eleazar snapped back, "Or cowards."

At the insult, Gischala placed his hand on his sword and moved toward Eleazar. Gischala had been rumored to have abandoned his own city to the plunder of the Romans before making his way to Jerusalem. Simon didn't doubt the rumor for a second. It was the creature's nature.

Glaring back at Gischala, Eleazar responded in kind, along with all the guards in the room. For a moment, they were all prepared to pounce on one another. End it all right here.

Then Simon raised his hands to calm everyone. "Back down. If we kill ourselves, there'll be no one to defend Jerusalem. Is that what you want?"

It was a stand-off. Neither would be the first to back down.

Simon asked, "Do you think I have any less complaint against the both of you?"

It struck Simon that the three of them had all been captains of the temple guard. Gischala had betrayed Simon to the Romans years ago, and then Eleazar had betrayed Gischala. Those two had united to kill Ananus and take over the city. Then Gischala had turned on Eleazar, driving him back into the inner temple and to their current stand-off.

It was an irredeemable situation of complex betrayal.

Eleazar backed down first. He had the fewest numbers and the smallest territory of control in the inner temple.

Gischala and his men lowered their arms.

One of the members of the sanhedrin, Jacob ben Mordecai, spoke up. Simon noticed he had a bruised face and split lip from some altercation. Jacob offered an option. "Though we may not find grounds for a coalition of forces, might we at least consider agreeing to a common interest. The civilian residents of this city have been victims to the plundering of all sides in this civil dispute. If you are not careful, you may find yourself creating a fourth faction that will ensure the demise of us all."

"I will support such a treaty," said Simon.

Gischala and Eleazar would not take their eyes off each other.

Eleazar said, "I cannot. My sacred cause takes precedence over the lives of the common man."

Gischala said, "Soon I will have the entire temple under my control."

Eleazar shook his head with disdain.

Gischala added, "And when I do, I will set free the captives and those imprisoned in a jubilee liberation. All citizens will have unhindered access to the temple services without violence."

"They have access now," argued Eleazar. "But you have been killing the priests inside and defiling the holy place with your catapults and missiles. You will never be allowed to defile it with your presence."

Gischala turned to his men. "Let us leave. This negotiation is over."

He marched past Simon with his men.

Simon watched him leave, contemplating the scripture that Gischala had referenced from Isaiah. It was a well-known messianic scripture. He could only conclude that Gischala thought he was helping to bring in the age of Messiah. With such delusions, Simon knew that there was no hope of a treaty with these three. There was only the need for defeating them both.

• • • • •

Cassandra and Thelonius helped Alexander with his rounds of the patients in the hippodrome. Rachel was next to Cassandra as they offered broth to some of the sick in their beds. They had used the last of their few vegetables soaked in water to create the broth. Tomorrow they would have nothing left.

But they were interrupted by the announcement of an arrival, a shipment of several carts guarded by soldiers.

Cassandra, Alexander, and Thelonius met them at the entrance to the stadium. They recognized the guards from Jacob's household. Cassandra noticed Nathan, the servant in charge. He was smiling nervously at her.

They pulled back the canvas to reveal stores of food: grain, vegetables, bread and oil. Four carts full of food.

Nathan announced, "Weekly rations from Jacob ben Mordecai."

Cassandra and Alexander embraced each other with joy.

Alexander said a soft prayer of thanksgiving for the provision.

295

Nathan approached the three of them with trepidation. He looked around to make sure none of the guards could hear him, then whispered, "All is not well."

They looked at him with interest. "My master conspires to force your adults into conscripted labor for the city."

Cassandra looked to Alexander. "But what about our threat to sue him?"

Nathan whispered again, "He intends to keep his promise regarding the food rations so you will not prosecute. But he will make the suggestion of labor to the sanhedrin under the pretense of emergency war preparations."

It took gall for Jacob to push back like this. Their battle with him was not over. Alexander felt it would never be over.

"Who will protect the children?" Cassandra's demand was fierce, but Alexander saw the dread in his wife's face.

He reassured her, "We will make an immediate appeal to the sanhedrin to remove the children from the city."

Alexander reached out his hand to clasp wrists with Nathan. "And thank you for your help."

"I'm so sorry," the pepper-haired servant said in return with regretful eyes. "I didn't know what to do. I froze in fear." Alexander knew he was guilt-ridden for having witnessed the attempted rape of Cassandra and had done nothing to stop it.

Cassandra spoke up. "I forgive you, Nathan. As Jesus Christ forgave me."

He looked at her, unable to understand the grace he was experiencing. He could produce no words.

Rain clouds gathered overhead, and the sound of rumbling thunder assured them that the drought was over.

Alexander saw Nathan look up into the sky with a smile and blink his eyes in the drops of water that began to drizzle upon him.

•••••

At the Huldah Gates, the Two Witnesses had finished their public prayer for rain to break the drought. They raised their hands into the air as the water fell down upon them in waves, washing them from the heat and dirt of the day.

God had heard them and had given them rain.

CHAPTER 65

The streets were still wet from the rain that had finally come the prior day. Cassandra, Alexander, and Thelonius wiped the mud off their sandals and entered the Hall of Unhewn Stones on the temple mount. The sanhedrin had allowed them in to make a request on behalf of the quarantined of the city.

Cassandra spotted Jacob in their midst as the thirty of them sat on their chairs of judgment surrounding the high priest. She felt better when she saw that his black eye and beaten lip matched her own. She had used make-up to cover the worst of her own injuries so they would not be readily observed and questions asked.

She didn't recognize the new high priest recently chosen for the office. She didn't care. Whatever his name, he was the False Prophet of this priesthood of harlotry that rode the Beast of Rome.

As the sanhedrin was led in prayer for their officiation, she prayed for grace to avoid being pulled into the hatred that stood crouching at her door. When they finished, Jacob looked up and noticed her. She saw the ever-slightest upturn of his bruised lip and turned away, placing her hand on her belly, holding in the urge to vomit.

The secretary of the sanhedrin announced, "Who stands before this sacred court to make his appeal?"

Alexander stepped forward into the middle of the semi-circle of chairs. "My lords, my name is Alexander Maccabaeus, and I am the physician in charge of the quarantine of the hippodrome with my wife Cassandra and colleague Thelonius under the overseer Jacob ben Mordecai."

How ironic, thought Cassandra, *that this court is in judgment over us. The day is at hand when the roles will be reversed. Soon their dominion will be taken away with the Beast they serve, and they will plead before us for mercy. But there will be no mercy for these who worshipped the Beast and took his mark.*[1]

Alexander continued, "As you know, we have performed our ministry for the past year since the outbreak of the first plague in the city. Since that time, we have also obtained upwards of two hundred children orphaned in the war and have organized close to a hundred adults to help us. And if this city is attacked, we will be here to bring aid and comfort to the wounded as well."

He paused and looked at each of the sanhedrin members to show his serious concern. "In light of the urgency of the loss of food stores in the city, as well as the impending danger of war, I request your authorization for the removal of the children from Jerusalem to a safe distance north in the city of Pella."

The sanhedrin mumbled to one another. They seemed accepting to Cassandra. But she saw the sour frown on Jacob's face. He nudged the Pharisee next to him, who cleared his throat and spoke out, "You are Christians, are you not?"

"Yes, my lord."

"You do know that it is illegal to proselytize in the city at this time?"

"Yes, my lord. We do not leave the quarantine except with express approval from the overseer. We give medical help, and we worship in private, but not outside the hippodrome."

"But you proselytize within the hippodrome."

"If people ask us why we do what we do, we answer with honesty, my lord. Nothing more."

Cassandra smiled to herself with satisfaction. Her husband was successfully deflecting the attempt to trap him.

The priest continued his interrogation, "I noticed that you started your ministry at the same time that the Two Witnesses began spreading their malicious doctrines. Have you been giving aid and comfort to those two demons?"

"My lords, I think the Two Witnesses have explained quite clearly to everyone that they conspire with no man. And they claim that God alone provides for them."

The whisperings amongst the sanhedrin increased with agitation. They hated the Witnesses, but they also feared them, and they were afraid to do anything to them lest they be struck down like others had been.

To justify themselves, the sanhedrin attributed the Witnesses' miraculous protection to demons just as they'd done to Jesus.

But they knew better than to try to stop the Witnesses.

Jacob broke in as though with a well-planned strategy. Standing, he paced the floor with a faux regal posture.

"Fellow sanhedrin members, as the overseer of the hippodrome on behalf of this august body, I feel it important to explain some things that cause me concern over the request of the Christians."

Christians. He was deliberately reminding everyone there that she and Alexander and their community were part of the despised and marginalized minority of contempt to the Jewish populace.

"I have been in charge of providing the rations for the poor children in their care as well as the necessary medical supplies for the sick in our midst. And I am honored to do so."

He wasn't honored when he took the rations and supplies away.

"On the one hand, I would be happy to support the removal of the children to safety. I always have."

Master of lies.

"However, I cannot support their passage at this time. We cannot afford to send security for their trip. And I do not think in this dangerous time that their adult supervision would be well-equipped to protect those children from the bandits and brigands that fill the desert."

A repeat of the lie he told us. As if they would even give a care for their survival.

"We must protect these orphans, not send them out into the hands of our enemies."

He hates those orphans because he knows many of them are Christians now.

"But I do have an alternative solution that I think all sides can agree upon. I suggest that we put the adults of Alexander's community to work in the quarry on the wall, helping to rebuild our defenses. There are a hundred and fifty of them, and they are able-bodied. And about half of the orphans are also old enough to begin working for the benefit of the city as well. Perhaps cleaning the drains within the city." Cassandra cringed in horror. He would send the children into the sewers? Another wave of nausea came over her.

He continued, "They are all receiving food rations from the government. It is only right and fair that they give back to the city that has been so generous to them. Should they not pay their fair share as do we all?"

So that is his diabolical plan: to enslave the Christians and the orphans. And they called the Two Witnesses demons!

Cassandra felt her breathing grow labored with fear.

She saw Jacob staring at her.

The high priest announced, "Thank you for your compassion toward the people of this city, Jacob. And for the sacrificial offering of your stone quarry. It has been of inestimable value in preparing to defend the holy city from the pagan hordes."

Jacob bowed with faux humility. "It is my honor and privilege. For Jerusalem."

For the Beast, thought Cassandra.

The high priest continued, "Unless there are any objections, I think we need waste no more time deliberating over this matter. It appears Jacob has it under control."

He turned to Jacob. "You have this sanhedrin's authority to do as you see fit in this matter. I know you will do what is best for Jerusalem."

Jacob had a contented smirk on his face. He said, "Thank you, my colleagues. We will begin conscription tomorrow morning."

Cassandra felt like vomiting.

CHAPTER 66

Alexander, Cassandra, and Thelonius returned to the hippodrome and met in their tent to discuss their plans.

"Can you not request an appeal to the sanhedrin?" Thelonius asked.

"Their decision is final," said Cassandra.

"We begin conscripted labor tomorrow," said Alexander. "We have to meet with Jacob to go to the quarry in the morning."

Cassandra could not countenance any of it. "He'll work us to death. He's putting the children in the sewers. We have to bring our charges of his crime before the sanhedrin."

"Cassie," said Alexander. "The risk is too great. He is following through on his promise of food rations. If he knows we intend to report him, our lives and the lives of those under our care will be in jeopardy."

Thelonius added, "In a short time, our claim will be worthless in the courts. How long will our threat have weight? A few weeks? A month or so?"

Cassandra could tell Alexander did not want to push that time any closer. He said, "Even so, it won't change the decision of the sanhedrin on this matter." He paused, thinking hard.

"You two should take the children to Pella tonight," he insisted.

"Tonight?" said Thelonius with incredulity.

"You can take the tunnels as we discussed previously."

Thelonius responded, "And we've also discussed that they would be upon us before we could get half-way to the Jordan."

Cassandra said, "If we leave, Jacob will try to bring us back and punish us. If we stay, he will punish us. Either way, he will seek to punish us. We must try."

Alexander said, "You are right. We are at the banks of the Red Sea. So let us pray that God will part the waters and drown those who are after us."

Thelonius sighed with unbelief.

Alexander added, "But I will stay behind."

Cassandra blurted out, "No!"

Alexander touched her shoulder reassuringly. "I must, Cassandra. It is my medical services he needs. I don't believe he'll want to hurt me if the three of you are gone. With no victim and only one witness left, I would not be a threat to him, only an asset."

She protested, "But I need you with me, Alex."

He smiled. "You used to say that I needed you. I do believe you have grown, my love."

She held her belly with eyes full of tears. "Alex, I'm with child."

Alex and Thelonius sat silently stunned.

"What?" exclaimed Alex.

"Several weeks now."

"Why didn't you tell me?"

"I don't know. I wanted a moment that we could rejoice."

He laughed with joy. "Dear wife, let us rejoice now!"

Alexander embraced her, and they kissed. He didn't want to let her go. But their time was running short. He pulled apart from Cassandra and said with a jubilant smile, "God has answered my prayers—as well as your arguments against leaving. You must go to Pella."

Her eyes pooled with sorrow that he was right.

"Thelonius will care for you." Alexander looked to the Roman for approval. He got it with a silent nod. "And I think the adults should stay here."

Thelonius said, "But the children will be vulnerable to bandits."

Alexander said, "We'll break them up into smaller groups, more capable of hiding."

Thelonius nodded with resignation.

Alexander concluded, "The adults are more important to Jacob than the children."

Cassandra began to show signs of acceptance. She said, "He loses the burden of the orphans but retains his labor force. And his quarantine doctor."

Alexander was already figuring the logistics, "You can take a dozen adults for chaperones. Jacob won't notice a handful missing. If you leave at midnight, that will give you six hours before sunrise."

"We'll have to move at a fast pace," said Thelonius.

"With some providence, you could make it to the foothills across the Jordan, where you can hide."

Cassandra said, "That's twenty-five miles. That will take us two days."

"We'll have to try," said Thelonius. "We have no other option."

Alexander added, "I can create a diversion that may give you the added hours you need."

"What kind of diversion?" she asked.

"I have no idea. But I pray God does."

"Then let us get moving," said Thelonius. "We have no time to spare."

CHAPTER 67

Jacob had awakened in his home shortly before sunrise. He ate his breakfast and prepared for his morning visit to his stone quarry to check on his workers. But first he would stop at the hippodrome to make sure the Christians would be following through on their promise.

Alexander and Cassandra were fanatical Christians, but he believed that they had begun to see the benefit to their cause as well. This cosmos was not heaven, it was earth. And on earth, reality was much more shaded and complex. There were exceptions to all morals. Compromise was necessary to accomplish the greater good. Even Christians had to accept that reality.

Jacob thought of Cassandra. He filled with anger at his thwarted attempt to dominate her. But it had the strange effect of increasing his desire to take her. He just had to find another way to do it. The right moment. Power and domination was titillating no matter where it manifested itself, in the sanhedrin or in the bedroom.

It would take some weeks before the claims of the three witnesses against him would carry little merit in court. He would make sure Nathan would not join in their accusations. He could be certain of that much. But regarding the three others, he had to be patient and wait it out. He began to calculate how he might still make Cassandra his mistress in due time. By force, if necessary. He grinned. By force, preferably.

He was interrupted in his thoughts by his servant Nathan. "My lord, you have visitors."

He came to the door to find Alexander and his hippodrome Christians waiting at his threshold.

Alexander said, "We are reporting for work in the quarry."

"Well," smiled Jacob. "One thing I do appreciate about you Christians is your enthusiasm for service and obedience to authority."

Jacob stepped outside to survey his new laborers. That was when he noticed the fog. There hadn't been a morning fog for days. And this one seemed extraordinarily thick.

He said, "Unusually cold morning with all this fog."

Alexander responded, "Unusual indeed."

Jacob noticed a satisfied look on Alexander's face. He thought that was odd.

He said, "Well the sun is almost up, it should burn off soon."

Jacob led his new working force in the cold morning air to the stone quarry north of the temple just outside the wall of the New City. Solomon had used this quarry for some of the building materials of the first temple. Jacob's family had acquired it and became rich using it to help build Herod's temple.[1]

Alexander and his group of Christians followed Jacob down the walkway into the deep ravine of cut rock. It was a mine for limestone, covering two acres and extending as far as seven hundred feet under the city.

The men were given kerchiefs, gloves, picks, and shovels. It would be backbreaking labor, just the kind of thing to domesticate these religious fanatics. Jacob would work them until they were too broken to spread their messianic propaganda.

"Every day, sunrise until sunset," Jacob informed Alexander. "Several breaks, including meals. The foremen will explain the details. Limestone is more demanding than you may think."

A foreman showed the new workers how to use their tools properly for extracting the stone as well as the rules of safety and order. Then they were led down into a darkness lit by torches. Though Alexander would not be participating in the labor, he went along to see what the workers were being subjected to.

Jacob rotated squads of workers between the quarry and the walls to balance the sweaty, depressing dark underground with some time in the sun working on the walls. It was all part of maintaining the morale for efficient productivity.

But he had determined to leave the Christians down in the mines. Sometimes it was more important to make a point to those who needed to learn a lesson.

He and Alexander followed the group further. At first the atmosphere was temperate as was the nature of caves and tunnels. But as they neared the laboring, the noise of metal on rock pierced their ears. The air became thick with limestone dust. Workers had to wear the kerchiefs over their mouths to protect their lungs. But the truth was, the longer men worked in the mines, the worse their health became.

It was a slow death.

A group of workers carried a fellow laborer past them on a stretcher.

Jacob and Alexander followed them back out of the mine.

Alexander examined the man's leg. It was partially crushed.

"We have occasional cave-ins," Jacob commented.

"How occasional?"

"Every week. It's part of the cost of doing business. The workers get used to it."

Alexander glared at Jacob before tending to the victim. The worker screamed in pain. The leg would probably have to be amputated.

Alexander said, "Tell that to those who pay the price and see what they think."

They arrived at the medic tent, and Alexander helped take care of the patient.

Jacob waited outside. The sun had risen, but it was still unusually cold and the fog had still not lifted. He thought it strange and pulled his cloak tighter around his shoulders to keep himself warm.

The screams of pain in the tent as the man had his leg sawed off pierced Jacob's musing. He wanted to get out of there.

When Alexander exited, Jacob saw that his hands and clothes were all covered with blood. He said, "Let us return to the hippodrome so you can get cleaned up and I can choose the orphans who are of working age at the theater."

They arrived at the hippodrome, where the doctor took his time cleaning up and checking on his remaining patients before they left. Then they made their way across the valley to the theater where the orphans resided.

When they entered the building, there was no one there.

"Where is everyone?" demanded Jacob.

"I don't know." Alexander yelled out, "Hello? Is anyone here?"

His voice echoed through a hollow empty stadium.

Jacob felt flush with mistrust. "What is this, a trick?"

"Jacob, you took away all our adults and put them in the mine. There is no one to watch over the children. They probably left and spread out into the city."

Jacob did not believe him. "Where is your wife and Thelonius, then?"

"Maybe they've gone to look for them."

Jacob had no patience left. "Where are the children, Alexander?!"

"Let's check the New City. They may be exploring up there. They're children after all."

Jacob said, "Nonsense! You are lying to me. You've sent them away to Pella, haven't you?"

Alexander's carefully blank expression gave it away. Jacob was right. He had been tricked. These lying scheming Christians had tricked him.

He said, "When did they leave, last night under cloak of darkness?"

Alexander nodded.

Jacob turned to his two guards at the entrance and shouted, "Gather a force of fifty armed men immediately! Ride toward Pella by way of the Jordan River, find the children and return them to Jerusalem. Now!"

"My lord," said the guard. "The fog…"

"I don't care about the fog! Just find those children and bring them back!"

"Yes, sir." He bolted off.

Jacob turned to Alexander. "How dare you defy me."

The Christian now relaxed with admission. "I have not defied you. I have stayed. The Christian men have stayed to fulfill your demands of labor. We removed the burden of the orphans from your food rations and medical supplies. And there are not enough witnesses to charge you with a crime. What more do you want, Jacob?"

Jacob considered his points. They were true. But Cassandra was gone. He wanted her. He wanted to take her and force her…

"You have defied me!" yelled Jacob. "You will pay for this deception, Alexander. You and all your men. You speak of burden and rations. I will multiply your burdens and lessen your rations. You will regret this."

He turned in a huff and tramped out of the theater, leaving the deceiver to consider the consequences.

Jacob returned to his home. It had taken longer than usual with the fog. He stomped into his atrium to tend to his flowers. It was one of the few ways he could calm his frustrations.

But it didn't work this time.

All he could think of was being bested by that two-shekel Christian and his whore wife. When he brought them back, he was going to make her his household slave and rub Alexander's nose in it.

No, he would make both Cassandra *and* the young girl his slaves.

He began formulating plans for them, plans for his gratification—and retribution.

Within an hour, he was alerted to the arrival of his guards.

He ran to the door to find the captain with his squad, empty-handed.

"Where is she?" he barked with panic.

The captain was downcast. "My lord, the fog was too thick. We could not get a thousand yards from the wall."

"What are you talking about? It's late morning. There should be no fog left." But he could see that there was, even in the city.

Another guard stepped up. "My lord, my captain tells the truth. I've never seen anything like it. The sun is hidden behind a cloudy sky and the fog is still hanging heavy. We may be able to try again in an hour or so."

The captain remained apologetic. "It was an act of God, my lord."

Jacob exploded at the sound of those words. "That was no act of God. That was sorcery! God curse that witch and her brood! She did this!"

He paced around, desperately trying to figure out any other option. There was none. They had left in the dark of night through the tunnels beneath the eyes of the nightwatch on the walls. That would give them about ten hours of travel. If they made it to the other side of the Jordan they could easily hide in the mountains and never be found. Another few days and they could make it to Pella.

But then again, these were children, not mature adults. They couldn't have made it that far. There was still time.

He ordered the captain, "Get out there and wait for the fog to lift. And bring me back those children!"

"Yes, my lord." The captain and guard left.

He mumbled to himself, "Cassandra will never be allowed to return to this city. And Alexander will never be allowed out. As long as I am alive, they will never see each other again."

CHAPTER 68

Jordan Valley

Cassandra wiped her brow and looked out onto the lush valley around her. The barren desert trail of the Judean highlands had given way to the fertile vegetation of this crossing point into the mountains of the Transjordan. She led her group of twenty children down the trail to the banks of the Jordan River where a couple of barges would ferry them across to the other side.

Noah and Rachel walked closely beside her. They were the first of ten groups of as many children who had slipped out of Jerusalem the night before. Thelonius was in the last group, and each one had an adult chaperone to guide them.

Sneaking two hundred children past guarded city walls was no easy task. They had briefed the children of their plan earlier in the day and given them each a water skin and a few days of food rations to carry with them.

At around midnight, they'd entered one of the many underground tunnels beneath the city, thanks to one of the adult volunteers who had worked as a civil engineer for the city. The children had been divided into ten bands of twenty, each with an adult. They left a distance between them of about ten minutes as they left the city. A single assembly of hundreds of children would simply be too large, too slow, and too loud to hide. As small traveling companies, the children moved swiftly and silently through the night.

They came out of the secret city tunnels some distance from the walls along some sheep trails and resumed their trek on the main road under the light of the moon. They would alternate between jogging and brisk walking. Cassandra had warned them that they would have to push themselves until they got across the Jordan. She suspected they knew she was lying. The truth was that they would have to push themselves beyond their breaking point for the next four days if they were going to survive.

But these were strong ones. They had endured the terror of Roman attacks and had made their way through the fierce, rugged wilderness to Jerusalem on their own, hiding and foraging. If anyone could make this journey alive, it would be these little survivors.

They took a half hour nap every four hours or so. It was hard on them, but they had to make the sixteen miles to the river before a search party could catch up with them. Across the river was their hope.

The evening had been unusually cool, and within a couple hours into their trek, Cassandra noticed a thick fog developing that would hopefully delay their trackers in the morning. God was helping them. But would it be enough? She only hoped Alexander's diversion would give them a few more hours of lead time they so desperately needed.

They came upon the river's edge and found a ferry crossing with two barges. Each was large enough to carry forty people or a dozen horsemen.

By now noon was approaching, and there was still no sign of a search party. Cassandra kept looking over her shoulder at the path that led down into the valley miles behind them. They had left Jerusalem over ten hours ago. Surely, Jacob would have found out by now of their absence. The fog might have delayed them a few more hours, but it was burned off by now. If a company of soldiers on fast horses left now from the city, they could traverse the sixteen miles in a half day.

Cassandra and her fleeing young fugitives had only six hours before that search party reached the river. And then only another three hours before the soldiers could catch up to them ten miles upriver.

They had waited for the second band of fugitives to catch up to them at the riverbank. She loaded both groups onto the barges and they crossed the river.

On the other side, she offered to buy the horse of one of the barge owners, who saw his opportunity and promptly sold it at three times the normal price. They had prepared for this. It was all the money she had with her. Thelonius at the rear had the rest. Cassandra had one of the adults who knew where Pella was take the horse to ride ahead.

It would be at least two or more days before they could return with help. Still they had to try.

Cassandra turned to Rachel and said, "Rachel, remember what I told you about becoming an adult?"

"Yes." The young girl looked like she knew what was coming.

"I need you to be an adult for me now. For the others. I need you to take over the group of children that the man who took the horse had been guiding. Can you do that for me?"

She looked uncertain. It would mean being on her own, separated from her brother and from Cassandra. But she said, "I can do it."

"I want to go with her!" interrupted Noah. Cassandra saw the Roman dagger held tightly in his little fist, ready to protect his big sister.

"Of course you can. You both know the plans. Ten minutes behind me. The bird whistle means spread out and hide. There is plenty of foliage for hiding spots along the river."

Noah asked, "Won't a search party be able to catch us easier along the river than in the mountains?"

Noah was right. If the children made it to the mountains a mere ten miles further east, they could conceal themselves in rocky terrain where horses simply could not follow.

"That is exactly what they will be expecting. So by the time they travel ten miles to the mountains, discover we are not there, and then travel ten miles back to the river, we'll be another ten miles upriver and closer to Pella."

Cassandra didn't say that they would still be twenty miles away from their destination. But she didn't know what else they could do. She just prayed that if they all broke up to escape, most of the children would find their way to Pella as they had to Jerusalem.

Rachel explained to Noah, "Thelonius is with the last group of children. He is going to bribe the ferries to stay across the river and leave their posts. That will delay the search party from crossing for several more hours."

"That is correct," said Cassandra. "We need all the time we can get. So get going." She hugged Rachel with a smile of encouragement, then whispered in her ear, "I'm so proud of you. Watch over your brother."

Rachel replied, "He's watching over me now." She turned to her company of children and gave a short whistle. "Let's get going."

Cassandra watched Rachel and Noah jog up the trail with their twenty wards following.

Dear Lord, she prayed, *please let these children survive, especially Rachel and Noah.*

• • • • •

It had been six hours of hiking, and Thelonius stopped his last company of children for rest and drinks of water along the river. They had traveled a good ten miles. The others were ahead of them all along the river.

The search party must have made it to the ferry crossing by now.

Thelonius had one of the boys with him climb the largest tree to look downriver and see what was happening. At this distance, it would be difficult to see individuals, but he should be able to spot any large group of horsemen by the dust cloud they would raise as they galloped.

The boy called down from thirty feet up, "I see them! They're at the river."

"How many do you guess?" Thelonius called up in return.

"It's hard to tell! Maybe fifty!"

"Only fifty?" asked Thelonius.

"About fifty!" the boy repeated.

That didn't make sense. Jacob should have sent at least a hundred just to be able to corral the children once they hunted them down. The pursuers would have to go on a hide-and-seek mission to catch all the young ones once they spread out and tried to escape.

This could be another advantage, Thelonius thought. Jacob was overconfident. *The arrogant fool.*

The boy called down again, "They're getting on the barges!"

"What?" muttered Thelonius. "I bribed the ferrymen not to be there."

They had been betrayed. Thelonius had used up the last of the funds they had cobbled together for this plan. The ferrymen were supposed to have left the barges on the opposite side of the river and be absent for several hours. But the ferrymen probably used the opportunity to ask for a higher bribe from the search party. It was a gamble the fugitives had risked. And apparently, they lost the bet.

Thelonius called up, "Keep watching them! Tell me which way they go after they cross the river!"

He looked ahead nervously as he waited for the news. His band was the rear guard. Cassandra and her lead company were a good hour ahead of them. They would communicate with whistles that would move down the line,

313

letting the other groups of children know when there was trouble, when to run, and when to hide.

Finally, the boy up in the tree shouted, "They're moving east toward the mountains!"

Thelonious sighed with relief. That ruse gave them another ten hours lead time. It still wasn't enough, but it was something.

He was about to tell the boy to come down the tree, when he heard from above, "Wait! They've stopped! They're turning around! They're coming north!"

"No," muttered Thelonius. "No, please." They must have had good trackers with them. They must have figured out the ploy. It would only be a matter of minutes, maybe a half hour by the time they caught up with them. They wouldn't even make it halfway to Pella.

But they had to try. He barked, "Come down, now!"

He turned to his whistler and said, "Alert the others ahead to run. We'll find a good location to spread out and hide."

The boy signaled ahead with a special whistle.

Thelonius could hear the response as the group ahead whistled to the next group and so on. The signals faded into the distance.

"Let's move!"

The children began jogging. Thelonius took up the rear, looking ahead for the best location to consider hiding. The problem was that their pursuers apparently had trackers so they probably wouldn't have a problem finding most of them.

He thought to himself, *Where was the miraculous deliverance that Cassandra and Alexander had prayed for? Where was God?*

They'd run for fifteen minutes when Thelonius noted the children slowing down with exhaustion. These small fugitives weren't athletes but children who had already pushed themselves beyond their limits. It was amazing they had made it this far.

A flush of hope filled Thelonius as they approached an area of much thicker brush. In fact, they had entered the edge of a small forest. They could spread out here.

The children ahead of him stopped running as if reading his mind. Or had they run out of strength?

As he rounded a bend in the path and caught up with them, he discovered why they had stopped. They were in a small ravine created by an escarpment on the right and the river on the left. All the other groups of children were there together. What had happened? Why had Cassandra's lead group stopped and let all the other groups catch up with them?

And then he saw why: Another group of fifty armed soldiers on horseback had them all corralled and tied together with ropes. Thelonius spotted Cassandra, and Noah and Rachel tied up with the rest.

He immediately figured out what their pursuers had done. They had split up early on, half went upriver to find another crossing, while the other half took the Transjordan side. Their chasers had anticipated the fugitives' naïve strategy and had wedged them in.

This ravine had created a trap for them. The children could not run and hide because of the high escarpment on one side and the river on the other. The few who could swim chose not to brave the strong current. It would have been futile to try.

Their escape to Pella had failed. Terribly. They had only made it halfway to their destination.

Still, he was proud of the children. They had been so brave, so obedient. They had truly done the best they could have.

And now it was all over. All was lost.

Some soldiers approached the children and began tying them onto the long rope of captives.

Thelonius saw Cassandra up ahead with sad face and bound wrists.

Out of the blue, a soldier slugged Thelonius, and he fell to the ground in a stupor. He heard the soldier say, "Troublemakers."

He felt the soldier pull him up roughly and tie his hands to the rope.

"Let's get you ready for your journey back to Jerusalem, where you belong—in custody." He spoke louder for all the children to hear, "If you try to escape, you will be punished! We will not tolerate disobedience!"

The sound of horses trampling their way from behind made Thelonius feel even worse.

315

The fifty soldiers of the rear search party arrived to lead them back to Jerusalem.

Thelonius's jaw ached with the pain of his injury. He felt one of his teeth loosened by the hit. He spit out some blood that had pooled in his mouth.

They had failed. He had failed.

But what no one knew was that this was not merely the ruin of an escape plan for the children. For Thelonius it was the ruin of another more important plan. A deep, dark secret that he carried. One that involved the most beloved person in his life.

It was late in the day. The deep valley was already in the shadows of the setting sun. Thelonius needed to sleep. They all did.

But they plodded on in their captive train, guarded in front and behind by their heartless captors.

The horses ahead stopped. The leader of the soldiers raised his hand in warning. Thelonius saw the soldiers stiffen with readiness.

He saw through the guard in the road just ahead a single man standing in their way. He was wearing strange armor Thelonius had never seen before.

They were on the edge of the forest where Thelonius had hoped to run and hide.

And that forest now exploded with its own hidden figures. All around them. Warriors.

Arrows split the air, taking down a dozen of the soldiers.

Thelonius turned and yelled to the captives, "Get down! We're under attack!"

The children obeyed and dropped to the dirt.

The brush burst open with what Thelonius thought were ghosts because they moved like phantoms. Their fighting technique appeared to be more like dance than battle. They moved with elegance and fluidity as they cut down the soldiers from their mounts.

They looked like a troop of dancing wraiths of death.

It had all been so quick. By the time the shock of the attack had settled on Thelonius, the battle was already over.

All hundred of the soldiers had been wiped out in mere moments. All lay dead on the ground, skewered, sliced, and hacked to death.

And none of the captives had been harmed. At least it seemed so.

"Cassandra! Cassandra?" Thelonius cried out. "Are you okay? Is everyone okay?"

He didn't hear her. He looked around for her.

But he was distracted by the phantom-like warriors that now surrounded the captives. There were about twenty of them. All in strange-looking armor that he could not tell if it was leather or metallic. But it was minimal and dark.

A mere twenty exotic warriors had wiped out an entire contingent of soldiers on horseback.

What in heaven had just happened?

"Thelonius."

The voice startled him. He turned to find Cassandra with Noah and Rachel, standing beside a handsome, dark warrior, apparently the leader of this band of ghost-warriors. They were already cut from their bonds.

He stared at her, unable to speak.

She said with a smile, "Allow me to introduce to you Captain Michael, the prince of these Kharabu warriors from Pella, and a friend of mine."

CHAPTER 69

Pella

Cassandra looked with joy over the congregation of Christians in the city who had gathered to celebrate with them. It had taken the fugitives two days to finish the trip to Pella from where the Kharabu had rescued them. It had not been enough time for the scout she'd sent to retrieve help, but she had learned that Alexander had sent a separate scout ahead of them from Jerusalem the day before on horseback.

Thank God for a wise husband and his over-planning! Cassandra chuckled to herself.

Now they were safely within the city, guarded by Michael and his Kharabu warriors. Cassandra had laughed and cried with old friends she'd thought she would never see again, especially the elder Boaz from Jerusalem. His white-haired, patriarchal presence reminded her of her heavenly father's lovingkindness. The protection of the Kharabu warriors enabled her to sleep peacefully at night. But the most emotional moment of all was the one she was in right now.

She stood with Noah and Rachel before the elder Boaz and the congregation of Pella in a converted synagogue, making public testimony.

Cassandra spoke first, fighting tears of joy with each word. "I, Cassandra, on behalf of my husband Alexander Maccabaeus do testify before this body of witnesses this legal action." She turned to Rachel and Noah. "Rachel, we accept you as our daughter. Noah, we accept you as our son."

The two children were beaming with happiness.

Rachel followed next. "I, Rachel, accept you, Cassandra, as my mother and Alexander as my father."

Noah's turn came. "I, Noah, accept you, Cassandra, as my father..." He paused, embarrassed at the gaffe. Everyone in the crowd laughed. He smiled.

"Sorry. As my mother. And I accept Alexander as my father. That sounds better."

The people applauded. Cassandra reached out and embraced the two of them with all her strength. She could not stop weeping at her joy. She whispered to them, "My son, my daughter."

Noah and Rachel said simultaneously, "Mother." They laughed at the coincidence and hugged even tighter.

The elder announced to the guests gathered around, "Let us enter the congregation hall and celebrate the feast!"

The people moved to the hall. Cassandra and the children stayed back. Thelonius approached them.

He spoke to Rachel first. "Rachel, you are becoming a lovely young woman." She blushed.

He held Noah's shoulders as one man would another. "And you, little troublemaker, remember what I told you in the temple. Honor your father— and mother."

Noah grinned. "I will."

"Now, off with you. Go eat and drink your fill." They ran off to the hall with the others.

Thelonius stopped and looked at Cassandra's belly. She was barely showing yet, but he smiled and hugged her gently.

"I am returning to Jerusalem," he said. "I will bring word of your safety— and family."

"You can't go, Thelonius," she resisted. "Jacob will throw you in prison."

"I have to go back. Alexander needs help, and without you, who will bother him?"

She slapped him playfully, then turned serious, holding her belly. "After I have this baby, I will return to Jerusalem as well."

"No," he scolded her. "Your children need you."

"You're right. Well, if you are half the man of your father, I know Alexander will be safe."

He nodded assent, picked up his pack, and prepared to leave. "Say goodbye to the children for me." He paused. "And pray for me."

She said, "I pray for you every single day, Thelonius Rufus Severus. And for the woman in your life whom you would not tell us about."

He stopped, speechless with surprise.

"I am a woman, Thelonius. We watch and listen closely, and we read between the lines where you men sometimes try to hide things."

"When did you know?"

She smiled. "When I first asked you that day you arrived in Jerusalem."

"I do not know what to say."

She held his arm reassuringly. "You need not say anything until you want to. Just know that I pray for whatever troubles your soul about the woman you love. Wherever she is."

He sighed deeply, looking troubled. "Thank you, Cassandra."

"You're very welcome, Thelonius. And may the Lord Jesus Christ be with you."

"And also with you."

He left her.

She watched him as he mounted his horse and faded into the black of the night.

And in her heart, she felt the pull of her love, for her husband far away and her children so near, tearing her apart.

CHAPTER 70

Panias

Apollyon led his entire force of Watchers through the Gates of Hades and deep into the cave where the crevice opened up as a shaft into the Abyss.

The gods of the nations and the two hundred ancient ones were gathered around the precipice for an occult ritual that would turn the tide of war.

Some of the two hundred had taken over the helms of some of the nations, such as Semyaza, Azazel, and Ba'al. But most of the seventy pantheons consisted of Apollyon's hand-picked divinities to rule those nations.

The cavern had been cleared of its rubble and widened for Apollyon's purposes, but the group of Watchers was large. They found themselves packed tightly into the crowded rock hollow.

Apollyon and a group of twelve "obs," female necromancers, led them in an ancient occult ritual of conjuring. The obs had their faces smeared with salve, and their bodies twitched with the habitation of demons.

Bread was placed around the ledge of the pit. Honey, milk, and wine was poured into the pit as a libation offering.

Chests of silver were then cast into the darkness below. They would not be heard hitting the black waters because all sound was swallowed up in the void.

Then a dozen Watchers carried a dozen black boars up to the ledge to have their throats cut and bled into the Abyss for sacrifice.[1]

But something happened at that moment that took the Watchers by surprise. As they held the boars in their arms, their hands were not free to defend themselves against the dozen other Watchers who slipped up behind them to slit their throats in place of the boars.

The choking, gagging Watchers were bound with cherubim hair and kicked into the shaft. They plunged to their imprisonment.

The other Watchers froze in confusion. Apollyon had just substituted some of his own minions for the sacrifice.

But why?

In rapid response, designated gods all over the cavern grabbed fellow Watchers and slit their throats and bellies with silent speed and accuracy.

One of those who had been so cut was Anat, the Canaanite goddess of sex and war. Three other Watchers held her firmly as she bled out. Apollyon stepped up behind her and whispered in her ear, "Virgin goddess, you really should have been more discreet with your plans of a coup."

Her eyes bulged with surprise. She could not speak through her sliced throat. She could only gurgle. She struggled in the arms of her captors, but her powerful strength had been drained onto the floor along with her intestines.

Apollyon had seen her contempt for Ba'al's humiliation, her mounting hostility against her master. He knew what she was planning all along.

"Vengeance for your brother, your lover. What heroic sacrifice."

He knew his sarcasm dug as deep as the knife blades.

The goddess was bound along with the other bleeding victims, and dragged to the ledge, where they were all cast into the crevice. They disappeared into the pitch black of the bottomless pit.

Two hundred of them suffered this fate, sacrificed by the gods of the seventy nations under Apollyon's authority. They were the two hundred ancient ones.

Previously in the divine council where the Adversary had filed his covenant lawsuit, the Son of Man had given Apollyon one contingency for the release of his four captive principalities. That contingency stipulated that before they would be freed, Apollyon would have to return the two hundred Watchers that he had freed. They would have to be returned to their captivity. Back to Tartarus. These were the ancient ones who had been imprisoned at the time of the Flood for their egregious violation of humanity.

It was a gamble for Apollyon. He was losing a significant part of his heavenly host. But it was worth it to him. He would receive his four mightiest principalities in return, and he would maintain all the gods of the seventy nations for his assault on the holy city. It was a trade of the two hundred for the seventy. But those seventy were the key to his victory.

The truth of the matter was that he would gladly betray all his allies if it helped him to crush the heel of the seed of the Woman.

And there was more than one purpose for the way he fulfilled the sentence. By sacrificing the Watchers in an act of conjuring, he enabled the ability to call up another army, one of greater proportions.

He led the remaining Watchers in an incantation. They sang an eerie lyric in a lost tongue. The sound of their unified voices reverberated through the walls and down into the pit of the Abyss.

Apollyon raised his arms to call up his new host.

"Arise, my children! Arise from the underworld to consume the living!"

The Watchers continued to chant.

A hideous, howling shriek pierced the black darkness of the shaft, followed by a bellowing roar of the opening of an ancient tomb of evil.

Smoke belched out of the shaft, and the Watchers could hear the buzzing sound of wings. So many of them that they felt the vibrations in their own bodies.

Apollyon laughed maniacally. The joy was too great to suppress. He was the angel of the Abyss, the bottomless pit. These were his subjects. He was their king.

Out of the smoky depth of the Abyss came a swarm of demons, hundreds of millions of them. Locust demons with faces of humans and tails of scorpions. Their teeth were like lions' teeth with breastplates of iron. The noise of their wings was like the noise of many chariots and horses rushing into battle. The sound penetrated the air with a deafening hum.

Pouring out of the shaft, they flowed in a torrent of evil past Apollyon and his Watchers.

The locusts burst out of the cave of Panias like a gushing stream of black pitch in the unseen world.

They sought the intent of their king: habitation in the legions of Rome.[2]

Then I looked, and I heard an eagle crying with a loud voice as it flew directly overhead, "Three woes to those who dwell in the land...

And the fifth angel blew his trumpet, and I saw a star fallen from heaven to land, and he was given the key to the shaft of the Abyss. He opened the shaft of the Abyss, and from the shaft rose smoke like the smoke of a great furnace, and the sun and the air were darkened with the smoke from the shaft.

Then from the smoke came locusts on the land, and they were given power to harm only those people who do not have the seal of God on their foreheads. They were allowed to torment them for five months.

They have as king over them the angel of the Abyss. His name in Hebrew is Abaddon, and in Greek he is called Apollyon.[3]

Apocalypse 8:13–9:11

EPILOGUE

Mount Bashar
The River Euphrates

The evening was pitch-black. There was no moon, and the skies thundered with storm clouds overhead. The Euphrates river flowed in the darkness past the mountain of the Amorites, where the angelic hostage exchange had previously taken place.

Lightning cracked the sky and hit the mountaintop with burning fury. All signs of animal and insect life had long since fled. The storm of war was rising.

The sound of a heavenly trumpet ripped the atmosphere. It resounded through all of creation in the unseen realm, announcing the first woe.

Four falling stars plummeted to the land and hit the base of the mountain with a concussion that could be felt for miles.

As the smoke cleared from the crash site, the figures of four shining ones pulled themselves from four steaming craters. They stood naked with heaving chests, tense muscles and eyes set like flint toward Jerusalem.

They were the gods Ba'al, Ares, Serapis, and Poseidon, the four bound angels of the legions, now freed to oversee the armies of Rome.

Free to launch Armageddon.

> Then an angel blew his trumpet, and I heard a voice saying to the angel who had the trumpet, "Release the four angels who are bound at the great river Euphrates." So the four angels, who had been prepared for the hour, the day, the month, and the year, were released to kill a third of the people of the land.
>
> Apocalypse 9:15

This story concludes with the next novel in the series, *Judgment: Wrath of the Lamb*.

• • • • •

If you liked this book, then please help me out by writing a positive review of it wherever you purchased it. That is one of the best ways to say thank you to me as an author. It really does help my sales and status. Thanks! — *Brian Godawa*

• • • • •

More Books by Brian Godawa

See www.Godawa.com for more information on other books by Brian Godawa. Check out his other series below:

Chronicles of the Nephilim

Chronicles of the Nephilim is a saga that charts the rise and fall of the Nephilim giants of Genesis 6 and their place in the evil plans of the fallen angelic Sons of God called, "The Watchers." The story starts in the days of Enoch and continues on through the Bible until the arrival of the Messiah, Jesus. The prelude to Chronicles of the Apocalypse. ChroniclesOfTheNephilim.com

Chronicles of the Watchers

Chronicles of the Watchers is a series that charts the influence of spiritual principalities and powers over the course of human history. The kingdoms of man in service to the gods of the nations at war. Completely based on ancient historical and mythological research. ChroniclesOfTheWatchers.com

Biblical & Historical Research

For additional free biblical and historical scholarly research related to this novel and series, go to Godawa.com > Chronicles of the Apocalypse > *Scholarly Research*.

BIBLIOGRAPHY OF BOOKS ON BIBLE PROPHECY THAT INFLUENCED AUTHOR BRIAN GODAWA

For additional biblical and historical research related to this series, go to www.ChroniclesoftheApocalypse.com and Click on Scholarly Research.

John L. Bray, *Matthew 24 Fulfilled*, (American Vision; 5th Edition, 2009).

David Chilton, *The Days of Vengeance: An Exposition of the Book of Revelation*, (Dominion Press; 1st Edition, 2006).

Gary DeMar, *10 Popular Prophecy Myths Exposed: The Last Days Might Not Be as Near as You Think*, (American Vision, 2010).

— *Last Days Madness: Obsession of the Modern Church* Wolgemuth & Hyatt Pub; 4th Revised edition (September 1999).

— *Left Behind: Separating Fact From Fiction*, (American Vision; First edition, 2010).

— *Why the End of the World is Not in Your Future: Identifying the Gog-Magog Alliance*, (American Vision; First edition, 2010)

Kenneth L. Gentry, Jr., *The Beast of Revelation*, (American Vision, 2002).

— *Before Jerusalem Fell: Dating the Book of Revelation*, (Victorious Hope Publishing, 2010)

— *The Book of Revelation Made Easy: You Can Understand Bible Prophecy*, American Vision (December 31, 2009).

— *The Divorce of Israel: A Redemptive-Historical Interpretation of Revelation Vol. 1 & 2*, (Liberty Alliance, 2016).

— *Navigating the Book of Revelation: Special Studies on Important Issues*, (GoodBirth Ministries, 2011).

— *The Olivet Discourse Made Easy*, (Apologetics Group. 2010)

— *Perilous Times: A Study in Eschatological Evil*, (Covenant Media Press, 1999).

Kenneth L. Gentry Jr., and Thomas Ice, *The Great Tribulation: Past or Future?: Two Evangelicals Debate the Question*, (Kregel Academic & Professional, 1999).

John H. Gerstner, *Wrongly Dividing the Word of Truth: A Critique of Dispensationalism 3rd Edition* (Nicene Council, 2009).

Hank Hanegraaff, *The Apocalypse Code: Find out What the Bible Really Says About the End Times and Why It Matters Today,* (Thomas Nelson, 2010).

George Peter Holford, *The Destruction of Jerusalem: An Absolute and Irresistible Proof of the Divine Origin of Christianity*, (Covenant Media Press; 6th American edition, 2001).

Peter J. Leithart, *The Promise of His Appearing: An Exposition of Second Peter* (Canon Press, 2004).

Keith A. Mathison, *Dispensationalism: Rightly Dividing the People of God?* (P & R Publishing, 1995).

Philip Mauro, *The Seventy Weeks and the Great Tribulation: A Study of the Last Two Visions of Daniel and the Olivet Discourse of the Lord Jesus Christ* (Hamilton Brothers, 1922).

R.C. Sproul, *The Last Days According to Jesus: When Did Jesus Say He Would Return? 2nd Edition,* (Baker Pub Group, 1998).

If You Like This Novel
Get This Free eBook
Limited Time Offer

FREE

The Research Notes behind the Novel Series
Chronicles of the Apocalypse

By Brian Godawa. Over one hundred pages of Biblical and historical
sources, with citations, addressing each verse in Matthew 24.

Download
Free eBook

https://godawa.com/matthew-24/

Get the Theology behind This Novel Series

The Biblical Theology behind Chronicles of the Apocalypse

By Brian Godawa

Brian Godawa reveals the Biblical and historical basis for the Last Days presented in the novel series *Chronicles of the Apocalypse*. Godawa unveils the biblical meaning of many End Times notions like the Last Days, cosmic catastrophes, the Abomination of Desolation, the antichrist, the Great Tribulation, and more!

Available in eBook, Paperback & Audiobook

https://godawa.com/get-end-times/

Are We Living in the Last Days?
Check out this Controversial Online Course!

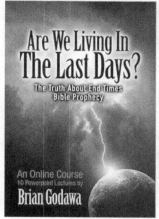

25% OFF!
Limited Time Only
10+ Intense Lectures on End Times

Powerpoint Videos with Powerful Visuals By Brian Godawa

There are so many Christians teaching outrageous things about Bible Prophecy these days. It's enough to frustrate the serious Bible student. What would you think if you found out most all of it is simply mistaken? What if you found out that the ancient mindset of the Jewish writers was influenced by the Old Testament imagery of the past, and not a crystal ball gaze into our modern future? What if you found out that everything that modern prophecy pundits are looking for—the antichrist, the Beast, the Tribulation, the Rapture—was not what they told you it was, but something different? Includes lots of colorful and helpful PowerPoint visuals, charts, pictures, and film clips for a much richer presentation of the material. PLUS a bunch of FREE Bonuses!

Check out the Free Introduction & Learn More
(Use Code NTBA84 for 25% Discount)

Click Here
For Details

LastDaysCourse.com

GET MORE BIBLICAL IMAGINATION

Get More Biblical Imagination

Sign up Online For The Godawa Chronicles

www.Godawa.com

Insider information on the novels of Brian Godawa
Special Discounts, New Releases,
Bible Mysteries!

We won't spam you.

CHRONICLES OF THE NEPHILIM

The Prequel Series to Chronicles of the Apocalypse. Nephilim Giants, Watchers, Cosmic War.

www.Godawa.com

CHRONICLES OF THE WATCHERS

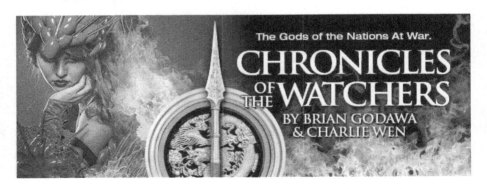

A Series About the Watchers in History.
Action, Romance, Gods, Monsters & Men.

The first novel is *Jezebel: Harlot Queen of Israel.*

www.Godawa.com

  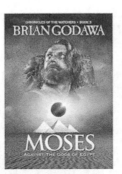

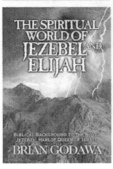 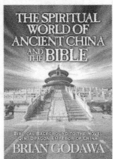 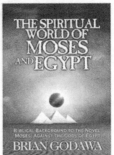

ABOUT THE AUTHOR

Brian Godawa is the screenwriter for the award-winning feature film, *To End All Wars*, starring Kiefer Sutherland. It was awarded the Commander in Chief Medal of Service, Honor and Pride by the Veterans of Foreign Wars, won the first Heartland Film Festival by storm, and showcased the Cannes Film Festival Cinema for Peace.

He previously adapted to film the best-selling supernatural thriller novel *The Visitation* by author Frank Peretti for Ralph Winter (*X-Men, Wolverine*), and wrote and directed *Wall of Separation*, a PBS documentary, and *Lines That Divide*, a documentary on stem cell research.

Mr. Godawa's scripts have won multiple awards in respected screenplay competitions, and his articles on movies and philosophy have been published around the world. He has traveled around the United States teaching on movies, worldviews, and culture to colleges, churches and community groups.

His popular book *Hollywood Worldviews: Watching Films with Wisdom and Discernment* (InterVarsity Press) is used as a textbook in schools around the country. In the Top 10 of Biblical Fiction on Amazon, his first novel series, *Chronicles of the Nephilim*, is an imaginative retelling of Biblical stories of the Nephilim giants, the secret plan of the fallen Watchers, and the War of the Seed of the Serpent with the Seed of Eve. The sequel series, *Chronicles of the Apocalypse*, tells the story of the apostle John's book of Revelation, and *Chronicles of the Watchers* recounts true history through the Watcher paradigm.

Find out more about his other books, lecture tapes and DVDs for sale at his website, **www.godawa.com**.

BLANK PAGE

BLANK PAGE

BLANK PAGE

BLANK PAGE

BLANK PAGE

END NOTES

[1] **Eleazar ben Simon**: Actually, Eleazar ben Ananias was captain of the temple who stopped the sacrifice. But a different Eleazar, son of Simon was a warrior who eventually took over the inner temple. So I combined both of these characters into one in order to simplify the story.

Eleazer stops the sacrifice, which is considered the final act of war: Flavius Josephus, *The Wars of the Jews* 2.17.2 §409-410 "Eleazar, the son of Ananias the high priest, a very bold youth, who was at that time governor of the temple, persuaded those that officiated in the divine service to receive no gift or sacrifice for any foreigner. And this was the true beginning of our war with the Romans; for they rejected the sacrifice of Caesar on this account; (410) and when many of the high priests and principal men besought them not to omit the sacrifice which it was customary for them to offer for their princes, they would not be prevailed upon. These relied much upon their multitude, for the most flourishing part of the innovators assisted them, but they had the chief regard to Eleazar, the governor of the temple." Flavius Josephus and William Whiston, *The Works of Josephus: Complete and Unabridged* (Peabody: Hendrickson, 1987), 624.

[2] Flavius Josephus, *The Wars of the Jews* 2.499-555.

[3] Flavius Josephus, *Wars of the Jews* 2.20.4 §566.

[4] The entire Jewish population of Damascus, numbering 10,000 was forced into a stadium and murdered by Syrian Greeks. (Wars 2.20.2)

Jewish forces attacked the city of Ashkelon twice and lost 18,000 men. (Wars, 3.1.2-3)

Word spread all the way to Alexandria, Egypt, where Jews and Greeks rioted, causing 50,000 Jewish deaths. (Wars 2.18.7-8)

[5] Josephus, *Wars of the Jews* 2.22.1 §651.

[6] Josephus, *Life* 45-47 §233-245.

[7] Josephus, *Life* 38-40; *Wars of the Jews* 2.21.8.

[8] Josephus, *Wars of the Jews* 3.1.1-3; 3.2.4.

[9] Josephus, *Wars of the Jews* 3.1.1-3.

[10] **The Abomination of Desolation in Matthew 24:15 is explained in Luke 21:20 as being Jerusalem surrounded by armies**. It is the same sermon. Matthew was written to Jews who understood the reference, Luke was written to Greeks who would not, so he interpreted it for them.

Matthew 24:15–16, 34 [15] "So when you see the abomination of desolation spoken of by the prophet Daniel, standing in the holy place (let the reader understand), [16] then let those who are in Judea flee to the mountains… Truly, I say to you, this generation will not pass away until all these things take place."

Luke 21:20–21 [20] "But when you see Jerusalem surrounded by armies, then know that its desolation has come near. [21] Then let those who are in Judea flee to the mountains.

The Roman armies surrounded Jerusalem twice within Jesus' generation. Once in AD 66 led by Cestius, and once in AD 70 led by Titus.

[11] **There are a few different interpretations of when the 1290 days of Daniel 12:11 occurs**: The ceasing of the daily sacrifice and the abomination being set up in the holy land are two starting points for the 1290 days that ends in the shattering of the power of the holy people. So the ceasing of the sacrifice on behalf of

Caesar, which started the war, is the first part in mid-AD 66. But the 1290 days does not start until the second part, the abomination of desolation, is "set up" in the holy land in AD 67. I am basically using the first one, but the second one is just as viable.

"TWO STARTING POINTS FOR THE 1,290 DAYS: Daniel 12:11 gives two starting points to the 1,290 days, seemingly without an end point: "And from the time that the daily sacrifice is taken away, and the abomination of desolation is set up, there shall be one thousand two hundred and ninety days." Because it is unusual to have two beginning points, some view the taking away of the sacrifice as the beginning of the 1,290 days, with the abomination of desolation happening at the end of the 1,290 days. J. E. H. Thomson notes the following on how the grammatical construction of this verse does not support this interpretation:

> And the abomination that maketh desolate set up. At first sight the reader is inclined to… regard this as a statement of the terminus ad quem [end point]. The grammatical difficulties against this view are forcible…Yet it seems strange that two termini a quo [starting points] should be assigned and no terminus ad quem.

That Daniel 12:11 gives two starting points for the 1,290 days (the daily sacrifice taken away and the abomination of desolation) is not as strange as it first seems. The end point has already been supplied in v. 7; it would be the shattering of Daniel's people. Thus, the glorious Man was saying from the time that the daily sacrifice was removed and the one who would make the Jewish nation desolate came (the abomination of desolation) to the shattering of the Jewish nation would be 1,290 days or 43 months.

"I believe the removal of the daily sacrifice that Daniel 12:11 speaks of is not the cessation of sacrifice that happened near the end of the Jewish war (in late July of AD 70) but the removal of the sacrifice the Jews offered twice a day on behalf of the emperor (Josephus, The Jewish War 2, 10, 4); this occurred in the summer of AD 66. This change in the sacrifice marked the beginning of the Jewish war with Rome."

McKenzie PhD, Duncan W.. *The Antichrist and the Second Coming: A Preterist Examination Volume I* (K-Locations 3672-3685). Xulon Press. K-Edition.

"The primary indicator of the Jewish rebellion involved the leaders of the revolt refusing to allow any sacrifices in the Temple from Gentiles. This resulted in the taking away of the daily sacrifice that was being offered for the emperor. According to Josephus, "This action laid the foundation of the war with Rome; for they renounced in consequence the sacrifices offered for Rome and the emperor."

"The outcome of this taking away of the daily sacrifice for the emperor was the coming of the one who would make the Jewish nation desolate; this was the abomination of desolation (Dan. 9:27). Responding to Nero's order to crush the Jewish rebellion, Titus marched the fifteenth legion from Egypt up the length of the Holy Land to rendezvous with his father at Ptolemais on the western border of Galilee. This coming of Titus happened around February of AD 67 as he marched a wing of the Roman army through the sacred land of Israel. This was the abomination of desolation that Jesus warned those in Judea to flee from; all hell literally broke loose at this time (Matt. 24:15-24; cf. Rev. 6).

"Titus' coming was the beginning of the great tribulation; this culminated in the shattering of the Jewish nation 1,290 days later, in August/September of AD 70 (Dan. 12:1-7).

I thus propose that the starting point for the 1,290 days of Daniel 12:11 involved two stages. The first stage was the taking away of the daily sacrifice for the emperor (c. August AD 66); this marked the beginning of the Jewish rebellion. The second stage (which happened about six months later, c. February AD 67) was the abomination of desolation, the coming of the one who would make Israel desolate (Dan. 9:27). It was 1,290 days after Titus' coming to the Holy Land that the Jewish nation was shattered and dispersed into the nations. We thus see the meaning of Daniel 12:11 as follows: From the time that the daily sacrifice is taken away and the abomination of desolation is set up [i.e., the coming of the one who would make Israel desolate, Dan. 9:27], [to the time of the end, the shattering of the Jewish nation, Dan. 12:6-8] there shall be one thousand two hundred and ninety days."

McKenzie PhD, Duncan W.. *The Antichrist and the Second Coming: A Preterist Examination Volume I* (K-Locations 3705-3714). Xulon Press. K-Edition.

A second possibility for the 1290 days:

"It is to be noted that the two measures of time here given, 1290 days and 1335 days, both fall within the period of three years and a part, given in verse 7 as the full measure of the time of the end. This tends still further to confirm the view that by "a time, times, and a part" is meant three full rounds of the annual feasts of the Jews, and part of a fourth.

"It will further be seen from this answer that Daniel's question had reference to the very last epoch of Jewish history; for it was in that very last stage of their national existence that the daily sacrifice was caused to cease, which was by them regarded (when it came to pass in the days of the siege of Jerusalem, as we shall presently show) the harbinger of some dire calamity.

"THE TAKING AWAY OF THE DAILY SACRIFICE

"We take the marginal reading (which is the more literal) as giving the sense, the words of the margin being "and to set up the abomination, " &c. This reading would make the 1290 days the measure of time between the two specified events. But we have lately seen an interpretation, based on the text of the A. V., which makes the taking away of the daily sacrifice, and the setting up of the abomination that maketh desolate, simultaneous events, both governed by the preposition "from." But this obviously leaves the verse without meaning; for it gives a measure of time from two specified events, without stating to what that measure brings us.

"The "daily sacrifice" was the sacrifice of a lamb every morning and evening. This was to be kept up by the children of Israel throughout all their generations, and a special promise was given upon condition that this offering be continued (Ex 29: 38-45). (It should be observed that the causing of the sacrifice and oblation to cease, as foretold in (Da 9: 27), is a very different thing.)

"Now, as a matter of historic fact, the daily sacrifice was taken away during the siege of Jerusalem; and this was counted by the Jews an event of such importance, and such a portent of approaching disaster, that Josephus has recorded the very date on which it occurred, saying: "And now Titus gave orders to his soldiers that were with him to dig up the foundations of the tower of Antonia, and make a ready passage for his army to come up, while he himself had Josephus brought to him; for he had been informed that, on that very day, which was the seventeenth day of Panemus, the sacrifice called 'the daily sacrifice' had failed, and had not been offered to God for want of men to offer it; and that the people were grievously troubled at it" (Wars, VI. 2.1.)."

"The Roman army, which, by comparison of the Lord's words in (Mt 24: 15,16 Lu 21: 20,21,) is clearly seen to be "the abomination which maketh desolate, " encompassed Jerusalem before the failure of the daily sacrifice; whereas it might appear from the wording of the prophecy that those events occurred in the reverse order. But Mr. Farquharson shows that "there is nothing whatever in the verbs of the sentence to indicate which of the events should precede the other; the interval of time between them only is expressed."

"The first approach of the Roman armies under Cestius is described by Josephus in his book of Wars, II 17, 10. This was in the month corresponding to our November, A.D. 66. The taking away of the daily sacrifice was in the month Panemus, corresponding to the Hebrew Tammuz, and our July, A.D. 70 (Hartwell Horne's Chronological Table). Thus the measure of time between the two events was three years, and part of a fourth.

"But more than this: the measure 1290 days is exactly 43 great months (30 days each, according to the Hebrew method of reckoning), and inasmuch as their practice was to reckon by even weeks, months, and years the fulfilment of this part of the prophecy is seen in the fact that it is just 43 even months between the two events, ignoring the parts of the two months in which the events severally occurred."

Mauro, Philip. *The Seventy Weeks and the Great Tribulation* (K-Locations 2288-2319). K-Edition.

A third view is that the Abomination of desolation being set up is the Roman armies surrounding Jerusalem:

"Around the 6th of Av of A.D. 66, Eleazar terminated the daily sacrifice to Caesar fulfilling part of v. 11.12 According to Josephus, this act "was the true beginning of our war with the Romans."13 Hearing about this act of sedition, Agrippa immediately dispatched three thousand horsemen who seized the upper city, Mt. Zion, where they attacked the Jewish rebels who possessed the lower city and Temple.14 The Roman army with their idols to Zeus, Caesar and Rome is the abomination that causes desolation… Thus immediately after Eleazar put an end to the daily sacrifice to Caesar, Roman auxiliaries, the abomination that causes desolation, entered Jerusalem. Thus the starting point of the 1,290 days is the termination of the daily sacrifice to Caesar and the consequent abomination that causes desolation which occurred immediately thereafter.

"Counting 1290 days from these two events ends on Shabat of A.D. 70. This is the month in which the Roman army arrived outside of Jerusalem to begin preparations for what would end up being the final siege of Jerusalem.15 Remember, the Roman army with their idols to Zeus, Caesar and Rome is the abomination that causes desolation. Here one can see that there appears to have been 1,290 days from the cessation of the daily sacrifice to Caesar and the resulting abomination that causes desolation when the Roman auxiliaries fought the rebels inside Jerusalem until the Roman army, the abomination that causes desolation, arrived outside of Jerusalem again in preparation for their final assault on the city."

Daniel Chapter 12: A Preterist Commentary online. http://revelationrevolution.org/daniel-chapter-12-a-preterist-commentary/

CHAPTER 1

[1] Serapis of Alexandria: Serapis was a god in Alexandria from where Titus brought the 15th Legion into Judea. Tacitus and Suetonius both claim Vespasian had an encounter with Serapis in Alexandria right before he was declared emperor after the death of Nero. Tacitus Histories 4.81-82; Suetonius, *Vespasian* 7.1.

A statue of Serapis in Alexandria "suitably depicted a figure resembling Hades or Pluto, both being kings of the Greek underworld, and was shown enthroned with the modius, a basket/grain-measure, on his head, since it was a Greek symbol for the land of the dead. He also held a scepter in his hand indicating his rulership, with Cerberus, gatekeeper of the underworld, resting at his feet. The statue also had what appeared to be a serpent at its base, fitting the Egyptian symbol of rulership, the uraeus.

"With his (i.e. Osiris's) wife Isis, and their son Horus (in the form of Harpocrates), Serapis won an important place in the Greek world. In his 2nd-century AD Description of Greece, Pausanias notes two Serapeia on the slopes of Acrocorinth, above the rebuilt Roman city of Corinth and one at Copae in Boeotia.

"Serapis figured among the international deities whose cult was received and disseminated throughout the Roman Empire, with Anubis sometimes identified with Cerberus. At Rome, Serapis was worshiped in the Iseum Campense, the sanctuary of Isis built during the Second Triumvirate in the Campus Martius. The Roman cults of Isis and Serapis gained in popularity late in the 1st century when Vespasian experienced events he attributed to their miraculous agency while he was in Alexandria, where he stayed before returning to Rome as emperor in 70. From the Flavian Dynasty on, Serapis was one of the deities who might appear on imperial coinage with the reigning emperor. The main cult at Alexandria survived until the late 4th century." https://en.wikipedia.org/wiki/Serapis

[2] **Sons of God as divine heavenly host**: Excerpt from Brian Godawa, *Psalm 82: The Divine Council of the Gods, the Judgment of the Watchers and the Inheritance of the Nations*.

A Definition

But what exactly is this messianic cosmic battle between Christ and the powers? And how does it affect us? It is sometimes called Christus Victor, and consists of the idea that mankind's Fall in the Garden resulted in a sinfulness of humanity that was so entrenched against God, that it led to universal idolatry as embodied in the tower of Babel story (Gen 11). As a result of man's incorrigible evil, God placed all of the nations and their lands under the authority of other spiritual powers, but kept one people and their land for his own: Israel. Those Gentile nations and their gods would be at war with the promised messianic seed of Israel. But in the fullness of time, Messiah would arrive, overcome those spiritual powers of the nations and take back rule of the earth in the kingdom of God.

Gods or Men?

344

Psalm 82 is a doorway into the Christus Victor narrative because it summarizes the three-act structure of that messianic story of allotment, judgment and inheritance. Here is the full text of the Psalm in all its simple and concise glory:

> Psalm 82:1–8
> ¹ God has taken his place in the divine council;
> in the midst of the gods he holds judgment:
>
> ² "How long will you judge unjustly
> and show partiality to the wicked? *Selah*
>
> ³ Give justice to the weak and the fatherless;
> maintain the right of the afflicted and the destitute.
>
> ⁴ Rescue the weak and the needy;
> deliver them from the hand of the wicked."
>
> ⁵ They have neither knowledge nor understanding,
> they walk about in darkness;
> all the foundations of the earth are shaken.
>
> ⁶ I said, "You are gods,
> sons of the Most High, all of you;
>
> ⁷ nevertheless, like men you shall die,
> and fall like any prince."
>
> ⁸ Arise, O God, judge the earth;
> for you shall inherit all the nations!

Much scholarly debate has occurred over the identity of these "gods" of the divine council. Are they human judges who merely represent divine justice or are they actual divine beings? I am convinced that they are Yahweh's heavenly host of divine beings surrounding his throne, referred to with the technical term, "Sons of God." Here's why…

Gods, Not Men

First off, the Psalm itself uses the Hebrew word "Elohim" which is accurately translated as "gods." As much as Christians have been conditioned to think that the Bible says there are no other gods that exist but Yahweh, this simply is not biblical. I have explained elsewhere, based on orthodox scholars smarter than me (see here and here and here), that the Hebrew word for "gods," *elohim*, is not a metaphor, and it is not polytheistic. It is a reference to created yet divine beings that we sometimes imprecisely refer to as "angels." They are biblically referred to as "holy ones" (Deut 33:2-3; Heb 2:2), "host of heaven" (1 King 22:19-23) or "Sons of God" (Job 1:6; 38:7).

Both the Old Testament and the New Testament refer to false gods as having demonic spiritual reality behind their earthly façade (Deut 32:17; Psa 95:5-6 LXX; Psa 106:37-38; 1 Cor 8:4-6; 10:18-20). It is not polytheistic or henotheistic to acknowledge this biblical reality. But it does open up a view of the world that includes supernatural agents other than Yahweh and "angels" who interact with humans in history.

Psalm 89 clarifies this "assembly of gods" as being divine, not human, because it is in the heavens, not on earth.

> Psalm 89:5–7
> ⁵ Let the heavens praise your wonders, O Yahweh,
> your faithfulness in the assembly of the holy ones!
>
> ⁶ For who in the skies can be compared to Yahweh?
> Who among the gods is like Yahweh,

 a God greatly to be feared in <u>the council of the holy ones</u>,
and awesome above all who are around him?

In this text, we see that there is an assembly of gods/holy ones who surround Yahweh in the heavens. The text explicitly calls the assembly of Yahweh's holy ones "gods." But it uses the hypothetical question of incomparability with Yahweh, "who among the gods is like Yahweh?" The implied answer is none of them. They are gods, but not in the same sense as Yahweh is God. So, there you have it. The Bible itself saying that there are gods, but they are not the same kind of divinity as Yahweh. But they are called "gods." Something that makes Evangelical Christians skittish, but something one must accept if one accepts the Evangelical principle of Sola Scriptura. If the Bible says it, it's true, regardless of where our pre-conceived biases may lean.

What Would Jesus Exegete?

Suffice it to say for this article, that if the Bible says it, I believe it and that settles it. I am fine with using the term "divine beings" if you want to feel more comfortable, but the bottom line is that the Sons of God who surround Yahweh's heavenly throne as his host are divine.

Jesus, God in the flesh, used this very Psalm 82 to justify his claims to deity in John 10:31-39. So if Jesus himself exegetes Psalm 82 gods to be divine, then we need to agree with the author and finisher of our faith.

> John 10:34–36
> [34] Jesus answered them, "Is it not written in your Law, 'I said, you are gods'? [35] If he called them gods to whom the word of God came—and Scripture cannot be broken— [36] do you say of him whom the Father consecrated and sent into the world, 'You are blaspheming,' because I said, 'I am the Son of God'?

Jesus did not claim to be a representative human judge like other Israelite judges as some propose. That would have been a denial of his deity. Jesus was claiming to be divine. He was defining Sons of God as actual divine beings, not mere human judges. And his point in reciting Psalm 82 was to prove to them that his own claim to divinity was not blasphemous because they already accepted other beings as having divinity.

Job

This heavenly courtroom scene of legal judgment is not an anomaly. It shows up in many places throughout the Bible that indicate a clear context of spiritual beings who engage in council with Yahweh and carry out his judgments. Job 1:6 and 2:1 describe an apparently regular occurrence of "Sons of God" (*bene ha Elohim* in Hebrew) presenting themselves before Yahweh, along with the satan as legal adversary in that heavenly court.

Satan operates as a spiritual prosecutor seeking indictment of righteous Job by accusing him of self-interest in serving God. We all know the rest of the story. But the important thing for this argument is that the Sons of God are defined in Job as being present at the creation of the heavens and earth, indeed as shouting for joy (Job 38:7). Those are not human judges that existed before man was created, those are God's heavenly host of divine beings.

There are plenty of other passages that describe the divine council around Yahweh of these heavenly beings who counsel with him and carry out his decisions with duly delegated legal responsibility (1 King 22:19-23; Deut 32:43 LXX; Zech 2:13-3:7; Isa 6:8ff). You can read more about this theological paradigm in my book <u>When Giants Were Upon the Earth</u>.

[3] **Ancient peoples believed divine principalities and powers ruled over earthly powers**: Philo, On the Giants 2:6-8 "II. (6) "And when the angels of God saw the daughters of men that they were beautiful, they took unto themselves wives of all of them whom they chose." Those beings, whom other philosophers call demons, Moses usually calls angels; and they are souls hovering in the air. (7) And let no one suppose, that what is here stated is a fable, for it is necessarily true that the universe must be filled with living things in all its parts, since every one of its primary and elementary portions contains its appropriate animals and such as are consistent with its nature;—the earth containing terrestrial animals, the sea and the rivers containing aquatic animals, and the fire such as are born in the fire (but it is said, that such as these last are found chiefly in Macedonia), and the heaven containing the stars: (8) for these also are entire souls pervading the universe,

being unadulterated and divine, inasmuch as they move in a circle, which is the kind of motion most akin to the mind, for every one of them is the parent mind. It is therefore necessary that the air also should be full of living beings. And these beings are invisible to us, inasmuch as the air itself is not visible to mortal sight." Charles Duke Yonge with Philo of Alexandria, The Works of Philo: Complete and Unabridged (Peabody, MA: Hendrickson, 1995), 152.

"Accordingly, so long as my eyes are not deprived of that spectacle with which they are never sated, so long as I may behold the sun, and the moon, so long as I may fix my gaze upon the other planets, so long as I may trace out their risings and settings, their periods, and the reason for the swiftness or the slowness of their wanderings . . . so long as I may be with these, and in so far as it is permitted to a man, to commune with celestial beings, so long as I may keep my mind directed ever to the sight of kindred things on high, what difference does it make to me what soil I tread upon? (Seneca Ad Helviam 8.5; LCL)

"Visions in the sky, Seneca promises, involve the following:

"You will see the gleaming of countless stars, you will see one star flooding everything with his light and the sun that marks off the spaces of day and night in his daily course, and in his annual course distributes even more equably the periods of summer and winter. You will see the moon taking his place by night, who as she meets her brother borrows from him a pale, reflected light, now quite hidden, now overhanging the earth with her white face exposed, ever changing as she waxes and wanes, ever different from her last appearance. You will see the five planets pursuing their different courses and sparkling down to earth from opposite directions; on even the slightest motions of these hang the fortunes of nations, and the greatest and smallest happenings are shaped to accord with the progress of a kindly or unkindly star. (Seneca Ad Marciam 18.5; LCL)

"A devoted sky student, often involved in alternate states of consciousness, advises that by contemplating the harmonious movements of the stars the devotee himself "participates in their immortality, and already, before his appointed hour, converses with the gods" (Vettius Valens 9.8)."

Bruce J. Malina and John J. Pilch, Social Science Commentary on the Deutero-Pauline Letters (Fortress Press 2013) 444.

Plato on the allotment of the gods: "Once upon a time the gods were taking over by lot the whole earth according to its regions,—not according to the results of strife: for it would not be reasonable to suppose that the gods were ignorant of their own several rights, nor yet that they attempted to obtain for themselves by means of strife a possession to which others, as they knew, had a better claim. So by just allotments they received each one his own, and they settled their countries; and when they had thus settled them...Like as we previously stated concerning the allotments of the Gods, that they portioned out the whole earth, here into larger allotments and there into smaller, and provided for themselves shrines and sacrifices"

Plato, Critias 109b, 113b-113c - Plato in Twelve Volumes, Vol. 9 translated by W.R.M. Lamb. Cambridge, MA, Harvard University Press; London, William Heinemann Ltd. 1925. http://classics.mit.edu/Plato/critias.html

[4] **The Allottment of the Nations to the Watchers**: Excerpt from Brian Godawa, _Psalm 82: The Divine Council of the Gods, the Judgment of the Watchers and the Inheritance of the Nations_.

In the previous footnote, I defined the biblical motif of Christus Victor as Christ's victory over the spiritual powers who ruled sinful mankind. I defined the divine council biblically as an assembly of gods, called "Sons of God," "holy ones," and "heavenly host" who surround Yahweh, engage in legal counsel with him and carry out his decisions.

But the next question is, how did man come under the rule and authority of these gods, these divine beings from Yahweh's heavenly host?

I am using Psalm 82 as a portal into this fascinating storyline of the Bible. So let's take a look again at what it says.

Psalm 82:1–8
[1] God has taken his place in the divine council;
in the midst of the gods he holds judgment:

[2] "How long will you judge unjustly
and show partiality to the wicked? *Selah*

[3] Give justice to the weak and the fatherless;
maintain the right of the afflicted and the destitute.

[4] Rescue the weak and the needy;
deliver them from the hand of the wicked."

So we see that for some reason, God has given some of these members from his divine council a responsibility to rule over mankind on earth. Where did this come from? Why would God do such a thing? Isn't God alone the judge of all the earth? And why is he blaming failure to rule on divine beings? Does that make them fallen angels?

To answer those questions, we need to go back to the beginning. Not Genesis 1, but rather, the beginning of the allotment of the nations to the gods. Back to the Tower of Babel. But rather than going straight to Genesis 11, that tells the story of Babel, we need to read what Moses reveals about Babel in Deuteronomy 32.

The Deuteronomy 32 Worldview

Deuteronomy is famously known as the Song of Moses. In it, Moses sings a song of the story of Israel and how she had come to be God's chosen nation. He begins by glorifying God and then telling them to "remember the days of old" (v. 7).

Deuteronomy 32:8–9
[8] When the Most High gave to the nations their inheritance,
when he divided mankind,

he fixed the borders of the peoples
according to the number of the sons of God.

[9] But the LORD's portion is his people,
Jacob his allotted heritage.

The context of this passage is the Tower of Babel incident in Genesis 11. It's the only "division of mankind" in the text of Genesis. Rebellious humanity sought divinity in unified rebellion, so God separated them by confusing their tongues, which divided them into the seventy nations described in Genesis 10. The incident at Babel led to the creation of nations and their ownership of those territorial lands as the "inheritance" of those peoples. Nations are essentially God's creation to protect mankind from destroying itself through idolatrous one world global unity in wickedness.

The apostle Paul referred to this allotment of national boundaries in Acts 17:26 when he said that God "made from one man every nation of mankind to live on all the face of the earth, having <u>determined allotted periods and the boundaries of their dwelling places</u>." That one man from whom every nation was made is not Adam, but Noah, because the allotment of nations occurred at Babel, not the Garden.

But that's not all. Deuteronomy 32 says that the borders of those nations were fixed "according to the number of the Sons of God." That is, the Sons of God are in authority over these nations, both geographically, and spiritually. This allotment is in contrast with Yahweh's allotment of Jacob. The seventy nations were allotted to the Sons of God, in the same way that Yahweh allotted to himself the nation of Israel, described as (the people of) "Jacob."

And allotment is used synonymously in the passage with inheritance and heritage. In fact, the inheritance or allotment of land is one of the major themes of the Old Testament. God promises the Land of Canaan as an inheritance to the twelve tribes of Israel.

Joshua 11:23
23 So Joshua took the whole land, according to all that the LORD had spoken to Moses. And Joshua gave it for an inheritance to Israel according to their tribal allotments.

Allotment and inheritance are covenantal words related to ownership of land.

Since Genesis 10 describes seventy nations, the number of the Sons of God here must be seventy to match those nations. Or maybe seventy groups of Sons of God. But who are these seventy chosen divine beings? They can't be the myriad of "ten thousands" of heavenly host usually described as being around Yahweh's throne (Deut 33:2-3; Dan 7:10). They are only seventy. Yet Psalm 82 clearly states that they are part of that divine council. Then, who are they?

Are the Sons of God in Psalm 82 Already Evil?

Psalm 82:3-4 describes these gods as being given responsibility to administer justice over the peoples. The commands that God gives them about not showing partiality, giving justice and rescuing the weak, are all expressions found in the Law and the Prophets (Deut 1:16-17; Jer 22:3; Prov 24:11). The gods of the nations were supposed to rule according to God's justice.

Another Psalm reflects the same injustice of the ruling gods and their guilt before God's Word.

Psalm 58:1–2
1 Do you indeed decree what is right, you gods? Do you judge the children of man uprightly? 2 No, in your hearts you devise wrongs; your hands deal out violence on earth.

A shallow reading of both Psalm 82 and 58, gives one the impression that these "gods" are good spiritual powers that are entrusted with authority, since God would not impose bad rulers, would he? And then it appears that they fail to rule justly and end in darkness, which leads to their punishment in 82:7 of "dying like men," or "falling" like any other earthly ruler. So they sound like good divine beings gone bad.

But I think this is not an accurate understanding. I will argue that the Sons of God who inherited the nations at Babel (Deut 32:8-9) and ruled those nations in antiquity (Psa 82:2-3) were already fallen and evil when they received their allotment. Here's why...

First, the dominant paradigm of the Old Testament is the single nation of Israel as set apart by Yahweh to be a light to the darkened world of the Gentile nations, considered as a whole to be against God (Isa 49:6; Psa 2:1-2). All the nations worshipped gods that were not Yahweh. And even by the time of the New Testament, the Jews considered the word Gentile to be synonymous with sinner (Matt 5:47; 10:5; 18:17; Act 4:25-26). Paul writes in Galatians 2:15, "We ourselves are Jews by birth and not Gentile sinners." So the biblical understanding of nations in Genesis 11, Deut 32 and Psalm 82 are Gentile nations who are generically idolaters.

Second, let us not forget that all the nations created at Babel consisted of people in rebellion against Yahweh at the very start. The confusion of tongues and division of mankind was a judgment for sinful man who had sought deity with their pagan temples to the gods. So the context of Deut 32:8-10 is division as judgment, not as neutral separation.

Third, earlier in Deuteronomy, Moses clarifies God's command not to worship the heavenly host, defined interchangeably as both gods and as astronomical bodies (sun, moon and stars). But he states that he allotted those gods to all the other peoples.

Deuteronomy 4:19–20
19 And beware lest you raise your eyes to heaven, and when you see the sun and the moon and the stars, all the host of heaven, you be drawn away and bow down to them and serve them, things that Yahweh your God has allotted to all the peoples under the whole heaven. 20 But Yahweh has taken you and brought you out of the iron furnace, out of Egypt, to be a people of his own inheritance, as you are this day.

This allotment of the gods/host of heaven to the peoples is reminiscent of the description of God "giving over" pagans to their idolatrous worship of creation in Romans 1:24-28. The contrast of God setting apart Israel "to be a people for his own inheritance" in Deut 4:20 after the allotment of the heavenly host in verse 19 is a reiteration of the allotment contrast in Deuteronomy 32. These verses refer to the same allotted inheritance.

In Deuteronomy 4 it's clear that Yahweh did not give the nations to be ruled by righteous heavenly host who then fell through accepting undeserved worship. Rather, Yahweh gave the host of heaven to all the peoples to worship as their gods because they were already idolaters. He was "giving them over" to their idolatry and giving the false gods their own people to rule over.

On first glance the phrase "to all the peoples under the whole heaven," would appear to mean everyone, including Israelites. But the context contradicts that inclusion when Moses says, "But Yahweh has taken you (Israel) to be a people of his own inheritance." "All the peoples under the whole heaven" is contrasted with Israel, not included with her.

Another passage in Deuteronomy reinforces this notion of sinful nations allotted to fallen gods. In Deuteronomy 29:26 Moses tells the Israelites that when they entered the land of Canaan, they "went and served other gods and worshiped them, gods whom they had not known and whom he had not allotted to them." So God allotted the fallen gods of the heavenly host to the Gentile nations of Canaan.

So, why does Psalm 82 read as if these Sons of God were righteous beings to start? Well, I don't think it does. I think it is the same principle involved with the giving of the Law of God to man. God did not give the Law to a righteous people, hoping they would keep it and then they failed to achieve that righteous obedience. Rather, God gave the law to an *already sinful* people to show them their sin and thus their need for atonement (Rom 5:12-14). In the same way, God gives those fallen gods their fallen humanity to rule over in their fallenness. And then the Law exposes the unrighteousness of their rule.

Though I am not dogmatic about the Sons of God being already fallen when they were allotted the nations, I would argue that if they were originally righteous, they must have fallen very quickly, maybe within a few years of Babel. The evidence of the earliest civilization after the Flood that we know of, ancient Sumer, already contains a highly developed sophisticated religion of idolatrous polytheism.

The earliest cultures referred to in the Bible after the Flood are all idolatrous and polytheistic to the core when we meet them: the Canaanites, the Egyptians, and the Amorites, from which God called Abraham (Gen 12). We simply have no historical or biblical evidence of a period of righteous spiritual rulers or righteous worship of Yahweh after Babel. If there was, it didn't last long enough to merit historical significance or inclusion in the Scriptures.

It makes more sense that Babel proved mankind's incorrigible depravity. Even after the Flood, they would not worship Yahweh. So Yahweh gave them over to the false gods they already worshipped. Since morality is inherently part of the creation, and is not relative or subjective, then even fallen angels who are awarded territory are still accountable for their behavior. The Sons of God could not claim they were just following orders or performing God's will at their spiritual Nuremburg Trial to come (Rom 9:19-23).

The Sons of God are Also Called Watchers

One last aspect of the divine council is necessary to understand the big picture in Scripture: the Sons of God who have been allotted the Gentile nations are also called "Watchers," for the very simple reason that they were given the responsibility of watching over the nations they were given.

In Daniel 10:4-7 the prophet receives a vision at the Tigris river that includes a "man" described in terms reserved in Scripture for divine beings (see Ezekiel 1). Some scholars even argue it could be a pre-incarnate Jesus Christ.

That divine holy one then describes a scenario of heavenly "princes" at war.

> Daniel 10:13; 20-21
> [13] The prince of the kingdom of Persia withstood me twenty-one days, but Michael, one of the chief princes, came to help me, for I was left there with the kings of Persia…
>
> [20] Then he said, "Do you know why I have come to you? But now I will return to fight against the prince of Persia; and when I go out, behold, the prince of Greece will come. [21] But I will tell you

what is inscribed in the book of truth: there is none who contends by my side against these except Michael, your prince.

In this passage, we see that the notion of national principalities and powers ruling over earthly kingdoms continued even past the exile into Daniel's period. The previous prophecies of Daniel 2 and 7-8 had predicted Persia and Greece to be at war, as one kingdom was replaced by the other. But these princes in Daniel 10 are not the earthly rulers, but rather their heavenly counterparts. There is a principality of Persia, a principality of Greece, and Michael the archangel is considered the principality of Israel.

The biblical picture is that the heavenly and earthly rulers were tied together in unity, so that when there was a war on earth, there was a corresponding war in heaven. So much so, that the fates of both heaven and earth were linked. Here are a couple examples from Scripture that reinforce this theme:

In the time of the Judges when Israel fought the pagan kings of Canaan, the battle with Sisera at the river of Megiddo was described within the same paragraph from both perspectives of heaven and earth.

Judges 5:19–20
[19] "The kings came, they fought; then fought the kings of Canaan, at Taanach, by the waters of Megiddo; they got no spoils of silver. [20] From heaven the stars fought, from their courses they fought against Sisera.

identical language is used to link the fighting of the kings on earth with the fighting of heavenly stars. Again, remember, the heavenly host were often considered interchangeably with the heavenly rulers over the earth. When the kings on earth were at war, so their allotted gods were at war.

Another strong example of this equivalence between heavenly and earthly rulers is found in the predicted judgment of them in Isaiah who describes a synchronized judgment of earthly kings and their heavenly rulers:

Isaiah 24:21–23
[21] On that day the LORD will punish
the host of heaven, in heaven,
and the kings of the earth, on the earth.

But where do I get the idea that these heavenly rulers are called Watchers? Well, jumping back to Daniel 4, he has another vision where he tells us Watchers are holy ones that come down from heaven.

Daniel 4:13, 17
[13] "I saw in the visions of my head as I lay in bed, and behold, a watcher, a holy one, came down from heaven…

[17] The sentence is by the decree of the watchers, the decision by the word of the holy ones, to the end that the living may know that the Most High rules the kingdom of men and gives it to whom he will and sets over it the lowliest of men.'

The Watchers are called "holy ones" (Deut 33:2-3; Jude 14), which we saw in a previous post, is another name for the heavenly host (1King 22:19) of the divine council (Psa 82:1), which are also called the Sons of God (Job 5:1; 15:15). So all these terms refer to the same divine beings. Though we do not see the term Watchers used specifically in Daniel 10, we see those ruling principalities of the nations that are also synonymous with the ruling gods/Sons of God/heavenly host of Psalm 82 and Deut 32.

I explain the ramifications of this in detail in my book When Giants Were Upon the Earth.

CHAPTER 2

[1] **Cassandra is ruminating over this passage**. It refers to the destruction of Jerusalem specifically for rejecting Jesus as Messiah, which would end in eternal separation as well.

2 Thessalonians 1:7–10 [7] and to grant relief to you who are afflicted as well as to us, when the Lord Jesus is revealed from heaven with his mighty angels [8] in flaming fire, inflicting vengeance on those who do not know God and on those who do not obey the gospel of our Lord Jesus. [9] They

will suffer the punishment of eternal destruction, away from the presence of the Lord and from the glory of his might, [10] when he comes on that day to be glorified in his saints, and to be marveled at among all who have believed, because our testimony to you was believed.

[2] **Consider the parables of Jesus, given to his contemporaries that were about rejecting him.** As already described elsewhere, the "end of the age" was not the universal end of the world, but the localized end of the old covenant age in that first century.

The "sons of the kingdom" who are thrown out are not Gentiles, but unbelieving Jews. Gentiles did not have the kingdom to lose, the Jews did.

> Matthew 8:11–12 [11] I tell you, many will come from east and west and recline at table with Abraham, Isaac, and Jacob in the kingdom of heaven, [12] while the sons of the kingdom will be thrown into the outer darkness. In that place there will be weeping and gnashing of teeth."

> Matthew 13:41–43 [41] The Son of Man will send his angels, and they will gather out of his kingdom all causes of sin and all law-breakers, [42] and throw them into the fiery furnace. In that place there will be weeping and gnashing of teeth. [43] Then the righteous will shine like the sun in the kingdom of their Father. He who has ears, let him hear.

> Matthew 13:49–50 [49] So it will be at the end of the age. The angels will come out and separate the evil from the righteous [50] and throw them into the fiery furnace. In that place there will be weeping and gnashing of teeth.

In this parable, Jesus describes, not the end of the world, but the Gospel as a wedding feast that the Jews reject, so God destroys their city (AD 70) and offers it to the Gentiles in response. This was exactly the message of Paul in the book of Acts.

> Matthew 22:6–14 [6] while the rest seized his servants, treated them shamefully, and killed them. [7] The king was angry, and he sent his troops and destroyed those murderers and burned their city. [8] Then he said to his servants, 'The wedding feast is ready, but those invited were not worthy. [9] Go therefore to the main roads and invite to the wedding feast as many as you find.' [10] And those servants went out into the roads and gathered all whom they found, both bad and good. So the wedding hall was filled with guests. [11] "But when the king came in to look at the guests, he saw there a man who had no wedding garment. [12] And he said to him, 'Friend, how did you get in here without a wedding garment?' And he was speechless. [13] Then the king said to the attendants, 'Bind him hand and foot and cast him into the outer darkness. In that place there will be weeping and gnashing of teeth.' [14] For many are called, but few are chosen."

The parable of the talents is not about all people at the end of the world, it is about the Jews who knew God was returning to Zion in Messiah, but did not invest in the New Covenant kingdom. They are the old wineskins that cannot contain new wine.

> Matthew 25:29–30 [29] For to everyone who has will more be given, and he will have an abundance. But from the one who has not, even what he has will be taken away. [30] And cast the worthless servant into the outer darkness. In that place there will be weeping and gnashing of teeth.'

The wrath to come:

Some believe that John the Baptist's call for repentance to avoid the "wrath to come" was a reference to hell. It was not. It was another reference to the destruction of Jerusalem because as Malachi predicted, Elijah would come right before the Day of the Lord. Jesus said John was Elijah, so his message was not merely about Messiah coming for salvation, but for judgment as well.

> Malachi 3:1–5
> [1] "Behold, I send my messenger, and he will prepare the way before me. And the Lord whom you seek will suddenly come to his temple; and the messenger of the covenant in whom you delight, behold, he is coming, says the LORD of hosts. [2] But who can endure the day of his coming, and who can stand when he appears? …[5] "Then I will draw near to you for judgment.

Malachi 4:5–6

[5] "Behold, I will send you Elijah the prophet before the great and awesome day of the LORD comes. [6] And he will turn the hearts of fathers to their children and the hearts of children to their fathers, lest I come and strike the land with a decree of utter destruction."

Matthew 11:13–14

[13] For all the Prophets and the Law prophesied until John, [14] and if you are willing to accept it, he is Elijah who is to come.

The first coming of Messiah involved both salvation AND judgment:

Isaiah 61:1–2

[1] The Spirit of the Lord GOD is upon me, because the LORD has anointed me to bring good news to the poor; he has sent me to bind up the brokenhearted, to proclaim liberty to the captives, and the opening of the prison to those who are bound; [2] to proclaim the year of the LORD's favor, and the day of vengeance of our God; to comfort all who mourn;

Many Christians point out that Jesus said he fulfilled this passage in Luke 4 but stopped and did not quote the part about the day of vengeance. But he DID quote that second part later in the Olivet Discourse when he prophesied about the destruction of Jerusalem in AD 70.

Luke 21:20–22

[20] "But when you see Jerusalem surrounded by armies, then know that its desolation has come near. [21] Then let those who are in Judea flee to the mountains, and let those who are inside the city depart, and let not those who are out in the country enter it, [22] for these are days of vengeance, to fulfill all that is written.

[3] **Elihu quotes:** Matthew 16:27; 25:31.

[4] **Qumran and the belief in angelic deliverance vs. human fighting**:

"Most intriguing of all is the relation between the militancy of the War Rule and the quietism of the Community Rule. As noted above at the end of Chapter 4, the Community Rule is pacificistic only up to a point: "I will not grapple with the men of perdition until the day of revenge." The mas`kîl is described as "a man zealous for the precept, whose time is for the day of revenge," who entertains "everlasting hatred in a spirit of secrecy for the men of perdition" (1QS 9). It is well known that the settlement at Qumran was destroyed by military assault during the revolt against Rome, and was apparently defended (see Cross 1995: 60–2). While it is impossible to prove who the defenders were, the simplest hypothesis is that they were the same people who had inhabited the site for a century and a half. While the war anticipated in the War Rule has many fantastic qualities, it also shows some knowledge of realistic military tactics. The preparation of such an elaborate War Rule strongly suggests that the community was prepared to implement it, if the members believed that the appointed time had arrived. That time may very well have arrived in the war against Rome."

"The hope of the Sons of light depended on the belief that "mighty men and a host of angels are among those mustered with us, the mighty one of war is in our congregation, and the host of his spirits is with our steps, and our horsemen are [like] rainclouds and like clouds of dew covering the earth" (1QM 12:7– 8)."

John J. Collins, *Apocalypticism in the Dead Sea Scrolls* (NY: Routledge, 1997),108-109.

CHAPTER 3

[1] **Elijah's contest with the prophets of Ba'al**: 1Kings 18:20-40.

[2] **Azazel and Semyaza were the leaders of the fallen Sons of God in Genesis 6**: 1Enoch 9:6-9 "You see what Azaz`el has done; how he has taught all (forms of) oppression upon the earth. And they revealed eternal secrets which are performed in heaven (and which) man learned. 7 (Moreover) Semyaz, to whom you have given power to rule over his companions, co-operating, they went in unto the daughters of the people on earth; 8 and they lay together with them—with those women—and defiled themselves, and revealed to them

every (kind of) sin. 9 As for the women, they gave birth to giants to the degree that the whole earth was filled with blood and oppression."

James H. Charlesworth, *The Old Testament Pseudepigrapha, vol. 1* (New York; London: Yale University Press, 1983), 17.

Azazel's and Semyaza's original binding in the earth: 1 Enoch 10:4, 11-13 "the Lord said to Raphael, "Bind Azaz`el hand and foot (and) throw him into the darkness!" And he made a hole in the desert which was in Duda`el and cast him there…And to Michael God said, "Make known to Semyaza and the others who are with him, who fornicated with the women, that they will die together with them in all their defilement. 12* And when they and all their children have battled with each other, and when they have seen the destruction of their beloved ones, bind them for seventy generations underneath the rocks of the ground until the day of their judgment and of their consummation, until the eternal judgment is concluded. 13* In those days they will lead them into the bottom of the fire—and in torment—in the prison (where) they will be locked up forever."

James H. Charlesworth, *The Old Testament Pseudepigrapha, vol. 1* (New York; London: Yale University Press, 1983), 17-18.

> 1Enoch 54:4-6 ""For whom are these imprisonment chains being prepared?" 5 And he said unto me, "These are being prepared for the armies of Azaz`el, in order that they may take them and cast them into the abyss of complete condemnation, and as the Lord of the Spirits has commanded it, they shall cover their jaws with rocky stones. 6 Then Michael, Raphael, Gabriel, and Phanuel themselves shall seize them on that great day of judgment and cast them into the furnace (of fire) that is burning that day, so that the Lord of the Spirits may take vengeance on them on account of their oppressive deeds which (they performed) as messengers of Satan, leading astray those who dwell upon the earth."

James H. Charlesworth, *The Old Testament Pseudepigrapha, vol. 1* (New York; London: Yale University Press, 1983), 38.

Apollyon has the key to the Abyss: Revelation 9:1 And I saw a star fallen from heaven to earth, and he was given the key to the shaft of the bottomless pit.

The Abyss: "The Abyss was believed to be the underworld prison of evil spirits. When the demons were cast out of the demoniac by Jesus, they pleaded with him not to send them to the Abyss (Luke 8:30–31). The Abyss was also considered the realm of the dead. Jesus, after his death, descended into the Abyss ("deep" NIV; Rom. 10:7 quoting Deut. 30:13 LXX). However, in Revelation the name Hades is used for the realm of the dead (cf. Rev. 1:18; 6:8; 20:13, 14), reflecting the Septuagint in which the Hebrew Sheol is translated by "Hades" rather than "Abyss."

Clinton E. Arnold, *Zondervan Illustrated Bible Backgrounds Commentary: Hebrews to Revelation., vol. 4* (Grand Rapids, MI: Zondervan, 2002), 304.

"While the key to the abyss is mentioned again in 20:1, the notion of a shaft that could be locked and unlocked is implied rather than explicitly stated. In the other two references, in Rev 11:7 and 17:8, the abyss is the place from which the beast is said to ascend. PGM XIII.169–70, 481–83 indicates a belief in a supernatural being who rules over the abyss: "a god appeared, he was put in charge of the abyss."

David E. Aune, *Revelation 6–16, vol. 52B, Word Biblical Commentary* (Dallas: Word, Incorporated, 1998), 526.

"In Job the "abyss" (41:23[22]–24[23]) is the abode of the cosmic sea dragon (40:17[12]; 40:25[20]; 41:10[9]); cf. also Isa. 27:1 and Ps. 73(74):12–13, with Amos 9:3), who has "the appearance of the morning star" (41:10[9]), is "king of all" in his realm (41:26[25]), and is antagonistic to God (e.g., 40:32[27]). This abode became symbolic for the forces of evil (Ps. 76(77):16). The "abyss" is synonymous with the concept of Hades (Job 38:16; Ezek. 31:15; Jonah 2:6) and is the realm of suffering (Ps. 70[71]:20) and death (Exod. 15:5 [ΑΣΘ]; Isa. 51:10; 63:13; Wis. 10:19). Isa. 24:21–22 says that God will punish angels and evil kings, and "they will be gathered together as prisoners in the pit [bôr], and will be confined in prison, and after many days will be punished. Fallen angels were said to be imprisoned in the pit to await final judgment (1 En. 10:4–14; 18:11–16; 19:1; 21:7; 54:1–6; 88:1–3; 90:23–26; Jub. 5:6–14; 2 Pet. 2:4; cf. 4 Ezra 7:36; Prayer of Manasseh 3)."

G. K. Beale, *The Book of Revelation: A Commentary on the Greek Text, New International Greek Testament Commentary* (Grand Rapids, MI; Carlisle, Cumbria: W.B. Eerdmans; Paternoster Press, 1999), 493.

"The "bottomless pit" translates the phrase tou phreatos tēs abussou which literally means: "the shaft of the abyss." The word phreatos means "a relatively deep pit or shaft in the ground" (L-N 12). It is apparently the narrow entryway to the abussos, which literally means "without bottom": the a is a negative and is attached to buthos ("depths"), i.e., the unfathomable deep… Wright (2011: 86) puts the matter picturesquely: "John's conception of the present creation includes a bottomless pit which, like a black-hole in modern astrophysics, is a place of anticreation, anti-matter, or destruction and chaos."

Kenneth L. Gentry, Jr., *The Divorce of Israel: A Redemptive-Historical Interpretation of Revelation Vol. 1* (Dallas, GA: Tolle Lege Press, 2016), 729.

[3] **Angels and Watchers have flesh**: While angels are multidimensional in their ability to traverse between the heavenlies and the earth, they are described as having flesh that eats food (Gen. 18; 19:1), and can have sexual congress with human beings (Gen. 6:1-4). This is a heavenly flesh that is different from human flesh (1 Cor. 15:39-40), but is flesh nonetheless. This would make angels or divine beings such as the Watchers unlike demons who are incorporeal spirits seeking flesh to inhabit or possess.

For the difference between angels, Watchers and demons, see Brian Godawa, *When Giants Were Upon the Earth: The Watchers, the Nephilim, and the Biblical Cosmic War of the Seed* (Embedded Pictures, 2014), 275-278.

[4] **Satan is called "the ruler of this world"**: (Jn. 12:31, 14:30-31, 16:11), in 2 Cor. 4:4, "the god of this world." In Eph. 2:2 he is called the "prince of the power of the air, the spirit that is now working in the sons of disobedience." In fact, when Jesus was tempted by the satan in the desert, he offered Christ all the kingdoms of the world for his own "domain and glory; for it has been handed over to me, and I give it to whomever I wish" (Luke 4:6). It seems as if the satan is the only Watcher god in authority over the nations, like he has all the power."

Brian Godawa, *When Giants Were Upon the Earth* (Embedded Pictures, 2014), 289.

"Much tradition identified Satan as the angel of Rome, thus adapting the angels-of-the-nations idea to the situation of Roman world-hegemony. Since Rome had conquered the entire Mediterranean region and much else besides, its angel-prince had become lord of all other angel-princes of the vanquished nations. This identification was already explicit at Qumran, where Rome and the Romans (the "Kittim" of the War Scroll) are made the specific allies and agents of Satan and his host. Similarly in the New Testament, Satan as the 'archon of this world' (John 12:31; 14:30; 16:11) or 'god of this aeon' (2 Cor. 4:4) could scarcely avoid being identified as the special patron of Rome."

Walter Wink. *Naming the Powers: The Language of Power in the New Testament* (The Powers : Volume One) (Kindle Locations 405-409). Kindle Edition.

The names of Satan: Apollyon/Abaddon: "This angel is named only here in Revelation [9:11 as Apollyon], and elsewhere in the OT and early Jewish literature is mentioned only in 4Q280 10 ii 7:"[Cursed be you Ange]l of the Pit, and Spir[it of Aba]ddon" (Kobelski, Melchizedek, 43–44). While in 4Q280 and related texts these two titles are alternate ways of describing Belial, in Revelation it is not at all clear that the angel of the abyss is a designation for Satan, for he is carefully named elsewhere with a selection of aliases in two different contexts (12:9; 20:2), and neither Abaddon nor the angel of the abyss is mentioned again. The fact that ἄγγελον is articular here, however, suggests that the author expected the readers to be familiar with this figure, i.e., that the angel of the abyss is none other than Satan-Belial." David E. Aune, *Revelation 6–16, vol. 52B, Word Biblical Commentary* (Dallas: Word, Incorporated, 1998), 534.

"The "Destroyer" in Rev. 9:11 is either the devil himself or an evil representative of the devil; either alternative receives confirmation from Jewish exegetical tradition on Exodus (see below). Rev. 12:3–4 and 13:1ff. are compatible with this conclusion, since there the devil and the Beast respectively are pictured wearing royal diadems and leading evil forces. This is also in line with the same conclusion already reached about the angel's identification in 9:1." G. K. Beale, *The Book of Revelation: A Commentary on the Greek Text*, New *International Greek Testament Commentary* (Grand Rapids, MI; Carlisle, Cumbria: W.B. Eerdmans; Paternoster Press, 1999), 503.

Belial: 2 Corinthians 6:14-15. "The personification of wickedness, treachery, or the like, as Belial. In most of its OT attestations, bĕliyya'al functions as an emotive term to describe individuals or groups who commit the most heinous crimes against the Israelite religious or social order, as well as their acts." S. D. Sperling, "Belial," ed. Karel van der Toorn, Bob Becking, and Pieter W. van der Horst, *Dictionary of Deities and Demons in the Bible* (Leiden; Boston; Köln; Grand Rapids, MI; Cambridge: Brill; Eerdmans, 1999), 169.

Helel ben Shachar: Isaiah 14:12-15. Though many scholars accept this passage as having two referents, one, a historical prophecy to the King of Babylon, and the other, a spiritual allusion to Satan's pre-Edenic fall, David Lowe makes a persuasive argument that it has nothing to do with Satan. See David W. Lowe, *Deconstructing Lucifer: Reexamining the Ancient Origins of the Fallen Angel of Light*, (Seismos Publishing 2011).

Mastemah: "Mastemah appears as a noun meaning 'hostility' in OT (Hos 9:7–8) and Qumran writings. In Qumran literature the word is mostly connected with an evil angel (Belial) and in Jub. Mastemah is always a proper name for the leader of the evil angels." J. W. van Henten, "Mastemah," ed. Karel van der Toorn, Bob Becking, and Pieter W. van der Horst, *Dictionary of Deities and Demons in the Bible* (Leiden; Boston; Köln; Grand Rapids, MI; Cambridge: Brill; Eerdmans, 1999), 553.

Satan as ancient serpent and dragon: "And the great dragon was thrown down, that ancient serpent, who is called the devil and Satan, the deceiver of the whole world." Revelation 12:9.

Job 1:6-12; Zechariah 3:1-2. "The Hebrew (satan) means something like "adversary," "prosecutor," or "challenger." It speaks of an official legal function within a ruling body—in this case, Yahweh's council. When Yahweh asks the satan where he has been, we learn that his job involves investigating what is happening on earth (Job 1:7). He is, so to speak, Yahweh's eyes and ears on the ground, reporting what he has seen and heard." Michael S. Heiser, *The Unseen Realm: Recovering the Supernatural Worldview of the Bible, First Edition* (Bellingham, WA: Lexham Press, 2015), 56–57.

[5] **Vespasian's forces in Palestine:**
Legion V Macedonia and X Fretensis from Antioch
Legion XV Apollinaris that Titus marched up from Egypt.
23 auxiliary infantry cohorts
The following client kings each sent 2,000 archers and 1,000 cavalry:
Agrippa II, Sohaemus of Emesa, Antiochus IV of Commagene
Malichus II of Nabatea provided 5,000 infantry (archers) and 1,000 horsemen

Si Sheppard, *The Jewish Revolt AD 66-74* (Oxford: Osprey Publishing, 2013), 35.

The gods of those Roman forces:

Legion V Macedonia: "The ancient Macedonians worshipped the Olympic Pantheon, especially Zeus, Artemis, Heracles, and Dionysus. Ancient Greeks regarded it as an essential element of Hellenic identity to share common religious beliefs and to come together at regular intervals at Panhellenic sanctuaries (Olympia, Delphi, Nemea/Argos, etc.) in order to celebrate Panhellenic festivals. Most of the gods who were worshipped in southern Greece can also be found in the Macedonian pantheon and the names of the most important Macedonian religious festivals are also typically Greek."
https://en.wikipedia.org/wiki/Ancient_Macedonians#Religion

Legion X Fretensis: Neptune (Poseidon in Greek) was a patron deity of Legion X.

https://en.wikipedia.org/wiki/Legio_X_Fretensis

Legion XII Fulminata: In Antioch, Syria. Baal Haddad was the chief storm god of Syria: "The tablets from Ebla contain a pantheon of Canaanite gods, but some of the names and relationships are different from those at Ugarit. Concerning the deity Baal, there were either two storm gods or one storm god with two names, Baal and Hadad. By the time of Ugarit, Hadad had definitely become another name for Baal, and some cultures (e.g., the Arameans) worshiped Baal by the name Hadad. The greater prominence of the god Dagon as head of the pantheon at Ebla may explain the Ugaritic reference to Baal as "Son of Dagon." Winfried Corduan, "Baal," ed. John D. Barry et al., *The Lexham Bible Dictionary* (Bellingham, WA: Lexham Press, 2016).

Legion XV Apollinaris: Serapis was a god in Alexandria from where Titus brought the 15th Legion into Judea. Tacitus and Suetonius both claim Vespasian had an encounter with Serapis in Alexandria right before he was declared emperor after the death of Nero. Tacitus Histories 4.81-82; Suetonius, Vespasian 7.1

Commagene Client King: Commagene's gods: "The restored freedom of Commagene, now allied to Rome, allowed Antiochus leisure for his great religious expression still visible atop Nemrud Dagh. His remarkable fusions of Greek and Iranian gods satisfied the composite population, which could now worship Zeus-Oromasdes (Ahuramazda), Heracles-Artagnes, and the grandly titled Apollo-Mithras-Helios-Hermes!" Richard D. Sullivan, "Commagene (Place)," ed. David Noel Freedman, *The Anchor Yale Bible Dictionary* (New York: Doubleday, 1992), 1096.

Nabatean Client King: Hubal and Allah, the Arabic pre-Islamic deities of Nabatea: "The Qurayshite pantheon was composed principally of idols that were in the haram of Makka, that is, Hubal (the most important and oldest deity), Manaf, Isaf, and Na'ila. The pantheon of the hums and other associations was superimposed on the Qurayshite one; their principal deities were Allah (the god who brought victory to Quraysh against Abraha at the Battle of the Elephant) and three goddesses, Allat, al-'Uzza, and Manat. Allah's shrine was the Ka'ba in Makka, but the three goddesses had neither idols nor a shrine in that city. To find a shrine consecrated to one of them, one must look as far as Buss, about 100 kilometers northeast of Makka, where there was a temple of al-'Uzza. The question has been raised whether Hubal (the main god of Quraysh) and Allah (main god of the entire tribal federation around Quraysh) were not one and the same deity under two successive names: indeed, Allah (which is probably a contracted form of al-Ilah, "the God") could be a designation that consecrated Hubal's superiority over the other gods." Scott Fitzgerald Johnson, *The Oxford Handbook of Late Antiquity* (Oxford University Press, 2012), 304.

The kings of the east whose angels are bound at the Euphrates: Ahura Mazda is the god of Commagene, Hubal of Arabia and Ba'al of Syria. All these gods were over the nations' forces that made up the Roman army that marched down upon Jerusalem. At this point, they are being bound by the angels until their appointed time.

"Contrary to dispensationalists, these kings do not represent modern-day, "Oriental rulers" (Walvoord 236). Rather, they are "kings from the east," who are mentioned in a book which declares its events are near (1:3; 22:10). We should recall that the Roman forces set against Israel were comprised not only of Roman legionary troops but others from various auxiliary kings. Josephus notes that in the initial imperial engagement of the war, Vespasian added to his legions, "a considerable number of auxiliaries... from the kings Antiochus, and Agrippa, and Sohemus, each of them contributing one thousand footmen that were archers, and a thousand horsemen. Malchus also, the king of Arabia, sent a thousand horsemen, besides five thousand footmen, the greatest part of whom were archers" (J.W. 3:4:2 §68). The same held true for the final stages of the war under Titus, beside "whom marched those auxiliaries that came from the kings, being now more in number than before, together with a considerable number that came to his assistance from Syria" (J.W.5:1:6 §42–44). So then, not only did Titus draw troops from the Euphrates in the east (J.W. 5:1:6 §44), but Antiochus IV is the king of Commagene, and "Samoseta, the capital of Commagene, lies upon Euphrates" (J.W. 7:7:1 §224). In addition, Titus called the tenth legion through Jericho (J.W. 5:1:6 §42; 5:2:3 §69), which is east of Jerusalem (cf. Jos 13:32; 16:1; 20:8)—though not near the Euphrates. These important troop movements from east of Jerusalem involved the tenth legion, one of "the most eminent legions of all" (J.W. 3:4:2 §65)."

Kenneth L. Gentry, Jr., *The Divorce of Israel: A Redemptive-Historical Interpretation of Revelation Vol. 2* (Dallas, GA: Tolle Lege Press, 2016), 360.

[6] **Foes of Israel coming from the Euphrates river and the north**: "That they have been held at "the great river Euphrates" evokes the OT prophecy of an army from beyond the Euphrates (from "the north") whom God will bring to judge sinful Israel (Isa. 5:26–29; 7:20; 8:7–8; 14:29–31; Jer. 1:14–15; 4:6–13; 6:1, 22; 10:22; 13:20; Ezek. 38:6, 15; 39:2; Joel 2:1–11, 20–25) and other ungodly nations around Israel (Isa. 14:31; Jer. 25:9, 26; 46–47; 50:41–42; Ezek. 26:7–11; cf. Assumption of Moses 3:1)."

G. K. Beale, *The Book of Revelation: A Commentary on the Greek Text, New International Greek Testament Commentary* (Grand Rapids, MI; Carlisle, Cumbria: W.B. Eerdmans; Paternoster Press, 1999), 506.

"Not only is the Euphrates Israel's ideal northern border, but it is also the extent of the power of Israel's two most powerful kings, David (2Sa 8:3; 1Ch 18:3) and Solomon (2Ch 9:26). Because it is an important marker of the northern border of Israel, Beale (506) notes that in the Old Testament the Euphrates long serves as an apocalyptic image of God's threatened judgment upon his covenant people by means of invading forces (Isa 7:20; 8:7–8; 27:12; Jer 1:14–15; 6:1, 22; 10:22; 13:20; Eze 38:6, 15; 39:2; Joel 2:20-25). This is because historically "from the River Euphrates had come Sennacherib and Nebuchadnezzar, destroyers of Samaria and Jerusalem; by now the Euphrates has become a mere symbol for the quarter from which judgment is to come on Jerusalem" (Carrington 165)."

Kenneth L. Gentry, Jr., *The Divorce of Israel: A Redemptive-Historical Interpretation of Revelation Vol. 1* (Dallas, GA: Tolle Lege Press, 2016), 758-759.

"The Bible often uses north as a designation for a geographical area that includes the north as well as the northeast. For example, Babylon was mostly east of Israel, but Jeremiah 4:6 warns that the disaster that came upon Judah would arrive "from the north," a reference to Babylon (Jer. 1:13–15; 3:18; 6:1, 22; 10:22; Zech. 2:6–7). Notice that "all the families of the kingdoms of the north will break forth on all the inhabitants of the land" (Jer. 1:15). Charles Dyer, who teaches that Ezekiel 38 and 39 are describing a future battle,5 makes the point that "from the north land" and "remote parts of the earth" (Jer. 6:22) are "an apt description of the Babylonians (cf. Hab. 1:6–11)"6 and their invasion of Israel in the sixth century B.C. If Babylon is said to invade Israel from the north when it is actually mostly east of Israel, and north is the "remote parts of the earth,"7 then "far north" can have a similar meaning in Ezekiel (38:6, 15; 39:2).

"The same is also the case when Israel was overrun by the Assyrians (Zeph. 2:13) and Persians (Isa. 41:25; Jer. 50:3). Consider this description of a northern invasion that was on the prophetic horizon, a battle fought with bows and arrows and javelins: "Behold, a people is coming from the north, and a great nation and many kings will be aroused from the remote parts of the earth" (Jer. 50:41). The "remote parts of the earth" seems like a description far beyond the then-known world, but it wasn't. Jeremiah was describing the judgment of Babylon (50:42). Is the Bible mistaken? Not at all. The language is typical of prophetic/poetry passages, and it's no different from the way Ezekiel uses the "remote parts of the north." As Timothy Daily concludes, "From the perspective of the Holy Land, the invaders came down from the north, even if their place of origin was actually to the east. Ezekiel is giving the direction of the invasion, not the place of the invader's origin."

"Archeologist Barry Beitzel confirms this analysis when he states that "the Bible's use of the expression 'north' denotes the direction from which a foe would normally approach and not the location of its homeland." 9 The same holds true for any invading army that was north and east of Israel. They, too, would have to bring a land army into Israel from the north since the Mediterranean Sea is directly west of Israel. Tanner concludes: "'North' refers not so much to the precise geographical direction from Israel, but rather to the direction of advance and attack upon Israel (armies came against Israel from the north). This is how Jeremiah viewed Babylonia, though Babylonia was technically to the east."

Gary DeMar, *The Gog and Magog End-Time Alliance*, (Powder Springs, GA: American Vision Inc., 2016), 90-91.

[7] **Armageddon:** "The correct (Hebrew) term John uses to describe the climactic end-times battle is *harmagedon*. This spelling becomes significant when we try to discern what this Hebrew term means. The first part of the term (har) is easy. In Hebrew har means "mountain." Our term is therefore divisible into har-magedon, "Mount (of) magedon...the Hebrew phrase behind John's Greek transliteration of our mystery Hebrew term is actually h-r-m-ʿ-d. But what does that mean? If the first part (h-r) is the Hebrew word har ("mountain"), is there a har m-ʿ-d in the Hebrew Old Testament? There is—and it's stunning when considered in light of the battle of "Armageddon" and what we discussed in the previous chapter about the supernatural north and antichrist.The phrase in question exists in the Hebrew Bible as har moʿed. Incredibly, it is found in Isaiah 14:13...the phrase har moʿed was one of the terms used to describe the dwelling place of Yahweh and his divine council—the cosmic mountain...When John draws on this ancient Hebrew phrase, he is indeed pointing to a climactic battle at Jerusalem. Why? Because Jerusalem is a mountain—Mount Zion. And if Baal and the gods of other nations don't like Yahweh claiming to be Most High and claiming to run the cosmos

from the heights of Zaphon/Mount Zion, they can try to do something about it." Michael S. Heiser, *The Unseen Realm: Recovering the Supernatural Worldview of the Bible, First Edition* (Bellingham, WA: Lexham Press, 2015), 369-373.

Spiritual war of cosmic mountains: Isaiah 14:13-15. For the fictional depiction of this spiritual war of cosmic mountains see Brian Godawa *Jesus Triumphant: Chronicles of the Nephilim Book 8* (Embedded Pictures, 2015). For an explanation of the theology behind that fiction see the appendix of that same book, pages 308-311. For the academic defense of the interpretation, see Michael S. Heiser, *The Unseen Realm: Recovering the Supernatural Worldview of the Bible, First Edition* (Bellingham, WA: Lexham Press, 2015), 288-295.

Armageddon as battle of cosmic mountains: Richard J. Clifford, *The Cosmic Mountain in Canaan and the Old Testament* (Wipf & Stock Pub, 2010).

[8] **War of the Seed**: Brian Godawa's *Chronicles of the Nephilim* series tells this storyline that extends through the entire Bible.

Genesis 3:15 "I will put enmity between you and the woman, and between your offspring and her offspring; he shall bruise your head, and you shall bruise his heel."

"The seminal promise is, of course, that God would send a seed of the woman who would crush the head of the seed of the serpent and in the process would have his heel bruised (Gen. 3:15). There is a predictive element in this, certainly, but there is no single one-time fulfillment of this. Instead, we see variations on this theme repeated all through Scripture:

> 1) The prophesied star of Jacob would "crush the forehead of Moab" (Num. 24:17).

> 2) Jael kills Sisera (and by proxy King Jabin, an oppressor of Israel) by driving a tent spike through his head (Judges 4).

> 3) After he learns his wicked sons were killed in battle and the ark was lost, wicked priest Eli falls over backwards and breaks his neck (1 Sam. 4).

> 4) David kills Goliath with a stone to the head, then cuts off his head (the stone, by the way, is a "smooth stone" from a brook—a stone cut out without hands) (1 Sam. 17).

> 5) The usurper-king Abimelech attacked and murdered his own brethren, but was killed when a woman threw a millstone from a tower window and "crushed his skull" (Judges 9).

> 6) Absalom, son of David, guilty of murdering his older brother and leading a conspiracy for the control of the government, is eventually routed in battle and flees into the woods, only to be caught by his head in a tree. He is killed while hanging there. (2 Sam. 18).

> 7) David enshrined the language of this promise in Ps. 68:21–22 (cf. 74:12–14).

> 8) Psalm 110:1 refers to making Christ's enemies His footstool. (This becomes by far the most referenced Old Testament passage in the New Testament.)

> 9) The seminal promise is repeated in a later context, Habakkuk 3:13.

> 10) Jesus alludes to it as something accomplished already (Luke 10:18–19).

"Now, the image is again mentioned by Paul in Romans 16:20 as something that was about to occur for his audience "soon." This is a highly probable reference to AD 70."

Joel McDurmon, *We Shall All Be Changed: A Critique Of Full Preterism And A Defense Of A Future Bodily Resurrection Of The Saints* (Atlanta GA: American Vision, 2012), 15-16.

CHAPTER 4

[1] **The Watchers revealed themselves less than in the past**: This is the notion that I applied to my entire series of both Chronicles. The stories that occur in the more distant primeval past, such as *Enoch Primordial* and *Noah Primeval*, display the gods in more visible manifestations with mythopoeic flair. This matches our own murky lack of knowledge of this more magical past. But as time goes on and mankind becomes more sophisticated and even more rational, so the gods become less visible and more in the background. I see this very thing in our modern world that is so infected by materialism that there is almost no supernatural awareness, while there is much more of it in more primitive cultures around the world. It's as if the more modern and more materialistic we become, the more blind we are to our sinful delusion, and the less need there is to deceive us any more. It is like that old adage that the best trick Satan got to play on us was to get us to believe he didn't exist.

[2] **Vespasian's consultation with the oracle of Carmel**:

Suetonius, *The Twelve Caesars, Vespasian* 5.6

"When [Vespasian] consulted the oracle of the god of Carmel in Judaea, the lots were highly encouraging, promising that whatever he planned or wished however great it might be, would come to pass."

http://penelope.uchicago.edu/Thayer/E/Roman/Texts/Suetonius/12Caesars/Vespasian*.html

Tacitus, *Histories* 2.78
"After Mucianus had spoken, the rest became bolder; they gathered about Vespasian, encouraged him, and recalled the prophecies of seers and the movements of the stars. Nor indeed was he wholly free from such superstitious belief, as was evident later when he had obtained supreme power, for he openly kept at court an astrologer named Seleucus, whom he regarded as his guide and oracle. Old omens came back to his mind: once on his country estate a cypress of conspicuous height suddenly fell, but the next day it rose again on the selfsame spot fresh, tall, and with wider expanse than before. This occurrence was a favourable omen of great significance, as the haruspices all agreed, and promised the highest distinctions for Vespasian, who was then still a young man. At first, however, the insignia of a triumph, his consulship, and his victory over Judea appeared to have fulfilled the promise given by the omen; yet after he had gained these honours, he began to think that it was the imperial throne that was foretold. Between Judea and Syria lies Carmel: this is the name given to both p287 the mountain and the divinity. The god has no image or temple — such is the rule handed down by the fathers; there is only an altar and the worship of the god. When Vespasian was sacrificing there and thinking over his secret hopes in his heart, the priest Basilides, after repeated inspection of the victim's vitals, said to him: "Whatever you are planning, Vespasian, whether to build a house, or to enlarge your holdings, or to increase the number of your slaves, the god grants you a mighty home, limitless bounds, and a multitude of men." This obscure oracle rumour had caught up at the time, and now was trying to interpret; nothing indeed was more often on men's lips. It was discussed even more in Vespasian's presence — for men have more to say to those who are filled with hope. The two leaders now separated with clear purposes before them, Mucianus going to Antioch, Vespasian to Caesarea. Antioch is the capital of Syria, Caesarea of Judea."

http://penelope.uchicago.edu/Thayer/E/Roman/Texts/Tacitus/Histories/2B*.html

CHAPTER 5

[1] **Paul's recommendation to avoid marriage during the great tribulation**:

1 Corinthians 7:26–35 [26] I think that in view of the present distress it is good for a person to remain as he is. [27] Are you bound to a wife? Do not seek to be free. Are you free from a wife? Do not seek a wife. [28] But if you do marry, you have not sinned, and if a betrothed woman marries, she has not sinned. Yet those who marry will have worldly troubles, and I would spare you that. [29] This is what I mean, brothers: the appointed time has grown very short. From now on, let those who have wives live as though they had none, [30] and those who mourn as though they were not mourning, and those who rejoice as though they were not rejoicing, and those who buy as though they had no goods, [31] and those who deal with the world as though they had no dealings with it. For the present form of this world is passing away. [32] I want you to be free from anxieties. The unmarried man is anxious about the things of the Lord, how to please the Lord. [33] But the married

man is anxious about worldly things, how to please his wife, [34] and his interests are divided. And the unmarried or betrothed woman is anxious about the things of the Lord, how to be holy in body and spirit. But the married woman is anxious about worldly things, how to please her husband. [35] I say this for your own benefit, not to lay any restraint upon you, but to promote good order and to secure your undivided devotion to the Lord.

CHAPTER 6

[1] **Corrupt priesthood through the eyes of Qumran**:

"The new apostates corrupted by power, wealth and Hellenism were Hasmonaean kings, Sadducean nobles and even Pharisees, 'seekers of smooth things," who had given up strict observance for an easier life. These formed 'an assembly of worthlessness and a Congregation of Belial," a false leadership that had broken the Holy Covenant, 'interpreters full of guile who led the people astray' and 'prevented the thirsty from drinking the draught of knowledge.'" Faulkner, Neil (2012-09-30). *Apocalypse: The Great Jewish Revolt Against Rome AD 66-73* (K-Locations 1544-1547). Amberley Publishing. K-Edition.

"Interestingly, the Qumranians also denounced Jerusalem's priestly system for its murderous conduct: "God will condemn [the wicked priest] to destruction even as he himself planned to destroy the poor. And as for that which He said, Because of the murders committed in the city and the violence done to the land, the explanation of this is (that) the city is Jerusalem, where the Wicked Priest committed abominable deeds and defiled the Sanctuary of God, and the violence done to the land, these are the towns of Judah where he stole goods of the Poor" (1QpHab 12:5-9).56 They also interpret Habakkuk 2:8 as follows: "Because you have plundered many nations, all the remnant of the people shall plunder you: interpreted this concerns the last Priests of Jerusalem, who shall amass money and wealth by plundering the peoples. But in the last days, their riches and booty shall be delivered into the hands of the army of the Kittim [Romans]" (1QpHab 9:5-7)." Kenneth L. Gentry, Jr., *The Divorce of Israel: A Redemptive-Historical Interpretation of Revelation Vol. 2* (Dallas, GA: Tolle Lege Press, 2016), 430-431.

[2] **Times of the Gentiles**:

Many Christians disagree over what the "times of the Gentiles" are referring to in Luke 24. But look closely at the passage and it is clear that the context indicates that it was connected to the fall of Jerusalem in AD 70.

> Luke 21:20–24 [20] "But when you see Jerusalem surrounded by armies, then know that its desolation has come near. [21] Then let those who are in Judea flee to the mountains, and let those who are inside the city depart, and let not those who are out in the country enter it, [22] for these are days of vengeance, to fulfill all that is written. [23] Alas for women who are pregnant and for those who are nursing infants in those days! For there will be great distress upon the earth and wrath against this people. [24] They will fall by the edge of the sword and be led captive among all nations, and Jerusalem will be trampled underfoot by the Gentiles, until the times of the Gentiles are fulfilled.

Consider these points: 1) Jesus is referring to the abomination of desolation as the pagan armies of Rome surrounding Jerusalem. We know this because the same exact sermon in Matthew 24 uses the term "abomination of desolation" where Luke here uses "Jerusalem surrounded by armies" as a substitute. So the context is Daniel's abomination that was to occur during the fourth successive "beast" kingdom. According to the statue dream of Daniel 2 and the corresponding vision of four beasts in Daniel 7, there would be four Gentile kingdoms that ruled the known earth, before the kingdom of God would arrive. Those kingdoms were Babylon, Medo-Persia, Greece and then Rome. They were all Gentile kingdoms. Then Daniel said,

> Daniel 2:44–45 [44] And in the days of those kings the God of heaven will set up a kingdom that shall never be destroyed, nor shall the kingdom be left to another people. It shall break in pieces all these kingdoms and bring them to an end, and it shall stand forever, [45] just as you saw that a stone was cut from a mountain by no human hand, and that it broke in pieces the iron, the bronze, the clay, the silver, and the gold.."

The stone that broke the other kingdoms is obviously the kingdom of God and his Messiah cornerstone. Then he reiterates this kingdom replacement in Daniel 7. The kingdom of God comes at the ascension of the Son of Man to his throne of glory and power:

> Daniel 7:13–14 [13] "I saw in the night visions, and behold, with the clouds of heaven there came one like a son of man, and he came to the Ancient of Days and was presented before him. [14] And to him was given dominion and glory and a kingdom, that all peoples, nations, and languages should serve him; his dominion is an everlasting dominion, which shall not pass away, and his kingdom one that shall not be destroyed."

All nations and peoples, all GENTILES should serve him. When the kingdom of God came in the first century, the Times of the Gentile kingdoms of Daniel was fulfilled.

[3] **Kittim as Romans**:

"The Qumran community identified the various Old Testament references to the Kittim with their own enemies, the forces of Belial or the Sons of Darkness, whom they expected to defeat in a final eschatological battle. Their enemies were likely either the Hellenistic kingdom of the Seleucids (and Ptolemies) or the Roman Empire (Pesher Nahum [4QpNah] 3–4.1.2–3; Pesher Habakkuk [1QpHab] 2.12, 14; 3.4, 9; 4.5, 10; 6.1, 10; 9.7; Pesher Psalms [1QpPs] 9–10.2, 3; Pesher Isaiah [4QpIsaa] 7–10.3, 7, 9, 11, 12; War Scroll [1QM] 1.2, 4, 6, 9, 12; 11.11; 15.2; 16.3, 6, 8, 9; 17.12, 14; 18.2, 4; 19.10, 13; 4QMa 10.2.2, 8, 9, 10, 12; 11.2.1, 5, 7, 8, 19, 20; 13.3, 5; 4QMb 1.9, 12; Sefer ha Milḥamah [4Q285] 5.6; [11Q14] 1.1.4, 6)."

Dale A. Brueggemann, "Kittim," ed. John D. Barry et al., The Lexham Bible Dictionary (Bellingham, WA: Lexham Press, 2016).

War of the Sons of Light Against the Sons of Darkness:

Gary A. Rendsburg Ph.D., "Lecture 10: The War Scroll and Other Apocalyptic Texts," The Great Courses, The Dead Sea Scrolls, (Rutgers University) Online: https://www.thegreatcoursesplus.com/the-dead-sea-scrolls

"The War Scroll (1QM). This scroll consists of nineteen badly deteriorated columns. It was originally somewhat longer, but how much is now impossible to determine. The work is ostensibly a manual to guide the self-styled "Sons of Light" in a final eschatological war, in which they are to face, and eventually vanquish, the "Sons of Darkness." Nevertheless, the text is essentially a theological, not a military, composition.

"Among the topics the War Scroll treats are: preliminary preparations for the war; rules for the sounding and inscription of trumpets used to guide the course of the battle; the dimensions and inscriptions of shields and standards used; the battle array, including who may and may not participate in the conflict; the role of the priests and Levites; and the ebb and flow of the final battle against the Kittim (probably the Romans)." M. O. Wise, "Dead Sea Scrolls: General Introduction," ed. Craig A. Evans and Stanley E. Porter, Dictionary of New Testament Background: A Compendium of Contemporary Biblical Scholarship (Downers Grove, IL: InterVarsity Press, 2000), 255.

1QM 1.1–7 indicates that the Sons of Light will return from the wilderness (probably Qumran) to encamp in the wilderness of Jerusalem (1.3), after which the armies of the Sons of Light will go forth from Jerusalem (3.11; 7.4).

[4] **Alexander quotes from**:

> Isaiah 40:3 A voice cries: "In the wilderness prepare the way of the LORD; make straight in the desert a highway for our God."

> Matthew 3:1–3 [1] In those days John the Baptist came preaching in the wilderness of Judea, [2] "Repent, for the kingdom of heaven is at hand." [3] For this is he who was spoken of by the prophet Isaiah when he said, "The voice of one crying in the wilderness: 'Prepare the way of the Lord; make his paths straight.' "

[5] **Qumran thought they were the voice crying in the wilderness**:

1QS 8.12b-16b: "...they *(community members) shall* separate from the habitations ungodly men and shall go into the wilderness to prepare the way of Him; as it is written, Prepare in the wilderness the way of... make straight in the desert a path for our God. This is the study of the Law which He commanded by the hand of Moses... and as the Prophets have revealed by His Holy Spirit."

[6] Elijah before the Day of the Lord:

Malachi 3:1; 4:5-8[1] "Behold, I send my messenger, and he will prepare the way before me. And the Lord whom you seek will suddenly come to his temple... [5] "Behold, I will send you Elijah the prophet before the great and awesome day of the LORD comes. [6] And he will turn the hearts of fathers to their children and the hearts of children to their fathers, lest I come and strike the land with a decree of utter destruction."

Many Christians fully embrace Jesus's claim that John the Baptist was the Messenger of Malachi, but they fail to realize that his ministry was not merely the proclamation of the Messiah, but of the Day of the Lord judgment upon Israel. That judgment occurred within a generation of Christ's ministry, just as he predicted (Matthew 23:36-24:2). The coming of Messiah was linked with both salvation and judgment. John said that the judgment to come was for Israel (Matt 3:8-9). He was not prophesying about the Gentiles, but about Israel. John said that the axe was at the root of the tree NOW, not thousands of years from now. He said the wrath to come was upon the Jews of the first century, not centuries later.

Matthew 3:7–12 [7] But when he [John the Baptizer] saw many of the Pharisees and Sadducees coming to his baptism, he said to them, "You brood of vipers! Who warned you to flee from the wrath to come? [8] Bear fruit in keeping with repentance. [9] And do not presume to say to yourselves, 'We have Abraham as our father,' for I tell you, God is able from these stones to raise up children for Abraham. [10] Even now the axe is laid to the root of the trees. Every tree therefore that does not bear good fruit is cut down and thrown into the fire. [11] "I baptize you with water for repentance, but he who is coming after me is mightier than I, whose sandals I am not worthy to carry. He will baptize you with the Holy Spirit and fire. [12] His winnowing fork is in his hand, and he will clear his threshing floor and gather his wheat into the barn, but the chaff he will burn with unquenchable fire."

[7] Transmigration of the soul (reincarnation):

"Plato taught that the immortal soul takes on a body only as punishment for some sin, for which suffering will be tenfold; the soul must leave the ideal realm and enter into the material world. Man is "a soul in a body, and his soul needs to grow toward the highest good, that it may no longer have to suffer continued rebirth but go into that state in which it may, like God, behold and enjoy forever the hierarchy of ideal forms, in all their truth, beauty, and goodness" (Noss, 52). Before this final blissful state is realized we may come back, even as animals."

Norman L. Geisler, "Reincarnation," Baker Encyclopedia of Christian Apologetics, Baker Reference Library (Grand Rapids, MI: Baker Books, 1999), 639.

[8] Alexander is paraphrasing from the following Scripture:

Luke 1:17 and he [John] will go before him [Messiah] in the spirit and power of Elijah, to turn the hearts of the fathers to the children, and the disobedient to the wisdom of the just, to make ready for the Lord a people prepared."

[9] Alexander is referring to John the Baptizer's theme of coming judgment on Israel:

Matthew 3:7–12 [7]But when he [John the Baptizer] saw many of the Pharisees and Sadducees coming to his baptism, he said to them, "You brood of vipers! Who warned you to flee from the wrath to come? [8] Bear fruit in keeping with repentance. [9] And do not presume to say to yourselves, 'We have Abraham as our father,' for I tell you, God is able from these stones to raise up children for Abraham. [10] Even now the axe is laid to the root of the trees. Every tree therefore that does not bear good fruit is cut down and thrown into the fire. [11] "I baptize you with water for repentance, but he who is coming after me is mightier than I, whose sandals I am not worthy to carry. He will baptize you with the Holy Spirit and fire. [12] His winnowing fork is in his hand, and he will clear his threshing floor and gather his wheat into the barn, but the chaff he will burn with unquenchable fire."

[10] **Alexander is paraphrasing from the following Scriptures**:

> Malachi 3:1–5 [1] "Behold, I send my messenger, and he will prepare the way before me. And the Lord whom you seek will suddenly come to his temple; and the messenger of the covenant in whom you delight, behold, he is coming, says the LORD of hosts. [2] But who can endure the day of his coming, and who can stand when he appears? For he is like a refiner's fire and like fullers' soap. … [5] "Then I will draw near to you for judgment.

Romans as God's instrument of desolation:

> Daniel 9:26–27 [26] And the people of the prince who is to come [Messiah] shall destroy the city and the sanctuary. Its end shall come with a flood, and to the end there shall be war. Desolations are decreed…. And on the wing of abominations shall come one who makes desolate, until the decreed end is poured out on the desolate."

> Luke 21:20 "But when you see Jerusalem surrounded by armies, then know that its desolation has come near.

> Luke 19:43–44 [43] For the days will come upon you, when your enemies will set up a barricade around you and surround you and hem you in on every side [44] and tear you down to the ground, you and your children within you. And they will not leave one stone upon another in you, because you did not know the time of your visitation."

> Matthew 22:6–7 [6] while the rest seized his servants, treated them shamefully, and killed them. [7] The king was angry, and he sent his troops and destroyed those murderers and burned their city.

Day of Vengeance:

> Isaiah 61:1–2
> [1] The Spirit of the Lord GOD is upon me, because the LORD has anointed me to bring good news to the poor; he has sent me to bind up the brokenhearted, to proclaim liberty to the captives, and the opening of the prison to those who are bound; [2] to proclaim the year of the LORD's favor, and the day of vengeance of our God…

[11] **Daniel's seventy sevens** are commonly referred to as seventy weeks, but it is actually "seventy sevens."

[12] **The decree in Daniel 9:25 of the restoration and rebuilding of Jerusalem**:

"Undoubtedly an initial problem confronting the interpreter is determining the identity of the "command" in Daniel 9:25: "Know therefore and understand, that from the going forth of the command to restore and build Jerusalem…"

"At first we might suspect Cyrus's decree in 538 B.C., which is mentioned in 2 Chronicles 36:22-23 and in Ezra 1:1-4; 5:13, 17, 6:3. Certainly Cyrus gives a command to rebuild the city (Isa. 44:28): yet the bulk of the references to his decree deal with the Temple's rebuilding. Daniel, however, specifically speaks of the command to "restore and build Jerusalem," which is an important qualification as Hengstenberg so capably shows.15 Though the Jews make half-hearted efforts to rebuild Jerusalem after Cyrus's decree, the city long remains little more than a sparsely populated, unwalled village.

"Yet Daniel speaks of the command to "restore" (root: *shub*, "return") Jerusalem (Dan. 9:25). This requires a return to its original integrity and grandeur as per Jeremiah's prophecy: "I will cause the captives of Judah and the captives of Israel to return, and will rebuild those places as at the first" (Jer. 33:7). This must involve the restoring of the city complete with its streets and protective wall: "the street shall be built again, and the wall, even in troublesome times" (Dan. 9:2516). The Jews did not seriously undertake this until the middle of the fifth century B.C. Hengstenberg points to the decree of Artaxerxes I in Nehemiah 2:1 (cf. v. 1817) as the beginning point, which he argues is in 455 B.C…

"The process of diligent rebuilding, which climaxed in a restored Jerusalem, seems to have begun either: (1) in seed in the spiritual revival under Ezra (Ezra 7); or (2) in actuality under the administration ofNehemiah (Neh. 2:1, 17-18; 6:15-16; 12:43).[30] There were several political commands preparing for the restoration of Jerusalem and one divine command: "So the elders of the Jews built, and they prospered through the prophesying of Haggai the prophet and Zechariah the son of Iddo. And they built and finished it, according to the commandment of the God of Israel, and according to the command of Cyrus, Darius, and Artaxerxes king of Persia" (Ezra 6:14).

"The first period of seven weeks must indicate something, for it is set off from the two other periods. Were it not significant, Daniel could have spoken of the sixty-nine weeks, rather than the "seven weeks and sixty-two weeks" (Dan. 9:25). This seven weeks (or forty-nine years) apparently witnesses the successful conclusion of the rebuilding of Jerusalem.[31] The city was rebuilt during this era, despite the opposition in "troublesome times" (cp. Neh. 4:18), which God ordained for them in this prophecy (Dan. 9:25).

"The second period of sixty-two weeks, extends from the conclusion of the rebuilding of Jerusalem to the introduction of the Messiah to Israel at His baptism at the beginning of His public ministry (Dan. 9:25), sometime around A.D. 26-30. This interpretation is quite widely agreed upon by conservative scholars, being virtually "universal among Christian exegetes" excluding dispensationalists. The third period of one week is the subject of intense controversy between dispensationalism and other conservative scholarship."

Kenneth Gentry Jr., "Daniel's Seventy Weeks," Covenant Media Foundation online. http://www.cmfnow.com/articles/pt551.htm

[13] **Aaron quotes from**: Daniel 9:24

[14] **Daniel's Seventy Weeks**:

> Daniel 9:24–27
> "Seventy weeks are decreed about your people and your holy city, to finish the transgression, to put an end to sin, and to atone for iniquity, to bring in everlasting righteousness, to seal both vision and prophet, and to anoint a most holy place. [25] Know therefore and understand that from the going out of the word to restore and build Jerusalem to the coming of an anointed one, a prince, there shall be seven weeks. Then for sixty-two weeks it shall be built again with squares and moat, but in a troubled time. [26] And after the sixty-two weeks, an anointed one shall be cut off and shall have nothing. And the people of the prince who is to come shall destroy the city and the sanctuary. Its end shall come with a flood, and to the end there shall be war. Desolations are decreed. [27] And he shall make a strong covenant with many for one week, and for half of the week he shall put an end to sacrifice and offering. And on the wing of abominations shall come one who makes desolate, until the decreed end is poured out on the desolate."

Many futurists, especially Dispensationalists, think that this prophecy was not fulfilled in the death, resurrection and ascension of Christ and the new covenant. They think that the Kingdom of God has not yet come until Christ returns. This is tantamount to a denial of the new covenant in Christ. See how the Scriptures say that each of these elements of Daniel's prophecy was fulfilled in Christ in his death, resurrection and ascension.

The following is excerpted from Kenneth L. Gentry, Jr., "Daniel's Seventy Weeks," paper PT551 (Covenant Media Foundation). http://www.cmfnow.com/articles/pt551.htm

The 7 weeks and 62 weeks to Messiah: "The first period of seven weeks must indicate something, for it is set off from the two other periods. Were it not significant, Daniel could have spoken of the sixty-nine weeks, rather than the "seven weeks and sixty-two weeks" (Dan. 9:25). This seven weeks (or forty-nine years) apparently witnesses the successful conclusion of the rebuilding of Jerusalem.[31] The city was rebuilt during this era, despite the opposition in "troublesome times" (cp. Neh. 4:18), which God ordained for them in this prophecy (Dan. 9:25). The second period of sixty-two weeks, extends from the conclusion of the rebuilding of Jerusalem to the introduction of the Messiah to Israel at His baptism at the beginning of His public ministry (Dan. 9:25), sometime around A.D. 26-30. This interpretation is quite widely agreed upon by conservative scholars, being virtually "universal among Christian exegetes"[32] excluding dispensationalists. The third period of one week is the subject of intense controversy between dispensationalism and other conservative scholarship.

The 6 messianic elements of Verse 24:

Finishing the transgression (v. 24): "Let us notice, first, that the Seventy Weeks will witness the finishing of the transgression. As just noted, Daniel's prayer of confession was regarding Israel's sins (Dan. 9:4ff) and the prophecy's focus is on Israel (Dan. 9:24a). Consequently, this finishing (Heb. kala) the transgression has to do with Israel's finishing, i.e., completing, her transgression against God. The finishing of that transgression occurs in the ministry of Christ, when Israel culminates her resistance to God by rejecting His Son and having Him crucified: "Last of all he sent his son to them, saying, 'They will respect my son.' But when the vinedressers saw the son, they said among themselves, 'This is the heir. Come, let us kill him and seize his inheritance'" (Matt. 21:37-38; cf. 21:33-45; Acts 7:51-52).

Put an end to sin (v. 24): "The second part of the couplet is directly related to the first: Having finished the transgression against God in the rejection of the Messiah, now the sins are sealed up (NASV marg.; Heb., chatham). The idea here is, as Payne observes, to seal or to "reserve sins for punishment."[41] Because of Israel's rejection of Messiah, God reserves punishment for her: the final, conclusive destruction of the Temple, which was reserved from the time of Jesus' ministry until A.D. 70 (Matt. 24:2, 34). The sealing or reserving of the sins indicates that within the "Seventy Weeks" Israel will complete her transgression and with the completing of her sin God will act to reserve (beyond the seventy weeks) their sins for judgment. This is a major point in the Lord's Olivet Discourse: Though just before His crucifixion Christ says, "Your house is left to you desolate" (Matt. 23:3[42]), He then reserves His judgment for one generation (Matt. 24:2, 34).

Atone for Iniquity (v.24): "The third result (beginning the second couplet) has to do with the provision of "reconciliation for iniquity."[43] The Hebrew word kaphar is the word for "atonement," i.e., a covering of sin. It clearly speaks of Christ's atoning death, which is the ultimate atonement to which all Temple rituals looked (Heb. 9:26[44]). This also occurred during His earthly ministry—at His death.

Everlasting righteousness (v. 24): "Because of this atonement to cover sin, the fourth result is that everlasting righteousness is effected. That is, the final, complete atonement establishes righteousness. This speaks of the objective accomplishment, not the subjective appropriation of righteousness. This was effected by Christ within the seventy week period, as well: "But now the righteousness of God apart from the law is revealed, being witnessed by the Law and the Prophets, even the righteousness of God" (Rom. 3:21-22a).

Seal up vision and prophecy (v. 24): "The fifth result (the first portion of the third couplet) has to do with the ministry of Christ on earth, which is introduced at His baptism: He comes "to seal up vision and prophecy." By this is meant that Christ fulfills (and thereby confirms) the prophecy. The careful dispensationalist resists the idea that this has to do with the sealing of prophecy in Christ's earthly ministry because He did not fulfill all prophecy at that time.[46] But neither does He within the seventy weeks (up through the Tribulation), nor in the "millennium"! For following these are the resurrection and the New Heavens and New Earth. Actually, the sealing of prophecy regards the subject of Daniel 9: the accomplishment of redemption from sin, i.e. atonement. This Christ accomplished: "Behold, we are going up to Jerusalem, and all [!] things that are written by the prophets concerning the Son of Man will be accomplished" (Luke 18:31; cp. Luke 24:44; Acts 3:18).

Anoint the Most Holy (v. 24): "Finally, the seventy years are for the following goal: "to anoint the Most Holy." This anointing [Heb. mashach] speaks of the introduction of "Christ" by means of His baptismal anointing. This seems clearly to be the case for the following reasons: (1) The overriding concern of Daniel 9:24-27 is Messianic. The Temple that is built after the Babylonian Captivity is to be destroyed after the seventy weeks (v. 27), with no further mention made of it. (2) In the following verses, the Messiah (Heb., mashiyach, "Christ," "Anointed One") is specifically named twice (vv. 25, 26). (3) Contrary to the dispensational interpretation, there is no evidence of an anointing of any Temple in Scripture—whether Solomon's original Temple, Zerubbabel's rebuilt Temple, Ezekiel's visionary Temple, or Herod's expanded Temple.

"(4) The "most holy" phraseology well speaks of the Messiah, who is "that Holy One who is to be born."[48] It is of Christ that the ultimate redemptive Jubilee is prophesied by Isaiah in these words: "The Spirit of the Lord GOD is upon Me, because the LORD has anointed Me to preach good tidings to the poor; He has sent Me to heal the brokenhearted, to proclaim liberty to the captives, and the opening of the prison to those who are bound; to proclaim the acceptable year of the LORD" (Isa. 61:1-2a; cp. Luke 4:17-21). It was at His baptismal anointing that the Spirit came upon Him (Mark 1:9-11). And this was introductory to His ministry, of which we read three verses later: "Jesus came to Galilee, preaching the gospel of the kingdom of God, and saying, 'The time is fulfilled [the Sixty-ninth week?[49]], and the kingdom of God is at hand. Repent, and believe in the gospel" (Mark 1:14-15). Christ is pre-eminently the Anointed One.

Messiah would confirm the covenant (v. 27): "The confirming of covenant (v. 27) refers to the prophesied covenantal actions of verse 24, which come about as the result of the Perfect Covenantal Jubilee (Seventy Weeks), and is mentioned as a result of Daniel's covenantal prayer (cf. v. 4). The covenant mentioned, then, is the divine covenant of God's redemptive grace.[53] Messiah came to confirm the covenantal promises: "to perform the mercy promised to our fathers and to remember His holy covenant" (Luke 1:72).[54] He confirmed the covenant by His death on the cross: "by so much more Jesus has become a surety of a better covenant" (Heb. 7:22b).[55] The word translated "confirm" (Heb: higbir) is related to the angel Gabriel's name, who brought Daniel the revelation of the Seventy Weeks (and who later brings the revelation of Christ's birth [Luke 1:19, 26]). "Gabriel" is based on the Hebrew gibbor, "strong one," a concept frequently associated with the covenant God.[56] The related word found in Daniel 9:27 means to "make strong, confirm."[57] This "firm covenant" brings about "everlasting righteousness" (Dan. 9:24) -- hence its firmness.

Messiah would put an end to sacrifice and offering (v. 27): "This confirmation of the covenant occurs "in the middle of the week" (v. 27). I have already shown that the seventieth week begins with the baptismal anointing of Christ. Then after three and one-half years of ministry—the middle of the seventieth week—Christ was crucified.[60] Thus, the prophecy states that by His conclusive confirmation of the covenant, Messiah will "bring an end to sacrifice and offering" (v. 27) by offering up Himself as a sacrifice for sin: "Now, once at the end of the ages, He has appeared to put away sin by the sacrifice of Himself" (Heb. 9:25-26; cp. Heb. 7:11-12, 18-22). Consequently, at His death the Temple veil was torn from top to bottom (Matt. 27:51) as evidence the sacrificial system was legally disestablished in the eyes of God (cf. Matt. 23:38), for Christ is the Lamb of God (John 1:29; 1 Pet. 1:19)."

[15] **Alexander quotes from:** Matthew 24:37–39 and Luke 17:22-27.

Some Christians believe that this passage is talking about the future second coming of Christ, not his judgment coming in AD 70. On this topic, Gary DeMar argues:

"A number of commentators (e.g., J. Marcellus Kik and Kenneth Gentry) argue that Matthew 24:35 is a "transition text." It's at this point, they argue, that Jesus is referring to a time period that is still in our future. Luke 17:22–37 describes five Olivet-Discourse prophetic events that are identical to those found in Matthew 24. The difference between Matthew 24 and Luke 17 is in the order of the events, a characteristic of the passages that few commentators can explain. Ray Summers writes:

"This is a most difficult passage. The overall reference appears to be to the coming of the Son of Man—Christ—in judgment at the end of the age. Some small parts of it, however, are repeated in Luke 21 in reference to the destruction of Jerusalem (A.D. 70), and larger parts of it are in Matthew 24, also in reference to the destruction of Jerusalem. The entire complex cautions one against dogmatism in interpreting.8

"Taking Matthew 24 as the standard, Luke places the Noah's ark analogy (Matt. 24:37–39) before the events of Matthew 24:17–18 ("let him who is on the housetop not go down"), verse 27 ("for just as the lightning comes from the east"), and verse 28 ("wherever the corpse is, there the vultures will gather"). If the five prophetic events of Matthew 24 that are found in Luke 17:22–37 are numbered 1–2–3–4–5, Luke's numbering of the same events would be 2–4–1–5–3.9 (See accompanying chart.)

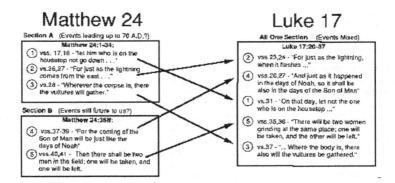

Matthew 24

Section A (Events leading up to 70 A.D.?)

Matthew 24:1-34:

1. vss. 17,18 - "let him who is on the housetop not go down . . ."
2. vs.26,27 - "For just as the lightning comes from the east . . ."
3. vs.28 - "Wherever the corpse is, there the vultures will gather."

Section B (Events still future to us?)

Matthew 24:35ff:

4. vss.37-39 - "For the coming of the Son of Man will be just like the days of Noah"
5. vss.40,41 - Then there shall be two men in the field; one will be taken, and one will be left.

Luke 17

All One Section   (Events Mixed)

Luke 17:20-37

2. vss. 23,24 - "For just as the lightning, when it flashes ..."
4. vss.26,27 - "And just as it happened in the days of Noah, so it shall be also in the days of the Son of Man"
1. vs.31 - 'On that day, let not the one who is on the housetop ..."
5. vss.35,36 - "There will be two women grinding at the same place; one will be taken, and the other will be left."
3. vs.37 - "... Where the body is, there also will the vultures be gathered."

"After A Long Time

"Another line of evidence offered by those who believe that events following Matthew 24:34 refer to a yet future personal and physical return of Jesus is the meaning given to "after a long time" (24:48; 25:19) and the "delay" by the bridegroom (25:5). On the surface these examples seem to indicate that two different events are in view, one near (the destruction of Jerusalem) and one distant (the second coming of Christ). This is the view of Stephen F. Hayhow.

"Both parables, the parables of the virgins (vv. 1–13), and the parable of the talents (vv. 14–30), speak of the absence of the bridegroom/master, who is said to be "a long time in coming" (v. 5) and "After a long time the master of the servants returned" (v. 19). This suggests, not the events of A.D. 70 which were to occur in the near future, in fact within the space of a generation, but a distant event, the return of Christ.10

"Notice that the evil slave says, "My master is not coming for a long time" (Matt. 24:48). The evil slave then proceeds to "beat his fellow-slaves and eat and drink with drunkards" (24:49). But to the surprise of the "evil slave" the master returned when he least expected him (24:50). The master did not return to cut the evil slave's distant relatives in pieces (24:51); he cut him in pieces. The evil slave was alive when the master left, and he was alive when the master returned. In this context, a "long time" must be measured against a person's lifetime. In context, two years could be a long time if the master usually returned within six months.

"The same idea is expressed in the parable of the "talents." A man entrusts his slaves with his possessions (25:14). The master then goes on a journey (25:15). While the master is gone, the slaves make investment decisions (25:16–18). We are then told that "after a long time the master of those slaves came and settled accounts with them" (25:19). In this context "a long time" is no longer than an average lifetime. The settlement is made with the same slaves who received the talents. In every other New Testament context, "a long time" means nothing more than an extended period of time (Luke 8:27; 23:8; John 5:6; Acts 8:11; 14:3, 28; 26:5, 29; 27:21; 28:6). Nowhere does it mean centuries or multiple generations.

"The delay of the bridegroom is no different from the "long time" of the two previous parables. The bridegroom returns to the same two groups of virgins (25:1–13). The duration of the delay must be measured by the audience.

"This brief analysis helps us understand the "mockers" who ask, "Where is the promise of His coming?" (2 Peter 3:3–4). Peter was aware that Jesus's coming was an event that would take place before the last apostle died (Matt. 16:27–28; John 21:22–23). The doctrine of the soon return of Christ was common knowledge (Matt. 24:34; 26:64; Phil. 4:5; Heb. 10:25; 1 John 2:18; Rev. 1:1, 3). It is not hard to imagine that the passage of several decades would lead some to doubt the reliability of the prophecy, especially as the promised generation was coming to a close. The horrendous events of A.D. 70 silenced the mockers."

Gary DeMar, "Just Like the Days of Noah," AmericanVision.org website (Jan 3, 2011).
https://americanvision.org/3889/just-like-the-days-of-noah/

Parousia:

"is used technically for the visit of a ruler or high official…The imperial period with its world ruler or members of his household, if it did not increase the cost, certainly invested the parousia of the ruler with even greater magnificence." Gerhard Kittel, Geoffrey W. Bromiley, and Gerhard Friedrich, eds., *Theological Dictionary of the New Testament* (Grand Rapids, MI: Eerdmans, 1964–), 860.

"The term parousia was widely used for the official visit of a potentate. If we accept Wilcken's explanation of the difficult Flinders Petrie Papyrus 2.39e, we may see there an early reference to enforced contributions to a fund for presenting golden stephanoi to officials at their parousiai. Deissmann finds in this practice a background for figurative language in the Pauline and Pastoral epistles: 'While the sovereigns of this world expect at their parusia a costly crown for themselves, "at the parusia of our Lord Jesus" the apostle will wear a crown—the "crown of glory" (1 Thess. 2:19) won by his work among the churches, or the "crown of righteousness" which the Lord will give to him and to all them that have loved His appearing (2 Tim. 4:8)" Colin J. Hemer, *The Letters to the Seven Churches of Asia in Their Local Setting* (Grand Rapids, MI; Cambridge, U.K.; Livonia, MI: William B. Eerdmans Publishing Company; Dove Booksellers, 2001), 74–75.

"The word 'parousia' is itself misleading, anyway, since it merely means 'presence'; Paul can use it of his being present with a church, and nobody supposes that he imagined he would make his appearance flying downwards on a cloud. The motif of delay ('how long, O Lord, how long?'69) was already well established in Judaism, and is hardly a Christian innovation, as is often imagined. The usual scholarly construct, in which the early church waited for Jesus's return, lived only for that future and without thought for anything past (such as memories of Jesus himself), only to be grievously disappointed and to take up history-writing as a displacement activity, a failure of nerve—this picture is without historical basis. The church expected certain events to happen within a generation, and happen they did." N. T. Wright, *The New Testament and the People of God, Christian Origins and the Question of God* (London: Society for Promoting Christian Knowledge, 1992), 462–463.

Christ coming on the clouds:

The following is drawn from Brian Godawa, *End Times Bible Prophecy: It's Not What They Told You* (Los Angeles, CA: Embedded Pictures Publishing, 2017), 131-134.

"Coming on the clouds" is used throughout the Old Testament as a figurative storm reference to God's judging presence upon a city, nation, or people. Clouds and storm are both metaphors for deity and for local judgment. Here is a brief survey of the instances.

When God judged the city of Nineveh in the days of Nahum the prophet…

> Nahum 1:2–3
> The LORD takes vengeance on his adversaries and keeps wrath for his enemies. 3…His way is in whirlwind and storm, and the clouds are the dust of his feet.

When God delivered David and judged Saul…

> Psalm 18:9–11
> He bowed the heavens and came down; thick darkness was under his feet. 10 He rode on a cherub and flew; he came swiftly on the wings of the wind. 11 He made darkness his covering, his canopy around him, thick clouds dark with water.

When God judged Egypt in the days of Ezekiel, he said,

> Ezekiel 30:3–4
> For the day is near, the day of the LORD is near; it will be a day of clouds… 4 A sword shall come upon Egypt.

In 721 B.C., Isaiah prophesied judgment against Egypt that occurred by about 701 B.C.

> Isaiah 19:1
> An oracle concerning Egypt. Behold, the LORD is riding on a swift cloud and comes to Egypt;

When God judged Assyria in 701 B.C. he described his anger. ..

Isaiah 30:30
And the Lord will cause his majestic voice to be heard and the descending blow of his arm to be seen, in furious anger and a flame of devouring fire, with a cloudburst and storm and hailstones.

Remember that passage in Joel about the last days that Peter said was being fulfilled in his day? You guessed it, more clouds of judgment.

Joel 2:1–2
[F]or the day of the LORD is coming; it is near, 2 a day of darkness and gloom, a day of clouds and thick darkness!

These are all local and limited judgments upon cities, nations, or peoples, and they all use the imagery of God coming on the clouds with the storm of judgment. This was a common ancient image of God's judgment. Did God literally come floating in on clouds in the sky to Nineveh, Saul, or Egypt? Of course not. Clouds and storm were figurative expressions, literary signs of his spiritual presence in the local and limited judgments upon those nations and cities. So, Jesus coming on the clouds of heaven in power and glory was an obvious figurative expression of Jesus's presence in the judgment upon Jerusalem, the sign of his power and the glory of the new covenant.

But there is one more thing. In each of these cases, God used a different nation or people as his tool to perform the judgment. In other words, the pagan people carried out God's will; they represented him spiritually.

God used Babylon to judge Assyria in Nahum. God used Babylon to judge Egypt in Ezekiel 30:10. God used the Egyptians against themselves (Isa 19:2) as well as the Assyrians to judge Egypt (Isa 19:4). And so, God would use the Romans to be his hand of judgment upon Israel in A.D. 70 when they destroyed the city and temple. God often used pagan forces of destruction to humble his people. But fear not, God then judged those pagans for their evil as well! God promised he would do this to the Romans after their desolation.

Daniel 9:27
And on the wing of abominations shall come one who makes desolate, until the decreed end is poured out on the desolator.

The Roman empire eventually did fall. A good historical argument has been made that though the barbarians ultimately invaded and overthrew Rome, its power first became crippled within, due to the growth of Christianity that subverted pagan devotion to the idolatrous authority of Caesar.

[17] **Two messiahs of the Dead Sea scrolls**:

"One central theme concerns the imminent arrival of a day of judgment and restoration, at which time worship in Jerusalem will be reestablished. It is then that the "anointed of Israel" (i.e., what we usually consider as the "Messiah") will take his stand alongside the "anointed of Aaron," the true High Priest, and when the ungodly of Israel will be punished and driven from power. This will also be a time of violent conflict with the Gentile enemies of Israel, the Kittim.

"A feature that has aroused much public and scholarly interest is the apparent expectation of two messiahs, one "of Aaron" and the other "of Israel." For example, the following passages anticipate and hope for the appearance of the "Messiah of Aaron and of Israel": CD 12:23-13:1; 14:18-19; 19:10-11; 20:1; 1QS 9:11; 4Q252 5:1-4.10 For several years this dual messianism has stood at the center of debate. Did the people of Qumran expect two messiahs, or a single messiah who may be described as the "anointed of Aaron and Israel"? One text puts "messiah" in the plural: "until the coming of the Prophet and the Messiahs of Aaron and Israel" (1QS 9:11). When we also take into account the messianic feast, at which the priest and the Messiah will preside (cf. IQSa 2:11-21), it seems best to understand Qumran's messianic expectation as diarchic (i.e., rule by two persons): a joint rule shared by a priestly Messiah, the "anointed of Aaron," and a Davidic Messiah, the "anointed of Israel."

"A royal descendant of David and a Zadokite high priest would rule side by side over restored Israel. It has also been plausibly suggested that the emphasis on two messiahs may have originated as a corrective of the merger of the high priestly and royal offices during the Hasmonean period."

John J. Collins, *Apocalypticism in the Dead Sea Scrolls* (NY: Routledge, 1997), 5-6.

[18] **Qumran belief that Messiah would purify and restore the temple to the sons of Zadok**:

"The so-called "Messianic Rule," 1QSa, is introduced as "the rule for all the congregation of Israel in the last days, when they shall join... according to the law of the sons of Zadok the priests and of the men of their covenant, who have turned aside [from the] way of the people." The hope, in short, is that all Israel will rally to the sectarian community in the end of days. The War Rule, accordingly is a rule for all Israel but the Israel it envisages is an entity of the eschatological future. Even the eschatological Israel can be reasonably described as a remnant, since the violators of the covenant, at least, will have been weeded out. The endorsement of the temple cult must also be seen in this context. The Rule envisages a cult that is regulated by a calendar of 52 weeks or 364 days, the sectarian calendar that was not observed in the Jerusalem Temple and was one of the main factors that led to the secession of the Dead Sea sect. The temple that is endorsed is not the actual temple of Maccabean or Hasmonean times, but the purified temple of the eschatological era."

John J. Collins, *Apocalypticism in the Dead Sea Scrolls* (NY: Routledge, 1997),108-109

[19] **The new covenant church is the new/heavenly Jerusalem, Mount Zion, not a physical Mount Zion**:

Hebrews 12:22–24 [22] But you have come to Mount Zion and to the city of the living God, the heavenly Jerusalem, and to innumerable angels in festal gathering, [23] and to the assembly of the firstborn who are enrolled in heaven, and to God, the judge of all, and to the spirits of the righteous made perfect, [24] and to Jesus, the mediator of a new covenant.

The heavenly Jerusalem of the new covenant receives God's promises. The earthly Jerusalem of the old covenant receives God's judgment:

Galatians 4:24–31 [24] Now this may be interpreted allegorically: these women are two covenants. One is from Mount Sinai, bearing children for slavery; she is Hagar. [25] Now Hagar is Mount Sinai [old covenant] in Arabia; she corresponds to the present Jerusalem, for she is in slavery with her children. [26] But the Jerusalem above [new covenant] is free, and she is our mother. [27] .. [29] But just as at that time he who was born according to the flesh [first century Jews] persecuted him who was born according to the Spirit [Jewish Christians], so also it is now. [30] But what does the Scripture say? "Cast out the slave woman and her son, for the son of the slave woman shall not inherit with the son of the free woman." [31] So, brothers, we are not children of the slave but of the free woman.

This eschatological temple was prophesied to be built by Messiah:

Zechariah 6:12–13 [12] And say to him, 'Thus says the LORD of hosts, "Behold, the man whose name is the Branch: for he shall branch out from his place, and he shall build the temple of the LORD. [13] It is he who shall build the temple of the Lord and shall bear royal honor, and shall sit and rule on his throne. And there shall be a priest on his throne, and the counsel of peace shall be between them both." '

The new covenant church is the new eschatological temple. Since Messiah is a spiritual cornerstone, his temple he builds is a spiritual temple, not a physical earthly one. Cornerstones are the standard rule upon which the building is built.

Ephesians 2:19–22 [19] So then you are no longer strangers and aliens, but you are fellow citizens with the saints and members of the household of God, [20] built on the foundation of the apostles and prophets, Christ Jesus himself being the cornerstone, [21] in whom the whole structure, being joined together, grows into a holy temple in the Lord. [22] In him you also are being built together into a dwelling place for God by the Spirit.

Torah and its elements are shadows that are fulfilled in Christ:

> Hebrews 10:1 For since Torah has but a shadow of the good things to come instead of the true form of these realities, it can never, by the same sacrifices that are continually offered every year, make perfect those who draw near.

The priest of the old covenant needed to sacrifice for himself, but Christ as heavenly high priest of the new covenant is sinless and without need of sacrifice for himself:

> Hebrews 7:23–28 [23] The former priests were many in number, because they were prevented by death from continuing in office, [24] but he holds his priesthood permanently, because he continues forever. [25] Consequently, he is able to save to the uttermost those who draw near to God through him, since he always lives to make intercession for them. [26] For it was indeed fitting that we should have such a high priest, holy, innocent, unstained, separated from sinners, and exalted above the heavens. [27] He has no need, like those high priests, to offer sacrifices daily, first for his own sins and then for those of the people, since he did this once for all when he offered up himself. [28] For the law appoints men in their weakness as high priests, but the word of the oath, which came later than the law, appoints a Son who has been made perfect forever.

[20] **Cassandra quotes from**:

> Hebrews 9:12 [12] he entered once for all into the holy places, not by means of the blood of goats and calves but by means of his own blood, thus securing an eternal redemption.

> Hebrews 9:8–9 [8] By this the Holy Spirit indicates that the way into the holy places is not yet opened as long as the first section is still standing [9] (which is symbolic for the present age). According to this arrangement, gifts and sacrifices are offered that cannot perfect the conscience of the worshiper...

[21] **Cassandra quotes from**:

> Hebrews 9:26–28 [26] for then he would have had to suffer repeatedly since the foundation of the world. But as it is, he has appeared once for all at the end of the ages to put away sin by the sacrifice of himself. [27] And just as it is appointed for man to die once, and after that comes judgment, [28] so Christ, having been offered once to bear the sins of many, will appear a second time, not to deal with sin but to save those who are eagerly waiting for him.

> Hebrews 8:13 [13] In speaking of a new covenant, he makes the first one obsolete. And what is becoming obsolete and growing old is ready to vanish away.

[22] **The Judaizers in Jerusalem**: These characters, including Jacob ben Mordecai were introduced in *Remnant: Rescue of the Elect*. The book of Galatians destroys the Judaizers as "cut off from Christ" because of their desire to place Torah requirements on Christians (Gal 5:4). Here are some of their beliefs mentioned in this paragraph as communicated in the New Testament:

Paul called the Judaizers, "the Mutilators":

> Philippians 3:2–3 [2] Look out for the dogs, look out for the evildoers, look out for those who mutilate the flesh. [3] For we are the circumcision, who worship by the Spirit of God and glory in Christ Jesus and put no confidence in the flesh.

"The force of Paul's rhetoric in this statement is nearly impossible to communicate in English translation. In Greek, the statement consists of three clauses all beginning with the same verb ("watch out"!) and each verb's direct object begins with a "k" sound. We can almost catch the rhetorical effectiveness of the phrase with the translation, "Beware the curs! Beware the criminals! Beware the cutters!" Paul is referring to Jewish Christians who teach that circumcision, dietary observance, and Sabbath-keeping are all necessary requirements, in addition to faith in Christ, for salvation. By calling them "dogs" Paul is turning their own advocacy of ritual purity back upon them. Because ancient streets were often home to dogs (Ps. 59:6, 14), who ate whatever they found, they may have been considered a symbol of nonobservance in matters of diet. The term "mutilators" (katatomē) is a play on the term "circumcision" (peritomē), which Paul uses in the next verse. Since circumcision was not necessary for salvation, those who promoted it were only mutilating the flesh, something that Leviticus 21:5 forbids as a pagan ritual." Clinton E. Arnold, *Zondervan Illustrated Bible Backgrounds Commentary: Romans to Philemon., vol. 3* (Grand Rapids, MI: Zondervan, 2002), 359–360.

The legal ordinances, such as dietary restrictions and sabbaths, of Torah are abolished: Paul clearly says that Christians died to Torah and are no longer under it's authority or obligations.

> Ephesians 2:14–15 [14] For he himself is our peace, who has made us both one and has broken down in his flesh the dividing wall of hostility [15] by abolishing the law of commandments expressed in ordinances, that he might create in himself one new man in place of the two, so making peace,

> Romans 7:4–6 [4] Likewise, my brothers, you also have died to the law through the body of Christ, so that you may belong to another, to him who has been raised from the dead, in order that we may bear fruit for God. [5] For while we were living in the flesh, our sinful passions, aroused by the law, were at work in our members to bear fruit for death. [6] But now we are released from the law, having died to that which held us captive, so that we serve in the new way of the Spirit and not in the old way of the written code.

> Colossians 2:16–23 [16] Therefore let no one pass judgment on you in questions of food and drink, or with regard to a festival or a new moon or a Sabbath. [17] These are a shadow of the things to come, but the substance belongs to Christ. [18] ... [20] If with Christ you died to the elementary principles of the world, why, as if you were still alive in the world, do you submit to regulations— [21] "Do not handle, Do not taste, Do not touch" [22] (referring to things that all perish as they are used)—according to human precepts and teachings? [23] These have indeed an appearance of wisdom in promoting self-made religion and asceticism and severity to the body, but they are of no value in stopping the indulgence of the flesh.

[23] Peter refers to Jewish heresy as "dog returning to its vomit"

> 2 Peter 2:20–22 [20] For if, after they have escaped the defilements of the world through the knowledge of our Lord and Savior Jesus Christ, they are again entangled in them and overcome, the last state has become worse for them than the first. [21] For it would have been better for them never to have known the way of righteousness than after knowing it to turn back from the holy commandment delivered to them. [22] What the true proverb says has happened to them: "The dog returns to its own vomit, and the sow, after washing herself, returns to wallow in the mire.

Returning to the elementary principles of a dead system:

> Galatians 4:9 But now that you have come to know God, or rather to be known by God, how can you turn back again to the weak and worthless elementary principles of the world, whose slaves you want to be once more?

The book of Hebrews and the return to old covenant Torah: Some Christians believe that the warnings of apostasy in Hebrews have to do with giving up one's faith. But that is an over simplification that does not take into account the context of Hebrews. The author is warning Jewish Christians not to cling onto the earthly temple and torah because they are shadows that have been transcended by Christ. So the apostasy referred to is not about giving up belief, but rather, continuing to maintain the old covenant law after it has been done away with. Thus the "recrucifying of Christ" is about maintaining a system that is obsolete, which would effectively deny the sacrifice of Messiah, which did away with it. This is theological apostasy, not mental apostasy.

Now read this chapter from Hebrews that Alexander is referring to in the light of Judaizing heresy and it becomes more clear:

> Hebrews 6:4–6 [4] For it is impossible, in the case of those who have once been enlightened, who have tasted the heavenly gift, and have shared in the Holy Spirit, [5] and have tasted the goodness of the word of God and the powers of the age to come, [6] and then have fallen away, to restore

them again to repentance, since they are crucifying once again the Son of God to their own harm and holding him up to contempt.

These are not Christians who "gave up believing in Jesus," they are Christians who returned to Torah as their obligation.

CHAPTER 9

[1] **Titus sought to destroy both Judaism and Christianity**:

Sulpicius Severus, *Sacred History* 2:30 (4th century)
"Titus himself thought that the temple ought specially to be overthrown, in order that the religion of the Jews and of the Christians might more thoroughly be subverted; for that these religions, although contrary to each other, had nevertheless proceeded from the same authors; that the Christians had sprung up from among the Jews; and that, if the root were extirpated, the offshoot would speedily perish."

http://www.preteristarchive.com/StudyArchive/s/severus-sulpicius.html

CHAPTER 10

[1] **Ten horns as ten client kings of Rome**: "Though provincial governors are quite possibly in view, I am inclined, however, to see them as does Aune (951): "Here the ten kings represent Roman client kings." Rome's system of client kingship was such that kings (including even ethnarchs, tetrarchs, etc.) were appointed by Roman authorities from within various localities. They were responsible for keeping the peace, assisting Rome with defense, and ensuring the flow of tribute money to Rome. They would provide soldiers "as part of tribute, or through friendships and alliances" (Gilliver 2001: 24). During Nero's rule "the client system of the East [including Judea] was then revealed at its most efficient" (Luttwak 1976: 112)…

"Archelaus himself recognized that "the power of disposing of it [his kingdom rule] belonged to Caesar, who could either give it to him or not, as he pleased" (Ant. 17:11:2 §312). Their rule was tenuous, so that John could say "they receive authority"; that authority was "with the beast"; and it was for "one hour."

"Client kings, such as the Antiochus, Agrippa, Sohemus, Malchus, and Alexander provided auxiliary forces for Rome during the Jewish War (J.W. 2:18:9 §499–501; 3:4:2 §68; 5:1:6 §45) (cf. Aune 951; Stuart 2:327). Dio Cassius (65:4:3) mentions that the Roman siege of Jerusalem included "many slingers and bows that had been sent by some of the barbarian kings." In fact, "a Roman army on campaign always included a complement of allies.… Rome relied very heavily on others for her cavalry forces" in that "such troops might have local knowledge of topography and the enemy, and could provide specialist fighting techniques appropriate to the situation" (Gillver 2001: 22; cp. Grant 1974: 77). The auxiliary forces in the empire after Augustus comprised about half of Rome's military might (cf. Luttwak 1976: 16; cf. Tac., Ann. 4:5)." Kenneth L. Gentry, Jr., *The Divorce of Israel: A Redemptive-Historical Interpretation of Revelation Vol. 2* (Dallas, GA: Tolle Lege Press, 2016), 474-475.

The Ten Client Kings Named: We do not know them all, but Wellesley lists 8 of them (assuming Berenice is not counted as a king). Malchus of Nabatea makes the 9th (*Wars of the Jews* 3.4.2), and Tiberius Alexander, governor of Egypt makes 10 (*Wars of the Jews* 4.10.6): "Mucianus, governor of Syria; Sohaemus of Emesa, Antiochus IV, ruler of Comagene, King Agrippa, sheikh of Anjar and Golan; Berenice, widow of Herod of Anjar. "We are not surprised to learn that the governors of all the provinces of Asia Minor, through disposing of no legionary garrisons, had promised such support in supplies, facilities and auxiliary forces as they could give and Vespasian might require. Among them were the proconsul of Asia, Gaius Fonteius Agrippa, and the legate of Galatia-with-Pamphylia, Lucius Nonius Calpurnius Asprenas. Both In addition, there was Cappadocia, still a procuratorial province governed by a knight without the legionary garrison which Vespasian himself was to give it; its governor in 69 is unknown, and equally unknown is the governor of Pontus, added to Bithynia five years before." Kenneth Wellesley, *Year of the Four Emperors* (Taylor and Francis, 2014) 123-124.

"According to David S. Clark

"These ten horns were ten kings, not kings sitting on the throne of Rome, as I understand, but those kings and countries subjected by Rome, and which made the empire great. We know that Rome embraced at that time the countries of Europe that bordered on the Mediterranean Sea, and the northern part of Africa and considerable territory in Asia, and also in central Europe. Rome had conquered the world.

Adams writes that

"the ten horns may represent the provincial governors and their provinces which at first gave support to Rome (vv. 12, 13), and in turn received their authority from her. They persecute Christians in carrying out her interdicts against them (v. 14). But in the end, it is these provinces which turned upon and destroyed Rome (v. 16).

According to Russell,

"on the whole, we conclude that this symbol signifies the auxiliary princes and chiefs who were allies of Rome and received commands in the Roman army during the Jewish war. We know from Tacitus and Josephus that several kings of neighboring nations followed Vespasian and Titus to the war.... It is not incumbent to produce the exact number of ten, which, like seven, appears to be a mystic or symbolic number.

Chilton writes:

"Rome actually had ten imperial provinces, and some have read this as a reference to them. It is not necessary, however, to attempt a precise definition of these ten subject kings; the symbol simply represents [quoting Terry] "the totality of those allied or subject kings who aided Rome in her wars both on Judaism and Christianity."

Steve Gregg, *Revelation, Four Views: A Parallel Commentary* (Nashville, TN: T. Nelson Publishers, 1997), 414–416.

[2] Revelation 17:12.

[3] Revelation 17:9-10.

[4] **The Beast as a manifold symbol for several things**:

The Beast as the individual man Nero:

Revelation 13:18 This calls for wisdom: let the one who has understanding calculate the number of the beast, for it is the number of a man, and his number is 666.

The Beast as the principality behind Nero:

Revelation 17:8 The beast that you saw was, and is not, and is about to rise from the bottomless pit and go to destruction. And the dwellers on earth whose names have not been written in the book of life from the foundation of the world will marvel to see the beast, because it was and is not and is to come.

The Beast as the collective empire of Caesars:

Revelation 17:9–10 [9] This calls for a mind with wisdom: the seven heads are seven mountains on which the woman is seated; [10] they are also seven kings, five of whom have fallen, one is, the other has not yet come, and when he does come he must remain only a little while.

Consider this interesting theory about the Beast as the spiritual principality behind Titus by Duncan McKenzie:

"One should also note that John was told the beast was "about to come up out of the abyss" (Rev. 17:8 NASB). The Antichrist was about to come in the first century, not thousands of years later. Those in John's first century audience with the required knowledge would be able to calculate the number of his name (Rev. 13:18). I shall argue that the Antichrist was the demonic ruler that would come out of the abyss at the end of the old covenant age to work through Titus in his AD 70 destruction of the Jewish nation. It was this demonic ruler, not the man Titus, who would be destroyed in the lake of fire at the time of the parousia (Rev. 19:20; cf. Dan. 7:11).

"In talking about the man of lawlessness, the one who would capture the Temple and be defeated by Jesus's Second Coming (2 Thess. 2:4, 8), Vine notes that the word translated as "destroy" in 2 Thessalonians 2:8 ("and then the lawless one will be revealed, whom the Lord will consume with the breath of His mouth and destroy with the brightness of His coming") does not necessarily mean to annihilate but rather to make inactive.

> Destroy: katarge, lit. to reduce to inactivity (kata, down, argos, inactive) . . . In this and similar words not loss of being is implied, but loss of well being . . . [Thus,] the Man of Sin is reduced to inactivity by the manifestation of the Lord's parousia with His people.

"It was the spirit of Antichrist working through Titus that was defeated and rendered inactive... It was the demonic king from the abyss, not Titus, that was destroyed in the lake of fire at Jesus's parousia (Rev. 19:11-21).

"Understanding that the Antichrist was ultimately a spirit helps to explain the somewhat strange wording in Daniel 9:

> And after the sixty-two weeks Messiah shall be cut off, but not for Himself; and the people of the prince who is to come shall destroy the city and the sanctuary. The end shall be with a flood, and till the end of the war desolations are determined. Daniel 9:26

Why does the text not simply say the prince to come would destroy Jerusalem and the Temple? The reason is because the prince to come, the Antichrist, would be a spiritual prince; it was his people that would destroy Jerusalem. Daniel 12 contains a similar statement of a spiritual ruler and his people. In verse 1 the angel Michael is said to be a prince of the Jewish people:

> At that time Michael shall stand up, the great prince who stands watch over the sons of your people and there shall be a time of trouble, such as never was since there was a nation, even to that time . . . . Daniel 12:1

It is the same with the prince to come in Daniel 9:26; he was a demonic prince of the Roman people. This was the beast from the abyss, the spirit of Antichrist. Consistent with this consider the angelic/demonic kings and princes spoken of in Daniel 10:

> Then he [the glorious Man of Daniel 10:5-6] said to me, "Do not fear, Daniel, for from the first day that you set your heart to understand, and to humble yourself before your God, your words were heard; and I have come because of your words. But the prince of the kingdom of Persia withstood me twenty-one days and behold, Michael, one of the chief princes, came to help me, for I had been alone there with the kings of Persia." . . . Then he [the glorious Man] said, "Do you know why I have come to you? And now I must return to fight with the prince of Persia; and when I have gone forth, indeed the prince of Greece will come. But I will tell you what is noted in the Scripture of Truth. (No one upholds me against these, except Michael your prince . . . .)" Daniel 10:12-13, 20-21 (underlined emphasis mine)

McKenzie PhD, Duncan W.. *The Antichrist and the Second Coming: A Preterist Examination Volume I* (K-Locations 455-486). Xulon Press. K Edition.

[5] **Punishment of earthly rulers along with their heavenly counterparts**: **On earth as it is in heaven or "as above, so below"**: "This concept as prayed by Jesus in the Lord's Prayer is rooted in the Deuteronomy 32 worldview. Deut 32:8-10 says that Yahweh divided the seventy nations according to the number of the fallen Sons of God and placed them under their authority. They became the "princes" (Dan. 10:13, 20-21) or "gods" of those pagan nations (Deut. 32:17; 4:19-21), rulers of those geographical territories.

"When earthly rulers battle on earth, the Bible describes the host of heaven battling with them in spiritual unity. In Daniel 10, hostilities between Greece and Persia is accompanied by the battle of heavenly Watchers over those nations (described as "princes").

"Daniel 10:13, 20-21 The prince of the kingdom of Persia withstood me twenty-one days, but Michael, one of the chief princes, came to help me, for I was left there with the kings of Persia." …Then he said, "Do you know why I have come to you? But now I will return to fight against the prince of Persia; and when I go out, behold, the prince of Greece will come. [21] But I will tell you what is inscribed in the book of truth: there is none who contends by my side against these except Michael, your prince.

"When Sisera fought with Israel, the earthly kings and heavenly authorities (host of heaven) are described interchangeably in unity.

"Judges 5:19–20 "The kings came, they fought; then fought the kings of Canaan…From heaven the stars fought, from their courses they fought against Sisera.

"When God punishes earthly rulers, he punishes them along with the heavenly rulers ("host of heaven") above and behind them.

"Isaiah 24:21–22 On that day the LORD will punish the host of heaven, in heaven, and the kings of the earth, on the earth. They will be gathered together as prisoners in a pit; they will be shut up in a prison, and after many days they will be punished.

"Though this notion of territorial archons or spiritual rulers is Biblical and carries over into intertestamental literature such as the Book of Enoch (1 En. 89:59, 62-63; 67) and others, it seems to lessen at the time of the New Testament.

"Walter Wink points out that the picture of Watchers over nations is hinted at in 1 Cor. 4:9 where the apostle explains their persecution has "become a spectacle (theatre) to the world, to angels and to men." He explains that "the image of the Roman theater conjures up hostile and jeering crowds," and the angels are "heavenly representatives of the Gentile nations and people, who watch, not without malicious glee, the tribulations endured by the apostle to their peoples."

"The epistles speak of the spiritual principalities and powers that are behind the earthly rulers and powers to be sure (Eph. 6:12-13), but it appears to be more generic in reference. And after the death, resurrection, and ascension of Christ, these spiritual powers have been disarmed and overthrown (Col. 2:15, Luke 10:18), at least legally losing their hegemony (Eph. 1:20-23). The fallen angelic powers are still around, but have been defanged with the inauguration of the Messianic kingdom of God." Brian Godawa, *When Giants Were Upon the Earth: The Watchers, the Nephilim, and the Biblical Cosmic War of the Seed* (Embedded Pictures, 2014), 278-279.

[6] Revelation 17:4–6; 18:24.

[7] **The description of the Harlot reflects the priesthood of Israel**: Revelation 17:4–6 [4] The woman was arrayed in purple and scarlet, and adorned with gold and jewels and pearls, holding in her hand a golden cup full of abominations and the impurities of her sexual immorality. [5] And on her forehead was written a name of mystery: "Babylon the great, mother of prostitutes and of earth's abominations." [6] And I saw the woman, drunk with the blood of the saints, the blood of the martyrs of Jesus.

"Her dress reflects her covenantal status as a kingdom of priests, particularly reminding the first-century reader of Jerusalem's central Temple and its prominent High Priest (note his great authority in Acts 23:4). In Exodus 28 we read of the High Priest's ritual attire:

And these are the garments which they shall make: a breast-piece and an ephod and a robe and a tunic of checkered work, a turban and a sash, and they shall make holy garments for Aaron your brother and his sons, that he may minister as priest to Me. And they shall take the gold and the blue and the purple and the scarlet material and the fine linen…. And the skillfully woven band, which is on it, shall be like its workmanship, of the same material: of gold, of blue and purple and scarlet material and fine twisted linen. And you shall take two onyx stones and engrave on them the names of the sons of Israel (Exo. 28:4–5, 8–9).

"His attire also matches the decor of the Tabernacle (the forerunner to the Temple): "Moreover you shall make the tabernacle with ten curtains of fine twisted linen and blue and purple and scarlet material; you shall make them with cherubim, the work of a skillful workman (Exo. 26:1). The Old Testament description of the Temple points out that the altar (which received the blood of sacrifices, Exo 24:6; 29:12; Lev 1:5) was gold —like the cup from which the Harlot drank the blood of the saints:

> The whole altar which was by the inner sanctuary he overlaid with gold (1 Kgs 6:22).

"Josephus provides us with an eyewitness description of the first century Temple, which also parallels the Harlot's dress: "The Temple's tapestry was Babylonian [!] tapestry in which blue, purple, scarlet, and linen were mingled" (War 5:5:4). He also mentions the prominence of gold in Temple vessels: "The greatest part of the vessels that were put in them was of silver and gold" (War 5:4:5).

"John's unusual focus on her forehead is significant not only in our present argument but later in another context, as well. In the description of the High Priest in the Old Testament we read:

> "You shall also make a plate of pure gold and shall engrave on it, like the engravings of a seal, 'Holy to the Lord'.... And it shall be on Aaron's forehead, and Aaron shall take away the iniquity of the holy things which the sons of Israel consecrate, with regard to all their holy gifts; and it shall always be on his forehead, that they may be accepted before the Lord (Exo. 28:36, 38).

"John dresses the Harlot in a way that draws our attention to her forehead. And when we look there, we see the opposite of what appears on the forehead of the High Priest, showing John's estimation of what the Holy City, Temple of God, and the priesthood have become. (Interestingly, Jeremiah also mentions the harlotrous forehead of Jerusalem in Jer. 3:3)." Kenneth L. Gentry Jr., *Perilous Times: A Study in Eschatological Evil* (Covenant Media Press, 1999), 77-79.

[8] **Den of thieves**: Jesus's cleansing of the temple was actually a prophetic drama foreshadowing the destruction of the temple in AD 70.

> Mark 11:15-17 [15] And they came to Jerusalem. And he entered the temple and began to drive out those who sold and those who bought in the temple, and he overturned the tables of the money-changers and the seats of those who sold pigeons. [16] And he would not allow anyone to carry anything through the temple. [17] And he was teaching them and saying to them, "Is it not written, 'My house shall be called a house of prayer for all the nations'? But you have made it a den of robbers."

"We must now return to this passage once more, this time to see the way in which Jesus's Temple-action is here, too, explained in terms of his Messiahship. So closely do they belong together, in fact, that the destruction of the Temple—predicted already in symbolic action, and here in prophetic oracle—is bound up with Jesus's own vindication, as prophet and also as Messiah. In the eschatological lawcourt scene, he has pitted himself against the Temple. When his prophecy of its destruction comes true, that event will demonstrate that he was indeed the Messiah who had the authority over it. Mark 13:2 and its parallels thus makes explicit the meaning of Mark 11:15-17. 'There will not be one stone upon another that will not be cast down.'

N. T. Wright, *Jesus and the Victory of God, Christian Origins and the Question of God* (London: Society for Promoting Christian Knowledge, 1996), 511.

[9] Matthew 23:29-36

"Woe to you, scribes and Pharisees, hypocrites! For you build the tombs of the prophets and decorate the monuments of the righteous, saying, 'If we had lived in the days of our fathers, we would not have taken part with them in shedding the blood of the prophets.' Thus you witness against yourselves that you are sons of those who murdered the prophets. Fill up, then, the measure of your fathers. [33] You serpents, you brood of vipers, how are you to escape being sentenced to Gehenna? Therefore I send you prophets and wise men and scribes, some of whom you will kill and crucify, and some you will flog in your synagogues and persecute from town to town, so that on you may come all the righteous blood shed on the land, from the blood of righteous Abel to the blood of Zechariah the son of Barachiah, whom you murdered between the sanctuary and the altar. Truly, I say to you, all these things will come upon this generation.

378

End of the age: The following is an excerpt from Brian Godawa, *End Times Bible Prophecy: It's Not What They Told You* (Embedded Pictures Publishing, 2016), 71-73:

I had always been taught that the end of the age was the end of history, the end of the world, and the final judgment of mankind. Surely such language was obvious in its huge scope. But remember what we have learned about the Old Testament imagery of worldwide and cosmic language used of covenants? Well, consider this: Jesus and the writers of the New Testament were ancient Jews steeped in the Old Testament, its imagery, language, and poetry. They were not modern, scientific Westerners like you and I. As I looked into the concept of the end of the age and the last days, I discovered a covenantal meaning that blew my mind.

My first hint was that the Greek word for "age" that Jesus used was *aion*, which Louw-Nida defines as "a unit of time as a particular stage or period of history—age, era."

This notion of the end of the age shows up in other teachings from Jesus. At the end of Matthew, Jesus said to his disciples, "Behold, I am with you always, to the end of the age" (28:20). In another place he said that those who followed him would receive both persecutions and spiritual family in this age, "and in the age to come eternal life" (Mark 10:30).

The notion of the present age and the messianic age to come was prevalent in Jewish understanding and in the New Testament as well. Paul wrote of the Christians living in "this age" (1 Cor 3:18), "this present evil age" (Gal 1:4) that had evil spiritual rulers of this age (1 Cor 2:8; 2 Cor 4:4); but there was the messianic "age to come" (Eph 1:21, Heb 6:4). When Messiah came, he would usher in a new covenant, a new age of spiritual transformation in the world.

Well, of course, Messiah had come. That "age to come" was not a reference to a second coming of Jesus, but his first coming, bringing the kingdom of God (the kingdom age to come), a kingdom that was both now and not yet. It was inaugurated but not consummated.

This "age to come" was the new covenant age. Paul wrote elsewhere that the gospel (the new covenant) was "hidden for ages, but now revealed to his saints (Col 1:26). In 1 Corinthians 10:11, he wrote that the old covenant events occurred as an example "for our instruction upon whom the end of the ages has come." Did you catch that? The temple had not yet been destroyed, and Paul was saying that his generation was at the end of the ages! He said that it *had come* upon that first century of believers. The end of the age is not a future event that hasn't happened yet; it occurred in the first century with the coming of the new covenant, confirmed in the destruction of the temple. But Paul isn't the only one who wrote that in the New Testament.

Hebrews 9:26 says that Jesus suffered on the cross, "once for all at the end of the ages to put away sin by the sacrifice of himself." The end of the ages is not the end of history or the end of the world as we understand it. The end of the ages had already occurred at the time of the crucifixion of Christ. The end of the ages was the end of the old covenant era and the beginning of the new covenant in Christ's blood!

But get this: that same writer of Hebrews talked about the new covenant in Christ being superior to the old covenant in Hebrews 8. He quoted Jeremiah confirming that the prophets predicted the arrival of the new covenant age. And then he said, "In speaking of a new covenant, he makes the first one obsolete. And what is becoming obsolete and growing old is ready to vanish away" (8:13).

What was growing old and ready to vanish at that time?

"It blew my theology when I realized that he was talking about the destruction of the temple as the final culmination of the new covenant replacement of the old covenant! He was writing in the time period after Christ's death and resurrection and right before the temple had been destroyed. So the new covenant had been established in Christ's blood, but it was not consummated with historical finality. Like Paul, the writer believed they were at the end of the ages. The new covenant would make the old covenant obsolete. But take a closer look at the language he used. He said that the old is "becoming obsolete and is ready to vanish away," as if the old covenant had not vanished yet. It was only in the process of *becoming* obsolete. "Becoming," not "had become," and not "would become" thousands of years in the future. What could that mean?

Well, the writer was writing within the generation that Jesus said would see the destruction of the temple. The temple had not yet been destroyed. Hebrews 8 says that they were in a time period of change between covenants and that change had not yet been fully or historically consummated. That first century generation was in the transition period between ages or covenants. So, what would be the event that would embody the theological claim that the old covenant was obsolete and the new covenant had replaced it? The destruction of the symbol of the old covenant, the temple! The old covenant would not be obsolete until its symbolic incarnation, the temple, was made desolate.

"I had to eventually admit that the "end of the ages" did not mean what I was taught it meant, or what we modern Westerners assume it means. It did not mean the end of history, or the second coming of Christ, but, rather, to the New Testament writers, it meant the end of God's old covenant age."

[10] Revelation 17:16

[11] Isaiah 10:12.

[12] **Rod of Yahweh's anger**: Isaiah 10:5–6 [5] Woe to Assyria, the rod of my anger; the staff in their hands is my fury! [6] Against a godless nation I send him, and against the people of my wrath I command him, to take spoil and seize plunder, and to tread them down like the mire of the streets.

[13] Isaiah 10:12-15.

[14] **God sovereignly uses pagan armies to judge peoples, cities and nations. Then he judges those pagan nations as well:**

These are two parables of the destruction of Jerusalem and the Jews for rejecting Jesus:

> Matthew 22:6–7
> [6] while the rest seized his servants, treated them shamefully, and killed them. [7] The king was angry, and he sent his troops and destroyed those murderers and burned their city. [It was the Romans that destroyed Jerusalem]

> Matthew 21:40–41
> [40] When therefore the owner of the vineyard comes, what will he do to those tenants?" [41] They said to him, "He will put those wretches to a miserable death and let out the vineyard to other tenants who will give him the fruits in their seasons." [The Jews were put to death by the Romans]

This Daniel prophecy about the "people of the prince" can be interpreted as the people of the Messiah, because Messiah is "the prince" in the rest of the passage. That would make the Romans referred to as Messiah's people for accomplishing his purpose, just like pagan Cyrus was God's "anointed" (messiah) to accomplish his purpose (Isa 45:1-2).

> Daniel 9:26
> [26] And after the sixty-two weeks, an anointed one shall be cut off and shall have nothing. And the people of the prince who is to come shall destroy the city and the sanctuary. Its end shall come with a flood, and to the end there shall be war. Desolations are decreed.

Notice in these Old Testament passages how God describes the pagan nations' actions as his own actions:

> Isaiah 10:5–6
> [5] Woe to Assyria, the rod of my anger; the staff in their hands is my fury! [6] Against a godless nation I send him, and against the people of my wrath I command him, to take spoil and seize plunder, and to tread them down like the mire of the streets.

> Isaiah 10:15
> [15] Shall the axe boast over him who hews with it, or the saw magnify itself against him who wields it? As if a rod should wield him who lifts it, or as if a staff should lift him who is not wood!

> Isaiah 45:1–2
> [1] Thus says the LORD to his anointed, to Cyrus, whose right hand I have grasped, to subdue

nations before him and to loose the belts of kings, to open doors before him that gates may not be closed: ² "I will go before you and level the exalted places, I will break in pieces the doors of bronze and cut through the bars of iron,

God uses Nebuchadnezzar as his tool to judge Egypt

Ezekiel 30:24–26
²⁴ And I will strengthen the arms of the king of Babylon and put my sword in his hand, but I will break the arms of Pharaoh, and he will groan before him like a man mortally wounded. ²⁵ I will strengthen the arms of the king of Babylon, but the arms of Pharaoh shall fall. Then they shall know that I am the LORD, when I put my sword into the hand of the king of Babylon and he stretches it out against the land of Egypt. ²⁶ And I will scatter the Egyptians among the nations and disperse them throughout the countries. Then they will know that I am the LORD."

God uses the Medes to destroy Babylon in 539 BC

Isa. 13:1
The oracle concerning Babylon ...The LORD of hosts is mustering the army for battle. 5 They are coming from a far country, From the farthest heavens, The LORD and His instruments of indignation, To destroy the whole earth. ...11 Thus I will punish the world for its evil..17 Behold, I am going to stir up the Medes against them..

God used Babylonians to perform his judgment destroying the first temple 587 BC

Jeremiah 4:12–27
Now it is I who speak in judgment upon them." ¹³ Behold, he comes up like clouds; his chariots like the whirlwind; his horses are swifter than eagles… Warn the nations that he is coming; announce to Jerusalem, "Besiegers come from a distant land; they shout against the cities of Judah…²⁷ For thus says the LORD, "The whole land shall be a desolation; yet I will not make a full end.

God used Babylon to judge Edom And The Nations surrounding them. (fulfilled in the Babylonian Invasion of Judah 587-586 BC -- Jer. 25, Ezek. 35, Obad 15, Mal 1:2

Isaiah 34:2–6
² For the LORD is enraged against all the nations, and furious against all their host; he has devoted them to destruction, has given them over for slaughter. ³ …⁵ For my sword has drunk its fill in the heavens; behold, it descends for judgment upon Edom, upon the people I have devoted to destruction. ⁶ The LORD has a sword; it is sated with blood; it is gorged with fat, …. For the LORD has a sacrifice in Bozrah, a great slaughter in the land of Edom.

God uses Babylon to judge Assyria and Israel

Habakkuk 1:5–6 ⁵ "Look among the nations, and see; wonder and be astounded. For I am doing a work in your days that you would not believe if told. ⁶ For behold, I am raising up the Chaldeans, that bitter and hasty nation, who march through the breadth of the earth, to seize dwellings not their own.

Then God judges Babylon

Habakkuk 2:16
¹⁶ You will have your fill of shame instead of glory. Drink, yourself, and show your uncircumcision! The cup in the LORD's right hand will come around to you, and utter shame will come upon your glory!

The Destruction of Samaria and the exile of 10 northern tribes by Assyria, 8th century BC

Micah 1:3–7 ³ For behold, the LORD is coming out of his place, and will come down and tread upon the high places of the earth. ⁴ And the mountains will melt under him, and the valleys will split open, like wax before the fire, like waters poured down a steep place. ⁵ All this is for the transgression of Jacob and for the sins of the house of Israel. What is the transgression of Jacob?

Is it not Samaria? And what is the high place of Judah? Is it not Jerusalem? [6] Therefore I will make Samaria a heap in the open country.

Against Assyria (fulfilled: 701 BC against Sennacherib Isa. 37:36)

Isaiah 30:25–28
on the day of the great slaughter, when the towers fall. [27] Behold, the name of the LORD comes from afar, burning with his anger, and in thick rising smoke; his lips are full of fury, and his tongue is like a devouring fire; [28] his breath is like an overflowing stream that reaches up to the neck; to sift the nations with the sieve of destruction, and to place on the jaws of the peoples a bridle that leads astray.

[15] Revelation 17:16–17 [16] And the ten horns that you saw, they and the beast will hate the prostitute. They will make her desolate and naked, and devour her flesh and burn her up with fire, [17] for God has put it into their hearts to carry out his purpose by being of one mind and handing over their royal power to the beast, until the words of God are fulfilled.

Examples throughout Revelation of God "allowing" or "giving power" to the wicked: Revelation 6:2, 4, 8; 9:1, 3; 13:5, 7, 14–15; 16:8.

[16] **Coming on the clouds referred to in this paragraph**:

Against Egypt by Assyria: Fulfilled: 701 BC Sargon?:

Isaiah 19:1 The oracle concerning Egypt. Behold, the LORD is riding on a swift cloud, and is about to come to Egypt;

Against Ninevah (By Babylon)

Nahum 1:2–3 [2] the LORD takes vengeance on his adversaries and keeps wrath for his enemies. [3] …. His way is in whirlwind and storm, and the clouds are the dust of his feet.

Against Assyria (fulfilled: 701 BC against Sennacherib Isa 37:36):

Isa. 30:30 And the LORD will cause His voice of authority to be heard. And the descending of His arm to be seen in fierce anger, And in the flame of a consuming fire, In cloudburst, downpour, and hailstones. 31 For at the voice of the LORD Assyria will be terrified, …31:4 So will the LORD of hosts come down to wage war on Mount Zion and on its hill."

Against Egypt:

Ezekiel 30:3-10 "For the day is near, Even the day of the LORD is near; It will be a day of clouds, A time {of doom} for the nations. 4 "And a sword will come upon Egypt…10 "Thus says the Lord GOD: "I will put an end to the wealth of Egypt, by the hand of Nebuchadnezzar king of Babylon.

Against Israel (Babylon) 586 BC:

Jeremiah 4:13, 16 [13] Behold, he comes up like clouds; his chariots like the whirlwind; his horses are swifter than eagles— woe to us, for we are ruined!…[16] Warn the nations that he is coming; announce to Jerusalem, "Besiegers come from a distant land; they shout against the cities of Judah.

[17] **Coming on the clouds**: The following is an excerpt from Brian Godawa, *End Times Bible Prophecy: It's Not What They Told You* (Embedded Pictures Publishing, 2016), 132-133:

I had always understood "coming on the clouds" as being an obvious, literal allusion to Jesus floating in on clouds in the sky in a climactic ending to history. What else could it mean? This seemed to be the biggest obstacle to surmount in understanding the Olivet Discourse as a prophecy of the first century coming of Christ at the end of the old covenant age.

Then I was shown in the Old Testament the very clear precedent of this metaphor. With a new understanding of the ancient Jewish mindset and how they interpreted these words, I began to see it as the very opposite of the wooden, literalistic event I used to see it as. Let me show you what changed my mind, and I'm sure it will begin to change yours.

"Coming on the clouds" is used throughout the Old Testament as a figurative storm reference to God's judging presence upon a city, nation, or people. Clouds and storm are both metaphors for deity and for local judgment. Here is a brief survey of the instances.

When God judged the city of Nineveh in the days of Nahum the prophet…

> Nahum 1:2–3
> The LORD takes vengeance on his adversaries and keeps wrath for his enemies. [3]…His way is in whirlwind and storm, and <u>the clouds are the dust of his feet</u>.

When God delivered David and judged Saul…

> Psalm 18:9–11
> He bowed the heavens and came down; thick <u>darkness was under his feet</u>. [10] He rode on a cherub and flew; he came <u>swiftly on the wings of the wind</u>. [11] He made darkness his covering, his canopy around him, <u>thick clouds dark with water</u>.

When God judged Egypt in the days of Ezekiel, he said,

> Ezekiel 30:3–4
> For the day is near, the day of the LORD is near; <u>it will be a day of clouds</u>… [4] A sword shall come upon Egypt.

In 721 B.C., Isaiah prophesied judgment against Egypt that occurred by about 701 B.C.

> Isaiah 19:1
> An oracle concerning Egypt. Behold, <u>the LORD is riding on a swift cloud</u> and comes to Egypt;

When God judged Assyria in 701 B.C. he described his anger. ..

> Isaiah 30:30
> And the Lord will cause his majestic voice to be heard and the descending blow of his arm to be seen, in furious anger and a flame of devouring fire, <u>with a cloudburst</u> and storm and hailstones.

Remember that passage in Joel about the last days that Peter said was being fulfilled in his day? You guessed it, more clouds of judgment.

> Joel 2:1–2
> [F]or the day of the LORD is coming; it is near, [2] a day of darkness and gloom, <u>a day of clouds and thick darkness</u>!

These are all local and limited judgments upon cities, nations, or peoples, and they all use the imagery of God coming on the clouds with the storm of judgment. This was a common ancient image of God's judgment. Did God literally come floating in on clouds in the sky to Nineveh, Saul, or Egypt? Of course not. Clouds and storm were figurative expressions, literary signs of his spiritual presence in the local and limited judgments upon those nations and cities. So, Jesus coming on the clouds of heaven in power and glory was an obvious figurative expression of Jesus's presence in the judgment upon Jerusalem, the sign of his power and the glory of the new covenant.

CHAPTER 11

[1] **Moshe quotes from**: Leviticus 26:3-13.

[2] **Elihu quotes from**: Leviticus 26:14-25.

[3] **Cassandra is referring to**: Leviticus 26 and Deuteronomy 28.

[4] **The plagues of Egypt are mentioned in**: Deuteronomy 28:27.

The four repetitions of seven-fold curses is in: Leviticus 26.

[6] **Revelation as a description of the fulfillment of Leviticus 26 curses:** "Once again in Revelation we must also recognize the Old Testament influence: "Revelation's four septets [oracles, seals, trumpets, bowls] derive from the second part of Lev 26" (G. Campbell 2004b: 72; cp. Chilton 16; Bandy 2010:13, 15). These four sevens reflect the legal-covenantal nature of the judgments. In Lev 26 (one of the two great covenant blessing and cursing chapters of the Old Testament, cp. Dt 28) we hear God warning Israel four times: "If also after these things, you do not obey Me, then I will punish you seven times more for your sins" (Lev 26:18, cp. also vv. 21, 24, and 28). The seals, trumpets and bowls are structured by this seven-fold (i.e., complete) judgment against Israel for breach of covenant (in Revelation the covenant is particularly a marriage covenant). Even before John's Revelation, the Lord himself warns of "seven other spirits" coming to beset Israel (Mt 21:45) and calls down seven woes upon her religious leaders (Mt 23)." Kenneth L. Gentry, Jr., The Divorce of Israel: A Redemptive-Historical Interpretation of Revelation Vol. 1 (Dallas, GA: Tolle Lege Press, 2016), 574-575.

"[Leviticus 26] concerns woes that God will send on the Israelites if they commit idolatry. Four times it is repeated that God will judge them "seven times" if they become unfaithful. Each sevenfold figurative expression introduces a successively worse ordeal that is conditioned on Israel's failure to repent after the preceding woe (drought and crop failure in 26:19–20, "wild beasts of the earth" in v 22, "sword ... death ... famine of bread" in vv 25–26, and desolation and "sword" in vv 29–33). The promise interwoven in these warnings is that if Israel does repent of idolatry (cf. 26:1, 30–31), God will bless Israel again (cf. likewise Deut. 32:24–25). Thus, these are warning judgments inducing repentance and so renewing faith and only permanently punishing apostate Israelites.

"If this background is in mind in Rev. 6:1–8, then the afflictions cited there not only purge and punish but also serve as warnings for people to repent. Could it also be that the four judgments of Leviticus, which are each summarized figuratively as consisting of seven punishments, serve as the model for the four sets of seven judgments that so dominate the Apocalypse? This is a viable consideration especially if the "seven thunders" in 10:3–4 are construed as one of these sets, though for some reason it remains unrevealed (see further on ch. 10)."

G. K. Beale, *The Book of Revelation: A Commentary on the Greek Text, New International Greek Testament Commentary* (Grand Rapids, MI; Carlisle, Cumbria: W.B. Eerdmans; Paternoster Press, 1999), 373.

[7] **The seals, trumpets, thunders and bowls is not chronological but conceptual/cyclical/spiral:**

"While the seventh element in each series represents the final judgment, the preceding six are not necessarily in chronological order. The primary intention of the numbering is to represent the order of John's visions, not necessarily the order of historical events, which would have to be only secondary. This is a crucial hermeneutical principle of the book that needs to be kept in mind, since it applies not only to the numbered elements in each series but also to the arrangement of the seals, trumpets, and bowls series and to the unnumbered visions. John's repeated use throughout the book of such transitional expressions as "after this," "after these things," and "I saw" provide the exegetical underpinnings of this all-important literary principle." G. K. Beale, The Book of Revelation: A Commentary on the Greek Text, New International Greek Testament Commentary (Grand Rapids, MI; Carlisle, Cumbria: W.B. Eerdmans; Paternoster Press, 1999), 129.

"John does not intend his storyline to unfold in terms of linear logic, but more "as a gestalt of simultaneous images" (Boring 58). He argues this partly on the basis of the fact that, the very means of John's receiving Revelation suggests the opposite, for "picture language is a better vehicle for dealing with ultimates than discursive propositional language, no one picture can capture or convey the reality of its subject matter. Thus a plurality of pictures of the same reality are found in Revelation, pictures that cannot be logically harmonized if reduced to statement" (Boring 58). He continues:
"While...there is some considerable parallelism between the series of events represented by the seals, trumpets and bowls, the material must again be forced to make it fit a neat scheme of recapitulation. This series of visions is not a chaos of disorder, but neither is it architectonically precise. It moves forward as a kind of impressionistic, interrelated spiral, bringing previous scenes before the imagination in new and intensified light, but never in some predictable, diagrammable way. John's style of communication is allusive and evocative, imaginative and pictorial, rather than rigidly logical and consistent.

"The dominant view today is some form of the recapitulation or spiral approach rather than strictly chronological progression…

"Beale observes that "the trumpets go over the same ground as the seal woes, but from a different perspective" and "the bowl woes are temporally parallel with the trumpets" Mounce puts it well when he notes: "While there is a rather clearly discernible literary development [between the seals, trumpets, and bowls], it is not to represent a corresponding chronological development. The three series cover the same period of travail…

"Revelation's movement is characteristically Johannine—it involves a spiraling motion (as do John and 1 John)108 which re-cast earlier prophecies, even though "each series is not simply a repetition of the previous one, but is a development of it" (Filho 2002: 215). This is "like the Gospel of John, the same theology is repeated over and over again, each time going a little deeper, and carrying the message further, like waves on a seashore" (Corsini 63). "The Gospel and epistles of St John stand out from the rest of the New Testament writings for their concentric or circular structure"…

Fiorenza (1998: 171) and Paulien (1995: 261) call Revelation's movement a conical spiral. Metzger (18) agrees, adding that "the book involves a series of parallel yet ever-progressing sections. These bring [matters] before the reader, over and over again, but in climacteric form." This style is called climacteric, based on a Greek word speaking of climbing stairs: the Greek word klimax means "ladder, flight of stairs". John's spiral structure allows parallel treatment of the events simultaneously with an upward progress within each cycle. Between the parallel cycles, the visions make rhetorical progress in terms of the judgments' growing intensity. Witherington argues that "the threefold '7' judgments are basically describing one reality (though perhaps in progressively more intense or complete ways) for they all conclude with the same final judgment. This is demonstrated by the repeated use of the terms 'thunder,' 'lightning,' 'earthquake,' and 'heavy hail' in varying order at 4.5; 8.5; 11.9 and 16.18–21." (I believe he is mistaken in declaring the "final judgment" as the goal of the cycles. Rather the destruction of the temple and the conclusion of the old covenant is their conclusion, as I am arguing in this commentary.) Elsewhere (18) he states: "The subsequent set of seven judgments do not merely repeat what has been said in the previous seven judgments. They evolve from and expand upon them. They then could be seen as increasingly precise or intense disclosures of the same reality."

Kenneth L. Gentry, Jr., *The Divorce of Israel: A Redemptive-Historical Interpretation of Revelation Vol. 1* (Dallas, GA: Tolle Lege Press, 2016),157-158.

The following chart showing the recapitulation or conceptual repetition of the seals, trumpets and bowls was taken from: G. K. Beale, *The Book of Revelation: A Commentary on the Greek Text, New International Greek Testament Commentary* (Grand Rapids, MI; Carlisle, Cumbria: W.B. Eerdmans; Paternoster Press, 1999), 129.

	Seals	Trumpets	Bowls
Four Catastrophes	6:1-2: white horse, bow, crown, conquer	8:7: hail, fire, blood	16:2: sores
	6:3-4: red horse, sword take peace from earth	8:8-9: fiery mountain in sea, 1/3 sea became blood	16:3: sea to blood
	6:5-6: black horse, balance	8:10-11: star falls on 1/3 of rivers wormwood > water	16:4-7: rivers to blood
	6:7-8: pale horse, sword, famine, plague, wild animals	8:12: 1/3 sun, 1/3 moon, 1/3 stars	16:8-9: sun
The Woes Intensify: The End Approaches	6:9-11: martyrs under altar, "how long," "little longer"	8:13: "woe, woe, woe" demon locusts from dark pit	16:10: darkness
	6:12-17: earthquake, sun and moon, stars fall, all fear	9:13-21: 200,000,000 demon cavalry from Euphrates	16:12-16: kings of east cross Euphrates to prepare for Armageddon
Interlude	{ 7:1-8: sealing 144,000 / great multitude }	{{ 10:1-11: eating scroll / 11:1-3: 2 witnesses	(pattern broken) {
The End	8:1: silence	11:15: end announced and celebrated but not described	16:17-21: theophany "God remembered great Babylon"
			17–18: then elaborate the 7th bowl Babylon as a continuation and elaboration of the fall of Babylon

How literalism corrupts Bible prophecy interpretation

After all, isn't the Bible supposed to be taken literally? Isn't it only liberals and apostates who deny the literal truth of the Bible? When you interpret the Bible nonliterally, don't you end up believing it's just a bunch of religious myths? Well, no, actually. As a matter of fact, nobody takes the *entire* Bible literally. Not even those who say they do. Let me explain.

Nobody believes the hybrid sea beast of Revelation 13—with its ten horns on seven heads like a leopard, with a bear's feet and a lion's mouth—is a literal, biological, hybrid creature. Everyone believes it is figurative (at least everyone I've checked. I suppose there may be someone on the fringe who doesn't). We may not agree on what it symbolizes, but *everybody* believes it *symbolizes* something other than what it appears to be.

386

Nobody thinks that in the last days this monster, or the land beast of Revelation 13:11, or the many hybrid creatures spoken of in Daniel's prophecies will roam the land as in a Godzilla movie. They are figurative symbols that represent evil kingdoms, as Daniel and the apostle John explained. Scripture says that God owns the cattle on a thousand hills (Psalm 50:10). Nobody believes that literally. Nobody believes that God *does not* own the cattle on the thousand-and-first hill or the two thousandth hill. Even literalists will admit that this is a figurative, poetic expression that God owns everything. Nobody believes that when Jesus said he was "the door" (John 10:7) that he was literally a wooden plank with hinges and a handle. This is a metaphor, a figure of speech that is not literally applicable, but operates as a symbol.

I could go on and on, and in this book I eventually will. But for now I just want to make the point that no right-thinking Christian believes that everything in the Bible is to be taken literally. It is a book full of figurative expression, poetry, hyperbole, symbol, allegory and metaphor. The question is not do we take the Bible literally, but *which parts* do we take literally and *which parts* do we take figuratively? The second question is the next obvious one: how do we know which parts are which? And that is not always an easy question to answer.

So when I say that literalism corrupts Bible prophecy, what I am really saying is that literalism taken to an extreme corrupts the *interpretation* of Bible prophecy by applying literalism where it was not intended by the biblical authors. I sometimes call this kind of excessive literalism "hyperliteralism." But again, no one, not even hyperliteralists, take everything in the Bible literally.

But in my earlier days, I didn't have that finer distinction. And as I dug deeper into Bible prophecy in particular, I discovered that the dispensational viewpoint did in fact have some awareness of the poetry or figurative language in the Bible. How could it not? But because of its bias of literal interpretation as a priority over figurative interpretation, this view forged a standard of Bible hermeneutics that favored that bias. One of the more popular expressions of the standard of literal interpretation of the Bible is embodied in an often-quoted paragraph by David Cooper.

> When the plain sense of Scripture makes common sense, seek no other sense; therefore, take every word at its primary, ordinary, usual, literal meaning unless the facts of the immediate context, studied in the light of related passages and axiomatic and fundamental truths, indicate clearly otherwise.

That made perfect sense to my Bible-believing reason. In order to avoid the anarchy and relativism of every man's interpretation being right in his own eyes, we must take the Bible at face value. We must use our common sense to understand the plain sense of Scripture. We can't just go turning anything we like, willy nilly, into esoteric symbols and arcane allegories. Ordinary and usual seemed superior to extraordinary and unusual. I agreed—and I still agree today—that words should not be taken out of context. They should be understood within their immediate context as well as the context of other Scripture. That remains a sound hermeneutic rule of interpretation: first and foremost, let Scripture interpret Scripture.

There was only one problem that I was about to discover: *my* plain and common sense, *my* ordinary and usual understanding is not at all the same as *the ancient Hebrew* plain and common sense, or ordinary and usual understanding. It wasn't until I began to study the ancient Hebrew mindset, steeped as it was in the Old Testament and influenced by a Near Eastern mindset, that I began to realize just how different that was from my mindset, steeped as it is in a modern American, Western worldview and in scientific categories of thinking.

The Genre of Prophecy and Apocalyptic

Most important is the genre of a piece of literature. You can get the translation right, but if you don't understand the genre you will get it completely wrong. Such is the nature of the genres of apocalypse, prophecy and dream visions. They are decidedly symbolic. The apostle John writes in the Greek of the very first verse of Revelation 1:1 that the angel "sent and signified" the Revelation to John. The images in Revelation are signs or symbols for something else. If the reader takes them literally or in their "plain sense," they will misinterpret the text. Literal isn't everything when it comes to genre.

Different genres of writing have different purposes and therefore should be interpreted through different lenses than the ordinary and usual. The genre of ancient Hebrew prophecy and apocalypse in the Bible is anything but ordinary and usual. It is actually extraordinary and unusual. It is certainly not driven by the notion of plain sense or literal meaning. It is a highly poetic genre expressed in visions and dreams of fantastic images and poetry of symbolism and metaphor.

And prophecy does not exist in a vacuum of our modern understanding. The Jewish writers of Scripture used repetitious images, motifs, and patterns of writing that have precedents in Scripture itself. Rather than interpreting the ancient prophecies through *our* eyes, we must seek to interpret it through *their* eyes and worldview. Before we try to envision the locusts with human heads and scorpion tails as modern Cobra helicopters, we should first see how locusts and human traits on animals and scorpions were used in the Old Testament, since that was the world within which they lived and breathed and had their very being.

It turns out that the commonly used standard we cited above of interpreting the Bible through our plain sense, common sense, ordinary and usual meaning is an act of cultural prejudice. Our Western plain sense literalism is simply not the priority in a very symbolic genre of a different culture with a different plain sense than ours, different colloquialisms and memes than ours, and a different sense of what is ordinary and usual.

It turns out that interpreting Bible prophecy with our modern, Western, hyperliteralistic plain sense will almost certainly result in a false interpretation of the text. If anything, the principle for interpreting poetic symbolic literature like Bible prophecy should be the opposite of the plain sense approach. So I herewith propose a rewrite of the hermeneutic principle applied to prophecy.

> When the plain sense of prophecy makes sense, beware your own bias and seek the genre sense. Take every word at its primary, extraordinary, symbolic meaning unless the facts of the immediate context, studied in the light of related passages and historical facts, indicate clearly otherwise.

[8] **Elihu quotes from**: Revelation 6:2.

[9] **Moshe quotes from**: Revelation 8:7.

[10] **Elihu quotes from**: Revelation 16:2.

[11] **The Mark of the Beast as symbolic of systemic and institutional identity with the Imperial Cult of Caesar:** "A number of scholars emphasize the Roman practice of marking slaves and soldiers to demonstrate ownership or loyalty, in that charagma (engraved, etched, or imprinted mark, BAGD 1077) is used in that way in the first century (Beale 715; Beasley-Murray 218; Stuart 2:289). Even in Scripture slaves literally receive a mark to demonstrate their loyalty to a master (e.g., Ex 21:6; Dt 15:17). The practice of physical marking is commonplace in ancient times, and is still practiced today in Hindu countries, especially among Vishnu and Siva devotees. The term is also used "often" as "an official stamp on writings . . , esp. the imperial stamp to attest the validity of decrees etc." (TDNT 9:416)…

We must note that the mark is on the "forehead" and/or "hand" (cp. 13:16 with 20:4). John's imagery source, which the beast parodies and reverses, appears ultimately to derive from Dt 6, a very important, well-known, and influential section of the Law containing the "Shema Israel" (Dt 6:4-9). This In Dt 6 the devout Jew is to keep "these words which I am commanding you today" (6:6) and to "bind them as a sign [sēmeion] on your hand and they shall be as frontals on your forehead" (6:8). The design of this Mosaic command is spiritual: the faithful must believe in one God and let his law govern their every thought (forehead) and deed (hand), for "you shall love the Lord your God with all your heart and with all your soul and with all your might" (Dt 6:5). "The 'forehead' represents ideological commitment and the 'hand' the practical outworking of that commitment" (Beale 717). The temple leadership (erroneously) see themselves as promoting the worship of the one true God and encouraging men to true faith and holy practice." Kenneth L. Gentry, Jr., *The Divorce of Israel: A Redemptive-Historical Interpretation of Revelation Vol. 2* (Dallas, GA: Tolle Lege Press, 2016), 277-278.

"By the end of the century, in the middle of which Paul came through the eastern empire preaching the message of Jesus, these developments had produced a new civic and religious reality. The highest honour a city could now hope for was to become neōkoros, temple-guardian for the Sebastoi, the Augustus-family. Worshipping the emperors was well on the way to becoming a central and vital aspect not only of life in general but of civic and municipal identity. Whatever we say about either the intentions or the effects of Roman rulers from Julius Caesar to Vespasian, the richly diverse phenomena we loosely call 'imperial cult'

388

were a vital part of a complex system of power, communication and control, in other words, of all the things empires find they need to do. The (highly variegated) imperial cult was an 'institutional metaphor' which supplied 'a brief formula for the fundamental structure of the social system, which otherwise could not be put into words," and which worked actively 'to transmit this system to future generations'" N. T. Wright, *Paul and the Faithfulness of God, vol. 4, Christian Origins and the Question of God* (Minneapolis: Fortress Press, 2013), 341.

"The evidence now available, including that from epigraphy and archaeology, appears to show that the cult of Caesar, so far from being one new religion among many in the Roman world, had already by the time of Paul's missionary activity become not only the dominant cult in a large part of the empire, certainly in the parts where Paul was active, but was actually the means (as opposed to overt large-scale military presence) whereby the Romans managed to control and govern such huge areas as came under their sway. The emperor's far-off presence was made ubiquitous by the standard means of statues and coins (the latter being the principal mass medium of the ancient world), reflecting his image throughout his domains; he was the great benefactor, through whom the great blessings of justice and peace, and a host of lesser ones besides, were showered outwards upon the grateful populace — who in turn worshipped him, honored him, and paid him taxes." N.T. Wright, "Paul's Gospel and Caesar's Empire," in Ed. Richard A. Horsley, *Paul and Politics: Ekklesia, Israel, Imperium* (Penn., Trinity Press, 2000), 161.

[12] **The mark of the Beast as rejection of Jesus as Messiah**:

The following is excerpted from Gary DeMar, "Are Embedded Microchips A Sign That We're Living In The Last Days?" GaryDeMar.com https://garydemar.com/embedded-microchips-sign-living-last-days/

Revelation 13:16-17 is not describing the control of financial transactions but access to the temple overseen by the Jewish anti-Christian religious establishment of the first century prior to the destruction of the temple that took place in AD 70 when the temple was destroyed by the Romans. The key to interpreting the passage is the prohibition "to buy or to sell" (13:17).

Jesus told the church of Laodicea, "I advise you to buy from Me gold refined by fire, that you may become rich" (Rev. 3:18). This shows that buying gold refined by fire is symbolic and is related to worship. It is reasonable, therefore, to assume that the reference to buying and selling in Revelation 13:17 is also symbolic and relates to worship. Once again, the Old Testament is helpful:

> Ho! Everyone who thirsts, come to the waters;
> And you who have no money come, buy and eat.
> Come, buy wine and milk
> Without money and without cost.
> Why do you spend money for what is not bread,
> And your wages for what does not satisfy?
> Listen carefully to Me, and eat what is good,
> And delight yourself in abundance. (Isa. 55:1-2; cf. John 4:13-15; Rev. 21:6)

Isaiah is describing something more significant than physical money, wine, milk, and bread.

Temple leaders controlled buying and selling to regulate access to the temple (Matt. 21:12). "This is established in [Revelation] 3:18 (and compare 21:6). When those who refuse the mark of the Beast are not allowed to buy and sell, it means that they are expelled from the synagogue and Temple. The merchants of the land in Revelation 18 are those who worshipped at the Temple and synagogue." Jesus foretold that this would happen: "They will make you outcasts from the synagogue, but an hour is coming for everyone who kills you to think that he is offering service to God" (John 16:2). Keep in mind that the "beast coming up out of the land" is involved in these events. The land beast is most certainly associated with first-century Israel, especially the priests who controlled access to the temple, which was finished during Nero's reign in AD 64.

Early in the church's history, the disciples went to the temple to preach the gospel (Acts 5:20-21, 24, 42; 24:12). At first, they were welcomed (2:46). Peter and John frequented the temple during "the hour of prayer" (3:1). Jewish Christians continued to use the temple, even participating in some of its rituals (21:26). After the temple officials learned that those Jews were preaching that Jesus was the Messiah — the Lamb of God who takes away the sin of the world — Paul was "dragged ... out of the temple; and immediately the doors were shut" (21:26-30).

During Jesus's ministry, the temple officials were "selling" and worshipers were "buying" access to the temple (Matt. 21:12), turning God's house into a "robbers' den" (Matt. 21:12-13). Only the Jews who aligned themselves with the priests (i.e., had the "mark of the beast"), the sacrificial system, and the temple buildings were allowed to enter the temple for worship.

To take the "mark of the beast" meant a person denied that Jesus was the Messiah, the true temple of God, the only sufficient sacrifice. Of course, Christian Jews avoided the "mark of the beast" and showed their true allegiance to Jesus, "having His name and the name of His Father written on their foreheads" (Rev. 14:1). They demonstrated that these names on their foreheads through their public professions of faith and allegiance to Jesus.

CHAPTER 12

[1] **Israel has become a symbolic Babylon, Sodom, Egypt**:

> Revelation 11:8 ...and their dead bodies will lie in the street of the great city that symbolically is called Sodom and Egypt, where their Lord was crucified.

Israel called by the name of Sodom: Isaiah 3:8–9; Jeremiah 23:14; Lamentations 4:6; Ezekiel 16:46, 48–49, 55–56; Amos 4:11; John 11:8 Matthew 10:15; 11:23–24).

Israel likened to Egypt: Amos 4:10-11.

The Great City of Babylon in Revelation 17 is Jerusalem:

> Revelation 18:21–24 [21] "So will Babylon the great city be thrown down with violence, and will be found no more;.. [24] And in her was found the blood of prophets and of saints, and of all who have been slain on the land."

The Great City was previously introduced as the place of the crucifixion, which is Jerusalem.

> Revelation 11:8 ...and their dead bodies will lie in the street of the great city that symbolically is called Sodom and Egypt, where their Lord was crucified.

Jerusalem was the one guilty of the "blood of all the prophets and saints who have been slain on the land." (Rev 18:24):

> Matthew 23:35–37 [35] so that on you [Jerusalem] may come all the righteous blood shed on the land.... [37] "O Jerusalem, Jerusalem, the city that kills the prophets and stones those who are sent to it!!

Old Testament prophets call Jerusalem the Great City: Jeremiah 22:8 " 'And many nations will pass by this city, and every man will say to his neighbor, "Why has the LORD dealt thus with this great city?"

Lamentations 1:1 How lonely sits the city that was full of people! How like a widow has she become, she who was great among the nations! She who was a princess among the provinces has become a slave.

Josephus calls Jerusalem a great city: "This was the end which Jerusalem came to by the madness of those that were for innovations; **a city otherwise of great magnificence**, and of mighty fame among all mankind." Flavius Josephus, *The Wars of the Jews*, 7.4.

"And where is now that **great city**, the metropolis of the Jewish nation, which was fortified by so many walls round about, which had so many fortresses and large towers to defend it, which could hardly contain the instruments prepared for the war, and which had so many ten thousands of men to fight for it? (376) Where is this city that was believed to have God himself inhabiting therein?" Flavius Josephus, *Jewish Wars* 7:8:7 §375.

Roman historians Tacitus and Pliny call Jerusalem a great city: "However, as I am about to describe the last days of a famous city, it seems proper for me to give some account of its origin." Tacitus, *Histories* 5.2

"Jerusalem, by far the most famous city, not of Judæa only, but of the East, and Herodium, with a celebrated town of the same name." Pliny the Elder, *The Natural History*, 15.15, ed. John Bostock (Medford, MA: Taylor and Francis, Red Lion Court, Fleet Street, 1855), 1428.

The Great City is Jerusalem. Extra biblical sources: Sibylline Oracles 5:154, 226, 413.

Babylon in Revelation 17 and 18 is Jerusalem, not Rome: "Several textual indicators suggest that John is focusing on Jerusalem rather than Rome (cp. Provan 1996: 94). (1) In this very Judaic book the language of religious defilement in 18:2 would suggest a Jewish city is in view. (2) Babylon's double punishment reflects the Old Testament prophetic witness against Jerusalem (18:6; see below). (3) The "great city" (18:10, 16, 18, 19, 21; cp. 18:2) was previously introduced as the place of the crucifixion (11:8). (4) In 18:24 the killing of the prophets by Babylon reflects a familiar sin of Jerusalem (Neh 9:26; cp. 1Ki 19:10, 14; 21:13; 2Ch 24:19, 21; 36:14-16; Isa 1:15; Jer 2:30; 25:4; 26:20-23). (5) The bowl judgments in Revelation 16 are being expanded upon in Revelation 17-18. In the latter bowls "Babylon the great" was distinguished from the cities of the nations (16:19)."Kenneth L. Gentry, Jr., *The Divorce of Israel: A Redemptive-Historical Interpretation of Revelation Vol. 2* (Dallas, GA: Tolle Lege Press, 2016), 506-507.

"It might be objected that the great city in Revelation appears too important among the nations to be identified with Jerusalem rather than Rome. However, Jerusalem was thought to be the "navel" or center of the earth (Gen R 59:5), "destined to become the metropolis of all countries" (Exod R 23:10), and the Psalms (e.g. 48:2–3, 50:2); Lamentations (e.g. 1:1, 2:15) and Prophets (e.g. Zech 14:16–21, Isa 2:2–4, Micah 4:1–3) speak in the loftiest terms of Jerusalem's place among the nations. Rev 17:18 is probably a similar hyperbole; cf. 4QLam which describes her as "princess of all nations." J. Massyngberde Ford, *Revelation: Introduction, Translation, and Commentary, vol. 38, Anchor Yale Bible* (New Haven; London: Yale University Press, 2008), 285

CHAPTER 14

[1] **Alexander quotes from**:

> Matthew 10:29 Are not two sparrows sold for a penny? And not one of them will fall to the ground apart from your Father.

[2] **Claudius' expulsion of the Jews**: Acts 18:2. This occurred in A.D. 49 "Because the Jews at Rome caused continuous disturbances at the instigation of Chrestus [Christ], he expelled them from the city." Suetonius, *Claudius* 25.4. See also Dio Cassius, *Roman History* 60:6. A similar expulsion of the Jews was ordered by Tiberius in A.D. 29. See Philo, *Embassy* 159–61; Suetonius, *Tiberius* 36. Clinton E. Arnold, *Zondervan Illustrated Bible Backgrounds Commentary: John, Acts., vol. 2* (Grand Rapids, MI: Zondervan, 2002), 397–398.

[3] **God's kingdom will overcome all other kingdoms on earth in history, not at the end of history**:

> Daniel 2:44–45 [44] And in the days of those kings the God of heaven will set up a kingdom that shall never be destroyed, nor shall the kingdom be left to another people. It shall break in pieces all these kingdoms and bring them to an end, and it shall stand forever, [45] just as you saw that a stone was cut from a mountain by no human hand, and that it broke in pieces the iron, the bronze, the clay, the silver, and the gold.

> Matthew 13:31–33 [31] He put another parable before them, saying, "The kingdom of heaven is like a grain of mustard seed that a man took and sowed in his field. [32] It is the smallest of all seeds, but when it has grown it is larger than all the garden plants and becomes a tree, so that the birds of the air come and make nests in its branches." [33] He told them another parable. "The kingdom of heaven is like leaven that a woman took and hid in three measures of flour, till it was all leavened."

CHAPTER 15

[1] **Phineas quotes from the War Scroll, of the Dead Sea Scrolls:**

1QM 12:7-8
Quoted from John J. Collins, *Apocalypticism in the Dead Sea Scrolls* (London, Routledge, 1997), 109.

1QM 1:15-16
Quoted from Michael O. Wise, Martin G. Abegg Jr., and Edward M. Cook, *The Dead Sea Scrolls: A New Translation* (New York: HarperOne, 2005), 148.

[2] **Aaron quotes from the War Scroll (1QM 1:10-12):**

I used a compilation of different translations of the same text from:

Florentino García Martínez and Eibert J. C. Tigchelaar, *The Dead Sea Scrolls Study Edition (translations)* (Leiden; New York: Brill, 1997–1998), 115.

Geza Vermes, *The Dead Sea Scrolls in English, Revised and extended 4th ed.* (Sheffield: Sheffield Academic Press, 1995), 126.

It is important to note the similarity between the Essene interpretation of the Eschatological War and Jesus's own statements of the day of vengeance. Both drew from Daniel. And both used similar language of the great tribulation and suffering unlike anything else in history for Israel. This shows that there is a tradition of understanding that both the Christians and Essenes shared.

Matthew 24:21–22 [21] For then there will be great tribulation, such as has not been from the beginning of the world until now, no, and never will be. [22] And if those days had not been cut short, no human being would be saved. But for the sake of the elect those days will be cut short.

1QM 1:10-12
And it shall be a time of [great] tribulation for the people which God shall redeem; of all its afflictions none shall be as this, from its sudden beginning until its end in eternal redemption.

Geza Vermes, *The Dead Sea Scrolls in English, Revised and extended 4th ed.* (Sheffield: Sheffield Academic Press, 1995), 126.

[3] **Daniel's prophecy of the temple destroyed**: More to come on this.

Daniel 9:26
[26] And after the sixty-two weeks, an anointed one shall be cut off and shall have nothing. And the people of the prince who is to come shall destroy the city and the sanctuary. Its end shall come with a flood, and to the end there shall be war. Desolations are decreed.

[4] **Isaiah's Day of Vengeance**:

Isaiah 61:1–2
[1] The Spirit of the Lord GOD is upon me, because the LORD has anointed me to bring good news to the poor; he has sent me to bind up the brokenhearted, to proclaim liberty to the captives, and the opening of the prison to those who are bound; [2] to proclaim the year of the LORD's favor, and the day of vengeance of our God...

Christians claim that Jesus fulfills the first part of this prophecy, but not the second part until his second coming. But they are wrong. Jesus does claim that the Day(s) of Vengeance is fulfilled in the Roman destruction of Jerusalem in AD 70:

First part of Isaiah 61 (Jubilee):

Luke 4:16–21
[16] And he came to Nazareth, where he had been brought up. And as was his custom, he went to the synagogue on the Sabbath day, and he stood up to read. [17] And the scroll of the prophet

Isaiah was given to him. He unrolled the scroll and found the place where it was written, [18] "The Spirit of the Lord is upon me, because he has anointed me to proclaim good news to the poor. He has sent me to proclaim liberty to the captives and recovering of sight to the blind, to set at liberty those who are oppressed, [19] to proclaim the year of the Lord's favor." [20] And he rolled up the scroll and gave it back to the attendant and sat down. And the eyes of all in the synagogue were fixed on him. [21] And he began to say to them, "Today this Scripture has been fulfilled in your hearing."

Second part of Isaiah 61 (Day of Vengeance):

Luke 21:20–22
[20] "But when you see Jerusalem surrounded by armies, then know that its desolation has come near. [21] Then let those who are in Judea flee to the mountains, and let those who are inside the city depart, and let not those who are out in the country enter it, [22] **for these are days of vengeance, to fulfill all that is written**.

[5] **The War Rule commanded soldiers be twenty-years of age**:

"Whereas Numbers gave the age of mobilization as twenty years, the youngest group in the scroll is twenty-five to thirty, and these are assigned to despoil the slain, collect the booty and cleanse the land. If practical military considerations took precedence, we should expect this age group to be involved in skirmishing, or in some military task where agility was important."

John J. Collins, *Apocalypticism in the Dead Sea Scrolls* (London, Routledge, 1997), 98.

1Q33 col vii
The men of the army shall be from forty to fifty years old.
The inspectors of the camps shall be from fifty to sixty years old.
The officers shall be from forty to fifty years old.
The despoilers of the slain, the plunderers of booty, the cleansers of the land, the keepers of the baggage, and those who furnish the provisions shall be from twenty-five to thirty years old.

Geza Vermes, The Dead Sea Scrolls in English, Revised and extended 4th ed. (Sheffield: Sheffield Academic Press, 1995), 132.

CHAPTER 16

[1] **Agrippa quotes from**: Zephaniah 1:2-4, 14-18

[2] **De-Creation as a prophetic motif**: This is an excerpt from Brian Godawa, *End Times Bible Prophecy: It's Not What They Told You* (Los Angeles, CA: Embedded Pictures Publishing, 2017), 39-41.

It all began with learning to appreciate the creation language in the Bible as a means of communicating the value of his covenant with his people. When God created the heavens and the earth in Genesis 1, he was creating order out of the chaos of Genesis 1:2, the formlessness and emptiness of creation. Part of that created order was the sun, moon, and stars. They were to separate light and dark and be for signs and seasons (1:14-15). In ancient Near Eastern religions, people pictured the gods fighting the sea (a symbol of chaos) as an expression of their rule and power to illustrate their creation of order out of chaos. The Hebrew scriptures do the same thing, only in a way that says Yahweh is the true God. He is the one who created his covenant order within the chaos of the world.

Psalm 74 is a good example of this creation and covenant motif out of the chaos of the sea. Read this passage and notice how God had power over the chaos of the sea when he established his covenant through Moses. But then read on and you will see the language of creation connected to that covenant.

Psalm 74:13–17
You divided the sea by your might; you broke the heads of the sea monsters on the waters. [14] You crushed the heads of Leviathan; you gave him as food for the creatures of the wilderness. [15] You split open springs and brooks; you dried up ever-flowing streams. [16] Yours is the day, yours also

the night; you have established the heavenly lights and the sun. [17] You have fixed all the boundaries of the earth.

The creation language of the sun, moon, and stars separating day and night is part of God fixing or establishing the boundaries of the earth. God's covenant with Israel is described in the language of creation of the universe. It is poetic metaphor, an image that stands for something else.

Isaiah also wrote about the Mosaic covenant beginning when God conquered the chaos of the Red Sea. Creating God's people, Zion, is expressed in terms of Genesis 1, establishing the heavens and earth.

> Isaiah 51:15–16
> I am the LORD your God, who stirs up the sea so that its waves roar— the LORD of hosts is his name. [16] And I have put my words in your mouth and covered you in the shadow of my hand, establishing the heavens and laying the foundations of the earth, and saying to Zion, "You are my people."

So we see that God described his covenantal relationship in the cosmic terms of creation, including the sun, moon, and stars. He created order out of chaos with his covenantal rule. Creating his covenantal order with his people was spiritually likened to the creation of the heavens and the earth.

It makes perfect sense then that when his covenantal relationship was violated, it would be described in the terms of the destruction of creation. Theologians call this "decreation."

When God destroyed the holy temple, the symbol of God's covenant, in 587 B.C. through the Babylonians, he used the cosmic terms of all of creation being undone. It's told in the terms of a reversal of Genesis 1.

> Jeremiah 4:23–28
> I looked on the earth, and behold, it was without form and void; and to the heavens, and they had no light. [24] I looked on the mountains, and behold, they were quaking, and all the hills moved to and fro. [25] I looked, and behold, there was no man, and all the birds of the air had fled. [26] I looked, and behold, the fruitful land was a desert, and all its cities were laid in ruins before the LORD, before his fierce anger. [27] For thus says the LORD, "The whole land shall be a desolation; yet I will not make a full end. [28] For this the earth shall mourn, and the heavens above be dark; for I have spoken."

These cosmic disturbances did not occur literally when this prophecy was fulfilled. The earth did not return to the original state of chaos, "without form and void"; men and birds did not vanish from the earth; the sun, moon, and stars did not literally go dark. These were all decreation terms to express the spiritual reality of God's covenantal relationship being violated.

[3] **Sun, Moon and Stars in prophecy**: This is an excerpt from Brian Godawa, *End Times Bible Prophecy: It's Not What They Told You* (Los Angeles, CA: Embedded Pictures Publishing, 2017), 41-43.

God used these same terms of a collapsing universe to describe the destruction of Babylon by the Medes in 539 B.C. If a nation's covenant order is like the "heavens and the earth," their destruction is like the destruction of the heavens and the earth.

> Isaiah 13:9–11
> Behold, the day of the LORD comes, cruel, with wrath and fierce anger, to make the land a desolation and to destroy its sinners from it. [10] For the stars of the heavens and their constellations will not give their light; the sun will be dark at its rising, and the moon will not shed its light. [11] I will punish the world for its evil, and the wicked for their iniquity.

These cosmic catastrophes were not literal. When the Medes overran Babylon as this prophecy predicted, the sun, moon, and stars did not go dark. If the sun went dark, the entire solar system would have been destroyed. Sun, moon, and stars are not merely creation metaphors, they are also symbols of the spiritual power and authority behind earthly rulers. The ancient Hebrews, like their Near Eastern neighbors, believed that behind the earthly power of human rulers was the power of the heavenly beings that they likened to stars in the heavens, calling them the heavenly host. So when a nation's rulers lost power that was described as if the sun, moon, and stars lost their light or their power.

When God said in Isaiah 34:4 that "all the host of heaven shall rot away, and the skies roll up like a scroll. All their host shall fall, as leaves fall from the vine, like leaves falling from the fig tree," he was poetically describing the fall of Edom's spiritual and earthly power in the light of God's judgment (34:5). He was not describing literal stars falling to earth. They would burn up the earth long before they got within the earth's orbit. Meteors are not stars, so you couldn't interpret that literally even if you wanted to. And the sky did not roll away in some kind of reverse gravity stargate wormhole in 587 B.C. when this prophecy was fulfilled.

When Egypt was destroyed by Babylon around 580 B.C., the prophet Ezekiel prophesied that event with the following description: "I will cover the heavens and make their stars dark; I will cover the sun with a cloud and the moon will not give its light. All the bright lights of heaven will I make dark over you and put darkness on your land" (Ezek 32:7-8, 11). You could say that dark clouds could achieve a certain amount of this effect, but certainly not all of it. The darkening of the heavenly host was a common metaphor for powers losing their authority.

When Israel was destroyed and led into captivity by Nebuchadnezzar in the 6th century B.C., Isaiah used the same poetic metaphor of sun, moon, and stars as symbols of spiritual powers linked to earthly powers.

> Isaiah 24:21–23
> On that day the LORD will punish the host of heaven, in heaven, and the kings of the earth, on the earth. [22] They will be gathered together as prisoners in a pit; they will be shut up in a prison, and after many days they will be punished. [23] Then the moon will be confounded and the sun ashamed.

In the Bible cosmic catastrophe or collapsing universe imagery, including the sun, moon, and stars losing their light, is a poetic device for figuratively describing the fall of earthly rulers and the spiritual powers behind them, not literal astronomical phenomena and not a literal end to the space-time universe. As N.T. Wright has explained, this view remained even into the first century time of the New Testament.

> Within the mainline Jewish writings of this period, covering a wide range of styles, genres, political persuasions and theological perspectives, *there is virtually no evidence that Jews were expecting the end of the space-time universe*. There is abundant evidence that they, like Jeremiah and others before them, knew a good metaphor when they saw one, and used cosmic imagery to bring out the full theological significance of cataclysmic socio-political events. There is almost nothing to suggest that they followed the Stoics into the belief that the world itself would come to an end; and there is almost everything—their stories, their symbols, their praxis, not least their tendency to revolution, and their entire theology—to suggest that they did not.
>
> What, then, did they believe was going to happen? They believed that *the present world order* would come to an end—the world order in which pagans held power, and Jews, the covenant people of the creator god, did not.

Day of the Lord as local judgment on any nation, city or people:

[4] **Legion V's revenge for their previous defeat under Cestius**: Though this passage describes the destruction of Gadara, I used it here with creative license.

Flavius Josephus, *The Wars of the Jews*, 3.7.1 §132-134
"So Vespasian marched to the city Gadara, and took it upon the first onset, because he found it destitute of any considerable number of men grown up and fit for war. (133) He came then into it, and slew all the youth, the Romans having no mercy on any age whatsoever; and this was done out of the hatred they bore the nation, and because of the iniquity they had been guilty of in the affair of Cestius. (134) He also set fire, not only to the city itself, but to all the villas and small cities that were round about it; some of them were quite destitute of inhabitants; and out of some of them he carried the inhabitants as slaves into captivity."

Flavius Josephus and William Whiston, *The Works of Josephus: Complete and Unabridged* (Peabody: Hendrickson, 1987), 645–646.

[5] **Vespasian was struck by a random arrow on his foot**:

Flavius Josephus, *The Wars of the Jews* 3.7.22, §235-236

"About the evening the Romans erected the battering ram again, against that part of the wall which had suffered before; (236) where a certain Jew that defended the city from the Romans, hit Vespasian with a dart in his foot, and wounded him a little, the distance being so great, that no mighty impression could be made by the dart thrown so far off."

Flavius Josephus and William Whiston, *The Works of Josephus: Complete and Unabridged* (Peabody: Hendrickson, 1987), 650.

[6] **The siege of Jotapata**: The details for this chapter were taken from Flavius Josephus, *The Wars of the Jews* 3.7.1-36, §132-339.

[7] **Daniel's forth empire beast was the ancient Roman empire**:

> Daniel 7:7 After this I saw in the night visions, and behold, a fourth beast, terrifying and dreadful and exceedingly strong. It had great iron teeth; it devoured and broke in pieces and stamped what was left with its feet. It was different from all the beasts that were before it, and it had ten horns.

> Daniel 7:19 "Then I desired to know the truth about the fourth beast, which was different from all the rest, exceedingly terrifying, with its teeth of iron and claws of bronze, and which devoured and broke in pieces and stamped what was left with its feet,

> Daniel 7:23 "Thus he said: 'As for the fourth beast, there shall be a fourth kingdom on earth, which shall be different from all the kingdoms, and it shall devour the whole land, and trample it down, and break it to pieces.

[8] **This mighty warrior was Eleazar ben Sameas**: His story can be found in Flavius Josephus, *The Wars of the Jews* 3.7.21, §229-232.

(229) And here a certain Jew appeared worthy of our relation and commendation; he was the son of Sameas, and was called Eleazar, and was born at Saab, in Galilee. (230) This man took up a stone of vast bigness, and threw it down from the wall upon the ram, and this with so great a force that it broke off the head of the engine. He also leaped down and took up the head of the ram from the midst of them, and without any concern, carried it to the top of the wall, (231) and this, while he stood as a fit mark to be pelted by all his enemies. Accordingly, he received the strokes upon his naked body, and was wounded with five darts; (232) nor did he mind any of them while he went up to the top of the wall, where he stood in sight of them all, as an instance of the greatest boldness: after which he threw himself on a heap with his wounds upon him, and fell down, together with the head of the ram."

Flavius Josephus and William Whiston, *The Works of Josephus: Complete and Unabridged* (Peabody: Hendrickson, 1987), 650.

CHAPTER 17

[1] **Vespasian's failure to get information out of a captive of Jotapata**:

Flavius Josephus, *The Wars of the Jews*, 3.7.33 §320-322
"But Vespasian had a suspicion about this deserter, as knowing how faithful the Jews were to one another, (321) and how much they despised any punishments that could be inflicted on them; this last, because one of the people of Jotapata had undergone all sorts of torments, and though they made him pass through a fiery trial of his enemies in his examination, yet would he inform them nothing of the affairs within the city, and as he was crucified, smiled at them! (322) However, the probability there was in the relation itself did partly confirm the truth of what the deserter told them, and they thought he might probably speak the truth. However, Vespasian thought they should be no great sufferers if the report was a sham; so he commanded them to keep the man in custody, and prepared the army for taking the city."

Flavius Josephus and William Whiston, The Works of Josephus: Complete and Unabridged (Peabody: Hendrickson, 1987), 654.

[2] **This story of the deserter who gave information can be found in**:

Flavius Josephus, *The Wars of the Jews* 3.7.33, §317-319
"on which day a certain deserter went to Vespasian, and told him, how few were left in the city, and how weak they were, (318) and that they had been so worn out with perpetual watching, and also perpetual fighting, that they could not now oppose any force that came against them, and that they might be taken by stratagem, if any one would attack them; (319) for that about the last watch of the night, when they thought they might have some rest from the hardships they were under, and when a morning sleep used to come upon them; as they were thoroughly weary, he said the watch used to fall asleep: accordingly his advice was, that they should make the attack at that hour."

Flavius Josephus and William Whiston, *The Works of Josephus: Complete and Unabridged* (Peabody: Hendrickson, 1987), 653–654.

[3] **Jotapata casualties**:

Flavius Josephus, *The Wars of the Jews* 3.7.36, §336-338
"This day the Romans slew all the multitude that appeared openly; but on the following days they searched the hiding places, and fell upon those that were underground, and in the caverns, and went thus through every age, excepting the infants and the women, (337) and of these there were gathered together as captives twelve hundred; and as for those that were slain at the taking of the city, and in the former fights, they were numbered to be forty thousand. (338) So Vespasian gave order that the city should be entirely demolished, and all the fortifications burnt down."

Flavius Josephus and William Whiston, *The Works of Josephus: Complete and Unabridged* (Peabody: Hendrickson, 1987), 654.

CHAPTER 18

[1] **This story of Joseph's capture at Jotapata was taken from**: Flavius Josephus, *Wars of the Jews* 3.7. It is important to understand that Josephus was spinning his story to justify himself. So the reader must read between the lines to figure out what his true actions might have been.

[2] **Joseph's fortification of Galilee**: Flavius Josephus, *The Life of Flavius Josephus* 14.77-79; *Wars of the Jews* 2.20.5 §570. *Life* 17; *Wars* 2.21.

Joseph vs. Gischala at Tiberias: Flavius Josephus, *The Life of Flavius Josephus* 17-18 §87-96; *Wars of the Jews* 2.21.6- §614-619.

Gischala's attempted assassination of Joseph: Flavius Josephus, *The Life of Flavius Josephus* 18 §94-96; *Wars of the Jews* 2.21.6 §615-619.

Placidus' armies take Sepphoris and Gabara on the way to Jotapata: Flavius Josephus, *Wars of the Jews* 3.6.1 §112-114.

Joseph goes to Jotapata and Vespasian prepares to face Joseph there: Flavius Josephus, *Wars of the Jews* 3.7.3 §141-144.

[3] **Joseph is referring to the following Scriptural passages about God using armies of pagan nations to chastise Israel**: Assyria: Isaiah 10:5-19 and Babylon: Jeremiah 4:12-27; Habakkuk 1:5-6.

[4] **These statements of Joseph are taken from**: Flavius Josephus, *The Wars of the Jews* 3.8.5, §362-366.

[5] **Josephs' mathematical trick**: This mathematical trick is not a creative addition by the author. It is a well-known math problem in history called The Josephus problem or The Josephus permutation based on the historic event. It would make sense that Josephus arranged for himself to survive until the end, since the odds of him being the last man standing are so ridiculous as to justify skepticism in the extreme. I drew the

mathematics from this article on the internet: "Josephus Problem," Wolfram Mathworld. http://mathworld.wolfram.com/JosephusProblem.html

CHAPTER 19

[1] **This story of Joseph before Vespasian is taken from**: Flavius Josephus, *The Wars of the Jews* 3.8.8-9, §392-408.

[2] **Joseph's interpretation of Daniel's prophecy applied to Vespasian**: Flavius Josephus, *The Wars of the Jews* 6.5.4, §312-313

"(312) But now, what did most elevate them in undertaking this war, was an ambiguous oracle that was also found in their sacred writings, how, "about that time, one from their country should become governor of the habitable earth." (313) The Jews took this prediction to belong to themselves in particular and many of the wise men were thereby deceived in their determination. Now, this oracle certainly denoted the government of Vespasian, who was appointed emperor in Judea."

Flavius Josephus and William Whiston, *The Works of Josephus: Complete and Unabridged* (Peabody: Hendrickson, 1987), 743.

Josephus believed that the Roman desolation of Jerusalem fulfilled Daniel's prophecy of the abomination of desolation:

Flavius Josephus, *The Antiquities of the Jews*, 10.11.7, §276

"And indeed it so came to pass, that our nation suffered these things under Antiochus Epiphanes, according to Daniel's vision, and what he wrote many years before they came to pass. In the very same manner Daniel also wrote concerning the Roman government, and that our country should be made desolate by them."

Flavius Josephus and William Whiston, *The Works of Josephus: Complete and Unabridged* (Peabody: Hendrickson, 1987), 285.

Flavius Josephus, *The Wars of the Jews* 6.2.1, §109

"And who is there that does not know what the writings of the ancient prophets contain in them,—and particularly that oracle which is just now going to be fulfilled upon this miserable city—for they foretold that this city should be then taken when somebody shall begin the slaughter of his own countrymen!"

Flavius Josephus and William Whiston, *The Works of Josephus: Complete and Unabridged* (Peabody: Hendrickson, 1987), 732.

[3] **Persian King Cyrus called "messiah"**:

Isaiah 45:1 Thus says the LORD to his anointed ['messiah'], to Cyrus, whose right hand I have grasped, to subdue nations before him and to loose the belts of kings, to open doors before him that gates may not be closed…"

[4] **Joseph quotes**: Daniel 7:14.

[5] **God has gone over to the Romans, and using them as his means to judge Israel**:

Flavius Josephus, *The Wars of the Jews* 3.8.3 §354
(354) and [Josephus] said [to God],—"Since it pleaseth thee, who hast created the Jewish nation, to depress the same, and since all their good fortune is gone over to the Romans…"

Flavius Josephus and William Whiston, The Works of Josephus: Complete and Unabridged (Peabody: Hendrickson, 1987), 655.

Flavius Josephus, *The Wars of the Jews* 6.2.1 §110
"(110) And are not both the city and the entire temple now full of the dead bodies of your countrymen? It is

God therefore, it is God himself who is bringing on this fire, to purge that city and temple by means of the Romans, and is going to pluck up this city, which is full of your pollutions."

Flavius Josephus and William Whiston, *The Works of Josephus: Complete and Unabridged* (Peabody: Hendrickson, 1987), 732.

CHAPTER 20

[1] **Garden imagery of the temple**:

"In the accounts of the furnishing of the Mosaic tabernacle (Ex 25:31–34; 37:17–20; Num 8:4) and the Solomonic temple (1 Kings 6:18, 29, 32, 35; 7:19, 22, 24, 26, 49; also 2 Chron 4:5, 21), flowers, particularly almond blossoms and lilies, figure prominently, justifying the later psalmic reference to the "beauty of holiness." The lampstands of the tabernacle, and later of the temple, were designed as almond trees and their "bowls" (i.e., cups holding the oil and wick) as almond blossoms. Additional almond blossoms decorated the "stems" of the lampstand, suggesting a graceful art-deco-like style. (For another view of the lampstands as representing an edenic *"tree of life," see Myers). We should also recall Aaron's rod that sprouted almond blossoms and even ripe almonds. It was placed in the ark of the covenant under the mercy seat. On the gold and cedar walls of Solomon's temple were engraved cherubim, palm trees and both open flowers and closed buds; and on the doors of olive and cypress were more open flowers. More spectacular, the bronze pillars were adorned with lilies and pomegranates four cubits (approximately six feet!) in size; and the sea of bronze, whose brim was shaped like a lily blossom, was further ornamented with two rows of lily buds around it."

Leland Ryken et al., *Dictionary of Biblical Imagery* (Downers Grove, IL: InterVarsity Press, 2000), 294.

"That the Garden of Eden was the first sacred space is also suggested by observing that Solomon's temple was described with botanical and arboreal imagery that gave it a garden-like appearance. The account in 1 Kings 6–7 of the temple construction includes a proliferation of garden-like descriptions of the interior, much of which are descriptions of carvings, structures or pieces of furniture covered with precious metals: wood-carved 'gourds and open flowers' (1 Kgs. 6:18), 'palm trees and open flowers' (1 Kgs. 6:29, 32, twice mentioned), 'pomegranates numbered two hundred in rows around both capitals' on the two doorway pillars (1 Kgs. 7:20; cf. likewise, 7:18–19), on the top of which were a 'lily design' (1 Kgs. 7:22); the bronze sea in the courtyard had two rows of 'gourds' under its brim, which was 'made ... like a lily blossom' (1 Kgs. 7:24–26); 'four-hundred pomegranates' around the two capitals of the pillars (1 Kgs. 7:42); ten (!) lampstands that were configured like trees with blossoms (1 Kgs. 7:49), thus resembling a small orchard (note the later Testament of Adam 4:7, which says that in Zech. 1:8–11 the prophet saw 'trees' in the heavenly 'tabernacle'; cf. also Ps. 74:3–7 which includes portrayal of a 'thicket of trees' in Israel's sanctuary; cf. similarly y. Yoma 4:4).

Accordingly, subsequent Old Testament literature identifies Solomon's temple (Pss. 52:8; 92:13–15; Lam. 2:6) and Israel's eschatological temple (Is. 60:13, 21) with a 'garden' or garden-like depictions in order to identify them with Eden."

G. K. Beale, *The Temple and the Church's Mission: A Biblical Theology of the Dwelling Place of God*, ed. D. A. Carson, vol. 17, New Studies in Biblical Theology (Downers Grove, IL; England: InterVarsity Press; Apollos, 2004), 71–72.

[2] Isaiah 27:6.

[3] Isaiah 28:1-4.

CHAPTER 21

[1] **The language of seas of blood and carnage that fulfill these verses of Revelation can be found in Josephus**:

Flavius Josephus, *The Wars of the Jews* 4.7.6, §437.
"Now this destruction that fell upon the Jews, as it was not inferior to any of the rest in itself, so did it still appear greater than it really was; and this, because not only the whole of the country through which they had

fled was filled with slaughter, and Jordan could not be passed over, by reason of the dead bodies that were in it, but because the lake Asphaltitis was also full of dead bodies, that were carried down into it by the river."

Flavius Josephus and William Whiston, *The Works of Josephus: Complete and Unabridged* (Peabody: Hendrickson, 1987), 685.

Flavius Josephus, *The Wars of the Jews* 3.10.9, §530-531.
"One might then see the lake all bloody, and full of dead bodies, for not one of them escaped. (530) And a terrible stink, and a very sad sight there was on the following days over that country; for as for the shores, they were full of shipwrecks, and of dead bodies all swelled; and as the dead bodies were inflamed by the sun, and putrefied, they corrupted the air, insomuch that the misery was not only the object of commiseration to the Jews, but to those that hated them, and had been the authors of that misery. (531) This was the upshot of the sea fight. The number of the slain, including those that were killed in the city before, was six thousand and five hundred."

Flavius Josephus and William Whiston, *The Works of Josephus: Complete and Unabridged* (Peabody: Hendrickson, 1987), 663.

[2] The murder of Jews in Tiberias stadium:

Flavius Josephus, *The Wars of the Jews* 3.10.10, §539-541.
"(539) Then came Vespasian, and ordered them all to stand in the stadium, and commanded them to kill the old men, together with the others that were useless, who were in number a thousand and two hundred. (540) Out of the young men he chose six thousand of the strongest, and sent them to Nero, to dig through the Isthmus, and sold the remainder for slaves, being thirty thousand and four hundred, besides such as he made a present of to Agrippa; (541) for as to those that belonged to his kingdom, he gave them leave to do what he pleased with them; however, the king sold these also for slaves."

Flavius Josephus and William Whiston, The Works of Josephus: Complete and Unabridged (Peabody: Hendrickson, 1987), 663–664.

[3] The results of the battle on the Sea of Galilee:

Flavius Josephus, *The Wars of the Jews* 3.10.9, §530-531.
"One might then see the lake all bloody, and full of dead bodies, for not one of them escaped. (530) And a terrible stink, and a very sad sight there was on the following days over that country; for as for the shores, they were full of shipwrecks, and of dead bodies all swelled; and as the dead bodies were inflamed by the sun, and putrefied, they corrupted the air, insomuch that the misery was not only the object of commiseration to the Jews, but to those that hated them, and had been the authors of that misery. (531) This was the upshot of the sea fight. The number of the slain, including those that were killed in the city before, was six thousand and five hundred."

Flavius Josephus and William Whiston, *The Works of Josephus: Complete and Unabridged* (Peabody: Hendrickson, 1987), 663.

The story of the battle on the Sea of Galilee: Flavius Josephus, *The Wars of the Jews* 3.10.9, §522-531

[4] Leviathan at the creation of the Mosaic covenant:

Psa. 74:12-17
Yet God my King is from of old,
working salvation in the midst of the earth.
You divided the sea by your might;
[A reference to the Exodus deliverance of the covenant at Sinai]
You broke the heads of the sea monsters in the waters.
You crushed the heads of Leviathan;...
You have prepared the light and the sun.
You have established all the boundaries of the earth;

Isa 51:9-16
Was it not You who cut Rahab in pieces,
Who pierced the dragon?
Was it not You who dried up the sea,
The waters of the great deep;
Who made the depths of the sea a pathway
For the redeemed to cross over?...
[Y]ou have forgotten the LORD your Maker,
Who stretched out the heavens
And laid the foundations of the earth...

"For I am the LORD your God, who stirs up the sea and its waves roar (the LORD of hosts is His name). "I have put My words in your mouth and have covered you with the shadow of My hand, to establish the heavens, to found the earth, and to say to Zion, 'You are My people.'"
[a reaffirmation of the Sinai covenant through Moses]

In these texts, and others, God does not merely appeal to his power of creation as justification for the authority of his covenant. More importantly, God uses the creation of the heavens and earth, involving subjugation of rivers, seas, and dragon (Leviathan), as poetic descriptions of his covenant with his people, rooted in the Exodus story, and reiterated in the Davidic covenant. The creation of the covenant is the creation of the heavens and the earth which includes a subjugation of chaos by the new order. The covenant is a cosmos—not a material one centered in astronomical location and abstract impersonal forces as modern worldview demands, but a theological one, centered in the sacred space of land, temple, and cult as the ancient Near Eastern worldview demands.

For an extended explanation of Leviathan, see Brian Godawa, *When Giants Were Upon the Earth: The Watchers, the Nephilim, and the Biblical Cosmic War of the Seed* (Los Angeles, CA: Embedded Pictures Publishing, 2014), 79-88.

[5] **Jesus walking on the sea and Leviathan?:** In my novel, Jesus Triumphant, I depict Jesus walking on the water as him walking on the back of Leviathan. Since Leviathan is a spiritual symbol of chaos and Jesus was showing his mastery over chaos, I used Leviathan as an expression of the spiritual reality behind the historical event. See Brian Godawa, *Jesus Triumphant* (Los Angeles: Embedded Pictures, 2016).

[6] **The sea as chaos and God's power over the sea as covenant metaphor**: "In ANE religious mythologies, the sea and the sea dragon were symbols of chaos that had to be overcome to bring order to the universe, or more exactly, the political world order of the myth's originating culture. Some scholars call this battle Chaoskampf—the divine struggle to create order out of chaos.

"Hermann Gunkel first suggested in Creation and Chaos (1895) that some ANE creation myths contained a cosmic conflict between deity and sea, as well as sea dragons or serpents that expressed the creation of order out of chaos. Gunkel argued that Genesis borrowed this idea from the Babylonian tale of Marduk battling the goddess Tiamat, serpent of chaos, whom he vanquished, and out of whose body he created the heavens and earth. After this victory, Marduk ascended to power in the Mesopotamian pantheon. This creation story gave mythical justification to the rise of Babylon as an ancient world power most likely in the First Babylonian Dynasty under Hammurabi (1792-1750 B.C.). As the prologue of the Code of Hammurabi explains, "Anu, the majestic, King of the Anunnaki, and Bel, the Lord of Heaven and Earth, who established the fate of the land, had given to Marduk, the ruling son of Ea, dominion over mankind, and called Babylon by his great name; when they made it great upon the earth by founding therein an eternal kingdom, whose foundations are as firmly grounded as are those of heaven and earth." The foundation of Hammurabi's "eternal kingdom" is literally linked to Marduk's foundational creation of heaven and earth.

"Later, John Day argued in light of the discovery of the Ugarit tablets in 1928, that Canaan, not Babylonia is the source of the combat motif in Genesis, reflected in Yahweh's own complaint that Israel had become polluted by Canaanite culture. In the Baal cycle, Baal battles Yam (Sea) and conquers it, along with "the dragon," "the twisting serpent," to be enthroned as chief deity of the Canaanite pantheon.

"Creation accounts were often veiled polemics for the establishment of a king or kingdom's claim to sovereignty. Richard Clifford quotes, "In Mesopotamia, Ugarit, and Israel the Chaoskampf appears not only in cosmological contexts but just as frequently—and this was fundamentally true right from the first—in political contexts. The repulsion and the destruction of the enemy, and thereby the maintenance of political order, always constitute one of the major dimensions of the battle against chaos."

God removing the sea from the earth: Revelation 21:1 Then I saw a new heaven and a new earth, for the first heaven and the first earth had passed away, <u>and the sea was no more</u>.

"But if we understand this literally, it makes no theological sense: Why would the sea not be a part of the eternal new creation order? Did not God re-create the "new earth"? Why would he not also re-create the sea? Did not he create and bound the sea in the original creation (thalassas, Ge 1:10; Ex 20:11),9 as one feature of creation which was "very good" (Ge 1:31; cp. Ps 104:24, 28)? Nor does it make contextual sense, for what becomes of the "river" that flows through the city (22:1–2)? Does it evaporate? Make a complete, endless circle around the globe? Rivers naturally and necessarily end—into a pool of some sort, such as a lake, sea, or ocean (Ecc 1:7; cp. Eze 47:8; Zec 14:8). Besides, Scripture can speak metaphorically by employing the drying up of a sea—as when God judged Old Testament Babylon (Jer 51:36; cp. 50:38). Why could not this sea absence be metaphorical (as even dispensationalist Thomas agrees) The literalistic approach is unworkable—and unnecessary.

"Many commentators understand the sea to represent the chaos and woe in the world. In the Old Testament the sea sometimes pictures the turmoil caused by the wicked, as in Isaiah 57:20: "But the wicked are like the tossing sea, / For it cannot be quiet, / And its waters toss up refuse and mud." Jeremiah 6:23 reads: "They are cruel and have no mercy; / Their voice roars like the sea" (cp. Ps 65:7; Isa 17:12; Jer 50:42; 49:23; 51:42; Eze 26:5; Da 7:2–3; Zec 10:11). In Revelation 13:1 the beast arises from the sea. Beale argues that "the evil nuance of the sea metaphorically represents the entire range of afflictions that formerly threatened God's people." This would point to the removal of opposition to God and his people in the new order, which would certainly fit the ultimate consummation order, as well as the postmillennial hope in redemptive-historical preterism's future victory and prosperity." Kenneth L. Gentry, Jr., *The Divorce of Israel: A Redemptive-Historical Interpretation of Revelation Vol. 2* (Dallas, GA: Tolle Lege Press, 2016), 736.

[7] **The story of the sea battle of Taricheae can be found here**: *The Wars of the Jews* 3.9.3 §419-427

[8] **The story of the battle of Joppa and those killed in the sea storm**: Flavius Josephus, *The Wars of the Jews* 3.9.3 §419-427.

"Although the greatest part of them were carried by the waves, and dashed to pieces against the abrupt parts of the rocks, insomuch that the sea was bloody a long way, and the maritime parts were full of dead bodies; for the Romans came upon those that were carried to the shore, and destroyed them; (427) and the number of the bodies that were thus thrown out of the sea was four thousand and two hundred"

Flavius Josephus and William Whiston, The Works of Josephus: Complete and Unabridged (Peabody: Hendrickson, 1987), 658.

[9] **Jesus's statement about throwing a mountain into the sea**: Notice that the context is Jesus condemning Jerusalem for not having faith in Messiah. It was like a tree that would not bear fruit, and therefore be cursed (judged). So the faith that old covenant Jews lacked was the faith that would end that old covenant system, that earthly Mount Zion.

> Mark 11:20–23 [20] As they passed by in the morning, they saw the fig tree withered away to its roots. [21] And Peter remembered and said to him, "Rabbi, look! The fig tree that you cursed has withered." [22] And Jesus answered them, "Have faith in God. [23] Truly, I say to you, whoever says to this mountain, 'Be taken up and thrown into the sea,' and does not doubt in his heart, but believes that what he says will come to pass, it will be done for him.

"Jesus, in other words, appears to be deliberately evoking the whole context in Jeremiah. The cursing of the fig tree is part of his sorrowful Jeremianic demonstration that Israel, and the Temple, are under judgment.

"The word about the mountain being cast into the sea also belongs exactly here. Though the existence of more than one saying in this group suggests that Jesus used to say this sort of thing quite frequently, 'this mountain," spoken in Jerusalem, would naturally refer to the Temple mount. The saying is not simply a miscellaneous comment on how prayer and faith can do such things as curse fig trees. It is a very specific word of judgment: the Temple mountain is, figuratively speaking, to be taken up and cast into the sea.200

"In addition to Isaiah and Jeremiah, the whole incident cries out to be seen, as various writers have recently argued, within the context of a deliberate reapplication of Zechariah. The quasi-royal entry into the city, and Jesus's messianic authority over the Temple (about which more anon), evokes Zechariah 9:9 and 6:12; the warning of a great cataclysm echoes 14:1–5. Further, the whole context speaks of the mighty acts whereby YHWH will set up his kingdom once and for all (14:9), whereupon the Gentiles will come in to worship (14:16–19)."

N. T. Wright, *Jesus and the Victory of God, Christian Origins and the Question of God* (London: Society for Promoting Christian Knowledge, 1996), 422.

Earthly Mount Zion vs. heavenly Mount Zion:

> Hebrews 12:22–24 22 But you have come to Mount Zion and to the city of the living God, the heavenly Jerusalem, and to innumerable angels in festal gathering, ···and to Jesus, the mediator of a new covenant.

CHAPTER 22

[1] **Day of Atonement four-fold duties**:

> Leviticus 23:27–28 (NASB95)
> 27 "On exactly the tenth day of this seventh month is the day of atonement; it shall be a holy convocation for you, and you shall humble your souls and present an offering by fire to the LORD.
> 28 "You shall not do any work on this same day, for it is a day of atonement, to make atonement on your behalf before the LORD your God.

[2] **The miracle of the perpetual light of the Menorah**:

> b. Menahot 86B
>
> A. "Outside the veil of the testimony in the tent of meeting" (Lev. 24:3)—
>
> B.This serves as testimony for everyone in the world that the Presence of God is in Israel.
>
> C. Now did they need a light? And is it not the case that all those forty years that the Israelites spent in the wilderness, they need no light?
>
> D. For it is said, "For over the tabernacle a cloud of the Lord rested by day, and fire would appear in the cloud by night, in the view of all the house of Israel throughout their journeys" (Ex. 40:38).
>
> E. If so, why is it said, "of the testimony:"
>
> F. This serves as testimony for everyone in the world that the Presence of God is in Israel [Sifra CCXL:I.14].
>
> II.6 A. What is the meaning of "the testimony"?
>
> B. Said Raba, "This refers to the western lamp, into which the same quantity of oil was poured as was poured into the others, and yet he kindled the others from it and ended up with it." [Cf. M. Tamid 6:1E: And if he found the two easternmost lamps still flickering, he clears out the eastern one and leaves the western one flickering, for from it did he kindle the candlestick at twilight].

Jacob Neusner, *The Babylonian Talmud: A Translation and Commentary, vol. 19* (Peabody, MA: Hendrickson Publishers, 2011), 454.

[3] **The four miracles recorded in Talmud that occurred between Christ's death and before the temple was destroyed in AD 70**:

y. Yoma 6:3, I.4.A–D (Jerusalem Talmud)

[I:4 A] It has been taught: Forty years before the destruction of the Temple the western light went out, the crimson thread remained crimson, and the lot for the Lord always came up in the left hand.

[B] They would close the gates of the Temple by night and get up in the morning and find them wide open.

[C] Said [to the Temple] Rabban Yohanan ben Zakkai, "O Temple, why do you frighten us? We know that you will end up destroyed.

[D] "For it has been said, 'Open your doors, O Lebanon, that the fire may devour your cedars!' " (Zech. 11:1).

Jacob Neusner, *The Jerusalem Talmud: A Translation and Commentary* (Peabody, Massachusetts: Hendrickson Publishers, 2008).

b. Yoma 4:1, II.5.A-C (Babylonian Talmud)

A. Our rabbis have taught on Tannaite authority:

 B. Forty years before the destruction of the sanctuary, the lot did not come up in the right hand, and the thread of crimson never turned white, and the westernmost light never shone, and the doors of the courtyard would open by themselves,

C. until Rabban Yohanan b. Zakkai rebuked them. He said, "Temple, Temple, why will you yourself give the alarm [that you are going to be destroyed? You don't have to, because] I know that in the end you are destined to be destroyed. For Zechariah b. Eldo has already prophesied concerning you: 'Open your doors, Lebanon, that fire may devour your cedars' (Zech. 11:1)."

Jacob Neusner, *The Babylonian Talmud: A Translation and Commentary, vol. 5a* (Peabody, MA: Hendrickson Publishers, 2011), 142.

[4] **Portents described here in Josephus**: Josephus writes of multiple omens that occur on several different festival occasions before the War began in AD 66. I have conflated them together here and placed them under the Feast of Dedication in AD 64 for the sake of the story. But the meaning of these alleged omens remains the same as in Josephus.

"Thus also, before the Jews' rebellion, and before those commotions which preceded the war, when the people were come in great crowds to the feast of unleavened bread, on the eighth day of the month Xanthicus [Nisan], and at the ninth hour of the night, so great a light shone round the altar and the holy house, that it appeared to be bright day time; which light lasted for half an hour. (291) This light seemed to be a good sign to the unskillful, but was so interpreted by the sacred scribes, as to portend those events that followed immediately upon it. (292) At the same festival also, a heifer, as she was led by the high priest to be sacrificed, brought forth a lamb in the midst of the temple. (293) Moreover, the eastern gate of the inner [court of the] temple, which was of brass, and vastly heavy, and had been with difficulty shut by twenty men, and rested upon a basis armed with iron, and had bolts fastened very deep into the firm floor, which was there made of one entire stone, was seen to be opened of its own accord about the sixth hour of the night. (295) This also appeared to the vulgar to be a very happy prodigy, as if God did thereby open them the gate of happiness. But the men of learning understood it, that the security of their holy house was dissolved of its own accord, and that the gate was opened for the advantage of their enemies. (296) So these publicly declared, that this signal foreshowed the desolation that was coming upon them." Flavius Josephus, *The Wars of the Jews*, 6.289-300.

[5] **Voice heard in the temple, "Let us remove ourselves"**: "Moreover at that feast which we call Pentecost, as the priests were going by night into the inner [court of the] temple, as their custom was, to perform their sacred ministrations, they said that, in the first place, they felt a quaking, and heard a great noise (300) and after that they heard a sound as of a great multitude, saying, "Let us remove hence." Flavius Josephus, *The Wars of the Jews*, 6.289-300.

Yosippon, another Jewish historian referred to armies being seen in the skies in AD 66:

"For one year before Vespasian came, a single great star shining like unsheathed swords was seen over the Temple. And in those days when the sign was seen it was the holiday of Passover and during that entire night the Temple was lit up and illuminated like the light of day, and thus it was all seven days of the Passover. All the sages of Jerusalem knew that it was a malevolent sign, but the rest of the ignorant people said that it was a benevolent sign. "…Now it happened after this that there was seen from above over the Holy of Holies for the whole night the outline of a man's face, the like of whose beauty had never been seen in all the land, and his appearance was quite awesome.

"Moreover, in those days were seen chariots of fire and horsemen, a great force flying across the sky near to the ground coming against Jerusalem and all the land of Judah, all of them horses of fire and riders of fire. When the holiday of Shavu'oth came in those days, during the night the priests heard within the Temple something like the sound of men going and the sound of men marching in a multitude going into the Temple, and a terrible and mighty voice was heard speaking: "Let's go and leave this House.""

Sepher Yosippon *A Mediaeval History of Ancient Israel* translated from the Hebrew by Steven B. Bowman. Excerpts from Chapter 87 "Burning of the Temple" cited in http://fulfilledtheology.ning.com/forum/topics/historical-records-with-some (9/16/2014)

Rushing wind as a symbol of the Holy Spirit: Acts 2:2.

[1] **Dramatic prophecies of Jeremiah**:

Hiding his girdle by the Euphrates (Jer 13:1-11)
Breaking a potter's bottle in the valley of Hinnom (Jer 19:1)
Walking through all the gates of Jerusalem (Jer 17:19-27)
Wearing a yoke on his neck (Jer 27:1-14)
Purchasing the deed to a field (Jer 32:6-15)
Burying stones in some pavement (Jer 43:8-13)
Casting a scroll into the Euphrates (Jer 51:59-64).

Theatrical prophecies of Ezekiel:

God told him to perform a war epic as a prophecy, complete with a miniature city besieged by battering rams (Ezek 4:1-3).
God told him to lay on his side for 430 days, tied up in ropes, eating food cooked over burning excrement, with an emblem of the sins of Israel on top of him (Ezek 4:4-8).
Cutting his hair and beard, and dispersing it in various ways to dramatically depict God's concluding judgment (Ezek 5:1-4).
Covering his face, dragging his baggage around day and night, and digging a hole in a wall to store it, as a sign of exile (Ezek 12:1-11).
Ezekiel then had to tremble and shudder while eating as another dramatic sign of the anxiety that Israel will feel in their exile

[2] **Alexander refers to**:

Revelation 11:1–3[1] Then I was given a measuring rod like a staff, and I was told, "Rise and measure the temple of God and the altar and those who worship there, [2] but do not measure the court outside the temple; leave that out, for it is given over to the nations, and they will trample the holy city for forty-two months. [3] And I will grant authority to my two witnesses, and they will prophesy for 1,260 days, clothed in sackcloth."

[3] **Elihu quotes from**:

Ezekiel 37:26–28
[26] I will make a covenant of peace with them. It shall be an everlasting covenant with them. And I will set them in their land and multiply them, and will set my sanctuary in their midst forevermore. [27] My dwelling place shall be with them, and I will be their God, and they shall be my people. [28]

Then the nations will know that I am the LORD who sanctifies Israel, when my sanctuary is in their midst forevermore."

[4] **Ezekiel's influence on Revelation**: "A sampling of the OT influence from Ezekiel is quite remarkable. The following few, clear samples illustrate how Ezekiel impacts Rev at significant points: (1) The all-important throne-room vision of God in Rev 4:1–11 draws from Eze 1. (2) In 5:10 the double-sided scroll in God's hand on the throne that initiates the divine judgments strongly reflects Eze 3:3. In addition, note: (3) the marking of the foreheads (Eze 9:4; Rev 7:3); (4) the coals thrown to the earth from heaven (Eze 10:2; Rev 8:5); (5) the four judgments related to the fourth seal (Eze 14:21; Rev 6:8); (6) Gog and Magog (Eze 38–39; Rev 20:7–10); (7) the birds flocking to their prey as symbols of divine judgment (Eze 39:17ff; Rev 19:17ff); (8) the glorified Jerusalem (Eze. 40–47; Rev 21); and more. According to Beale and Carson (2007:1086) "Goulder (1981: 343–49) has argued that broad portions of Ezekiel have been the dominant influence on at least twelve major sections of Revelation (Rev. 4; 5; 6:1–8; 6:12—7:1; 7:2–8; 8:1–5; 10:1–7; 14:6–12; 17:1–6; 18:9–24; 20:7–10; 21:22).

"Carrington goes so far as to declare that "the Revelation is a Christian rewriting of Ezekiel. Its fundamental structure is the same. Its interpretation depends upon Ezekiel." Goulder observes even further that "these uses of Ezekiel are a dominant influence on the structure of Revelation, since they are placed to a marked extent in the same order as they occur in Ezekiel itself." Vogelgesang agrees that "the order of Ezekelian passages used in Revelation approximate the order of Ezekiel itself."

"Boxall provides us with a helpful table demonstrating Ezekiel's influence on Revelation:
Rev 1 = Eze 1
Rev 4 = Eze 1
Rev 5 = Eze 2
Rev 6 = Eze 5–7
Rev 7:1–2 = Eze 7:2–3
Rev 7–8 = Eze 9–10
Rev 10 = Eze 2–3 (cp. Rev 5)
Rev 10–13 = Eze 11–14 (echoes)
Rev 11:1–2 = Eze 40
Rev 13:11–18 = Eze 14
Rev 17 = Eze 16, 23
Rev 18 = Eze 26–28
Rev 19:11–21 = Eze 29, 32 (39)
Rev 20:1–3 = Eze 29, 32
Rev 20:4–6 = Eze 37
Rev 20:7–10 = Eze 38:1–39:20
Rev 10:11–15 = Eze 39:21–29
Rev 21–22 = Eze 40–48"
Kenneth L. Gentry, Jr., *The Divorce of Israel: A Redemptive-Historical Interpretation of Revelation Vol. 1* (Dallas, GA: Tolle Lege Press, 2016), 121.

[5] **Ezekiel prophesies the jealousy of God (and therefore, the ark of God's presence) departing when Babylon destroys the ark**:

> Ezekiel 10:18–19 [18] Then the glory of the LORD went out from the threshold of the house, and stood over the cherubim. [19] And the cherubim lifted up their wings and mounted up from the earth before my eyes as they went out, with the wheels beside them. And they stood at the entrance of the east gate of the house of the LORD, and the glory of the God of Israel was over them.

> Ezekiel 16:41–42 And they shall burn your houses and execute judgments upon you in the sight of many women. I will make you stop playing the whore, and you shall also give payment no more. 42 So will I satisfy my wrath on you, and my jealousy shall depart from you.

[6] **Jesus describes God leaving the temple and destroying it**:

> Matthew 23:37–24:2 [37] "O Jerusalem, Jerusalem, the city that kills the prophets and stones those who are sent to it! How often would I have gathered your children together as a hen gathers her

brood under her wings, and you were not willing! [38] See, your house is left to you desolate. [39] For I tell you, you will not see me again, until you say, 'Blessed is he who comes in the name of the Lord.' " [1] Jesus left the temple and was going away, when his disciples came to point out to him the buildings of the temple. [2] But he answered them, "You see all these, do you not? Truly, I say to you, there will not be left here one stone upon another that will not be thrown down."

[7] Elihu is quoting from:

Zechariah 6:12–14 [12] And say to him, 'Thus says the LORD of hosts, "Behold, the man whose name is the Branch: for he shall branch out from his place, and he shall build the temple of the LORD. [13] It is he who shall build the temple of the LORD and shall bear royal honor, and shall sit and rule on his throne. And there shall be a priest on his throne, and the counsel of peace shall be between them both." ' [14] And the crown shall be in the temple of the LORD as a reminder to Helem, Tobijah, Jedaiah, and Hen the son of Zephaniah.

[8] The eschatological temple is the body of Christ, not a future physical building:

Revelation 21:22 [22] And I saw no temple in the city, for its temple is the Lord God the Almighty and the Lamb.

Revelation shows how the eschatological temple of Ezekiel is transformed into a spiritual reality, not a physical one. Jesus is the temple of God, that is why John sees no physical temple. And Christians are the body of Christ (therefore, the temple) (Rom 12:5; 1 Cor 10:17; 1 Cor 12:27; Eph 4:12).

The following is an excerpt from Brian Godawa, *Israel in Bible Prophecy: The New Testament Fulfillment of the Promise to Abraham* (Los Angeles, Embedded Pictures Publishing, 2017), 48-51.

Despite the fact that the New Testament nowhere says that the physical temple will be rebuilt, there is the promise of an eschatological temple in Ezekiel 40-48. Futurists (those who believe the last days are in our future) assume it is a physical temple, though the description of that temple is in a vision of obvious spiritual symbols, such as a trickle of living water, becoming an uncrossable river that flows out of the temple into the sea, turning the entire sea into freshwater (Ezke 47:1-12). Milton Terry, renowned expert on Biblical Apocalyptics concludes,

Ezekiel's temple is no more explicable as a model of real architecture than are his cherubim and wheels possible in mechanics…this vision of restored and perfected temple, service, and land symbolizes the perfected kingdom of God and his Messiah."

In line with Terry's messianic interpretation of Ezekiel's eschatological temple, the Messiah is prophesied to build that temple:

Zechariah 6:12–13
[12] And say to him, 'Thus says the LORD of hosts, "Behold, the man whose name is the Branch: for he shall branch out from his place, and he shall build the temple of the LORD. [13] It is he who shall build the temple of the LORD and shall bear royal honor, and shall sit and rule on his throne." '

In the New Testament, Jesus is revealed as that "branch of Jesse" (Acts 13:22-23). So, Jesus, as Messiah, is the builder of the eschatological temple. But what kind of temple is it? The answer is to be found in the cornerstone.

The cornerstone of a temple is the "perfect" foundational stone upon which a temple is based. It is usually buried in the corner of the building, and all the rest of the structure is built upon it's perfect angles and measurements. The biblical prophecies describe that perfect cornerstone of the eschatological temple as Messiah himself:

Isaiah 28:16
[16] therefore thus says the Lord GOD, "Behold, I am the one who has laid as a foundation in Zion, a stone, a tested stone, a precious cornerstone, of a sure foundation: 'Whoever believes will not be in haste.'

407

Now, is that a spiritual metaphor or not? Obviously the text is not promising that the body of Messiah would literally be buried in the ground of a physical temple as its cornerstone. So if the very cornerstone of the eschatological temple is spiritual, then the entire temple, that is based upon it, would have to be a spiritual temple, not a physical one.

Acts 4:11
[11] This Jesus is the stone that was rejected by you, the builders, which has become the cornerstone.

Isaiah 8:14
[14] And he will become a sanctuary and a stone of offense and a rock of stumbling to both houses of Israel, a trap and a snare to the inhabitants of Jerusalem.

The Jews who rejected that cornerstone of the new temple would be judged when God came and destroyed their physical temple to replace it with the spiritual one in AD 70 (Matt 21:40-43). The simple biblical fact is: the new temple of God in the New Covenant era is not an earthly temple built with hands, but a heavenly one built by the Spirit.

But don't take my word for it, the apostles who wrote the Scriptures also told us that the temple was transformed into the spiritual reality of Jesus Christ himself. Jesus is the New Temple.

John 1:14
[14] And the Word became flesh and dwelt [tabernacled] among us, and we have seen his glory, glory as of the only Son from the Father, full of grace and truth.

In this passage, Jesus is described using the term for tabernacle, which was the precursor to the temple. As argued above, the "New Jerusalem" is a spiritual metaphor for the New Covenant (Heb 12:22–24; Gal 4:22–31). In that New Covenant "city," there is no physical stone temple, because Jesus is God's true and spiritual temple:

Revelation 21:22
[22] And I saw no temple in the city [New Jerusalem], for its temple is the Lord God the Almighty and the Lamb.

This revelation of the New Jerusalem in Revelation is not a future reality, but a present one. New Jerusalem is the New Covenant (Heb 12:22) described as a spiritual building.

The apostle Paul makes that spiritual temple connection crystal clear when he speaks of the new holy temple of God, "being built on the foundation of the apostles and prophets, Christ Jesus himself being the cornerstone" (Eph 2:20).

Ephesians 2:19–22
[19] So then you are no longer strangers and aliens, but you are fellow citizens with the saints and members of the household of God, [20] built on the foundation of the apostles and prophets, Christ Jesus himself being the cornerstone, [21] in whom the whole structure, being joined together, grows into a holy temple in the Lord. [22] In him you also are being built together into a dwelling place for God by the Spirit.

The new temple of God here is not a physical one rebuilt with stone, but a spiritual house consisting of the body of Christ. This is not mere "spiritualizing," as if it doesn't have any tangible reality. No, the Church of Jesus Christ is a real presence of people in this world, and it is the true presence of Jesus Christ as well, not a mere metaphor. In the Bible, "spiritualization" does not mean something is any less real, in fact, it is in some ways *more* real. The Body of Christ as God's "spiritual" temple is a very real and tangible presence of God on the earth.

Peter affirms this same notion of the body of Christ being God's "spiritual" holy temple in this new covenant.

1 Peter 2:4–6
[4] As you come to him, a living stone rejected by men but in the sight of God chosen and precious,

⁵ <u>you yourselves like living stones are being built up as a spiritual house</u>, to be a holy priesthood, to offer spiritual sacrifices acceptable to God through Jesus Christ. ⁶ For it stands in Scripture: "Behold, I am laying in Zion a stone, a cornerstone chosen and precious, and whoever believes in him will not be put to shame."

2 Corinthians 6:16
¹⁶ For <u>we are the temple of the living God</u>; as God said, "I will make my dwelling among them and walk among them, and I will be their God, and they shall be my people.

⁹ **The New Jerusalem is the New Covenant Church right now, not in some future**:

Hebrews 12:22–23
²² But you have come to Mount Zion and <u>to the city of the living God, the heavenly Jerusalem</u>, and to innumerable angels in festal gathering, ²³ and <u>to the assembly of the firstborn</u> who are enrolled in heaven, and to God, the judge of all, and to the spirits of the righteous made perfect,

Revelation 21:1–3
¹ Then I saw a new heaven and a new earth, for the first heaven and the first earth had passed away, and the sea was no more. ² And I saw the holy city, <u>new Jerusalem</u>, coming down out of heaven from God, prepared as a bride adorned for her husband. ³ And I heard a loud voice from the throne saying, "<u>Behold, the dwelling place of God is with man. He will dwell with them, and they will be his people, and God himself will be with them as their God.</u>

Hebrews 11:8–16
⁸ By faith Abraham obeyed when he was called to <u>go out to a place that he was to receive as an inheritance</u>… ¹⁴ For people who speak thus make it clear that they are seeking a homeland. ¹⁵ If they had been thinking of that [physical] land from which they had gone out, they would have had opportunity to return. ¹⁶ But as it is, they desire a better country, <u>that is, a heavenly one. Therefore God is not ashamed to be called their God, for he has prepared for them a city</u>.

The Body of Christ is the New Jerusalem

Revelation 21:9–10
⁹ Then came one of the seven angels who had the seven bowls full of the seven last plagues and spoke to me, saying, "Come, <u>I will show you the Bride, the wife of the Lamb</u>." ¹⁰ And he carried me away in the Spirit to a great, high mountain, and showed me <u>the holy city Jerusalem coming down out of heaven from God</u>,

¹⁰ **Alexander is referring to**: Ezekiel 37.

¹¹ **Micah passage referred to here**:

Micah 2:12–13 ¹² I will surely assemble all of you, O Jacob; I will **gather** the **remnant** of Israel; I will set them together like sheep in a fold,

¹² **Hosea's writings referred to here**:

Hosea 8:8 Israel is swallowed up; already they are among the nations as a useless vessel.

Hosea 1:10–11, ¹⁰ Yet the number of the children of Israel shall be like the sand of the sea, which cannot be measured or numbered. <u>And in the place where it was said to them, "You are not my people," it shall be said to them, "Children of the living God."</u> ¹¹ <u>And the children of Judah and the children of Israel shall be **gathered** together,</u>

¹³ **Isaiah's remnant**:

Isaiah 11: 10–12
¹⁰ In that day the root of Jesse, who shall stand as a signal for the peoples—of him shall the nations inquire, and his resting place shall be glorious. ¹¹ In that day the Lord will extend his hand yet a second time to recover the **remnant** that remains of his people, from Assyria, from Egypt, from Pathros, from Cush, from Elam, from Shinar, from Hamath, and from the coastlands of the

sea. [12] He will raise a signal for the nations and will assemble the banished of Israel, and **gather the dispersed of Judah from the four corners of the earth**.

This remnant of Isaiah 11 is said to be fulfilled in the New Covenant by Paul:

Romans 15:8–9, 12
[8] For I tell you that Christ became a servant to the circumcised to show God's truthfulness, in order to confirm the promises given to the patriarchs, [9] and in order that the Gentiles might glorify God for his mercy. As it is written, "Therefore I will praise you among the Gentiles, and sing to your name."
[12] And again Isaiah says, "The root of Jesse will come, even he who arises [resurrection] to rule the Gentiles; in him will the Gentiles hope."

[14] **Christian believers are now the biblical remnant**:

Romans 11:5–6
[5] So too at the present time there is a remnant, chosen by grace. [6] But if it is by grace, it is no longer on the basis of works; otherwise grace would no longer be grace.

[15] **Gentiles gathered with the regathering of the Jews**: This is Paul's exact argument in Romans 9.

Romans 9:24–29 [24] even us whom he has called, not from the Jews only but also from the Gentiles? [25] As indeed he says in Hosea, "Those who were not my people I will call 'my people,' and her who was not beloved I will call 'beloved.' " [26] "And in the very place where it was said to them, 'You are not my people,' there they will be called 'sons of the living God.' " [27] And Isaiah cries out concerning Israel: "Though the number of the sons of Israel be as the sand of the sea, only a **remnant** of them will be saved, [28] for the Lord will carry out his sentence upon the earth fully and without delay." [29] And as Isaiah predicted, "If the Lord of hosts had not left us offspring, we would have been like Sodom and become like Gomorrah."

See also:

Zechariah 2:6–11 [6] For I have spread you abroad as the four winds of the heavens, declares the LORD… for behold, I come and I will dwell in your midst, declares the LORD. [11] And many nations shall join themselves to the LORD in that day, and shall be my people. And I will dwell in your midst…

Isaiah 49:6 [6] he says: "It is too light a thing that you should be my servant to raise up the tribes of Jacob and to bring back the preserved (remnant) of Israel; I will make you as a light for the nations, that my salvation may reach to the end of the earth."

Jesus is the Messiah who brings together both Jew and Gentile into one:

John 10:14–17 [14] I am the good shepherd. I know my own and my own know me, [15] just as the Father knows me and I know the Father; and I lay down my life for the sheep. [16] **And I have other sheep that are not of this fold. I must bring them also, and they will listen to my voice. So there will be one flock, one shepherd**. [17] For this reason the Father loves me, because I lay down my life that I may take it up again

[16] Hosea 1:11, 23.

[17] **Alexander is quoting from**:

Ephesians 3:4–6 [4] When you read this, you can perceive my insight into the mystery of Christ, [5] which was not made known to the sons of men in other generations as it has now been revealed to his holy apostles and prophets by the Spirit. [6] This mystery is that the Gentiles are fellow heirs, members of the same body, and partakers of the promise in Christ Jesus through the gospel.

[18] **Pentecost as the beginning of the regathering of the Jews from all the nations**:

The following is an excerpt from Brian Godawa, *Israel in Bible Prophecy: The New Testament Fulfillment of the Promise to Abraham* (Los Angeles, Embedded Pictures Publishing, 2017), 59-61.

410

In Acts 2, we read about the first explosion of the Gospel with the first baptism of the Holy Spirit. It was the thing that Jesus had told them to wait for, which would launch them into all the world with the Good News (Acts 1:4). Pentecost would be the historical inauguration of the heavenly New Covenant achieved by the death, resurrection and ascension of Christ. It would be the pouring out of God's Spirit upon his people (Isa 32:12-19; 44:5; Ezek 36:25-28; 37:14).

The disciples asked Jesus if this was the time of the restoration of Israel (1:6), the very thing we have been discussing in this work. Jesus told them that the restoration of Israel would begin occurring when the Holy Spirit came upon them, but they were not to worry themselves with the timing (1:8).

And what was the restoration, but the pouring out of God's Spirit and the regathering of Jews from all over the known earth in a spiritual metaphorical resurrection? (Ezek 37). So when the disciples were baptized with the Spirit at Pentecost and began to speak in foreign tongues, that was the fulfillment of God's pouring out of his Spirit. Pouring is a form of baptizing (Heb 9:10, 13, 19, 21). But it was also the beginning of the regathering of Jews because "there were dwelling in Jerusalem Jews, devout men from every nation under heaven" (Acts 2:5). The list of nations that are described (Acts 2:9-11) just happens to be a representative sampling of the seventy nations of Genesis 10. To the ancient Jew, those seventy were "all the nations" to which the Jews were scattered (Amos 9:9). According to the apostle Luke, Pentecost of AD 30 was transformed into the beginning of the gathering of Jews from all the nations.

And that gathering of Jews included the Gentiles. It was a gathering of two bodies into one that was occurring all throughout the book of Acts. Notice these passages that say that the evangelism of Acts is the very fulfillment of the promise to gather the Gentiles with the Jews as his people:

Acts 15:13–19
[13] After they finished speaking, James replied, "Brothers, listen to me. [14] Simeon has related how God first visited the Gentiles, to take from them a people for his name. [15] And with this the words of the prophets agree, just as it is written.

Acts 26:23
[Paul:] [23] that the Christ must suffer and that, by being the first to rise from the dead, he would proclaim light both to our people and to the Gentiles."

The "ingathering" was based upon the unity of belief in Jesus as Messiah. Isaiah had prophesied that when Messiah first came (the branch of Jesse), *in that very day*, the Lord would "recover the remnant that remains of his people," from all the nations. "In that day," the root of Jesse would be "raised (resurrected) as a signal for the nations," and would "assemble the banished of Israel and gather the dispersed of Judah from the four corners of the earth" (Isa 11:1-2, 10-12). According to the prophecy, the gathering of the remnant and the Gentiles would occur at the *first coming* of Messiah, when Jesus was resurrected, not the second coming. *In that day* of Messiah's arrival and resurrection (his raising as a signal), he would draw both the remnant of Israel as well as Gentile believers. This will not start in our future, it already started in the book of Acts! Paul likened that raising of the signal to Christ's resurrection, and confirmed this Isaianic promise as already being fulfilled *during his ministry*:

Romans 15:8–9, 12
[8] For I tell you that Christ became a servant to the circumcised to show God's truthfulness, in order to confirm the promises given to the patriarchs, [9] and in order that the Gentiles might glorify God for his mercy... [12] And again Isaiah says, "The root of Jesse will come, even he who arises to rule the Gentiles; in him will the Gentiles hope.

What were the promises given to the patriarchs that Paul says were confirmed ("verified") in Christ's resurrection? All of them, including the regathering (Acts 3:24; 32; 15:13-15; 24:24; 26:6). In fact, most of the prophecies about the regathering of Israel almost always add the inclusion of Gentiles as a simultaneous event (See more below). But the point is that the book of Romans says explicitly that the Isaianic prophecy about the gathering of the remnant along with the Gentiles was already being fulfilled *in his own day*. This is not an eschatological system demanding something must be fulfilled in the future, this is the New Testament itself saying the prophecy was fulfilled in the first century, *in that day*.

One of the ways that Dispensationalists seek to deny the fulfillment of the regathering is to suggest that the inclusion of the Gentiles has been fulfilled in Christ, but the gathering of Israel has not yet been fulfilled. They argue that "confirmation" of promises to the patriarchs is not the same as "fulfillment." God only verified the promises to Israel, not fulfilled them. They see this split because they do not see an earthly nation called Israel regathered into the land in the way that they expect it to be. But their problem is that, as we have seen, the gathering of the Jews was simultaneous with the gathering of the Gentiles. If we return to Acts 2, the holy Scripture says again that both the gathering *and* Gentile inclusion were being fulfilled *in their day*.

[19] Ezekiel 37:24-28; 36:26.

[20] **Ezekiel's vision of the dry bones fulfilled in the new covenant**:

The following is an excerpt from Brian Godawa, *Israel in Bible Prophecy: The New Testament Fulfillment of the Promise to Abraham* (Los Angeles, Embedded Pictures Publishing, 2017), 70-74.

Ezekiel 37:7-14 describes a vision that Ezekiel was given about the regathering and restoration of Israel depicted as a massive resurrection. Then in his further explanation of everything that restoration entailed, he writes this from the mouth of God:

> Ezekiel 37:21–28
> [21] then say to them, Thus says the Lord GOD: Behold, I will take the people of Israel from the nations among which they have gone, and will gather them from all around, and bring them to their own land. [22] And I will make them one nation in the land, on the mountains of Israel. And one king shall be king over them all, and they shall be no longer two nations, and no longer divided into two kingdoms… [24] "My servant David shall be king over them, and they shall all have one shepherd. They shall walk in my rules and be careful to obey my statutes. [25] They shall dwell in the land that I gave to my servant Jacob, where your fathers lived. They and their children and their children's children shall dwell there forever, and David my servant shall be their prince forever. [26] I will make a covenant of peace with them. It shall be an everlasting covenant with them. And I will set them in their land and multiply them, and will set my sanctuary in their midst forevermore. [27] My dwelling place shall be with them, and I will be their God, and they shall be my people. [28] Then the nations will know that I am the LORD who sanctifies Israel, when my sanctuary is in their midst forevermore."

In an expansion of that prophecy earlier in the text, God adds another promise that he will place his spirit within them and give them a heart of flesh to replace their heart of stone (remember the "outpouring of the Spirit" fulfilled in Acts?).

> Ezekiel 36:24–28
> [24] I will take you from the nations and gather you from all the countries and bring you into your own land. [25] I will sprinkle clean water on you, and you shall be clean from all your uncleannesses, and from all your idols I will cleanse you. [26] And I will give you a new heart, and a new spirit I will put within you. And I will remove the heart of stone from your flesh and give you a heart of flesh. [27] And I will put my Spirit within you, and cause you to walk in my statutes and be careful to obey my rules. [28] You shall dwell in the land that I gave to your fathers, and you shall be my people, and I will be your God.

On every level, this entire prophecy is about the arrival of the New Covenant, not some distant future reinstitution of the Old Covenant shadows of physical temple and land. Each of the prophecy's constituent elements are fulfilled in the New Testament Scriptures *at the time of the first century*. Let's take a look at those elements:

1. The gathering of Israel from all the nations (v. 21): This was already explained above as starting to occur in AD 30 at Pentecost (Acts 2). The New Covenant fulfilled in the first century.

2. One nation with one king, David (v. 22-25): It was already detailed above that this messianic reference was Jesus seated on David's throne at his resurrection and ascension (Acts 2:30-33) and uniting his sheepfolds (Jn 10:16). That's the New Covenant fulfilled in the first century.

3. The everlasting covenant of peace with Israel (v. 26): The New Testament says that this everlasting covenant of peace is the New Covenant brought through Christ fulfilled in the first century.

Hebrews 13:20
[20] Now may the God of peace who brought again from the dead our Lord Jesus, the great shepherd of the sheep, by the <u>blood of the eternal covenant</u>,

Colossians 1:20
[20] and through him to reconcile to himself all things, whether on earth or in heaven, making <u>peace by the blood of his cross</u>.

4. God's dwelling place shall be with them (v. 27-28): In multiple places in the New Testament the Church of believers in Jesus are described as God's temple (1Cor 3:16-17; Eph 2:19-22), but Paul explicitly quotes the Ezekiel prophecy of the regathering and God's dwelling as fulfilled in the New Covenant Church beginning in the first century.

2 Corinthians 6:16
[16] What agreement has the temple of God with idols? For we are the temple of the living God; as God said, "I will make my dwelling among them and walk among them, and I will be their God, and they shall be my people.

5. Remove the heart of stone, replace with a heart of flesh (36:26): Paul wrote that this promise of heart replacement was fulfilled in the arrival of the New Covenant of Christ fulfilled in the first century.

2 Corinthians 3:3
[3] And you show that you are a letter from Christ delivered by us, written not with ink but with the Spirit of the living God, <u>not on tablets of stone but on tablets of human hearts</u>.

6. God will put his Spirit in them and causing them to obey (36:27)

7. He will be their God and they will be His people (36:27): Not only does the Old Testament link these two phrases to the New Covenant (Jer 31:31-34), but the New Testament also claims this promise was fulfilled beginning in the first century with the arrival of the New Covenant.

Ephesians 1:13
[13] In him you also, when you heard the word of truth, the gospel of your salvation, <u>and believed in him</u>, <u>were sealed with the promised Holy Spirit</u>. (see also Jn 7:37-39, 1Cor 6:19)

Hebrews 8:6–13
[6] "Behold, the days are coming, declares the Lord, when I will establish a new covenant with the house of Israel and with the house of Judah... <u>I will put my laws into their minds, and write them on their hearts, and I will be their God, and they shall be my people...</u>[13] <u>In speaking of a new covenant, he makes the first one obsolete. And what is becoming obsolete and growing old is ready to vanish away</u>.

Notice how the Holy Spirit-authorized writer of Hebrews says right up front that the promise to the house of Israel and Judah is fulfilled in the arrival of the New Covenant in the first century, *not* in a future time yet to come. God places his Spirit in all believers in Jesus, they are his people of the New Covenant.

Dispensationalists claim that the gathering of the Gentiles occurred with the coming of Jesus but not the promised gathering of Judah and Israel, which has yet to take place. But the New Testament over and over again claims that the New Covenant fulfills that promise to Judah and Israel of their gathering. If the New Testament claims a prophecy has been fulfilled, then it is literally anti-biblical to deny that fulfillment.

Ezekiel 36-37 is pregnant with motifs and promises of the New Covenant arrival of Messiah, not a second coming and reinstitution of Old Covenant shadows. It is important to remember that the Old Testament contains no theology of the second coming of Messiah. It's all about the first coming for them. The second coming is a New Testament doctrine, not an Old Testament one. The whole point to the prophets was that when Messiah came, he would fulfill the promises and usher in the messianic age to come. The New

Covenant is that messianic age, complete with Jesus seated on the throne of David (Eph 1:20-23), the regathering of Israel, and the inclusion of the Gentiles, the pouring out of God's Spirit, the new eternal covenant, the replacement of stoney hearts with flesh and God causing his people to walk in his statutes. The whole package is fulfilled in Christ. So when Christians read these prophecies as if they are intended to be split into pieces of fulfillment, the last of which will occur at a second coming of Christ, they are quite simply imposing their preconceived theology onto the text that has already been fulfilled instead of reading it within its original Old Covenant context.

[21] **The number fifty in Ezekiel as poetic reference to Jubilee**:

"The preamble to the temple vision opens with a complex date notice containing three distinct elements. First, the twenty-fifth year of our exile relates the vision to Ezekiel's own deportation to Babylon in 597 B.C. As noted earlier, the number twenty-five (multiples of which appear repeatedly in the vision) alludes to the midpoint of the Jubilee cycle. According to Israelite tradition, every fiftieth year on the Day of Atonement the horn (yōbēl) was to be blown throughout the land proclaiming release (dĕrôr) to all enslaved Israelites. The application of the term dĕrôr to the return from exile in Isa. 61:1 indicates that after the Babylonian captivity Jubilee language was appropriated for this event. The possibility that Ezekiel looked on the return from captivity as a Jubilee kind of experience finds support in his own reference to the year of liberty (šĕnat haddĕrôr) in 46:17."

"Whereas Ezekiel's contemporary, Jeremiah, applied the term dĕrôr to the "release" of persons (Jer. 34:8, 15, 17), the present usage is inspired by Lev. 25, which established the Israelite custom of "proclaiming release" (qārā' dĕrôr) every fiftieth year. In this "Year of Jubilee" all enslaved Israelites were to return (šûb) to their patrimonial holdings ('ăḥuzzâ). Ezekiel modifies the Mosaic ordinance by prescribing the return (šûb) of the land to the original owners' hands."

Daniel Isaac Block, *The Book of Ezekiel, Chapters 25–48, The New International Commentary on the Old Testament* (Grand Rapids, MI: Wm. B. Eerdmans Publishing Co., 1997–), 512, 680.

"But if the date in 40:1* is understood as the day in the middle of the period of captivity leading up to the great liberation, then the whole system of the temple measurements, whose inner structure is built on the numerals twenty-five, fifty and their multiples, acquires a hidden depth of significance with regard to the occurrence of the great liberation in the "year of fifty years.""

"The introductory date of the middle year of the period culminating in the great release seems to give to this figure in its present context a new, immediately significant emphasis. Already in the measurements of the gates and then of the temple building, which. in a bold increase on the sacred measurements of Solomon's temple, is oriented on the number fifty, there is reflected at the same time the number of the year of the great release. Under the symbol of these measurements, the one who comes to worship in the temple, in the event that access to the sacred house is granted to him as a priest, climbs by means of twenty-five steps to the site of what is holy."

"Thus two things are revealed in these figures. It becomes clear, on the one hand, that the details of the guidance vision with regard to the temple building very cautiously endeavor to preserve the measurements known from Solomon's temple. On the other hand, however, they try to accommodate these to the total plan of chapters 40f, which is determined by the figures twenty-five, fifty and their multiples."

Walther Zimmerli, Frank Moore Cross, and Klaus Baltzer, Ezekiel: *A Commentary on the Book of the Prophet Ezekiel, Hermeneia—a Critical and Historical Commentary on the Bible* (Philadelphia: Fortress Press, 1979–), 347, 362, 358–359.

[22] **Alexander is quoting**: Luke 4:14-21. See also Luke 7:18-23 for the same Jubilee language fulfilled in Christ.

Luke 7:18–23
[18] The disciples of John reported all these things to him. And John, [19] calling two of his disciples to him, sent them to the Lord, saying, "Are you the one who is to come, or shall we look for another?" [20] And when the men had come to him, they said, "John the Baptist has sent us to you, saying, 'Are you the one who is to come, or shall we look for another?' " [21] In that hour he healed many people of diseases and plagues and evil spirits, and on many who were blind he bestowed sight.

[22] And he answered them, "Go and tell John what you have seen and heard: <u>the blind receive their sight, the lame walk, lepers are cleansed, and the deaf hear, the dead are raised up, the poor have good news preached to them.</u> [23] <u>And blessed is the one who is not offended by me."</u>

[23] **Alexander remembers**: Luke 21:20–22.

[24] **Alexander remembers**: John 3:6.

[25] **Moshe is summarizing the metaphorical picture of Ezekiel 47.**

"Ezekiel's vision of the stream also lives on in the NT. One may recognize a veiled allusion in Jesus's words in John 7:38: "As the scripture has said, 'Out of the believer's heart shall flow rivers of living water,' " presumably as a life-giving agent of divine grace and blessing. The expression ὕδατος ζῶντος, "living waters," points immediately to Zechariah's mayim ḥayyîm, but secondarily to Ezekiel. Some have seen a connection with Ezekiel's En-eglaim in the 153 fish caught in John 21:11. B. Grigsby has carried this interpretation still further, suggesting that the evangelist sees the resurrected Christ as fulfilling the role of Ezekiel's temple, dispensing living water to a barren world.71 Whereas these interpretations are far from certain, the Ezekielian connection in Rev. 22:1–2 is obvious: "Then he [the interpreting angel] showed me a river of the water of life, as clear as crystal, coming from the throne of God and of the Lamb through the middle of the street of the city. On either side of the river was the tree of life, with its twelve kinds of fruit, which it produces every month, and the leaves of the tree, which offer healing for the nations."

Daniel Isaac Block, *The Book of Ezekiel, Chapters 25–48, The New International Commentary on the Old Testament* (Grand Rapids, MI: Wm. B. Eerdmans Publishing Co., 1997–), 698–699.

"That the description given of this stream and its effects, must be understood in an ideal manner, not of any actual river, but like all the rest of the vision, of spiritual things shadowed forth under it, is so evident as scarcely to require any proof. The source of it alone (the summit of an elevated mountain), and the manner of its increase, should put this beyond a doubt with all who would not convert the Bible into a nursery of extravagance and credulity. For a natural river like this would of necessity be in contravention of the established laws of nature, and could only exist as a perpetual miracle.

"Issuing as this stream does from the threshold of the temple, from the very foot of the throne of God (comp. Rev. xxii. 1), it must be, like all the special manifestations of God to his church, itself of a spiritual nature, and only in its effects productive of outward material good. It is just the efflux of that infinite fulness of life and blessing, which is treasured up in his spiritual temple, and continually pours itself forth as the operations of his grace proceed among men. It is emphatically a river of life. Wherever it is experienced, the barren soil of nature fructifies, the dead live again, the soul is replenished with joy and ^ gladness. And instead of spending, like the streams of nature, as it advances through the moral deserts of the world, it still multiplies and grows;

"A life-giving and ever-increasing stream of heavenly influence, proceeding from the centre of the Divine kingdom, and diffusing itself far and wide among men, is what the prophet intends to exhibit to our mind; and to give this idea form and shape to our apprehensions, he must fill up the picture with the appropriate signs and manifestations of life. But to take these up, one by one, and adapt them to particular things in the present or future dispensations of God, can only be an exercise of fancy, as likely to mislead as to conduct to sound and legitimate conclusions. Let us rest in the great reality. Let us rejoice in the thought, that the Spirit of God should have coupled, with all the other exhibitions of the Divine kingdom given to the prophet, so encouraging a prospect of its vivifying, restorative, and expanding energies. And let it deepen the blessed conviction in our bosom, that the purpose of God in grace is fixed; and that mighty as the obstacles are, which everywhere present themselves to withstand its progress, it shall certainly not fail to make good its triumph over all the disorders and corruption of the world"

Fairbairn, Patrick. *Commentary on Ezekiel* (K-Locations 7317-7321, 7327-7333, 7340-7348). Titus Books. K-Edition.

CHAPTER 25

[1] **The siege of Gamala**:

Flavius Josephus, *The Wars of the Jews* 4.1.10, §80-82

"The Romans slew but four thousand, whereas the number of those that had thrown themselves down was found to be five thousand: (81) nor did anyone escape except two women, who were the daughters of Philip, and Philip himself was the son of a certain eminent man called Jacimus, who had been general of king Agrippa's army; (82) and these did therefore escape, because they lay concealed from the sight of the Romans when the city was taken, for otherwise they spared not so much as the infants, of whom many were flung down by them from the citadel."

Flavius Josephus and William Whiston, *The Works of Josephus: Complete and Unabridged* (Peabody: Hendrickson, 1987), 668.

The entire story of the siege and fall of Gamala can be found in Flavius Josephus, *The Wars of the Jews* 4.1.1-10, §1-83.

CHAPTER 26

[1] **The story of the fall of Gischala and John's escape in this chapter can be found in**: Flavius Josephus, *The Wars of the Jews* 4.2.1-5, §84-120.

[2] **The conflicts between John of Gischala and Joseph can be found in detail in**: Flavius Josephus, *The Wars of the Jews* 2.21.1-10, §585-646.

[3] **Cydessa**:

Flavius Josephus, *The Wars of the Jews* 4.2.3, §104-105

"Titus was prevailed with by his pretense for a delay, and that he pitched his camp farther off the city at Cydessa. (105) This Cydessa was a strong mediterranean village of the Tyrians, which always hated and made war against the Jews; it had also a great number of inhabitants, and was well fortified; which made it a proper place for such as were enemies to the Jewish nation."

Flavius Josephus and William Whiston, *The Works of Josephus: Complete and Unabridged* (Peabody: Hendrickson, 1987), 669.

[4] **Titus did exactly that**:

Flavius Josephus, *The Wars of the Jews* 4.2.5, §115

"...but Titus, not so much regarding the supplications of the people, sent part of his horsemen to pursue after John, but they could not overtake him, for he was gotten to Jerusalem before; they also slew six thousand of the women and children who went out with him, but returned back and brought with them almost three thousand."

Flavius Josephus and William Whiston, *The Works of Josephus: Complete and Unabridged* (Peabody: Hendrickson, 1987), 669.

It is obvious that Josephus had contempt for Gischala and painted the worst picture he could of his antagonist. But there are contradictions in the text that requires one to read between the lines as this chapter does. In Wars 4.110, Josephus says that John left the women and children while they were being destroyed by the Romans. But then in 4.115, he writes that Titus sent cavalry after John but could not overtake him because he had arrived at Jerusalem before they could. But this would not have been possible had John been there in the battle. They would have easily been caught. Josephus was probably trying to make John look worse by leaving them in the heat of battle. Of course, leaving them before battle was just as bad, but less personal.

CHAPTER 27

[1] **Water from the pools of Solomon in the south flowed to Jerusalem in the upper and lower aqueducts**:

"Between the altar and porch of the Temple, but placed towards the south, was the immense laver of brass, supported by twelve colossal lions, which was drained every evening, and filled every morning by machinery, and where twelve priests could wash at the same time. Indeed, the water supply to the Sanctuary is among the most wonderful of its arrangements. That of the Temple is designated by Captain Wilson as the 'low-level supply,' in contradistinction to the 'high-level aqueduct,' which collected the water in a rock-hewn tunnel four miles long, on the road to Hebron, and then wound along so as to deliver water to the upper portion of the city. The 'low-level' aqueduct, which supplied the Temple, derived its waters from three sources—from the hills about Hebron, from Etham, and from the three pools of Solomon. Its total length was over forty miles."

Alfred Edersheim, *The Temple, Its Ministry and Services as They Were at the Time of Jesus Christ*. (London: James Clarke & Co., 1959), 55–56.

[2] **The molten sea**:

"Near the altar, on the southeast corner of the temple, stood an immense cast metal water-basin or laver called the "brazen sea" or the "molten sea." This reservoir, 45 feet in circumference (14 m), 7.5 feet high (2.3 m), 3 inches thick (7.6 cm), and 15 feet (4.6 m) from brim to brim, held 11,000 gallons (41,640 liters) of water. It rested on the backs of 12 bronze oxen three facing north, three facing west, three facing south and three facing east (2 Chronicles 4:2–3). Two rows of 300 gourds encircled the sea below the rim. The purpose of the laver was to provide a source of water for the ritual cleansing of the priests who would officiate and the cleansing of vessels used in the sacrificial system."

The Rose Guide to the Temple (Rose Publishing, 2012), 72.

"The priests were to wash their hands and feet in it to prepare for presenting burnt offerings on the altar or entering the temple. This was done by allowing water from faucets set into the laver to run over their hands and feet while holding their feet with their hands. Thus, this vessel was the first of the service vessels to be used each morning by the priests. The Mishnah speaks about a wooden device designed by a priest named Ben Katin which seems to have been a waterwheel mechanism that drew water for filling the laver from a large underground cistern. According to these sources, the sound of this device in operation could be heard as far as the city of Jericho (located some 20 miles away; 32 km). The use of this waterwheel in the early morning officially began the priestly service in the Temple Court."

The Rose Guide to the Temple (Rose Publishing, 2012), 211.

[3] **Altar hearth symbolizes the "mountain of El"**: Bible scholar Michael Heiser talks of this phrase altar hearth (*ha ari-el*)in Ezekiel 43 as meaning "mountain of El" and "bosom of the earth," in The Naked Bible Podcast #157 Ezekiel 40-48 Part 2 https://www.nakedbiblepodcast.com/naked-bible-157-ezekiel-40-48-part-2/

"The identification of the outer court as the visible earth and sea is suggested further by the Old Testament description, where the large molten wash-basin and altar in the temple courtyard are called respectively the 'sea' (1 Kgs. 7:23–26) and the 'bosom of the earth' (Ezek. 43:14; the altar also likely was identified with the 'mountain of God' in Ezek. 43:16). The altar was also to be an 'altar of earth' (in the early stages of Israel's history) or an 'altar of [uncut] stone' (Exod. 20:24–25), thus identifying it even more with the natural earth. Thus both the 'sea' and 'altar' appear to be cosmic symbols that may have been associated in the mind of the Israelite respectively with the seas and the earth."

G. K. Beale, *The Temple and the Church's Mission: A Biblical Theology of the Dwelling Place of God*, ed. D. A. Carson, vol. 17, New Studies in Biblical Theology (Downers Grove, IL; England: InterVarsity Press; Apollos, 2004), 33.

Molten sea symbolizes the primordial sea:

"One of the features of ANE temples was their utilization of artistic and architectural elements relating to the idea of the temple as the cosmic center of the world. The great deep, or cosmic waters, is one aspect of the array of cosmic attributes of such a holy spot. The temple of Marduk at Babylon, for example, had an artificial sea (ta-am-tu) in its precincts; and some Babylonian temples had an apsû- sea, a large basin. Such features symbolize the idea of the ordering of the universe by the conquest of chaos; or they represent the presence of the "waters of life" at the holy center. Ancient Israel shared in this notion of watery chaos being subdued by

Yahweh and of the temple being built on the cosmic waters. The great "molten sea" near the temple's entrance would have signified Yahweh's power and presence."

Carol Meyers, "Sea, Molten," ed. David Noel Freedman, *The Anchor Yale Bible Dictionary* (New York: Doubleday, 1992), 1062.

[4] **Jerusalem and temple the center of the earth**:

> Ezekiel 38:12 …the people [Jews] who were gathered from the nations, who have acquired livestock and goods, who dwell at the center of the earth.

"Jerusalem was thought to be the "navel" or center of the earth (Gen R 59:5), "destined to become the metropolis of all countries" (Exod R 23:10), and the Psalms (e.g. 48:2–3, 50:2); Lamentations (e.g. 1:1, 2:15) and Prophets (e.g. Zech 14:16–21, Isa 2:2–4, Micah 4:1–3) speak in the loftiest terms of Jerusalem's place among the nations. Rev 17:18 is probably a similar hyperbole; cf. 4QLam which describes her as "princess of all nations." J. Massyngberde Ford, *Revelation: Introduction, Translation, and Commentary, vol. 38, Anchor Yale Bible* (New Haven; London: Yale University Press, 2008), 285.

"These two passages from the Talmudic tractate Yoma present Mount Zion as the point from which creation proceeded, in other words, the one place of a genuinely primordial character in our world. The following midrash shows that the notion of increasing orders of centrality can be found even on the mountain itself:

> Just as the navel is positioned in the center of a man, thus is the Land of Israel positioned in the center of the world, as the Bible says, "dwelling at the very navel of the earth" (Ezek. 38:12), and from it the foundation of the world proceeds.... And the Temple is in the center of Jerusalem, and the Great Hall is in the center of the Temple, and the Ark is in the center of the Great Hall, and the Foundation Stone is in front of the Ark, and beginning with it the world was put on its foundation.

In short, the Temple is a visible, tangible token of the act of creation, the point of origin of the world, the "focus" of the universe." Jon D. Levenson, "The Temple and the World," *The Journal of Religion*, Vol. 64, No. 3 (Jul., 1984), 283.

The temple as cosmic mountain: "The Temple of Yahweh in Israel was naturally associated with a cosmic mountain dwelling like Sinai because it was situated in Jerusalem on Mount Zion, the new Sinai. Psalm 48 makes this quite clear:

1 Great is the LORD and greatly to be praised
in the city of our God!
His holy mountain, 2 beautiful in elevation,
is the joy of all the earth,
Mount Zion, in the far north [Lit.: heights of the north],
the city of the great King (Psa 48:1–2 ESV).

"Zechariah 8:3 (ESV) echoes the same notion: "Thus says the LORD: I have returned to Zion and will dwell [literally, "will tabernacle"; shakan] in the midst of Jerusalem, and Jerusalem shall be called the faithful city, and the mountain of the LORD of hosts, the holy mountain."

"As anyone who has been to Jerusalem knows, Mount Zion isn't much of a mountain. It certainly isn't located in the geographical north—it's actually in the southern part of the country. So what's meant by "the heights of the north"?

"This description would be a familiar one to Israel's pagan neighbors, particularly at Ugarit. It's actually taken out of their literature. The "heights of the north" (Ugaritic: "the heights of tsaphon") is the place where Baal lived and, supposedly, ran the cosmos at the behest of the high god El and the divine council. The psalmist is stealing glory from Baal, restoring it to the One to whom it rightfully belongs—Yahweh. It's a theological and literary slap in the face, another polemic.

"This explains why the description sounds odd in terms of Jerusalem's actual geography. This is why Isaiah and Micah used phrases like "the mountain of the house of Yahweh" (Isa 2:2; Mic 4:1). The description is designed to make a theological point, not a geographical one. Zion is the center of the cosmos, and Yahweh and his council are its king and administrators, not Baal." Michael S. Heiser, *The Unseen Realm: Recovering the Supernatural Worldview of the Bible*, First Edition (Bellingham, WA: Lexham Press, 2015), 226–227.

[5] **Genesis 1 as a ritual temple dedication**:

"If the cosmos is to be viewed as a temple, then it is possible that a cosmological text could adopt the metaphor of temple building and dedication. This course of analogy and logic results in the understanding that Genesis 1 is framed in terms of the creation of the cosmos as a temple in which Yahweh takes up his repose. A fresh look at the Gudea temple building and dedication text offers some intriguing comparisons that might commend seeing Genesis 1 in these terms.

"First, we encounter the common idea that the sanctuary is being constructed in order to provide a resting place, in Gudea's case for Ningirsu and his consort, Bau. Genesis 1 likewise finds its conclusion in Yahweh's taking up his rest. As developed earlier, "rest" does not imply relaxation, but more like achieving equilibrium and stability. He is making a place of rest for himself, a rest provided for by the completed cosmos. Inhabiting his resting place is the equivalent to being enthroned—it is connected to taking up his role as sovereign ruler of the cosmos. The temple simply provides a symbolic reality for this concept as demonstrated by its role in the Akitu enthronement festival in Babylon. Psalm 104:2–4 captures this as the elements of the cosmos serve as functionaries for Yahweh's rule. Further confirmation exists in the presence of the ark in the most sacred area of the temple representing the footstool of God's throne (Ps. 132:7–8).

"Second, we find that the dedication ceremonies sometimes last seven days. This element in Gudea can also be seen in various biblical accounts that have to do with sanctuary building and dedication.6

"In Genesis 1 we have the provision of rest for the deity occurring after a six-day period during which functions are established and functionaries installed through a procedure that has striking similarities to the decreeing of destinies, itself deeply embedded in temple dedications.

"The focus on decrees for functions and functionaries constitutes the third item of significance. The dedication ceremony in Gudea Cylinder B: vi–xii touches on many of the pertinent elements that we recognize from Genesis 1. The Sabbath element in Genesis not only helps us to recognize the temple-cosmos equation in Genesis, but also to realize the contextual significance of the functions (days 1–3) and functionaries (days 4–6) in the creation narrative. Just as Gudea's account established functions for the temple and then supplied functionaries that operate in it, the Genesis account set up functions (days 1–3) and functionaries (days 4–6) for the cosmic temple. Genesis 2:1 indicates this as it refers to the creation of heaven and earth (the cosmos with its functions) and all their hosts (the functionaries in the various realms of the cosmos). In a temple construction project, the structure would be built, and the furniture and trappings would be made in preparation for the moment when all was ready for the dedication of the temple. On this occasion, often a seven-day celebration, the functions of the temple would be declared, the furniture and hangings would be put in place, the priests would be installed, and the appropriate sacrifices would be made to initiate the temple's operation. Somewhere in the process, the image of the deity would be brought into the temple to take up his repose in his new residence. On the basis of all of this, Genesis 1 can be viewed as using the metaphor of temple dedication as it portrays God's creation (= making functional/operational) his cosmos (which is his temple, Isa. 66:1)."

John H. Walton, *Ancient Near Eastern Thought and the Old Testament: Introducing the Conceptual World of the Hebrew Bible* (Grand Rapids, MI: Baker Academic, 2006), 197–198.

"This connection is further substantiated by the fact that the rest takes place on the seventh day. Several examples of temple inaugurations from ancient Near Eastern literature, cited above, show that these rites took place in the course of seven days and that the deity entered the temple to take up his rest on the seventh day. Mark Smith, in his discussion of the motif of seven days in Genesis 1, concludes, with Hurowitz, that "creation in Genesis 1 uses the language of temple-building." Regardless of whether Genesis 1 is understood as reflecting a temple-building account (like the building of Baal's Temple in seven days) or a temple-inauguration account (like the temple inauguration in Gudea Cylinder B), the connection between Genesis 1 and temple imagery is confirmed.

Seven-day temple inaugurations are the norm in biblical temple-building accounts. In the account of the construction of Solomon's temple, a seven-day dedication, to which was added a seven-day feast/banquet (2

Chr 7:9; 1 Kgs 8:65), followed the completion of construction. Levenson observes the repeated use of the number seven in the account and concludes that the account is modeled on the seven days of creation.

"1 Kings 6:38b tells us that it took Solomon seven years to build his Temple. According to 1 Kings 8, he dedicated it during the Feast of Booths (Sukkot), which occurs in the seventh month (verse 2) and which, in the Deuteronomic tradition, is a festival of seven days' duration (Deut 16:13–15).... Can the significance of the number seven in this Temple dedication be coincidence? In light of the argument on other grounds that Temple building and creation were thought to be congeneric, this is improbable. It is more likely that the construction of the Temple is presented here as a parallel to the construction of the world in seven days.

"However, because the number seven occurs frequently in texts reflecting the ancient Near Eastern cognitive environment, it might be more likely that the association is the reverse—namely, that the Genesis 1 account is modeled after a temple-inauguration account."

John H. Walton, *Genesis 1 as Ancient Cosmology* (Winona Lake, IN: Eisenbrauns, 2011), 181–182.

[6] **Simon bar Gioras and the battles in Idumea**:

Flavius Josephus, *The Wars of the Jews* 2.22.2, §652-654.
"Simon, the son of Gioras, got a great number of those that were fond of innovations together, and betook himself to ravage the country; nor did he only harass the rich men's houses, but tormented their bodies, and appeared openly and beforehand to affect tyranny in his government. (653) And when an army was sent against him by Ananus, and the other rulers, he and his band retired to the robbers that were at Masada, and staid there, and plundered the country of Idumea with them, till both Ananus and his other adversaries were slain; (654) and until the rulers of that country were so afflicted with the multitude of those that were slain, and with the continual ravage of what they had, that they raised an army, and put garrisons into the villages, to secure them from those insults."

Flavius Josephus and William Whiston, *The Works of Josephus: Complete and Unabridged* (Peabody: Hendrickson, 1987), 638–639.

For the full story of Simon's plunder of Idumea, see Flavius Josephus, *The Wars of the Jews* 4.9.3-8 §503-544.

[7] **The language of seas of blood and carnage that fulfill these verses of Revelation can be found in Josephus**:

Flavius Josephus, *The Wars of the Jews* 4.7.6, §437.
"Now this destruction that fell upon the Jews, as it was not inferior to any of the rest in itself, so did it still appear greater than it really was; and this, because not only the whole of the country through which they had fled was filled with slaughter, and Jordan could not be passed over, by reason of the dead bodies that were in it, but because the lake Asphaltitis was also full of dead bodies, that were carried down into it by the river."

Flavius Josephus and William Whiston, *The Works of Josephus: Complete and Unabridged* (Peabody: Hendrickson, 1987), 685.

Flavius Josephus, *The Wars of the Jews* 3.10.9, §530-531.
"One might then see the lake all bloody, and full of dead bodies, for not one of them escaped. (530) And a terrible stink, and a very sad sight there was on the following days over that country; for as for the shores, they were full of shipwrecks, and of dead bodies all swelled; and as the dead bodies were inflamed by the sun, and putrefied, they corrupted the air, insomuch that the misery was not only the object of commiseration to the Jews, but to those that hated them, and had been the authors of that misery. (531) This was the upshot of the sea fight. The number of the slain, including those that were killed in the city before, was six thousand and five hundred."

Flavius Josephus and William Whiston, *The Works of Josephus: Complete and Unabridged* (Peabody: Hendrickson, 1987), 663.

CHAPTER 28

[1] **Moshe quotes from**: Revelation 8:10-11.

[2] **The Trial by Ordeal or Law of Jealousy**: Is described in Numbers 5:11-31.

"Since Revelation relates the divorce of God's unfaithful Old Testament wife (Israel; cf. Exc. Rev 5), these bitter waters could also allude to "the law of jealousy" (Nu 5:29), which is used for determining whether a wife had committed adultery. In Numbers 5:11–31 we have the procedures for a priest's ritual examination of a woman charged with adultery. In that trial he gives the accused "holy water in an earthenware vessel" with "some of the dust that is on the floor of the tabernacle" (Nu 5:17). This is called "the water of bitterness that brings a curse" (Nu 5:18, 23, 24). In several Old Testament passages we have references to bitterness in contexts alluding to Israel's judgment due to her adultery against her husband the Lord God, for example, Jeremiah 4:18 (cp. 4:17, 30–31; cf. Jer 2:2; 3:1–2, 8–10, 20) and Lamentations 1:4 (cp. La 1:9, 19). Perhaps Jeremiah 9:15 alludes to Numbers 5 as Israel forsakes her law and breaks covenant with God (Jer 9:13)."

Kenneth L. Gentry, Jr., *The Divorce of Israel: A Redemptive-Historical Interpretation of Revelation Vol. 1* (Dallas, GA: Tolle Lege Press, 2016), 718.

[3] **Elihu quotes from**: Revelation 16:4-6.

Drinking the blood:

"We should remember that this is hyperbolic drama. We should not expect that anyone is literally going to drink blood. Josephus speaks of Israel's miseries during the Jewish War in terms similar to John's imagery: Of the Idumeans Josephus writes that they "their thirst was chiefly after the blood of valiant men, and men of good families" (J.W. 4:6:1 §357). Regarding the wicked rebels leading the revolt "they had fed themselves out of the public miseries, and drank the blood of the city" (J.W. 5:8:2 §344). And "they drank the blood of the populace to one another, and divided the dead bodies of the poor creatures between them" (J.W. 5:10:4 §440)."

Kenneth L. Gentry, Jr., *The Divorce of Israel: A Redemptive-Historical Interpretation of Revelation Vol. 1* (Dallas, GA: Tolle Lege Press, 2016), 340-341.

[4] **Elihu quotes from Jesus**: Matthew 23:34-36.

[5] **Babylon in Revelation 17 and 18 is Jerusalem, not Rome**: "Several textual indicators suggest that John is focusing on Jerusalem rather than Rome (cp. Provan 1996: 94). (1) In this very Judaic book the language of religious defilement in 18:2 would suggest a Jewish city is in view. (2) Babylon's double punishment reflects the Old Testament prophetic witness against Jerusalem (18:6; see below). (3) The "great city" (18:10, 16, 18, 19, 21; cp. 18:2) was previously introduced as the place of the crucifixion (11:8). (4) In 18:24 the killing of the prophets by Babylon reflects a familiar sin of Jerusalem (Neh 9:26; cp. 1Ki 19:10, 14; 21:13; 2Ch 24:19, 21; 36:14-16; Isa 1:15; Jer 2:30; 25:4; 26:20-23). (5) The bowl judgments in Revelation 16 are being expanded upon in Revelation 17-18. In the latter bowls "Babylon the great" was distinguished from the cities of the nations (16:19)."Kenneth L. Gentry, Jr., *The Divorce of Israel: A Redemptive-Historical Interpretation of Revelation Vol. 2* (Dallas, GA: Tolle Lege Press, 2016), 506-507.

"It might be objected that the great city in Revelation appears too important among the nations to be identified with Jerusalem rather than Rome. However, Jerusalem was thought to be the "navel" or center of the earth (Gen R 59:5), "destined to become the metropolis of all countries" (Exod R 23:10), and the Psalms (e.g. 48:2–3, 50:2), Lamentations (e.g. 1:1, 2:15) and Prophets (e.g. Zech 14:16–21, Isa 2:2–4, Micah 4:1–3) speak in the loftiest terms of Jerusalem's place among the nations. Rev 17:18 is probably a similar hyperbole; cf. 4QLam which describes her as "princess of all nations." J. Massyngberde Ford, *Revelation: Introduction, Translation, and Commentary, vol. 38, Anchor Yale Bible* (New Haven; London: Yale University Press, 2008), 285.

[6] **Elihu quotes from**: Revelation 18:10, 20, 24, 21.

[7] **Moshe quotes**: Revelation 18:4–5.

CHAPTER 30

[1] **Jacob quotes from**: James 1:27 and Psalms 82:3-4.

[2] Romans 5:18–20.

[3] John 5:24–25.

[4] John 5:28–29.

[5] 1 Corinthians 15:51–55.

CHAPTER 31

[1] **Imprecatory Psalms and the forgiveness of Christ**:

"Among the Israelites the imprecatory psalms attest that the pardoning of enemies was not esteemed as a virtue. This is not to say that the Hebrews were being vindictive or sadistic when they prayed that the young children of the enemy might be dashed against the rocks (Ps. 137:9). They were supplicating for the extinction of God's enemies, represented by a generation that might well live to rise against Him in the future, a contingency that would not occur were they to be exterminated forthwith. The Torah discouraged the Hebrews from seeking either the peace or prosperity of their enemies (Dt. 23:6), lest these conditions should lead the Hebrews to imagine that following a pagan way of life would make them equally prosperous also. The law thus made it legitimate for a follower of the covenant ethic to hate rather than to forgive his enemy.

III. The Teaching of Christ

"Jesus summed up this attitude broadly by contrasting the love of one's friends with the hatred of one's enemies (Mt. 5:43). In expounding the ethic of the New Covenant, Christ taught that forgiveness is a duty. No limit can be set to the extent of forgiveness (Lk. 17:4), and it must be granted without reserve. Jesus will not admit that there is any wrong so gross nor so often repeated that it is beyond forgiveness. To Him, having an unforgiving spirit is one of the most heinous of sins. Jesus sought to displace the pagan spirit of implacability by a generous, forgiving spirit. It is so far the essence of His teaching that in popular language "a Christian spirit" is not inappropriately understood to be synonymous with a forgiving disposition. His answer to Peter that one should forgive not merely seven times in a day but seventy times seven (Mt. 18:21f) not only shows that He thought of no limit to one's forgiveness, but shows also that the principle could not be reduced to a definite formula.

IV. Conditions of Forgiveness

"Jesus recognized that there are conditions to be fulfilled before forgiveness can be granted. Forgiveness is part of a mutual relationship; the other part is the repentance of the offender. God does not forgive without repentance, nor is it required of mankind. The effect of forgiveness is to restore to its former state the relationship that was broken by sin. Such a restoration requires the cooperation of both parties. There must be both a granting and an acceptance of the forgiveness. Sincere, deep-felt sorrow for the wrong, which works repentance (2 Cor. 7:10), is the condition of mind that insures the acceptance of the forgiveness. Hence Jesus commands forgiveness when the offender turns again, saying, "I repent" (Lk. 17:3f.). It was this state of mind that led the father joyfully to welcome the Prodigal before he even gave utterance to his newly formed purpose (15:21)."

R. K. Harrison, "Forgiveness," ed. Geoffrey W. Bromiley, The International Standard Bible Encyclopedia, Revised (Wm. B. Eerdmans, 1979–1988), 341.

CHAPTER 32

[1] **The Tower of Babel**:

The following is an excerpt from Brian Godawa, *When Giants Were Upon the Earth: The Watchers, the Nephilim, and the Biblical Cosmic War of the Seed* (Los Angeles, CA: Embedded Pictures Publishing, 2014), 191-196.

The Tower of Babel incident is also an event that has a long history of as many interpretive possibilities as there are scholars. The standard ancient interpretation was that Babel and its tower were simply the city of Babylon in mid-Mesopotamia that had been started, then stopped by the confusion of tongues, only to be reborn a thousand years later under Hammurabi's predecessors.

Contrarily, Anne Habermehl has argued that it was in the far northeastern part of Syria; David Rohl argued that Babel was actually the oldest known city of Eridu in the southernmost region of Sumeria on the gulf, and its tower was the famous ziggurat called Nunki.

Again, with so many different interpretations possible, spanning thousands of miles of geography, no one really knows. But I went with the traditional interpretation on this one because it was still a sensible option. Unfortunately, because the water table is so high in the modern region of the ruins of Babylon, we will never be able to excavate any layers of sediment below to discover its more ancient past.

Babel Inheritance

Another key element of the storyline of Chronicles of the Nephilim is the allotment of nations to the sons of God as punishment for humanity's rebellion. While I wrote a bit about this in the appendices of Noah Primeval, Abraham Allegiant is where this fascinating Biblical theological legal concept takes place at the Tower of Babel incident.

A brief look at the original full text of the Tower of Babel pericope in the Bible will help set the stage for a closer look at the theological ramifications of what it was all about.

> Genesis 11:1-9
> 1 Now the whole earth had one language and the same words. 2 And as people migrated from the east, they found a plain in the land of Shinar and settled there. 3 And they said to one another, "Come, let us make bricks, and burn them thoroughly." And they had brick for stone, and bitumen for mortar. 4 Then they said, "Come, let us build ourselves a city and a tower with its top in the heavens, and let us make a name for ourselves, lest we be dispersed over the face of the whole earth." 5 And the LORD came down to see the city and the tower, which the children of man had built. 6 And the LORD said, "Behold, they are one people, and they have all one language, and this is only the beginning of what they will do. And nothing that they propose to do will now be impossible for them. 7 Come, let us go down and there confuse their language, so that they may not understand one another's speech." 8 So the LORD dispersed them from there over the face of all the earth, and they left off building the city. 9 Therefore its name was called Babel, because there the LORD confused the language of all the earth. And from there the LORD dispersed them over the face of all the earth.

So we see that within a short time after the Flood, mankind had proven to be corrupt once again in seeking to unite in a headlong pursuit of self-deification. They decidedly used kiln-burned brick with bitumen for mortar most likely because of their memory of the Flood wiping away their mud brick buildings and temples. This waterproofing technique was the first expression of their devious attempt to circumvent God's future judgment.

Then they seek to build a city and a tower "with its top in the heavens." The Hebrew word for tower no doubt referred to the ziggurat temple-tower at the heart of every Mesopotamian city. To discover the idolatrous meaning of this reference, John Walton explains that the function of the ziggurats came from the names given to them:

For instance, the name of the ziggurat at Babylon, Etemenanki, means "temple of the foundation of heaven and earth." One at Larsa means "temple that links heaven and earth." Most significant is the name of the ziggurat at Sippar, "temple of the stairway to pure heaven." The word translated "stairway" in this last example is used in the mythology as the means by which the messenger of the gods moved between heaven, earth, and the netherworld.

So the temple-tower of Babylon was a religious incarnation of their attempt to create a forbidden link between heaven and earth by building their own stairway to heaven for the gods, a violation of God's monarchic authority.

Then they seek to "make a name for themselves," which is a common Biblical and ancient Near Eastern idiom for greatness. By uniting together, their pride was so great that there would be no limit to their hubris. This blasphemous self-deification would be a real threat because, remember, mankind was God's image, his representative ruler over creation. So, if man would unite in this kind of rebellion, imagine the evil that would result, an evil that might rival what happened before the Flood.

So the confusion of tongues and dispersion of mankind breaks apart the tyrannical potential of this global one world government.

We are told twice that God "dispersed them over the face of the earth" in order to stop the megalomaniacal and totalitarian potential of mankind unified in rebellion against God.

The seventy nations described in Genesis 10 are the resultant new boundaries allotted to mankind that came from this Dispersion."

[2] **Make a name for themselves**:

This phrase (a name) used of the builders of the tower of Babel, was the same phrase in Hebrew used of the Nephilim:

> Genesis 6:4
> [4] <u>The Nephilim</u> were on the earth in those days, and also afterward, when the sons of God came in to the daughters of man and they bore children to them. <u>These were</u> the mighty men who were of old, the <u>men of the name</u> (*ha shem*).

> Genesis 11:4
> [4] Then they said, "Come, let us build ourselves a city and a tower with its top in the heavens, and <u>let us make a name (*shem*) for ourselves</u>, lest we be dispersed over the face of the whole earth."

[3] **"God gave them up"**:

This passage interweaves Romans 1:21-32 with Deuteronomy 32:8-11.

The allotment of the nations to the Sons of God:

The following is an excerpt from Brian Godawa, *When Giants Were Upon the Earth: The Watchers, the Nephilim, and the Biblical Cosmic War of the Seed* (Los Angeles, CA: Embedded Pictures Publishing, 2014), 47-50.

> Deut. 32:8-9
> When the Most High gave to the nations their inheritance, when he divided mankind, he fixed the borders of the peoples according to the number of the sons of God. But the LORD's portion is his people, Jacob his allotted heritage.

The reference to the creation of nations through the division of mankind and fixing of the borders of nations is clearly a reference to the event of the Tower of Babel in Genesis 11 and the dispersion of the peoples into the 70 nations listed in Genesis 10.

But then there is a strange reference to those nations being "fixed" according to the number of the sons of God. We'll explain in a moment that those sons of God are from the assembly of the divine council of God. But after that the text says that God saved Jacob (God's own people) for his "allotment." Even though Jacob was not born until long after the Babel incident, this is an anachronistic way of referring to what would become God's people, because right after Babel, we read about God's calling of Abraham who was the grandfather of Jacob (Isa. 41:8; Rom. 11:26). So God allots nations and their geographic territory to these sons of God to rule over as their inheritance, but he allots the people of Jacob to himself, along with their geographical territory of Canaan (Gen. 17:8).

The idea of Yahweh "allotting" geographical territories to these sons of God who really existed and were worshipped as gods (idols) shows up again in several places in Deuteronomy:

Deut. 4:19-20
And beware lest you raise your eyes to heaven, and when you see the sun and the moon and the stars, all the host of heaven, you be drawn away and bow down to them and serve them, things that the LORD your God has allotted to all the peoples under the whole heaven.

Deut. 29:26
They went and served other gods and worshiped them, gods whom they have not known and whom He had not allotted to them.

"Host of heaven" was a term that referred to astronomical bodies that were also considered to be gods or members of the divine council. The Encyclopedia Judaica notes that, "in many cultures the sky, the sun, the moon, and the known planets were conceived as personal gods. These gods were responsible for all or some aspects of existence. Prayers were addressed to them, offerings were made to them, and their opinions on important matters were sought through divination."

But it was not merely the pagans who made this connection of heavenly physical bodies with heavenly spiritual powers. The Old Testament itself equates the sun, moon, and stars with the angelic "sons of God" who surround God's throne, calling them both the "host of heaven" (Deut. 4:19; 32:8-9). Jewish commentator Jeffrey Tigay writes, "[These passages] seem to reflect a Biblical view that... as punishment for man's repeated spurning of His authority in primordial times (Gen. 3-11), God deprived mankind at large of true knowledge of Himself and ordained that it should worship idols and subordinate celestial beings."

There is more than just a symbolic connection between the physical heavens and the spiritual heavens in the Bible. In some passages, the stars of heaven are linked interchangeably with angelic heavenly beings, also referred to as "holy ones" or "sons of God" (Psa. 89:5-7; Job 1:6).

Daniel 10:10-21 speaks of these divine "host of heaven" allotted with authority over pagan nations as spiritual "princes" or rulers battling with the archangels Gabriel and Michael.

Daniel 10:13, 20
13 The prince of the kingdom of Persia withstood me twenty-one days, but Michael, one of the chief princes, came to help me... 20 "But now I will return to fight against the prince of Persia; and when I go out, behold, the prince of Greece will come.

Some Second Temple non-canonical Jewish texts illustrate an ancient tradition of understanding this interpretation of the gods of the nations as real spirit beings that rule over those nations:

Jubilees 15:31-32
(There are) many nations and many people, and they all belong to him, but over all of them he caused spirits to rule so that they might lead them astray from following him. But over Israel he did not cause any angel or spirit to rule because he alone is their ruler and he will protect them.

Targum Jonathan, Deuteronomy 32, Section LIII
When the Most High made allotment of the world unto the
nations which proceeded from the sons of Noach [Noah],
in the separation of the writings and languages of the
children of men at the time of the division, He cast the lot among the seventy angels, the princes
of the nations with whom is the revelation to oversee the city.

In conclusion, the entire narrative of Deuteronomy 32 tells the story of God dispersing the nations at Babel and allotting the nations to be ruled by "gods" who were demonic fallen divine beings called sons of God. God then allots the people of Israel for himself, through Abraham, and their territory of Canaan. But God's people fall away from him and worship these other gods and are judged for their apostasy

[4] **Marduk's location**:

"First, the Bible refers to the notion that the images of the gods represented their empowered presence. So the capture of the image indicated the capture of that god, and the destruction of its image as the disempowering of the god.

Isaiah 30:22 Then you will defile your carved idols overlaid with silver and your gold-plated metal images. You will scatter them as unclean things. You will say to them, "Be gone!"

"Defile your idols … and your images … throw them away (30:22). Destruction or removal of a cultic statue could make the attendant god depart or lose power. Esarhaddon claims in one of his campaigns that "gods and goddesses dwelling within it [the captured town] fled to heaven above like birds," while Ashurbanipal, destroying temples and statues of Susa, wrote that "their gods, their goddesses I reckoned among the phantoms." Many inscriptions record destruction or capture of the enemy's gods."

John H Walton, *Zondervan Illustrated Bible Backgrounds Commentary (Old Testament): Isaiah, Jeremiah, Lamentations, Ezekiel, Daniel, vol. 4* (Grand Rapids, MI: Zondervan, 2009), 110–111.

"Marduk the protector was so important to Babylon's sense of security and personal identity that when the city revolted against Persian rule c. 485 BCE, the Persian king Xerxes had the statue destroyed when he sacked the city. After Alexander the Great defeated the Persians in 331 BCE, he made Babylon his capital and initiated efforts to restore the city to its former glory but died before this could be accomplished. By the time the Parthians ruled the region in 141 BCE, Babylon was a deserted ruin and Marduk had been forgotten."
Joshua Mark, Ancient History Encyclopedia online http://www.ancient.eu/Marduk/

[5] **Esagila and the Abyss**:

"The Ésagila, ("temple whose top is lofty") was a temple dedicated to Marduk, the protector god of Babylon. It lay south of the ziggurat Etemenanki. In this temple was the cult image inhabited by Marduk, surrounded by cult images of the cities that had fallen under the hegemony of the Babylonian Empire from the 18th century BC; there was also a little lake which was named Abzu by the Babylonian priests. This Abzu was a representation of Marduk's father, Enki, who was god of the waters and lived in the Abzu that was the source of all the fresh waters. The Esagila complex, completed in its final form by Nebuchadnezzar II (604–562 BC) encasing earlier cores, was the center of Babylon. It comprised a large court (ca. 40×70 meters), containing a smaller court (ca. 25×40 meters), and finally the central shrine, consisting of an anteroom and the inner sanctum which contained the statues of Marduk and his consort Sarpanit."

"According to Herodotus, Xerxes had a statue removed from the Esagila when he flooded Babylon in 482 BC, desecrated the Esagila and sacked the city. Alexander the Great ordered restorations, and the temple continued to be maintained throughout the 2nd century BC, as one of the last strongholds of Babylonian culture, such as literacy in the cuneiform script, but as Babylon was gradually abandoned under the Parthian Empire, the temple fell into decay in the 1st century BC."

"Esagila," Wikipedia https://en.wikipedia.org/wiki/Esagila

[6] **Marduk's weapons**:

Enuma Elish Tablet IV:27-59:

When the gods his fathers saw what he had commanded,
Joyfully they hailed, "Marduk is king!"
They bestowed in full measure scepter, throne, and staff,
(30) They gave him unopposable weaponry that vanquishes enemies.
"Go, cut off the life of Tiamat,
Let the winds bear her blood away as glad tidings!"
The gods, his fathers, ordained the Lord's destiny,
On the path to success and authority did they set him marching.
(35) He made the bow, appointed it his weapon,
He mounted the arrow, set it on the string.
He took up the mace, held it in his right hand,
Bow and quiver he slung on his arm.
Thunderbolts he set before his face,
(40) With raging fire he covered his body.
Then he made a net to enclose Tiamat within,
He deployed the four winds that none of her might escape:

South Wind, North Wind, East Wind, West Wind,
Gift of his grandfather Anu; he fastened the net at his side.
(45) He made ill wind, whirlwind, cyclone,
Four–ways wind, seven–ways wind, destructive wind, irresistible wind:
He released the winds which he had made, the seven of them,
Mounting in readiness behind him to roil inside Tiamat.
Then the Lord raised the Deluge, his great weapon.
(50) He mounted the terrible chariot, the unopposable Storm Demon,
He hitched to it the four–steed team, he tied them at his side:
"Slaughterer," "Merciless," "Overwhelmer," "Soaring."
Their lips are curled back, their teeth bear venom,
They know not fatigue, they are trained to trample down.
(55) He stationed at his right gruesome battle and strife,
At his left the fray that overthrows all formations.
He was garbed in a ghastly armored garment,
On his head he was covered with terrifying auras.
The Lord made straight and pursued his way,

William W. Hallo and K. Lawson Younger, *The Context of Scripture* (Leiden; New York: Brill, 1997–), 397.

A different translation:

(45) He brought forth Imhullu "the Evil Wind," the Whirl-wind, the Hurricane,
The Fourfold Wind, the Sevenfold Wind, the Cyclone, the Matchless Wind;
Then he sent forth the winds he had brought forth, the seven of them.
To stir up the inside of Tiamat they rose up behind him
Then the lord raised up the flood-storm, his mighty weapon.
(50) He mounted the storm-chariot irresistible [and] terrifying.
He harnessed (and) yoked to it a team-of-four,
The Killer, the Relentless, the Trampler, the Swift.
(Their) lips were parted, their teeth bore poison.
They were tireless and skilled in destruction.
On his right he posted the Smiter, fearsome in battle,
On the left the Combat, which repels all the zealous.
For a cloak he was wrapped in an armor of terror;
With his fearsome halo his head was turbaned.
The lord went forth and followed his course,

James Bennett Pritchard, ed., *The Ancient Near Eastern Texts Relating to the Old Testament*, 3rd ed. with *Supplement* (Princeton: Princeton University Press, 1969), 66.

Enuma Elish **tablet III:31-34**:

She has set up the Viper, the Dragon, and the Sphinx,
The Great-Lion, the Mad-Dog, and the Scorpion-Man,
Mighty lion-demons, the Dragon-Fly, the Centaur—
Bearing weapons that spare not, fearless in battle.

James Bennett Pritchard, ed., *The Ancient Near Eastern Texts Relating to the Old Testament*, 3rd ed. with *Supplement* (Princeton: Princeton University Press, 1969), 64.

[7] **These names of Marduk are taken from:** the fifty names of Marduk in *Enuma Elis*, tablet VII v. 19-22.

James Bennett Pritchard, ed., *The Ancient Near Eastern Texts Relating to the Old Testament*, 3rd ed. with *Supplement* (Princeton: Princeton University Press, 1969), 70–71.

CHAPTER 33

[1] **The facts about Gischala's and Eleazar's subterfuge of Ananus in this chapter is from**: Flavius Josephus, *The Wars of the Jews* 4.3.14, §216-223.

[2] **The high priest Phannias**:

Flavius Josephus, *The Wars of the Jews* 4.3.7-8, §153-157.
"In order to try what surprise the people would be under, and how far their own power extended, they undertook to dispose of the high priesthood by casting lots for it, whereas, as we have said already, it was to descend by succession in a family. (154) The pretense they made for this strange attempt was an ancient practice, while they said that of old it was determined by lot, but in truth, it was no better than a dissolution of an undeniable law, and a cunning contrivance to seize upon the government, derived from those that presumed to appoint governors as they themselves pleased.

8. (155) Hereupon they sent for one of the pontifical tribes, which is called Eniachim, and cast lots which of it should be the high priest. By fortune, the lot so fell as to demonstrate their iniquity after the plainest manner, for it fell upon one whose name was Phannias, the son of Samuel, of the village Aphtha. He was a man not only unworthy of the high priesthood, but that did not well know what the high priesthood was; such a mere rustic was he! (156) Yet did they hale this man, without his own consent, out of the country, as if they were acting a play upon the stage, and adorned him with a counterfeit face; they also put upon him the sacred garments, and upon every occasion instructed him what he was to do. (157) This horrid piece of wickedness was sport and pastime with them, but occasioned the other priests, who at a distance saw their law made a jest of, to shed tears, and sorely lament the dissolution of such a sacred dignity."

Flavius Josephus and William Whiston, *The Works of Josephus: Complete and Unabridged* (Peabody: Hendrickson, 1987), 671.

[3] **Gischala betrayed Ananus by secretly siding with Eleazar and telling him that Ananus sent for Vespasian**: Flavius Josephus, *The Wars of the Jews* 4.3.14, §216-219; and 4.4.1 §224-227.

[4] **Gischala and others sent messages to the Idumeans and lied to that Ananus had sent for Vespasian. So the Idumeans came to render help against Ananus**: *The Wars of the Jews* 4.4.1-2, §228-235;

CHAPTER 34

[1] **The death of Ananus and the nobles of the city is described here**:

Josephus on Ananus the high priest: Consider Josephus' bias toward the pro-Roman faction of high priests. His praise becomes a reflection of his own corrupt spin, making him a part of what the New Testament considered the Harlot (corrupt priesthood) that rode the land beast of Jewish aristocracy. The high priest as office or individual was the False Prophet that the Harlot empowered.

Flavius Josephus, *The Wars of the Jews*, 4.5.2 §314-325
"2. (314) But the rage of the Idumeans was not satiated by these slaughters; but they now betook themselves to the city, and plundered every house, and slew everyone they met; (315) and for the other multitude, they esteemed it needless to go on with killing them, but they sought for the high priests, and the generality went with the greatest zeal against them; (316) and as soon as they caught them they slew them, and then standing upon their dead bodies, in way of jest, upbraided Ananus with his kindness to the people, and Jesus with his speech made to them from the wall. (317) Nay, they proceeded to that degree of impiety, as to cast away their dead bodies without burial, although the Jews used to take so much care of the burial of men, that they took down those that were condemned and crucified, and buried them before the going down of the sun. (318) I should not mistake if I said that the death of Ananus was the beginning of the destruction of the city, and that from this very day may be dated the overthrow of her wall, and the ruin of her affairs, whereon they saw their high priest, and the procurer of their preservation, slain in the midst of their city. (319) He was on other accounts also a venerable, and a very just man; and besides the grandeur of that nobility, and dignity, and honor, of which he was possessed, he had been a lover of a kind of parity, even with regard to the meanest of the people; (320) he was a prodigious lover of liberty, and an admirer of a democracy in government; and did ever prefer the public welfare before his own advantage, and preferred peace above all things; for he was thoroughly sensible that the Romans were not to be conquered. He also foresaw that of

necessity a war would follow, and that unless the Jews made up matters with them very dexterously, they would be destroyed: to say all in a word, if Ananus had survived they had certainly compounded matters; for he was a shrewd man in speaking and persuading the people, and had already gotten the mastery of those that opposed his designs, or were for the war. And the Jews had then put abundance of delays in the way of the Romans, if they had had such a general as he was. (322) Jesus was also joined with him; and although he was inferior to him upon the comparison, he was superior to the rest; (323) and I cannot but think that it was because God had doomed this city to destruction, as a polluted city, and was resolved to purge his sanctuary by fire, that he cut off these their great defenders and wellwishers, (324) while those that a little before had worn the sacred garments, and had presided over the public worship, and had been esteemed venerable by those that dwelt on the whole habitable earth when they came into our city, were cast out naked, and seen to be the food of dogs and wild beasts. (325) And I cannot but imagine that virtue itself groaned at these men's case, and lamented that she was here so terribly conquered by wickedness. And this at last was the end of Ananus and Jesus."

Flavius Josephus and William Whiston, The Works of Josephus: Complete and Unabridged (Peabody: Hendrickson, 1987), 679–680.

[2] **They fed Ananus to the dogs**: Flavius Josephus, The Wars of the Jews 4.5.2, §324.

[3] **A huge storm actually did occur during this takeover by the Idumeans**:

Flavius Josephus, *The Wars of the Jews* 4.4.5, §286-287
"For there broke out a prodigious storm in the night, with the utmost violence, and very strong winds, with the largest showers of rain, with continual lightnings, terrible thunderings, and amazing concussions and bellowings of the earth, that was in an earthquake. (287) These things were a manifest indication that some destruction was coming upon men, when the system of the world was put into this disorder; and anyone would guess that these wonders foreshowed some grand calamities that were coming."

Flavius Josephus and William Whiston, *The Works of Josephus: Complete and Unabridged* (Peabody: Hendrickson, 1987), 678.

[4] **Gischala's forces and Idumeans turned on Eleazar after they turned on Ananus**: Eleazar turned against Gischala because he considered him a tyrant. But he did barricade himself back in the inner temple.

Flavius Josephus, *The Wars of the Jews* 5.1.2, §5-8
"For Eleazar, the son of Simon, who made the first separation of the zealots from the people, and made them retire into the temple, appeared very angry at John's insolent attempts which he made every day upon the people; for this man never left off murdering: but the truth was, that he could not bear to submit to a tyrant who set up after him. (6) So he being desirous of gaining the entire power and dominion to himself, revolted from John, ... these seized upon the inner court of the temple, and laid their arms upon the holy gates, and over the holy fronts of that court."

Flavius Josephus and William Whiston, *The Works of Josephus: Complete and Unabridged* (Peabody: Hendrickson, 1987), 696.

CHAPTER 35

[1] **12,000 killed in the pillage and plunder of the Idumeans and Gischala**: Flavius Josephus, *The Wars of the Jews* 4.5.3, §333.

[2] **Cassandra quotes from**: Revelation 18:2.

[3] **Israel/Jerusalem is a 7x-demon-infested land**:

Matthew 12:43–45 "When the unclean spirit has gone out of a person, it passes through waterless places seeking rest, but finds none. 44 Then it says, 'I will return to my house from which I came.' And when it comes, it finds the house empty, swept, and put in order. 45 Then it goes and brings with it seven other spirits more evil than itself, and they enter and dwell there, and the last state of that person is worse than the first. So also will it be with this evil generation."

Revelation 18:2 And he called out with a mighty voice, "Fallen, fallen is Babylon the great [Jerusalem]! She has become a dwelling place for demons, a haunt for every unclean spirit, a haunt for every unclean bird, a haunt for every unclean and detestable beast.

Revelation 18:2 is a quotation of Isaiah 13 taunt about the historical city of Babylon that uses the metaphors of false gods (like satyrs and Lilith) as demons. So John, by quoting Isaiah in Revelation 18, he is saying that Jerusalem, the new Mystery Babylon is full of demons AND uncleanness, like the Babylon of old.

Isaiah 34:13-14 (LXX) 11 and for a long time birds and hedgehogs, and ibises and ravens shall dwell in it: and the measuring line of desolation shall be cast over it, and satyrs shall dwell in it...13 And thorns shall spring up in their cities, and in her strong holds: and they shall be habitations of monsters, and a court for ostriches. 14 And devils shall meet with satyrs, and they shall cry one to the other: there shall satyrs rest, having found for themselves a place of rest.

Isaiah 13:21-22 (LXX) But wild beasts shall rest there; and the houses shall be filled with howling; and monsters shall rest there, and devils shall dance there, 22 and satyrs shall dwell there.

"The madness of the seditious did also increase together with their famine, and both those miseries were every day inflamed more and more...

The Bible writers considered these pagan seirim deities to be demons and thus called them "goat demons." So prevalent and influential were these satyr gods that Yahweh would have trouble with Israel worshipping them as idols.

Leviticus 17:7 7 So they shall no more sacrifice their sacrifices to goat demons (seirim), after whom they whore. This shall be a statute forever for them throughout their generations.

2 Chronicles 11:15 15 [Jeroboam] appointed his own priests for the high places and for the goat idols (seirim) and for the calves that he had made.

Not only did Israel fall into worshipping the seirim in Canaan, they were even committing spiritual adultery with them while in the wilderness! It is no wonder Yahweh considered them demons, a declaration reiterated in Moses' own prophecy that after Israel would be brought into Canaan by the hand of God, she would betray Yahweh by turning aside to other gods, redefined as demons.

Deuteronomy 32:17 17 They sacrificed to demons that were no gods, to gods they had never known, to new gods that had come recently, whom your fathers had never dreaded.

For more explanation of this demonization of pagan deities see: Brian Godawa, *When Giants Were Upon the Earth: The Watchers, the Nephilim, and the Biblical Cosmic War of the Seed* (Los Angeles, CA: Embedded Pictures Publishing, 2014), 204-210.

Josephus describes the Jewish War in demonic terms as well: "It is therefore impossible to go distinctly over every instance of these men's iniquity. I shall therefore speak my mind here at once briefly:—That neither did any other city ever suffer such miseries, nor did any age ever breed a generation more fruitful in wickedness than this was, from the beginning of the world...

Flavius Josephus, *The Wars of the Jews*, 5.10.2, 5 §424; 442,7.8.1 §259–62; 4.3.3 §135; 4:9:8 §541; 5:11:1 §446-449; 4:9:10 §560–61
"And indeed that was a time most fertile in all manner of wicked practices, insomuch that no kind of evil deeds were then left undone; nor could any one so much as devise any bad thing that was new, (260) so deeply were they all infected, and strove with one another in their single capacity, and in their communities, who should run the greatest lengths in impiety towards God, and in unjust actions towards their neighbors, the men of power oppressing the multitude and the multitude earnestly laboring to destroy the men of power. (261) The one part were desirous of tyrannizing over others; and the rest of offering violence to others, and of plundering such as were richer than themselves. (262) They were the Sicarii who first began these transgressions, and first became barbarous towards those allied to them, and left no words of reproach unsaid, and no works of perdition untried, in order to destroy those whom their contrivances affected."

"the captains of these troops of robbers, being satiated with rapines in the country, go all together from all parts, and became a band of wickedness, and all together crept in Jerusalem...

"[Simon] caught all those that were come out of the city gates, either to gather herbs or sticks, who were unarmed and in years; he then tormented them and destroyed them, out of the immense rage he was in, and was almost ready to taste the very flesh of their dead bodies. (542) He also cut off the hands of a great many, and sent them into the city to astonish his enemies...

"He then sent a party of horsemen, and ordered they should lay ambushes for those that went out into the valleys to gather food. (447) Some of these were indeed fighting men, who were not contented with what they got by rapine...so they were first whipped, and then tormented with all sorts of tortures before they died, and were then crucified before the wall of the city...

"while their inclination to plunder was insatiable, as was their zeal in searching the houses of the rich; and for the murdering of the men, and abusing of the women, it was sport to them. They also devoured what spoils they had taken, together with their blood... and were guilty of such intolerable uncleanness, and they invented unlawful pleasures of that sort. And thus did they roll themselves up and down the city, as in a brothel house, and defiled it entirely with their impure actions."

CHAPTER 36

[1] **On Ba'al's two weapons**:

One as a hammer like mace and the other "Ginsberg (1935:328) identified ṣmdm with the two-pieced maces excavated at Ugarit. The weapon consists of two pieces, a head latched onto a handle, specifically in Ginsberg's words (1935:328) "a mace with a stone head drilled through to adjust the wooden shaft, to which it is lashed tightly with thongs; and hence the name from the root ṣmd, 'to bind.' Such mace heads are found frequently in excavations."...

"A famous stele from Ugarit, sometimes called the "Baal au foudre" stele and housed in the Louvre, depicts Baal wielding two weapons. The weapon in his right hand is sometimes characterized as a mace (Amiet 1980:201).204 In his left hand Baal holds "tree-lightning" (Vanel 1965:84; Williams-Forte 1983:28, 30). Other examples of second millennium iconography of the storm-god depict him with a weapon (Vanel 1965:esp. 108; Seeden 1980:esp. 102), which appears at times as "branch-like lightning" (Williams-Forte 1983:26)."...

Comparative evidence drawn from Mediterranean and Near Eastern myths comports with the meteorological character of ṣmdm (Thespis 164–65). Zeus pelts Typhon with thunderbolts at Mons Cassius, the Latin name for Mount Sapan (Apollodorus, The Library, 1.6.3; Frazer 1921:48–49). Zeus's thunderbolts made by Cyclopes, the son of the craftsman-god Hephaistos, have been compared with Baal's weapons fashioned by Kothar (Walcot 1969:115)...."

Mark S. Smith, *The Ugaritic Baal Cycle: Introduction with Text, Translation and Commentary of KTU 1.1-1.2, vol. 1* (Leiden; New York; Köln: E.J. Brill, 1994), 339–340.

The actual text of the Baal cycle where Kothar-wa-Hasis crafts the two weapons, Yagarrish/Yagrush ("Driver") and Ayyamarri/Ayamur ("Expeller") for Baal to defeat Yamm (Sea) and River (Nahar) is KTU 1.2.11-25:

Kothar fashions the weapons,
And he proclaims their names:
"Your name, yours, is Yagarrish:
Yagarrish, drive Yamm,
Drive Yamm from his throne,
[Na]har from the seat of his dominion.
"Your name, yours, is Ayyamarri:
Ayyamarri, expel Yamm,
Expel Yamm from his throne,
Nahar from the seat of his dominion.
Leap from Baal's hand,
Like a raptor from his fingers.

Strike the head of Prince Yamm,
Between the eyes of Judge River.
May Yamm sink and fall to the earth."
The weapon leaps from Baal's hand,
[Like] a raptor from his fingers,
It strikes the head of Prince [Yamm,]
Between the eyes of Judge River.

Mark S. Smith and Simon B. Parker, *Ugaritic Narrative Poetry, vol. 9, Writings from the Ancient World* (Atlanta, GA: Scholars Press, 1997), 103–104.

"The most important textual witnesses to the weapons of the storm god of Aleppo [Ba'al] are found in the Old Babylonian letters from the Mari archives From these letters we learn that the weapons that were housed in the temple of the storm god in Aleppo were brought to the Mariote city of Terqa during Zimri-Lim's reign. While the letters seem to allude to the conflict myth that we find in fuller form later on in the Baal-Cycle from Ugarit, the weapons in the letters appear to be real weapons used as cultic objects." Joanna Töyräänvuori, "Weapons of the Storm God in Ancient Near Eastern and Biblical Traditions," Studia Orientalia, volume 112 (Helsinki, Finnish Oriental Society, 2012), 154, 160.

"In the text of the Ugaritic Baal-Cycle, the weapons forged by the smith Kothar-wa-Ḥasis, and wielded by Baal in the battle against Yamm, were clubs called by the names ygrš and aymr and translated as 'driver' and 'chaser," respectively. A club (or a hammer, also a smiting weapon) could certainly have been one of the storm god's weapons, as the association seems to have had a cross-cultural mythological foundation. Many Syrian and Anatolian reliefs depict the weather god (Adad or Tarhunt) holding a lightning weapon in one hand and a hammer or a smiting weapon in the other hand."\

Joanna Töyräänvuori, "Weapons of the Storm God in Ancient Near Eastern and Biblical Traditions," *Studia Orientalia, vol. 112*, (Finnish Oriental Society, 2012) 166

[2] **Ares' weapons**:

> A Hymn to Ares [1] Ares, exceeding in strength, chariot-rider, golden-helmed, doughty in heart, shield-bearer, Saviour of cities, harnessed in bronze, strong of arm, unwearying, mighty with the spear, O defence of Olympus, father of warlike Victory, ally of Themis, [5] stern governor of the rebellious, leader of righteous men, scepterd King of manliness, who whirl your fiery sphere among the planets in their sevenfold courses through the aether wherein your blazing steeds ever bear you above the third firmament of heaven; hear me, helper of men, giver of dauntless youth!"

Anonymous. *The Homeric Hymns and Homerica with an English Translation by Hugh G. Evelyn-White. Homeric Hymns.* Cambridge, MA.,Harvard University Press; London, William Heinemann Ltd. 1914. The Annenberg CPB/Project provided support for entering this text.

CHAPTER 37

[1] **Johanan Ben-Zakkai's escape from Jerusalem**:

"This most important expounder of Jewish law in the A.D. 60s is supposed to have spent forty years in business, forty in study and forty in teaching (Sanh. 41a), a 120-year life span that too closely mirrors that of Moses for full credibility. In 68, during the first Jewish War with Rome, he outwitted the extremists and made his way to Vespasian's camp, where he successfully asked the Roman general to spare Jamnia and its sages. There he founded the famous Jewish academy, served as its first president and worked for the continuation of Judaism before his death in the 80s."

Paul L. Maier, "Chronology," ed. Ralph P. Martin and Peter H. Davids, *Dictionary of the Later New Testament and Its Developments* (Downers Grove, IL: InterVarsity Press, 1997), 186.

"the original story of Yohanan's escape "runs from his being carried out of Jerusalem in a coffin to his meeting with Vespasian where he predicts that Vespasian will be emperor and Vespasian grants him a school in Jamnia"… Although we cannot know what actually happened or whether Yohanan and Vespasian ever actually met, Saldarini states that "a reasonable hypothesis is that Vespasian had ordered escaping Jews to be quartered in Jamnia and that once there Johanan did the natural thing and began teaching. Only gradually did his school become authoritative and central for Judaism. The story of the meeting with Vespasian explains that gradual development by one, critical meeting"

Gary G. Porton, "Yohanan Ben Zakkai," ed. David Noel Freedman, *The Anchor Yale Bible Dictionary* (New York: Doubleday, 1992), 1025.

[2] **Rabbi Yohanan ben Zakkai's blessing to Vespasian**:

This actually happened a little later in the historical account, when Nero died.

> b. Gittin 56a-b (Babylonian Talmud)
> "When he reached the Romans he said, Peace to you, O king, peace to you, O king. He [Vespasian] said: Your life is forfeit on two counts, one because I am not a king and you call me king, and again, if I am a king, why did you not come to me before now? He replied: As for your saying that you are not a king,in truth you are a king, since if you were not a king Jerusalem would not be delivered into your hand, as it is written, And Lebanon shall fall by a mighty one. 'Mighty one' [is an epithet] applied only to a king, as it is written, And their mighty one shall be of themselves etc.; and Lebanon refers to the Sanctuary, as it says, This goodly mountain and Lebanon. As for your question, why if you are a king, I did not come to you till now, the answer is that the biryoni among us did not let me. He said to him; If there is a jar of honey round which a serpent is wound, would they not break the jar to get rid of the serpent?"

http://www.come-and-hear.com/gittin/gittin_56.html

[3] **Rabbi Yohanan ben Zakkai at Yavneh**:

"Around the time that Titus was taking over the responsibilities of finishing the Jewish war from his father, the two of them allowed the equivalent of a new Sanhedrin to be established in the city of Yavneh (Jamnia). The result of this was a changing of both the times (of religious observation) and law by this new Flavian-approved Sanhedrin. Goldwurm writes the following on this:

"Before the destruction of Jerusalem, Rabban Yochanan ben Zakkai and his disciples were able to leave the doomed city and settle in Yavneh. Rabban Yochanan had asked of the Roman emperor [Vespasian]: "Give me Yavneh and its Sages," a request that was granted. Yavneh became the spiritual center of the people, and the secret of its survival. Rabban Yochanan ben Zakkai reorganized the Sanhedrin, which fixed the date of each new month and the time of each leap year. From Yavneh he sent instructions to the scattered Jewish communities in matters of law and observance, and Jews from all over the Diaspora turned to Yavneh for answers and advice."

Hersh Goldwurm, *History of the Jewish People: The Second Temple Era, ArtScroll History Series*, eds., Nosson Scherman and Meir Zlotowitz (Brooklyn: Mesorah Publications, 1982), 200-201. Quoted in McKenzie PhD, Duncan W.. *The Antichrist and the Second Coming: A Preterist Examination Volume I* (K-Locations 7501-7503). Xulon Press. K-Edition.

"Yohanan ben Zakkai is a transitional figure who helped oversee the birth a new epoch of Jewish history. He is understood in light of the Jewish revolt against the Romans in AD 66, the subsequent destruction of Jerusalem and its temple in AD 70, and the emergence of rabbinic Judaism at Yavneh in the wake of this catastrophe. Most of his historical and religious significance relates to his role in helping reconfigure Jewish practice and religious expectation after the loss of the sacred city and the temple (Herscher, "Zakkai at Yahveh," 36). Yohanan sought to console a distraught populace after a brutal defeat (Herscher, "Zakkai at Yahveh," 42) and to rethink what Judaism might look like without the sacrificial system (Neusner, "Historical Rabban Yohanan," 396).

"The traditional story concerning Yohanan's migration to Yavneh involves an elaborate escape from Jerusalem and an appearance before Vespasian (Alon, Judaism and the Classical World, 269). According to this account, Yohanan flees Jerusalem with the help of his disciples and asks Vespasian to grant him Yavneh as a gift (Alon, Judaism and the Classical World, 269, 295). Yohanan, recognizing the inevitable destruction of Jerusalem and the temple, wanted a place that would serve as a spiritual center for the study of Torah—a place "where shattered Judaism might be resuscitated" (Alon, Judaism and the Classical World, 269). In the legend, Vespasian grants this request, thereby assuring the continuation of Judaism even after the war.

"Yohanan is remembered as the founding rabbi of the school that eventually produced the Mishnah (Cohen, "Significance of Yavneh," 29; Fischer, et al., "Settlement in the Vicinity of Yavneh," 17). Neusner contends that Yohanan's revision of Temple rites for use in the synagogues, is an example of the ways he helped to rearticulate the Jewish faith for a religious community that had lost the holy city and temple (Neusner, "Historical Rabban Yohanan," 396)."

Robert Jones, "Yohanan Ben Zakkai," ed. John D. Barry et al., *The Lexham Bible Dictionary* (Bellingham, WA: Lexham Press, 2016).

[4] **Joseph's interpretation of Daniel's prophecy applied to Vespasian**: Flavius Josephus, *The Wars of the Jews* 6.5.4, §312-313

"(312) But now, what did most elevate them in undertaking this war, was an ambiguous oracle that was also found in their sacred writings, how, "about that time, one from their country should become governor of the habitable earth." (313) The Jews took this prediction to belong to themselves in particular and many of the wise men were thereby deceived in their determination. Now, this oracle certainly denoted the government of Vespasian, who was appointed emperor in Judea."

Flavius Josephus and William Whiston, *The Works of Josephus: Complete and Unabridged* (Peabody: Hendrickson, 1987), 743.

[5]**Titus changing the times and laws**:

> Daniel 7:25
> [25] He shall speak words against the Most High, and shall wear out the saints of the Most High, and shall think to change the appointed times and the law...

"Looking at the scriptures related to the Antichrist, one finds a common thread: the Antichrist's attack on the Temple. For example, the little eleventh horn changes the times and law (Dan. 7:25). The setting of the religious calendar as well as legal judgments was the responsibility of the Temple in the first century. The Flavians changed these when they set up the equivalent of a new Sanhedrin at Yavneh in AD 69. The prince to come destroys Jerusalem and the Temple (Dan. 9:26) and makes the Jewish nation desolate (Dan. 9:27). Titus accomplished this in AD 70. The king of the North invades the Holy Land (Dan. 11:41) and attacks God's holy mountain on which the Temple stood (Dan. 11:45), resulting in the shattering of the Jews' power (Dan. 12:7). This happened in AD 70 with Titus's destruction of the Jewish nation. The length of time that Titus spent warring against the Jews was three-and-a-half years ("a time, times and half a time," or "forty-two months"); this was the span of the Antichrist's persecution (Dan. 12:1,7; Dan. 7:25; Rev. 13:5)."

McKenzie PhD, Duncan W.. *The Antichrist and the Second Coming: A Preterist Examination Volume I* (Kindle Locations 589-597). Xulon Press. Kindle Edition.

"The following is a summary of the prophecies of Daniel 7 concerning the little eleventh horn of the fourth beast and how they were fulfilled in the spirit of Antichrist that worked through Titus:

1. The little eleventh horn would come on the scene when the tenth ruler of the fourth beast (Rome) was on the throne (Dan. 7:20; cf. Dan. 2:40-45). Titus's father, Vespasian, was the tenth Caesar of Rome (AD 69-79) and emperor when his son shattered the Jewish nation in AD 70. At this time, Titus (who would become the eleventh Caesar) was a general and not yet emperor, hence his designation as a little eleventh horn. We see a parallel between Jesus being the Son of God and Titus being the son of the then ruler of the world, Christ and Antichrist.

2. Three rulers (symbolized by three horns) would be removed before the little horn (Dan. 7:8). These were the three short-lived emperors (Galba, Otho, and Vitellius) that fell (v. 20) before Vespasian and Titus in AD 69, the year of four emperors. Notice that this left the little eleventh horn as an eighth ruler (11 – 3 = 8). This is

how the Antichrist is pictured in Revelation, as an eighth demonic king (who was about to come out of the abyss, Rev. 17:8-11; cf. Dan. 10:13). This points to the fact that the little horn was ultimately a demonic ruler.

3. The little eleventh horn would speak pompous and blasphemous words against God (Dan. 7:8, 11, 20, 25). Evidence of the fulfillment of this can be found in rabbinic writings that attribute incredible blasphemies to Titus when he destroyed the Temple (e.g., claiming that he had single-handedly killed the God of Israel).

4. The little horn would intend to change "times and laws" (Dan. 7:25). This was fulfilled in Titus and Vespasian's allowance (and possible direction) of a reorganized Sanhedrin set up in Yavneh. This resulted in changes to the Jewish calculation of the times of the annual religious observations as well as changes in Jewish law.

5. The little horn would be allowed to persecute Daniel's people for "a time and times and half a time" (Dan. 7:25), a time period of three-and-a-half years. This is confirmed in Revelation where this time of persecution by the Antichrist (the beast) is given as forty-two months (Rev. 13:5-7; cf. 11:2). This was fulfilled during Titus's three-and-a-half-year campaign against the Jews (March/April of AD 67 to August/September of AD 70). This timing is confirmed in Daniel 12:7, where the angel identifies the conclusion of "a time, times and half a time" as when the power of the holy people was "completely shattered." This happened at the AD 70 destruction of the Jewish nation by Titus."

McKenzie PhD, Duncan W.. *The Antichrist and the Second Coming: A Preterist Examination Volume I* (Kindle Locations 2486-2506). Xulon Press. Kindle Edition.

[6] **The revolt of Julius Vindex**:

The revolt of Vindex and the Gauls actually occurred a year later than I have in this timeline, and while Nero was in Naples. I moved it a bit earlier for the sake of creative license and fitting as many issues into the one sequence before I moved back to Jerusalem. For the story of Vindex and Nero see Suetonius, *Lives of the Twelve Caesars, Nero* 40-45.

Hellias had called Nero back to Rome with the report that there was a great conspiracy to assassinate him. Cassius Dio, *Roman History*, 63.19.

"Nero seemed to think he could adequately prevent revolt in the provinces by summoning suspected commanders to Greece and executing them. Nothing more is heard of this urban conspiracy: it is possible that what had really alarmed Helius were the first rumblings of revolt in Gaul... As all this must have occurred before Vindex finally rose in arms just before the middle of March in 68,"

Edward Champlin, *Nero* (Massachussetts, Harvard University Press, 2003), 180.

"Vindex's emissaries killed: "Plutarch says that, with the exception of Galba in Tarraconensis, the governors whom Vindex approached sent word of his treason to Nero (x). Presumably his emissaries did not return. From this alone he must have inferred that he had been delated."

P. A. Brunt, "The Revolt of Vindex and the Fall of Nero," *Latomus, T.* 18, Fasc. 3 (JUILLET-SEPTEMBRE 1959), 533.

CHAPTER 39

[1] **Becoming Sons of God**: The modern tendency to translate "sons of God" into "children of God" is cultural imperialism that destroys the glorious meaning of the original meaning of the phrase "sons of God." In the Bible, it was the sons who were the primary receivers of the inheritance. Also, sons of God is a concept that refers to the divine beings of God's council. Yes, we are children of God, but more importantly, to say that women can become "sons of God" is a legal theological concept that means they equally inherit the kingdom AND will also equally become divine beings of God's council. The generic term "children of God" does not embody those truths and therefore guts the true Biblical meaning given by God.

CHAPTER 41

¹ **El Shaddai called Abraham**:

> Exodus 6:2–3
> ² God spoke to Moses and said to him, "I am the LORD. ³ I appeared to Abraham, to Isaac, and to Jacob, as God Almighty, but by my name the LORD I did not make myself known to them.

² **Mount Bashar and the Amorites**:

"Scholars haven't reached a consensus over just where the Amorites came from. The Ebla texts refer to an Amorite LU.GAL, or king, named Amuti, in the 2300s B.C. The Amorite kingdom, MAR.TUki in Sumerian, seems to have been centered in Syria around Jebel Bishri, a mountain on the west bank of the Euphrates about thirty miles west of Deir ez-Zor. The mountain of the Amorites, called Bašar back in the day, was the site of a military victory led by the Akkadian king Narām-Sîn…"

Derek Gilbert, *The Great Inception: Satan's PSYOPs from Eden to Armageddon* (US: Defender Publishing, 2017), 141.

"The next and last occurrence of the royal title "king of the Amorites" occurs in the biblical references to Sihon, who associated with Heshbon in Transjordan, and who was defeated in the earliest recorded battle of the newly established Israelite federation (Numbers 21)."

George E. Mendenhall, "Amorites," ed. David Noel Freedman, *The Anchor Yale Bible Dictionary* (New York: Doubleday, 1992), 201.

³ **The lim ilani or "thousand gods"**:

"The theophoric element "Līm" used by several rulers in northwest Mesopotamia seems to be based on the Akkadian līm ilāni, the "thousand gods." The līm ilāni were invoked as witnesses to treaties, and scholars think the term probably means the entire pantheon of gods—in other words, the divine assembly."

Derek Gilbert, *The Great Inception: Satan's PSYOPs from Eden to Armageddon* (US: Defender Publishing, 2017), 143-144.

CHAPTER 42

¹ Hebrews 6:4–6.

CHAPTER 43

¹ **Satan's fall from heaven was in the ministry of Christ**:

"In Revelation 12, we see the origin of the notion that one third of the angels fell to earth with Satan at his fall. The only problem is that this event did not occur before the garden of Eden in a cosmic rebellion, it happened at the birth of Jesus Christ! Revelation 12:1-6 describes an apocalyptic parable of the cosmic war of the Seed of the Serpent (a dragon of chaos) and the Seed of the Woman (Israel/the Church). It describes one third of the angelic stars (Watchers?) joining Satan with the swipe of his serpentine tail. The dragon and his minions seek to devour the male seed (offspring) of the woman, but they fail and the child becomes king. And then the passage tells of a heavenly war:

Revelation 12:7–10 Now war arose in heaven, Michael and his angels fighting against the dragon. And the dragon and his angels fought back, 8 but he was defeated, and there was no longer any place for them in heaven. 9 And the great dragon was thrown down, that ancient serpent, who is called the devil and Satan, the deceiver of the whole world—he was thrown down to the earth, and his angels were thrown down with him. 10 And I heard a loud voice in heaven, saying, "Now the salvation and the power and the kingdom of our God and the authority of his Christ have come, for the accuser of our brothers has been thrown down, who accuses them day and night before our God." Most Christians believe this is a reference to Satan's fall before the Garden of Eden incident, where he takes one third of the angels in heaven with him. But a closer look at the context reveals that this is not the case at all, but rather the opposite. The war in heaven does not happen before the Garden, it happens at the time of the incarnation of Messiah on earth! The woman (Israel) gives birth to a male child (Messiah, v. 5), who the dragon (Satan) seeks to devour (from Herod's slaughter of the innocents all the way to the Cross). That Messiah ascends to the throne in authority after his resurrection (v. 5; Eph 1:20-22), during which time that woman (Israel) flees to the wilderness (time of tribulation under the Roman Empire)." The war in heaven we see cannot be before the Garden because it says that the throwing down of Satan occurs with the coming of the kingdom of Christ! (v. 10). He is thrown down to earth and then seeks to kill the Christ (v. 13). Satan then seeks to make war with the rest of her offspring (God's people) which we see in history.

"Revelation 12 is an apocalyptic parable that is describing the incarnation of Messiah, his ascension to the throne of authority over all principalities and powers, and his suppression of Satan's power as the Gospel goes forth into the world." Brian Godawa, *When Giants Were Upon the Earth: The Watchers, the Nephilim, and the Biblical Cosmic War of the Seed* (Embedded Pictures, 2014), 149-150.

CHAPTER 44

[1] **Throne above the heavenly waters**:

Psalm 104:2-3
Stretching out the heavens like a tent. He lays the beams of his chambers on the waters;

Psalm 148:4
Praise him, you highest heavens, and you waters above the heavens!

[2] **Earthly temple a shadow of the heavenly temple reality**:

Hebrews 8:5
[5] They serve a copy and shadow of the heavenly things. For when Moses was about to erect the tent, he was instructed by God, saying, "See that you make everything according to the pattern that was shown you on the mountain."

Hebrews 10:1
[1] For since the law has but a shadow of the good things to come instead of the true form of these realities, it can never, by the same sacrifices that are continually offered every year, make perfect those who draw near.

Hebrews 9:24
[24] For Christ has entered, not into holy places made with hands, which are copies of the true things, but into heaven itself, now to appear in the presence of God on our behalf.

[3] **Satan's fall at the time of Christ**: The Revelation passage below ties the fall of Satan with his loss of the ability to accuse or condemn. Romans 8 states that with the death of Christ, there is no longer any condemnation of sin (Romans 8:1). Jesus had bound the strong man in his ministry and plundered his territory (Matt 12:28-30).

Revelation 12:9–10
[9] And the great dragon was thrown down, that ancient serpent, who is called the devil and Satan, the deceiver of the whole world—he was thrown down to the earth, and his angels were thrown down with him. [10] And I heard a loud voice in heaven, saying, "Now the salvation and the power and the kingdom of our God and the authority of his Christ have come, for the accuser of our brothers has been thrown down, who accuses them day and night before our God.

[4] **The heavenly temple description**: The description in this chapter is drawn from several sources, The first in this passage is 1 Enoch 14:8-25. The others are Ezekiel 1:4-28 and Isaiah 6:1-3.

[5] **Throne guardians**: To see images of these throne guardians see the artwork at ChroniclesOfTheApocalypse.com. http://godawa.com/books/chronicles-of-the-apocalypse/story-art/

[6] **Apollyon/Satan as a Seraph**: There is a long tradition of this in Christian legends and traditions, but precious little in the Bible. I only draw on this because seraphim is a word that has serpentine characteristics, and Satan is portrayed as the serpent of old and the great dragon who fell from heaven as one of God's

angels (Rev 12:7-9). So I speculate, but I would not be dogmatic about it. I don't believe Ezekiel 29 is about Satan. See David Lowe, *Deconstructing Lucifer: Reexamining the Ancient Origins of the Fallen Angel of Light* (Amazon, 2011). Also, Norman C. Habel, "Ezekiel 28 and the Fall of the First Man," http://www.godawa.com/chronicles_of_the_nephilim/Articles_By_Others/Habel%20-%20Ezekiel%2028%20and%20the%20Fall%20of%20the%20First%20Man.pdf

[7] Psalm 82:1

[8] **The herald's praise comes from**: Psalm 89:5-7.

[9] **The herald's praise comes from**: Psalm 89:11-14.

[10] **Apollyon quotes**: Genesis 3:15.

[11] **Apollyon quotes from**: Deuteronomy 32:1, 8-9. For the allotment of the nations to the Watchers, see also:

Deuteronomy 4:19–21
[19] And beware lest you raise your eyes to heaven, and when you see the sun and the moon and **the stars, all the host of heaven,** you be drawn away and bow down to them and serve them, things that the LORD your **God has allotted to all the peoples** under the whole heaven. [20] But the LORD has taken you and brought you out of the iron furnace, out of Egypt, to be a people of **his own inheritance**, as you are this day.

Deuteronomy 29:26
They went and served other gods and worshiped them, gods whom they have not known and whom **He had not allotted to them**.

Jubilees 15:31-32
(There are) many nations and many people, and they all belong to him, but over all of them he caused spirits to rule so that they might lead them astray from following him. But over Israel he did not cause any angel or spirit to rule because he alone is their ruler and he will protect them.

Targum Jonathan, Deuteronomy 32, Section LIII
When the Most High made allotment of the world unto the
nations which proceeded from the sons of Noach [Noah],
in the separation of the writings and languages of the
children of men at the time of the division, He cast the lot among the seventy angels, the princes of the nations with whom is the revelation to oversee the city..

See also 1 Enoch 89:59; 90:25, 3Enoch 48C:9, DSS War Scroll 1Q33 Col. xvii:7, Targum Jonathan, Genesis 11, Section II; Philo, On the Posterity of Cain and His Exile 25.89; Concerning Noah's Work as a Planter 14.59; On the Migration of Abraham 36.202; 1 Clement 29; Origen, First Principles 1.5.1. Thanks to Don Enevoldsen for some of these passages.

Walter Wink footnotes a plenitude of texts about the 70 angel "gods" over the 70 nations in the Targums in Walter Wink. *Naming the Powers: The Language of Power in the New Testament* (The Powers : Volume One) (K-Locations 2235-2242). K-Edition.

[12] **The mystery of the Gospel**:

Ephesians 3:3–10
[3] how the mystery was made known to me by revelation, as I have written briefly. [4] When you read this, you can perceive my insight into the mystery of Christ, [5] which was not made known to the sons of men in other generations as it has now been revealed to his holy apostles and prophets by the Spirit. [6] This mystery is that the Gentiles are fellow heirs, members of the same body, and partakers of the promise in Christ Jesus through the gospel. [7] Of this gospel I was made a minister according to the gift of God's grace, which was given me by the working of his power. [8] To me, though I am the very least of all the saints, this grace was given, to preach to the Gentiles the unsearchable riches of Christ, [9] and to bring to light for everyone what is the plan of the mystery

hidden for ages in God, who created all things, [10] so that through the church the manifold wisdom of God might now be made known to the rulers and authorities in the heavenly places.

CHAPTER 46

[1] Revelation 11:6.

[2] **Ba'alzebub as Lord of the Flies**:

"The decipherment of the Ugaritic texts brought to light the frequent epithet "Prince Baal" or "Exalted Baal" (zbl b'l) or "The Prince, the Lord of the earth" (zbl b'l arṣ) (Albright 1936:17–18). Armed with this new information from Ugarit, scholars almost unanimously saw in 2 Kings 1 another example of a pejorative rendering of an original ba'al zĕbûl with ba'al zĕbûb, "Lord of flies," similar to the well-known euphemistic substitution of bōšet, "shame," for an original ba'al in such personal names as Mephiboshet and Ishboshet."

Theodore J. Lewis, "Beelzebul," ed. David Noel Freedman, *The Anchor Yale Bible Dictionary* (New York: Doubleday, 1992), 639.

[3] **What Jesus said about Ba'alzebub**:

Matthew 12:27–29
[27] And if I cast out demons by Beelzebul, by whom do your sons cast them out? Therefore they will be your judges. [28] But if it is by the Spirit of God that I cast out demons, then the kingdom of God has come upon you. [29] Or how can someone enter a strong man's house and plunder his goods, unless he first binds the strong man? Then indeed he may plunder his house.

Israel will be possessed by seven times the demons that Jesus cast out:

Matthew 12:43–45
[43] "When the unclean spirit has gone out of a person, it passes through waterless places seeking rest, but finds none. [44] Then it says, 'I will return to my house from which I came.' And when it comes, it finds the house empty, swept, and put in order. [45] Then it goes and brings with it seven other spirits more evil than itself, and they enter and dwell there, and the last state of that person is worse than the first. So also will it be with this evil generation."

[4] **Jerusalem as Egypt, and her plagues as the plagues of Egypt**:

"Elijah's drought in Israel happens to last for three and one-half years (Lk 4:25; Jas 5:17) thereby matching the time frame of our two witnesses (11:2–3). When John states that they "have power over the waters to turn them into blood, and to smite the earth with every plague, as often as they desire" (11:6bc), we recall that Moses called down plagues against the Egyptians (Ex 11:1; 12:13; Jos 24:5; 1Sa 4:8; Am 4:10), and turned water into blood (Ex 4:9; 7:17-21; Ps 105:29)...

"The two prophets also have power over the waters to turn them into blood, and to smite the earth [tēn gēn, "the Land"] with every plague, as often as they desire (11:6b). Later I will show in the exposition of 14:20 how the battles with the Romans caused the waterways to become choked with Jewish corpses and polluted with their blood. Josephus records for us that "the sea was bloody a long way" (J.W. 3:9:3 §426) and "one might then see the lake all bloody, and full of dead bodies" (J.W. 3:10:9 §529). Lupieri (177) notes regarding the tēn gēn that the prophets "will be directed with particular attention to the Holy Land. Moreover, the fact that they strike this land with 'plagues' suggests to the reader and hearer that it somehow corresponds to ancient Egypt."

Kenneth L. Gentry, Jr., *The Divorce of Israel: A Redemptive-Historical Interpretation of Revelation Vol. 2* (Dallas, GA: Tolle Lege Press, 2016), 92, 103.

The plague of flies and frogs in this chapter are fictional creative license. I believe that the frogs described in Revelation 16:13-14 is a metaphor that communicates the demonic nature of the unholy trinity as well as John's literary connection to the plagues.

[5] **The false prophet as the high priest of first century Israel**:

"Corsini (333) perceptively observes that "the beast-prostitute pair... constitute a repetition of the two beasts of ch. 13, described here not only in their complementary aspect, but also in the complexity involved in the symbol." On the same page he continues: "The symbol of the prostitute, like the beast from the land / false prophet, also points to Judaism. The symbol signifies Judaism's perversion, through the metaphor of prostitution. Prostitution means idolatry and Judaism has become idolatrous because it adores the beast and its statue, political authority. This is the case not because it accepts the political domination of the Romans.... Judaism adopts their mentality, their means and their goals."

"The angelomorphic Christ now declares that Babylon-Jerusalem has become a dwelling place of demons (18:2b). Here we see Babylon-Jerusalem associated with "demons" — and "every unclean spirit" (18:2c). This is not surprising in that the "false prophet" (the high-priestly aristocracy) issues death decrees against Christ and Christians (Ac 9:1-2, 21) when prompted by "unclean spirits," the "spirits of demons" (cf. 16:13-14). Kenneth L. Gentry, Jr., *The Divorce of Israel: A Redemptive-Historical Interpretation of Revelation Vol. 2* (Dallas, GA: Tolle Lege Press, 2016), 492.

[6] **Moshe quotes from**: Revelation 16:13–14.

The frog spirits in the mouths of the beast, the dragon and the false prophet:

The frogs are another literary allusion by John to the plagues of Egypt. But in relation to the False Prophet, I have argued that the False Prophet is symbolic of the high priesthood of Israel. The demonic presence in this apostate body of men, and the evil that their teachings bring is likened to frog spirits.

"We have already been informed that the dragon is Satan (12:9) who functions as the accuser of the brethren (12:10) and who seeks to pour water like a river "out of his mouth" in order to destroy the Jewish church and her seed (12:15; cp. 1Pe 5:8b). And the dragon empowers and directs the sea beast (13:2b) who has "a mouth speaking arrogant words and blasphemies" (13:5). John even emphasizes the speech of the Land beast (false prophet) in that he "spoke as a dragon" (13:11b) and "exercises all the authority of the first beast in his presence" (13:12; cp. Ac 17:7; 25:7-8). Each of these has coming from their mouths "unclean spirits," showing the evil intent of their directives. Ultimately, they contrast with the Messiah who has a sword in his mouth (1:16; 2:16; 19:15, 21) and who eventually conquers them thereby (19:20; 20:1, 10).

"These three are in "demonic concord joined" (Terry 421). As we have seen, John links the Jews and their synagogue system with Satan (Jn 8:44; Rev 2:9; 3:9) and Rome (13:11ff; 17:3ff). But how would it be that the false prophet, which represents the apostate Jewish high priestly system, joins with Rome to destroy the great city Jerusalem?...

"The high priestly system was not only corrupt in itself but sold out to Rome. Obviously they would not have wanted to destroy their own wealth, status, and position by joining with Rome to wage war against Jerusalem and the temple, the very loci of their authority (Jn 11:48, 50). But though this was certainly not their purpose, it nevertheless became the result of their actions. After all, by using Rome to oppose Christ (Jn 19:12, 15), they brought about the judgment-coming of Christ (16:15a; cp. 1:7; Mt 26:65) which effected "the great day of God" (16:14b). It was partly through the priestly rulers' corruption and abuse (Ant. 20:8:8 §180; 20:9:2 § 206–7; Pesah. 57a)—along with the abuses of the Roman procurators Albinus and Florus (Ant. 20:11:1 §252–58; J.W. 2:14:1 §271–76; 2:16:1, 4, 5 §333, 351, 353–54, 402)—that perpetually restive Israel was finally provoked to revolt against Rome."

Kenneth L. Gentry, Jr., *The Divorce of Israel: A Redemptive-Historical Interpretation of Revelation Vol. 2* (Dallas, GA: Tolle Lege Press, 2016), 361-362.

[7] **Armageddon**:

> Revelation 16:13–16
> [13] And I saw, coming out of the mouth of the dragon and out of the mouth of the beast and out of the mouth of the false prophet, three unclean spirits like frogs. [14] For they are demonic spirits, performing signs, who go abroad to the kings of the whole world, to assemble them for battle on the great day of God the Almighty. [15] ("Behold, I am coming like a thief! Blessed is the one who

stays awake, keeping his garments on, that he may not go about naked and be seen exposed!") [16]
And they assembled them at the place that in Hebrew is called Armageddon.

"The correct (Hebrew) term John uses to describe the climactic end-times battle is *harmagedon*. This spelling becomes significant when we try to discern what this Hebrew term means. The first part of the term (har) is easy. In Hebrew har means "mountain." Our term is therefore divisible into har-magedon, "Mount (of) magedon…the Hebrew phrase behind John's Greek transliteration of our mystery Hebrew term is actually h-r-m-'-d. But what does that mean? If the first part (h-r) is the Hebrew word har ("mountain"), is there a har m-'-d in the Hebrew Old Testament? There is—and it's stunning when considered in light of the battle of "Armageddon" and what we discussed in the previous chapter about the supernatural north and antichrist.The phrase in question exists in the Hebrew Bible as har mo'ed. Incredibly, it is found in Isaiah 14:13…the phrase har mo'ed was one of the terms used to describe the dwelling place of Yahweh and his divine council—the cosmic mountain…When John draws on this ancient Hebrew phrase, he is indeed pointing to a climactic battle at Jerusalem. Why? Because Jerusalem is a mountain—Mount Zion. And if Baal and the gods of other nations don't like Yahweh claiming to be Most High and claiming to run the cosmos from the heights of Zaphon/Mount Zion, they can try to do something about it." Michael S. Heiser, *The Unseen Realm: Recovering the Supernatural Worldview of the Bible, First Edition* (Bellingham, WA: Lexham Press, 2015), 369-373.

"The rulers of the empire": I use this phrase because the translation "kings of the whole world" is a bad translation that gives a false picture of the original language. In Greek, the word for "whole world" is *oikoumene*, which contextually in the New Testament means the Roman empire.

The same Greek word is used in Luke 2:1: "Now it came about in those days that a decree went out from Caesar Augustus, that a census be taken of all the inhabited earth." In the New American Standard Version, the marginal note in Luke 2:1 reads "the Roman empire" (also see Acts 11:28, 24:5)." Gary DeMar, *Last Days Madness: Obsession of the Modern Church*, Fourth revised edition (Powder Springs, GA: American Vision, 1999), 88.

In NT thinking the Roman empire is the world (Ac 11:28; 17:6; 24:5; Col 1:6, 24). This is true among non-biblical writers, as well (Jos., J.W. 2:16:4 §361, 380, 388; 4:3:10 §78; Ap. 2:4 §8; Tac., His. 2:78).

And the Greek word for "kings" mean rulers of all kinds, not merely kings as in monarchies.:

"The NT has 115 occurrences of βασιλεύς. "king" a) As in the LXX, references to the secular ruler predominate with 72 occurrences (25 in the Synoptics, 19 in Acts, 17 in Revelation, 7 in Hebrews, and 2 Cor 11:32; 1 Tim 2:2; 1 Pet 2:13, 17). b) 38 occurrences refer to Jesus (19 in the Synoptics and 16 in John, of which 26 are in the Passion narrative; Acts 17:7; Rev 17:14; 19:16)."

Horst Robert Balz and Gerhard Schneider, Exegetical Dictionary of the New Testament (Grand Rapids, Mich.: Eerdmans, 1990–), 206.

Spiritual war of cosmic mountains: Isaiah 14:13-15. For the fictional depiction of this spiritual war of cosmic mountains see Brian Godawa *Jesus Triumphant: Chronicles of the Nephilim Book 8* (Embedded Pictures, 2015). For an explanation of the theology behind that fiction see the appendix of that same book, pages 308-311. For the academic defense of the interpretation, see Michael S. Heiser, *The Unseen Realm: Recovering the Supernatural Worldview of the Bible, First Edition* (Bellingham, WA: Lexham Press, 2015), 288-295.

Armageddon as battle of cosmic mountains: Richard J. Clifford, *The Cosmic Mountain in Canaan and the Old Testament* (Wipf & Stock Pub, 2010).

Armageddon and the Coming of the Lord: Revelation 16:16; 19:11-21; 1Thessalonians 4:13-17.

[8] **Elihu quotes from**: Zechariah 14:1–5.

[9] **Zechariah on the Day of the Lord and the splitting of the Mount of Olives**:

"These verses are dark and hard to be understood; but divers good expositors take this to be the meaning of them. [1.] God will carefully inspect Jerusalem, even then when the enemies of it are laying it waste: His feet shall stand in that day upon the mount of Olives, whence he may take a full view of the city and temple, Mk. 13:3. When the refiner puts his gold into the furnace he stands by it, and has his eye upon it, to see that it receive no damage; so when Jerusalem, God's gold, is to be refined, he will have the oversight of it. He will stand by upon the mount of Olives; this was literally fulfilled when our Lord Jesus was often upon this mountain, especially when thence he ascended up into heaven, Acts 1:12. It was the last place on which his feet stood on this earth, the place from which he took rise.

"[2.] The partition-wall between Jews and Gentiles shall be taken away. The mountains about Jerusalem, and particularly this, signified it to be an enclosure, and that it stood in the way of those who would approach to it. Between the Gentiles and Jerusalem this mountain of Bether, of division, stood, Cant. 2:17. But by the destruction of Jerusalem this mountain shall be made to cleave in the midst, and so the Jewish pale shall be taken down, and the church laid in common with the Gentiles, who were made one with the Jews by the breaking down of this middle wall of partition, Eph. 2:14. Who art thou, O great mountain? And a great mountain the ceremonial law was in the way of the Jews' conversion, which, one would think, could never have been got over; yet before Christ and his gospel it was made plain. This mountain departs, this hill removes, but the covenant of peace cannot be broken; for peace is still preached to him that is afar off and to those that are nigh.

"[3.] A new and living way shall be opened to the new Jerusalem, both to see it and to come into it. The mountain being divided, one-half towards the north and the other half towards the south, there shall be a very great valley, that is, a broad way of communication opened between Jerusalem and the Gentile world, by which the Gentiles shall have free admission into the gospel-Jerusalem, and the word of the Lord, that goes forth from Jerusalem, shall have a free course into the Gentile world. Thus the way of the Lord is prepared, for every mountain and hill shall be brought low, and plain and pleasant valleys shall come in the room of them, Isa. 40:4."

Matthew Henry, *Matthew Henry's Commentary on the Whole Bible: Complete and Unabridged in One Volume* (Peabody: Hendrickson, 1994), 1592–1593.

"Zechariah 14:4–5 speaks of Israel's god standing on the Mount of Olives, and of a great earthquake, after which 'YHWH your god will come, and all the holy ones with him.' There is no earthquake in the synoptic account (though compare Matthew 27:51–2), and Jesus is sitting, not standing; this is enough to suggest that the evangelists have not deliberately invented the scene merely to 'fulfil' Zechariah. Nor does Matthew add, as he might have done, a note saying 'this was done to fulfil the prophecy ...' But this therefore points all the more to the likelihood of Jesus's choice of the Mount of Olives as the appropriate place from which to utter his last solemn oracles of judgment upon Jerusalem, and his last solemn predictions of the vindication of himself and his followers. He was at least as capable of acting in a symbolically resonant way as the great Hebrew prophets had been; and at least as alert to symbolic resonances, not least the symbolism of place, as were Christian writers a generation or so later. The Mount of Olives was a natural place for Jesus to be, anyway, half-way between the city itself and Bethany, where he and his followers were spending the nights. The force of the setting then seems to be that this was Jesus's paradoxical retelling of the great story found in Zechariah 14: in predicting Jerusalem's last great struggle, the 'coming' of YHWH, and the final arrival of the divine kingdom, he was acting to fulfil, in his own reinterpreted fashion, the prophecy of Zechariah."

N. T. Wright, *Jesus and the Victory of God, Christian Origins and the Question of God* (London: Society for Promoting Christian Knowledge, 1996), 344–345.

[10] **Elihu quotes from**: Revelation 16:15-16.

[11] **Isaiah and Jeremiah preached to a people who did not listen**: God's directives sounded eerily reminiscent of the time of AD 70.

Isaiah 6:8–12
[8] And I heard the voice of the Lord saying, "Whom shall I send, and who will go for us?" Then I said, "Here I am! Send me." [9] And he said, "Go, and say to this people: " 'Keep on hearing, but do not understand; keep on seeing, but do not perceive.' [10] Make the heart of this people dull, and their ears heavy, and blind their eyes; lest they see with their eyes, and hear with their ears, and understand with their hearts, and turn and be healed." [11] Then I said, "How long, O Lord?" And he said: "Until cities lie waste without inhabitant, and houses without people, and the land is a

desolate waste, [12] and the LORD removes people far away, and the forsaken places are many in the midst of the land.

Isaiah 30:9–11
[9] For they are a rebellious people, lying children, children unwilling to hear the instruction of the LORD; [10] who say to the seers, "Do not see," and to the prophets, "Do not prophesy to us what is right; speak to us smooth things, prophesy illusions, [11] leave the way, turn aside from the path, let us hear no more about the Holy One of Israel."

Jeremiah 7:25–28
[25] From the day that your fathers came out of the land of Egypt to this day, I have persistently sent all my servants the prophets to them, day after day. [26] Yet they did not listen to me or incline their ear, but stiffened their neck. They did worse than their fathers. [27] "So you shall speak all these words to them, but they will not listen to you. You shall call to them, but they will not answer you. [28] And you shall say to them, 'This is the nation that did not obey the voice of the LORD their God, and did not accept discipline; truth has perished; it is cut off from their lips.

CHAPTER 47

[1] **The story of Gadara's surrender and the escaping rebels can be found in**: Flavius Josephus, *The Wars of the Jews* 4.7.3, §413-418.

[2] **Vespasian actually sent the general Placidus to hunt the rebels from Gadara**: Flavius Josephus, *The Wars of the Jews* 4.7.4-6, §419-439.

This was a choice of creative license to minimize characters.

[3] **Agrippa's elbow wound**:

Actually, this happened at the city of Gamala. See Flavius Josephus, *The Wars of the Jews* 4.1.3, §14-16.

CHAPTER 48

[1] **Vespasian actually sent the general Placidus to hunt the rebels from Gadara**: Flavius Josephus, *The Wars of the Jews* 4.7.4-6, §419-439.

This was a choice of creative license to minimize characters.

[2] **The description of the Jordan plugged with dead bodies of 15,000**:

Flavius Josephus, *The Wars of the Jews* 4.7.5-6, §435-437

"…fifteen thousand of them were slain, while the number of those that were unwillingly forced to leap into Jordan was prodigious. (436) There were besides, two thousand and two hundred taken prisoners. A mighty prey was taken also, consisting of asses and sheep, and camels, and oxen.

"6. (437) Now this destruction that fell upon the Jews, as it was not inferior to any of the rest in itself, so did it still appear greater than it really was; and this, because not only the whole of the country through which they had fled was filled with slaughter, and Jordan could not be passed over, by reason of the dead bodies that were in it, but because the lake Asphaltitis was also full of dead bodies, that were carried down into it by the river."

Flavius Josephus and William Whiston, *The Works of Josephus: Complete and Unabridged* (Peabody: Hendrickson, 1987), 685.

CHAPTER 49

[1] **Jesus quotes** Psalm 58:1-2.

[2] **Jesus quotes from**: Psalm 2:6-8; Isaiah 11:12 (Romans 15:8-12); Colossians 2:15; Ephesians 4:8-10.

[3] **Jesus quotes from**: Psalm 110:1-2 and 1 Corinthians 15:25-27.

[4] **This is taken from**: Ephesians 1:20-22.

CHAPTER 50

[1] **Research for this chapter was drawn from the lone account of Nero's death in**: Suetonius, *Lives of the Twelve Caesars, Nero* 44-49.
http://penelope.uchicago.edu/Thayer/E/Roman/Texts/Suetonius/12Caesars/Nero*.html

See also Cassius Dio, *Roman History* 63.26-29.

[2] **The kingdom of the Beast plunged into darkness**:

"The throne of the beast does not here mean merely the emperor's chair of state, but the metropolis, i.e. the place where the throne was, the central point of the empire. Darkness overspreads this, which is the emblem of doom and terror. From the metropolis this spreads out over all parts of the empire."

Moses Stuart, *A Commentary on the Apocalypse, vol. 2* (Andover; New York: Allen, Morrill and Wardwell; M. H. Newman, 1845), 312.

"The fifth angel therefore pours out his Chalice upon the throne of the Beast; and, even as the sun's heat is scorching those who worship the Beast, the lights are turned out on his kingdom, and it becomes darkened – a familiar Biblical symbol for political turmoil and the fall of rulers (cf. Isa. 13:9-10; Amos 8:9; Ezek. 32:7-8). The primary significance of this plague is still the judgment on Israel, for (in terms of the message of Revelation) that was the throne and kingdom of the Beast. Moreover, as we shall see, the people who suffer from the Fifth Chalice are identified as suffering as well from the First Chalice, which was poured out upon the Land, upon the Israelite worshipers of the Beast (v. 2).

"It is also likely, however, that this judgment partially corresponds to the wars, revolutions, riots, and "worldwide convulsions" that racked the Empire after Nero committed suicide in June 68. F. W. Farrar writes in this connection of "the horrors inflicted upon Rome and Romans in the civil wars by provincial governors – already symbolized as the horns of the Wild Beast, and here characterized as kings yet kingdomless. Such were Galba, Otho, Vitellius, and Vespasian. Vespasian and Lucianus deliberately planned to starve the Roman populace; and in the fierce struggle of the Vitellians against Sabinus and Domitian, and the massacre which followed, there occurred the event which sounded so portentously in the ears of every Roman – the burning to the ground of the Temple of the Capitoline Jupiter, on December 19th, A.D. 69. It was not the least of the signs of the times that the space of one year saw wrapped in flames the two most hallowed shrines of the ancient world – the Temple of Jerusalem and the Temple of the great Latin god.'"

David Chilton, *The Days of Vengeance: An Exposition of the Book of Revelation*, (Texas: Dominion Press, 1987, 1990), 405-406.

"During the period of the Jewish War (AD 67–70) judgments befell Rome: the specific manifestation of the beast, Nero, committed suicide (June, AD 68) and the Roman civil wars erupted (AD 68-69) causing the death throes of the generic concept of the beast. Tacitus records the (generic) beast's circumstances:

> The history on which I am entering is that of a period rich in disasters, terrible with battles, torn by civil struggles, horrible even in peace. Four emperors fell by the sword; there were three civil wars, more foreign wars and often both at the same time. There was success in the East [i.e., the Jewish War], misfortune in the West. Illyricum was disturbed, the Gallic provinces wavering, Britain subdued and immediately let go. The Sarmatae and Suebi rose against us; the Dacians won fame by defeats inflicted and suffered; even the Parthians were almost roused to arms through the trickery of a pretended Nero. Moreover, Italy was distressed by disasters unknown before or returning after the lapse of ages.... Rome was devastated by conflagrations, in which her most ancient shrines were consumed and the very Capitol fired by citizens' hands. Sacred rites were defiled; there were adulteries in high places. The sea was filled with exiles, its cliffs

444

made foul with the bodies of the dead. In Rome there was more awful cruelty. High birth, wealth, the refusal or acceptance of office—all gave ground for accusations, and virtues caused the surest ruin. The rewards of the informers were no less hateful than their crimes; for some, gaining priesthoods and consulships as spoils, others, obtaining positions as imperial agents and secret influence at court, made havoc and turmoil everywhere, inspiring hatred and terror. Slaves were corrupted against their masters, freedmen against their patrons; and those who had no enemy were crushed by their friends... Besides the manifold misfortunes that befell mankind, there were prodigies in the sky and on the earth, warnings given by thunderbolts, and prophecies of the future, both joyful and gloomy, uncertain and clear. For never was it more fully proved by awful disasters of the Roman people or by indubitable signs that gods care not for our safety, but for our punishment. (Hist. 1:2–3)

Josephus himself observes that "about this time it was that heavy calamities came about Rome on all sides" (J.W. 4:10:1 §585) with thousands dying (J.W. 4:9:9 §545–555; 4:11:4 §645–55; Tac., Hist. 1:2). General Vespasian was tormented by the horrible news: "And as this sorrow of his was violent, he was not able to support the torments he was under, nor to apply himself further in other wars when his native country was laid waste" (J.W. 4:10:2). In addition, the Jewish War was extremely costly to the Romans, requiring four legions (which sustained thousands of casualties) and more than three years of effort and resources (Barker 311)."

Kenneth L. Gentry, Jr., *The Divorce of Israel: A Redemptive-Historical Interpretation of Revelation Vol. 2* (Dallas, GA: Tolle Lege Press, 2016), 619-620.

[3] **Nero's plan to kill all the senate and other atrocities mentioned here**: Sueonius. *Nero* 37. 3; Tacitus *Histories* 4. 42. Aquillius' victims: *Histories* 4. 42, 1; Cassius Dio 63. 18, 2; Pliny *Ep*. 1. 5, 3

Sueonius. *Nero* 37. 3

"At the very beginning of the revolt it is believed that he formed many plans of monstrous wickedness, but in no way inconsistent with his character: to depose and assassinate the commanders of the armies and the governors of the provinces, on the ground that they were all united in a conspiracy against him; to massacre all the exiles everywhere and all men of Gallic birth in the city: the former, to prevent them from joining the rebels; the latter, as sharing and abetting the designs of their countrymen; to turn over the Gallic provinces to his armies to ravage; to poison the entire senate at banquets; to set fire to the city, first letting the wild beasts loose, that it might be harder for the people to protect themselves."

http://penelope.uchicago.edu/Thayer/E/Roman/Texts/Suetonius/12Caesars/Nero*.html

[4] **The Beast thrown into the lake of fire**:

"Even though we read of the violent historical deaths of Nero and the high priests, John states that they were "thrown alive into the lake of fire" (19:20c). The syntax here emphasizes their being alive when thus condemned: zōntes eblēthēsan hoi duo eis tēn limnēn tou puros ("alive they were cast, the two, into the lake of fire"). He is underscoring the fact of conscious punishment—prohibiting any idea of simple annihilation: they were tormented grievously. Though the bodies of their armies were eaten by birds as a temporal punishment (19:18), the penalty for the beast and false prophet was more than that. "The burning of dead bodies inflicts no pain; the burning of living ones implies pain indescribable" (Stuart 2:350). As Smalley (499) observes, "the thought of being alive while burning intensifies the fierceness of the punishment." They do not simply die and have their bodies ignobly destroyed, but they die, personally and consciously descending into the "lake of fire which burns with brimstone.""

Kenneth L. Gentry, Jr., *The Divorce of Israel: A Redemptive-Historical Interpretation of Revelation Vol. 2* (Dallas, GA: Tolle Lege Press, 2016), 623-624.

CHAPTER 51

[1] This chapter is a condensation of events that occurred over a longer period of time. I've taken some creative license in the interest of simplifying a complex situation. For Josephus' version of the events, see: Flavius Josephus, *The Wars of the Jews* 4.9.3-12, §503-577.

CHAPTER 52

[1] **Apollyon is reading from**: Detueronomy 28:15-68.

[2] **Israel was Yahweh's wife**:

"Most scholars would agree with Mathewson (45) that: "Israel was considered married to God at Sinai, where God established his covenant with his people (Jer. 2.2; 31.32; Hos. 2:14–15; cf. 13.4–5)." Rabbinic Judaism picked up on this imagery and spoke of the Mount Sinai covenant as being Israel's "Day of Espousal" with the Shekinah cloud's descent upon the tabernacle deemed the marital consummation."

Kenneth L. Gentry, Jr., *The Divorce of Israel: A Redemptive-Historical Interpretation of Revelation Vol. 1* (Dallas, GA: Tolle Lege Press, 2016), 523.

[3] **Apollyon quotes from**: Ezekiel 16:8.

[4] **The spiritual harlotry of Israel**: "Ortlund points out regarding this harlotry theme that "what begins as Pentateuchal whispers rises later to prophetic cries and is eventually echoed in apostolic teaching." Eventually this harlotry image is especially employed by the prophets Hosea, Jeremiah, and Ezekiel who "exploit it to the fullest". Hosea develops the theme of harlotry throughout his entire book, even marrying a harlot himself to illustrate Israel's sin (Hos 1:2; 3:1–3). For instance, Hosea 2:2 reads: "Contend with your mother, contend, / For she is not my wife, and I am not her husband; / And let her put away her harlotry from her face, / And her adultery from between her breasts." Jeremiah 3:6 speaks similarly: "Then the Lord said to me in the days of Josiah the king, 'Have you seen what faithless Israel did? She went up on every high hill and under every green tree, and she was a harlot there'" (Jer 3:6). Jeremiah and Ezekiel particularly develop it "into elaborate images". The harlot metaphor is applied to Israel dozens of times in the Old Testament.18 The prophets speak of Israel's unfaithfulness through idolatry as hurtful to her husband: "Then those of you who escape will remember Me among the nations to which they will be carried captive, how I have been hurt by their adulterous hearts which turned away from Me, and by their eyes, which played the harlot after their idols" (Eze 6:9a). Consequently, "in a number of passages in the Old Testament, therefore, the 'lovers' after whom Israel went were other deities who were making a bid for her allegiance" (J. Thompson 1997: 476).

We must realize that although the charge of Israel's spiritual harlotry tends to focus on its most egregious manifestation in idolatry, it is not limited to idol worship. In the biblical view of marriage, the wife's faithfulness involves a wholesale relationship of loving obedience to her husband (Nu 5:29; Jer 31:32; Eph 5:22–23; 1Pe 3:1, 6), not just the avoidance of adulterous relations. Consequently, there are places where charges of harlotry against Israel speak of situations not involving actual, formal idolatry. For instance, when lawlessness (not idolatry) prevails in Jerusalem, the "faithful city" becomes a "harlot" (Isa 1:21–23). Here Isaiah declares that the "faithful city has become a harlot" because she was "full of justice" and "righteousness" but "now murderers." The "faithful [Heb., amen] city" is now acting like a "harlot," the most unfaithful of women."

Kenneth L. Gentry, Jr., *The Divorce of Israel: A Redemptive-Historical Interpretation of Revelation Vol. 1* (Dallas, GA: Tolle Lege Press, 2016), 526-527.

[5] **Apollyon quotes from** Malachi 2:11.

[6] **God's promise to divorce Israel for her unfaithfulness**:

Jeremiah 3:1
[1] "If a man divorces his wife and she goes from him and becomes another man's wife, will he return to her? Would not that land be greatly polluted? You have played the whore with many lovers; and would you return to me? declares the LORD.

Isaiah 50:1
[1] Thus says the LORD: "Where is your mother's certificate of divorce, with which I sent her away? Or which of my creditors is it to whom I have sold you? Behold, for your iniquities you were sold, and for your transgressions your mother was sent away.

Hosea 2:2

² "Plead with your mother, plead— for she is not my wife, and I am not her husband— that she put away her whoring from her face, and her adultery from between her breasts;

The expulsion from God's house:

"As noted above Jerusalem is the City of God wherein Yahweh dwells in his house (2Ki 23:27; Ps 68:29). Thus, when God issues his covenantal wife a divorce decree, he follows the Mosaic divorce legislation and "sends her out from his house" (Dt 24:1).

"Thus, in the Old Testament when Israel sinned against God and he judged her, she had no right to remain in his house: "They have turned back to the iniquities of their ancestors who refused to hear My words, and they have gone after other gods to serve them; the house of Israel and the house of Judah have broken My covenant which I made with their fathers.... Therefore do not pray for this people, nor lift up a cry or prayer for them; / for I will not listen when they call to Me because of their disaster. / What right has My beloved in My house / When she has done many vile deeds?" (Jer 11:10, 14–15). Documents from Elephantine, Egypt, show that this was actually practiced among the Jews in that "the divorced woman had to leave the matrimonial home" (J. Collins 1997: 116)."

Kenneth L. Gentry, Jr., *The Divorce of Israel: A Redemptive-Historical Interpretation of Revelation Vol. 1* (Dallas, GA: Tolle Lege Press, 2016), 532.

⁷ **Apollyon quotes from the parable of the tenants**: Matthew 21:33-43.

⁸ **Apollyon quotes from**: Matthew 23:34-35.

⁹ **Michael is drawing from**: Isaiah 10:5-19.

God providentially uses pagan armies to accomplish his will: Isa 10:5-7, 25-27; 44:27–45:7; Hab 1:6-11; Jer 51:11, 28. Note especially that though God calls Nebuchadnezzar "My Servant" (Jer 25:9), he nevertheless destroys his kingdom (Jer 25:12).

God's providential control of the pagan destruction of Jerusalem and the temple: "Revelation emphasizes the divine governance over and again: Its very theme shows Christ's vengeance against Israel (1:7; 6:16; 19:2). The first vision in the opening of the judgment material shows God on his throne above the history that he controls (4:1ff) and through which he avenges himself (6:10-11, 16-17; 11:8; 14:19; 15:1,7; 16:1, 7, 19; 19:2, 15). His throne is repeatedly emphasized throughout the drama (1:4; 3:21; 4:2-10; 15:1, 6, 11, 13; 6:16; 7:9, 10-11, 15, 17; 14:3; 16:17; 20:11; 21:5; 22:1, 3). We see this also in the abundant use of divine passives (e.g., 6:2, 4, 8; 9:1, 3; 13:7) and judgments falling from heaven upon men (8:2, 5, 7; 9:1; 12:9, 12; 16:1-2, 8). This reminds us of an earlier reference to Israel and Rome in Acts 4:27-28: "For truly in this city there were gathered together against Your holy servant Jesus, whom You anointed, both Herod and Pontius Pilate, along with the Gentiles and the peoples of Israel, to do whatever Your hand and Your purpose predestined to occur." Kenneth L. Gentry, Jr., *The Divorce of Israel: A Redemptive-Historical Interpretation of Revelation Vol. 2* (Dallas, GA: Tolle Lege Press, 2016), 486.

CHAPTER 53

¹ **The cosmic collapse described here**:

"As the Sixth Seal is broken, we are more clearly brought into the closing events of the Last Days. The Lamb reveals the next great aspect of His covenanted judgments, in a symbol often used in Biblical prophecy: de-creation. Just as the salvation of God's people is spoken of in terms of creation (cf. 2 Cor. 4:6; 5:17; Eph. 2:10; 4:24; Col. 3:10), so God's judgments (and the revelation of His presence as Judge over a sinful world) are spoken of in terms of de-creation, the collapse of the universe — God ripping apart and dissolving the fabric of creation, Thus St. John uses the fundamental structures of creation in describing the fall of Israel:
1. Earth
2. Sun
3. Moon
4. Stars

5. Firmament
6. Land
7. Man

"These seven judgments are detailed in terms of the familiar prophetic imagery of the Old Testament. First, destabilization: a giant earthquake (cf. Ex. 19:18; Ps. 18:7, 15; 60:2; Isa. 13:13-14; 24:19-20; Nab. 1:5).

"Second, the eclipse and mourning of Israel: The sun became black as sackcloth made of hair (Ex. 10:21-23; Job 9:7; Isa. 5:30; 24:23; Ezek. 32:7; Joel 2:10, 31; 3:15; Amos 8:9; Mic. 3:6).

"Third, the continued image of an eclipse, with the idea of defilement added: The whole moon became like blood (Job 25:5; Isa. 13:10; 24:23; Ezek. 32:7; Joel 2:10, 31).

"The fourth judgment affects the stars, which are images of government (Gen. 1:16); they are also clocks (Gen. 1:14), and their fall shows that Israel's time has run out: The stars fell to the earth, as a fig tree casts its unripe figs when shaken by a great wind (Job 9:7; 13ccl. 12:2; Isa. 13:10; 34:4; Ezek. 32:8; Dan. 8:10; Joel 2:10; 3:15); the great wind, of course, was brought by the Four Horsemen, who in Zechariah's original imagery were the Four Winds (Zech. 6:5), and who will be reintroduced to St. John in that form in 7:1; and the fig tree is Israel herself (Matt. 21:19; 24:32-34; Luke 21:29-32).

"Fifth, Israel now simply disappears: The heaven vanished like a scroll when it is rolled up21 (Isa. 34:4; 51:6; Ps. 102:25-26; on the symbolism of Israel as "heaven," see Isa. 51:15-16; Jer. 4:23-31; cf. Heb 12:26-27).

"Sixth, the Gentile powers are shaken as well: Every mountain and island were moved out of their places (Job 9:5-6; 14:18-19; 28:9-11; Isa. 41:5, 15-16; Ezek. 38:20; Nab. 1:4-8; Zeph. 2:11). God's "old creation," Israel, is thus to be de-created, as the Kingdom is transferred to the Church, the New Creation (cf. 2 Pet. 3:7-14). Because the rulers in God's Vineyard have killed His Son, they too will be killed (Matt. 21:33-45). The Vineyard itself will be broken down, destroyed, and laid waste (Isa. 5:1-7). In God's righteous destruction of Israel, He will shake even heaven and earth (Matt. 24:29-30; Heb. 12:26-28) in order to deliver His Kingdom over to His new nation, the Church."

David Chilton, *The Days of Vengeance: An Exposition of the Book of Revelation,* (Texas: Dominion Press, 1987, 1990), 196-197.

[2] **The huge storm and earthquake during battle**: This actually happened earlier when the Idumeans first attacked the city. But it did happen.

Flavius Josephus, *The Wars of the Jews* 4.4.5, §286-287
"286) for there broke out a prodigious storm in the night, with the utmost violence, and very strong winds, with the largest showers of rain, with continual lightnings, terrible thunderings, and amazing concussions and bellowings of the earth, that was in an earthquake. (287) These things were a manifest indication that some destruction was coming upon men, when the system of the world was put into this disorder; and anyone would guess that these wonders foreshowed some grand calamities that were coming."

Flavius Josephus and William Whiston, *The Works of Josephus: Complete and Unabridged* (Peabody: Hendrickson, 1987), 678.

"First, as a practical matter it seems virtually impossible that a quake could literally divide a city into three parts. Actual earthquakes do not divide cities, they desolate them by toppling buildings (Jer 51:29; Eze 38:19-20; Nah 1:5-6; Ac 16:26). Besides, this quake occurring in Jerusalem is called "a great earthquake, such as there had not been since man came upon the earth, so great an earthquake was it, and so mighty" (16:18b). Surely if literal (or even hyperbolical), this would not merely divide the city into three different parts. Interestingly, Josephus records an earthquake during Herod's reign using similar hyperbolic language, and it certainly does not merely divide the city: "Then it was also that there was an earthquake in Judea, such a one as had not happened at any other time, and which earthquake brought a great destruction upon the cattle in that country. About ten thousand men also perished by the fall of houses" (Ant 15:5:2 §121–22; cp. J.W. 1:20:3 §370).

"Second, as a literary matter we note that every island and mountain disappears, which cannot be literal (see discussion below). The islands are even personified as fleeing away (ephugen), not collapsing into the sea (cf. Ps 46:2). All of them. And if all mountains disappeared, Jerusalem would have been absolutely devastated (not divided) because it was built on a mountain: "The city was built upon two hills, which are opposite to one another, and have a valley to divide them asunder; at which valley the corresponding rows of houses on both hills end" (J.W. 5:4:1 §136).

"Third, we find the fuller description of Babylon's fall in Revelation 17–18, and "since the fall of Babylon takes place already in 16.19, it appears that Revelation 17:1–18.24 serves as a parenthetical expansion to describe and explain the Babylon theme in more detail"

"Revelation speaks of a three-fold division in the city (16:19). We learn from Josephus (J.W. 5:1:4 §21) that "there were three treacherous factions in the city, the one parted from the other. Eleazar and his party, that kept the sacred firstfruits, came against John in their cups. Those that were with John plundered the populace, and went out with zeal against Simon. This Simon had his supply of provisions from the city, in oppositions to the seditious" (cp. Witherington 2001b: 359; Buchanan 119, 431, 530). This division was significant enough that even the Roman historian Tacitus mentions that "there were three generals, three armies" fighting inside Jerusalem (Hist 5:12:3). In fact, Josephus (J.W. 5:1:1 §3) sees this as "the beginning of the city's destruction." The problem of factionalism which eventually led to the three-fold division in Jerusalem."

Kenneth L. Gentry, Jr., *The Divorce of Israel: A Redemptive-Historical Interpretation of Revelation Vol. 2* (Dallas, GA: Tolle Lege Press, 2016), 376-378.

[3] **Alexander quotes from**: Revelation 16:17–19.

CHAPTER 54

[1] **Qumran Jews believed in annihilation of the wicked after some punishment**:

"[Qumran's] distinctive doctrines are found particularly in the War Rule (1QM), Community Rule (1QS), Thanksgiving Hymn (1QHa) and Damascus Document (CD)…

> • Hell is a place of burning (CD 2.5; 1QM 14:17–18; 1QS 2:7, 15; 4:13; 1QHa 4:25, 19; 4Q174 f1_3ii:1).
> • At the same time it is a place of darkness (1QM 14:17, "fire burning in the dark places of the damned";14 1QS 2:8, "eternal flame, surrounded by utter darkness"; 4:13; 4Q287 f6:4;14 Unless otherwise indicated, all translations of the Dead Sea Scrolls are from Wise, Abegg, and Cook, Dead Sea Scrolls. 4Q418 f69ii:7). This is especially significant at Qumran because their enemies are called the Children of Darkness (e.g. 1QS 1:10).
> • Being in hell presumably involves torment, but there is no specific reference to this, except that the angels will afflict them (1QS 4:12).
> • The result of being in hell is eternal destruction. (CD 2:6; 1QS 2:15; 4:14; 5:13; 1QHa 14:21–22, "a fire which burns up all the men of guilt completely"; 4Q174 f1_3ii:1–2, "consuming fire and destroying all the children of Belial"; 4Q287 f6:6,9; 4Q286 f7ii:10; 4Q418 f69ii:6,8; 4Q491 f1_3:4 "eternal annihilation"; 4Q496 f3:5)…

"At the start of the Community Rule, they describe the fate of all those who fail to keep their strict version of Judaism:

> [EXT]The judgment of all who walk in such ways will be multiple afflictions at the hand of all the angels of perdition, everlasting damnation in the wrath of God's furious vengeance, never- ending terror and reproach for all eternity, with a shameful extinction in the fire of Hell's outer darkness. For all their eras, generation by generation, they will know doleful sorrow, bitter evil, and dark happenstance, until their utter destruction with neither remnant nor rescue. (1QS 4:12 14; duplicate at 4Q257 5:12–13, and the ending is similar to 4Q286 f7ii:10)[/EXT]…

"The Qumran Jews therefore emphasized that their punishment is: [BL 1-7]

> • "everlasting . . . never-ending . . . for all eternity, with a shameful extinction . . . for all their eras, generation by generation, . . . until their utter destruction with neither remnant nor rescue." (1QS 4:12–14)

- "eternal destruction" (1QS 2:15)
- "eternal destruction with none spared" (1QS 5:13)
- "eternal annihilation" (4Q491 fl_3:4; 4Q496 f3:5)
- "[disgra]ces of destruction wi[thout remnant . . . for all eternit]y. (4Q286 f7ii:7)
- "eternal destruction . . . the children of evil will no longer exist" (4Q418 f69ii:4–8)
- "burn [the damned of Sh]eol, as an [eternal] burning" (1QM 14:18) [/BL 1-7]

David Instone-Brewer, "Eternal Punishment in First Century Jewish Thought," *Edward Fudge Festschrift, A Consuming Passion* ed by C. Date and R. Highfield, 2015.

[2] **Goyim means**: Gentiles.

CHAPTER 55

[1] **The third seal and the price of food during the siege of Jerusalem**:

"Josephus actually mentions that during the siege, the Jews paid a talent for a measure of wheat (J.W. 5:13:7 §571). A talent "was the largest unit of weight" (ISBE2 4:1052) and therefore represents enormously high prices. In fact, Josephus speaks much about famine prices for food during the siege (J.W. 5:10:2 §427; 6:3:3–5 §198–219; cp. Dio 66:5:4). He even specifically notes the difference in wheat and barley, as per Revelation 6:6: "Many there were indeed who sold what they had for one measure; it was of wheat, if they were of the richer sort; but of barley, if they were poor" (J.W. 5:10:2 §427). This removal of food from Jerusalem during the Jewish War seems to be another feature of God's divorce judgment against her. After all, "the responsibility of the husband is to provide his wife with the necessities of life, such as food, clothing, and dwelling."

Kenneth L. Gentry, Jr., *The Divorce of Israel: A Redemptive-Historical Interpretation of Revelation Vol. 1* (Dallas, GA: Tolle Lege Press, 2016), 588.

[2] **The burning of the granaries and storehouses in Jerusalem**:

Flavius Josephus, *The Wars of the Jews* 5.1.4, §21-26
"4. (21) And now there were three treacherous factions in the city, the one parted from the other. Eleazar and his party, that kept the sacred firstfruits, came against John in their cups. Those that were with John plundered the populace, and went out with zeal against Simon. This Simon had his supply of provisions from the city, in oppositions to the seditious…

(24) and this he did always in such parts of the city as he could come at, till he set on fire those houses that were full of corn, and of all other provisions. The same thing was done by Simon, when, upon the other's retreat, he attacked the city also; as if they had, on purpose, done it to serve the Romans, by destroying what the city had laid up against the siege, and by thus cutting off the nerves of their own power. (25) Accordingly, it so came to pass, that all the places that were about the temple were burnt down, and were become an intermediate desert space, ready for fighting on both sides, and that almost all the corn was burnt, which would have been sufficient for a siege of many years. (26) So they were taken by the means of the famine, which it was impossible they should have been, unless they had thus prepared the way for it by this procedure."

Flavius Josephus and William Whiston, *The Works of Josephus: Complete and Unabridged* (Peabody: Hendrickson, 1987), 697–698.

[3] **Elihu quotes from**: Revelation 6:7-8.

CHAPTER 56

[1] **Jesus quotes from**: Romans 3:1-20.

[2] **Jesus quotes from**: Romans 3:21-26.

[3] **Jesus quotes from**: Romans 8:1; 4.

[4] **Jesus quotes from**: Galatians 4:24-30.

[5] **The saints' quote is from**: Revelation 6:10.

Why "land of Israel"?: The word in the English translation of this quoted verse is "Those who dwell on the earth." But the Greek word for "earth" does not mean globe, but is better translated as "land." And that phrase, "those who dwell on the land" or "land-dwellers" in the LXX refers to Israelites.

"As he comments on the first appearance of "Land-dwellers" in Revelation 3:10, Hort suggests that John derives this phrase from Hosea 4:1 (LXX). Other commentators recognize its general Old Testament backdrop. Hosea 4:1 clearly speaks of rebellious Israel (though Hort applies 3:10 to the wider world): "Listen to the word of the LORD, O sons of Israel, / For the LORD has a case against the inhabitants of the land [tous katoikountas tēn gēn], / Because there is no faithfulness or kindness / Or knowledge of God in the land [epi tēs gēs]."

"In the LXX, references to Israelites as the Land-dwellers occur often, with the phrasing including epi (as generally in Revelation) in Jeremiah 1:15; 6:12; Ezekiel 7:7; Zephaniah 1:8; Zechariah 11:6 (though without epi in Hos 4:1a; Jer 10:18; Joel 1:2, 14; 2:1). The phrase frequently applies to idolatrous pagans—although specifically to those dwelling in the Land of Israel (Nu 32:17; 33:52, 55; Jos 7:9; 9:24; Jdg 1:32; 2Sa 5:6; 1Ch 11:4; 22:18). Buchanan (128) observes that "the great majority of cases, however, identify [the Hebrew phrase] as those who lived on the land of Palestine (Exod 23:31; 34:12, 15; Josh 2:9, 24; 6:12; 7:9; 9:14; 10:18; 13:21; 24:18; 25:29, 30; Judges 1:32–33; Ezek 7:7; Hos 4:1; Joel 1:2, 14; 2:1; Zech 11:6) and should be rendered 'inhabitants of the land' rather than 'inhabitants of the earth.'" Thus we see how the Land-dweller phrase speaks of people in the Land, that is, the Promised Land."

Kenneth L. Gentry, Jr., *The Divorce of Israel: A Redemptive-Historical Interpretation of Revelation Vol. 1* (Dallas, GA: Tolle Lege Press, 2016), 602.

[6] Michael is remembering Jesus' words of condemnation: Matthew 23:35.

[7] **Jesus quotes from**: Revelation 18:24, 29, 9.

[8] **Jesus quotes from**: Revelation 9:20-24.

[9] **Jesus quotes from**: Romans 9:27-29.

CHAPTER 57

[1] **Josephus describes the threefold division of civil war within Jerusalem**:

Josephus, *The Wars of the Jews* 4.9.12, §577-584
"12. (577) And thus did Simon get possession of Jerusalem, in the third year of the war, in the month Xanthicus [Nisan]; whereupon John, with his multitude of zealots, as being both prohibited from coming out of the temple, and having lost their power in the city (for Simon and his party had plundered them of what they had) were in despair of deliverance. (578) Simon also made an assault upon the temple, with the assistance of the people, while the others stood upon the cloisters and the battlements, and defended themselves from their assaults. (579) However, a considerable number of Simon's party fell, and many were carried off wounded; for the zealots threw darts easily from a superior place and seldom failed of hitting their enemies; (580) but having the advantage of situation, and having withal erected four very large towers aforehand, that their darts might come from higher places."

Flavius Josephus and William Whiston, *The Works of Josephus: Complete and Unabridged* (Peabody: Hendrickson, 1987), 691.

Josephus, *The Wars of the Jews* 5.1.2-3, §5-13
"2. (5) For Eleazar, the son of Simon, who made the first separation of the zealots from the people, and made them retire into the temple, appeared very angry at John's insolent attempts which he made every day upon the people; for this man never left off murdering: but the truth was, that he could not bear to submit to a tyrant who set up after him. (6) So he being desirous of gaining the entire power and dominion to himself, revolted from John, and took to his assistance Judas the son of Chelcias, and Simon the son of Ezron, who were

among the men of greatest power. There was also with him Hezekiah the son of Chobar, a person of eminence. (7) Each of these were followed by a great many of the zealots; these seized upon the inner court of the temple...

"(9) Now as to John, what advantage he had above Eleazar in the multitude of his followers, the like disadvantage he had in the situation he was in, since he had his enemies over his head; and as he could not make any assault upon them without some terror, so was his anger too great to let them be at rest; (10) nay, although he suffered more mischief from Eleazar and his party than he could inflict upon them, yet would he not leave off assaulting them, insomuch that there were continued sallies made one against another, as well as darts thrown at one another, and the temple was defiled everywhere with murders.

"3. (11) But now the tyrant Simon, the son of Gioras, whom the people had invited in, out of the hopes they had of his assistance in the great distresses they were in, having in his power the upper city, and a great part of the lower, did now make more vehement assaults upon John and his party, because they were fought against from above also; yet was he beneath their situation, when he attacked them, as they were beneath the attacks of the others above them. (12) Whereby it came to pass, that John did both receive and inflict great damage, and that easily, as he was fought against on both sides; and the same advantage that Eleazar and his party had over him, since he was beneath them, the same advantage had he, by his higher situation over Simon. (13) On which account he easily repelled the attacks that were made from beneath, by the weapons thrown from their hands only; but was obliged to repel those that threw darts from the temple above him, by his engines of war."

Flavius Josephus and William Whiston, *The Works of Josephus: Complete and Unabridged* (Peabody: Hendrickson, 1987), 696-697.

[2] **I got this apt description from Josephus**:

Flavius Josephus, *The Wars of the Jews* 5.1.1, §4
"But for the present sedition, one should not mistake if he called it a sedition begotten by another sedition, and to be like a wild beast grown mad, which for want of food from abroad, fell now upon eating its own flesh."

Flavius Josephus and William Whiston, *The Works of Josephus: Complete and Unabridged* (Peabody: Hendrickson, 1987), 696.

CHAPTER 58

[1] **Jacob quotes from**: Psalms 137:5-6 and 122:6-8.

[2] **Cassandra quotes from**: Matthew 23:37–39.

[3] **Jacob quotes from**: Jeremiah 22:30.

[4] **The problem of the curse of Jeconiah and the lineage of Jesus**:

"JEREMIAH 22:30—Was Jehoiachin childless or did he have heirs?

"PROBLEM: Jeremiah was told here to "write this man down as childless." However, Jechoiachin had a son, Shealtiel, who is listed in Matthew 1:12.

"SOLUTION: First of all, the verse does not say he would actually be childless. Jeremiah was simply told to write him down "as if childless" (NIV). Further, this is explained by the last part of the verse, namely, "none of his descendants shall prosper, sitting on the throne of David, and ruling anymore in Judah." This is true of His immediate successors. And it is even true of his long-range successor, Christ, who was not an actual son of Jehoiachin but only a legal son through his legal father, Joseph (see comments on Matt. 1:17). Jesus, however, was the actual son of David through Mary, His actual mother (cf. 2 Sam. 7:12ff; Luke 3:23, 31)."

Norman L. Geisler and Thomas A. Howe, *When Critics Ask : A Popular Handbook on Bible Difficulties* (Wheaton, Ill.: Victor Books, 1992), 277.

"A command is given (v. 30) in the pl. (kitbû, write!) to record that he will be 'arîrî, childless (see Gen 15:2, and note esp. Lev 20:20–21, where being 'arîrî is a curse for an unauthorized union), yet v. 28 spoke of his offspring while 1Ch 3:16–17 states that he had seven sons. The explanation for this is found in the rest of v. 30, which should be understood in light of the presumed ardent hope and desire of the people of Judah—in their land and in exile—that this son of David, or one of his sons, would be restored to the throne. God says it will not happen, the emphasis being on "his lifetime" (in which he'll not succeed) and the lifetimes of his sons, none of whom would reign on the throne, making it as if he was childless (so NIV). In keeping with this, the divine promises to the line of David are not renewed until the days of Zerubbabel, his grandson (see Hag 2:20–23, and... Jer 52:31–34)...

According to 1 Chronicles 3:16–17, Jehoiachin had seven descendants. These, however, were hauled off into Babylon and there, according to an archaeological finding on a Babylonian tablet in the famous Ishtar Gate, all seven were made eunuchs. In this manner, Jehoiachin became "as if childless," as no man of his seed prospered, nor did any sit on David's throne."

Michael L. Brown, *Answering Jewish Objections to Jesus: New Testament Objections., vol. 4* (Grand Rapids, MI: Baker Books, 2007), 98.

[5] **Cassandra is quoting from and making the argument of** Hebrews 7. The Psalm she quotes is Psalm 110:4.

[6] **Cassandra quotes from** Hebrews 7:26-28 and 9:26-28.

CHAPTER 59

[1] **The events cited in this chapter of the civil war in Rome at Nero's death**:

Flavius Josephus, *The Wars of the Jews* 4.9.2, §491-496
2. (491) Now as Vespasian was returned to Cesarea, and was getting ready, with all his army to march directly to Jerusalem, he was informed that Nero was dead, after he had reigned thirteen years and eight days. (492) But as to any narration after what manner he abused his power in the government, and committed the management of affairs to those vile wretches, Nymphidius and Tigellinus, (493) his unworthy freedmen; and how he had a plot laid against him by them, and was deserted by all his guards, and ran away with four of his most trusty freedmen, and slew himself in the suburbs of Rome; and how those that occasioned his death were, in no long time, brought themselves to punishment; (494) how also the war in Gaul ended; and how Galba was made emperor, and returned out of Spain to Rome; and how he was accused by the soldiers as a pusillanimous person, and slain by treachery in the middle of the marketplace at Rome, and Otho was made emperor; (495) with his expedition against the commanders of Vitellius, and his destruction thereupon; and besides what troubles there were under Vitellius, and the fight that was about the Capitol; as also how Antonius Primus and Mucianus slew Vitellius, and his German legions, and thereby put an end to that civil war,—(496) I have omitted to give an exact account of them because they are well known by all, and they are described by a great number of Greek and Roman authors."

Flavius Josephus and William Whiston, *The Works of Josephus: Complete and Unabridged* (Peabody: Hendrickson, 1987), 688.

See also: Cassius Dio, *Roman History* 63-64;Tacitus, *The Histories* 1.2.

[2] **Severing Josephus' chains**: This event occurred in AD 69 when Vespasian was declared emperor. This timing is for creative license.

Flavius Josephus, *The Wars of the Jews* 4.10.7 §622-629
[Vespasian:] "It is a shameful thing (said he) that this man who hath foretold my coming to the empire beforehand, and been the minister of a divine message to me, should still be retained in the condition of a captive or prisoner." So he called for Josephus, and commanded that he should be set at liberty; (627) whereupon the commanders promised themselves glorious things from this requital Vespasian made to a stranger. Titus was then present with his father, (628) and said, "O father, it is but just that the scandal [of a prisoner] should be taken off Josephus, together with his iron chain; for if we do not barely loose his bonds, but cut them to pieces, he will be like a man that hath never been bound at all." For that is the usual method as to such as have been bound without a cause. (629) This advice was agreed to by Vespasian also; so there

came a man in, and cut the chain to pieces; while Josephus received this testimony of his integrity for a reward, and was moreover esteemed a person of credit as to futurities also."

Flavius Josephus and William Whiston, *The Works of Josephus: Complete and Unabridged* (Peabody: Hendrickson, 1987), 694.

CHAPTER 60

[1] **Cassandra refers to Rahab:**

> James 2:25
> [25] And in the same way was not also Rahab the prostitute justified by works when she received the messengers and sent them out by another way?

> Hebrews 11:31
> [31] By faith Rahab the prostitute did not perish with those who were disobedient, because she had given a friendly welcome to the spies.

[2] **Cassandra quotes from:** Matthew 6:25-34.

[3] **Cassandra quotes from:** Philippians 2:5–8.

[4] **Cassandra draws from:** 2 Corinthians 5:21.

CHAPTER 61

[1] **These statements are taken from Jesus:** Luke 21:12-19.

[2] **The Jews diverting Nero away from them to the Christians:** Regarding Nero's search for scapegoats on which to blame the Roman fires of July, AD 64 (Tac., Ann. 15:41), Gibbon sees the Jews behind Nero's choice of Christians. He notes that the Jews "possessed very powerful advocates in the palace, and even in the heart of the tyrant: his wife and mistress, the beautiful Poppaea, and a favourite player of the race of Abraham." These two suggest to Nero "the new and pernicious sect of Galileans," the Christians...

Clement (1 Clem 6:5) claims that the Neronic persecution was prompted "through envy [dia zēlos pathontes]," which many scholars believe refers to the Jews...

(2) Suetonius (Claud. 25:4; cp. Dio 60:66:6) shows that the Jews were expelled from Rome under Claudius around AD 50 for causing riots in their confrontations with Christians (cp. Ac 18:2; 24:5). The Romans disliked the Jews (Jos., Ap 2:66-92) even declaring that "the Jews regard as profane all that we hold sacred; on the other hand, they permit all that we abhor" (Tac., Hist 5:4). Tacitus (Hist. 5:5) adds that "the other customs of the Jews are base and abominable, and owe their persistence to their depravity" and that toward the non-Jewish "they feel only hate and enmity." Romans saw the Jews as troublemakers frequently stirring riots in Rome. Such conduct caused the Romans to expel them from Rome on several occasions (Suet., Tib. 36; Tac. Ann. 2:85; Jos. Ant. 18:3:5 §81). The Jews could rightly fear that blame for the AD 64 fires in Rome might fall upon them and would therefore be motivated to deflect attention to the Christians...

Schaff (HCC 1:383) comments that "it is not unlikely that in this (as in all previous persecutions, and often afterwards) the fanatical Jews, enraged by the rapid progress of Christianity, and anxious to avert suspicion from themselves, stirred up the people against the hated Galileans." Kenneth L. Gentry, Jr., *The Divorce of Israel: A Redemptive-Historical Interpretation of Revelation Vol. 2* (Dallas, GA: Tolle Lege Press, 2016), 220-223.

[3] **The Parable of the Sheep and Goats can be found in:** Matthew 25:31-46.

CHAPTER 62

[1] Romans 8:28.

CHAPTER 63

[1] **Cassandra is quoting from**: Esther 4:14.

CHAPTER 65

[1] **Cassandra is drawing from**: 1 Corinthians 6:3 and Daniel 7:26.

CHAPTER 67

[1] **Solomon's quarries**:

"Some of the stone for Hezekiah's building projects was probably taken from a quarry located north of the Temple Mount near the present-day Damascus Gate, now called Solomon's Quarry or Zedekiah's Cave. This quarry was used through the Roman period (63 B.C.-A.D. 324)."

Paul J. Achtemeier, Harper & Row and Society of Biblical Literature, *Harper's Bible Dictionary* (San Francisco: Harper & Row, 1985), 467.

"A tradition that the stone for the temple was quarried in the area near the modern Damascus Gate, known as Solomon's Quarries, Royal Quarries, Royal Caves, King Solomon's Mines, and the cave of Zedekiah, is without archeological support, but the tradition is not unreasonable (cf. 1 K. 6:7)."

W. S. Lasor, "Jerusalem," ed. Geoffrey W Bromiley, *The International Standard Bible Encyclopedia, Revised* (Wm. B. Eerdmans, 1979–1988), 1008.

"Quarry under Jerusalem: This quarry, called Zedekiah's Cave or Solomon's Quarries, is a 2.2-acre (9,000 m2), underground limestone quarry that extends for about 755 feet (230 m) under the Old City of Jerusalem. Herod the Great used stone from this quarry for building blocks when he built the Second Temple and its retaining walls, including what we now call the Wailing Wall."

Richard Myers, *Images from The Temple Dictionary of the Bible.* (Bellingham, WA: Logos Bible Software, 2012).

CHAPTER 70

[1] **Necromancers as "obs" and ancient conjuring ritual used in this chapter**:

"Necromancy was practiced throughout the ancient Near East. In Mesopotamia, the necromancer rubbed salve on his or her face in an effort to contact or perhaps embody the spirit of the dead, or used "skulls or figurines as temporary houses for the spirit which was being summoned."517 Although evidence of specifics is sparse, similar practices took place in Hittite Anatolia, where a distinguishing feature was the prominent role played by "old women.""

John H. Walton, *Zondervan Illustrated Bible Backgrounds Commentary (Old Testament): Joshua, Judges, Ruth, 1 & 2 Samuel, vol. 2* (Grand Rapids, MI: Zondervan, 2009), 380–381.

"The word for "spirit" is ʾôb (see first comment on v. 7). The etymological origin of this term is much debated, but one attractive proposal in the light of the present context (note, e.g., the spirit coming up "out of the ground," v. 13) is that the word derives from a non-Semitic loanword meaning "sacrificial pit." Proposed by Hoffner first on the basis of the occurrence of a cognate word meaning "pit" in Hittite religious texts, he finds additional cognates in Sumerian, Akkadian, Hurrian, and Ugaritic.525 He argues that the Hebrew term, like its Hittite cognate, is to be understood as designating a pit dug in the ground, which served as a means of access between infernal spirits of gods or deceased persons and the upper world. Among the Hittites, rituals were carried out which involved the opening up of such pits in places selected by oracle, the lowering of offerings into the pits, and the luring up of spirits out of the pit to eat the sacrifices and drink the blood libations and show their favour and superior knowledge to the sacrificers.

"Among the offerings lowered in the pit were foodstuffs, often including a black sacrificial animal (a hog or a dog), silver objects such as a model of a human ear (symbolizing the practitioner's desire to hear from the underworld), and a ladder or staircase (to encourage the spirit to ascend). Sumerian and Akkadian versions of the Gilgamesh Epic also attest the use of pits or holes in the ground as portals through which the dead could ascend from the underworld; Gilgamesh used such a pit to summon his departed companion Enkidu.528 In the Old Testament, the Hebrew term 'ôb is extended to connote not only the "ghost" that comes out of the pit but also the necromancer who calls forth the spirit."

John H. Walton, *Zondervan Illustrated Bible Backgrounds Commentary (Old Testament): Joshua, Judges, Ruth, 1 & 2 Samuel, vol. 2* (Grand Rapids, MI: Zondervan, 2009), 381–382.

[2] **The demon locusts in the armies of Rome**:

Ken Gentry makes a strong argument for the case that these demons are described this way in order to link them to the Roman legions that would besiege Jerusalem for 5 months in AD 69-70.

1. **"Their appearance was like horses prepared for battle"** (Rev 9:7) is a reference to the war horses of the legion.

2. **"On their heads appeared to be crowns like gold"** (9:7) Crowns are symbols of victorious march. These could be symbolic of the spiritual powers and authorities of darkness.

3. **"And their faces were like the faces of men"** (9:7).

"This may also imply that these demons inhabit those Jews—particularly the Idumeans, zealots, and Sicarii—within the city during the final five month siege. They lead these men to act in a bestial manner, for as Josephus writes of that period: the trapped citizens are "like a wild beast [thērion] grown mad, which, for want of food from abroad, fell now upon eating its own flesh" (J.W. 5:1:1 §4). Thus, those men operate "without mercy, and omitted no method of torment or of barbarity" (J.W. 5:1:5 §35)."

4. **"These demon-locusts also had hair like the hair of women"** (9:8a).

"This additional anthropomorphism may indicate the demonically-enhanced, shameful crimes committed within Jerusalem of this period. According to Paul long hair (such as women have) on men may picture that which is dishonorable: "even nature itself teaches you that if a man has long hair, it is a dishonor to him" (1Co 11:14). Or this image may even more particularly anticipate the demonic actions of John of Gischala's men:

> They also devoured what spoils they had taken, together with their blood, and indulged themselves in feminine wantonness, without any disturbance, till they were satiated therewith; while they decked their hair, and put on women's garments, and were besmeared over with ointments; and that they might appear very comely, they had paints under their eyes, and imitated not only the ornaments, but also the lusts of women, and were guilty of such intolerable uncleanness, that they invented unlawful pleasures of that sort. And thus did they roll themselves up and down the city, as in a brothel-house, and defiled it entirely with their impure actions; nay, while their faces looked like the faces of women, they killed with their right hands; and when their gait was effeminate, they presently attacked men. (J.W. 4:9:10 §561–563)

5. **"Their teeth were like the teeth of lions"** (9:8b)

"This not only picks up again from the Joel backdrop (Joel 1:4, 6; cf. Rev 13:2), but enhances the terror imagery. It is a proverbial image denoting the frightening and destructive power of lions (Job 4:10; Ps 7:2; 57:4; 58:6; Jer 2:30; Joel 1:6; Sir. 21:1–3; cp. 2Sa 1:23) from whom "none can deliver" (Pr 30:30; Isa 5:29; Hos 5:14)…Not only does this add to the fear John is evoking, but may indicate their insatiable appetite which is used in Scripture as a metaphor of destructive war: "Behold, a people rises like a lioness, / And as a lion it lifts itself; / It will not lie down until it devours the prey, / And drinks the blood of the slain" (Nu 23:24; cp. Job 38:39; Ps 17:12; 22:13; 104:21; Eze 19:6; Na 2:12; 1Pe 5:8)."

6. **"They had breastplates like breastplates of iron"** (9:9)

"This is a part of their look as "horses prepared for battle" (9:7a): fully dressed for battle in their protective plated armor."

7. **"The sound of their wings was like the sound of chariots, of many horses rushing to battle"** (9:9b).

"The visual image (along with its audial element) also is designed to impart fear, for in antiquity the attack of war horses and chariots was a signal of approaching devastation (1Sa 13:5; 1Ki 20:1; Isa 2:7; 5:28; Jer 6:23; 46:9; 47:3–4; 50:42; Eze 23:24; 26:7, 10; Nah 3:1–4)."

8. **"They have tails like scorpions, and stings; and in their tails is their power to hurt men for five months"** (9:10).

"Here in 9:10 John repeats the "five months" time frame from 9:5b which emphasizes this particular period of the Jewish War. This five-month period represents the last days of Israel's temple and the death throes of her holy city."

Kenneth L. Gentry, Jr., *The Divorce of Israel: A Redemptive-Historical Interpretation of Revelation Vol. 1* (Dallas, GA: Tolle Lege Press, 2016), 742-750.

[3] **Apollyon as Satan**: "This angel is named only here in Revelation [9:11 as Apollyon], and elsewhere in the OT and early Jewish literature is mentioned only in 4Q280 10 ii 7:"[Cursed be you Angel of the Pit, and Spirit of Abaddon" (Kobelski, Melchizedek, 43–44). While in 4Q280 and related texts these two titles are alternate ways of describing Belial, in Revelation it is not at all clear that the angel of the abyss is a designation for Satan, for he is carefully named elsewhere with a selection of aliases in two different contexts (12:9; 20:2), and neither Abaddon nor the angel of the abyss is mentioned again. The fact that ἄγγελον is articular here, however, suggests that the author expected the readers to be familiar with this figure, i.e., that the angel of the abyss is none other than Satan-Belial." David E. Aune, *Revelation 6–16, vol. 52B, Word Biblical Commentary* (Dallas: Word, Incorporated, 1998), 534.

"The "Destroyer" in Rev. 9:11 is either the devil himself or an evil representative of the devil; either alternative receives confirmation from Jewish exegetical tradition on Exodus (see below). Rev. 12:3–4 and 13:1ff. are compatible with this conclusion, since there the devil and the Beast respectively are pictured wearing royal diadems and leading evil forces. This is also in line with the same conclusion already reached about the angel's identification in 9:1." G. K. Beale, *The Book of Revelation: A Commentary on the Greek Text, New International Greek Testament Commentary* (Grand Rapids, MI; Carlisle, Cumbria: W.B. Eerdmans; Paternoster Press, 1999), 503.

"The title "angel of the abyss" is not found anywhere else in antiquity except in 2Q280. The demons this trumpet unleashes upon Jerusalem are under the dominion of a king whose name in Hebrew is Abaddon, and in the Greek he has the name Apollyon (9:11b). ...The following evidence suggests to me that this "king" is Satan: (1) John describes him both as a "king" as well as "the angel of the abyss" (from which come the demons; 9:1–3). In Scripture, Satan functions as an evil ruler of great power in the fallen world (Mt 4:8; Jn 12:31; 14:30; 16:11; 1Jo 5:19), and even as the ruler of demons (Mt 9:34; 12:24–27; Lk 10:17–18; Eph 2:2; cp. Jub. 11:15; 17:16; 18:9, 12; 48:2–15). In fact, the Bible calls fallen angels (demons) "his angels" (Mt 25:41; Rev 12:9). Later in Revelation, we see Satan appearing as a dragon with diadems, showing his kingship (12:3).

"(2) John refers to him as "the angel of the abyss [ton aggelon tēs abussou]," where the definite article suggests this angel is well-known. Satan is certainly a well-known figure in Scripture and in first-century Judaism. John even mentions him in Revelation four times before now (2:9, 13, 24; 3:9). (3) The symbolic names given to him, "Apollyon" and "Abaddon" (9:11b), both mean "destroyer," which fits Satan's character and work (1Co 5:5; Eph 6:11; Heb 2:14; 1Pe 5:8). This is true even in Revelation where he seeks to destroy Jesus at his birth (12:3–4) and then his saints (12:12–13, 17). Indeed, the name "Satan" means "adversary" which comports with the concept of "destroyer"—since he seeks a legal means to destroy God's people (e.g., 2:9–10). So once again we see Satan's work among the Christ-denying Jews, as per Christ's declaration that their father is the devil (Jn 8:44) and that they are a "synagogue of Satan" (Rev 2:9; 3:9). They are now receiving their just desserts: Satan sends his demon army to sorely afflict them.

457

"John's Greek abbadōn is a transliteration of the Hebrew 'baddōn, which appears in the Old Testament only in the Wisdom literature (Job 26:6; 28:22; 31:12; Ps 88:11; Pr 15:11; 27:20). It also appears four times in the DSS (NIDOTTE 1:226). It means "destruction" and in the LXX is always translated by apōleia ("destruction, annihilation), except in Job 31:12 which translates it apolluein. In Job 31:12 it is the place of destruction, whereas elsewhere it parallels Sheol (Job 26:6; Pr 15:11; 27:20), death (Job 28:22), or the grave (Ps 88:11), and is thus strongly associated with death. The word "Apollyon" is apolluōn in the Greek: it is the present participle of apollumi, which means to "destroy." Like the Hebrew 'baddōn it is often used to refer to killing (Mt 2:13; 12:114; 27:20; Mk 3:6; 9:41; 11:18; Lk 11:51; 12:33; 15:17; 17:27; 19:47). Satan himself virtually personifies death in Heb 2:14b: "who had the power of death, that is, the devil" (cp. 1Co 5:5).

"In addition to the designation "Apollyon" referring to Satan as the "destroyer," the term has an "etymological connection" with the name of Apollo the sun god and may therefore allude to him (Smalley 234; cp. Caird 120; Sweet 170; TDNT 1:397; Beagley 54; Ford 152; Morris 128; Lupieri 163; M. Wilson 2002: 305; Boxall 145; Osborne 374). If so, Apollo would serve as a link to the Roman emperor Nero who held Apollo as his patron deity. Suetonius notes that Nero drove a chariot in the games (Nero 24:2) mimicking Apollo. Nero "was acclaimed as the equal of Apollo in music and of the Sun in driving a chariot" (Nero 53)." Kenneth L. Gentry, Jr., *The Divorce of Israel: A Redemptive-Historical Interpretation of Revelation Vol. 1* (Dallas, GA: Tolle Lege Press, 2016), 750-752.

Made in the USA
Las Vegas, NV
27 December 2023